CLASH OF CULTURES

Faith's searching gaze stopped abruptly, her heart beginning an erratic pounding as her eyes touched on a familiar figure outlined against the shadows of the wooded glade. She gasped as the figure moved forward to approach her in a steady, unhesitant step.

Faith's angry protest was instinctive.

"What are you doing? Can't you see . . . ?" Suddenly at a loss for words, Faith clutched her dress more tightly against her. "I . . . I need to get dressed. I . . ."

Faith's words trailed off as Black Wolf continued his intense perusal. A surging heat moved to the cooled surface of her cheeks as a strangely unrecognizable emotion was exhibited briefly in his eyes. The bold savage! He was enjoying his power over her!

When Black Wolf finally spoke, contempt edged his voice. "You clutch the garment as if it were a shield. You need not hide your body from my gaze. I will take what I want anyway. . . ."

Untamed Captive

Elaine Barbieri

ZEBRA BOOKS
KENSINGTON PUBLISHING CORP.

ZEBRA BOOKS

are published by

Kensington Publishing Corp.
475 Park Avenue South
New York, NY 10016

First printing: September 1987

Printed in the United States of America

To Siobhan Rhiannon Fitzpatrick,
a new life to cherish,
with my deepest love.

Chapter I

The deadly circle tightened. Pounding hooves thundered around the clustered wagons, filling Faith's eyes and throat with a choking cloud of dust as she strained to penetrate the grainy mist with her gaze. Savage war cries rent the terrifying din caused by gunshots, frantic shouts, and the moans of the wounded.

The bark of gunfire intensified and a body thudded to the ground a few feet from the wagon under which Faith had found refuge. Blood streamed from its bare unmoving chest, tinting russet skin an even deeper hue. Gunfire barked again, but this time the body which fell was inside the defensive circle. Turning, Faith met the light, unseeing gaze of the wagon master. Gasping, she covered her eyes against his lifeless stare.

The sound of a low wail raised Faith's head from her hands. It came from beneath a wagon a short distance away. Mary . . . it was Mary Cummings. Faith looked with a sense of growing horror to the still form beside the terrified four-year-old, and a numbing cold spread through her veins. Mrs. Cummings . . . her eyes were open, sightless, like the wagon master's. . . .

Faith quickly glanced toward her mother. Crouched beneath the wagon a few feet away, Lydia Durham met Faith's questioning gaze. She did not need to speak. Faith read it in her eyes. Mrs. Cummings was dead.

The appeal in Faith's glance went unheeded, and Faith

7

was suddenly conscious of her mother's unnatural expression. Mama was afraid . . . even more terrified than she. An instinct, advanced for her fourteen years, told Faith she could do nothing to help her mother now. But Mary . . . someone must see to Mary.

Faith sent a quick glance around the area within the circled wagons. Bodies littered the dry, dusty ground as gunfire rang from behind hastily assembled shelters. A few brave women, their faces stiff with fear, scrambled between the fallen men.

Papa . . . where was Papa?

Faith's wildly searching gaze jerked to a halt, touching with relief on a graying red head as it poked out from behind temporary shelter to return a hail of fire. She released a tense breath. Papa was all right.

The frantic wail from the nearby wagon grew louder.

Torn by the memory of her father's words as he had thrust her beneath the wagon at the beginning of the attack, Faith looked back in her mother's direction. Papa had glanced toward her mother, already barricaded, his worried expression darkening with a flush. His voice had been tight, his words concise.

"Stay here, under the wagon, Faith. It's the safest place for you and your mother. Don't move away from here for any reason—any reason, do you hear me?" When she had nodded, Wallace Durham had added in a lower tone meant for her ears alone, "You're the strong one, Faith. I'm depending on you to take care of your mother."

The ring of war cries and the pounding of hooves had then jerked her father from her side, and the horror had begun.

Bullets snapped the ground around her, jerking Faith from her thoughts, and once more she quickly glanced toward her mother. Obviously in tenuous control of her emotions, Lydia Durham returned her gaze in shuddering silence.

A short cry from the Cummingses' wagon turned Faith's attention back toward Mary. Tears streaking her small face, the child had raised herself to her knees. Her red-rimmed eyes were focused on a spot at the far end of the inner circle, where her father was fighting desperately to push back an attempted breakthrough. Crying out anew as another round of gunfire struck the ground near her, Mary was poised to run.

Faith knew a moment of blinding panic. Mary would never make it to her father. The frightened child would be running to her death!

Faith's response was spontaneous as she shouted over the deadly confusion.

"No, Mary! Stay where you are! I'm coming!"

Pulling herself to a crouching position, Faith took a deep breath. Deaf to her mother's warning shout, she burst out from under the wagon, breaking into a run.

She was nearing the Cummingses' wagon when she heard hoofbeats pounding the ground behind her. A quick glance to her rear turned her blood cold. An Indian had jumped a break between the wagons and was coming up behind her! Her heart thundering in her ears, Faith ran faster.

Abruptly a brutal arm slipped around her waist, jerking her upward. Struggling furiously against the unyielding grip, Faith caught a glimpse of a fierce, painted face as she was lifted high into the air and thrust astride the savage's horse. Out of the corner of her eye, Faith saw little Mary scramble back under the Cummingses' wagon to hide her head against her mother's lifeless form.

Someone was calling her name! Helpless against the viselike grip which held her prisoner, Faith turned toward the sound of her mother's voice as her captor roughly wheeled his horse around. Her mother had scrambled out from beneath the wagon! She was running toward them, screaming Faith's name.

A low shout sounded from behind the hastily constructed barrier a short distance away as Wallace Durham moved out into the open. Unexpectedly, two more Indian ponies jumped the break between the wagons. Mindless of the gunfire raging around him, the first Indian leaned over in a swift, graceful movement to scoop her mother from the ground. Wallace Durham was only a few feet away when the second Indian raised his gun and fired.

Shock jarred all action to a sudden halt in Faith's mind, freezing in it the picture of her father's startled face in the moment before he fell lifelessly to the ground.

The shattering scene was lost to her sight as Faith's captor abruptly spurred his horse. Within moments, they were sailing back over the break and away from the circle of wagons. A short, guttural command was barked into her ear as they hit solid ground and headed into open country.

They were traveling at breathtaking speed when Faith heard the sound of horses' hooves to their rear. Darting a quick look behind her, she caught a glimpse of her mother, held captive by the painted savage on the second horse. Incredulous grief and terror shone in her mother's eyes, and Faith shuddered, knowing full well her mother's glance mirrored her own.

Chapter II

Captain William Potter struggled to maintain an impassive façade. He squared his uniformed shoulders, pulling his fit, well-honed physique to a militarily correct posture, then squinted his eyes against the smoke which filled his nostrils and burned his eyes as he evaluated the devastation of the civilian wagon train. Low sounds of pain and grief accompanied the frantic scene. He steeled himself against the anguished tableau. The sober, precise mind of this professional soldier argued against his instinctive shock and rage. He had seen destruction like this too many times since he had been assigned to this savage frontier. He could not afford to allow it to affect him.

His men were moving amongst the burning wagons as he dismounted, responding to his quick, efficient commands. His rapid assessment had determined the train had originally consisted of approximately thirty wagons. It had obviously been surprised by the attack, if he were to judge from the loose circle which had been the main defense against the marauding Indians who had overwhelmed it. He supposed that meant he should direct his men to locate the body of the wagon's scout who was certain to be lying dead somewhere in advance of the train. But first things first. The wounded and dying here were his first priority.

Captain Potter surveyed the shocked, exhausted faces of the survivors. Where was the wagon master—someone in authority with whom he could speak? His eyes moved amongst the bodies which littered the ground and the grief-stricken figures attending to them. He frowned. The casualty count was obviously high. He had no doubt it would have been higher still had he and his troop not happened to be patrolling the area when gunshots in the distance had drawn him. He had not arrived in time to be able to do more than drive the Indians off. Despite his desire to pursue them, he had realized full well he could not abandon the survivors.

"Sergeant!"

His low command raised the head of the short, brawny soldier moving amongst the survivors.

"Yes, sir, Captain."

"Have you located the wagon master?"

"He's dead, sir."

"Is there someone else who can give me some information?"

"What do you want to know, Captain?"

The low, uneven voice to his rear turned Captain Potter toward a tall, slender fellow standing weakly behind him. A young child clutched his hand, her pale face streaked with tears as she pressed herself against his side. Captain Potter instinctively closed the distance to them as his eyes moved to the bloody gash on the fellow's forehead. Taking the injured man's arm, he lowered him to a seated position on the ground and crouched beside him. A quick assessing glance revealed that the wound had all but stopped bleeding. The man's eyes appeared to be clear, but Captain Potter hesitated, unwilling to press him for details so soon after the ordeal he had obviously undergone. His response was low, filled with concern.

"Are you sure you're all right, sir?"

"I'm in better shape than most, Captain." With a shaking hand the fellow pointed to a nearby wagon. "My wife's under the wagon over there. I just left her. She's past help now."

Captain Potter's eyes jerked to the covered, motionless form to which the man gestured. Not waiting for his reaction, the man continued resolutely.

"My name's Martin Cummings, Captain. This train's out of Hanibal, Illinois, heading for Montana. Sheldon Grimsby was our wagon master. He was one of the first ones killed. Sheila and me was going to hit it rich in the gold fields and provide a good life for ourselves and Mary." Cummings's face twitched as he paused for a deep breath. "Sheila won't never see those gold fields now."

"Mr. Cummings, you don't have to—"

"No, Captain." Martin Cummings lifted his hand in a brief, silencing gesture, allowing it to fall to his daughter's head as she burrowed her face against his arm. Stroking her fair hair gently, he raised his pain-filled eyes once again.

"We didn't have no idea those Indians was coming. Our scout was out since dawn, but we didn't hear a word from him. It was lucky little Jimmy Pierce sneaked one of the horses off the back of his family's wagon and rode out ahead of the train, because he saw the Indians all painted up and riding over the rise like the devil was after them, and he rode back to warn us. We hardly had time to circle the wagons before they attacked."

Captain Potter nodded, experiencing little satisfaction at the confirmation of his suspicions.

"We had thirty-five wagons starting off, Captain." Cummings's voice quaked revealingly. "We don't have nowhere near that number left now. The fire them Indians started spread real fast. We would've been surrounded by it if you hadn't arrived when you did."

Nodding, Captain Potter averted his gaze to assess the little girl's terrified expression. She was so young, hardly more than three or four. So young to lose her mother.

Turning his gaze back toward the grief-stricken man, Captain Potter took a deep breath. Arapaho . . . he was certain the train had been attacked by Arapaho. But Sioux, Arapaho, Cheyenne . . . what was the difference? They were all savages with a lust for blood. In the three years since he had graduated from West Point to come to this frontier, he had learned that lesson only too well.

Realizing full well that words were inadequate in the face of Martin Cummings's sorrow, Captain Potter hesitated. His response was simple and sincere.

"You have my sympathy for your loss, Mr. Cummings.

My men will help you prepare your wife to be brought to the fort. We'll be moving the salvagable wagons as soon as possible, and—"

"That ain't what's important now, Captain." Martin Cummings's narrow face was beginning to pale noticeably. Little beads of perspiration appearing on his forehead and upper lip, he reached out to grasp Captain Potter's arm with surprising strength. "You have to go after the Indians . . . they took captives."

"Captives?"

Startled, Captain Potter frowned. He hadn't thought there had been time for the Indians to penetrate the circle of wagons.

"They took two, Captain. Mrs. Durham and her daughter."

Captain Potter suppressed a spontaneous shudder. A woman and a child. Only the week before he had found the body of a woman the Indians had taken. Tortured . . . mutilated . . . He had been physically sickened by the sight. It returned still to haunt him in the darkness of the night.

"The girl—Faith Durham—she's only about thirteen or fourteen. She was trying to help Mary after Sheila . . ." Biting down tightly on his trembling lower lip, Martin Cummings paused in an attempt to retain control of his emotions. "She was running toward Mary when a few of the Indians jumped the breach between the wagons. They grabbed Faith, swept her right off her feet, and when her mother ran out to stop them, they took her, too."

His breathing becoming erratic as unconsciousness threatened to overwhelm him, but Cummings continued with sheer strength of will.

"Wally Durham tried to stop them, but one of them shot him. He can't do nothin' to help his family now."

"Don't upset yourself any further, Mr. Cummings."

"You have to go after them, Captain. Faith is a pretty little girl . . . long, bright red hair, the same color as her Pa's. I can't close my eyes for thinking of that red hair hanging on a scalp pole somewhere."

Sobbing softly anew, Mary Cummings drew her father's

14

attention for a few moments as he comforted her weakly. The eyes he raised back to the young captain were filled with grief.

"Lydia Durham is a small, kinda fragile woman, Captain. I'm thinking she won't last long under rough treatment. I don't want to think she'll go the way of my Sheila. You got to do something."

The anxiety inside him raised to a stronger pitch than he cared to admit by Martin Cummings's earnest plea, Captain Potter nodded. Reaching out to grab the man's arm as he appeared ready to collapse, he shouted a quick command over his shoulder.

"Sergeant!"

A quick step at his side raised his gaze to the burly campaigner's concerned expression.

"Get this man into a wagon and readied for transportation with the rest of the wounded as soon as possible." Turning back, Captain Potter looked hard into Martin Cummings's eyes.

"I'll find them, Mr. Cummings. I give you my word on that."

His softly spoken pledge going unacknowledged as Martin Cummings slipped off into unconsciousness, Captain Potter lifted the sobbing child into his arms. Closing his eyes momentarily, he whispered in soft consolation into her small ear. He had seen too much suffering and death, been too ineffective against it. The faces of the innocent dead haunted him. But not this time. He would not abandon those two innocent captives to the savages who had taken them. He would find them and bring them back, whatever the cost. Those brutal heathens would not win out again . . . not again.

Chapter III

The heat of the afternoon sun was relentless and searing. Faith stumbled as the sharp stones of the trail cut into her bared feet. Stifling the spontaneous grunt of pain which rose to her lips, she pulled herself upright and forced herself forward. Calling upon her dwindling reserve of strength, she brushed away the gleaming red-gold strands of hair which adhered to her face and neck due to perspiration, and lifted the brilliant blue of her eyes to the afternoon sky. The sun was well past the zenith, and their captors had driven them at a ruthless pace since sunup. Neither her mother nor herself had been given more than a small sip of water to sustain them, and she was truly uncertain how much longer they would be able to go on.

She did not need to turn around to see that the mounted Indians who pushed them inexorably forward were thoroughly enjoying their captives' exhaustion. Low snickers and the babble of voices were frequently provoked by her mother's stumbling gait and by hers. They had shown no sympathy when her mother had fallen a short time before. Instead, Lydia Durham's temporary inability to regain her feet had seemed to stir them to an angry frenzy which had resulted in their raining unsparing blows on both her mother and herself. Faith knew there was no use in protesting their inhuman treatment. The fact that they had demanded their captives' shoes at the beginning of the drive, only to throw them into the bushes on the side of the trail, revealed that their cruelty was deliberate.

Darting a quick look to her side, Faith sent her mother an assessing glance. Lydia was staggering, the smooth skin of her cheek swollen and darkened by an ugly bruise. But it was not her mother's physical pain which worried Faith. It was the blankness of her mother's expression which sent little tremors of fear down her spine.

Unexpected tears suddenly welled in her eyes, and Faith fought to control them. Papa's last words to her had been spoken in concern for her mother. He had known Mama was not strong, not in the way she herself was; but Papa had not loved Mama any the less for it. He had patiently explained to Faith a few years before that her mother had not been raised to withstand hard work and deprivation. Her mother had been the daughter of a wealthy and powerful man who had disowned her when she had declared her intention to marry Papa, but Wallace Durham had told Faith that he had promised her mother he would see to it that she would one day again live a luxurious life. It had been her father's greatest disappointment that he had not yet been able to keep his pledge.

Papa's decision to join the wagon train West had been influenced by that same driving desire to return to her mother all she had sacrificed for him. Mama had not wanted to go into such a "savage" land. She had been afraid. But Papa had been driven by tales of the fortunes to be made in the gold fields, and by the chance to fulfill his promise. He would be driven no longer. . . .

The vision of her father's fallen, bloodstained body returned to her mind, and Faith struggled to control her trembling. He was dead. Papa was dead. She would never again see the sun glint on the graying red hair so similar to her own, see his pale blue eyes crinkle with laughter. She would never again feel his strong arms around her, would never again hear his deep voice ring with pride when he said her name. Her love for Papa had been tinged with that same pride—a pride in his handsome, smiling face and the great, comforting size of him; in his gentleness and concern, his wisdom and his strength—in all the things he was . . . things

17

that would never be again.

Papa was free of his promise now, but she was not free of hers. Papa had said she was the strong one and she had promised him she would take care of Mama. It was up to her now.

Faith darted another glance up toward the cloudless sky. She was beginning to find it difficult to think. The heat of afternoon was strong on her unprotected head, dizzying, and her mind was beginning to whirl in slow, confusing circles. She glanced beside her again. Mama's ragged step was slowing to a stop. Mama's beautiful face, in which her father had held so much pride, was bruised and smeared with dirt, but its former flush was gone. Now it was a starkly white, frightening in its total absence of color. Mama was going to fall!

Covering the few steps between them, Faith reached out to take her mother's arm, only to have her hand roughly knocked away as the Indian behind her spurred his pony between them. Faith looked up to see the painted savage smile wickedly the moment before he urged his pony forward to bump roughly against her mother's side. The result was instantaneous. Her mother fell roughly to her knees, a low whimper of pain escaping her lips as she broke her fall with her hands.

Directing his horse with a skillful hand, the Indian maintained his position between them as Faith sought to go to her mother's side. His low laughter at her frantic bid to sidestep him being more than she could bear, Faith felt a true fury suffuse her. Breathing heavily, tears of frustration filling her great eyes, she stepped back. In desperation, she glanced around her. Her eyes touched on a jagged rock to the side of the trail. Making a frenzied dash in its direction, she picked it up and hurled it with all her strength. It struck the Indian in the chest, momentarily doubling him over as it knocked the breath from his lungs.

Taking advantage of the Indian's momentary disability, Faith darted around his startled pony's legs to her mother's side. In the back of her mind she made a mental note that the other two Indians were watching in stolid silence as their companion sought to regain his breath.

Her hands trembling, Faith reached down to draw her mother to her feet, only to hear her gasp.

"Faith . . . you shouldn't have. . . . He's inhuman. He'll kill you."

"No . . . no, Mama. Don't worry. Please get up."

Faith darted a look over her shoulder, and her heart leaped in her chest as the silent Indians spurred their horses forward. Fear drying the last remaining moisture from her mouth, Faith jerked frantically at her mother's arm.

"Mama, quickly, get up! They'll beat you."

"No . . . Faith. I can't . . ."

Panic flushed through Faith's racing mind. Her mother's heavy lids were fluttering weakly. The woman was helpless, near the point of unconsciousness. She could not get up . . . go on any longer.

Realization of her mother's supreme helplessness sent a new strength surging through Faith's limbs. Jumping to her feet, she turned her back to her mother, shielding her with her slender form. Her eyes were blazing.

"Stay away from us, both of you! She can't go on, can't you see that? She needs rest, something to eat and drink! She—"

Faith's angry harangue came to a sudden halt as the first Indian grated a low, gasping command which stopped the other two in their tracks. Halted, the Indians turned toward the enraged man Faith had struck. His grotesque war paint paling in contrast to the fury in his eyes, the savage charged toward her.

An unexpected thrashing in the brush beside the trail abruptly halted the Indian's momentum, bringing him up short as four mounted Indians emerged from the foliage. The savagery in her captor's face dimmed to caution at their appearance.

Faith turned quickly, making use of the time to raise her mother to her feet. Holding Lydia tightly by the arm, she surveyed the exhausted woman with alarm. Her gleaming black hair, always meticulously groomed, hung from what had been an upswept coiffure in ragged, tangled strands. Her

19

smooth, unlined skin, blemished by the ugly bruise on her cheek, retained its unnatural pallor beneath its sun-touched surface. The lack of color darkened the deep circles under her weary gray eyes, emphasizing their size and the obvious pain reflected within them.

But her mother's gaze was fixed on the leader of the Indians who had appeared so unexpectedly. Faith turned sharply in his direction. If she must face a further threat, she was determined to be ready.

Abruptly, Faith realized that these Indians were not of the same tribe as the first. They were of like size and stature, their skin bearing the same russet hue, their appearance just as menacing; but there was a subtle difference which she was temporarily unable to identify.

The leader was a man of massive shoulder and chest whose body was scarred with the marks of many battles. The two Indians directly behind him were less imposing in stature, but appeared to be of similar age and appearance. The fourth was more youthful. Despite his apparent height and wide expanse of shoulder, he had not yet realized his full muscular potential. But for all his youth, his eyes were sharp and quick as his gaze moved from one of their captors to the other. He turned unexpectedly, catching Faith in avid perusal. Unprepared for the feral intensity of his gaze, she started, and a warning sounded somewhere in the back of her mind as a voice raised in anger jerked her gaze from his.

Her heart pounding, Faith assessed the progress of the Indians' conversation as they spoke in the harsh tones of their native tongue. His fury unabating, her captor objected angrily to a word spoken by one of his companions, and a heated discussion raged between the two before her captor turned back once more to resume his conversation with the other group. He spoke in short, stilted sentences, the stiffness in his demeanor indicating that the new arrivals were not friends or even acquaintances.

The conversation grew intense. Her captor snapped his eyes in her direction, the heat in his gaze burning a new fear into her heart. Then he turned to converse with his companions. A low, furious babble continued for long moments before her captor turned back to the other Indians once more.

His expression supremely controlled, her captor finally nodded his head. Folding his arms across his chest, he waited as the leader of the other group motioned to the young brave. The young Indian turned his mount into the foliage beside the trail, emerging within moments, trailing a hardy chestnut mare behind him.

The exchange was brief as her captor took the animal's lead and barked a short guttural command to his companions. Within moments the three painted savages had disappeared up the trail, dragging the horse behind them.

Confused, Faith turned toward her mother. The clatter of hooves behind her snapped her back in time to see the remaining Indians spurring their ponies toward them.

Instinctive fear drove Faith into spontaneous action. Ignoring the exhaustion which deadened her limbs, she broke into a run, dragging her mother behind her. Realizing they stood no chance of eluding the Indians on open ground, she turned unexpectedly and plunged into the brush beside the trail. Gasping with pain as her lacerated feet struck one sharp surface after another, Faith held a tight grip on her mother's hand in her blind race for escape. But her mother was weakening, slipping and falling even as the thrashing behind them came closer.

Realizing her mother could not face much more of the tortuous route they pursued, Faith broke out onto the trail once more. Momentary elation soared in her mind. Mama was running more easily now and the Indians had not emerged from the foliage. If only Mama and she could make it as far as the next stand of trees before the Indians reached the trail, they could hide . . . escape . . . they could . . .

The sudden clatter of hooves on the trail behind them crushed the hope which had begun to flourish inside her. Jerking harder at her mother's arm, Faith gasped a breathless plea.

"Mama, please . . . run faster! They're coming!"

Refusing to surrender to her fate, Faith ignored the hoofbeats sounding behind her, the barbarous cries which rent the heavy air. Abruptly, her mother's hand was pulled from her grasp as the woman went tumbling head over heels onto the dusty, sunlit trail. Not realizing the terrified scream echoing in her ears was her own, Faith had just reached her mother's side when she was pulled abruptly from her feet. Snatched high into the air, she caught a brief glimpse of a dark, enigmatic gaze before she was roughly deposited astride the laboring Indian pony that had overtaken her.

Struggling fiercely against the unyielding strength of the brutal arm which held her prisoner, she gritted tightly from between clenched teeth, "Let me go! My mother is hurt! She needs me!"

The only response was the painful tightening of the young Indian's hold. Frantic, Faith turned back toward her mother as the leader of the group dismounted and dropped to her mother's side. Quivering with fear, Faith watched as the Indian signaled another to do the same. Within moments, the leader had remounted and had taken her mother's unconscious form onto his horse in front of him.

The sight of her mother's still, colorless face as she lay motionless in the broad Indian's arms evoked a new panic inside Faith. She was struggling frantically to break free of her captor's imprisoning grip when his unexpected rasp brought her battle to a startled halt.

"If you value your life and the life of the other woman, you will be still!"

Faith turned sharply to meet her captor's gaze. The menace on his youthful face confirmed the truth of his ruthless statement, and a few fear was born inside her. In her panic she had given no thought to the fact that her mother's only hope was that Faith remain well enough to care for her once she regained consciousness. Faith had no choice but to obey this young savage's commands. None at all.

She glanced back toward her mother in helpless despair. Blood streamed from a bruise on Lydia Durham's temple, but a thread of hope came alive inside Faith as her mother's eyes flicked open momentarily, as if in answer to her silent plea. The muscular arms supporting her mother tightened as the leader spoke a few unintelligible words on command to the other Indians. Turning, the massive Indian spurred his mount to a more rapid pace.

The horse beneath her surged forward at her captor's urging, and unexpectedly a bitter consolation brought a choking sob to Faith's throat. At least Mama would not have to walk anymore.

The burning afternoon sun had slipped below the horizon, and the darkening trail was steeped in soundless twilight when Faith realized through the haze of exhaustion which numbed her mind that the horses were slowing to a stop. The sound of a nearby stream registered unconsciously in the back of her mind and she stirred. Water . . . If she could splash some water on her face, refresh herself, perhaps then she would be able to clear her mind . . . be able to think.

An aching fatigue touched every bone in her body. Her bruised and lacerated feet were throbbing painfully. With deep humiliation, Faith realized that during the last few hours of their journey she had relied completely on the support of the young Indian who held her captive. She was ashamed of her weakness.

The horses drew to a halt, and Faith's blurred gaze moved toward her mother. Lydia Durham lay limply against the lead Indian's chest, and Faith's fear stirred anew. If her mother's condition did not improve, these savages would abandon her here to die: or worse, they might even kill her.

Fear drew her up stiffly within her captor's arms just as the leader of the Indians spoke a few short words to his men. Within seconds the strong arm which supported her relaxed, and her captor dismounted. Reaching up, the young Indian swung her down from the pony's back and stood her on her feet.

Her pain acute when her swollen feet touched the ground, Faith took a short, gasping breath. But her eyes were on her mother, who was being swung to the ground a short distance away. Mama's eyes were open. She was swaying uncertainly. She was going to fall!

Faith's compulsive step toward her mother was stopped

by the short command the leader snapped. Responding to it immediately, the young Indian reached out and jerked her back to his side.

Struggling under his unrelenting grip, Faith turned toward him, seething with fury.

"Let me go! My mother needs help, can't you see that? She's hurt!"

The young Indian's only response was a tightening of the imprisoning hand on her arm.

Darting a helpless glance back toward her mother, Faith watched as the exhausted woman sank slowly to a seated position on a nearby log. Her face was still a ghastly white, frighteningly stiff. She did not speak, but raised a dazed expression in Faith's direction. Faith's heart began to pound rapidly. Her mother needed her.

Suddenly struggling fiercely under the young savage's hand, Faith managed to break free. She had taken a few steps toward her mother's side when she was jerked to a halt and turned roughly to face the young Indian's fury. Without a word, he swung her up and over his shoulder. She was pounding at his back and shoulders in protest of his treatment as he walked off into the deepening foliage.

The sound of the gurgling stream grew louder, but Faith's fury made her insensible to its call. She was still screaming her rage when she was dumped unceremoniously onto the ground. Her heated outburst came to a shuddering halt as the menace in the young Indian's gaze registered fully in her mind. His low tone was filled with venom.

"Do not test my patience! You are a child, and it is your youth and Broken Hand's command which saves you. But Broken Hand will not save you from the weight of my anger if you press me further!"

"You don't frighten me with your threats!"

The young savage sneered his contempt.

Reaching down, he dragged Faith to her feet, and pulled her to stand uncertainly at the edge of the stream.

"You will bathe your feet so they will once again support you without pain, and then you will return to camp." His eyes narrowing, the young Indian continued harshly, "The

24

other woman is watched carefully by Broken Hand. Should you try to escape, Broken Hand's wrath will fall on her."

Reading the veracity of his words in the young Indian's eyes, Faith took a deep breath. She was unable to withhold her next question despite her fear of its response.

"What . . . what do you intend to do with us?"

A dismissing glance his only response, the young Indian turned in silence and walked back in the direction from which they had come.

Rage and frustration brought a new trembling to Faith's aching frame. Despite his youth, her captor was no less a barbarian than the others of his race. Perhaps she was a child, but the events of this day had forced upon her a maturity far beyond her years. She had seen her father shot down, and she and her mother had been beaten and tormented by ruthless savages. Mama was all she had left now. She would not see Mama suffer the same fate as Papa, not while she still had a breath left in her body.

Taking a painful pace forward, Faith stepped down off the bank. She emitted a low gasp as the rippling water touched the burning cuts. A low sob escaped her throat. Haunting, terrifying visions returned to play on her young mind, reviving horrendous tales of the torture and hardship inflicted upon Indians' captives. Fear of such treatment had been her mother's most stringent reason for protesting their migration West. And now Papa was dead and Mama was faced with the realization of her nightmare.

Faith bit down sharply on her lower lip to halt its trembling, and took a deep breath. She would do as the arrogant savage demanded, for in truth she had no choice. She would nurse her wounds, until Mama and she were both strong again, and then . . .

Lydia Durham sat motionlessly on the narrow log. She had no other choice. It took all of her strength to accomplish the rudimentary task of holding herself upright. A small laugh echoed somewhere in the back of her mind, amongst the whirling thoughts and fragmented pictures which deluged her. Her mind, as disoriented as those pictures, refused to function except to register the deadening ache in her temple and the numbness in her limbs which all but incapacitated her.

Her eyes moved around the small clearing, following the movements of the men preparing camp. It was twilight, would soon be dark. A small fire was blazing and one of the men was mixing flour or grain in a small pouch and forming it into small, flat cakes. Another was securing the horses, as a third, a much younger fellow, emerged from the trees with an angry step.

Lydia frowned, and a new throbbing began in her head. These men were strange to her sight. Their skins were a deep, rich hue, totally unlike the pale color of her own trembling hands. They wore little clothing, their slender, hairless bodies naked above the waist, and their hair was long, longer than hers would be if she indeed wore it hanging down as did they. But she preferred a different style of dressing her hair . . . did she not?

Raising a tentative hand to her temple, Lydia touched her aching head. Drawing her fingers away, she saw they were covered with a sticky substance, and a deep trembling began to shake her limbs. It was blood. She was bleeding. . . .

Abruptly, Lydia became aware of the multitude of pains assaulting her body, the burning pain in her feet. She looked down and gasped! Her feet were bare, lacerated and swollen! Suddenly aware of the stinging in her palms, she turned them upward. The soft, well-tended skin was torn and scratched, unrecognizable as her own. Her cheek was throbbing, and when she raised tentative fingers to press it gently, her hand snapped back in spontaneous reaction to the pain of contact. Something was wrong . . . terribly wrong!

Trembling wildly, Lydia turned to search the clearing for a familiar face. She did not know these people! Who were they? What were they doing here? Why was she with them? She was wounded . . . terribly hurt . . . and they were ignoring her and her pain! She needed someone to help her, someone to . . .

A step sounded beside her and Lydia turned responsively

26

toward it. A man resembling the others looked down at her in silence. But no, he was not like the others. He was taller, broader. His chest was massive, bearing the scars of many wounds. His arms were strong, bespeaking tremendous power. She remembered . . . remembered the strength in those arms. As she had ridden on horseback to this place, they had supported her, had held her protectively close.

She raised her eyes to meet the man's intense gaze. Yes, she remembered those eyes, too. They were the first she had seen when she had awakened from her frightening dream, a dream she could not quite remember. She allowed her eyes to move over the man's hard expressionless demeanor, noting that his face was strong, broad, sharply planed. In close proximity, she saw that the long hair fastened at the back of his neck with little strings and ties was streaked with gray. Yet he appeared to be a man in his prime. He studied her emotionlessly, and a flicker of apprehension moved across her mind.

But no, she did not need to fear this man. He was the one who had helped her . . . carried her on his horse. Yes, his was the chest which had supported her as she had swayed with weakness. It had been his hand which had reached up to lift her from the horse to the ground. He was looking at her, waiting for her to speak. She would ask him to help her.

Drawing herself slowly to her feet, making a supreme effort to overcome the pain and throbbing which began anew inside her head, Lydia turned to the silent stranger. Uncertain how much longer her trembling legs would support her, she reached out and touched the corded muscles on his forearm, offering him a tentative smile. The sound of her own voice rang strangely in her ears, hoarse and rasping as she spoke.

"I . . . I am unwell. I would appreciate it if you could help me. I . . . I would like to bathe my face." Her smile trembled. "My head is bleeding. I should like to rinse away the blood. . . ."

Her voice trailing away, Lydia found herself unable to break the hold of the big man's mesmerizing gaze. Dark, intense, it seemed to penetrate her jumbled mind, driving away the painful scraps of memory which taunted her. There was power in his eyes . . . and a strange, elusive peace.

The strong arm tensed under her fingertips, and Lydia felt a moment's trepidation. Silently shaking off her touch, the man grasped her arm, steadying her as her legs became less stable beneath her. Taking her arm firmly, he began to walk her rapidly into the foliage.

Out of the circle of light from the campfire, Lydia was suddenly unable to make out more than the man's massive shadow in the darkness. She was gasping as he dragged her onward at a fast pace. Weakness almost overwhelmed her when he stopped abruptly, and her eyes were scanning his dark shadow in an attempt to fathom the reason for his abrupt halt, when she heard the sound of water moving close-by. Turning, she saw a small stream glinting in the waning light, and she released a deep relieved breath. Taking the few steps to the stream's edge, she sank to her knees and reached down to touch the rapidly moving ripples. The water was cool, refreshing, and she cupped her hand to raise some to her lips. She swallowed and closed her eyes as the welcome moistness slipped down her throat.

Reaching into the pocket of her dress, she withdrew a dainty handkerchief and dipped it into the stream, then raised it to her temple and carefully sponged away the sticky wetness. It was growing darker, but she worked carefully, slowly. The big man stood silently behind her and she was glad. She knew she did not need to fear the darkness in his presence. He would protect her.

Black Wolf squinted across the fire, absentmindedly noting that Broken Hand had led the woman into the foliage ringing the camp. He frowned. He was confused by Broken Hand's consideration of the woman. The girl had not yet returned from the stream. He had given her enough time to attend to herself, and he had already decided he would go after her shortly if she did not return of her own accord.

Black Wolf's dark-eyed gaze moved along the edge of the clearing as he waited the girl's reappearance. He noted with a peculiar tensing of his stomach muscles that Spotted Elk's eyes followed the same course as his. Black Wolf's frown darkened. He was only too aware that Spotted Elk jealously coveted his captive.

Black Wolf gave a low snort. A warrior who had counted many coups, Spotted Elk had doubtless anticipated with enjoyment the reception he would have received had he entered the village with the girl as his captive. But Black Wolf gave no thought to his reception in the village or to the attention his captive would afford him. He cared even less for Spotted Elk's jealousy.

In truth, Black Wolf was not certain what demon had possessed him when he had seen the girl seeking to escape. He had known only that despite his hatred for those of her race, he could entertain neither the thought of her escape, nor the vision of her as Spotted Elk's captive.

An unrest deep inside nagged him viciously. It was the same unrest which had come strangely to life the moment his eyes had touched on the young, bright-haired captive. Even now her image hovered stubbornly in the depths of his mind . . . brilliant hair that glowed with an inborn fire, meeting the blazing sun with a color that rivaled its brilliance; eyes the color of the morning sky, alive with a spirit which would not be subdued.

His dark gaze flickered. He remembered the Arapaho's fury at the girl's well-aimed attack. The girl's arm had been strong, her aim true as she had hurled that rock at her captor, striking him in the chest. He remembered still the low whoosh which had escaped the Arapaho's lips as she had succeeded in robbing him of breath. Had Broken Hand not directed them out onto the trail at that time, he was certain the girl would not have escaped the Arapaho's vengeance.

His unexpected concern continued to plague him. What did he care if the girl, indeed, breathed her last? His hatred and distrust of all whites was deeply engrained. His eyes narrowing into slits, Black Wolf endured a revisitation of the memory of the horrendous deed which had brought his bitterness to full fruition only a few months before.

An unprotected camp of women and children, attacked by

soldiers while the men were away hunting. His mother had survived the attack for a few hours. Her words were still clear in his ears. . . .

. . . Gunshots, smoke, screams of dying anguish as soldiers raced between the lodges, setting them afire . . . escape from the flames only to face indiscriminate death at the hands of stone-faced soldiers . . . and then, in the choking, silent aftermath of destruction, words of praise heaped upon the dealers of death by the military commander who had claimed a job well done . . .

Black Wolf's mouth tightened into a straight, unrevealing line. He had found his mother wounded and left for dead amongst the dead. He remembered still the warmth of her blood as it had drained onto his flesh. He remembered the cries of the dying fading into stillness and death in the dark of night. Those voices echoed still in his mind. They gave him little peace.

All other members of his family had been killed by the white man's plague many years before. He had returned to Black Kettle's village with the other braves, to the lodge of his mother's sister, Walking Woman. A widow of many years, she had welcomed him. Many moons had passed, but he had not forgotten. Vengeance was his responsibility alone.

He had been kept from his vow to avenge the blood shed that night by Black Kettle's desire for peace, and the fact that his own youth kept him from a voice in the council. He was bound to the decisions of that council . . . for now.

Black Wolf frowned as a sound at the edge of the camp jerked him back to the present. The bright-haired girl stood hesitantly in the shadows, her pale face stiff with uncertainty. A surge of a heated emotion for which he had no name rose within him and Black Wolf observed her in silence. Her eyes darted to the spot where the woman had been sitting and panic touched her gaze. The light of the fire reflected in her great light eyes as they searched the shadows. Her slender frame began to shudder, and Black Wolf felt a new tension touch his sense. Shaken, she snapped her eyes back in his direction. Hesitating only momentarily, she walked toward him, her step uneven and pained.

Drawing himself to his feet as she neared, Black Wolf looked down into her face. The dirt of the trail had been washed from her skin. It was smooth, flawless, despite a surface tint caused by the sun and the bruise which marked one cheek. He felt a strong desire to touch that skin, to feel it under his fingertips.

His unexpected reaction brought a new surge of anger to his mind, and he stiffened.

"Mama . . . where is she? What happened to her?"

His eyes narrowing, Black Wolf responded to the girl's agitated question with a silence which raised a new flush on her thin cheeks. Incensed, the girl raised her voice a notch higher.

"Where is she? What have you done with her? Tell me! I want to know!"

The girl's small hands gripped his arm. No sign of fear was evident in her demeanor despite the threat of his silent presence as he towered over her meager form. Her slender fingers dug cuttingly into his arm.

"Tell me . . . tell me where she is!"

Abruptly realizing the girl had drawn the disapproving gazes of Spotted Elk and Tangle Hair in their direction, Black Wolf pulled away from the girl's tenacious grip. Taking a firm hold on her arm, he forced her into a seated position on the ground. His voice was low with warning.

"The woman is no longer of concern to you. Broken Hand attends to her."

"Broken Hand attends. . . ."

Her eyes widening as her voice trailed to a halt, the girl was suddenly on her feet. Grasping her arms as she attempted to brush past him, Black Wolf jerked her around to meet his vicious gaze. Forcibly restraining her, he grated harshly, "Think well before you act. Your life may be forfeit."

The girl held his gaze, a new resolution lighting briefly in her eyes before the stiffness left her slender frame. His eyes narrowing with suspicion, Black Wolf watched in silence as she lowered herself to a seated position on the ground.

She had not moved from that position when the sound of

movement in the foliage minutes later raised both their glances to the two figures who emerged into the clearing. Jumping unexpectedly to her feet, the girl called out sharply in a voice torn between pain and relief.

"Mama!"

Grasping her shoulder as the girl took a step in the woman's direction, Black Wolf felt her shock as the woman turned briefly in her direction, no sign of recognition on her pale, startled face. Stricken into a stunned silence, the girl stood motionless and incredulous as the woman turned away.

Black Wolf was acutely aware that this time there was no resistance when he urged the girl to assume a seated position and then took his place beside her.

The campfire popped and crackled, sending a shower of sparks into the heavy night air. Hardly noticing its brief display, Faith huddled in tense wakefulness as the steady breathing of sleep echoed in the silent camp. Shock and incredulity resounded within her mind. Mama . . . coming out of the foliage with the tall Indian, Broken Hand . . . She had called out to her, but Mama had made no response. Instead Mama had stared toward her confusedly, as if she had not recognized her and was uncertain what to make of her anxiety.

The young Indian, her keeper, had then taken control. She had been unable to approach Mama, unable to talk to her since.

Her gaze moving once more across the camp, Faith appraised her mother's sleeping form. Mama rested quietly, as if completely at ease, protected from the damp night air by the blanket Broken Hand had given her. Faith shuddered. Her keeper had not been so generous. Using the blanket to cover his own nakedness, he had left her to spend the night in shivering discomfort.

But Faith's anger at her captor's thoughtless cruelty was long since spent. Determined to use her wakefulness to full advantage, she sent a brief glance around the sleeping camp

32

before raising herself slowly to a seated position. It appeared now was the best time to make a soundless path to her mother's side. She would rouse Mama and talk to her. Mama had obviously been more shaken by her fall than she had realized, but she would explain to her that everything would be all right . . . that they would soon be free.

Resolution providing her with new strength, Faith pulled her shaking frame to her knees. She turned a last, assessing glance behind her toward the young Indian. He was asleep. Gradually, with utmost care, Faith pulled herself to a standing position. She had taken her first stealthy step forward when an arm snaked out to curve around her knees, pulling her roughly to the ground.

Struggling violently as the young Indian's firm, hard body pinned her tightly against the ground, as his broad hand clamped over her mouth, Faith heard his voice grate harshly into her ear.

"Fool! You cannot escape!"

Faith shook her head violently. He was the fool, not she! Did he really think she would attempt to escape, leaving her mother behind?

"Be still!"

This time the young Indian's voice was menacing. Reacting more to the threat in the dark eyes glaring into hers than the words he spoke, Faith was suddenly still. She reasoned that it would do no good to anger the young Indian any further. Her time would come.

The muscular chest pressing tightly against hers heaved with agitation, and Faith could feel the rapid pounding of the Indian's heart echoing the quickened beating of her own as he continued to confine her with the weight of his body. He lifted his hand slowly from her mouth, studying her silent subservience to his command with obvious suspicion. Satisfied at last that she had surrendered to his threat, he drew his body from hers and raised himself to a seated position. Not waiting for her reaction to her sudden freedom from his weight, the Indian pulled her back the few feet to the spot they had formerly occupied in the circle around the campfire.

He drew her unexpectedly close, and Faith was about to protest when his harsh rasping hiss shocked her into silence.

"If you value your life, be still."

His eyes sparking with menace, the young Indian drew her down beside him, holding her captive in his embrace as he reached for the blanket he had discarded minutes before. Carefully wrapping it around them both, he settled her against him. His warm breath against her ear sent a chill down her spine as he spoke.

"You cannot escape."

Adjusting her carefully in the circle of his imprisoning arms, the young Indian closed his eyes. Freed of the contact of his raking gaze, Faith released a deep, silent breath. There had been no mistaking the hatred burning in the young Indian's eyes. She knew it well, recognized its strength, for it clearly mirrored her own.

Night was on the wane when the girl's breathing finally slowed to the shallow breaths of sleep. Satisfied that he was at last free to study her without interruption, Black Wolf raised his head, his lips tightening as he looked down into her small, motionless face. The immaturity obvious in her sleeping features brought a frown to his brow. She was a child in years, but he had no doubt she would be a formidable enemy despite her youth. Her brave spirit glowed with the same fire that was reflected in the color of her hair. For all her tender years, she possessed more courage than the silent, weak woman whom Broken Hand guarded so closely. Black Wolf gave a low, unconscious snort. It was indeed difficult for him to believe that faint, shadow woman had borne this fire child.

The girl stirred in her sleep, grating out a muttered word of protest to an unseen enemy. Black Wolf's frown darkened at the anger that flitted momentarily across the girl's face before it faded into the oblivion of her dreams. His eyes trailed the fine line of her cheek, noting the thick, golden brown lashes which lay in full half-moons against her clear skin. Then his gaze drifted to the little tendrils of red-gold hair curled against her temples, swept to the gleaming swirls of the same lush mass which curled against his shoulder. Her tresses were smooth and warm against his skin.

He did not tire of studying her. His eyes followed the line of her straight, slender nose, the curve of her lips as they formed a whispered, unintelligible word. Succumbing to impulse, he touched the white skin of her cheek. It was soft, softer than he had thought possible.

But the girl's dreams were taking a painful course. Her smooth face moved suddenly into an expression of deep sorrow. Her lips trembled and a low tearful sob escaped them. She was shuddering in his arms. The fear which her pride had withheld from view was exposed in the vulnerability of sleep, and Black Wolf was strangely affected.

She was a child after all, lost from her people and afraid. Drawing her more closely into his arms, Black Wolf settled her against him. She was helpless and vulnerable in sleep, and she was a child. The hatred for her people which lived inside him had not yet driven him to prey on children. She was safe with him . . . for now.

Chapter IV

Faith raised her gaze toward the intense midday sun. Her eyes dropped momentarily closed against the glare as she swayed with the steady gait of the pony beneath her. She was tired . . . oh, so tired. Traveling since dawn with the silent Indian band, she had come to realize the effects of the enforced march Mama and she had endured the day before were with her still. Her head ached, her stiff muscles cried out in pain as she attempted to adjust her seat on the tireless animal. She glanced down. Her one consolation was that her cut and bruised feet appeared to be healing. She could only hope Mama fared as well.

Extremely conscious of the strong young chest supporting her back, Faith raised her arm to brush the beads of perspiration from her forehead. Fatigue had long since forced her to abandon her stubborn independence. She had finally acknowledged to herself her temporary need to rely on the strength of the young Indian who held her captive. She had determined that the sensation of his warm breath against her hair and the brush of his beardless chin against her temple were necessary parts of her temporary captivity. She had also determined that she would not be forced to bear it much longer.

Faith shot a hopeful glance toward the lead horse on which her mother rode in silence. Mama had not spoken a word to her since awakening—had, in fact, had eyes for no one but the savage who held her captive. She had not strayed from his side as they had eaten their meager morning meal. She had left him only to slip off into the foliage for a few short minutes. Faith's attempt to do the same so Mama and she might speak had been thwarted by the young Indian's quick, restraining hand.

A sudden instinct snapped Faith from her thoughts, turning her toward the Indian who rode his pony close beside them. His scrutinizing gaze added yet another fear to her overburdened mind, and she jerked her eyes from him with discomfort.

The tensing of the strong body which supported her raised Faith's apprehension. Lifting her eyes to the young Indian's face, she saw that he stared at a point just beyond the next rise. She followed the line of his gaze, her heart beginning to pound anew as an Indian village abruptly came into view.

Pitched in a broad bottom a short distance from a river, the village appeared to be peaceful and orderly. The lodges stood in a great circle, gleaming white in the brilliant sun, a large herd of horses grazing idly nearby. Women worked in silent industry around the fires as gray columns of smoke rose on the still air.

A call sounded, raising all heads to view their approach, and with startling suddenness the tenor of the tranquil picture changed. Figures scurrying between the scattered lodges increased the crowd which quickly gathered to witness their approach.

Broken Hand turned toward them, speaking a low guttural command. The young Indian tightened his imprisoning grip as he spurred his horse to a position second to the lead. Waiting only until he had taken the place behind him, Broken Hand urged his horse to a more rapid pace.

Her heart racing with fear, Faith shot a quick glance toward her mother. A thickness rose in her throat at the confusion in her mother's eyes, at the lack of recognition as she turned briefly in Faith's direction. A few Indian children separated from the crowd as they approached and began to run in their direction. Their hoots and shouts appeared to confuse Lydia Durham all the more and she shrunk back visibly against Broken Hand's chest.

The restrictive pressure around her waist tightened, became almost painful, and Faith snapped her gaze up toward her captor in protest. But the young Indian's eyes were fixed on Broken Hand, his expression stiff.

Broken Hand's strong features were soberly composed. A war chief of renown, he was accustomed to leading large numbers of men, but this war party had been different from the others since its inception.

The desire for revenge against the people who had killed his son in battle had raged hot and deep within him, not allowing him time to wait for the arrow-renewal ceremony which would have brought more men to his side. But he had been dedicated to his sense of purpose, and had prepared well for this venture, despite the small size of his party.

With the medicine man, he had taken his men to the sweat lodge. They had consecrated their weapons and offered prayers that neither bullet nor arrow might hinder them. The night before they had started out, he had made camp with his men. He had lit the pipe and offered it to the sky, the earth, and the four cardinal points. They had smoked, sung, and chanted a prayer. He had talked to Black Wolf, Spotted Elk, and Tangle Hair, had told them what he expected of them. He had not despaired because Spotted Elk's desire to add to his stature within the tribe overshadowed his true devotion to the cause of revenge, and he had not worried over Black Wolf's youth. Spotted Elk had gone to war many times, as had Tangle Hair. They had both proved their bravery. But of them all, Broken Hand had looked to Black Wolf to distinguish himself, for it was in Black Wolf that he saw a spirit which would one day make him a leader of his people.

When all had gone to sleep, he had sung to himself a song for help and wisdom. Afterward, he had lain down to rest, and it had been then that the dream vision had come to him. The vision filled his mind as clearly now as it had that night, and he rejoiced in the revisitation.

He had been seated in the shadowed mist of dreams. He had been singing no longer, but his song for guidance from the Great Power had echoed in his ears, filling the raised plane to which he had ascended. A woman had approached him out of the mists. She had been small and slender. The smooth line of her form, the manner in which she had moved lightly across the ground as she approached him, had set her apart from the women of his tribe. Her skin had been fair . . . white. Her hair, black and gleaming, had streamed unbound past her shoulders, and her eyes had been the color of the shadows from whence she had come. She had spoken to him in the white man's language, but her words had filled his heart.

She had spoken to him of Tall Ree. She had told him that he had not lost his son in vain. She had told him that his son had been the sacrifice which had prepared him for the place he was to fill in the destiny of his people. She had said she had come to him to help him fulfill that destiny. She had said she would teach him, and he would learn. She had said she would give to him that which he had never known, and he would give to her in return. She had held out her hand. He had taken it, and she had smiled. He remembered her touch, and he remembered her smile.

Broken Hand was abruptly drawn from the revisitation of his dream by the trembling of the woman who sat before him on his horse. He adjusted her more firmly against his body, and she reacted immediately to his touch, allowing his strength to support her as she leaned more fully against him. Broken Hand was suffused with a strange emotion for which he had no name. He knew only that he had recognized this woman the moment his eyes had touched upon her. His heart had cried out to her as she had stood shielded by the red-haired girl who called her mother.

His vision come to life, this woman had raised her gaze and his heart had joined with hers. He had known immediately that she had been the true reason his raging spirit had forced him from camp a few days before. He had known that destiny had brought him to the time and place of their meeting. He had also been certain it had been predestined that one of the horses he had captured would be used to gain her freedom from the Arapaho warrior,

White Eagle.

Broken Hand adjusted the woman more comfortably against him as a deep sense of peace swelled within him. The truth of his dream vision, the knowledge that this was truly the woman who had appeared to him, had been completely confirmed in his mind when the past had been stricken from her memory the moment he had taken her into his arms. She had emerged from the shadows fresh and new, looking to him and him alone. Trust and tranquillity were in her gaze, and he had felt her draw from within him a part of his soul which he had never touched before. She had given him peace, in the knowledge that Tall Ree had also fulfilled his destiny. He looked with joy to the total realization of his dream prophecy and all she would teach him.

The sound of hoofbeats to his rear brought Broken Hand back to a present uncertainty. The red-haired girl . . . She wished to approach Shadow Woman, to speak to her, to revive a memory of hatred for his people. Fire burned in the red-haired one's eyes as well as her hair. It was the same fire which had burned within his heart when Tall Ree had fallen. He did not wish to have it touch Shadow Woman. He wished Shadow Woman's gaze to remain pure when she looked to him, as pure as his gaze when he looked to her. Yet the girl was of Shadow Woman's flesh. He could not shed her blood.

Black Wolf rode close behind him, and Broken Hand's momentary anxiety calmed. He had called Black Wolf to that position. It was fitting. Black Wolf's pony had passed Spotted Elk's superior animal to take the girl. It was a sign, and he bowed to it. He also knew that Black Wolf's spirit was a match for the girl's. He need have no fear for the purity of Shadow Woman's regard while Black Wolf kept the girl under his care.

They were drawing close to the crowd which awaited them, and Broken Hand reined his horse to a slower pace. His powerful frame erect, Broken Hand assessed the tenor of those gathered. He clutched his captive instinctively close. The reception his people would give to the captives was uncertain, despite Black Kettle's bids for peace with the white man. But he was sure of one thing. Shadow Woman would not suffer in this village, not while he lived; and because of the tie of blood, the fiery-haired girl would also know his protection.

A familiar visage in the crowd drew Broken Hand's glance. Owl Woman observed him closely, her small eyes keen in her narrow face, but Broken Hand's expression remained impassive. Owl Woman, wife to him and mother of Tall Ree . . . Owl Woman's sorrow had turned her from all consolation, even his own. Broken Hand had honored her choice and had accepted a life filled with little else but revenge for the death of his son.

But all was changed now.

Broken Hand quickly glanced to the rear. Black Wolf awaited instructions as to the captive he carried. Broken Hand nodded in acknowledgment of the silent bond between him and this brave young warrior. It was strong, had become stronger still in the many moons since Tall Ree's death. Black Wolf, his family taken from him by the white man, and Broken Hand, his son a victim of the white man's deceit, shared a deep common sorrow which united them with wordless bond.

A silent gesture brought Black Wolf up behind him as they reached Broken Hand's lodge. Dismounting as his people gathered around him, Broken Hand lifted his captive from his mount. He instructed Black Wolf to do the same.

His dark eyes assessing, Broken Hand observed the girl's appealing glances toward Shadow Woman as Black Wolf stood her on her feet. The fear in the girl's eyes did not overshadow her hatred. She would allow Shadow Woman no rest in her desire to return to the white man's world. She would slowly force the peace from Shadow Woman's eyes, just as she would attempt to force Shadow Woman from his side. This he could not allow.

Broken Hand spoke to Black Wolf, his voice deep with command.

"You will find a lodge which will accept the girl as one of us. She will perform as a daughter of the lodge and will be taught in the ways of the Cheyenne. But she will have no contact with this woman until her heart is Cheyenne. I give

41

that word to you and hold you to its course."

Black Wolf was nodding his head in silent acceptance when an unexpected voice to his rear turned Broken Hand toward Spotted Elk.

"I will take the girl into my lodge. My wife will accept her . . . teach her."

His eyes narrowing as Black Wolf's young face tightened revealingly, Broken Hand observed the two warriors carefully. A new tension existed between them. Spotted Elk was proud. He had not accepted the fact that Black Wolf had outshone him in apprehending the girl. Or perhaps it was more than that. . . .

Black Wolf spoke evenly in response.

"No, I will take the girl to the lodge of Walking Woman."

Spotted Elk's face darkened. "Walking Woman is old, too old to teach the girl as Broken Hand instructs."

"The girl will go to Walking Woman."

Spotted Elk turned hotly to Broken Hand as he spoke. Reading the futility of argument in Broken Hand's firm gaze, Spotted Elk made no response, other than to turn sharply on his heel and lead his mount away.

Satisfied that the matter had been settled, Broken Hand dismissed the gathered crowd. He was drawing Shadow Woman to his lodge when Owl Woman appeared suddenly at his side.

Her small, black eyes tight and piercing, she faced Broken Hand stiffly.

"This woman is of the blood of the men who killed Tall Ree. I do not want her in my lodge."

"This woman will be Cheyenne."

"She will not."

Holding Owl Woman's gaze as firmly as he held the white woman's arm, Broken Hand spoke in a tone of finality.

"This woman will be Cheyenne, and she will be my second wife."

Brushing Owl Woman aside, Broken Hand drew the white woman into his lodge. He was intently aware of the long hesitation before Owl Woman entered behind them.

*　　*　　*

The young Indian's hand cut fiercely into her arm as he pushed her firmly in front of him, but Faith subdued her instinctive protest. Her heart pounding, she knew she had been the subject of the intense conversation which had been conducted in the short, halting tones of the Indian tongue a few minutes before. She had felt the young Indian's strong reaction to Broken Hand's words. She had also sensed his instinctive protest to the interjection of the Indian known as Spotted Elk.

Faith darted a quick look around her. Unfriendly eyes were everywhere, studying her, assessing her; and fear pushed her heartbeat to a new, escalated tempo. Swallowing against the dryness in her throat, she attempted a glance to her rear. Mama was being ushered into a lodge a short distance away. Broken Hand was following, the silent, bitter-looking Indian woman walking behind him. Instinctively, she sensed her mother faced a greater threat from the Indian woman than she did from Broken Hand.

Faith made a quick mental note of the location of the lodge into which her mother had disappeared. Somehow she would find her way there later and speak to Mama. She would tell her . . .

An unexpected jerk on her arm almost lifted Faith from her feet, and she turned sharply in the young Indian's direction. Pulling her so close to his side that the strong muscles of his thigh moved against hers, the young Indian forced her to a faster pace. His expression fierce, he directed a heated glance down into her eyes.

"Your thoughts of escape are useless. The shadow woman has been taken into Broken Hand's lodge. There she will remain. You will not look to her or talk to her. For you she is dead."

"Dead!" A hot rush of fury overwhelmed Faith's fear. "You mean dead like my father . . . killed by savages."

Black Wolf's gaze tightened. Without a response, he jerked her to an abrupt halt. A short, warning glance silenced her in the moment before he turned to the lodge before which they stood and called out in greeting. Within moments, the flap lifted to reveal a small, round-faced woman with graying hair. The spark that lit her tired eyes as

43

they touched on Black Wolf momentarily erased the years from her aging face. She spoke warmly in her native tongue before turning to regard Faith warily.

When he spoke, Black Wolf's face was sober, his words obviously chosen with care.

"Our party has returned in safety, Walking Woman. Your greeting warms my heart as your prayers have guided my way. At Broken Hand's instruction, I have brought you a new daughter to lighten the burden of your many years. She will share your lodge and you will instruct her in the ways of our people until her heart is one with the Cheyenne."

Faith gritted her teeth tightly shut against the spontaneous words which formed in her throat. These people were fools as well as savages! Teach her the ways of the Cheyenne . . . She had no desire to become like them—barbarians and murderers.

The aging Indian woman observed Faith's carefully withheld response. When she spoke her words were low and filled with caution.

"This young one bears no desire for guidance. And my heart is too filled with thoughts of the child who has been brought to me for care to overcome her resistance."

His handsome face immediately concerned, the young Indian pulled the flap back farther, his eyes touching on a boy of six or seven who lay in fevered silence within the lodge. His hand dropping from Faith's arm, Black Wolf moved immediately inside to touch the child's flushed face. The boy reacted weakly to Black Wolf's appearance and the warrior turned with a frown.

"Why was Young Hawk brought to you?"

"Young Hawk has been with me for three days, because his mother fears his sickness will overcome the child she now nourishes at her breast. She has asked me to look after him as I did for others, until he is well." Turning a quick, worried glance toward the boy, Walking Woman shook her head. "Three days . . . For three days White Bull has come to my lodge and sung. He has lit the fires of purification and filled my lodge with prayers to the Great Power, but still the boy sickens."

44

Realizing she had been all but forgotten in Black Wolf's concern for the boy, Faith stood hesitantly in the doorway of the lodge. Her eyes drifted to the boy's wasted frame, and she grimaced inwardly at the sound of his labored breathing and racking cough. She remembered vividly the sound of that same cough. Her mother had suffered and come close to dying with a similar ailment. Her father had brought in several doctors to tend to her, the last being Dr. Coulter who had ultimately cured her simply by filling her room with steam from boiling pots.

As the boy's breathing grew more ragged, Faith hardened her heart. If the boy died, it would be one less savage to shed the blood of innocent settlers.

Appearing suddenly to remember her presence, Black Wolf turned toward her. Walking quickly to her side, he pulled her into the lodge. His voice was low with concern as he spoke.

"You will not be welcomed to this lodge while Young Hawk sickens. You will remain silent and obey Walking Woman."

When silence met his harshly whispered instructions, Black Wolf grated tightly, "You will do well to heed my words."

Stifling her response, Faith abruptly sat on the ground. Heed his words . . . yes, she would heed them. And she would watch carefully for the moment she would be able to hurl them back in his face. Cheyenne . . . she would never be Cheyenne.

A sound of movement in the doorway turned Faith toward the ancient Indian who paused there. His graying hair hanging lankly against his narrow shoulders, his wrinkled face unrevealing, he appeared to study her intently with his small, birdlike eyes. Grunting something in his native tongue, he walked toward her. He reached down to touch her hair. Steeling herself against his touch, Faith faced the old man's unrelieved scrutiny as he extended his other hand to place his fingertips against her temple. After long moments the old man turned to address Black Wolf in low, guttural tones.

Jerking his eyes in her direction, Black Wolf frowned.

"White Bull says he has seen you before. He says your face came to him in the fire, the same fire which burns in your hair. He says the fire told him of your coming . . . that you have the power to cure Young Hawk. He asks that you release the spirits needed to cure the boy or the boy will die."

Startled, Faith turned toward the old man. A shudder moving down her spine at the intensity of his stare, she turned back to Black Wolf's scrutiny.

"I don't know anything about spirits, and I'm not a healer. The old man is mistaken."

Hesitating for long moments after Black Wolf's translation of her reply, White Bull finally turned away from her in silence. He walked toward the boy and sat on the ground beside him. Leaning forward, he took a live coal from the fire. He then reached into a small pouch at his side, withdrew some herbs, and sprinkled them liberally upon it. A pale smoke rose, immediately filling the lodge with a sharp fragrance. The old man held his hands over the smoke, washing them in the cleansing heat and fumes. Turning, he pressed his palms against the boy's chest as he prayed.

The boy's wracking cough continued. Reaching again into his pouch, White Bull withdrew a hide rattle. Drawing himself to his feet, he began to chant a low, droning song, pacing and shaking his rattle to its rhythm as he walked around the dwelling. At intervals, he stopped singing and spoke low words of prayer.

Watching his strange incantations with a frown, Faith was aware that Walking Woman followed the old man's movements, an expression of great hope in her small, dark eyes. Faith shot a short look in the boy's direction as his breathing became increasingly irregular. Hating herself for the pity which welled inside her, she assessed the beads of perspiration which covered the child's forehead and upper lip, his struggle for each breath. The boy's small face, surrounded by black, lifeless hair, was pale beneath the russet color of his skin, and he was thin to the point of emaciation. The child coughed again, his body jerking helplessly with the painful spasms.

Seated beside her, Black Wolf watched in silence as the old man sprinkled more herbs over the coal. The pungent fumes became stronger, and Faith's breath caught in her throat as White Bull again passed his hands through the smoke, palms held carefully upward. Pausing to rub his hands on the ground in fulfillment of his ritual, the old man placed his hands on the boy once more. But the boy continued to gasp for breath.

Unable to control her protest any longer, Faith muttered in a tone loud enough to be heard by the silent Black Wolf.

"The boy is choking. The old man is only making things worse."

Black Wolf's upper lip curled in suppressed anger.

"Young Hawk acted unwisely. He jumped across the spring at its source. The spirits within took offense and shot their arrows into his body. The arrows remain inside him, causing his sickness. Gifts have been made to the spirits, but they have not been accepted. White Bull attempts to withdraw those arrows so he may survive."

Faith frowned as the old man resumed his pacing and his song. She remembered well Dr. Coulter's whispered comment when Mama had been so sick the year before. He said Mama's lungs had been severely affected, that they could not take much more punishment. Even in her inexperience, she could see the boy suffered from a condition frighteningly similar to her mother's desperate illness. Whatever the reason for the boy's sickness, she was all but certain this method of healing would not help him to get well.

Unable to watch the boy's suffering any longer, Faith drew herself to her feet. Unexpectedly, a broad hand clamped around her ankle, staying her attempt to move. Faith's eyes jerked downward to met Black Wolf's intense, slitted gaze.

"I . . . I would like to go outside." Lifting her unfettered foot to expose the lacerations on the sole which had again begun to throb painfully, she offered in quiet explanation, "I would like to bathe my feet."

Slowly releasing her ankle, Black Wolf raised himself to stand beside her. Taking her by the arm, he ushered her outside. His steps rapid despite her obvious difficulty, he directed her down the incline toward the river's edge. Then, turning abruptly, he walked away.

Relief flooded Faith's senses. Seating herself carefully on the sandy bank near the shallows, she lowered her feet into the water, gasping as the cool liquid touched the ragged cuts. She closed her eyes against the sweep of the red-gold late afternoon sky and the growing shadows of evening beginning to darken the uneven terrain. The sounds of the coming night echoed in her ears. Behind her, she heard the chanting drone of the medicine man's prayers as he continued his attempt at healing, and she released a shaken breath.

Unexpectedly, her father's smiling, handsome face returned to mind, and Faith gasped in pain at the visitation. Just yesterday her beloved father had been killed by savages like these. She and Mama had been taken captive, beaten and abused, and refused the consolation of each other's company. The memory of her mother's dazed expression returned to haunt her, and Faith's despair increased. She was frighteningly uncertain as to the full extent of Mama's injuries, whether Mama would ever recognize her again as her own flesh and blood. And now, for a strange reason unknown to her, she was expected to live among these savages, to have sympathy for one of them who was ill? No. Never!

Refusing to submit to tears, Faith took a deep breath. These savages would overcome her resistance with neither threats, kindnesses, nor sympathetic appeals. To escape the pity which had swelled in her heart at the sight of the sick Indian child, she need merely remember her father's face the moment before he had fallen lifelessly to the ground.

Imploring that painful implement to firm her resolve, Faith took another deep breath. She would follow Black Wolf's instructions. She would make no attempt to contact

Mama, not for a while. She would allow Black Wolf to become confident of her obedience. She would observe him as he grew lax in his surveillance of her. She would prepare carefully, and when the time was right, she would make her move. Mama's mind would clear again once her head wound healed. She would speak to Mama then, and they would make plans. She would not live out her life a captive of the barbarians who had killed her father. She would not.

Her determination renewed, Faith reached down and gently washed her feet free of the gritty substances which had caused her pain. She hoped Mama had had the opportunity to do the same.

Faith covered her ears in an attempt to shut out the rasp of the boy's labored breathing, the harsh, wracking cough. Night had fallen over the camp, but sleep had not come within the lodge of Walking Woman. Reclining on the sleeping robe provided by her captor, Faith fought to subdue her increasing anxiety. The boy Young Hawk was surely dying. White Bull had left only a few moments before, his last ritual of healing knowing no further success than his previous efforts.

Her eyes moving to the bed on which the boy lay, Faith watched Walking Woman as she attempted to afford the boy comfort. The old woman turned unexpectedly in her direction, catching her eye. The pain in the old woman's expression resounded deep within her and Faith closed her eyes against it, only to be shaken abruptly from her attempted escape by a hard, unyielding hand.

Her eyes snapping open, Faith observed the fury in Black Wolf's gaze. A similar fury was reflected in his grating voice.

"Young Hawk dies. White Bull has read the fire. You possess the medicine to help him, but your heart is closed to Young Hawk's pain."

Unable to bear Black Wolf's accusation, Faith shook her head vigorously.

"I'm not a doctor! White Bull didn't see me in the fire. He

49

saw someone else."

"Young Hawk dies."

Another fit of coughing wracked the boy's frame, jerking Faith's head in his direction. Unrestrainable pity choked her throat. Surely the child was too ill to benefit from the simple procedure employed for Mama. . . .

Without conscious realization, Faith rose to her feet. Moving toward the boy, she reached out and touched his forehead. She swallowed tightly against the heat which burned her palm. No, she could not bear to watch this child suffer any longer. She had to do something . . . something. . . .

Turning back, Faith caught Black Wolf's intense stare. "The fire—we must build it up higher. We must get a pot of some kind, so that we may boil water, fill the air with heat and mist."

"White Bull has already taken Young Hawk to the sweat lodge. It was to no avail."

Walking Woman's quiet interjection turned Faith toward her in confusion.

"Sweat lodge?"

"The lodge where our people go to cleanse themselves, body and spirit, in vapor."

Not quite certain what to make of Black Wolf's response, Faith frowned. Vapor . . . certainly the same method employed by Dr. Coulter.

Even as she hesitated in confusion, Young Hawk's grating cough again splintered the silence. Faith took a short decisive breath.

"Then we must take him there again—now. He must be allowed to stay there until he is no longer coughing so painfully."

Faith held her breath as Black Wolf appeared to study her statement. She was intensely aware of the small flicker of suspicion in the depths of Black Wolf's eyes the moment before he issued Walking Woman a short command. Drawing herself to her feet in silence, Walking Woman immediately turned and slipped from the lodge. Black Wolf moved to Young Hawk's side. Whispering a soft, comforting phrase which turned the boy toward him with an attempted smile, Black Wolf wrapped Young Hawk in his blanket and lifted him into his arms.

Realizing she was expected to follow, Faith took up behind as Black Wolf walked from the lodge and turned onto the well-used trail to the river. A sharp turn brought them to a low structure, no more than three or four feet high, outside of which Walking Woman had already raised a fire. Gently placing the child on the ground, Black Wolf lifted the door flap and slipped inside. Turning, he drew the child in behind him, his quick glance clearly instructing that Faith follow.

Taking a firm hold on her trepidation, Faith slipped into the semidarkness. Her eyes scanned the primitive interior of the lodge as Black Wolf strove to situate Young Hawk more comfortably. She shook her head in confusion. The lodge was nothing more than a crude shell with a rectangular hole dug in the center of the floor. No attempt was being made to light a fire. She shook her head. How did they intend to induce the steam . . . ?

As if in answer to her thoughts, Walking Woman appeared at the opening of the lodge, in her hands two forked sticks on which she held a heated stone. Within moments several of the heated stones had been placed in the rectangular hole in the center of the lodge, and Black Wolf was brushing them with water from a small horn container. A fine mist rose immediately from the heated rocks, and Faith released a short breath. Well, they would soon know if Young Hawk would respond.

If he did not . . . ?

The first gray light of dawn marked the night sky as Walking Woman handed yet another heated stone through the low doorway of the sweat lodge. The heat and steam within the low structure was now intense. Perspiration soaked Faith's clothes, temporarily dying the silken strands of her hair a darker hue as they adhered wetly to her scalp. Glittering beads dotted her forehead and upper lip, clinging to her heavy dark lashes like a residue of tears. She brushed them away with an impatient hand as she turned once more to the young Indian boy.

She assessed him briefly, then met Black Wolf's gaze. His dark eyes registered a confirmation of her own thoughts. Yes, the child breathed easier. His coughing spells were less frequent, his slender body less plagued by the shuddering which had all but torn him apart. Young Hawk's eyes had dropped closed, and his chest was moving in slow, even breaths. He slept.

Exhaustion apparent on her countenance, Faith spoke softly.

"I think we can take the boy back now."

Black Wolf shook his head.

"No, first we must take him to the river so that he may be submerged."

"No!" Her objection instinctive, Faith shook her head. "No, the boy is too weak."

"It is the custom."

Her resistance firm, Faith shook her head. "Not this time. You can do whatever you want for yourself, but you must wrap the boy in his blanket and draw him back to the lodge first. Walking Woman and I can bathe him there, where the cool breezes will not affect him."

Watching as Black Wolf appeared to consider her words, Faith released a short, tense breath as he finally turned to wrap the boy in a blanket once more.

A few minutes later, Black Wolf stepped back after restoring Young Hawk to his sleeping bench in Walking Woman's lodge. Turning in silence, he disappeared through the doorway. Not allowing herself time for contemplation of the Indian's behavior, Faith worked steadily beside Walking Woman as they cleansed the boy's thin body with cool water.

Too tired to do more than collapse against her sleeping robe and close her eyes when the boy was finally resting quietly, Faith drifted off immediately into sleep. She did not hear Black Wolf's step as he slipped back into the lodge, fresh from the river in which he had bathed. She did not hear him walk to her side or feel his gentle hand stroke the flaming

52

tendrils from her brow. She did not awaken when he moved to lie beside her, and she started only briefly as his cool flesh touched against hers, as his arms reached out to draw her close. She did not see the glimmer that lit the depths of his dark eyes in the moment before he adjusted her within his embrace and closed his eyes to sleep.

Chapter V

Dawn was beginning to streak the dark night sky as Lydia moved restlessly on her sleeping bench. A fear, dark and shattering, would give her no rest. Her eyes darted across the small structure toward the woman who slept a short distance away. The woman's name was Owl Woman. Broken Hand had explained that they would soon move from Owl Woman's lodge to a lodge which he would share with her alone. Lydia frowned. Broken Hand's eyes had been filled with a warmth which had soothed the ragged fear inside her, but she was again uneasy.

Broken Hand called her Shadow Woman, but the name was unfamiliar to her . . . as unfamiliar as the life with which she was now faced and the people who surrounded her. She was uncertain, troubled. This world was strange to her . . . but she had no memory of a world other than this. Every attempt at recall caused a resurgence of the throbbing pain which blocked her memory. Reaching up, she touched the wound on her temple. She shuddered again. She was confused, frightened.

No longer able to face her fears, Lydia turned in her blanket, her delicate hand covering her eyes in an attempt to sleep. She could not still her shuddering, a shuddering which grew stronger until it threatened to shake her apart. She could not stop. . . .

Strong hands closed on her shoulders, and Lydia's eyes snapped open to see a dark, shadowed form crouching

54

beside her. The sheer breadth of the masculine shoulders, the carriage of the nobly shaped head were unmistakable, as unmistakable as the warmth of the strong body which moved to lie beside her. Strong arms enfolded her, and Lydia allowed herself to be drawn into a familiar circle of strength and consolation. She lay her head against the smooth, hairless chest and smiled as a now-familiar scent allowed peace to engulf her.

Broken Hand. She was safe once more.

Faith snapped suddenly awake, and her gaze touched on the rough hide shelter over her head. Momentarily disoriented, she turned to survey the interior of Walking Woman's lodge, her eyes coming to rest on the still figure of Young Hawk as he lay unmoving on his sleeping bench. An inexplicable fear rising in her throat, she scrambled to her feet and moved to the young boy's side, brushing past Walking Woman in her position of silent observance at the foot of the boy's sleeping blanket.

Young Hawk's eyes were closed, his body was still, and Faith stifled a sob. But his chest was rising and falling in barely discernible breaths, in sharp contrast to his labored breathing of the night before. Reaching out, Faith touched her hand lightly to the boy's forehead. The raging heat of fever had abated. The boy was improved.

Sitting back on her heels, Faith released a relieved breath. Young Hawk was resting. She was uncertain whether he had turned the curve toward recovery, but he was doubtless free of much of his former pain. In any case, she had done all she knew. The rest would be up to the old man and his songs of prayer.

Turning back toward her robes, Faith met Walking Woman's appreciative gaze. She hardened her heart against the old woman's gratitude. Momentarily uncertain as to what was expected of her, she glanced around the lodge. Black Wolf was nowhere to be seen. She had no desire to exceed the boundaries up set for her . . . not yet. If she were to judge from Walking Woman's expression, she had won a favorable position in this lodge with her actions of the night before. She would use it well when the time was right.

Unexpectedly, Faith's stomach gave a hungry growl. Out of the corner of her eye, Faith saw a smile touch Walking Woman's mouth. Taking a small cake baked in the ashes of the fire, Walking Woman offered it to her, and Faith accepted it eagerly. She could not remember when she had been so hungry.

Brushing the last crumbs from her hands a few minutes later, Faith looked to the doorway of the lodge. Drawing herself to her feet, she walked in its direction.

Emerging into the brisk morning air a few seconds later, Faith looked carefully around the camp. The position of the sun in the morning sky indicated it had risen only a short time before, but the camp was alive with activity. Cooking fires raised faint columns of smoke from the circle of lodges as women scurried back and forth to the river for water. A few men and boys returned from that same direction, their bodies gleaming wetly from their baths, while other boys galloped out from the camp toward the horses on the hillside. In the distance she saw an Indian boy, not much older than Young Hawk, driving a few horses toward camp. Several warriors awaited the horses' arrival and Faith frowned in contemplation of the planned activity which had roused them so early.

It was obvious to her that she had been allowed to sleep far later that day than the average Cheyenne woman, and she wondered at the unexpected generosity which had allowed her that comfort. Her eyes darting toward the lodge where she had last seen her mother, Faith felt the knot of anxiety tighten in her stomach. Gray smoke rose from the outlet in the center of the lodge, but aside from that, there was no sign of activity within. She dared not take a step in its direction. Her disobedience of Broken Hand's instructions would only negate any advances she had made.

As Faith surveyed the unfamiliar terrain, a figure emerged over the rise from the river. Squinting into the bright morning glare, she strained to make out the features of the

Indian as he approached. There was no mistaking the tall, slender outline. Black Wolf's broad expanse of shoulder, not yet filled out to its massive potential, was distinctive, as were his noble carriage and the smooth, almost animal-like grace of his soundless stride. He continued directly toward her, and Faith felt an inexplicable tightening in her stomach. It was akin to fear, but far more breathtaking. Her heart began an uneven pounding.

Black Wolf's even features were now clear to her eye, and she appraised him openly as he approached. She noted grudgingly that he was a handsome savage. His features were clear, fine; his profile strong. The planes of his smooth, beardless face were so pure that they would appear almost beautiful were it not for the intensity in his dark eyes which lent him the air of savagery so characteristic of his demeanor. Her eyes dropped to his bared, well-muscled chest, heaving from his recent exertion, to the long length of his well-formed body covered only by a breechcloth. An unexpected color tinged her cheeks. She remembered the strength of that chest supporting her, the pressure of his muscular thighs against the backs of her legs while they had ridden those long, exhausting miles.

When at last he stood at her side, Faith saw that the midnight black of Black Wolf's hair glistened wetly in the sun. She was suddenly conscious of her own disheveled state. Raising her eyes to his, Faith swallowed against the strange lump which had arisen in her throat. He appeared to observe the heat in her cheeks, and Faith's color deepened. His eyes were still moving over her face when she spoke hesitantly in an attempt to avert his intense perusal.

"I . . . I will return shortly." Not willing to further explain her need, Faith did not wait for his response. Turning sharply in the direction of the wooded area a short distance away, she reasoned that even a savage such as he would understand her need for privacy. Faith continued steadily forward until she slipped out of sight within the dense foliage. Only then did she turn back, her face flushing an even deeper hue as she realized Black Wolf had slipped into the lodge without a glance in her direction.

Humiliation suffused her face with a fresh flood of color. Yes, Black Wolf need not fear that she would try to escape . . . not yet. He knew only too well she would attempt nothing while Mama remained the prisoner of Broken Hand. Facing her thoughts of a few moments before, Faith raised her chin in silent defiance. Yes, Black Wolf was truly an impressive savage despite his youth. She gave a small, choked laugh. He would doubtless regard her lightly, believing her a frightened young girl who would succumb to Cheyenne ways out of fear, but she would never take him lightly. The eventual success of Mama's and her escape hinged on her realization that Black Wolf's youth was no barrier to the savage spirit which she had seen reflected in the dark mirror of his eyes. She would not forget it. It was the same savagery she had seen in the eyes of her father's murderers when they had turned their gazes toward her. That savagery was burned into her mind and would never be forgotten.

Turning abruptly, Faith made an attempt to dismiss her surging rage. Breathing deeply, she walked absent-mindedly into the wooded copse. Uncertain how deeply she had walked a few minutes later, she stopped short as a small, shaded pool met her eyes. Glancing around, she saw she was completely alone, and she marveled that such a tempting spot was not preferred to the sun-baked bank of the river.

Faith stepped to the pond's edge and glanced down into the still water. Unconsciously, she raised a hand to her hair. The thick, curling mass was heavy with the grime of her enforced march and the perspiration which had accompanied the long night's ordeal. Faith took a last cursory glance around the silent glade. Her hands moved to the buttons on the front of her dress, and within moments she was pulling it over her head and tossing it onto the moss-covered bank. Free of her clothing at last, she walked cautiously into the pool. Caution deserting her as the cool water reached her waist, Faith flung herself into its shimmering depths. The water closed over her head, and Faith raised herself gasping to the surface. Elation filled her, temporarily dispossessing her of care, and she struck out for the center of the pool.

The hot morning sun beat down unmercifully on Lydia's head. The heavy, deadening ache which dulled her senses was growing. A piercing pain stabbed her temple, weakening her knees. She glanced down at the dressed skins stretched out on the ground, and at the lodge poles assembled nearby. A sober-faced woman was already standing over them, cutting them and preparing them for sewing. Bundles of sinew thread lay on the ground, brought by the women who had gathered to raise the lodge for Broken Hand's new wife.

Lydia shot a quick glance in Owl Woman's direction. Hostility . . . she read it in the stiff-faced squaw's dark eyes, in the unsmiling expressions of the other women. Broken Hand had explained that it was not unusual for a man of his stature to take a second wife, but his explanation had not clarified the reason for the women's hostility. She did not want to be abandoned to them.

Her brief glance toward Broken Hand carried the full weight of her silent appeal. Her plea registered in the dark depths of his eyes as he stepped forward to take her by the arm. He led her to a spot a short distance from the women who conversed in low, muffled tones. The strength of his hand held her upright as he spoke softly.

"You need not fear, Shadow Woman. You have come out of the shadows to me, and I will keep you safe. Owl Woman does not want you in her lodge. It is fitting that a new lodge be erected for you, and in her anxiety to have you gone, Owl Woman has consented to raise it for you. The women come to help her and, in helping her, help you. You must be patient and endure their anger. It is temporary."

Realizing full well that Broken Hand sought to relieve her anxiety, Lydia reached out tentatively to touch his hand. Her growing unrest was tied to her memory of the red-haired girl who had traveled with them to this place. She had not seen the girl since their arrival. She wished to speak to her. Perhaps the girl could free those memories which inundated her mind in warring fragments. A dimple flickered tentatively in her soft cheek as she attempted a smile.

"Broken Hand, I'm uncertain and confused. I . . . I would like to talk to the girl. Perhaps she can help me."

His rough features hardening unexpectedly, Broken Hand shook Lydia's hand from his arm. He stepped back, his gaze suddenly cold.

"The girl is dead."

"Dead!"

Shaken, Lydia swayed, only to feel Broken Hand's hand grasp her arm more tightly than before. His expression held little sympathy for her plight.

"Dead only to you. You will not speak to her. She will do you harm."

"No . . . no, the girl will not harm. me. I saw her face. She—"

His hand abruptly tightening almost to the point of pain, Broken Hand grated from between tight lips, "You do not need the girl. I will bring you the peace you seek. Before the sun goes down this day, our lodge will be raised. I will comfort you in the darkness of the night, and your spirit will know rest. Your mind is free of the past, and so it will remain. The Great Power has divined that it should be so."

His strong features suddenly softening, Broken Hand raised his other hand to her cheek. His crooked fingers trailed across its smooth surface as he continued in a lower tone, "Last night you slept in my arms and all care slipped away. Tonight I will take you to wife. My body will join with yours and our union will be complete. That is the future for which you were destined. In that future you will be secure."

Lydia's heart began a ragged pounding. Something was wrong. . . . Broken Hand's words echoed in her ears, competing with a roaring sound which grew louder as she sought to expel the new anxiety his statement had evoked. Even as she looked into Broken Hand's face, her vision became clouded by shards of shattered pictures which pierced her mind with needles of pain. An unexpected darkness began to descend, choking out the light of morning. The pain in her head grew stronger. She was breathless against it. A lightless void moved to enclose her. It was drawing her in . . . drawing her in. . . .

Broken Hand's strong arms caught her close. His low entreaties faded from her hearing. Abruptly, all was dispelled as the soft wings of oblivion swept her away.

Nodding his head absent-mindedly to Wounded Eye's low narration, Black Wolf found his eyes straying back to the line of trees a short distance away. The girl had been gone too long. It had not been his desire to follow her when she had announced her desire for privacy, despite the nagging doubt which had clung to the back of his mind. He had not fooled himself that the girl had given up hope for escape. He knew only too well that the spirit which burned in the girl's eyes would not easily be subdued. An Arapaho warrior had killed her father, but her heart held tight to a hatred which knew no distinction between tribes.

The same could not be said for Shadow Woman. Her name declared the place to which she had dispatched all memories which caused her pain. She was Broken Hand's woman now.

Black Wolf darted a look toward the camp crier as he approached. As custom demanded, the old man rode slowly, calling out the news in a droning voice which the camp anticipated eagerly each day. He had already covered the southern part of the circle of lodges with his low recitation. Black Wolf listened with a furrowed brow.

Their chief, Black Kettle, had spoken. He had received a letter from William Bent, urging them to make peace with the whites. Black Kettle would hold a council with other chiefs and decide the course they would take.

Black Wolf gave a low snort of disapproval. The white man's Governor Evans had sent a proclamation, calling all Indians who wished peace to come to Fort Lyon where they would be watched by the troops. The governor had said in that way those peaceful Indians would not suffer for the depredations of their warrior brothers. Black Wolf shook his head. Black Kettle was too eager for peace. He believed the white man to be as honest as he. But many of the other war chiefs, including Broken Hand, knew the white man's traitorous heart. As for himself, Black Wolf knew the sting of the white man's serpent's tongue, and his heart cried out for vengeance.

But the crier's following words were not concerned with the progress of peace. His next announcement turned heads and brought women from their lodges in surpise. Owl Woman was raising a new lodge for Broken Hand. When it was done, Broken Hand would take the white woman captive as his wife.

Black Wolf suppressed his shock. A man of Broken Hand's stature within the village often took a second wife, but Broken Hand's open desire for this captive woman would cause a scandal which would set idle tongues wagging. Black Wolf's frown deepened. He had read Broken Hand's desire for the woman in his eyes from the first, had seen the change the woman had elicited within Broken Hand. And he had suspected Broken Hand would not allow the woman to be separate from him for long, but he had not anticipated that Broken Hand would openly take the woman to wife.

Black Wolf paused in his raging thoughts. He also had not anticipated that responsibility for the white girl would fall to him. He had been honored by the trust Broken Hand had placed in him, but he knew Broken Hand's decision would not be accepted freely by some. He expected he would suffer doubly from the honor Broken Hand had bestowed on him. He suspected Spotted Elk would not allow the matter to lie, and he was already certain there was far more to the young girl than first appearances would seem to allow. She would not easily submit to his authority.

Black Wolf grated his teeth tightly shut. The white man was his sworn enemy. Yet, the night before he had taken the sleeping red-haired girl into his arms and held her close as he had slept. He had yet to determine the reason for his own unexpected action. He knew only that a force inside him had drawn him to her side. Strangest of all was his realization that while the girl had slept peacefully in his arms, he had known peace as well.

A sound behind him turned Black Wolf in White Bull's direction in time to see White Bull emerge from Walking Woman's lodge and turn away. The old healer had arrived a short time before to find Young Hawk sleeping easily, his frail young body no longer straining for breath. White Bull had bowed to the power of the girl. He had named the girl Fire Spirit because her face had appeared to him in the fire, and because her hair bore the color of the flames which gave her power. White Bull had named her well.

But Fire Spirit had still not emerged from the stand of trees into which she had disappeared, and Black Wolf's unrest was growing. He had joined a casual gathering of young men in conversation so that he might be able to observe her approach unawares, but he had little interest in their conversation. Nodding to Wounded Eye's persistent questioning tone, Black Wolf turned with a frown in realization that the eyes of the group were full upon him.

Wounded Eye pressed him relentlessly.

"It is my thought that, like Broken Hand, your interest is deep in the captive you have brought to camp . . . a girl of the people who are your sworn enemy. Perhaps Broken Hand and Black Wolf will both forsake the warpath to follow at their white women's heels, as is the white man's custom."

Black Wolf's frown darkened, and a few snickers sounded within the group.

Wounded Eye persisted, his eyes tight on Black Wolf's face.

"Is that not so, Black Wolf?"

Disdaining to answer Wounded Eye's question, Black Wolf returned in a low voice, "I owe no man here a response, but I will tell you now that the girl has been turned over to my care by our war chief, Broken Hand. If there is one among you who would not respect Broken Hand's word or his judgment, I ask that he step forward so I might see him."

Black Wolf's eyes flicked over each man in the group, observing their silence. His parting glance speaking more eloquently than words, Black Wolf turned slowly and walked away. He was tired of this foolish taunting, and tired of the tension Fire Spirit had induced within him. He would go after her and find her, wherever she had gone. She would feel the weight of his censure, and she would not stray far from his sight again.

His handsome face still creased in a frown, Black Wolf approached the stand of trees which had held his attention for so long. He moved quietly into the foliage, instinct forcing a stealthy silence despite his growing annoyance. If the girl was hiding in an attempt to avoid him, he would take her by the hair which glowed with a fire of its own, and he would prove to her that while he was insensible to its pain, she was not. He would drag her back and he would assure that she would not attempt any measure of disobedience again.

The air within the shaded copse was cool against his skin. Uncertain in which direction to proceed, Black Wolf paused. A silence broken only by the buzz of insects and the trill of birds was soon tempered by another stirring . . . water lapping in a steady, even pattern. The tranquil sound drew him to its source, to the edge of the small pond his people had spurned for the sunlit banks of the river below. He stood in the shadows, his eyes searching for a sign of the girl. Widening circles ringed the smooth surface of the water and set Black Wolf's heart to racing. The girl—she had sunk below the surface, was perhaps at that moment fighting to survive.

Black Wolf's frantic step forward snapped to a halt as abruptly, the surface of the pond was broken. There was a short hesitation before one slender arm and then another rose from the water in rhythmic strokes to carry the pale shadow of a white form steadily toward the bank. Despite himself, Black Wolf remained silently concealed in the foliage, fascinated by the grace of the girl's movement as she reached the shallows and drew herself to her feet.

Black Wolf's breath escaped in a gasp as he viewed the purity of her slender beauty. Long hair, temporarily darkened a deeper hue, clung to her scalp, accenting her delicate features. He perused those features in silence, wondering at the fondness with which the Great Power had set them in her flawless face. Eyes blue as the summer sky glowed within the perfect setting, accented by a lush fringe of lashes darkened and curled by the water of the pool. Long spirals of hair hung past narrow, gracefully curved shoulders, down a straight, slender back. She turned to reach for the dress which lay on the bank, exposing the smooth, rounded curve of her buttocks, and no sooner had he caught his racing breath when she turned again to complete his unfettered view of her magnificence.

Black Wolf's eyes moved from the shining beauty of the girl's face, down the slender column of her throat. His gaze trailed the white breasts only beginning to bud with womanhood, the narrow rib cage and waist, and the flat, unmatured female hips. He swallowed against the emotion which tightened his throat. Fire Spirit was a girl on the brink of womanhood, too old to be called child, too young to be called woman. He remembered the warmth of her slenderness as he had held her against him in sleep. He had left her that morning before she had awakened, and he knew in her utter exhaustion, she had not realized his body had cradled hers throughout the night.

But a hatred for his people burned inside this beautiful child. It was a hatred similar to his own. He struggled to keep it foremost in his mind. He could not forget. . . .

The girl stiffened unexpectedly, snapping him from his thoughts. Her dress still in her hand, she tensely surveyed the foliage surrounding him.

The water had been cool against her skin, invigorating. Faith frowned. She had dallied too long, but the temptation had been too great to ignore. She had dived beneath the surface of the water, leaving her nagging fears behind her. The silent world where swaying plants danced on the cool currents and the small, gentle inhabitants of the placid pool brushed against her in tentative exploration had been the only escape she had been able to effect, and she had welcomed it.

But conscience had not allowed her further respite. Rising

to the surface, she had stroked to the bank, aware that her prolonged absence was severely testing the new acceptance she sensed within Walking Woman's lodge.

About to reach for her clothes, Faith frowned. Her body was clean, if still damp. She did not relish the thought of putting anything but freshly laundered undergarments against her skin. Submitting to impulse, Faith scooped her dress from the ground. She would take a few moments longer to launder at least a portion of her clothes. At least then she would . . .

A peculiar uneasiness interrupted Faith's trend of thought. The niggle of apprehension trailing up her spine caused her to dart a quick, assessing glance around the small clearing. She saw nothing, no one, but her discomfort was unappeased. Clutching her dress against her chest, she strained her eyes to penetrate the shadows of the foliage which surrounded her. Surely no one could . . .

Faith's searching gaze stopped abruptly, her heart beginning to pound erratically as her eyes touched on a familiar figure outlined against the shadows of the wooded glade. She gasped as the figure moved forward to approach her with a steady, unhesitant step.

Faith's angry protest was instinctive.

"What are you doing? Can't you see . . . ?" Suddenly at a loss for words, Faith clutched her dress more tightly against her. "I . . . I need to get dressed. I . . ."

Faith's words trailed off as Black Wolf continued his intense perusal. A surging heat moved to the cooled surface of her cheeks at the strangely unrecognizable emotion exhibited briefly in his eyes. The bold savage! He was enjoying his power over her!

When Black Wolf finally spoke, contempt edged his voice.

"You clutch the garment as if it were a shield. You need not hide your child's body from my gaze."

Angry humiliation loosened Faith's carefully guarded tongue. Her tone was scathing.

"I suppose nakedness is accepted by savages, but I tell you now that an invasion of privacy such as this is not accepted by my people. My people show more respect for their bodies.

66

They respect . . ."

Anger lit the depths of Black Wolf's eyes. Unconsciously relieved at the presence of that recognizable emotion, Faith held his gaze stiffly.

"Respect . . ." Black Wolf's lips twisted in a sneer. "You forget, I know the white man, and I know what he respects. He respects his people's ways, and those alone. He respects the food he eats, but not the animals who would give food and clothing to others. He kills them for the joy of killing and leaves them to rot in the sun. He respects the yellow ore he pulls from the land, but not the land itself. That he leaves barren, or filled with holes so it can no longer support those who would live upon it. He respects his gods and the ways in which his people speak to them, but he ridicules our gods and defiles our holy places. He respects his own given word, but does not hold fast to it when it is given to 'savages' such as we. Yes, I know the white man, and what he 'respects.'"

His chest heaving with agitation, Black Wolf raked her with his gaze as he continued in a low, grating voice.

"And your people respect women and children, but only if those women and children bear white skin. But you do not need to fear. Savage that I am, I do not make war on children. Nor do I abuse them unless they prove to be disobedient."

Faith pulled herself up stiffly against Black Wolf's verbal assault. "I do not accept your authority."

Black Wolf directed a menacing glance into her defiant expression.

"You will live in Walking Woman's lodge with me, and you will follow my commands. It is as Broken Hand wishes."

Stepping back, his chest heaving with a new agitation, Black Wolf ordered tightly, "Clothe yourself. The white skin you value so greatly is still valued for another reason by many in this village. Until you are more firmly accepted by my people, you will do well to follow Walking Woman's and my directions closely, and see that you do not stray. There are many who take the opportunity to prove that a white girl is not to be trusted. You will not be accepted easily as Cheyenne."

67

Faith could not restrain a sneer of her own.

"And if I do not choose to be Cheyenne?"

A deadly stillness dropped over Black Wolf's handsome features.

"You will be Cheyenne, or you will not 'be' at all."

Allowing her a moment to absorb the full weight of his warning, Black Wolf repeated his terse command.

"Clothe yourself."

Clamping her lips tightly shut, Faith lowered her dress to the ground. Unaware of the responsive tensing of Black Wolf's frame as her smooth white flesh was again exposed intimately to his gaze, Faith reached over and snatched up her undergarments. She drew them on with trembling hands, breathing a silent sigh of relief when her body was covered once more. Moments later she slipped her dress over her head.

Turning back even as she fastened the buttons on her bodice, Faith faced Black Wolf's stiff expression. She suppressed a shudder at the light that burned in his dark eyes, vowing to keep foremost in her mind the assessment of this young Indian she had made only a short time before. Savagery was deeply engrained in his heart. She would have to be extremely cautious so that she might reclaim Mama and escape.

Turning without a word, Black Wolf began walking back toward the village. Falling in behind, Faith walked in stiff silence. Caution and patience. She knew now that she must practice them . . . live them . . . if she wished to live at all.

Lydia stood beside the newly constructed lodge. It was large, reflecting Broken Hand's importance within the village. Owl Woman and the other women had worked steadily throughout the day, their glances turning time and again to touch her with open animosity.

She was uncertain exactly when she had succumbed to her uncertainty and pain earlier, but she had awakened in the lodge of Owl Woman. The first face she had seen had been Broken Hand's, and she had not truly realized that a man of such great size and noble bearing could be so tender.

She had emerged from the lodge a short time later, under Broken Hand's cautious eye, and had attempted to help in the sewing of the skins. But the other women had been impatient with her incompetence. Even had they not, she had found that each time she had leaned over to adjust a skin as they were being sewn together on the ground, a wearying light-headedness had assailed her. At Broken Hand's gruff command she had assumed a seat to observe the women at their work, and the animosity had grown.

She was observing in silence once more. The dedication ceremony . . . Strange . . . it was all so strange to her eyes.

Lydia turned toward the spectators engrossed in the ritual. Owl Woman stood in silence, banked by the women who had supported her. Lydia's gray eyes dropped closed, and she raised a hand to her throbbing head. Wrong . . . somehow this was wrong. . . .

Lydia turned unsteadily, desperately seeking a familiar face in the crowd of onlookers, but there were none. A brave Cheyenne warrior, Ridge Bear, had been honored at the ceremony. He was droning a recitation in his native tongue, commanding the attention of those around him. All except herself. Instead, a sense of panic was beginning to overwhelm her.

She turned away from the lodge, from the people surrounding it. She felt the need to escape, but she knew not where. To run . . . The world was quaking around her and her heart was pounding. The need grew stronger. She must run, quickly, from this place.

Her body trembling, Lydia had taken her first frantic step when a hand closed on her arm. Strong and firm, it stayed her, infusing her with its strength. She looked up.

In silence Broken Hand drew her back into the circle of intent listeners. But Lydia was not listening to Ridge Bear's words. She was aware only of the strength of the man who held her close at his side, the power that reached out to enclose her. Her heartbeat slowed, regaining its normalcy. Her trembling lessened until she was still, once more secure.

*   *   *

Faith reached out a tentative hand to touch Young Hawk's glistening forehead. It was cool to the touch. The boy's weak, responsive smile touched her heart, and she smiled in return. It was difficult to think of this child as an enemy, to believe that the savages who had murdered her father had once been children such as this.

Faith turned back to the fire. If the boy began to cough again, she would signal the resumption of the treatment of the night before. A flicker of amusement touched her mind. White Bull had returned earlier to again purify the lodge. His muttered instructions to Walking Woman had been translated by Black Wolf. White Bull had told Walking Woman to follow her instructions in treatment of the boy, saying that the boy was in Fire Spirit's hands.

Fire Spirit . . . She had been given a new name. Her protest had died on her lips. To demand the use of her Christian name was of little use. She would not be here long enough to make the effort worthwhile.

Faith lifted her head, her gaze drifting to the smoke outlet at the center of the lodge; it allowed a limited glimpse of the darkening sky overhead. The sun was setting. All was quiet in the camp, except for the droning recitation at the ceremony being conducted close-by. She had heard the camp crier earlier in the day and had inquired of Walking Woman why the man's words turned harsh glances toward her. The crier had been announcing the raising of a lodge. Broken Hand was to take a second wife. Shadow Woman . . . Mama.

Unable to endure her thoughts a moment longer, Faith turned and walked quickly toward the doorway. Within moments she was standing in the darkening twilight, her eyes moving toward the crowd which was just now dispersing from the newly raised lodge to the south of her. As Faith watched, her mother turned in her direction, but she did not see her. Mama's face was calm, her eyes solely for the man who stood at her side. The last of the women were moving away, and Broken Hand was urging her inside. Mama smiled . . . she smiled and disappeared from sight.

The pain inside her almost more than she could bear,

Faith choked back a sob. Papa's handsome face returned to her mind's eye and she sobbed again. Mama could not remember Papa, and she herself could not forget him.

Faith was still struggling to overcome the debilitating emotion which shook her, when she sensed a presence behind her. A broad palm touched her shoulder, attempting to draw her back, and Faith turned in rage to Black Wolf's scrutiny. Her voice was a low, venomous hiss.

"Don't touch me! You're savages, all of you! Mama and I will never be part of you! Never!"

Roughly brushing off Black Wolf's hand, Faith turned back into the lodge she had left only moments before. Without a glance toward Walking Woman's concerned expression, or to the child who turned weakly toward her, she threw herself onto her sleeping robe and closed her eyes. She would sleep . . . she would sleep long and deep, and when she awakened she would realize this had all been a terrible dream. A terrible dream . . .

Lydia stood in silence in the center of the lodge. She looked around its freshly swept interior, the furnishings put meticulously in place, the fire which burned in the center, illuminating the completed project. Owl Woman had labored long and hard to accomplish its completion, despite the hatred which had shone in her eyes each time she had glanced in Lydia's direction. She did not understand that hatred. Broken Hand had told her it should not be so.

Lydia's eyes moved to the lodge bed which rested against the far wall. She had watched the construction of the mattress . . . if that was what it was called. Willow rods, almost as thick as a man's forefinger, strung on long lines of sinew and covered with a mat of woven bulrush. And on top of that a sleeping robe and other soft skins. Owl Woman had made certain Broken Hand would be comfortable this night and any other he chose to spend in this lodge.

A small niggle of apprehension moved down Lydia's spine, setting her to trembling. Her eyes moved along the wall, searching for another similarly prepared spot. There was none. Where was she to sleep?

The sound of movement behind her turned Lydia to Broken Hand's sober expression. Looking down at her from his great height, his dark eyes assessed her trembling, the growing fear in her gaze. She saw a flicker of emotion cross his strong face and she attempted to still her quaking, but it was to no avail. Broken Hand moved closer. Their bodies almost touching, Faith could feel the heat generated by his massive form, smell the familiar, musky scent of his body, feel the rapid rise and fall of his chest as the spark of emotion in his eyes grew to flame.

She was trembling still as Broken Hand raised his hand to her cheek to trail his twisted fingers along its surface. The tense silence was shattered by his low, even tone.

"I touch you with my broken hand, Shadow Woman. The pain of the injury is long gone, but its memory is with me still. On the day that it was incurred, I was a child in the white man's fort. We were at peace with the white man, and my father had taken me there to trade. I was much enthused by the splendid uniforms of the soldiers, their marching, their glorious weapons. Camped outside the fort with my father's people, I found my curiosity was not yet appeased. I managed to sneak away from our camp and into the fort when all were asleep. I had remembered where I had seen the rifles of the soldiers, bright, shining weapons, and I wanted to hold one in my hands.

"I stole into the room in the darkness. A small lamp outside the door illuminated the storage area clearly enough so that I was able to take one of the guns from the wall. I was holding it with awe, smoothing its cool surface, when a soldier appeared in the doorway. I was frightened. I dropped the rifle at the soldier's command, but he did not care for my obedience. He raised his hand and knocked me to the ground. I was stunned, unable to move, and he came to tower over me. I remember his face well. It was filled with hatred, a hatred I have seen often since in the eyes of whites when they look to me. But I was a child and I was frightened. He smiled. He said I would never attempt to steal a rifle again; he would see to that. He picked up the rifle I had

72

dropped to the ground. Raising it, he crashed the hardwood butt into my hand again and again. The pain brought a scream to my lips, but I refused to release it. The soldier continued to strike me thus until I lost consciousness.

"When I awakened, I was lying outside the gates of the fort. In my pain, I crawled back to the side of my parents in silence. I knew I should not have left them, and I refused to tell them how I had received the wound.

"My hand was broken. The priest prayed over me, attempting to reduce my pain. He told me that I would not use my hand again unless the Great Power used his influence to make it so. That night I had a dream. A voice came to me from the shadows. It told me that I was facing the trial which would make me a man. If I overcame the pain, turned the newly borne hatred of the white man which raged inside me to strength, I would become a great warrior. I would no longer fear the white man. It would be he who feared me.

"I overcame my pain. I turned my hatred to strength, and my hand healed. I became a great warrior, as the dream prophesied."

Pausing, Broken Hand dropped his hand back to his side. His breathing ragged, he looked deeply into her eyes.

"I had another dream such as that, several nights ago. In it you came to me. Out of the shadows, you appeared, your face white and clear. Your eyes, the color of the mists from whence you had come, looked clearly into mine. You spoke to me of Tall Ree. You told me you had come to help me fulfill my destiny. You promised me you would teach me and I would learn. You told me you would give to me that which I had never known, and I would give to you in return."

Broken Hand paused, his strong features moved by the great emotion of his words as he drew her close.

"You have already fulfilled your promise. You have restored the life inside me which died with Tall Ree. You have filled me with the knowledge that destiny calls. It is an unknown destiny. It fills my heart. I wish to share it with you, Shadow Woman."

Broken Hand's broad palm moved to Lydia's breast. He stroked her gently, raising a swell of emotion inside her as he grated softly, "Now I wish to give to you. I am that which the Great Power has made me, and I offer it to you, Shadow Woman."

Broken Hand's gaze was unwavering. Stepping back, he leaned down and slowly stripped away his leggings and breechcloth to expose the full extent of his masculine splendor for the first time. Her heart pounding, Lydia stood unmoving as Broken Hand took her hand in his. He placed it against his cheek, curving her fingers so that she felt the grooves and lines fashioned by time on his impressive countenance. He trailed her fingertips across his mouth as he spoke.

"These are the lips which seek to taste your flesh, Shadow Woman, to give it homage." Trailing her hand down to place her palm against the surface of his broad chest, he continued raggedly, "Feel the strength I wish to give to you. It is borne of a heart which knows no fear in the presence of the enemy. Yet it is a heart which pounds at your nearness . . . at your touch. It is a heart which expands to take you in, Shadow Woman, to make you a part of it."

Holding firm to her hand despite its trembling, Broken Hand moved it slowly against his rib cage, then his flat, hard-muscled stomach. Without hesitation her hand curved over the full staff of his passion, and a flame flickered in the depths of his dark eyes as he continued in a gasping tone, "And this is the power I wish to give to you, Shadow Woman. It is the power to control my heart as well as the living force that moves within me. I give it to you as my wife and as my destiny."

Holding her mesmerized with his gaze, even as the warmth of his manhood pulsed against her, Broken Hand continued softly.

"And now I ask that you give to me in return." Taking her hand from him, Broken Hand raised it to the buttons on her bodice. Watching as her fingers appeared to work with a will of their own, he followed the opening of her bodice with his eyes, the smooth line of her shoulders as they were exposed to his gaze. His quick intake of breath broke the intimate silence of the lodge as her hands moved to slip her dress past

74

the soft curve of her hips, taking with it the last fragile wisps of cloth which shielded her flesh from his eyes.

The broad hands Broken Hand reached out to her were trembling, and a strangely wild emotion pulsed to life within Lydia. She accepted the warm heat of his body as his arms closed around her, was absorbed by his swift, eager strength as he swept her up into his arms. She allowed the soft litany of promises meant for her alone to sweep over her as he carried her to his sleeping bench. Feeling the softness of the fragrant mattress against her back, breathing in its sweet scent, she closed her eyes to the hungry lips which tasted her flesh, closed her arms around the strong back which curved over her in loving ministration. She murmured soft words of unintelligible response as he whispered her name again and again in her ear.

Shadow Woman . . . Shadow Woman . . . she was as he said, a woman with no past beyond the day she had opened her eyes to his. She was a woman born, come to life, from the shadows only to become a part of this man.

She felt the probing pressure of Broken Hand's manhood firm against her. Her heart began a ragged pounding, and she opened herself to him, welcomed him in. He filled her with his strength, with his eagerness; and an exultation came alive in her. His body moved demandingly against hers and she lifted herself to him. The moisture of his perspiration was damp against her skin, blending with her own, and she urged him onward, thrilling as he filled her totally, completely, with his burgeoning passion.

The first warning ripple shook Broken Hand's massive frame, and Lydia grasped him closer still. The rhythm of his movements became stronger, more rapid, and she felt a panic begin to assail her. She was gasping, quaking, floundering on a strange, unfamiliar plane of emotion.

Unexpectedly, Broken Hand's strong body jerked in great, shuddering spasms. He carried her with him on the wings of his passion, soaring gloriously for long moments in a spontaneous, irreversible burst of emotion, until she fell, careening into a great, spiraling void, to lie unmoving in the circle of his arms.

Her breathing was still labored as Broken Hand's deep voice registered in the confused depths of her mind.

"Shadow Woman . . . keeper of my destiny . . . you are mine."

Owl Woman looked to the woman who sat beside her. Unlike her own, Calf Woman's bowl was empty. The quickness with which Calf Woman had emptied that bowl, and the silent testimony of Calf Woman's broad, expanding girth precluded Owl Woman's question. Rising to her feet, Owl Woman took Calf Woman's empty bowl without comment and filled it again. Nodding absent-mindedly in response to Calf Woman's smile, she resumed her seat.

Owl Woman glanced toward Calf Woman once more, grimacing at the woman's gluttony as she eagerly consumed her food. Abruptly angry with herself, she made an effort to hide her annoyance. She supposed she should be grateful to Calf Woman. It had been Calf Woman who had so quickly organized the women to build Broken Hand's new lodge when Owl Woman had explained her need. And her need had been great. She had been unable to bear the thought of the white woman sleeping in her lodge—a woman of the same people who had killed Tall Ree.

Tall Ree . . . Owl Woman's small eyes narrowed with her silent pain. Her son had been a beautiful man. Tall and strong, handsome of face and friendly in manner, he had been both well liked and respected by all in the tribe. He had proved himself in battle, had counted many coups in his times against the enemy. Antelope Woman and he had been promised in marriage, and Owl Woman's thoughts had begun to turn with joy to thoughts of children from that joining, children to warm her arms and heart in the years to come. But the white man had killed Tall Ree, and all joy had ceased. Two summers had passed since that time, but pain and grief were with her still.

Owl Woman raised her hand to her hair and fingered the black braid just beginning to streak with gray. At Tall Ree's death, she had testified to her grief by cutting her hair short. Tall Ree's blood had been shed, and she had shed hers by cutting her face and legs and allowing the blood to run freely from the wounds. She had carried Tall Ree's war bonnet in procession around the camp while his horse, fully painted as for war, feathers in his tail and mane, had run loose near by. She had not washed away the blood which had streamed from her self-inflicted wounds, but had wailed at Tall Ree's grave, refusing to eat until Broken Hand had sent women to forcibly remove her. She had done all these things to honor Broken Hand and her son.

She remembered well Broken Hand's pain. His hair unbound, covering his wide expanse of shoulder, he had mourned his son as a brave man should, and he had avenged Tall Ree in battle. Both of them had honored the memory of Tall Ree, just as Broken Hand had honored the emptiness which had filled her, the emptiness which had kept them apart since their son's death.

But Broken Hand honored Tall Ree's memory no longer. He had awakened from a dream vision the night before he had left for his last encounter with the enemy. She had seen a strangeness in his eyes, but her questions had been met with silence. He had returned from that encounter with two captives and had brought the white woman into their lodge. He had told her the white woman had come to him from the shadows of his dream. Shadow Woman . . .

A sudden rage filling her mind, Owl Woman took her barely touched food and threw it into the fire. Calf Woman turned sharply in her direction, stared silently at her livid face for long moments before turning back to the fire with short, clucking sounds of disapproval. Owl Woman was shuddering, her small, thin body lost to her fury. She cared little for Calf Woman's disapproval. She cared only that Broken Hand had brought an enemy into her lodge, a woman of the people who had killed her son.

She had been outraged when Broken Hand had told her that he would take the white woman to wife. She had been the sole wife of Broken Hand for most of her life. He had needed no other woman. He had held himself celibate while he had respected her grief. She had not expected this last betrayal.

But Broken Hand had been adamant, and in her anger she had told him she would construct the lodge for him to use with his second wife. At that time she had had no doubt that separate quarters would be the perfect solution. She had been certain that Broken Hand would follow the usual custom of living with his first wife, with only occasional visits to the second. She had performed her wifely duties well. She had raised a splendid lodge for Broken Hand and the white woman. It was only now, after night had fallen, that she had begun to have her doubts.

Memory brought back to mind the expression of keen anticipation which had lit Broken Hand's noble face as he had ushered the white woman into her lodge. Owl Woman's stomach tightened with anxiety. She had experienced a strange sense of finality as the flap had fallen over the doorway of the new lodge. Why was it she had not realized that in shutting out the white woman, she would be shutting out Broken Hand as well?

Owl Woman searched her mind. Where had she gone wrong? She had only honored her son by indulging her grief. Broken Hand had done the same. She had gone over and over it in her mind without finding the answer she sought.

Owl Woman was pondering the burning question still when a seed of realization sprang to life in her mind. Pausing in her thoughts, she allowed it long moments to grow in frustration. The difference . . . the difference was that while Broken Hand had grieved, he had also put aside his grief to resume the course of his life. She had not. She had laid open the path for the white woman, her enemy, to make her way into Broken Hand's heart.

Slurping sounds echoed within the silent lodge, and Owl Woman snapped her head toward Calf Woman's greedy display. Now, instead of Broken Hand's noble presence, she need satisfy herself with the dubious pleasure of Calf Woman's company.

As if sensing Owl Woman's hostile thoughts, Calf Woman

drew herself unexpectedly to her feet. Her expression sober, she spoke, her words careful, grateful, and encouraging. Waiting only for Owl Woman's brief response, she turned and made a silent exit to return to her own lodge. Owl Woman gave a short, harsh laugh. Now she did not even have Calf Woman to distract her from her despair.

Raising herself to her feet, Owl Woman walked to the doorway and stepped outside. Her eyes moved to the newly constructed lodge a respectable distance from hers, and a flush of pure hatred surged to life inside her.

Shadow Woman . . .

The fire burned low inside the new lodge. She had no doubt Shadow Woman now lay in Broken Hand's arms. She remembered the strength of those arms, the wonder of the joinings Broken Hand and she had shared. Jealousy brought new life to the flames of hatred consuming her.

Owl Woman breathed deeply, striving to gain control of her raging spirit. On the honor of her son, she would make a vow. She would rid the camp of this white woman Broken Hand had taken to wife. She would see Shadow Woman gone—in any way she could. She cared not what means she would be forced to employ. And she would have Broken Hand back in her lodge once more. She would be his only wife.

Yes, she would fulfill her vow . . . no matter whose blood she need spill to achieve it.

Chapter VI

Captain William Potter raised his hand in a short, unconscious salute, his stride unbroken as he continued across the parade ground of Fort Lyon. The fort had been in turmoil ever since the arrival of the survivors from the wagon train, several days before. Their wagon master dead, the majority of the wagons either destroyed or disabled, the survivors still wandered aimlessly around the fort, in a shocked daze, searching for direction. Major Wynkoop had directed that the burials be accomplished quickly, with simple ceremony, due to the heat of summer and the lack of proper facilities to handle the number of casualties. Captain Potter suppressed a grimace. The silent graveyard close by the fort was all that remained of the great hopes and dreams of far too many of these good people.

Captain Potter took a deep breath and unconsciously squared the shoulders of his leanly muscled frame. A full year in this godless wilderness, and he still had not been able to accept the barbarity of the red-skinned savages who inhabited it. He resisted the urge to shake his head at the futility of it all. He had not been trained for this type of warfare. His days at the academy had taught him a far more noble way in which to conquer the enemy. It did not include attacking from ambush, mindless slaughter, and the taking of scalps. He was strangely out of place in the midst of these atrocities with which he was being faced.

Major Wynkoop, in command of the fort, continued to

work strongly for peace with the red man, and he was well aware that the honest, straightforward major was under heavy attack for his policies. The U.S. Army had been all too ineffective against these red men, and his own silent fear that in order to emerge victorious over them, it would be necessary to slip to their level of ruthless barbarism. He was a strong and fearless fighter, and had proved himself in many campaigns, but he knew with a deep inner certainty, he could never live with that solution. And he knew with that same certainty, that there were many men, both below his rank and above it, who could.

Captain Potter hastened his step, his fine-featured face set in a light frown. He was meticulous as always, the deep blue of his uniform without blemish, his boots shined to a mirrorlike glow. His recently trimmed, pale blond hair rested just above his collar, and except for his neat, light brown mustache, he was clean-shaven. He had steadfastly refused to allow his standards of personal grooming to lapse, even temporarily, no matter the circumstances with which he was presented. It was a method he unconsciously used to retain the thought that he had come to this land to advance civilization, not to allow its wildness to overwhelm him.

Stiffening with spontaneous concern, he approached the emergency hospital facilities set up in the building adjoining Dr. Holstan's quarters. He had just received a summons to the bedside of a survivor who had been unconscious since the raid. His haste was twofold. He had been all too ineffective in his post not to feel obliged to offer whatever aid was asked of him by these poor people, and it had been subtly intimated that the fellow might not last much longer.

Not bothering to knock, Captain Potter pushed open the door to the temporary facilities. His searching gaze moved between the cots which crammed the small room in search of Dr. Harvey Holstan. Finding the slumped, gray-haired figure he sought, he stepped immediately forward to make his way between the narrow rows. He touched the man's shirt-sleeved arm.

"Harvey, you sent for me?"

Harvey Holstan's bloodshot eyes rose to his. His

momentary disorientation was abruptly replaced by recollection as he nodded briefly.

"Oh, yes, I forgot." He released a weary sigh. "Martha Collins . . . the blond woman with the head wound . . . just passed away. There wasn't much I could do for her. Her skull was practically split in two. Someone said she was trying to save her husband when she was struck down, but the poor fellow was already dead. Young woman she was, William . . . not more than twenty-eight or twenty-nine. She left an infant behind. Captain Hemmings's wife, Sally, is taking care of the little thing. I guess the Hemmingses will be adding the child to their family. Doesn't look like Sally's got much choice but to do it now."

Captain Potter shook his fair head in silent acknowledgment of Dr. Holstan's words, and made a positive effort to harden his heart against the news of yet another death. Mrs. Collins was beyond his help now. But he had not been summoned to talk about her.

"Harvey, about the fellow who asked for me—"

"Oh, yes." Turning wearily, Harvey Holstan scanned the cots along the wall. "The second cot from the left . . . that fellow over there. I'd say you'd better hurry if you intend to talk to him."

Captain Potter turned quickly in the direction indicated. Within moments he was standing at the appointed bedside, his eyes moving over the injured man's still face. It was gray under the stubble of several days' growth of beard. The man appeared to be sleeping. The captain knew he dared not wait for the fellow to awaken. It was all too probable that he would not.

Taking a short breath, Captain Potter cleared his throat. The injured man's stubbly lashes fluttered against his pale cheek, and the captain took the opportunity to stir him even further.

"Sir . . . you asked to speak to me?"

The shaggy red head lightly peppered with gray moved against the pillow. The heavy lids lifted slowly. Pale blue eyes fought to focus on the captain's face. It was obvious that the injured man had been strong and fit, that he was in the prime of life. Pity and despair mingled within Potter as he pressed, "Mr. Durham, you asked for me?"

Wallace Durham stared toward him in silence. His gaze, finally focused, became suddenly intense.

"My . . . my wife . . . my daughter . . ."

Captain Potter removed his hat in a slow, diversionary move as he sought to find an easy way in which to deal the cruel blow. There was none.

"According to reports, they were taken captive by the Arapaho who raided the train; Mr. Durham. I've personally led two patrols in an attempt to find their trail, but neither I nor our scouts have been able to turn up anything."

Wallace Durham's breathing was becoming increasingly agitated, and Captain Potter swallowed hard against the man's obvious despair. He continued with an attempt at encouragement, "We haven't given up hope, Mr. Durham. The simple fact that your wife and daughter were taken instead of being struck down like so many of the others would seem to indicate that those particular savages had no intention of killing them. But whatever their intentions, they . . ."

Suddenly reaching up, the injured man grasped Captain Potter's arm tightly. He was struggling to speak and William paused, startled at the strength of the dying man's grip.

"You . . . must find them. Lydia . . . she isn't strong. Faith is a child."

His throat constricting at Wallace Durham's obvious anguish, William nodded. His hand closed over Durham's as it clutched his arm. His words were deep with sincerity.

"You may set your mind at rest, sir. Neither Major Wynkoop nor I will give up until your wife and daughter are located and returned. I give you my word."

But the pale eyes staring into his were glazing over, the frantic grip was loosening. Lowering Wallace Durham's hand back to the bed beside him, Captain Potter swallowed with considerable difficulty. A step at his side turned him toward Harvey Holstan the moment before the doctor leaned anxiously over the still figure. A short, cursory examination elicited from Dr. Holstan a low, incredulous snort.

"Just passed out, that's all. By all rights, this fella should've been dead two days ago. I've never seen a man survive a chest wound like that, especially after losing so much blood. Hell, he'd all but stopped bleeding when you brought him in here. The only thing that's keeping him alive is stubbornness. I'd say this here Wallace Durham is a hard man to come up against under normal conditions." Harvey Holstan gave a short, exhausted laugh. "Hell, he's so stubborn, he damned well just might make it."

Unable to share Harvey Holstan's dubious amusement, Captain Potter nodded.

"If he wakes up soon, just tell him I heard what he said, and I won't let him down."

The last trace of a smile left the aging practitioner's face. He shook his head.

"William, I wouldn't go making promises I might not be able to keep. This is a big country. Chances are them Indians have already—"

"Just tell him what I said, sir." At the doctor's raised brow, Captain Potter added in a more conciliatory tone, "If you please."

"Well, I don't know if *I please,* William, but I'll give the man the message, if he lives long enough to hear it."

Nodding, Captain William Potter turned toward the doorway. Replacing his hat squarely on his head, he strode forward. He was only a few, short steps away from the doctor's door when he spotted a familiar figure.

"Sergeant Lawson!"

The burly sergeant immediately snapped to.

"Sir."

"I want the men assembled for patrol in fifteen minutes."

"But, sir, we've just—"

"Fifteen minutes, Sergeant!"

"Yes, sir."

Hardly hearing his sergeant's response, Captain William Potter continued toward Major Wynkoop's office with new determination. If Harvey thought Wallace Durham was stubborn, he hadn't seen anything yet. Thus far in this savage land he had functioned according to orders, in the best manner of his military training. He had led his men well, nobly—and with total impotence. He was not going to see another failure on this damned barbaric frontier! He was going to find the Durham woman and child and bring them home. He was going to do it, damn it, or die trying!

Chapter VII

The sound of stirring within the lodge penetrated Faith's dreams and she turned restlessly, her eyes fluttering open to the new day. Her gaze moved to the short, matronly figure that worked beside the fire before it rose to view the sky visible through the smoke outlet in the top of the lodge. Cloudless, and an intense blue . . . It would be another clear, beautiful day spent in utter frustration.

Drawing herself to a seated position, Faith allowed her eyes to move around the lodge in thoughtless assessment. Young Hawk had regained his health and had moved back to the lodge of his family a week before. A spot of warmth stirred inside her. The boy had made no secret of his appreciation for her care during his sickness, nor had his grateful parents. Due to them, the hatred and suspicion which had followed her in the camp from the time of her arrival had lessened. Also due to them, she no longer walked the camp barefooted. Instead, she wore a pair of well-fashioned and beaded moccasins which were more comfortable than any footwear she had ever worn.

Faith grimaced at her realization of the direction her thoughts were taking. No, the warmth inspired by a child and appreciation for consideration received from a grateful mother would not make her forget. She would never be Cheyenne, no matter how forceful Black Wolf's insistence.

Faith's brow tightened into a frown. The departure of Young Hawk had given her more freedom both within the

86

camp and within the lodge. She had not appreciated sharing her sleeping bench with Black Wolf. She had argued inside her mind that a civilized man would have slept on the ground, allowing her the sleeping bench while the child used his. But Black Wolf had obviously not considered such a sacrifice for a moment. She remembered the first time she had awakened within the lodge with the warm strength of Black Wolf's body pressing against hers in sleep. She had been startled, had attempted to draw away, only to feel Black Wolf's arm tighten around her. Then his sharp command had halted her struggles, and she had eventually drifted back to sleep beside him.

Black Wolf and she had shared the same sleeping bench for the week of Young Hawk's recuperation, and if she were to be totally honest, she would have to admit she had begun to become accustomed to the sensation of Black Wolf's strong, young body steretched out against hers, to the warmth of his breath stirring her hair throughout the long hours of the night. It was a casual intimacy, but it was still a measure of intimacy of which she had wanted no part.

Faith's frown darkened. She remembered the first night after Young Hawk's departure. When the darkness of night had closed over the lodge, she had walked with open deliberation to the bench Young Hawk had recently vacated, and had lain down, turning her back to the fire. She remembered still the tension which had invaded her frame while she had pretended sleep. She had not needed to turn back to assess Black Wolf's reaction. She was all too attuned to the heat of his gaze not to feel its intensity as it had burned into her back. But she had eventually slipped off into sleep. In the time since, Black Wolf had voiced no objection to the new sleeping arrangements, and she had managed to all but dismiss her discomfort under his lingering glances when she retired to her sleeping bench at night.

Faith stirred again and stretched her cramped limbs. As was his custom, Black Wolf had risen early and left the lodge before she had opened her eyes to morning. She knew he followed the custom of all Cheyenne men in allowing a morning bath to start his day. She was only too familiar with the sight of males of all ages, some of an age barely able to walk, streaming from their lodges at the first light of dawn to make their way toward the river. The ritual was not shared by Cheyenne women. For that reason she had adhered strictly to her practice of visiting the sheltered pool in the wooded area nearby for a morning ritual of her own. As long as she did not abuse the time taken, Black Wolf silently accepted the practice, and she was inordinately grateful.

Faith pulled herself to a seated position on the side of her sleeping bench and acknowledged Walking Woman's morning greeting. Guilt flickered across her mind. Allowing her to sleep a little longer, Walking Woman had already dispensed with the "dead" drinking water of the night before and had returned from the river with "living" water to begin the morning meal. Quiet, industrious and generous, Walking Woman had done all in her power to welcome Fire Spirit to the lodge, and the girl had been unable to suppress her own responsive swell of affection in return for the aging woman's kindness.

Faith's eyes snapped to the doorway of the lodge. Through the opening she could see the first few stragglers coming back from the river. Black Wolf would be among them, but he would not return directly to the lodge. Instead, he would untie his horse from its post nearby and take it to the hill to graze. He would return with another, recently taken in a raid, and secure it there for easy access in the event of trouble. Walking Woman had explained that the procedure guaranteed a measure of safety in the event of a need for escape, and most of the men had adopted the practice.

A good portion of Black Wolf's day would be spent in hunting to provide food for Walking Woman and herself and for the widows and their children who depended on the generosity of those like him to survive. But Faith had seen the fire that burned in his eyes. Vengeance was the game Black Wolf sought, and she knew he was deeply opposed to Black Kettle's policy of peaceful negotiation.

Faith's fair brow knit in a frown. Many of Black Wolf's days of late had been spent in deep conference with Broken

Hand and other braves. She feared a new raid was being planned, and a new measure of frustration grew inside her. Her only consolation was the fact that only in the event of an extended absence on Black Wolf's and Broken Hand's part would she have the opportunity for which she had been waiting. But no, she was getting ahead of herself.

Drawing herself to her feet, Faith walked to the doorway of the lodge. She stepped outside and walked to a small rise a distance from the surrounding lodges, where she might enlarge her view of the camp. Her eyes moved directly to the lodge on which her anxious thoughts centered. Smoke was not yet streaming from the outlet in Broken Hand's lodge, as it did from the others in the village. Mama had obviously not awakened. Faith felt the pressure of tears close her throat and she swallowed against them. Three weeks . . . it had been more than three weeks since their arrival in camp, and she still had not been able to confront her mother, to even make an attempt to penetrate the shield of forgetfulness which her mother's mind obviously used to protect her from her grief.

A thought which had occurred to her more often of late reentered Faith's mind, unsettling her as she stared with determination toward Broken Hand's lodge. She had considered Mama's affliction, her inability to recognize her or remember the past, as a temporary disability. But . . . what if it was not? What if the blow to Mama's head had erased forever the memory of her former life . . . of herself . . . of Papa? She longed desperately to slide her arms around Mama's slenderness, to hear Mama's soft voice whisper a gentle reassurance that all would be well. She longed to, again, see the love in Mama's eyes, a love exhibited for her alone.

But there was no love for her visible in Mama's eyes now. There was not even recognition. Instead, Mama had eyes for no one but Broken Hand; and it was obvious, to the scandal of the whole camp, that Broken Hand had eyes for no woman but her. Although Broken Hand continued to support Owl Woman by bringing her the first proceeds from the hunt, he had not returned to Owl Woman's lodge. He had seen fit, instead, to spend each night in his new lodge with Mama. Faith had seen the women's resentment, and knew they gossiped about Broken Hand's absorption in his new bride. She had heard their low, whispered tones and had noticed their obvious deference to Owl Woman. She had also felt the weight of their disapproving glances when she had accompanied Walking Woman on the group-foraging treks for firewood and roots.

A familiar fury suffused her. Broken Hand was taking advantage of Mama's disability, the confusing mental sickness which had stolen her memory. She had no doubt it was intentional on his part, for she was certain only the orders of a war chief as powerful and respected as Broken Hand could have been so successful in keeping her and Mama apart. Faith did not fool herself. Despite the freedom within the camp she appeared to be afforded, she knew there was not a moment during the day when she was not closely observed. Each attempt to go to Mama, to speak to her, had been efficiently thwarted. On the one occasion when she had been able to speak a word to Mama while they had been in the field gathering roots, her heart had ached at the confusion exhibited in Mama's soft, gray eyes. But Black Wolf's quick intervention had brought that confrontation to a quick end. Her anger at Black Wolf's interference had been met with fear and confusion on Mama's part.

Black Wolf had been furious with Faith for her disobedience. Her punishment had been three days of confinement to the lodge, with her brief outings of necessity supervised by Black Wolf himself. But Faith had not allowed herself to become disheartened. She had determined during her days of confinement that she would not allow Black Wolf to intimidate her.

A week had passed since that incident, and Black Wolf's intense scrutiny was beginning to lessen. The thought that Deer Woman might have had something to do with the sudden relaxation of Black Wolf's vigilance stirred her to a strange discomfiture. Young and extremely cunning, Deer Woman had been able to effectively alert Black Wolf to her interest in him without abandoning the shy posture of the well-behaved Cheyenne maiden. Faith had been witness to the assessing glances Black Wolf had sent Deer Woman in return.

The heat of an unnamed emotion joined Faith's anger, flushing her face revealingly. Deer Woman's resolve had accomplished another feat as well. The noble, young Black Wolf, not so obsessed by the affairs of the Indian nation as he would have her think, had actually *smiled* at Deer Woman's flirting, covert glances! Faith had refused to admit to her own intense reaction to the power of Black Wolf's smile. Finally drawn lips parting over straight, white teeth she had formerly only seen bared in a warning hiss . . . The effect had been astounding, a complete transformation of Black Wolf's savage mien into one of stunningly warm appeal.

Faith gave a low snort. Fine. It would suit her fine if Black Wolf took Deer Woman to wife. Black Wolf would move to a new lodge with Deer Woman, and she would be allowed to stay in this lodge with Walking Woman, spared Black Wolf's incessant surveillance. Ignoring the strange tightening in her stomach that possibility induced, Faith lifted her chin with determination. Yes, then she would have greater opportunity. . . .

"You waste your anxious glances toward Broken Hand's lodge. You will not change what has come to pass, what Broken Hand has decreed."

Faith's attention snapped behind her to meet Black Wolf's gaze. She had not heard his silent approach, and she fought to control her anger at his attempted reading of her mind. Did she have no privacy from this persistent savage?

Refusing to allow him satisfaction, Faith responded with a slight shrug of her shoulder.

"I don't know what you're talking about."

"Untruth settles uneasily upon you. It shows in the color which flows into your face."

Coloring all the more darkly as Black Wolf called attention to her momentary flush, Faith allowed annoyance to sharpen her tongue.

"It's anger, not untruth that you see. And if you were a

gentleman, you'd have the good sense not to mention the color in my face."

Black Wolf's well-shaped lips pulled into a sneer.

"I do not aspire to be a 'gentleman.' I aspire to be only what I am—a warrior of my people."

This time it was Faith's turn to sneer.

"Dedicated to war and killing! My people don't consider killing a virtue to be admired."

"It is my thought that you do not truly know what is esteemed in the adult world of your people. In your world, 'gentlemen' receive medals for the slaughter of women and children . . . as long as those women and children are not of his race."

"That's not true! Our soldiers don't—"

"Do not speak to me of truth!" His handsome face darkening, Black Wolf took Faith roughly by the shoulders. "You speak as a child, not as one who knows the world. But I speak with the tongue of a man who has seen much. I have seen women and children who have fallen under the guns and knives of your soldiers. I have felt the blood of my mother draining onto my flesh as she lay dying from an attack by your soldiers on an unprotected camp. I saw her grow weaker, felt the life slowly slip from her body, heard the deep rattle within her throat as she released her last breath. But before she died, she told me of the man who had ordered the slaughter of the camp—Major Downing of the United States Army. She heard him praise his men. She heard his laughter and ridicule of the 'savages' who would breathe no more.

"It mattered little to Major Downing that the camp had been asleep when he had attacked, or that the 'savages' had been unprotected women and children whose men were away on the hunt. This man was a 'gentleman' in your sense of the word. He received the praise of your people for his great victory over those who were helpless against them." Black Wolf gave a low, bitter laugh. "I have no desire to achieve his status."

Steeling herself against the pain of Black Wolf's steely grip on her shoulders, Faith scoffed in disbelief.

"You lie! Our soldiers don't kill women and children."

Black Wolf's low laugh in response was as cutting as his words.

"You are a fool, as well as a child."

Releasing her unexpectedly, Black Wolf stepped back to view her with open contempt.

"Go to the pool and bathe. Perhaps then you will cleanse your mind as well, and make it free of the childish illusions which makes you slave to a world which exists only in your mind. It has made you blind to the kindness you have received here, and made you a fool. You should be glad that Shadow Woman does not share your debility. Instead, she has found happiness and contentment in Broken Hand's lodge. She is a young woman. She will bear him a son—"

"No . . . no!" Staggering backward as if she had been struck a blow, Faith shook her head in violent negation of Black Wolf's words. "Mama is sick. She doesn't know—"

"Shadow Woman is wife to Broken Hand."

"Broken Hand has another wife! He doesn't need Mama! I will *never* accept—"

"Then you will never again know Shadow Woman's company. The choice is yours."

Black Wolf waited until the weight of his words had registered fully on Faith's pale face before speaking again in terse command.

"Go to the pool and bathe. I wish to speak no more."

Turning blindly to follow his command, Faith staggered toward the familiar stand of trees and the trail worn by her daily ritual. She released a slow, silent breath as the coolness of foliage closed around her. Realizing she was no longer visible to Black Wolf's eye, she stopped short in an attempt to gain control of her rioting emotions.

No! She would not abandon Mama to the strange sickness which had stolen her mind! Suddenly shuddering, Faith closed her eyes against the thought of Mama's humiliation when she once again became herself and became aware of the life she had lived in this village. For a short moment, Faith was almost uncertain if it would, indeed, be better if Mama was never restored to reality. But, no. Mama's mind was hiding from her sorrow and grief. Her memory would one day return. It was up to her to make sure it would be soon—very soon—before it was too late.

Filled with a new determination, Faith took a deep breath and squared her slender shoulders. Today . . . she would talk to Mama today. She would make certain that within the week they would make their plans. Mama and she would leave the village . . . escape . . . and they would put their short time here behind them, strike it and all those with whom they had come into contact from their minds. They would go back East and start again. Yes, they would leave all this behind them forever.

Having arrived at the edge of the pool without consciously realizing it, Faith stared down onto its shiny, mirrored surface for long, silent moments before she began to undress.

Bold features, roughly hewn on a sharply chiseled face . . . skin like fine, old leather, creased with the deep grooves and lines of time and maturity, beautiful lines . . . black eyes which had seen much, wisdom and sadness clearly reflected within them . . . full lips which need not speak for the dark eloquence of those eyes . . . It was a powerful face filled with character and nobility.

Lydia raised her hand to Broken Hand's face, tracing those noble lines on which her eyes dwelled. Her fingers moved with easy familiarity along the path they had followed many times. She was fascinated by Broken Hand. She could not remember her life previous to this time, but she was certain she had never before met a man like him.

Her fingers trailed along the firm outline of Broken Hand's lips and they separated. She felt the warm flick of his tongue against their surface and she smiled. She was comfortable wrapped in this big man's arms, his naked flesh intimately close to hers. She enjoyed the scent of his body, the thrill of his touch. She enjoyed feeling the muscular wall of his chest against her breasts, his hard rib cage cushioning her more delicate softness as he pulled her closer, his flat stomach pressed flush to hers as the hardening rise of his manhood probed the warm nest he sought.

Turning in a quick, efficient maneuver, Broken Hand slipped atop her, pressing her firmly against the softness of their sleeping robes. She opened herself to him and he slid himself inside her. His low gasp reverberated in the silence of the lodge and she slid her arms around his naked back. As he lifted himself to begin a slow, subtle movement, his taut muscles rippled smoothly under her hands. He held himself above her, his long, black hair unbound, streaming over his shoulders in a wildly virile display. He was studying her, and she wished she knew what he saw. He moved again inside her and her heart set to racing. A smile curved his lips as Broken Hand lowered his head to whisper against her mouth.

"Shadow Woman, my body finds but a temporary peace within yours. Even as it comes to rest in your softness, it seeks to taste your full wonder once more. But I am not alone in my unrest. I have read the deep shadows in your eyes. A light glows in their endless m ists, a light that summons me. I must answer that summons, Shadow Woman, for it is the echo of a voice I hear inside myself, an echo of my own need for you."

Broken Hand withdrew for a moment, only to plunge deep and true within her once more. A wealth of emotions flashed clearly in the dark mirrors of his eyes just before they closed. When he looked at her again his eyes were filled with wonder.

"See . . . see how your body speaks to mine, Shadow Woman. Feel how it answers my call. Most truly we are one in this world of our lodge, when our bodies meet in joining."

Not waiting for a response he knew she could not give, Broken Hand again dove deep and sure within her. Her low gasp raising him to a quaking level of emotion he could not restrain, he plunged again and again, the rhythm of his lovemaking accelerating, growing stronger, more demanding. Within minutes he had lifted her high onto a plane of brilliant ecstasy. He held her there, soaring with him, glorying as she grasped him tight to share his exhilarating, shuddering descent from the world they alone had created.

He was lying atop her, his massive body pinning her

breathless, against their sleeping bench, but Lydia welcomed the loving pressure of his weight. In the time since she had come to Broken Hand, she had known many times of indecision and fear, many hours of insecurity. The hostile eyes which followed her still had the power to shake her, for she knew not the cause for their scrutiny. The silent appeal in the red-haired girl's gaze stirred another, nameless emotion inside her, a tension which brought a fierce, pounding ache to her temples.

Broken Hand had ordered her to hold herself aloof from the girl and from all who did not look at her with warmth. She had obeyed his command because it was only when Broken Hand's eyes touched on her that her unknown fears subsided; it was only when Broken Hand's arms were around her that she felt secure; and it was only when Broken Hand was buried deep inside her that she felt totally whole.

Lifting himself from her at last, Broken Hand looked down into her eyes, appearing to read her glance. He withdrew from her with reluctance and slid to the sleeping bench beside her. Obviously unwilling to separate fully from her, he pulled her flush against him as he whispered against the throbbing pulse in her temple.

"Were these other times, Shadow Woman, I would take you far from here, away from the people of my village. I would take you to a place where we might stay alone under the sun and moon, indulging our desires for each other at will, until each touch, each glance, no longer had the power to shake all other thought from our minds but the joining of our flesh. But we are not free to do this. Instead, I must force my mind to thoughts of other things, matters which stir other passions inside my breast."

Broken Hand released her so that he might take her hand. Grasping it tightly, he drew it close to her face so that she might clearly view their hands tightly entwined. He noted the manner in which she considered the contrast of his russet skin against the light coloring of her own hand.

"Yes, it is thus as your pale body is joined to mine, Shadow Woman. But in that joining has come the fulfillment of the vision which brought me hope when there was nothing but despair in my heart. Such are the feelings you inspire within me; such is the life you have returned to me."

Unable to speak past the emotion which filled her throat, Lydia reached up with her free hand to draw Broken Hand's face to hers. Slowly, she placed her mouth against his, brushing, tasting, fondling the uncompromising curve of his lips until they moved in response. Accepting the full wonder of her kiss, Broken Hand joined in her passionate assault, the fires of desire so recently sated, stirring visibly once more.

An unexpected sound of passing footsteps outside their lodge drew Broken Hand back from Lydia's tender response to his words. A quick glance upward toward the small patch of sky visible through the roof brought a frown to his brow. He looked back to regard her silence, a small smile finally turning up the corners of his lips.

"The day intrudes upon us once more, Shadow Woman. We are not free to indulge ourselves as we would prefer, but must conform to the schedules of those around us. Already the women of the camp have lit their fires and begun to prepare the morning meal. The men go to bathe and attend to their daily duties. But we lie together in a world which we seek to keep to ourselves. Such was not meant to be, Shadow Woman. Despite my desire, I must arise and face the new day."

Releasing her with obvious reluctance, Broken Hand drew himself to his feet. He remained staring down at her pale naked splendor for silent moments before extending a hand to help her rise. Her head barely reaching the height of his broad shoulder, Lydia looked up to the supreme tenderness exhibited in Broken Hand's dark eyes.

"Dress now, Shadow Woman. I would be spared the temptation which makes me reluctant to leave you. And you must stir the fire so that we may stave off the gossip which even now abounds, of the brave war chief who allows the world to pass by in order to remain a few minutes more in the arms of his woman."

The light flush that rose to Lydia's face brought a smile to Broken Hand's lips. Leaning over, he slipped into his breechcloth and took his leggings in hand. When he turned back he offered softly, "Come, woman. If you will quickly cover your nakedness, we may approach the river together as you go to get the living water with which to do your daily chores, and I go about my manly affairs."

Lydia did not need to consider Broken Hand's suggestion. Yes, she would prefer to face the first hostilities of the new day at his side. Moving quickly she slipped her dress over her shoulders and hastily buttoned the bodice. Not stopping to bind the dark, shining length of her hair, Lydia fell into step behind him as he walked to the doorway. At Broken Hand's side, she emerged into the world once more.

Black Wolf's gaze followed the flaming color of Faith's hair until it faded into the cover of trees. Her slender form was no longer visible, but her image remained fixed in his mind. Still intent on the fringe of foliage into which she had disappeared, he frowned. Hers was an image he had been unable to escape of late, and he was uncomfortable with his confused feelings.

Unconsciously, as he had many times in the past month, Black Wolf passed a moment in anger at the cruel trick the fates had played upon him. Allowing him a temporary honor in outdistancing Spotted Elk's pony to catch the fleeing Fire Spirit, the fates had also awarded him responsibility for the fiery vixen. It had been a dubious honor indeed. Had it not been for that same interference of fate, Fire Spirit would doubtless be living in Spotted Elk's lodge right now. A perverse agitation stirred Black Wolf further at the thought.

Spotted Elk's interest in the girl had been obvious from the first, and his interest had not waned. Black Wolf felt a familiar tensing in the pit of his stomach. Despite the fact that she was little more than a child, Spotted Elk's gaze followed Fire Spirit without relief. He had seen Spotted Elk approach the girl several times. Each time the girl's responses to his words had been short to the point of being curt, and Black Wolf had experienced a strange satisfaction. But he had not been at rest because of the flashes of anger her curtness had elicited in Spotted Elk's eyes. He knew he could not relax his vigilance if he hoped to spare Fire Spirit the brunt of Spotted Elk's wounded pride.

But somehow he knew it was not only wounded pride which provoked Spotted Elk's interest in the girl. The silent brave's eyes carried a heat far too intense. The annoying knots in Black Wolf's stomach tightened.

Unbidden, he recalled Faith's slenderness pressed against the hard wall of his body as they had lain together on his sleeping bench. The smoothness of her pale skin, its distinctively sweet scent, haunted him. He remembered the texture of her hair as it had curled around his fingers with a life of its own. The color of fire, the silken strands had been cool to the touch, but they burned him still in memory. Allowing him little respite from his feelings, he recalled the warm brush of her breath against his skin as she had lain so close to him; the manner in which she had curved her child's body to his in sleep. He remembered the warm, conflicting emotions which had assaulted him as he had pulled her closer still.

He had known little rest from those memories since she had boldly abandoned his sleeping bench to assume Young Hawk's vacated sleeping robes. In the long, wakeful hours of night as he had lain alone, staring at her sleeping form, it had taken the most severe control to restrain himself from moving to her side, from taking her back to lie beside him as he so desired. Acknowledging her to be the child that she was, and respecting her obvious innocence, he still felt the call of her warmth, and he was at a loss for a way to combat it.

But Fire Spirit was an assault on his emotions in other ways as well. Anger and frustration had soared to new heights within him in dealing with the spirited girl. He had also experienced an unexpected sympathy upon noting the sadness in her eyes as she had watched Shadow Woman from afar. He had determinedly kept them apart, realizing full well that Broken Hand would suffer no interference in the life Shadow Woman had accepted so freely. But he was intensely aware that he was motivated more by a desire to spare Fire Spirit Broken Hand's wrath than he was by the desire to follow Broken Hand's command.

The admission of his growing vulnerability where the girl was concerned shocked him. He had considered his hatred for the people of her race all-consuming. There was no room inside him for the protective, proprietary feelings she inspired. They confused him, interfered with the drive for revenge which had formerly filled his mind. Surely, it would have been better if Spotted Elk had been the one to assume responsibility for the girl. Had that been the case, he would now be free to . . .

His thoughts coming to an abrupt half as Spotted Elk appeared at the edge of the clearing, Black Wolf's eyes moved to the foliage into which Faith had disappeared a short time before. Had he needed proof as to the futility of his raging thoughts, one glance at Spotted Elk's surveillance of the wooded copse was sufficient. His chest beginning to heave in silent agitation, Black Wolf felt a new tension invade his stiff frame. He would not suffer Spotted Elk's attentions to Fire Spirit. He knew with a deep certainty that he was not beyond using physical force should Spotted Elk attempt to follow her, no matter how great Spotted Elk's stature was within the tribe. No man . . . *no man* would touch Fire Spirit while she was under his protection, and no eyes but his would touch on her naked beauty. He would not al—

The sudden clatter of hoofbeats to his rear snapped Black Wolf around in time to see the approach of a pony as it attempted to make its way past him into the hills. A quick glance revealed a slight figure running in pursuit, and he reached instinctively for the line which hung loosely from the animal's neck. The animal resisted his interference only mildly before submitting to restraint, and Black Wolf turned to the soft voice which sounded behind him.

"Many thanks, Black Wolf. In my carelessness, I allowed my father's horse to escape. You have saved me from suffering White Horse's wrath. For this I thank you."

Her delicate face creased in a smile, Deer Woman regarded Black Wolf warmly. Her large, dark eyes traveled his features with bold admiration as she accepted the line he relinquished. She held the animal with a firm hand that lent little credence to her statement that the docile animal had escaped her, and Black Wolf felt disbelief touch his mind. Despite her fragile appearance, Deer Woman was as determined as she was pleasing to the eye. Conflicting emotions assailed him. Several young men of the tribe had begun to pay her court, but Deer Woman had favored none of them. Instead she openly smiled upon him. He was warmed by her favor, despite his lack of desire to act upon it.

Black Wolf's response was short and unsmiling.

"Perhaps it would be best if you allowed another to tie the horse so it will not again escape you so easily. You might not be so fortunate the next time it breaks free."

Deer Woman smiled coyly at his sober statement.

"Perhaps that would be a good idea. I would not like to impose upon you again should this persistent animal escape his tether, although I admit I am happy that his errant ways have brought us together to talk. I do enjoy talking with you, Black Wolf." Pausing briefly after her bold statement, Deer Woman offered in a softer tone, "Singing Woman and I will be walking by the river before the sun sets. We would enjoy the company of a strong young man to protect us from possible threat in the shadows."

A reluctant smile flicked across Black Wolf's lips at the girl's blatant invitation. He had no doubt this one would make some brave a good wife. But he was not presently looking for a wife. Other things pressed too firmly for his attention.

A quick glance back toward the fringe of trees in the distance furrowed his brow in a frown. Fire Spirit had emerged from the foliage. Spotted Elk was standing at her side, speaking with obvious intensity. Spotted Elk's attention was full on her face, not allowing him awareness of the growing anger in Black Wolf's scrutiny.

"Silent Woman is with child and Spotted Elk wishes to take the white girl into his lodge so she might help with Silent Woman's womanly duties." Her dark eyes noting the heat in Black Wolf's gaze, Deer Woman continued boldly, "It would be fitting for you to allow her to do so. Walking Woman does not instruct the girl properly in the ways of the

Cheyenne, but spoils her shamefully. The fire-haired one will never make a good Cheyenne wife."

Having little patience for Deer Woman's unwanted interference in his affairs, Black Wolf snapped his response in an open display of short temper.

"I care not if the girl makes a good Cheyenne wife. I care only that Broken Hand's orders are followed in her regard. Broken Hand has given her to Walking Woman, and that is where she will stay."

Immediately repentant when discomfort touched Deer Woman's sensitive young face, Black Wolf said in a softer tone, "But perhaps Walking Woman has been too easy on her. I shall have to instruct Fire Spirit to observe the conduct of our women more closely, so that she may improve herself."

Deer Woman's smile returned for she obviously chose to consider Black Wolf's words an indirect compliment to herself. Her invitation more direct than before, she offered softly, "Singing Woman and I will welcome your company tonight, Black Wolf."

Deer Woman then jerked on the docile pony's lead with a firm hand. Drawing him with her, she walked back toward the village.

Dismissing Deer Woman from his mind the moment she was out of his sight, Black Wolf turned back toward the fringe of trees. Faith's intense, blue-eyed gaze met his, but he paid it little mind as he diverted his perusal to the man who stood boldly at her side. Agitation welled inside him. He started toward them in a rapid step, only to be brought to a halt as Faith spoke a short word to Spotted Elk and started back in his direction.

Fire Spirit's step drew her abreast of him, but she appeared to be ready to pass him without comment. Black Wolf's anger flared.

"You have been neglectful of your duties, Fire Spirit. Walking Woman works at the morning meal in our lodge, while you waste time in idle conversation."

A hard smile lifted Faith's lips as she met his gaze unblinkingly.

"Yes, I suppose it's only the men of the village who are allowed time for 'idle conversation.' You needn't waste time watching me, Black Wolf. Instead, you can concentrate on entertaining Deer Woman." Faith's smile became more brittle. "She's very pretty, isn't she? She would make a very good wife for a brave like you."

The heat of Black Wolf's anger increased.

"I need no advice from you. Your boldness is typical of your race. Rather, you would do well to devote your time to learning the quiet, obedient, and retiring ways of Cheyenne women."

"Quiet, obedient, and retiring . . . like Deer Woman?"

Shooting him a scornful glance, Faith did not allow him time for a response. Turning on her heel, she walked rigidly back toward the lodge.

Black Wolf's gaze was still trained on Faith's stiff retreating figure when he felt the inexplicable urge to laugh. He could not understand the reason. He was not truly amused.

Spotted Elk watched the red-haired girl as she walked stiffly toward Walking Woman's lodge. A furious heat burned deep inside, all but consuming him. He pulled himself to his full, slender height and lifted his chin with determination. He was a respected warrior who had counted many coups. He was well built and well groomed, and he was aware that the women of the village considered his even features of extraordinary appeal. He had many horses, a lodge with many poles. Silent Woman, his wife of five years, was with child, but his lodge was large enough to accommodate more than three within it.

Silent Woman had well earned her name. She was a good wife, subservient to his needs and wants. She would not speak out even if she did not desire the fire-haired girl to come into their lodge . . . and he had determined that the girl would.

She was young. He doubted if her slender body had yet made the passage from childhood to womanhood, but the challenge in her peculiarly light eyes showed a maturity far beyond her meager years. He chose to accept that challenge, and it was to his endless dismay that he was not free to do so. A familiar fire coming to life inside him, Spotted Elk fought to suppress his frustration. A momentary hesitation had allowed Black Wolf the edge needed to reach the girl ahead of him that first day. It was a hesitation for which he had suffered ever since.

Burning jealousy had come alive inside him as Black Wolf had held the girl seated before him on his horse during their return to camp. It had soared to new heights when Black Wolf had taken the girl under his blanket the first night they had camped on the trail. Each time he had seen her since, Spotted Elk had felt the growing weight of his desire for the girl. She was still a child, and it mattered little to him that she wanted no part of him. She was ignorant of the ways of the Cheyenne. Were she under his guidance, she would not disobey *his* commands. The heavy weight of his hand would instruct her well, and she would come to value his approval, to seek it out. And when she came of age, he would take her to wife. Until that time, he would keep her close, near him at all times.

Yes, his desire for the red-haired girl was full and deep inside him. It filled his mind, taking precedence over matters pertinent to his status within the tribe. He need convince Broken Hand that the girl should be turned over to him. Broken Hand's infatuation with his new wife was well known. It would aid Spotted Elk in his plan. He had but to be patient. The girl would provide him the opportunity he sought. The girl would be his, for only her fire could quench the internal heat which scorched him. Yes, she would soon be his.

The tranquil morning air was beginning to absorb the heat of day as Owl Woman stood outside her lodge in silence. She had little interest in the steady passage of people as they moved around the circle of lodges seeing to their morning chores, or in their friendly greetings. She had waited with growing impatience for Broken Hand's departure with the hunting party. Now that he had finally disappeared over the hill, her interest lay in the small party of women in the distance who were fast moving in the opposite direction. Quickly, she turned back to her lodge to emerge moments later with the ropes needed for the tying of the wood. Her call to the lodges close-by brought several women to their doors, and she forced a smile of invitation. Waiting with limited forbearance until they joined her, she issued a short summons to Shadow Woman.

Shadow Woman appeared obediently in the doorway to the lodge she and Broken Hand had shared for the past moon, and Owl Woman fought to suppress her burning hatred. But no, it would not do to reveal herself now. Broken Hand would not stand for mistreatment of his new wife, and she did not wish to be cast aside in disgrace. Instead, it was her lot to teach Shadow Woman the skills of a good Cheyenne wife. Her hatred burned hotter. But she would not be able to teach Shadow Woman if Shadow Woman was no longer willing to learn.

Motioning Shadow Woman to join the party, Owl Woman started off in the same direction in which the previous group of women had disappeared. Yes, it was time. It would be many hours before Broken Hand and the other men returned from the hunt, and by that time she would have achieved her purpose. Yes, by then she would have taken the first step in her plan.

The merry, laughing group of women and young girls gathered sticks lying on the ground and broke off low-lying branches to fling them into a growing pile of firewood. Faith had participated in the morning foraging parties many times, and she was relieved that Walking Woman had chosen a group which accepted her presence without protest. Hatred of whites still flourished within the camp. She had been witness to the protests against Black Kettle's peaceful policies, and she was distinctly uncomfortable when the subject of heated stares.

A burst of laughter sounded above her and Faith lifted her

eyes to Little Deer's smiling face. Perched on the limb of a tall tree, the child was enjoying herself tremendously as she reached out to snap off a dead branch and throw it to her mother below. Leaf Woman called out a short warning for her daughter's safety, which was met with another burst of laughter. An amused smile turned up the corners of Faith's lips as Leaf Woman voiced her concern sharply once more.

Faith's smile was erased by the inevitable direction of her rambling thoughts. Mama no longer evidenced that loving concern—not for her. Now it was she who was burdened by her concern for Mama's confused state of mind. Unbidden, the memory of Black Wolf's dark expression as he had described his own mother's death came to mind. A tremor of uncertainty shook her. Could it have been true what he had said? Could soldiers actually have been ordered to slaughter a camp of women and children such as these with whom she was now working? Could they actually have been praised and decorated for such a horrendous deed? She had no doubt that Black Wolf had been telling the truth when he had described the ghastly manner in which he had witnessed his mother's death. But to think that it was deliberate . . .

Uncomfortable with her thoughts, Faith moved into the surrounding bushes in an attempt to locate wood which might have been overlooked. They had been gathering firewood for a short time, but the ground was almost picked clean. The supply was becoming exhausted, and they had been forced to walk out farther and farther each time to find an adequate amount. If they remained camped in this location much longer, it would be difficult to collect enough.

The sound of voices to her rear turned Faith toward another group of women approaching from the village. They were obviously out on the same mission. Surely they realized they would have to . . .

Her mind freezing as she spotted Owl Woman leading the second group, Faith flicked her gaze quickly over those trailing into view behind her. Her heart began a rapid pounding as she saw Mama walking with them in silence.

Instinctively, Faith returned to Walking Woman's side and resumed her foraging. There was the possibility that Owl

Woman would allow her party to join theirs; they might progress farther afield as a larger group. Should Walking Woman suspect that she was entertaining any thoughts of attempting to speak to Mama, Walking Woman would immediately insist that they return to camp.

As Faith watched covertly, Owl Woman turned to speak to the women behind her. The women immediately disbursed through the bushes and began to gather wood, and Faith let out a tense breath. Sensing Walking Woman's scrutiny, she devoted herself to the chore before her. Patience . . . she need have a little more patience. . . .

Suffering from her own anxiety and the slow passage of time, Faith painstakingly worked her way in a cautious circle. Having arrived at the point she sought, she lifted her head and darted a slitted gaze to the women who worked around her. Laughing, involved in a casual game, they paid her scant attention, and she released a short, relieved breath. In a slow, discreet movement, she slipped behind a wall of foliage and immediately crouched down so she might peer back through the swaying leaves.

Mama . . . Mama . . . Was Mama not aware how carefully she had worked her way around the women and into a position close to her? Was Mama totally unaware that she was trying to speak to her? Even if Mama truly viewed her as a stranger due to her bewildered state of mind, surely she experienced some curiosity about her. Surely she would . . . But no, Mama was not even attempting to approach the thicket behind which she was hiding.

Taking a deep, shaky breath, Faith stepped out from behind the foliage. Cautiously, her heart pounding loudly in her ears, she worked her way to her mother's side.

"Mama . . ."

Lydia's head snapped sharply in Faith's direction. Confused apprehension apparent in her gaze, she took a short, spontaneous step backward.

"No. I . . . I don't know you. I'm not your mother. I'm not anyone's mother. I am wife to Broken Hand."

"Please, I only want to talk to you."

"I cannot speak to you. Broken Hand has forbidden it."

Another glance toward the women working in the bushes surrounding them satisfied Faith that they were engrossed in their task. She tried once more.

"Just a few minutes, please. Broken Hand isn't here right now. He can't hurt you."

Lydia's chin rose with dignity.

"I'm not afraid of Broken Hand. He wouldn't hurt me."

"Then surely there's no harm in talking."

Lydia appeared to consider Faith's words, and the girl anxiously held her breath, her eyes moving assessingly over her mother. There was no longer any trace of the bruised swelling which had disfigured Mama's clear cheek the day they had been captured. All that remained was a light scar in the area of her temple. Faith winced at the memory of the blood that had streamed from the jagged cut. Other than that, Mama appeared to be in good physical health.

The sun had tinted Mama's unguarded complexion a golden hue, accenting the pale shade of her frightened eyes until they appeared an almost luminous silver. Her former carefully tended coiffure was no more. Instead, she wore her hair pinned back behind her ears and streaming over her shoulders, in a style similar to Faith's own. The abused gingham dress she still wore showed the marks of a primitive laundering and Faith felt relief touch her senses. Obviously, Mama's instincts for personal hygiene had not faded along with her memory.

Faith shot a quick look around her. The two foraging parties of women had intermingled and spread out to cover a larger area. Walking Woman had worked her way far in advance of the group, and Owl Woman was talking with another woman as she worked. She and Mama would not be immediately missed. Realizing the chance she took because of her mother's obviously fragile mental condition, Faith reached out a tentative hand. A tremor shook Lydia Durham's slender frame as she touched her, and Faith fought the debilitating emotion that assailed her.

"Mama . . . please."

Holding her mother's gaze in an attempt at reassurance, Faith drew her slowly behind a nearby wall of foliage. As she did so, the older woman's anxiety intensified. She was shuddering, her delicate frame quaking so hard she could barely stand. Carefully, Faith eased her to a seated position on the ground. Seating herself beside her, Faith took her hand. Compassion for her mother's obvious distraction brought a bright flush of tears to Faith's eyes.

"Oh, Mama . . ."

"I . . . I don't know you." Lydia's voice trembled as she attempted to withdraw her hand. "My . . . my name is Shadow Woman. I am wife to Broken Hand. Broken Hand said he—"

"No, Mama, please." Desperation forced a tear from Faith's brimming eyes, and she brushed it away with an impatient hand. "Don't pull away. Let me talk to you. What do you remember before you saw Broken Hand for the first time?"

"I . . . I had no life before Broken Hand. Broken Hand told me I was born anew to be his wife . . . that I am the fulfillment of a vision which came to him in a dream."

"A vision?"

"Yes. He told me that I must not attempt to sort out the pictures which torture my mind . . . that give me pain. He said I must ignore all that happened before we came together. He said that I will soon be accepted within the village . . . that the women will not continue to look at me with disapproval."

"I don't look at you with disapproval."

"No." Lydia shook her head. "But you're not like the others."

"That's right, Mama. I'm not like them. I'm like you."

"No . . . no." Lydia shook her head again, her confusion growing. She raised a trembling hand to the scar on her temple, her eyes fluttering momentarily closed. "My head . . . it hurts. It hurts again."

"Mama, I don't want to hurt you." Tears streaming uncontrollably from her eyes, Faith reached up to stroke her mother's cheek. "I just want you to remember. We're not from this place. We're from a civilized world, far from here. Papa—your husband—was killed."

"No!"

"Yes, he was. We both saw him fall. And then we were captured. Those Indians drove us mercilessly and beat us."

"No, you're lying! Broken Hand is good and kind! *He* is my husband. He has joined his spirit to mine. He will take care of me, keep me close to him. I'll be a good wife to him. I—"

"You're not his wife! You're the wife of Wallace Durham, Mama. Try . . . try to remember! You must remember so we can get away from here!"

"No, I won't leave. Broken Hand will—"

"Neither of you will leave."

Both women jumped with alarm at the masculine voice which sounded unexpectedly to their rear. Startled, Faith gripped her mother's hand spontaneously tighter as she turned. Spotted Elk!

Taking advantage of their silence, Spotted Elk crouched down beside Faith. His low tone attempted to reassure her.

"No, Fire Spirit. Do not be afraid. Neither you nor Shadow Woman need fear me. I have attempted to tell you that I am your friend, but your ears have been closed to my words. I am not hindered by a need for obedience to Broken Hand's commands. I am a man, a respected warrior who will soon be a war chief. I am not as Black Wolf, bound to Broken Hand's words because of my youth. Were you living in my lodge, I would not forbid you to speak to Shadow Woman."

"Broken Hand won't let Mama speak to me because he's afraid." Finally regaining her voice, Faith continued shakily, "He . . . he fears Mama will remember everything and begin to hate him."

Lydia shook her head in violent denial.

"No, I could not hate Broken Hand! I could not!"

Pulling her hand unexpectedly from Faith's grasp, Lydia struggled shakily to her feet.

"I must go back to work now. I . . . I don't want to talk anymore."

Scrambling to her feet beside her mother, Faith attempted to shake off Spotted Elk's restraining hand. Annoyance

110

darkening his glance, he tightened his grip as he directed his words to the obviously shaken Lydia.

"If you wish to spare this girl the fury of Black Wolf's wrath, you will keep silent about this meeting."

Lydia's eyes darted to Faith in confusion.

"I . . . I don't want to hurt this girl."

"Then return to the other women now, and say nothing."

Lydia hesitated as Faith attempted to take a step toward her, but Spotted Elk stood firmly between them.

"Go now, before you are missed."

Shooting Faith a quick, stressed glance, Lydia turned and stepped back into the open once more. Watching until she had silently resumed her place amongst the women, Faith turned to Spotted Elk's intense perusal.

"I must return, too, before Walking Woman realizes I'm gone."

Spotted Elk's hand remained firmly on her arm. His eyes moved slowly over her face. His words were spoken in a low, conciliatory tone.

"You do not have words of gratitude for my silence in your behalf?"

"Silence?" Faith's eyes narrowed with suspicion. She did not trust Spotted Elk. "Why should you remain silent so that I may be spared?"

Pausing in response, Spotted Elk raised a hand to touch the flaming tendrils of hair that rested against Faith's cheek. His carefully controlled expression did not reveal the desire that flamed to life within him at the contact.

"Because I would prove to you that I am your friend. I would have you come to trust me so that I may tell Broken Hand it is your desire to come to my lodge to help Silent Woman with the child soon to be born to her."

Faith pulled back from his touch, and Spotted Elk suppressed his instinctive anger.

"I would not forbid your contact with Shadow Woman."

"It would make little difference to Broken Hand if I said I wanted to go to your lodge."

"You are wrong. Young Hawk is son of Broken Hand's brother. He is indebted to you for saving the boy. He would consider your request."

Faith hesitated. She could think of no reason for this man to lie, but instinct refused to allow other than a tight-lipped response.

"I must return before Walking Woman misses me."

Ignoring Spotted Elk's annoyance at her curt response, Faith again attempted to pull free of his restraining hand. Her effort to no avail, she glanced up sharply. A flicker of an unreadable emotion moved across Spotted Elk's countenance as he released her unexpectedly.

"We will speak again."

Spotted Elk's hand dropped from her arm, and Faith turned without further comment. She made her way through the foliage, the weight of Spotted Elk's perusal heightening the tension within her. She did not trust Spotted Elk in spite of his reassurances. But she did need to talk to Mama, to help her to remember before it was too late. Perhaps it would be best if she allowed Spotted Elk to speak to Broken Hand—to convince him that she be placed under Spotted Elk's custody.

Emerging into the clearing once more, Faith shot a furtive glance toward those around her. No, she had not been missed. She chanced a quick look in her mother's direction. Mama was working steadily, her head down. Faith's throat constricted with emotion and she swallowed against unwanted tears. Mama was confused and afraid. Mama wanted no part of her. But she would *make* Mama remember her! She must. . . .

Still concealed within the foliage, Spotted Elk controlled his rage at Fire Spirit's abrupt dismissal of him. He followed her slender, girlish figure as she worked her way back inconspicuously into the group of women and resumed her work. His eyes moved over the brilliant fire of her hair, and it brought to mind the similar fire which had burned in her peculiarly light eyes. Yes, he would have this girl in his lodge, and he would have her for his own. Nothing or no one would stop him. He would win her over with soft words and promises, and when she was under his control, he would satisfy his outrage at her disrespectful conduct.

It would not be long before she became a woman. She would be fully broken to his command by then. He would join his body with hers. His eagerness all but consumed him.

Owl Woman shot a furtive glance to the scene unwinding behind her. Shadow Woman had emerged from the cover of trees, her expression shaken. A short time later the girl had silently returned to work at Walking Woman's rear. Something was wrong.

Movement in the foliage drew her keen eyes in its direction in time for her to see Spotted Elk turn and disappear from sight. Fury flushed her face with heat. Spotted Elk's interest in the girl did not bode well for her plan.

Owl Woman took a deep breath and paused in contemplation. Moments later, her expression settled into deep, determined lines. Spotted Elk's interference would matter little. The woman and the girl would soon be gone from the village. Broken Hand's shame and her humiliation would come to an end. She had already determined that she would sacrifice her life to that end if need be, as long as that sacrifice was shared by the white woman as well.

Chapter VIII

The warm, afternoon sun beat down on his uncovered head as Black Wolf held his horse in line behind Broken Hand's gray. They had traveled far in search of game and were making their way back to camp. He looked to the men who rode with him; White Frog, Ridge Bear, Tangle Hair, and Broken Hand riding in the lead. The hunt had been successful in two ways. Their horses were loaded with meat, and the arduous pursuit of game had taken their minds from plans for the war party they had been forced to abandon while Black Kettle argued his plans for peace.

Satisfaction welled inside Black Wolf. He looked with pleasure to the arrival of their hunting party at the village, to the welcome the successful hunters would receive. He would dismount before his lodge, and Walking Woman would take the meat from his horse and smile her appreciation.

Black Wolf's lips quirked at the thought that followed. Fire Spirit would not join in the welcome but would stand stiffly nearby. He knew he would then instruct her to take his horse to the river to cleanse the animal's skin of the blood and dirt of the hunt. Fire Spirit would not accept the task with grace, but she would follow his orders. And he knew he would follow her as he had many times before, to make certain the task was performed well. He also knew the assignment of the task allowed him the opportunity to further ponder the enigma which was Fire Spirit and his own disturbed feelings toward her.

114

In the long, silent hours preceding the hunt, Black Wolf had examined his thoughts. He had finally admitted to himself the attraction of Fire Spirit's sharp mind, her undaunted spirit. He had also admitted that he found her small featured face extremely pleasing to his eye, and her unusual coloring particularly stimulating. He remembered with specific vividness the shades of silver and blue which mingled into a glowing frost within her eyes; and the red and gold hair which came to glowing life in the sun to dance and glimmer before his gaze. He also remembered the fine line of her lips and the manner in which they stretched wide over her evenly matched teeth, and the manner in which her one cheek moved into a tempting crease which winked and flirted with her smile.

He remembered other things, too—the fine, proud lift of her chin, her erect carriage. He remembered the promise of her slender lithe body, the smoothness of her velvet skin. That smooth white skin called to him; his longing to hold Fire Spirit's slenderness against him was at times too compelling for comfort. Her resistance to his authority enraged him, but, perversely, her courage and spirit also stirred both admiration and amusement within him. He had not yet come to terms with his strange rage at Spotted Elk's interest in the girl; but the fact that the girl was bound to him, not Spotted Elk, was a point of silent comfort in his perplexed state.

Black Wolf raised his face to the sun, allowing it to warm him for long, silent moments, to soothe his mind. He was truly uncertain if he would . . .

Hoofbeats to the rear of their small party interrupted his thoughts, and turned all heads in the party toward them. Black Wolf assessed the approaching mounted figures, immediately noting the men were not of his tribe. His eye caught the familiar gait of the horse in the lead. He snapped a quick glance in Broken Hand's direction. Broken Hand, too, had recognized the animal which he had traded several weeks before for the two women hostages. Broken Hand's frown revealed his distaste for another meeting with the men who had abused his wife so cruelly. Remembering the bruise which had marked Fire Spirit's smooth cheek, Black Wolf tensed, sharing his feelings. But the arrogant Arapaho in the lead did not appear to share their aversion as he approached and drew up alongside.

Black Wolf studied the three men intently as the leader prepared to speak. They were indeed the same three who had taken Shadow Woman and Fire Spirit captive, and a ripple of apprehension moved up his spine. The leader was the Arapaho, White Eagle, who had been struck by the rock thrown by Fire Spirit and who had been attempting to ride her down at the time Broken Hand had intervened. Anger remained in White Eagle's slitted gaze. He had not yet forgiven Broken Hand for cheating him of his revenge.

His eyes assessing their heavily laden horses, White Eagle addressed Broken Hand without preamble.

"Once again our paths cross, Broken Hand. The hunt has been good to you. Those who follow me have not been as fortunate this day, but our stomachs are filled with sated vengeance."

Broken Hand extended a wary greeting. His dark eyes assessing the victorious glow which illuminated White Eagle's eyes, he turned to remove a portion of the meat from his horse's back. White Eagle had not approached him to speak idle words and Broken Hand knew it was worth making the gift to determine his motives.

"We offer you a portion of our hunt to fill your stomachs this night, White Eagle. And our ears are eager for the tale which brings you pleasure."

Accepting the meat with a smile that was almost a leer, White Eagle secured it on his horse's back. He shot a short glance toward his men, noting their obvious discomfort as he lifted his head once more.

"My men do not feel you will share in our pleasure. They feel we will suffer your disapproval." He gave a short laugh. "I confess to you a truth, Broken Hand. I am not pleased with the bargain struck between us when last we met. Our raid on the wagon train has been costly, and it was my desire to vent my anger for the loss of lives on the two captives we had taken. Had it not been for the superior animal you offered in trade and the pressure of Little Bear and Black Crow, I would have refused your offer, so wild was my rage. Many days passed, and the wild unrest remained within me."

Broken Hand regarded White Eagle with caution, and Black Wolf felt the tension within him grow.

"But the Great Power looked down upon me with favor. He guided Little Bear, Black Crow, and me in our hunt to game we had not expected. He led us to a white man's cabin, a place where many good things had been stored to provide comfort during the long days of winter. The men were away, and the women provided little resistance to our attack. We took their bounty back to camp. Their scalps we sent to Fort Lyon with a message for the army there. My rage has been sated, and for that reason I can once again look upon you easily as friend."

Broken Hand's expression remained guarded.

"The Arapaho are brother to the Cheyenne. Our bargain was struck in good faith and was not meant to discomfort you in any way."

White Eagle's slitted gaze narrowed.

"The discomfort is no more, but I offer you a thought in warning. I will not again suffer the loss of a captive to the Cheyenne, no matter the price of the bargain struck, and no matter the threat in the eyes of the man who offers it." Pausing so that Broken Hand might take in the full weight of his pronouncement, White Eagle added with stiff courtesy. "I thank you for the sharing of your hunt. We will meet again."

The Arapahos' horses were fading into the distance when Broken Hand met Black Wolf's gaze in silence. Their understanding exchanged, they turned their horses in the direction of camp to make their way home.

The great circle of lodges loomed below them as their hunting party came over the final hill, but Black Wolf's former sense of well-being had vanished with the last sight of the Arapaho horses hours before. Darting a quick glance toward Broken Hand, Black Wolf saw that the older man's brow was also furrowed in a frown. He did not need to question the cause for Broken Hand's silent preoccupation. White Eagle's narration had been sobering indeed.

Aware that the other members of his party did not share in their dampened enthusiasm, Black Wolf pulled his horse aside to allow Tangle Hair to precede him. Tangle Hair was in high spirits. It was his desire to take Dancing Woman to wife, and the impressive proceeds from their hunt would add immeasurably to his stature in her eyes. Holding back as Ridge Bear, and White Frog followed Tangle Hair in close pursuit, Black Wolf noted that Broken Hand moved to accommodate their accelerated pace. Not wanting to trail behind, Black Wolf heeled his mount forward.

Their arrival in camp minutes later drew admiring comments and shouts of welcome, but Black Wolf's demeanor remained somber. His eyes scanned the faces of those surging to meet them. He dismounted, frowning his disappointment as a familiar voice turned him to Deer Woman's smiling face.

"The Great Power has smiled upon you today, Black Wolf. No other party has brought back the bounty with which yours returns. See . . . Walking Woman stands beside your lodge, awaiting you. She smiles with pride. Great will be the feast she prepares for you this night."

Nodding a response to Deer Woman's praise, Black Wolf was preparing to brush past her when Deer Woman's small hand stayed him. Her slender fingers gripped his forearm, drawing his attention back to her face as she spoke in a softer tone.

"The glow of the evening sky reflects with great beauty on the rippling waters of the river, Black Wolf. Singing Woman and I will keep to our intention to walk before darkness falls."

Amused by Deer Woman's boldness, Black Wolf smiled down into her expectant face.

"The beauty of the falling sun suffers in comparison to your smiling face, Deer Woman."

Turning away as Deer Woman acknowledged his compliment with lowered eyes, Black Wolf made his way toward

118

Walking Woman. He had appeased the very determined Deer Woman and salved her vanity without making a promise he did not wish to keep. He had settled that matter for the present.

Black Wolf's frown returned as his eyes sought his lodge and the waiting figure of Walking Woman. Fire Spirit was nowhere to be seen.

Anticipating his question, Walking Woman offered quickly, "Fire Spirit has gone to the river for water." Her brow furrowed into worried lines, she shook her graying head in dismay. "She doubtless heard your approach being called in camp. I cannot understand her delay in returning."

Not wishing to cause the gentle woman discomfort, Black Wolf managed a short smile.

"It is not difficult for me to reason the cause for Fire Spirit's delay. It is yet another small rebellion with which I must deal."

Walking Woman's open concern caused Black Wolf to pat her rounded shoulder with open affection as he offered in a softer tone, "It is my thought that Fire Spirit fills a place in your heart held empty for many years. It is for that reason that she is able to conduct herself almost as she wills."

"Oh, no!" Vigorously denying Black Wolf's statement, Walking Woman shook her head. "Fire Spirit behaves well and dutifully in the lodge. She works hard and with great dedication to learn the tasks to which she is set. She speaks to me with the respect due my position. . . ."

Black Wolf's raised brow drew Walking Woman's voice to a halt. Her glance again turned to dismay at his unexpectedly amused response.

"She speaks to you with the respect due your position? Then I must assume it is only myself to whom she addresses herself so willfully."

Walking Woman's work-roughened hand slipped up to cover her lips at the same moment the sound of a light step turned his head toward an approaching figure. Fire Spirit's pale-eyed glance dismissed him insultingly as she moved toward Walking Woman with the long awaited water.

Fire Spirit's slender brows drew into a frown as Walking

Woman turned to remove the first of the heavy meat from the waiting horse. Quickly placing the filled container on the ground, she stepped to Walking Woman's side.

"No, Walking Woman. I will carry the meat into the lodge. Your arms are still tired from the heavy burdens of the day. My arms are younger."

"And shorter." His own brow drawing into a frown, as the girl struggled to unload his mount, Black Wolf brushed her aside. "It seems that women's chores must fall to me as well, in the absence of strong arms within my lodge to meet the task with ease."

Unloading the meat efficiently, Black Wolf allowed Walking Woman to carry it inside. When the girl made an attempt to help, he shook his head.

"No. Walking Woman suffers at your inference that she is too feeble to do a woman's work."

Her eyes snapping to Walking Woman's retreating figure with alarm, Faith shook her head.

"No, I didn't mean that. I only meant that unloading such a heavy burden is not women's work."

A familiar annoyance quirked Black Wolf's well-shaped lips.

"It is not your place to decide which is women's work and which is not." His gaze moving pointedly to the lodge at the other side of the circle, he nodded in approval. Faith's eyes followed his to the sight of Shadow Woman as she struggled to aid Owl Woman in unloading Broken Hand's horse. A bright flush followed her expression of obvious distress as Shadow Woman faltered under the heavy burden she attempted to carry, and Black Wolf felt his satisfaction drain away. What was it about this girl that forced him to question the wisdom of some things he had accepted as right and just for the greater part of his life?

Fire Spirit turned back toward the dwindling pile of meat. Halting her as she attempted to help Walking Woman in her chore, Black Wolf shook his head.

"Walking Woman does not need your help here. Rather, you will save her steps by taking my animal to the river and washing him free of the stains of the hunt."

The girl turned suddenly to face him, the cool blue of her eyes snapping unexpected fire.

"You can wash your own animal in the river. You're the one who made him dirty in the first place."

Black Wolf met her anger with a cool, meaningful retort.

"That is true. I made him dirty in hunting and bringing back the meat which you will eat in the days to come. If you are not willing to share the work, you will not share in the proceeds from that work."

Fire Spirit's angry retort was halted by the small, worried sound that escaped Walking Woman's lips as the older woman observed their angry confrontation. Her mouth twitching revealingly at Walking Woman's anxiety, Fire Spirit hesitated before turning to snatch the horse's lead from his hand. Turning without another word, she started toward the river, pulling the animal behind her.

Lingering long enough to make certain Walking Woman's aging arms were up to the task at hand, Black Wolf followed the winding path toward the river. His encounter with the irritating girl had left him even more unsettled than the arrival of the Arapaho, White Eagle. Silently, he acknowledged that the Fire Spirit's rebellion was in part due to his leniency in handling her. He had no doubt that the covetous Spotted Elk would have shown no hesitation in halting her sharp retorts with the flat of his hand, had he been able to succeed in taking the girl into his lodge. Black Wolf's frown darkened. No, he had seen the last of bruises which would mark Fire Spirit's fair skin. He would not raise his hand in anger against her. Black Wolf gave a low snort. But neither would he allow the girl to flaunt her disrespect.

His step firm with determination, Black Wolf was making his descent to the river when his eyes caught a flash of red-gold sparkling against the backdrop of shimmering ripples. He paused, his eyes narrowing into assessing slits. Fire Spirit was standing in the shallows of the river, holding his horse's lead. The skirt of her dress was turned up and tied around her waist as she stood thigh-deep in the water. She was attempting to splash water on the animal's back, and was succeeding in getting herself far more wet than the animal she attempted to wash. Her low groan of frustration reached his ears as she assessed the gory slime that covered the animal's back. In her haste to avoid him, she had neglected to take the needed container with which to wash the horse. She was obviously too angry to return to the lodge and admit her oversight. As it was, she was attempting an impossible task.

Amusement tempered Black Wolf's angry resolve. Seating himself in silence, he watched perplexity cross Fire Spirit's irritated expression. She turned and the sun caught and reflected anew in the red-gold strands streaming down her back. Realization tightened his expression. Had he and his companions stumbled upon White Eagle's raiding party a few minutes later that first day, he had no doubt it would have been Fire Spirit's brilliant hair which would have been sent to Fort Lyon as White Eagle's message of revenge.

A peculiar thickness made it difficult for Black Wolf to swallow as his eyes moved over the girl's slender figure. He would not have known the challenge that sparked at him from within Fire Spirit's brilliant eyes, the beauty of her small-featured face; her keen mind or quick tongue; the unexpected skill with which she had treated Young Hawk; the tender care she had lavished upon the boy; her instinctive consideration for Walking Woman's advancing years. All would have been lost to him. He would not have experienced the courage and determination which was so much a part of her, which refused to allow her to submit to his authority. He suddenly realized how great would have been his loss.

His eyes still followed Fire Spirit's struggle, and a smile picked up the corners of his lips. Fire Spirit was fast losing patience with her impossible task. She shot a quick glance back toward the village. In her frustration, she did not see him sitting in his position of observance. For a long moment she obviously considered returning for a container, but abruptly, she turned back to the waiting horse. Determination in the set of her narrow shoulders, she gripped his mount's long mane firmly. A short gasp of surprise escaped Black Wolf's throat as she swung herself up and onto the animal's back. Jerking himself to his feet as she turned the horse in toward the center of the river, Black Wolf began moving toward the sandy bank.

His eyes on the girl's back as she heeled the animal forward, Black Wolf stumbled and slid as he raced down the uneven trail. Unsettling thoughts assailed his mind. The girl was not an experienced rider, and she was not familiar with the snagging current which became surprisingly swift near the river's center. His horse was exhausted from the long day's journey and unaccustomed to the girl's commands.

His chest heaving with anxious anger, Black Wolf reached the riverbank. He shouted her name, his deep voice carrying across the water to snap Fire Spirit's head in his direction.

An obstinate grimace flashed across her face, and she dug her bare heels into the animal's sides once more. Responding to her command, the stalwart pony struck out, swimming now, into the water. The girl glanced toward him with satisfaction, and Black Wolf read her glance. She was telling him that the animal was being washed, as he had ordered. And she was telling him that she was accomplishing it with little effort on her part.

But his tired horse was faltering. Black Wolf shouted quick, corrective commands, but the girl was either unwilling or unable to follow them. The horse was twisting in an attempt to break free of her direction. He was going to roll! Fire Spirit was being thrown from his back!

As he watched in horror, Black Wolf saw Fire Spirit's slender body hit the water with a loud crack and then disappear from sight. Within moments Black Wolf was in the water. A quick glance revealed that his horse had righted himself and was swimming toward him, but Fire Spirit was nowhere to be seen! Panic choked him and Black Wolf began to swim faster. He was nearing his swimming mount when he saw a small head bobbing to the animal's rear. Black Wolf caught a flash of brilliant blue eyes as the girl struck out toward the shore behind him with a strong stroke.

Treading water until the girl drew abreast of him, Black Wolf swam beside her until she touched down and drew herself to her feet in the shallows. The clatter of horse's hooves as his pony walked ashore a few feet down the bank did not deter Black Wolf's fury. Gripping Fire Spirit's narrow shoulders forcefully, he gave her a hard shake.

"Foolish child! Is the simple task of washing my horse so far above you that you cannot complete it without endangering your life?"

"I'm not a fool, and I'm not a child!" Her anger flaring in return, Faith attempted to break free of Black Wolf's biting grip. "I swim very well. I was in no danger, and if you will look at your mount, you will see that he is clean and refreshed as well."

Not to be swayed by the heat of Faith's response, Black Wolf tightened his grip. His fingers digging into her soft flesh, he shook her one more time before holding her stiffly so she could not avoid the full force of his angry stare.

"You will never attempt such a rash act again. I saw the danger, even if you did not. The horse twisted as you fell. He could just as easily have rolled on you, forcing you under, and you would not be here to glare at me now with foolish anger. I will not warn you again. In the future you will wash my horse in the same manner as the other women."

"Like a good Cheyenne woman."

Black Wolf gritted his teeth at her softly grated sarcasm.

"I fear you will never be a good Cheyenne woman."

The victorious smile which curved the girl's lips increased his vexation, and Black Wolf released her abruptly.

"You will return to the lodge now. Walking Woman is preparing the evening meal while you are busy with your senseless rebellions. Once more you leave the work to the generous woman who defends you with her every word."

"I do not! I do not take advantage of Walking Woman!"

The last of his forbearance vanishing in the wake of yet another rebellion, Black Wolf raised his hand and pointed toward the village.

"Go back to the lodge. I will tend to the horse!"

A wealth of protest registering momentarily in her light eyes, Fire Spirit abruptly turned on her heel and began stamping up the trail.

Watching as Fire Spirit continued her angry ascent, Black Wolf realized he had struck a tender chord inside her with his accusation as to her lack of consideration for Walking Woman. He nodded in satisfaction. If the girl had stirred his fury, he had stirred hers in return.

Closing the distance between his horse and himself, Black Wolf snatched up the trailing lead and began drawing his horse up the trail behind him. He was suddenly struck with the thought that the victory had gone to neither of them in this encounter. Fire Spirit was, indeed, moving to his command at last . . . while *he* completed the chore he had set for her to do!

At his last glimpse of Fire Spirit, the flash of her water-darkened hair as she slipped through the doorway of the lodge, Black Wolf shook his head and a flicker of a reluctant smile touched his lips. It was a game in which they were well matched, and he had no doubt it was a game they would play many more times. It came to him suddenly, with instinctive insight, that it had not been meant to be that Fire Spirit's glorious hair should be taken by the Arapaho and returned to Fort Lyon as a token of retribution. That conviction was deep and firm within him.

In silence Broken Hand watched from his vantage point beside his lodge as darkness settled over the camp. The bright lights of fires shone a deep, fluttering gold through the skins of the lodges, while sparks rose through the smoke holes to dance in a glorious, fluttering display on the night air. Broken Hand raised his head to the sound of dancing from a distant lodge. He frowned as several young men emerged from their lodges and moved instinctively in its direction. It was not a dance which called for peace. In his heart he feared Black Kettle's council would be to little avail.

Turning his mind from those disturbing thoughts, Broken Hand continued to peruse the sounds of camp . . . a woman's musical laughter, the voice of an old man as he raised his voice in summons, the barking of dogs on a nearby hill, a colt's frightened whinny in the distance, and its mother's answering neigh. The first shrill howl of the coyote sounded, and Broken Hand turned toward his lodge once more. The familiar sounds of night could not ease the unrest within him.

He entered the lodge, his eyes touching on the dark shining head of the woman who sat by the fire, intent on the garment she fashioned. He walked to her side and stroked the gleaming strands. Pale silver eyes rose to his, the shadows shifting as her lips curved in a smile. Leaning down, Broken Hand drew Shadow Woman to her feet and took the garment from her hand. Without a word he enfolded her in his arms.

A low sigh escaped his lips and Broken Hand took her slenderness up into his arms and carried her to his sleeping bench. He placed her upon it and crouched beside her to peruse her unblemished countenance. Under his scrutiny, the shadows returned to her gaze. The fine line of her lips parted with her whispered words.

"Broken Hand, today I—"

But Broken Hand's mind was far from the cause of her seeming disquiet. He silenced her with his hand. His words were low, fraught with feeling.

"Today I met a figure from the past. He spoke to me, and his words brought to my mind a glimpse of my life as it would have been had not the Great Power directed me to the time and place of our first meeting. It was a dreary picture, my life as it had been. Loneliness, hatred, and a need for revenge . . . There was room for no other emotion in my heart. I was an empty man, the man I would still be if it were not for the living spirit you restored within me."

Broken Hand paused in his solemn declaration. His dark eyes held hers, dispelling the shadows in her gaze. "You are the life within my soul, Shadow Woman. You have made me whole. I give myself to you, Shadow Woman, as you give yourself to me. We are part of each other, never to be separated."

Drawing himself up, Broken Hand stripped away his clothes and lay beside her. His broken hand moved to the buttons on her dress and he unfastened them with gentle care. He touched her silken flesh, and his heart sang.

Chapter IX

Captain William Potter followed Major Wynkoop's stiff, military figure across the darkened parade ground of the fort. His gaze was intent on the crowd rapidly gathering around Standing Buffalo, their Pawnee scout. His conference with Major Wynkoop had been interrupted a few moments before by a breathless corporal and the news that Standing Buffalo had just arrived at the fort. Not stopping to question the reason for the young soldier's anxiety, Major Wynkoop had made his way outside, and he had followed. Standing Buffalo had been dispatched almost a week earlier to make another attempt to track the Arapahos who had attacked the wagon train almost a month before. Sharing the same obsession as Potter, Major Wynkoop was unwilling to accept the loss of the Durham women and he had spared neither time nor effort in that regard.

Standing Buffalo turned at their approach, and Captain Potter felt a tug of apprehension. He had seen that particular expression on the scout's usually impassive face before. The peculiar sense of excitement in his dark eyes sent a chill moving down his spine.

The crowd of mumbling soldiers parted at their advance, and Major Wynkoop addressed the scout with undisguised concern.

"You have been gone for many days, Standing Buffalo. What do you have to report that brings you back to the fort at such an unexpected hour?"

Standing Buffalo's words were terse, spoken without expression.

"I return with a message from those who raided the wagon train."

"A message!" All trace of his military detachment vanishing, Major Wynkoop snapped with annoyance, "Damn, man, where are they? You were hired to find them, not act as their courier!"

Standing Standing Buffalo nodded in response.

"I was captured by White Eagle and his braves. I have been spared my life in order to bring you his greetings."

Raising his hand from the shadows, Standing Buffalo held up two bloodstained scalps. The long strands of hair, stuck together with blood and dirt, were almost unrecognizable in color and Captain Potter suppressed a spontaneous grimace. Major Wynkoop flicked his gaze back to the Pawnee scout, aware that the eyes of his men were fastened tight upon him.

"What is this message supposed to mean?"

"White Eagle gives you greetings. He reveals the fate of these two white women whom he took captive. He offers you the warning that there will be many more such scalps if the white man continues to violate Indian lands."

His eyes on the scalps in Standing Buffalo's hand, Captain Potter felt the blood slowly drain from his face. No . . . After all this time, after all the searching, it could not end like this.

Momentarily at as great a loss for words as he, Major Wynkoop hesitated in response. Shaking his head wearily, the major mumbled a few words to the sergeant standing close-by, and waited until the bloodied scalps exchanged hands. Then he raised his eyes to Standing Buffalo's measuring gaze. A few short words turned the Indian back toward the mess hall and dispersed the crowd.

Turning to Captain Potter at last, Major Wynkoop muttered quietly, "William, what is there to say that hasn't been said a hundred times before? There's only one thing now left to be done."

Surprising himself with his reply, Captain Potter offered softly, "I'll take care of it, sir."

Nodding his assent, Major Wynkoop turned wearily back toward his office.

Momentarily alone in the center of the parade grounds, Captain Potter took a deep, shaky breath. Strangely, his shock and grief were so strong that they almost reached proportions usual in a personal loss. Finding the Durham woman and child had become far more than just another facet of his military responsibility. He ached with their loss. And he was only too conscious of the task that lay before him. Dreading it more with every step he took, Captain Potter turned and started toward the temporary hospital facilities.

Most of the survivors from the wagon train had recuperated and gone on. One man still remained. Dr. Holstan had said that sheer determination had allowed Wallace Durham to cling to a life which should have ended the moment the bullet had entered his chest. Despite the severity of Durham's wounds, he had hung on in the hope of news of his wife and child. But Durham had waited long enough. It was time to end the pain of his uncertainty. It was the least Potter could do.

The long, restless night was rewarded by the brilliant sunshine of a new day. Captain Potter walked resolutely across the parade grounds toward the man who stood in silence beside his horse, his mind assailed by the thought that it was strange, indeed, how the sun continued to shine in the face of the horrors perpetrated in this barbaric land. He was only too aware that life had all but come to an end for Wallace Durham the night before as he had learned of the outcome of the month-long search for his wife and child.

Lydia and Faith Durham, two more names to add to the list of the lost. But somehow, those two were different. He had sensed it, felt it in his bones, although he had never met them. He had wanted terribly to bring them home.

Captain Potter's long stride brought him abreast of the lone horseman. His gaze touched on the unnatural pallor of the man's face; it contrasted so vividly with the brilliant red of his hair, the sadness in his pale eyes. The fellow's broad, well-built frame had suffered during his long recuperation. He was now unnaturally thin, his handsome face marked by deep hollows in his cheeks. The traces of his suffering were even more pronounced than the day before, and Captain Potter was only too aware of the cause for this most recent deterioration.

The sympathy in Captain Potter's gaze was evident in his voice as he spoke in a subdued tone.

"Wally, you shouldn't leave yet. Harvey said you really need another week or two before you'll be in condition for an extended journey. Where the hell are you going, anyway? You shouldn't be traveling alone in this country, especially now."

Wallace Durham shrugged his broad shoulders. "It doesn't make much difference, does it, William? Traveling in a group didn't help me much the last time. As for where I'm going . . . well, I don't have any reason to go back East. Come to think of it, I don't have much reason to continue west, either."

A suspicious moisture glazing over his eyes, Wallace Durham extended his hand. "You're a good man, William. Take care of yourself."

Captain Potter accepted his hand with a tentative smile. "You'll let me know where you end up, won't you, Wally? I've gotten kind of used to you this last month. I consider you a friend. I'd like to keep in touch."

"Yeah . . . sure. I'll drop you a note when I strike it rich."

Unable to miss the bitterness in Wallace Durham's gaze, William Potter watched as the man mounted up and turned his horse. Snapping him a short salute, Durham spurred his mount toward the gates, and within minutes, he had disappeared from sight.

Realizing he was still standing and staring at the open gates, Captain Potter turned toward his quarters. He suddenly realized there was no time for mourning.

Chapter X

The breeze that brushed Broken Hand's face in gentle gusts was fresh with the scent of sweet grass and prairie flowers, but he was unconscious of its gentle relief. He had little thought for the gradual waning of summer or the oncoming season. Instead, his mind was intent on the scene below him.

The circle of lodges spread before his eyes had gradually widened within the last month. Camped beside the Cheyenne now were their brothers the Arapaho and the Sioux, under Spotted Tail and Pawnee Killer. The gradual deterioration of affairs between the white man and his people was now such that a state of undeclared war existed between the white man and some of the tribes. Each day war parties left to attack the overland route used by stage and freight wagons to bring supplies to the white man's posts. Well coordinated, these raids meant the Indians held the road within their grasp allowing no traffic to pass.

Broken Hand frowned. The plunder taken from captured wagon trains was everywhere within camp. Warriors strutted about wearing shining capes of the white man's cloth; and Indian women worked to make shirts from fine material for the young men. Peace had left their village, and Broken Hand was filled with bitterness and confusion as he honored the stubborn peace of his own chief, Black Kettle.

His eyes narrowing into slits, Broken Hand watched as a tall, well-built man ended his council with Black Kettle.

With a brief motion of farewell, he strode away and mounted his horse.

George Bent was a man of mixed blood and a friend of the Cheyenne. He had brought a message from his father, William Bent, who had spoken to the white commander of the soldiers. Broken Hand's frown darkened. It was believed that the white man's message urged peace for all the tribes. Black Kettle had listened well. He would now call a council of the chiefs to discuss the white commander's words.

The figure of George Bent faded into the distance, and Broken Hand breathed deeply in an effort to clear the confusion from his mind. He was well aware of Black Kettle's thoughts. Black Kettle looked far into the future to a time when the buffalo would no longer roam the plains in great numbers as they did now. Many did not believe the buffalo would disappear, but Broken Hand saw the truth of Black Kettle's vision. He had seen the destruction the white hunters had brought upon the land, the thousands of carcasses left to rot in the sun. He knew that to the south the buffalo were already becoming scarce.

Black Kettle had called for land to be put aside for his people, so that they might hunt and live as those before them without interference by the white man. A treaty had been signed by many of the chiefs. It had been confusing, had not been honored by the white man, and had eventually been cast aside by his people as well. Black Kettle had not acknowledged the failure of the white man to keep his word. He refused to see that their treaty had lasted only until the change of season in the new year, when other white men had again invaded their land in great numbers to dig the yellow ore from the ground. A man of honor, Black Kettle maintained that once the peace was truly understood, it would be observed.

The turmoil within Broken Hand's mind grew greater. Tall Ree . . . the son of his body . . . dreams of a future which was gone forever . . . In his agony of despair he had sworn vengeance. Along with the younger war chiefs of the tribe, he had advocated driving the white man from the land. In his bitterness over the loss of Tall Ree, the price paid for vengeance had mattered little to him.

But the Great Power had sent Shadow Woman to him. In the months since her coming, he had searched his heart and mind for the reason. A new doubt filled his mind as to the wisdom of the former course he had advocated with the white man. Was that doubt, his own growing desire for a peaceful settlement with the white man, the message Shadow Woman had been meant to convey?

Broken Hand shook his head. A part of him was content to be bound by Black Kettle's peace, while another part of him still raged. His vacillation had held him immobile, but that immobility was threatening to destroy him. He was uncertain of the path to take . . . unsure.

A light step to his rear turned Broken Hand to the accusing gaze of Owl Woman. Her eyes, dark and angry, assaulted him as her low voice broke the silence between them.

"The white man, George Bent, has left. Even now Black Kettle calls for a council of the chiefs. He will call for peace among the tribes." Owl Woman's gaze narrowed as she appeared to read his mind. A small sneer curled her fine lips.

"I do not know the man who stands before me. He wears the body and face of my husband of many years, Broken Hand, but his heart has changed. He is tied to a woman of white skin, and his heart has turned to hers. He is white, just as she, and Tall Ree remains unavenged. My heart mourns the death of my husband while he still walks the earth before me. My heart mourns—"

"Silence, woman!" Broken Hand's eyes filled with the shadows of the tumult which tore him apart even as his voice rang with the remembered pain of Tall Ree's death. "You are ignorant of the ways of a man. You think only of the life which is gone from you forever. You care little for the future, for you feel it is not for you. You forget that many of our people will live and suffer for many years for the war you advocate so coldly this day."

"It is a war you called for as loudly as I!"

Broken Hand nodded his head, memories of days long past touching his eyes with a remembered heat.

"Yes, my heart cried out as did yours. I cared little for a future in which neither I nor my son would live. I cared little for the sons of other men, the daughters who would bear their children. I cared only for the blood I would shed to avenge my son. My eyes were closed to all but my own grief. And in my grief, I called others to me that shared my pain. We shed the blood of my enemies, and I was glad. But then I had a dream . . ."

"I care not for your dreams. Visions have replaced your strength with weakness!"

Broken Hand ignored Owl Woman's interruption to continue in a voice which grew strong with conviction.

"That dream challenged my vision of the enemy, showed me that the enemy was not solely represented by the skin of the white man. I saw that, in my hatred, I had closed my eyes to the future to my people. I have begun to realize that perhaps I was the true enemy of my people, that I drove them to destruction with my desire to kill. For in killing, I will be killed, and my people will follow to avenge me with more killing. It will go on and on until there are no more men to avenge, and no more women to bear their children."

"Fie . . . fie on you! The woman has made you weak!"

"The woman has made me strong! I will be strong enough to dismiss the hatred within my heart if it will save my people. I will walk behind Black Kettle in his effort for peace."

Owl Woman's thin face distorted with rage. Running to Broken Hand's side, she raised her fists and pounded heatedly on his chest, forcing Broken Hand to restrain her with his strength. Tears streamed from Owl Woman's eyes, and Broken Hand's heart wept. Memories of a time long gone gave him little peace, and he strove to console her.

"You rage now, Owl Woman, but you will come to see the wisdom of peace with the white man. When our land is again free, filled with buffalo—"

"That day will never come! It lives only in your mind and in the minds of others as weak and cowardly as you!"

The impact of her words provoking an undesired violence inside him, Broken Hand released Owl Woman abruptly.

The heart of a warrior, no matter how restrained, would not suffer such insult. His voice shaking with rage, he raised his hand and pointed to the lodge from which she had emerged.

"Return to your lodge, Owl Woman. It is only my memory of that which you were to me and the realization of the grief which drives you that restrains the weight of my hand. Someday you will see the wisdom of the course which Black Kettle advocates. It is the course I will follow. Now, go!"

His gaze following Owl Woman as she turned abruptly and fled down the hill toward her lodge, Broken Hand felt the full weight of the words he had spoken for the first time. He had come to this hill to make a decision, and in the confrontation which had passed, it had been made.

Broken Hand took a deep breath. He raised his gaze to the afternoon sky. The brilliance of the glowing sun blinded his eyes, but in its radiance he saw the image of the Great Power who had seen fit to set him on this difficult path. Peace would be long and hard, but the reason for Shadow Woman's coming was now clear to him.

In the distance a familiar, slender figure emerged from his lodge and looked in his direction. Broken Hand felt the weight of Shadow Woman's light-eyed gaze and saw in it the mirror of his destiny.

"Come! Come quickly!"

Her soft voice shaking with trepidation, Walking Woman took Faith by the arm and pulled her inside the lodge. Responding more to the aging woman's fear than her own, Faith crouched alongside her shaking form as she stared out through the doorway.

With a start, Faith saw the reason for Walking Woman's warning as the Arapaho, White Eagle, rode past the doorway at a rapid pace. Turning, he rode back in their direction to rein his mount in sharply before the lodge. He paused to shoot a sinister look into her eyes. His gaze then flashed to a place just out of her line of vision, and Faith held her breath in silent expectation.

A ragged trembling beset her slender frame. The coming

of White Eagle to the village a few weeks before had added a new complication to her life in the formerly peaceful village. Now, surrounded by the warring Arapaho and Sioux, she was the recipient of more intense hostility. White Eagle had not forgotten her assault upon him the day of her capture, and she had no doubt that were it not for Black Wolf's unswerving protection, he would have visited his vengeance upon her in the swiftest and most destructive terms.

The coming of the Sioux and Arapaho had caused another complication which Faith had not anticipated. Black Wolf's increased surveillance of her and Broken Hand's preoccupation with the protection of his new wife had frustrated all efforts to talk to Mama as she had planned. Now, a month later, she was no closer to helping Mama remember.

In the long hours of the night, Faith had come to the realization that escape had become all but impossible. Bound by the word of Black Kettle's tenuous peace, Black Wolf and Broken Hand left the camp only for short hunting trips. She had come to realize with bitter irony that the very peace they maintained would hold her more firmly a captive.

She had also come to accept the fact that escape was not feasible in any case. Still unable to recall her past, Mama clung to Broken Hand, visiting upon him all the love and attention she had once shown to Papa. Faith's heart wrenched at the perverse twist fate had accomplished, but she was determined that her mother's devotion to Broken Hand would come to an end. She would make it so.

Walking Woman suddenly was startled, and Faith curled her own shaking arm around the older woman's shoulders. Faith no longer questioned the true affection which had grown between Walking Woman and her, and she was only too aware that the fear Walking Woman displayed was not for herself. But what was it that had set Walking Woman to trembling anew? Had she seen . . . ?

Her silent question abruptly answered, Faith stiffened. Staggering into her line of vision, driven by the same two Indians who had assisted White Eagle to capture Mama and herself, were five more captives! As she watched, two middle-aged women and three children of assorted ages were herded roughly into a small circle a short distance from the doorway. The agony on the captives' faces as they staggered and sometimes fell under the brutal treatment caused a gasp of remembered pain to escape her lips.

Faith took an instinctive step forward, only to be restrained by Walking Woman's arm.

"No, Fire Spirit. You must not. White Eagle hopes to drive you to their aid. In that way he hopes to afford himself the opportunity for the vengeance he seeks."

Faith paused at the wisdom of Walking Woman's statement, and a low sob escaped her throat at the realization that these captives were suffering additional torment because of her. But she could not afford to fall into White Eagle's plan. That would do the captives little good, and it would endanger her own position within the tribe.

The blond woman was struggling to draw herself to her feet with the aid of the terrified children, and Faith held her breath. Turning his horse abruptly, White Eagle heeled him forward, deliberately knocking the woman to the ground once more. His low laugh accompanied the woman's cry of pain. Realizing her own despair would only encourage White Eagle to new assaults against his helpless captives, Faith forced herself to present an impassive façade.

Catching her eye, White Eagle called out in a taunting voice.

"So, your heart is truly Cheyenne. You do not share this woman's pain, but enjoy it much as we. It is plain to see that you have put aside the memories of a time you traveled under my guidance in just such a way as these. But I shall refresh your memory."

Reaching down, White Eagle dug his fingers into the woman's hair and lifted her cruelly to her feet. Laughing, he called out once more, "We will meet again, Fire Spirit, and then we will see if your heart remains truly Cheyenne."

Heeling his horse unexpectedly, White Eagle dragged the exhausted woman out of her line of vision. The screams of the other woman and of the horrified children as they raced in pursuit echoed in her ears, and Faith dropped her

137

eyes closed.

But Faith knew little respite from the horror for memories of Mama's torment, and her own, returned to her with paralyzing vividness. She was shaking with remembered terror when Walking Woman moved from her side.

Within moments, strong arms enclosed her in their protective grip. Unable to open her eyes against the memories which assailed her, Faith recognized the scent of Black Wolf's skin, the strong wall of his chest. She heard his low words of consolation as he held her close, felt the stroking touch of his hands against her back and hair.

Opening her eyes at last, Faith gasped between shaken breaths, "White Eagle . . . he was purposely tormenting those women and children because of me. They suffered for *my* resistance to him, and for his vengeance—"

"They suffer because they have fallen into White Eagle's hands, not because of you as he would have you believe!" Anger hardening his voice, Black Wolf looked sternly into Faith's guilt-ridden countenance. "You will strike the captives from your mind, and you will stay away from the Arapaho camp. White Eagle hopes to draw you there so he may take his vengeance. You will not afford him the opportunity he seeks."

Her natural resistance to Black Wolf's autocratic tone began to surface beneath her guilt and Faith shook her head. "I . . . I cannot abandon them to White Eagle's cruelty."

Abruptly withdrawing his comforting warmth, Black Wolf gripped her rigidly by the upper arm.

"You will do as I command, or you will suffer the consequences!"

Faith's chin rose stubbornly despite Walking Woman's warning glance, and Black Wolf continued, "If you choose to consider yourself as one of the hostages and to act in their behalf, you will assume that status within this lodge. You will be bound, hand and foot, and confined until you bow to my authority!"

"Your authority?"

"You will obey my commands!"

Faith held Black Wolf's furious gaze for long moments as

a question began to surface despite her racing thoughts. How had they again come to this heated anger when only moments before Black Wolf had sought to comfort her? No, she could stand no more of this torment . . . not now.

Faith's eyes fell under Black Wolf's stare, and Black Wolf's hands dropped from her arms.

"You will remain close to the lodge. Walking Woman." His hard-eyed stare shifting to the silent woman at his side, Black Wolf instructed tightly, "I leave Fire Spirit in your care. Responsibility for her actions falls to you."

Her eyes shifting to take in Walking Woman's sober acceptance of Black Wolf's words, Faith shook her head.

"No, you cannot . . ."

"But I can." His eyes dark and knowing, Black Wolf continued tightly, "If you wish to spare Walking Woman shame and embarrassment, you will behave as the Cheyenne woman you are."

"I am not a Cheyenne!"

"If you are not Cheyenne, you are a hostage. The choice is up to you."

Black Wolf turned sharply and walked from the lodge, leaving Faith to consider the full intent and warning in his words. Moving with an angry step to the doorway, Faith followed his tall erect figure, fighting the sense of inevitability which began to engulf her.

Black Wolf strode away from the lodge, furious. Fire Spirit continued to defy him, and frustration soared anew within him. He took a deep breath in an attempt to rein his anger under tight control. He could afford little time for thoughts of the fiery-haired girl that filled his mind.

With a rapid step, Black Wolf joined the steady stream of men as they made their way to a central spot within the circle of lodges. Black Kettle had called a council. He had no doubt as to the reason. George Bent had just left the camp to return to Fort Lyon. He had doubtless come with a call for peace, either from the commanding officer there or from the Indian agent, Major Colley. In any case, the result would be the same.

The months which had passed had been long and difficult. Restraint conflicting with the need for revenge which burned hot and deep within him, he had refused to join the war parties which had left the camp on a daily basis to raid the overland trail. His loyalty to the esteemed word of Black Kettle, his chief, and to Broken Hand, who had been as a father to him, had held him inactive. He had seen frustration evidenced in Broken Hand's pensive gaze, and he knew Broken Hand suffered a similar torment.

Many of the other young men had not practiced the same adherence to Black Kettle's word. He had endured Wounded Eye's taunting words in silence, consoling himself with the knowledge that his contribution to the camp had been greater than Wounded Eye's. Their camp on this river called the Solomon had doubled in size with the addition of the Arapaho and the Sioux, causing a scarcity of meat in the vicinity. Each day hunting parties had been forced to travel farther and farther to feed their people. Broken Hand and he had labored hard and long to fill that need.

But even in hunting, his mind had not been free. The coming of the Arapaho and the Sioux had heightened feeling against the whites. Unwarranted attacks against their people by the whites had driven them to seek retribution and had also caused his people to look with growing disfavor on Fire Spirit and Shadow Woman. Shadow Woman's silent acceptance of her new life had afforded her no more approval than Fire Spirit's rebellion. The arrival of White Eagle with the last band of Arapaho had turned Black Wolf's growing discomfort to apprehension. He had come to the point at which his time in camp was spent with one eye on the task at hand, and the other on Fire Spirit's safety.

Black Wolf's expression darkened. It was an intolerable situation. He did not need this problem to complicate his already confused feelings for the girl. His thoughts were tied too tightly to her glowing face, her slender form, the smile which so infrequently flashed across the fine line of her lips. Her strength, the purpose with which she passed her day,

140

seemed to call out to him, to draw him to her. In the silence of night he had stolen to her sleeping bench many times. He had crouched beside her, studied her face in the semidarkness, in an attempt to fathom the reason for his annoying preoccupation with her. The result had always been the same. A longing to touch her, to comfort her in the despair she suffered due to her continued estrangement from Shadow Woman.

And now, with the advent of White Eagle's new, aggressiveness toward her, Black Wolf's feelings were even more intense. He knew not what he truly felt, but of one thing he was certain. No one—not White Eagle, with his desire for vengeance; nor Spotted Elk, with his covetous glances—would touch the girl while she was in his care. And she would remain in his care. He would not give her up.

Aware that a growing crowd had begun to accumulate in the center of camp where Black Kettle sat in conference with Arapaho and Sioux chiefs, Black Wolf slowed his step. He needed to free his mind of all thoughts but the proceedings which were about to take place. On them rested the future of the tribe as well as the future of the one whose welfare had become more important to him than his own.

Drawing himself up to a spot of silence observance, Black Wolf paused to listen. The council had begun.

Lydia stood in silence within the lodge she and Broken Hand shared. She looked down onto the garment she had finished sewing so carefully only moments before. She was extremely proud. It was made of a deer skin she had painstakingly dressed and prepared until it was soft and pliable beneath her hands, and it had a soft, appealing color. With extreme care, she had cut the garment so that it would hang softly from her figure, gently swaying fringes descending from her arms and at the hemline. With a skill she had not realized she possessed, she had matched the parts and sewn the seams until the finished product was far superior to those of the other women. Completely engrossed in her task, she had taken the beads from a broken necklace she had found in camp, and had decorated the front of the graceful garment.

She glanced to the soft moccasins which lay beside it, and she smiled. The poor coverings she had formerly worn had been a begrudging gift from Owl Woman, prompted by a word of rebuke from Broken Hand. They had been no more than adequate. But these moccasins, fashioned by her own hand, were lovely.

A light frown creased Lydia's brow. Her preoccupation with her appearance had not been merely a matter of vanity. No, it was more than that. She was intensely aware of the growing animosity toward her in camp. It was the result of the influx of Arapaho and Sioux, and their heated feelings. And it was also due to the fact that she stood out from the other members of the tribe for her clothing was so different from theirs. It was not her wish to remain apart from the tribe. It was her wish to be absorbed within it, so that she might spare Broken Hand the censure of his brothers.

With shaking hands, Lydia stripped away the despised dress which marked her an outsider. Raising her new garment over her head, she allowed it to slip down over her shoulders and against her body. She smiled at its softness against her skin. She lifted one small foot and slipped it into a moccasin, then the other. Perfect . . . they were perfect.

Lydia raised her hands to her hair. She frowned. No, she would not fashion her hair into the braids accepted by the other women of the tribe. Broken Hand spoke often of the vision in which she had appeared to him, her hair streaming over her shoulders. He preferred it thus, and thus she would allow it to remain.

Securing the gleaming strands behind her ears with the small fasteners which were the only reminders of her former life, Lydia then paused. Broken Hand would be proud. She wished she could see her reflection. Perhaps later, when she went down to the river for water, she would be able to see her transformation to a true Indian wife. But until then she would wait in the lodge for Broken Hand's return.

Lydia's brow again moved into a frown. Broken Hand had

142

been deeply concerned about the council being conducted between Black Kettle and the chiefs of the other tribes. A chill slipped down Lydia's spine. Thoughts of the war parties which now left camp each morning had only succeeded in arousing the familiar, blinding pain in her head which all but incapacitated her. His concern stirring him to a deep anger, Broken Hand had instructed her to put aside all thoughts which caused her pain. Able to do little else, Lydia had agreed.

The painful reminder of her confused state brought the image of the red-haired girl, Fire Spirit, to her mind. The advent of the Arapaho and Sioux had caused a tightening of the restrictions imposed upon her. She had not come into close contact with the girl in many weeks, but she had not forgotten her. The girl was little more than a child, and very upset. Perhaps she would make a dress similar to her own for the girl as well, so that she might more easily be assimilated into the tribe. Perhaps then the girl would accept her circumstances and cease to torment her with references to a past she could not remember—a past she had no wish to recall. Perhaps then . . .

A familiar throbbing in the area of her temple put a quick halt to Lydia's wandering thoughts. No, she would not allow herself to be overcome by haunting shadows of the past tonight—not tonight. Walking stiffly to the door of her lodge, Lydia looked outside toward the crowd of men gathered in the center of the ring of lodges. She sought Broken Hand's tall, broad form, but he was hidden in the midst of the milling figures. She smiled, clearing her mind of thought. All would be well. She was Shadow Woman, wife of Broken Hand and he would return to her soon. All was always well when Broken Hand held her in his arms. . . .

Owl Woman's eyes touched on the doorway of the lodge she had raised for Broken Hand and his new wife. Hatred so powerful that it stole her breath surged to life inside her. The white woman stood poised, deep in thought as she surveyed the ongoing council. Shadow Woman . . . the cause of her husband's desertion of her lodge . . . the reason for his weakness . . . the chain which imprisoned Broken Hand's spirit. She would see that woman gone. The prospect of war with the white man had interrupted her plan to rid Broken Hand of Shadow Woman's presence, but she would allow it to disrupt her plan no longer. She would see that woman gone, one way or another. She would wait no longer.

Black Wolf maintained his position to Broken Hand's right. His eyes assessed the men seated in the center of the gathered crowd. Black Kettle's low narration of the message brought to him by George Bent was finished.

The white man wanted peace. The white man's Governor Evans would talk in good faith with the chiefs of their tribes. He would offer them land for their people alone, land where they would be free to hunt in the old ways. The white man would have no place on this land, and would no longer slaughter the buffalo and tear up the ground in search of the yellow ore. Peace would again reign amongst their people and no more would the sounds of mourning be heard within the camp.

The arguments had been vigorous on each side. The older men, their eyes looking to a future where the white man would come in such great numbers as to swallow the land, sought a solution other than war. The younger warriors knew only the need to revenge the blood of their brothers, spilled in treachery and deceit. They did not trust the white man to keep his word. The older men felt they had no choice but to try.

Black Wolf had not spoken at the council. His youth did not allow him a voice, but it was of little consequence. Broken Hand had spoken. His deep vibrant tones had at first been met with scorn and derision. The great warrior chief . . . now speaking peace . . . But the fire in Broken Hand's eyes had revealed a spirit which remained true and proud. Broken Hand had raised his voice in an eloquent demand that all warriors look to their wives and children, to see the widows and orphans they would become at the hands of the wave of white men which would wash over them undiminished, even as their people dwindled in number and ceased to exist. He had asked them not to consider the heat of vengeance which burned in their veins, but a future in which their children would starve and grow weaker while the white man grew stronger. He had declared that he had experienced the death of a son, that the pain was with him still. He had declared his will to fight to his death if the council so decided, but he had also declared that the death of the white man did no more than mirror their own.

Broken Hand had paused, the force of his words ringing in the hearts and minds of those surrounding him. The hush that followed had allowed him time to touch the eyes of all within the circle with his own before he spoke again. With great feeling he had continued to state that to save their people they must look to a peace which would guarantee that they could ride strong and proud in the land, that their children could grow strong, that they no longer need shed their blood to live. He had said that now was the time to seek such a peace, that we could not allow this time to escape us.

His words spent, Broken Hand had stepped back to allow Black Kettle to lead them further. The tenseness inside him growing stronger, Black Wolf assessed the miens of the chiefs around him. The question was raised, the vote received.

Peace . . . there would be peace.

Chapter XI

Wally Durham raised his head from the stream at which he worked. The unrelenting sun had raised beads of perspiration on his forehead and upper lip, and had marked his shirt with dark stains at his underarms and back. Straightening stiffly, he lifted his wide-brimmed hat from his head and wiped his forearm across his forehead. Exhausted by long hours of labor, he released a ragged sigh. Turning at a sudden thought, he assessed the condition of his horse and mule which stood idly by a few feet away in his temporary camp, realizing his life depended on their well-being. He gave a low laugh. He need not worry. Those animals were far more protected from the blazing sun than he under the temporary shelter he had erected the night before.

Wally glanced to the pale sky overhead. It was a cloudless blue that promised no relief from the scorching, rainless weeks he had spent in the wilderness. But the solitude, the silence, the heat which seared him were the only therapy for the bleakness which reigned inside him.

Not bothering to step out of the rippling stream in which he stood, he allowed his mind to drift back in painful memory. Lydia . . . his beautiful, fragile Lydia. Her father had opposed their union from the first. He had maintained that a working man without a personal fortune could not maintain his daughter in the style to which she had become accustomed, could not provide the luxuries which had become necessities by reason of her dependence upon them.

146

But Lydia had been adamant. She had loved him almost as much as he loved her. She had told him she needed little to be happy, little besides his love.

Wally gave a low tired laugh and began to walk upstream. And that was what he had given her—pitifully little in addition to his overwhelming love. A roof over her head, necessities instead of luxuries . . . and Faith. The heat of tears burned his lids anew, and Wally brushed a wide, sun-reddened hand across his eyes. Faith, with the blazing mane of his mother, a far deeper hue than his own, had inherited Lydia's beauty and sensitivity, and her grandmother's strength. Faith had been quick, clever, determined. Had been . . .

Lydia had been true to her word to the last. Quiet and forbearing, she had remained at his side without complaint. But he had been determined to restore to her all she had sacrificed for him. He had told her that he would build a house for her, far bigger than the one in which she had been born, that she would recapture the place in society she had sacrificed to marry him. And when all else had failed but their love, he had told her that he would take her west. He had said he had felt in his bones that their future lay in that direction. He had felt the conviction so deep and sure within him that he still could not believe it had all gone so wrong.

Lydia had not wanted to leave New York, but she had followed him, loving him. And he had loved her and the child they had produced from their love. God, how he had loved them. Even now he could not picture a future in which they did not play a part. Perhaps that was the reason he had wandered off into this godless wilderness, alone.

Wally stretched his aching back and flexed his cramped shoulders. His strength had returned, and he was aware that his broad frame was once again hard and firm. Yes, he was well again.

Wally dropped the pan he held to his side. Prospecting for gold . . . He had needed some reason to wander off into the wilderness, and this had been as good a reason as any. He didn't expect to find any, and he didn't really care. It had been just his luck that he had not seen an Indian, hostile or friendly, in all the weeks he had spent wandering from stream to dwindling stream. He was well aware that his supplies were short, that water was becoming more difficult to find. He had spent several days carefully limiting the contents of his rapidly emptying canteen before stumbling on this ravine and stream a day before. But the water here was cool and fresh, coming in direct descent from the hills close-by. He would stay a little longer. . . .

A sudden rattling sound interrupted his thoughts and Wally froze. His pale eyes jerked to the side. There it was, coiled near the edge of the stream and ready to strike. He must have frightened it with his thrashing.

In a flash, Wally's hand slipped to his hip, and the bark of his gun reverberated in the stillness. Dead . . . it was dead with one shot. He gave a low laugh. Hell, he had more lives than a cat. He had been spared again.

Dropping the pan into the water, Wally stepped out of the stream and leaned down to pick up the limp coil. He had heard somewhere that rattlesnake meat was tasty. Well, he'd find out tonight if that was just idle talk. But not now . . .

Tossing the body of the snake onto the ground a few feet away, Wally leaned down to pick up his pan. It was stuck in the mud at the bottom of the stream. He picked it up and made an attempt to wash it free of the gravelly stones adhering to it. He paused. The stone had a peculiar sparkle. It was bright, golden. . . . Wally's breath caught in his throat.

Taking the time to jam the stone into his pocket, Wally leaned down and dug his pan deep into the same muddy spot. He shook his pan rapidly and swallowed at the sight of the large, bright rocks which surfaced. He gave a low, disbelieving laugh and dug again and again.

The sun had begun to slip below the horizon, but Wally had not budged from the spot he had occupied in the stream for the greater part of the afternoon. He had stripped away his hat and shirt in deference to the heat. His careless disregard for his fair skin had resulted in the heavy freckling

148

and angry color which appeared on the rise of his cheeks and the bridge of his wide, straight nose. His broad, bared shoulders glistened with sweat and were tinted a similar hue, but he had been unconscious of the sun's sting.

Suddenly realizing he was having difficulty seeing the rocks that remained in his pan, he took the few steps out of the water and sat abruptly beside the pile he had accumulated so voraciously within the past few hours. The last pink rays of the setting sun glinted on the uncomely pile and he shook his head in disbelief. Reaching out, he took a large nugget and brought it closer to his face. Yes, there was no mistaking it . . . it was gold. He had indeed found what he had set out to find when he had come west.

He had struck gold.

Suddenly he was laughing, long and loud. The deep, rich tone of his voice echoed against the nearby hill, reverberating back in his ears in the eerie stillness. He was still laughing when he carelessly tossed the nugget back onto the ground beside him.

Rich . . . he was a wealthy man at last. He had no doubt he would be able to locate the source of his find, and then he could have more money than he would ever need. He had fulfilled his promise to Lydia. It was just too bad that he had done it too late.

Too late . . . The last dying rays of sun slipped below the horizon. Without their glow, the nuggets turned dark again, became rocks indistinguishable from the many others which lay on the ground around him. Just like his life without Lydia and Faith . . . no sparkle . . . dark . . . dead.

Tears, silent and unbidden, slipped out the corners of his light eyes and he sat in silence. They were not tears of joy. He had no joy in him.

Chapter XII

Owl Woman walked to the doorway of her lodge and looked to the brilliant afternoon sky. A clear blue, it showed no trace of clouds which might bring the rain needed to the rapidly drying plain, but she cared not. Her eyes moved to the distance, searching the sweep of land before her. In her bitterness, she cared for little—very little. Her thoughts, her dreams, the driving force of her day were centered on the woman who resided in the lodge with Broken Hand. Shadow Woman . . . Shadow Woman was true to her name, for in her coming Shadow Woman had cast the shadow of blight on Owl Woman's life. She had no purpose left but to see that woman gone.

But Owl Woman's perusal of the distant plain was not idle. Her eyes moved amongst the familiar rises, amongst the figures of mounted warriors as they slipped into the distance, seeking . . .

Abruptly, Owl Woman's gaze froze. Straining, she sought to make out the figure which had just come into her line of vision. Her heart leaping in her breast, Owl Woman began to breathe rapidly with excitement. Yes . . . yes, it was he! Her long-awaited opportunity had come! It was now arriving on the horse and mules which were becoming gradually clearer to her eye. Yes, the time was near!

Walking Woman labored in silence over the moccasins

she fashioned with care, but Faith knew a deep restlessness. She ran her eyes around the confines of the lodge and leaned forward to stir the pot which cooked over the low fire. She had lost track of the number of times she had stirred it within the last hour. She was certain she would stir it countless times more.

Drawing herself to her feet, Faith took a few, limited steps. Turning, she took the same steps back. Prison . . . she was confined in a hide prison with an open door, and it was all the fault of Black Wolf and his demands!

Her mind giving her cause to regret her unfair accusation of a moment before, Faith frowned. If she were to be more just, she would have to admit Black Wolf's caution, his instructions to Walking Woman to see that she remained in the lodge, only reflected his concern. A letter had been sent to Fort Lyon a day before, to which Black Kettle was still awaiting a reply, and the tenuous peace had made the warriors restless. White Eagle had ridden by the lodge on many occasions. She had seen the fury in Black Wolf's eyes as he had held the arrogant Arapaho's leer. She did not wish to become the cause of a conflict betwen those two men. Refusing to admit her concern for the younger, more slender Black Wolf, she had maintained that a conflict between them would only call attention to her. With the unsettled state of affairs, she did not wish to endanger Mama, herself or any of the other hostages in any way.

Faith looked through the open doorway into the glare of the midday sun. Sounds of movement came from all sides of the camp. It was only she who remained restless and confined since early morning. How she longed to go outside and feel the sun on her head, the breeze on her face. She could take a walk along the river. There she might be able to find some flowers which had not been trampled. Then she could pick them, and if Broken Hand did not see her, she could take them to Mama's lodge.

A familiar thickness rose in Faith's throat and she brushed her hand over her eyes. Her heart twisting painfully, Faith remembered her glimpse of Mama a few days before. Mama wore Indian dress now. Even at first glimpse, she had been able to see the garment had been carefully fashioned by her mother's own hands. Mama did those things so well. Faith remembered well the pride on Papa's face when Mama had fashioned a beautiful new dress for her thirteenth birthday. Papa had appreciated Mama's skill all the more because Mama had been forced to develop it due to their scant financial circumstances. If Papa could see her now . . .

Papa . . . she had lost him forever, and now she was beginning to believe that Mama was just as lost to her as he.

Faith was unaware of Walking Woman's perusal until Walking Woman's soft voice broke the silence of the lodge.

"The restlessness within you burns clearly in your eyes. Your youthful spirit wishes to be free of this place, Fire Spirit. My heart goes out to you, but I cannot afford you the permission you seek. Even now White Eagle waits."

"I know." Raising her hand with a motion that silenced Walking Woman's words, Faith was turning to reply when a step at the doorway of the lodge abruptly spun her back toward Black Wolf's unexpected appearance. His tall, youthful frame was in dark relief against the sunlight streaming through the doorway behind him, and she was unable to see his face as he hesitated briefly.

"Walking Woman's fingers are never idle, but you walk the lodge with the freedom of a child. Can your hands not aid Walking Woman in her work?"

Faith fought to control the spontaneous anger Black Wolf's remark raised inside her.

"There is little I can do here, confined as I am. I am not trained in the ways of making clothes out of animal hides."

"Shadow Woman finds no difficulty there."

His response cutting all the more deeply in view of her own thoughts of a moment before, Faith raised her chin bravely.

"Mama would not be so malleable to your ways if she were capable of memory."

Again Black Wolf hesitated. "Shadow Woman has chosen to forget the past. She is content to pass the remainder of her life as Broken Hand's wife."

"No. It is just that she is unwell. She—"

Black Wolf's small gesture silencing her halting response,

he took a step toward her, extending his hand in invitation. Faith was startled by the gesture, even more startled by the unexpected softness in his voice.

"Come, we will not speak of these things now. Since Walking Woman does not have need of your aid, you may accompany me as I complete a task which I have long neglected. It is of considerable importance, and I fear I have already put it off too long."

Faith hesitated at the odd note in his tone. His abrupt change in attitude had caught her off guard, and she searched her mind for its cause. But the desire to be free of the lodge, if only for a short time, overcame her caution. In a sudden decision she reached out to take the hand Black Wolf extended. The touch of his long, slender fingers sent a peculiar tingle down her spine and she lifted her eyes to Black Wolf's face. Shadowed as it was by the light behind him, she was unable to make out his expression. Annoyed, she shrugged off her temporary lapse, determined that she would accept the opportunity for some fresh air and exercise while it was offered.

Turning unexpectedly as they emerged through the doorway of the lodge, Black Wolf untied the horse he had secured nearby. Within a moment he was mounted. His gaze met hers with great sobriety for a few short seconds as she raised the crystal blue of her eyes to his.

Answering her silent question in a sweeping movement, he lifted her up and seated her across his horse, in front of him. Taken completely unawares by Black Wolf's unexpected action, Faith maintained her silence as Black Wolf heeled his horse into movement.

Black Wolf guided his horse carefully through the crowded camp. His arm wrapped around Fire Spirit's waist, he held her protectively close. Shoulders squared, he kept his gaze forward, aware of the many eyes which followed him. A small muscle ticked revealingly in his cheek as he passed the lodge of Spotted Elk and felt the weight of the frowning Cheyenne's stare. He was well aware that Spotted Elk had

153

been persistent in his attempt to pay his attentions to Fire Spirit, but he was also aware that they had been to no avail. Fire Spirit continued to avoid Spirited Elk, and he was glad. Had it not been so, he would have forbidden her the small freedom left to her within the camp.

With great deliberation, Black Wolf turned his horse up between yet another row of lodges. He rode slowly in order that White Eagle might view Fire Spirit and him together. He was wearying of White Eagle's attempts to force Fire Spirit into an unwise act which would put her at his mercy. This slow ride around camp was calculated to impress even more clearly than before upon two of Fire Spirit's most persistent pursuers that she was firmly under his protection.

But Black Wolf had another motive as well. Content at last that his message had been conveyed as White Eagle turned in anger and disappeared into his lodge, Black Wolf urged his horse abruptly out toward the freedom of the open plains.

Black Wolf kicked his horse into a full gallop as they headed across the yellowed, swaying grass spread out before them. A spontaneous smile of excitement moved across Faith's lips as the animal beneath them stretched out its powerful legs, consuming the ground in long, even strides. The sweetly scented air buffeted her face, sweeping away the restlessness which had tormented her so relentlessly a short time before. It whipped her hair into streaming red flames which licked the bared flesh of the strong chest which supported her. Faith laughed, reveling in the freedom of the plains which lay before her as far as her eyes could see, in the golden glow of the sun which warmed her, in the thrill of the robust animal beneath her, as Black Wolf urged him to an even faster pace.

They were racing over the land and the thrill inside Faith grew. Faith had watched Indian maidens as they had occasionally taken the mounts of their fathers and raced up into the hills. Had Black Wolf known how she had envied that freedom? Surprisingly, her envy had not been tied to a longing for escape, for she had long ago settled in her mind that she would not attempt escape without Mama. Instead, it came from a suppressed desire to experience the joys of this native race, their freedom and their appreciation of the earth around them which shone in eyes too often clouded with hatred.

But the strong arms which held her fast, even as they guided the racing pony with effortless grace, were reining him to a slower pace. A low sound of protest escaped her lips. Looking up, she caught the flash of pleasure in Black Wolf's eyes the moment before he responded by heeling his mount to its former rapid pace.

The strong animal was blowing heatedly when Black Wolf reined him to a slower gait once more. Black Wolf's strong arms tightened around her momentarily as he turned the horse toward a small shaded copse in the distance. They approached it in a silence which bespoke appreciation for the beauty of the cloudless day, the peace of the land around them, and the brief respite granted by its soundless solitude.

Their horse was breathing more evenly as they neared the brief foliage. Black Wolf reined to a stop beside a low tree and dismounted. Turning, he reached up, his strong hands closing around her waist as he lifted her easily from the saddle. Allowing his horse to wander toward the small trickle of water appearing unexpectedly from beneath a nearby boulder, Black Wolf urged Faith toward a shaded spot. He smiled unexpectedly as she dropped to the ground on the sweet-smelling grass and looked up to him with a spontaneous smile.

Standing towering over her for long moments, he looked down at her until the smile slowly faded from his lips. Lowering himself to sit beside her, Black Wolf stared with great pensiveness into her face. His silence allowed Faith unanticipated time to study the clarity of his sharply chiseled features, the intensity in his expressive dark eyes. She marveled at the smoothness of the richly colored, hairless skin of his cheeks, the fine line of his lips, and the appealing manner in which they had moved into his smile. He did not touch her, but she could feel the strength of his broad

155

shoulders, knew he would someday surpass even Broken Hand with the size and breadth of his well-muscled body. She was silently incredulous that in the months of their daily living, she had so seldom considered the true extent of his appeal.

Faith was suddenly grateful for this brief interlude where she could look upon him without the influence of malevolence and remembered pain. She had needed this respite desperately. Her spontaneous smile raised Black Wolf's hand to her cheek, and he gently stroked back the fiery wisps which had adhered to her temple. He spoke softly, his voice unusually deep in tone.

"It is quiet here. It is a place where the mind and heart run free of the weight of care. It is good to talk in a place such as this."

Black Wolf's touch slipped to her throat, where he traced its slender curve before allowing his hand to move into the fiery cloud resting against her shoulders. His fingers tangled in the windblown silk and she saw a responsive flicker in the deep velvet of his eyes.

"It was a place such as this, on a peaceful, sun-swept plain long ago, where Sweet Medicine restored the buffalo to my people when they were hungry."

Faith shook her head, her brow creasing in confusion.

"Sweet Medicine?"

"He who walked and moved among us . . . the giver of all good things to my people. The buffalo had disappeared from the land. My people hunted for many moons, but could not find them. The men suffered badly for their failure to provide for their families, and the women and children cried with hunger. It was then that Sweet Medicine came.

"Sweet Medicine instructed my people to wait four days while he sang. As he had predicted, a few buffalo appeared the first day, but they were allowed to pass. There were more the second and third day, and they, too, were allowed to pass. Still Sweet Medicine sang. On the fourth day, as Sweet Medicine had declared, the buffalo were all around camp. Sweet Medicine called to the people to go out among them and kill only what was needed and bring it back. The people did as they were told, and there was feasting and celebration. The buffalo have remained among us since that time, and we have not gone hungry."

Black Wolf moved his hand in Faith's hair. He stroked the silken spirals before entangling his hand within them once more.

"My people are beginning to go hungry again. The buffalo are moving from the land, from the white hunters who seek them for their hides."

Noting the tension that began to beset her, Black Wolf moved his soothing caress to the stiffening curve of Faith's shoulder.

"But the white commander has called for peace, and the chiefs have sent a letter to the fort which speaks their intentions to hold council with him. The coming of peace will restore the buffalo to the land and our people will thrive and grow."

Black Wolf's low, intimate tone left Faith unexpectedly without response. She wanted to tell him that she, too, wished for peace, for the cessation of the vicious cycle of hatred and death which had caused so much pain, but she could not find the words.

Black Wolf drew closer. She could feel his breath against her cheek, the warmth his body exuded.

"Sweet Medicine remained among my people for many years. He took a wife, and he had great pride in her. He combed her hair and painted her face, and kept her in fine clothes. And when he left for another place, he took her with him. She remained with him and lived with him, and they gave comfort to each other."

Cautiously, his eyes intent on her face, Black Wolf drew Faith into his arms. She could feel the rapid pounding of his heart against her chest, the youthful strength he carefully restrained even as he clutched her close against him. His words were soft against her hair.

"You are yet a child, Fire Spirit, but you are soon to be a woman. I saw your body, and in it I saw the promise of the woman you would soon become. You live among us as one of us, although you do not yet acknowledge that you will be

157

Cheyenne. Your father is gone, a victim of the same hatred which took my mother, Tall Ree, and many others whose lives have left us mourning their loss. Shadow Woman has entered a vale where she is as lost to you as she would have been had she met the same fate as the father you loved. You are without parents to whom I might send my emissaries and bring my gifts, so I must speak directly to you."

Faith was suddenly trembling. The ardor in Black Wolf's voice left no room for confusion of the thoughts he wished to convey. Shaken by the feelings its throbbing tone awoke within her, Faith remained motionless, silent. Her bemused state did not go unnoted by Black Wolf. He drew back so he might see her face to judge her reaction to his words. Supreme tenderness softened his expression as he held her eyes with his.

"My words surprise you. Anger, sadness, mourning has stood long and hard between us. We are sworn enemies of each other, and the war has raged hot and deep between us, even though I was sworn your protector. It masked the warmth that grew inside me, the warmth fed by your courage, your strength, and your unwilling compassion. Your beauty is not of our people, but it fills my eyes so that I can see no other. The fire of your spirit has burned into my soul, never to be released from its place there. I would wait for your childhood to fully pass from you, Fire Spirit. I would wait for the bloom of the beauty which now only begins to show its face. I would keep you safe, within the lodge we share with Walking Woman, until the time that I may take you to myself and make you one with my spirit."

Black Wolf paused. He breathed deeply against the emotions which filled his eyes and heart before he spoke once more.

"The peace which is about to come has allowed me to think of a time when the white man will no longer be my enemy, when I must put aside the vengeance which has driven me. I forced the vengeance and hatred from my heart and looked inside. In there I saw you had already found a place, and I knew it was there that you would stay."

Faith's lips trembled as she fought to form a response, but

Black Wolf covered them with his fingers.

"No, the child does not answer, for the woman who will someday be. I but wished to declare my intentions. By doing so I set my claim so no other can come before me."

Releasing her unexpectedly, Black Wolf reached down to retrieve a small bag at his waist. He pulled it open and removed two carved rings. He held one up to her.

"It is the custom of my people to exchange rings as a sign of a future promise. I offer this ring to you now."

Taking her small hand in his, Black Wolf slid the carved circle onto her finger. His lips curving in a smile, he held the other ring out to her.

"If you respect my words and the wish that no other will come before me, you must place this one on my hand."

Her eyes on the small, carved circle, Faith swallowed hard. She was confused, disoriented. In this silent place, away from the world around them, she did not recognize Black Wolf as her enemy. Instead, she felt the strength of the bond between them growing, and she knew not what to do. Black Wolf saw her perplexity, and the love he had only recently acknowledged within his mind swelled inside him.

Taking her hand, Black Wolf placed the ring between her fingers. Carefully, he guided her hand to slip the ring onto his. When it was done, he raised her small hand to his lips. Their warmth seared her and she gasped.

"You need not fear the power of these rings, Fire Spirit. Until such time as you are truly a woman, they will bring little change between us. You will continue to live as before, in Walking Woman's lodge, under my instruction. But the protection the rings afford will be twofold. They will protect you from Spotted Elk and White Eagle, and they will protect me from the very determined Deer Woman."

The annoyed quirk of Fire Spirit's lips at the mention of Deer Woman's name raised a flicker of satisfaction within Black Wolf. He knew that feeling was magnified a hundredfold in his own breast each time Spotted Elk followed Fire Spirit with his eyes. The presence of the same emotion within her heart gave him hope.

Black Wolf was suddenly amused. For the first time, Fire

Spirit refused to meet his eyes. So, where fear of his wrath and even death could not force the lowering of her brave chin, the weight of two small rings and the uncertain feelings they raised inside her could. Extending his hand, Black Wolf gently tipped Fire Spirit's face up to his.

"Our bond is sealed, Fire Spirit, but now we will think of other things. We will lie back against the grass, and we will speak of times when our worlds were unknown to each other, a time when peace reigned in both our hearts. First, you must speak."

Pressing her firmly backward until she reclined, staring up at the swaying foliage overhead, Black Wolf did the same. The warm flesh of his arm pressed against hers, forging their bond as she began to speak. The swell of memories, once released, knew no bounds, and Fire Spirit was soon speaking freely of former times.

Black Wolf's hand moved to covers hers as she spoke. He felt the ring against his palm, and his heart raced in anticipation of a time when the girl beside him would be a woman, and he could make her his own.

Her voice continued on, and its music filled his heart.

The movement of the sun in the afternoon sky marked the passing hours, and Black Wolf drew his words to a halt. Fire Spirit was lying on her stomach beside him, her eyes searching his face as she listened to the tales of his youth with obvious fascination. He was much relieved at the return of normalcy between them, but her nearness, the appeal in her beautiful face looking so innocently into his, disturbed him greatly. It was time to leave this place of solitude. He was only a man, after all.

Drawing himself hastily to his feet, Black Wolf reached down to assist Fire Spirit. The warmth in her small hands, the openess of her smile was too much to withstand. In a quick movement, unexpected even to himself, he drew her close against him. His arms held her as his mind fought his raging feelings. Child that she was, Fire Spirit stirred him more than any woman he had ever known. He trembled to

160

think of his reaction to the woman she would one day become.

He drew back, paying little attention to the hesitation on her face as he slowly dropped his mouth to hers. His lips played slowly against hers, the inadequacy of her untutored response stirring him more than he had thought possible. He withdrew from the kiss, knowing he could not afford more. Placing his trembling hands on her waist, he swung her up onto his horse and mounted behind her.

He clutched her close, and as a defense against his shaken feelings, heeled his horse into a gallop.

They were racing across the plains once more. The glorious red-gold of Fire Spirit's hair whipped against his neck and chest and Black Wolf sensed the thrill their wild ride raised within her. His own elation grew. The certainty within him set his heart to pounding, and he clutched her closer still. This girl, this fiery, fearless girl of white skin, would be his woman. No one else would do.

Owl Woman's round face was filled with bitter frustration. She looked to the last of the crowd still milling in a circle around the white trader and his wares. Her frustration soared anew. She had long awaited this man's coming to their village, and now the afternoon was on the wane and time was growing short. Soon . . . soon it would be too late. . . .

Owl Woman's eyes moved to the distance, her heart leaping as they touched on a mounted figure coming into sight. Yes, it was Black Wolf and the girl. . . . She took a deep, shaky breath and darted a quick glance toward the lodge Broken Hand and Shadow Woman shared. Broken Hand had kept his new wife carefully secreted against the white trader's inquisitive gaze, and Black Wolf's unexpected departure from camp with the girl had added a complication she had not expected to her plan. The white trader was beginning to gather his wares. He would soon withdraw from camp, and with him would go her opportunity to alert the white man's fort to the presence of Shadow Woman and the red-haired girl in their midst.

Owl Woman gave a low snort. Her plans for ridding Broken Hand and their camp of the white captives had run into one problem after another from the start. Broken Hand's close scrutiny of his much cherished wife had allowed her little freedom. She had been unable to arrange more than a few, brief opportunities for the girl to speak to Shadow Woman. She had at first thought that the girl could be successful in driving the cloud from Shadow Woman's mind in those limited meetings. She had hoped, with the return of memory, the white woman would cleave to her child and turn from Broken Hand. But the event had not come about, and she now knew that Shadow Woman's memory was too deeply buried to be so easily unearthed.

The arrival of the Arapahos at their camp had brought the news that the commander at Fort Lyon had searched with great eagerness for the girl and her mother. The searching had been abandoned because the commander there now thought them to be dead. Based on that knowledge, Owl Woman's new plan had been born. It was well known to her people that the trader, Samuel Marsh, moved easily between both white and Indian camps. She had heard Broken Hand speak of his distrust of the man, claiming him to be the eyes and ears of the white man's fort within their midst. It had been her intention to use this man well. She had realized that Shadow Woman, in her assumed Indian dress, might go unrecognized by this man, but she knew for certain the blazing hair of Fire Spirit would not. It had seemed it would be so easy to make certain Samuel Marsh saw the two of them together, so he might make certain in his mind who they were. She now realized that her plan was not so simple as she had thought.

A flicker of movement to her side jerked Owl Woman's gaze back toward Broken Hand's lodge. Broken Hand had moved to the door of the lodge in response to a summons. He spoke for a few brief moments before departing behind the slender youth who had obviously arrived with a message. Almost disbelieving her sudden reversal of luck, Owl Woman turned back to watch as Black Wolf reined his horse up before his lodge and followed Fire Spirit inside.

Her breathing ragged, Owl Woman hastened to the lodge beside hers. Pausing, she called out her request. within seconds a small, quick-footed child was scampering across the camp. The message that Broken Hand wished Black Wolf's appearance at the talks presently being conducted with the Arapaho would keep Black Wolf from interfering. It would keep him away long enough for her to accomplish her task.

A quick call to Shadow Woman sent her obediently to Owl Woman's lodge to attend to the food cooking there. Smiling, Owl Woman made two more requests, sending two more children on their way, and then she slipped silently back into her lodge. A satisfied glance through her open doorway showed her that Walking Woman, the red-haired girl, and the white trader had all but bumped into each other in their effort to respond to her summons. Her quick move to the doorway brought Shadow Woman up behind her, and Owl Woman did not miss the quick startled glance the trader shot at the red-haired girl and Shadow Woman. Recognition flashed in his eyes.

Elation suffused Owl Woman, only to disappear at the sound of a step to the side of her lodge, at her first glimpse of Black Wolf's livid anger.

"Walking Woman, Fire Spirit, you will return to your lodge."

Black Wolf's quick command sent Shadow Woman moving rapidly back toward her own lodge as well. Dismissing the trader with a gruff word, Black Wolf turned back to Owl Woman once more.

His rage tenuously controlled, he grated heatedly, "Owl Woman, it is only my respect for the mother of my friend, Tall Ree, which will allow me to keep from Broken Hand your flaunting of his wishes. But be warned. Do not again attempt a similar trick, or I will see that Broken Hand learns of your treachery."

Watching as Black Wolf strode back toward his lodge in anger, Owl Woman slowly brought her anxious breathing under control. She had not expected her plan to be discovered, but it mattered little what fate befell her. The woman who had stolen her husband's brave heart and replaced it with softness would soon be gone. The white man's fort would now be alerted to her presence here. She had accomplished her task. It was done.

Turning, Owl Woman reentered her lodge. Her mind and her heart were at rest.

Watching from the doorway of her lodge, Shadow Woman fought to dispel the quaking which had beset her. Owl Woman's hatred for her and for the red-haired girl had driven her to an act of disobedience. She was uncertain what had truly happened, but Black Wolf's barely restrained fury had shaken her.

But it had not been Black Wolf's anger which had raised the rapid beat of her heart to a pounding in her ears, caused the dryness in her throat and the shuddering which wracked her. The ring on Black Wolf's hand—white and carved—had been in sharp contrast to the russet tone of his skin. The matching ring on the girl's finger had not contrasted so sharply with her fair skin, but its presence there had jumped out at Shadow Woman, shaking her severely. Waves of shock again assailed her. She knew the significance of those rings.

Shadow Woman shook her head. No, the girl was a child. It could not be. It *should* not be.

The pain, the pain was returning, the fierce pounding in her temple that signaled a resumption of the shattered memories which would give her no rest. She did not want to remember . . . but those rings . . . those rings . . . No, it should not be. . . .

S. G. Colley, U.S. Indian Agent for the Upper Arkansas, again read the missive in his hand. His heavy brow furrowed in a frown, he lifted his eyes at last to the two military men impatiently awaiting his reaction.

"Yes, this letter is an exact copy of the one I received from Black Kettle and the other chiefs."

"Well, what is your reaction, man?" Major Wynkoop's

164

impatience exploded in a sharp question which shattered the unnatural silence of his small office. Pinning the pensive Indian agent with his stare, he continued tightly, "Captain Potter and I admit to being greatly encouraged by this letter, but, frankly, we're also suspicious. You know damned well those Indians have been more than successful in their raids on the Overland Trail. I've received too many communications from the governor not to be aware that food supplies are growing disastrously short in Denver—flour going from nine dollars to twenty-five dollars a hundredweight. And with that plague of locusts devouring the crops on the South Platte . . ." Major Wynkoop shook his head. "So why do you suppose the Indians are suing for peace now?"

His eyes lowering to the letter once more, Colley paused in response. His patience all but expired, Major Wynkoop shot Captain Potter a tight glance. "Come on, out with it, Colley! You're supposed to be the expert here. We want your opinion—some guidance, damn it!"

"Keep your pants on, Major." Raising his eyes to the exasperated Wynkoop, Colley continued with irritating hesitation. "Those Indians aren't as stupid as people would like to believe. They realize these are changing times. Their brothers farther south have seen the buffalo disappearing, and as much as their hearts cry out for blood, they also see the toll this war is taking on their nation. It seems to me Bent took just the right tack with Black Kettle, and persuaded him to lend his influence to push the cause of peace. He must have been doing some hefty talking. It says here that they want to make peace, providing you also make peace with the Kiwoa, Comanche, Arapaho, Apache, and the Sioux."

"I read the letter, Colley. I know what it says. It also says that they have prisoners they're willing to give up in exchange for the Indian prisoners being held in Denver."

"The prisoners aren't the important issue here. As I see it—"

"To hell, they aren't!" No longer able to restrain his annoyance with Colley's hesitation, Major Wynkoop pressed hotly, "Those savages took a woman and a boy near Plum Creek, and two women and three children from

165

Liberty Farm. I'll be damned if I want to have their scalps delivered to this fort like the scalps of those Durham women."

"I don't want that anymore than you do, Major!" Obviously roused to a similar anger by the major's statement, Colley waved the letter in his hand emphatically. "But I don't want to take responsibility for sending more soldiers out there and risking any more lives."

"I'll take the responsibility, Colley. That's what they pay me for. All I want to know from you is whether you think I can trust Black Kettle to keep his word about exchanging prisoners."

"It usually isn't the Indian who doesn't keep his word in an agreement, Major. I think you know that."

"That's all I wanted to know." Turning abruptly toward Captain Potter, Major Wynkoop instructed briskly, "Get the men ready, Captain. We'll take as many as we can— about one hundred and thirty should do it. We'll take one section of battery and we'll take the Indian messengers who brought the letter back with us under guard."

"Use your head, Major!" His head snapping up with disbelief, Colley waved the letter once more. "It also says here in this letter that three Cheyenne and two Arapaho war parties are still out—expected back soon. That means they don't know about Black Kettle's letter! You're liable to be leading your men into—"

"I'm going to get those prisoners back, Colley, while Black Kettle's still of a mind to return them. But I'm not stupid nor foolhardy. I don't intend to go charging out into Indian country while five war parties are still roaming, looking for a fight. I'll give those war parties a reasonable time to return."

"A reasonable time? How long's reasonable?"

Refusing a specific answer, Major Wynkoop regarded the Indian agent with a slitted gaze. "I haven't decided. In any case, it's what they call in the academy a 'calculated risk,' Colley. I've taken them before, and as a good soldier, I'll take them again. And now I'd suggest you draft a letter to Governor Evans, telling him about this communication."

"Of course, you want me to delay sending it until *after*

you've left."

"I didn't say that, Colley."

"You don't have to."

A small smile cracked Major Wynkoop's lips. He extended his hand.

"You're a good man, Colley."

Accepting Wynkoop's hand, Colley shook it firmly. Turning to the young captain who had observed the exchange in silence, he then extended his hand to him with a tight smile.

"Good luck, William. With this crazy man in command, you're going to need it."

His expression sober, Captain Potter accepted Colley's hand.

"Major Wynkoop and I share similar views on this situation, Colley. And the men and I are just as anxious as he to do something positive for a change."

"Well, let's hope this whole thing works out to be the positive measure you're expecting."

With a casual salute, Colley walked toward the door. His hand on the knob, he turned back briefly.

"I'll start writing that letter. I'll write real slow."

Waiting until the door closed behind Colley, Major Wynkoop turned abruptly toward Captain Potter.

"William, get the men ready. We'll leave tomorrow."

Captain Potter could not suppress his smile.

"Yes, I'd say that's a reasonable time, Major."

"Damned reasonable."

With a quick salute, Captain Potter walked briskly toward the doorway. He had only taken a few steps outside when a broad figure moved out of the shadows of the walk.

"William . . ."

At the low summons, Captain Potter turned. His eyes snapped toward the familiar, sunburned face topped with shaggy red hair, to meet the pale eyes riveted to his.

"What's going on, William? What did those Indians have to say in that letter? What the hell's the secret?"

"There's no secret, Wally." His expression softening, William Potter paused. "I thought you were going back to

Denver this morning. Your claim's all duly registered. You're going to be a rich man. I'd think you'd be anxious to get work started on it."

"My claim can wait. Being rich has lost its importance to me somehow. Right now I'd like to know what has this fort on tenterhooks."

Captain Potter's handsome young face creased with hesitation. He didn't want to stir this man up. It was obvious Wally Durham would be a long time in getting over the death of his family. This talk of returning hostages—

"Damn it, William, something's in the wind. The men have been buzzing all morning, and Colley just left Wynkoop's office looking like he had the weight of the world on his shoulders. Is there going to be an attack? If there is, I want you to know you can count on me to—"

"No, Wally." Fully realizing the big, red-headed man ached for retribution, Captain Potter shook his head. "The fact is, Black Kettle has sent letters to both Colley and the major telling them he wants to talk peace."

"Peace!" Wally Durham's face flushed darkly. "It's a little late to talk peace, isn't it? They've been raiding and killing for—"

"They're holding the hostages from Plum Creek and Liberty Farm. They said they're willing to exchange them for—"

"Hostages. They're going to exchange hostages—"

"I'm sorry, Wally. I'm damned sorry it's too late for your family, but Major Wynkoop isn't going to let the same thing happen to these women and children, not if he can help it. We're riding out tomorrow."

Wally took a deep breath. His voice obviously affected by emotion, he responded hoarsely.

"I'm going with you, William."

"Oh, no, you're not! Major Wynkoop will have enough problems on his hands. He can't afford to worry if you—"

"Do you really think I'd do anything to jeopardize the return of those hostages, William? What in hell do you think I am? I just want to know—to see with my own eyes—that those women and children are all right."

"And if they aren't?"

"I have to go. If I can't travel with the troop, I'll follow behind it."

"You could get yourself killed."

Wally Durham's only reply was a short shrug of his broad shoulders. Captain Potter stared at him in silent frustration. When he spoke again, his voice was resigned.

"You'll have to talk to Major Wynkoop about that, Wally. I have to get the men started."

Captain Potter's brow pulled into a tight frown as Wally Durham nodded and turned abruptly in the direction of Major Wynkoop's office. After staring at his retreating back for a few seconds, William Potter turned just as abruptly. He had a feeling Wallace Durham was going to be in on this encounter, whether they liked it or not. Squaring his shoulders, he lengthened his stride. Hell, he couldn't think of better company.

Once more confined in the lodge, Faith strained her eyes into the falling dusk outside the doorway. She was still shaken by Black Wolf's rage. In truth, she was uncertain as to the cause for it. Walking Woman and she had merely responded to a summons from Owl Woman. It was still a mystery to her why Owl Woman had sent the boy with the message that her mother, Shadow Woman, was ill and wished to see her. The memory of the fear Owl Woman's message had induced within her was so strong that it shook her once more in retrospect. Neither Walking Woman nor she had suspected Owl Woman of treachery.

But whatever Owl Woman's plan, it most certainly had been thwarted by Black Wolf's quick intervention. There had been no more than a look exchanged between the four women and the trader who had blundered into the affair, before the women had suffered Black Wolf's wrath.

Following Black Wolf's orders, Walking Woman and she had returned immediately to their lodge, and they had not seen Black Wolf since. Faith frowned, her mind slipping back to the day they had spent together on the endless prairie. Somehow it seemed so long ago, so unreal. The two people they had been were entirely unlike the two who had participated in that dramatic confrontation a short time later.

The angry, autocratic brave had not been the same Black Wolf who had smiled into her eyes, whispered words which had turned her strangely weak, pressed his mouth to hers. Faith's hands slipped down to finger the small, carved band which still adorned her finger. It had not escaped Walking Woman's notice, but she had made no comment, and Faith had offered no explanation. Indeed, she was uncertain whether the band should remain where Black Wolf had placed it. He had explained it was for her protection against Spotted Elk's leers and White Eagle's threatening glances. He had said it was for his protection as well. She gave a small grimace. Deer Woman . . . of course.

A sudden step outside the doorway of the lodge drew Faith's eyes in its direction just as a familiar outline appeared in the opening. Her expression sober, Faith met Black Wolf's gaze. She hesitated as he stretched out a hand in invitation.

Black Wolf's deep voice broke the uneasy silence which followed.

"Come, Fire Spirit. Do you so easily forget the bands we wear? I would walk with you beside the river before darkness falls. The path to that spot passes many lodges where our bands will be duly noted. I would set in the minds of all who wish to challenge our bond that we are promised to each other."

"Black Wolf . . . I'm not sure—"

"Come, Fire Spirit."

Yielding to his words, Faith rose to her feet. When she did not reach for his hand, Black Wolf took hers. His fingers intertwining with hers, he held their hands and the matching bands up toward Walking Woman.

"See here, Walking Woman. This child is promised to the warrior who is your dead sister's son. But she will not be a child much longer, and the woman she becomes will be my wife."

170

A low gasp escaped Faith's lips. Why was the statement, spoken aloud in such definite terms, so shocking to her ears? She had known what Black Wolf had been intending, yet the words sounded so final. And she was so confused. Only a few days before she had been certain she hated this tall, handsome Indian who ruled her life so unyieldingly. She had been planning her escape. . . .

The strong hand enclosing hers tightened, and she raised her eyes to Black Wolf's face once more. Understanding flashed in his eyes.

"Come, Fire Spirit. We will talk and your heart will cease its frightened clamoring."

"I'm not frightened!"

A hint of a smile touched Black Wolf's lips.

"That is good. I do not wish to inspire fear within you, Fire Spirit."

Tugging gently on her hand, Black Wolf drew her through the doorway. Relieved to be outside the lodge once more, Faith took a deep, unconscious breath which did not go unnoted by Black Wolf.

"You chafe at the confinement enforced upon you, and my heart is sad. Your spirit was not meant to know restrictions of any kind. I seek to give you freedom, Fire Spirit, but in that freedom I will bind you closer to me. It is my hope you will come to enjoy the tie that binds you. It is a bond I seek willingly for myself."

Dropping her hand, Black Wolf began to walk slowly beside her toward the river. Faith made a stringent effort to ignore the many curious glances their stroll drew. She strove to hide her confusing satisfaction as they passed Deer Woman's lodge. The bold young woman stopped dead in her tracks at their appearance, and Faith could not control a small flutter of her hand which drew the girl's attention to the band she wore there. She did not need to look to see the girl's quick assessment of Black Wolf's hand. In her preoccupation with Deer Woman's reaction, she missed the revealing twitch which jerked at the corner of Black Wolf's mouth.

She did not pass Spotted Elk's lodge with as much

enjoyment. Nodding briefly to Spotted Elk, she quickened her step and avoided more than a brief glance at Silent Woman's grotesquely bloated size. Surely the woman would have her child soon and Spotted Elk would cease his leering. She held her head stiffly averted as they passed White Eagle's lodge, and she was truly uncertain whether they had gone past unnoted.

The shadows of evening were deep when they reached the river. Faith stumbled and Black Wolf's hand reached out to steady her. His hand remained on her arm as they walked. Then it moved up to smooth her back in a caressing gesture which sent little shivers down her spine. They were alone beside the water when Black Wolf stopped their leisurely stroll and turned to her at last.

Startled at his seriousness, Faith shook her head. Perhaps Black Wolf was beginning to become as unsure as she of this surprising twist their lives had taken. But the touch of his hand was gentle as he raised it to her cheek. His sober gaze, traveling her face, appeared to note her confusion.

His voice was low, intimate.

"At first this afternoon, when I saw Walking Woman and you approaching Owl Woman's lodge, I was angry. I was certain you had some part in the deception arranged by Owl Woman. The afternoon we had spent together loomed fresh in my mind, and I felt betrayed. I avoided the lodge and your company and went to the hills to think. It was there that I remembered your expression, the confusion in your eyes, and I came to believe you innocent of any part in the affair. In any case, I reminded myself that you are yet a child and have not severed your ties to your past life. I knew it was my place to instill in you a desire to forget that life so you might put it aside forever."

"I . . . I do not wish to put my old life aside. I want to go back . . . with Mama. This ring is—"

"These rings are your true future, Fire Spirit, not the life you cling to in your mind. Shadow Woman has accepted her future here."

"No, Mama does not accept it. She is sick."

Black Wolf dropped his hand to her arm, gripping it

172

gently to pull her closer. The small smile which moved across his lips stirred her strangely and she waited for him to speak.

"Fire Spirit, we will speak only of ourselves this night. It is a need I feel deep inside me, and it is a need I cannot ignore."

Black Wolf took her hands in his. He raised them to his chest, to press her warm palms flat against the firmly muscled flesh there. His eyes flickered briefly closed at the contact and he gave a short laugh.

"Feel the pounding of my heart, Fire Spirit. It races from your touch, even when your touch is casual, unknowing."

Black Wolf slid her hand across his chest, lifted it to his mouth. The touch of his lips seared her as he kissed her fingers and the small band she wore. His chest was beginning to heave with emotion, and Faith felt her own breath quickening. She swallowed tightly as he raised her hands to lock them around his neck. He pulled her close against his lean length, allowing her to feel the lithe strength of his body, his stirring warmth as he adjusted her against his hard, male contours. Black Wolf's breathing was becoming ragged, and Faith felt a small tremor shake him. His unexpected debility awoke a similar reaction within her as well, and she swallowed tightly against her uncertain feelings.

His features tightening, Black Wolf lowered his head to whisper against her cheek.

"This afternoon, when I realized Owl Woman had sent me on a fool's errand with her message, I raced back to her lodge. It was my thought to chastise her and you as well for your part in whatever treachery was planned. When I arrived I saw the white trader standing beside you. I was uncertain if words had been exchanged, if devious plans were being attempted. The specter of losing you loomed great and threatening in my mind, and my heart knew a new kind of fear. I was enraged by its presence."

Pausing, Black Wolf drew back enough that she might feel the full power of his impassioned gaze. "But my rage has turned to need, Fire Spirit. This afternoon after we spoke together—after I took you into my arms—I drew myself away from you. It is my desire to honor your innocence, cherish it. We were alone and I did not trust my feelings. But here we are not truly alone, and there is safety from the passions which rule my mind. Walking Woman awaits us in the lodge, and it is not unlikely that we could be disturbed here, for many such as we walk this portion of the river. For that reason I would now take you into my arms as I could not dare this afternoon. I would feel you close to me, would assuage the need you have raised within me."

Raising his hand, Black Wolf cupped her cheek while still holding her fast against him, his eyes intent on her trembling lips, his voice a low rasp.

"Part your lips for me, Fire Spirit. I wish to taste your mouth, to savor it deeply."

A low, inaudible word of protest escaped Faith's throat, and Black Wolf pulled her closer still.

"Come, Fire Spirit, give your mouth to me. I would claim it for my own."

Black Wolf's hand moved to her lips. His fingertips trailed against their soft, trembling surface, and Faith released a low gasp at the stirring sensation that ensued. A low, feral response sounded deep in Black Wolf's throat the moment before he covered her parted lips with his own.

Crushed tight against his slender strength, Faith yielded to the seeking pressure of Black Wolf's kiss, the rioting sensations which came alive inside her as he moved his mouth against hers with a driven, voracious hunger. She was reeling from the heat of his claim, lost in the unfamiliar world of Black Wolf's searing touch, his low, passionate murmurs, and the ardent frenzy which soared to life within him. Black Wolf's mouth pressed deeper into hers, his lips worshiping. His tongue explored her mouth, caressing intimately, bringing hers into responsive play. He was drawing lovingly from her, swallowing deeply. His hand slid into her hair, his fingers twisting in the silken strands and clutching her more fiercely to him. He was gasping, grating her name through the increased ardor of his kisses.

Trembling violently, Faith gave herself up to the riotous world of careening colors, soaring sensation, and unknown expectation. She moved instinctively against him as Black Wolf crushed her to the hard wall of his body, as his fervor increased. Abruptly, Black Wolf tore his mouth from hers. His hand tightened in her hair almost to the point of pain as he jerked her head back so she might look into his passion-ravaged face. His chest heaved with ragged breaths as his other hand moved to the warm curves of her buttocks, cupping them to hold her firmly against the hard swell of his body.

"Feel the passion you raise within me, Fire Spirit. Your child's body moves me to a wonder which far surpasses anything I have known before. Your heart, your flesh calls out to me, and I ache to respond to its summons. I ache to take you, make you a part of me, but I cannot violate the youth which yet holds you outside my reach. But if it is an agony, a test I must suffer to make myself worthy of that which is to come, I suffer it gladly. For I will have you, Fire Spirit, make you my own. After many sunsets, the warm days will come to an end. The cold will come, but when the warmth again returns to the land, our waiting will be over. Your child's body will be gone, and I will take you, a woman, to my wife. I will cherish you, Fire Spirit. I will worship you with my body and my heart. You will be with me always."

Swallowing against the emotion apparent in the depths of his eyes, Black Wolf moved her body from his with conscious deliberation. His control obviously tenuous, he held her a distance from him. The darkening shadows of evening played across his handsome face, and Faith swallowed at the wealth of feelings displayed there.

"We must return now, Fire Spirit. A battle rages within me. I dare not test the outcome, for the need within me is great."

Slowly releasing her, Black Wolf turned, urging her to his side as he began walking back in the direction of camp. Her eyes held straight before her, Faith was conscious of the warmth of Black Wolf's perusal. Strangely, she felt lost, alone, deprived without the warmth of his touch.

As if sensing her thoughts, Black Wolf took a step closer, sliding his arm around her shoulders so he might draw her against his side. He pressed his face momentarily to her hair before resuming his slow pace back toward the village.

Her momentary discomfort vanishing as the warmth of his arm encircled her, Faith leaned full into his embrace, allowing herself to enjoy the comfort it entailed. She had determined she would not question her confused feelings, her raging thoughts now. Tomorrow would be soon enough to face them. Tonight she would lean on Black Wolf, and let him love her.

Chapter XIII

Snowing . . . it was snowing and bitter cold. Shivering, Lydia looked down upon a frozen, rolling prairie covered with short grass. Lodges, at least a hundred of them, were clustered in the bend of a river. Cheyenne . . . Arapaho. It was a large camp, but she had never seen this place before.

Lydia looked closer. She recognized the shields of War Bonnet, White Antelope, Lone Bear, Left Hand . . . she saw Black Kettle's lodge. The American flag he had received at council with the soldiers flew on a lodgepole before it. Below that flew a white flag, signifying their peaceful presence on this land.

Dawn was beginning to crease the night sky, and a frigid wind blew against her face. Heavily bundled women were beginning to emerge from the lodges to make their way toward the river.

Lydia shivered again, her confusion great, and a strange panic assailed her. What was she doing up here, away from Broken Hand's lodge? She wanted to return to Broken Hand. She wanted to run to him, to escape this strange, forced observance, but she found she could not move from the spot in which she stood.

The light of morning was growing brighter and she looked to the distance. Her heart beginning to pound rapidly, she saw two lines of cavalry moving furtively toward the camp. There were so many soldiers in those long, trailing lines. She was uncertain . . . could it be five hundred, six or even seven hundred men? As she watched, one group paused while the other moved around to the far side of camp. A small detachment broke off to secure the herd of Indian horses which stood nearby.

She was still watching as the commanding officer raised his hand. He brought it down in an abrupt, silent signal, and the soldiers began a wild, unexpected charge toward the camp. The earth shook with the thunder of racing hooves; the air rang with bloodthirsty shouts. Panic began to mount in the camp below her . . . women running to their lodges, men emerging, incredulous, as the cavalry rode into sight and began to fire.

Frantic women and children were running, scattering in all directions in the frigid morning cold in a frenzied attempt to escape. The soldiers bore down upon them relentlessly, firing, cutting them down as they ran. Screaming . . . gunshots . . . men, women, children falling to the ground, their bodies pounded into the frozen earth by the hooves of the cavalry; cries for mercy ignored as the arm of death descended again and again.

Blood! The ground was covered with blood!

Lydia shuddered, crying out her despair, but her voice was without sound. Helpless—impotent—she watched as the slaughter continued unabated for hours in which no one was spared.

Horror . . . she could not stand the horror any longer. She cried out again, her voice echoing in her ears and she gasped at its grating sound. She sobbed, tasting the salt of her tears as they flowed down her cheeks and trickled against her lips. No . . . no more, no more. . . .

A voice . . . she heard a voice, low and familiar in her ear. It sought to draw her back from the scene of pervading horror. Its deep tone was compelling, penetrating the growing mists, growing louder. A callused hand caressed her cheek, stroked her, comforted her; and she fought to open her eyes.

Broken Hand . . . He was lying beside her, his strong body curved to her trembling slenderness. Lydia jerked a panicked glance around her. She was in her lodge. It was warm, the scent of summer still in the air. The fire she had laid the night before still smoldered.

A low, grateful sob escaped her lips and Broken Hand's frown darkened. His whisper was filled with concern.

"You have been visited by a shadow vision which caused you pain. I sought to bring you back, but I could not awaken you. You were deep within its throes, consumed by its terror."

Lydia wrapped her arms tightly around Broken Hand's neck as she sought his comforting warmth. She buried her face agains this shoulder, sobbing out her despair at the horror which would not leave her. Broken Hand's arms wrapped tightly around her in return. His voice was low in her ear, murmuring soft words of comfort which were to no avail.

Her trembling stilled at last, Lydia lay silent in his arms. She glanced up through the smoke outlet at the top of the lodge to see that the darkness of night still engulfed them. A shudder shook her once more. She was afraid to close her eyes. This long night . . . would it never end?

Broken Hand's broad palm was stroking her hair. His whispered word turned her to his searching gaze. As she had many times before, Lydia raised her hand to Broken Hand's cheek, her fingers tracing the familiar lines now tightened into furrows of concern. His eyes probed the fear in her gaze, looking deeply within her. His expression grew darker.

"I see it in your eyes, the terror which shook you. It was a vision which will give you no peace until its horror is shared with another. I would share that vision, Shadow Woman, and lift the burden of its pain from your shoulders."

"No, I . . . I cannot speak of it. It was terrible . . . blood and death everywhere."

Lydia turned away, once more burying her face against Broken Hand's broad shoulder, but she found no respite. Within moments, broad, callused hands cupped her face, drawing it up to his. The strange light that burned in Broken Hand's pensive gaze seemed to meld to her shadowed stare. She could not escape it or his low entreaty.

"You are a part of me, Shadow Woman, and that part of

me feels pain. Allow the words to flow freely so that I, too, might see this vision which impales you. Come, look to me. Allow the picture to enfold in my eyes and you will be free."

Lydia's first words were a low stammer. A chilled memory of the bitter cold assailed her and she trembled anew. But Broken Hand's strength stilled her shuddering. Slowly, the words unwound, trailed from the terrorized depths of her mind.

With great attention to detail she described the night, the cold, the rolling prairie, the peace of the camp nestled in the curve of the winding river. She paused, recalling vividly that she had counted the number of lodges erected there. Yes, a hundred, over a hundred lodges . . . She was transported back to the eerie cold, war bonnets flashing before her eyes. White Antelope, Standing Water, One Eye, War Bonnet, Spotted Crow, Two Thighs, Bear Man, Yellow Shield, Yellow Wolf. Somehow, it did not seem strange in the silence of the night that these names emerged from her mouth in the native tongue of the Cheyenne . . . Wokaihwokomais, Mapevanists, Nahkuukiyuus. . . .

She looked closer. She saw mounted officers give the order to fire . . . saw soldiers again riding into the midst of the bewildered men and women who had emerged from their lodges, their guns blazing. Cannon, she saw cannon being fired into the fleeing groups of Indians who sought to escape the wholesale slaughter. She saw some seeking to escape in pits dug into the riverbank. She watched them fight bravely until soldiers overran them with their horses. Dead . . . they were all dead.

She saw Black Kettle. He was standing in front of his lodge in a daze. His calls for peace had gone unheeded; the flag he had raised had been blatantly ignored. White Antelope stood beside him. She saw the dawn of realization in Black Kettle's eyes. The white man would not listen. He was bent on killing all Indians in his sight.

Black Kettle began to run, calling out to White Antelope to do the same. White Antelope would not run. He stood bravely, singing his death song:

"Nothing lives long,
Except the earth and the mountains . . ."

And then he was dead! Lydia gasped in an attempt to catch her breath, her heart pounding as White Antelope's blood-spattered body was trampled into the dust by the relentless soldiers.

Great numbers of the people were fleeing up the dry bed of the creek. The soldiers were chasing them, firing at will. Black Kettle's wife fell. Soldiers rode by, firing more shots into her body as she lay wounded. They were being killed, defenseless people driven from their beds at the break of dawn . . . little and big trampled into the dust. . . .

The dust had settled. Captured children were dragged before the commanding officer. His mien was unaffected.

"Kill them. I said kill them all. There will be no exceptions."

The lieutenant raised his gun. He fired into the first child's head, and the child fell to the ground.

Lydia could speak no more. Shock and hysteria had merged to render her incapable of speech.

Shaken, Broken Hand drew her close against his chest. He curved his strong body around hers so she might draw herself into him, meld with his strength. He had seen the vision as Shadow Woman had described it to him, and his heart cried at the futility of Black Kettle's peace. He wondered in which fleeing, panic-stricken group he would be struck dead. He pulled Shadow Woman closer. She had seen it all from afar. She had not been part of the desperate scene. She had not been with him in the camp. The realization shook him greatly. No, he would not lose her. . . .

Broken Hand turned Shadow Woman's face up to his. His mouth covered hers, stifling her sobs. He tasted the sweet moistness there, drinking deeply. He stroked her flawless white skin, fondled the smooth line of her body. He slid himself atop her, loving her even as he entered her intimately. Her low gasp preceded the slow rising of her swollen lids. She looked into his impassioned face as he began to speak.

"I have gone into your heart and mind. I have witnessed and experienced the pain of your vision. From grief such as that which we have shared, there is no consolation save the joining of our souls. I seek to give you all that my heart and body have to offer. When it is done, we will find peace. It is a peace we will give each other, for I fear we will find it in no other way."

The light of understanding was bright in Shadow Woman's eyes as he plunged deep inside her. She rose to meet his thrust, her quaking body giving fully to him. They met again and again in the total melding of their bodies, each plunge relieving them more, numbing their pain. They were gasping on the isolated plane created by their joining when Broken Hand drove deeply one last time. Together they soared from its heights, spiraling as they fell from their ecstatic escape into the reality of their lodge once more.

Shadow Woman lay in Broken Hand's arms, silent and still at last. The perspiration of their mutual passion fused them still, and Broken Hand released a small sigh. She was drifting off to sleep, no longer fearing the darkness of uncertainty which surrounded them. She had trusted him to heal her, and in her trust had found peace.

Broken Hand drew her passionately closer, breathing deeply of the scent which was hers alone. He feared—how strongly he feared—this was the only peace they would ever know.

Chapter XIV

The endless prairie stretched out around them, the yellowing grass undulating gracefully in the brisk, hot wind. The morning sun, unabating, beat down in golden warning of the heat of the day to come, but the winding column of cavalry paid no heed to the relentless assault of waning summer.

Squinting against the glare, Captain Potter sent a quick, assessing glance around him. Satisfied that the horizon in all directions was devoid of threat, he released a short, relieved breath. Pursuant to Major Wynkoop's orders, they had left at dawn of that day, their objective the Cheyenne and Arapaho camp, and Black Kettle. Unspoken, but foremost in the mind of all the men, was the thought that there had not been time to notify war parties known to be out from the Indian camp and therefore ignorant of Black Kettle's imposed, temporary peace. But their journey so far had been uneventful, and he was extremely grateful for their good fortune.

Captain Potter moved his eyes to the man leading their impressive force. Major Wynkoop was a good man and a good soldier, and he was grateful to be serving under his command. From the beginning, Major Wynkoop had refused to dismiss hope of recovering the captives taken by the Indians. In their combined efforts, they had spared not a day in attempting to find the Durham woman and child and to bring them home. The memory of those bloodied scalps

183

and of the sense of failure which had accompanied their delivery to the fort was with him still.

A familiar sense of loss assailed him, and Captain Potter frowned. Major Wynkoop shared the same sense of failure; and he was certain, had it not been for the proof of the Durham women's deaths, they would be searching still.

Now, offered an opportunity to reverse that failure, to bring back the captives of more recent Indian raids, Major Wynkoop had not hesitated to act. He had totally ignored the risk to his personal career which a move such as this entailed. It was his hope that the effort would not be in vain.

Captain Potter turned to cast a short, assessing glance on the man who rode at his side. Wally Durham, his broad shoulders erect, his sunburned face composed into sober lines, had ridden in silence since dawn. He did not need to stretch his mind to fathom the direction Wally's thoughts were taking. One hundred thirty men and two officers, riding into a possibly hostile Cheyenne and Arapaho camp of undetermined size for the sole purpose of rescuing seven hostages . . . Wally was doubtless suffering the assault of painful memories, the aching need for revenge, and the unacknowledged, hopeless wish that among them he would find his wife and child.

Had it been any other man but Wally Durham, Captain Potter was certain Major Wynkoop would have refused permission to accompany the column. But there was one thing of which both Major Wynkoop and he were sure. Wally Durham could be trusted to do nothing which would threaten the safety of those hostages.

Captain Potter's trailing surveillance of the horizon jerked to a sudden stop. Coming over a rise of land in the distance was a small pack train, and it was heading in their direction. Major Wynkoop was drawing himself stiffly alert, as was Wally Durham. Captain Potter did not need to look behind him to know that the same could be said for the rest of the men in the command.

Abruptly recognizing the lone figure slowly approaching, Captain Potter glanced with disbelief toward Major Wynkoop. The same sense of incredulity was reflected on his sober face. Samuel Marsh . . . ! It made no sense at all that the old man was traveling completely unhindered and untouched in country where the tribes were fiercely at war.

Signaling a halt as the buckskin-clad trader finally drew up alongside the advancing column, Major Wynkoop frowned.

"What are you doing out in this country, Marsh? Don't you have any sense at all? The Cheyenne and the Arapaho have cut this trail to bits. Nothing is getting through."

The old man shook his shaggy head. His lips separated in a crooked smile.

"Oh, them Indians won't hurt me none, Major. I'm their friend . . . just like I'm the friend of the white man. I bring them Indians the things they want and I trade fairly."

Major Wynkoop was openly incredulous.

"They don't need 'things.' They've been raiding enough wagon trains to start selling merchandise to you."

"I know. I seen all the junk they was paradin' around camp."

"You saw . . . ?" Major Wynkoop's heavy brows lifted with growing astonishment. "Are you telling me that you just came from their camp?"

"That's right, I did. And it's a real big one, all right. There's Arapaho, Cheyenne, Sioux . . ."

Major Wynkoop nodded, his eyes darting to Captain Potter for the briefest second before turning back to the sharp-eyed old man.

"What was your assessment of the camp, Marsh? Are the Indians still hostile?"

"Some of them. It's the same old story, I'd say, the young ones wantin' to fight and the older warriors seein' a need for peace. The talk was that Black Kettle was lookin' to talk peace, and that William Bent had a heavy hand in convincin' him that now was the time to do it." The old man's eyes moved down the column, picking out the Indian messengers being held under guard. "Looks to me like Black Kettle's made his move, all right."

Refusing to acknowledge Marsh's sharp observation, Major Wynkoop prompted carefully.

"White captives, Marsh, what do you know about them? There's talk that there are seven of them at that camp."

"I'd say that's right." Marsh's deeply lined face screwed into thoughtful creases. "I seen a few. Children mostly, being held to the far side of the camp, away from the others. And then I saw a woman and a girl. I would've missed them, but one of the squaws called me to her lodge. I'm thinkin' she wanted me to see them. There's talk that she's jealous of the one captive. Hell, I wouldn't even have recognized that one as a white woman if that squaw hadn't called my attention to her. She was wearin' buckskins. Her hair was as black as any Indian's, and her skin was kinda darkened, from the sun, I guess. But them eyes . . . there was no mistakin' them, as big and gray as they was, starin' at me. But with the girl it was different. I never could've mistook that girl for no Indian. Hell, I ain't never seen hair so red or eyes so blue. When that young buck came up, a hollerin' and chasin' the lot of them back to their lodges, them eyes opened up as big as saucers. I'm thinkin' that old squaw really caught it for—"

Samuel Marsh's rambling recitation drew to a halt as shock registered on the face of the man in command and a spontaneous gasp issued from the throat of the big man in civilian dress. The big man's interjection turned Marsh's head in his direction.

"Red hair . . . you said the girl had red hair?"

Sam Marsh shook his shaggy gray head.

"That's right, blazin' red. I'd say a few shades brighter than your own, fella."

Noting the paling of the big man's face, the trader added without prompting, "I'd say the girl was about thirteen or fourteen years old—a real pretty thing, too. Come to think of it, she looked kinda like the woman in buckskins I was talkin' about, with them real fine features. Except for the hair and—"

"How old was the woman, the one with the gray eyes?"

"Young . . . I'd say about early thirties or thereabouts. Hell, that old squaw didn't stand no chance at all if her husband had took a shine to that woman."

The big man's face went from a colorless shade to a deep red in the space of a second, and the trader stammered in his sudden suspicion of the true situation.

"Well, they . . . anyways they both looked to be treated real well—not like some of the other captives I seen."

"Marsh." His tone snapping the trader's head back in his direction, Major Wynkoop pressed the man further. "Where was this camp? As far as I can tell from what these Indians are saying, it's on the south branch of Smoky Hill River, on Hackberry Creek."

"That's dead right, Major."

"That's all I wanted to know." His expression setting into determined lines, Major Wynkoop nodded. "We're going straight on, Marsh. I understand there are several war parties still in the area. I'll send some men back with you."

"No, Major." Marsh wagged his head in emphatic refusal. "If them war parties are in the area like you said, that'd be the best way to get me killed. They ain't goin' to hurt me if I'm travelin' alone. But if I'm travelin' with soldiers . . ."

The major's heavy brows knotted in a frown.

"You're sure of that, Marsh? I wouldn't want to come across that wild gray hair of yours flapping on some brave's scalp pole."

"Don't you worry about me, Major."

There was a brief hesitation before Major Wynkoop nodded in acceptance of the trader's choice. Snapping him a brief salute, the major signaled the column forward once more. Within moments the long, wavering line was progressing forward at a rapid pace.

Silent through the whole exchange, Captain Potter shot a quick look toward Wallace Durham. Incredulous as it seemed, there was suddenly little doubt in his mind that the woman and child were indeed Lydia and Faith Durham. His own anticipation sharply accelerated with this latest news, Captain Potter sympathized with the disbelief and hope that doubtlessly warred behind Wallace Durham's frozen façade. But it would not be much longer . . . not at this pace . . . not much longer until they faced those savages and found out for sure.

Soldiers approaching! The warning call had reverberated

within the vast camp, stirring a furor of activity and striking fear into Faith's heart. Quaking so hard she could barely stand, she stood beside Walking Woman at the entrance to their lodge, watching as warriors dashed madly from their lodges, rushing to reach their horses.

Armed and ready to fight, they were mounted and mobilized within moments. Falling in behind their chiefs, they moved like well-trained soldiers, and Faith marveled at the sudden change which had come over the lazy afternoon camp of a few minutes before.

The size of the approaching force was uncertain. Remaining behind in the lodges, the women were in a state of frenzied excitement as they prepared to evacuate and move their children to a point of safety. Black Wolf's instructions to her had been brief and sharp.

"Obey Walking Woman. She will take you to safety."

Confusion attacked Faith's mind, immobilizing her. She remembered the look on Black Wolf's face and her heartfelt wish to see him emerge safely from this encounter. She was confused. She did not need to seek safety as Black Wolf had instructed. The soldiers were her own people. They would not hurt her.

Mama . . . she must go to Mama.

Faith strained her eyes in the direction of Broken Hand's lodge. Mama was standing in the entrance, her eyes on Broken Hand's broad figure as he rode off with his warriors. Her own eyes had followed the same course a few minutes before as Black Wolf had moved up to ride at Broken Hand's side.

Faith's perplexity grew. Black Wolf, riding out to fight the enemy, the people who would come to rescue her if they indeed knew she was here. Mama did not suffer the same confused loyalties. She had no memory of a time when she had looked to these soldiers for protection.

But Mama was alone and frightened. Owl Woman had abandoned her, was nowhere to be seen. Dressed as Mama was in Indian clothes, Mama would easily be mistaken for one of the squaws, and if the soldiers did indeed come . . .

Her eyes shooting to Walking Woman's concerned

188

expression—the older woman stood silently beside her—
Faith knew another fear. The soldiers . . . she could not let
them hurt Walking Woman if the camp was overrun. She
could no more stand the thought of Walking Woman being
injured than she could stand to see Mama alone and
unprotected.

As Faith watched, the women of the camp began to
emerge from their lodges. In their anxiety to find a vantage
point from which to watch the expected battle, they walked
swiftly, blending in a great, swelling mass which moved
toward the nearby hill. Taking her hand, Walking Woman
pulled her out of the lodge into the frantic stream.

Running to keep up with the pace of the women around
her, Walking Woman made a sharp, unexpected deviation
from their course, drawing Faith along with her as she made
her way to Broken Hand's lodge. Mama . . . Walking
Woman was taking her to Mama!

Faith's anxiety grew when she saw the fear and confusion
glimmering brightly in her mother's eyes as they approached. She did not want to panic Mama, to lose her in the
ensuing pandemonium. Her mother's eyes shot to the ring on
her hand, back to her face, and then batted momentarily
closed. Faith took a hesitant step forward, her throat
choking with sorrow as her mother took a spontaneous step
backward.

Her gratitude profound, Faith watched as Walking
Woman moved toward her mother, extending her hand.
Her low words cleared the panic from the huge gray eyes
which regarded her intently.

"Come, Shadow Woman. I would save you for Broken
Hand, take you to a point of safety. I have promised Black
Wolf that I would care for you as I would care for Fire Spirit.
Come quickly, you must follow me."

Faith waited tensely, the seconds stretching into hours
before her mother slowly raised her hand to place it into
Walking Woman's small palm. Within moments they were
running toward a vantage point to the right of camp where a
rise would afford them a view of the conflict to come.

Pushing forward, her heart pounding wildly in her ears,

Faith was aware that Walking Woman and Mama were behind her as she struggled into a position that allowed clear observance. A low gasp escaped her throat! She could not believe her eyes!

Numb, Wally Durham was completely numb. He'd ridden the last miles as if in a dream, while the trader's words had drummed over and over in his mind. A red-haired girl, with light blue eyes . . . a dark-haired woman with gray eyes—alive in the Cheyenne camp. A choked sound escaped his tight throat. Afraid . . . he was afraid. . . .

In all his time spent alone in the past month, in a wild, hostile wilderness, he had never been truly afraid. Fear was for a man who had something to lose. He had not been such a man.

He had been driven to accompany Major Wynkoop on this mission by a force within him for which he could find no reason. But now the reason was only too clear. It had been the hand of fate which had seen fit to put him back in Fort Lyon at the time the letter from Black Kettle had been delivered.

The hand of fate had also struck a harsh and shattering fear in his heart. He dared not allow himself to believe the two captives Samuel Marsh had described were indeed Lydia and Faith. Oh, God, could it be true? And if it was not, would he be able to bear losing them again?

His heart pounding raggedly in his chest, Wally's eyes moved to the terrain before them. The column was moving at a rapid pace. Without pressing forward with unwise haste, Major Wynkoop had nevertheless speedily driven horses and men to the Indian encampment. They would soon be arriving at their destination.

A sign of movement on the rolling landscape before them caught Wally's eyes, pulled him from his thoughts. There it was again. . . .

A sudden motion from Major Wynkoop caused Captain Potter to signal a quick halt to their forward progress, and Wally gasped. Before his incredulous eyes a long, unending line of Indians emerged from the landscape in a tightly drawn line of battle. On and on the human chain stretched, extending almost as far as his eyes could see. His mind made a quick, mental calculation—six, seven . . . possibly eight hundred warriors, silent and waiting.

"Captain, tell the men to keep their hands away from their guns, and get one of those Indian messengers up here, quickly!"

His gaze remaining strictly forward, Major Wynkoop murmured under his breath in a tone meant for Wally Durham alone, "Well, what do you think, Durham? Eight to one good enough odds for you?"

Wally's response was equally dry.

"I've had better."

The clatter of horses' hooves to their rear turned Major Wynkoop's eyes from the opposing force for the first time. His glance touched on the Indian messenger who drew up at his side.

"All right, Standing Grass, I want you to take a message to Black Kettle for me. He's in that line somewhere, isn't he?"

The Cheyenne messenger's face was expressionless. "He is there."

Major Wynkoop nodded. "Then I want you to tell Black Kettle we have read his letter and would like to approach him to talk. Tell him we will fight if necessary, but it is our hope that we may speak of the peace he desires."

His expression unchanged, Major Wynkoop watched as the Indian turned without response and heeled his horse toward the silent, unmoving line. He directed a softly spoken comment to the two men beside him as the messenger drew up sharply and began speaking to the Indian obviously in command.

"They're a damned calm lot, aren't they? But then, I guess I'd be calm too if I knew I could cut my enemy down any time I wanted. I'm hoping Black Kettle wields as strong an influence as some would have us believe. I have a feeling he's our only ally."

His heart beginning to pound anew, Wally took a deep silent breath. He did not need to respond to the major's low statement. His response was clearly written in the stiff features of his face. No, fate could not be so cruel. It could not have brought him all this way, to this time and place, only to allow him to die without seeing Lydia and Faith again. It could not.

Wally's eyes remained strictly trained on the sober Indian whose bearing signified him the leader. He sensed rather than saw the first flicker of movement before Black Kettle turned fleetingly in their direction. Turning back to the Indian beside him, Black Kettle spoke briefly. Within moments a small entourage headed in their direction, and Major Wynkoop released a short, relieved breath which echoed the sentiments of the men to his rear.

"Captain, we'll ride forward slowly to meet them. Sergeant Wilson . . ."

A brief acknowledgment from the rear allowed Major Wynkoop to continue.

"Sergeant Wilson, you'll be in charge. You know what to do if we don't make it back."

His mind heard the conversation which progressed in low undertones, but Wally found himself completely entranced by the sight of the approaching Indian chiefs. Major Wynkoop spurred his horse into a slow forward pace. Captain Potter followed behind. Without conscious realization, Wally spurred his horse forward as well. The low protest of the sergeant behind him alerted the two officers to Wally's unexpected presence behind them, but it was too late. He was already a part of the council . . . whether they liked it or not.

Wally was beginning to twitch. The brilliant afternoon sun had beat unmercifully on the dramatic tableau of blue sky; vast, rolling prairie; and long, unmoving lines of opposing forces. But the outcome of the meeting was still in question. Gradually, one by one, additional chiefs had ridden forward to join the council, each listening in turn to Major Wynkoop's flat, unemotional statements.

He had come to hold consultation with the Cheyenne and

Arapaho; he did not wish to fight. He was not authorized to conclude terms of peace, but if they would bring in and turn over to him their prisoners, he would take such chiefs as they might select to the governor of Colorado and try to make peace for them.

The chiefs had been in sharp disagreement, their arguments conducted in their native tongue. Wally had been unable to comprehend more than the fact that a few of the chiefs did not wish to talk at all. Their eyes glittered with the prospect of the new scalps they could so easily take, the victory which was within their grasp.

But Black Kettle had remained adamant. His deep voice low, his argument untiring, he faced down each one of the opposing chiefs. When he turned back toward Major Wynkoop at last, the afternoon sun was beginning to drop toward the horizon, but Black Kettle showed no sign of stress. His countenance impassive, he addressed Major Wynkoop directly.

"It is the decision of our council to accept your terms. We will choose the chiefs you would take to the white man's governor, and we will talk peace."

Major Wynkoop's strict military bearing remained unchanged. His response was a flat statement.

"First the return of the prisoners."

Chief Black Kettle nodded.

"They are not all in this camp. We will return to you those presently with us, and the others as soon as we are able to procure them. With us now are four children, taken on the Little Blue River and the South Platte."

Wally stiffened, his spontaneous movement not going unobserved by Major Wynkoop's observant eye. Major Wynkoop's response was immediate.

"I am told you also have a woman and a girl . . . taken in a raid on a wagon train."

Black Kettle turned to the big Indian who had stood at his side for the duration of the council. Their gazes clashed in silence. Black Kettle returned his gaze to the unsmiling military man, his statement flat.

"The woman and girl of whom you speak are not captives

193

in our camp. They have been taken into the tribe and hold no desire to be returned to the white man's world."

Major Wynkoop's response precluded the protest that rose in Wally's throat.

"We will have *all* our people returned. The peace talk cannot progress until this is done."

His heart beginning a heavy pounding, Wally looked to the big Indian at Black Kettle's side. He considered the warrior carefully for the first time. Taller than most, the man had the breadth of shoulder and chest which bespoke great physical strength. His face was hard, heavily lined, but without the heaviness of feature characteristic of so many of his race. His expression was stoic. It was only in his dark, intense gaze that the major saw the violent protest the Indian suppressed, the frustrated anger.

Turning, Black Kettle addressed the warrior in their native tongue. The man gestured tightly in return. Black Kettle spoke again, a low finality in his tone. The warrior hesitated briefly, his eyes filled with challenge, before turning his horse abruptly and riding back toward the silent line of braves. Sparing the departing warrior no more than a second's glance, Black Kettle returned his gaze to Major Wynkoop.

"It is done."

Wally's eyes shot toward the big Indian's retreating back. The man had reached the silent line and given a few brief instructions. Several Indians moved immediately to obey his command, but a young brave challenged him openly, turning his horse to block the big Indian's attempt to ride through the line.

A slow flush began to suffuse Wally's face as he exerted a stringent effort to maintain control. The big Indian spoke gruffly to the young Indian, and the young brave's stance became belligerent.

The confrontation was coming to a head. Uncertain exactly what was happening, Wally was sure of only one thing. He would leave this place today with Lydia and Faith, or he would not leave at all.

*　　　*　　　*

Anger was apparent in the deep furrows of Broken Hand's brow. His voice was low as his eyes bore darkly into Black Wolf's stiff countenance.

"It is the decision of the council that the captives will be returned—all of them. They are to be turned over to the army major now."

Black Wolf's response was harsh, grating from the pressure of suppressed hostility.

"I hold no captive in my lodge. With me reside Walking Woman, sister of my mother; and Fire Spirit, who wears the ring symbolizing her promise to me. She wears it willingly."

Broken Hand's tight expression hardened.

"You must take the girl to Black Kettle as I will take Shadow Woman. Their time with us is done, to be put aside in the path of peace."

"I will not give up the girl."

Broken Hand paused, anger sparking in his gaze as he trailed it over Black Wolf's young, adamant face. "The choice is no longer yours. If you refuse to get the girl, another will bring her." Broken Hand lifted his eyes to scrutinize the warriors mounted nearby. "Spotted Elk waits anxiously to do my bidding, but it is not my choice that it be so." Broken Hand's voice softened. "You must decide now if you would speak to the girl one last time."

Broken Hand watched emotions play across Black Wolf's young face. The torment he saw there reflected his own inner sense of rage. Shadow Woman, wife to him, part of his body and his soul, was to be taken from him in the cause of a peace he knew in his heart would be short-lived.

Memories of the haunted vision Shadow Woman and he had shared returned to Broken Hand's mind to plague him. Would this choice, this sacrifice he was about to make, spare his people the fate which had been only too clearly revealed to Shadow Woman in that vision? He knew not. He had realized as he had shared that vision with her, that Shadow Woman had witnessed the horror from afar. Her position had been that of observer. It was then he had realized that the time would come when Shadow Woman would be separated from him . . . but he had not realized the time would come so soon.

195

His eyes still intent on Black Wolf's face, Broken Hand saw the realization of the futility of protest dawn in Black Wolf's eyes. Broken Hand waited no longer. Wheeling his horse, he rode around Black Wolf, relieved when the young warrior made no move to stop him. Black Wolf was as a son to him. He suffered Black Wolf's pain. He did not wish to chastise him openly, to order him restrained and to give Spotted Elk the satisfaction he so obviously sought.

Turning his eyes to the women clustered at a point of safety from which they might observe the proceedings, Broken Hand heeled his horse forward. His concentration intense, he noted the clatter of hooves as Black Wolf's horse was spurred into movement behind him. But all thought soon faded from Broken Hand's mind as his gaze touched on a slender figure within the silent group. Shadow Woman . . .

Faith had not been able to believe her eyes! Cavalry in a well-disciplined line had been advancing upon the well-protected camp. But the size of the force had been minute in terms of the great number which opposed them. Her heart had raced and despair had choked her heart. Slaughter . . . she would witness slaughter. . . .

But the slaughter had not come. She had watched as three men had separated from the military column and ridden forward to consult with Black Kettle and the other chiefs. Two officers and a civilian. She had been unable to make out more than the fact that the representatives of the opposing forces were talking quietly, with great restraint.

The day had dragged, long and hot, in their point of observance. Seated on the ground, the women had remained as silent and still as the warriors they watched.

Faith was uncertain of the first moment when she had become aware of her mother's strange distraction. The experience of the past months had taught her a hard lesson. If she wished to remain in her mother's presence without causing a resumption of her mother's panic, she need remain silent and not press her. With the potential danger of their situation, she had wished only to inspire confidence in her mother's troubled mind.

Aware that her mother's gaze was intent upon her, Faith had turned to see that her mother stared at the carved band Black Wolf had placed on her finger. Faith's hand had twitched spontaneously, and tears had filled her throat at her mother's pained confusion. Her mother had reached out to touch the hand which bore the ring. Her words had been low, rasping.

"No, this should not be. . . . It should not be. . . ."

Her mother's eyes had closed, had remained that way as myriad, painful emotions had flashed across her beautiful face. Unable to bear the sight of her mother's torment any longer, Faith had reached out a tentative arm to support her. Her mother had neither pulled away nor acknowledged her touch, and Faith had eventually returned her gaze to the silent tableau below her.

But something was happening now. . . . Broken Hand was leaving Black Kettle's side, his large pinto moving toward the line of waiting warriors. A short command dispatched several men toward the camp. Then Broken Hand turned to Black Wolf, and Faith sensed the conflict in their words as Black Wolf turned his horse to block Broken Hand's path.

The rustle of whispers around her confirmed her thoughts, and Faith touched Walking Woman's arm. A similar concern was reflected in Walking Woman's expression, and Faith's frustration soared. Something was wrong. . . .

Abruptly, Broken Hand turned his horse. He rode through the line of men . . . in their direction. Beside her, Mama stiffened and drew herself to her feet. Relief, joy shone in her eyes. Black Wolf rode at Broken Hand's rear, his expression tense. Faith's apprehension mounted.

The two horses were climbing the gradual rise toward them. Standing, awaiting their arrival, Faith's heart thudded in her breast. The two warriors drew their horses up alongside, and Faith shot a quick glance between them. Without a word, Broken Hand reached down and drew Mama up onto his horse. Faith's brow knit in concern, her confusion mounting as Black Wolf moved his horse closer and reached down toward her. Responding automatically, she lifted her arm and he swung her up in front of him. His lips were pressed in a tight, straight line, his eyes hard with anger.

"Black Wolf, wh-what is happening."

Black Wolf's arms closed tight around her. He turned his horse to follow as Broken Hand started back toward the waiting chiefs. They were drawing closer to the mounted council when Faith noticed the Indians dispatched to camp a few minutes earlier were returning with the captive children seated on their saddles in front of them. Her heart leaped. They were being released!

Broken Hand reined his mount to a slower pace and Black Wolf followed suit. His gaze remaining fixed on Broken Hand, Black Wolf pulled Faith closer until his chin rested against the throbbing pulse in her temple. His words were soft, spoken roughly through barely moving lips.

"These people, neither mine nor yours, do not acknowledge my claim upon you. But my claim is just. We will not be separated long."

Faith swallowed with difficulty. Her conflicting emotions warred, creating total confusion in her mind. She looked toward the mounted men waiting at the midpoint between the two opposing forces. Two officers . . . but the civilian, just to their rear . . .

Faith gasped, refusing to believe her eyes. Yes, the hair beneath that large, wide-brimmed hat was red, touched with gray. It was the same broad, handsome face. They were the same pale eyes. . . . Oh, God, Papa was alive!

Faith darted a quick look toward her mother. Her mother's eyes were frozen on Papa. She had gone rigid, unmoving in Broken Hand's arms. Broken Hand's composure slipped and he whispered a soft word into Mama's ear, but Mama did not respond. Broken Hand looked in momentary confusion toward Faith, realizing the significance of Lydia's distraction as Faith glanced toward her father once more.

Held immobile by shock and emotion, Faith watched as the captive children were lowered to the ground and released. Within moments, several soldiers had taken them up on their horses and turned back toward the column. Faith was unconscious of the words the commanding officer spoke. Instead, she watched as Papa dismounted and stood beside his horse, his eyes on Mama. Releasing Mama momentarily, Broken Hand dismounted. Reaching up, he lowered her carefully to the ground. Mama was swaying, her eyes riveted to Papa's face, and Broken Hand raised a supportive hand.

Black Wolf dismounted. Reaching up, he lifted Faith to the ground, but the grip he maintained on her arm was proprietary rather than supportive. She attempted to go to her mother's side, but he stayed her. She turned to hear his parting whisper.

"We will not be separated long."

The emotion in Black Wolf's voice brought a low sob to Faith's lips as he suddenly released her.

Realizing Broken Hand had also released her mother, Faith ran instinctively toward her. She reached her mother at the same moment as her father, sobbing as his familiar arms closed around them both.

But Mama would not accept Papa's embrace. Fighting to be free, she finally succeeded in stepping back, her eyes wide, incredulous as she stared at him in silence.

Her heart breaking, Faith saw disbelief flash across her father's face. He glanced to her for explanation. Realizing there was none forthcoming, he looked back to Mama. His low tone was filled with pain.

"Lydia . . . darling . . . what's wrong? Don't you know me?"

A strangled, choking sound escaped Mama's throat when Papa spoke for the first time. Her hand snapped to her neck as she appeared to make a frantic bid for breath. With startling abruptness, Mama's body went limp, and she fell toward the ground.

Gasping as her father managed to catch her mother in time to break her fall, Faith watched as he scooped Lydia's unconscious body up into his arms.

Within moments the second officer had dismounted. With

dispatch, he assisted in raising Mama's limp form onto Papa's horse. The officer then turned in her direction. A brief smile flicked across his handsome, light-skinned face.

"Miss Durham, my name is Captain William Potter. I'd be honored to have you ride back to Fort Lyon with me."

The thickness in her throat precluding speech, Faith nodded. Within moments, she was seated before him on his large sorrel, and they were following Papa back toward the main column when Faith turned a brief glance behind her.

Black Kettle, the other chiefs, Broken Hand, had all begun riding back toward the silent line of warriors. Only Black Wolf remained unmoving. His dark eyes caught hers in a silent promise which echoed loudly across the distance between them.

We will not be separated long. . . .

Chapter XV

"Please . . . please don't touch me."

Her wide-eyed gaze intent, Lydia backed up as she spoke. Halted in her stumbling retreat as she came firmly up against the table in the corner of the room, Lydia gave a low, panicked gasp. She turned her head to shoot a quick glance around the small bedroom, her unfamiliarity with the military quarters in which she had awakened earlier that morning adding yet another facet to her growing desperation. She jerked her head forward once more, shaking it against the silent plea in Wallace Durham's eyes as he drew nearer.

"No, don't come any closer! I . . . I don't want you to touch me."

Under tenuous control, Wally swallowed with visible discomfort. He slowed his step. His broad chest heaved with the emotions he strove to keep in check, but he feared he was fast losing the fight.

"You . . . you do remember me now, don't you, darling?" His big hands nervously clenching and unclenching at his sides, Wally continued softly, "Dr. Holstan just left. He said you were mentally alert, that you had total recall."

"Total recall . . ." Lydia's short laugh held a hysterical note. "Yes, I remember you. I remember that you're my husband. I remember that Faith and I were captured in a raid on the wagon train we joined to get to the gold fields. I remember that we both thought you had been killed. And I

201

remember everything that happened after that, too." Lydia's lips trembled with her inner torment. "That's the trouble, I remember everything . . . too much."

"Lydia . . ."

Wally took a step closer, only to be stopped by the panic in Lydia's eyes.

"No! How can you bear to touch me? You saw what I looked like when you took me back here!"

Lydia's trembling fingers moved against the demure cotton dress supplied to her by one of the soldiers' wives, but her mind replaced the simple garment with the buckskin dress she had discarded a short time before. Her hand shakily smoothed her upswept coiffure, her eyes closing at the memory of the flowing, wanton style she had worn for so long.

"A squaw . . . that's what I was. I was Broken Hand's wife, completely, exclusively. Do you know what that means?"

Her words driving him past restraint, Wally closed the distance that separated them, his hands clamping onto her arms to give her a small shake.

"Stop that, do you hear? Stop torturing yourself . . . and me. I don't have to hear any more, or know any more. Faith told me all I need to know. We had a long talk while you were still unconscious. She told me everything—how you fell and struck your head, that you were dazed and couldn't remember anything that had happened. She told me you didn't recognize her all the while you were both captives."

A low sob escaped Lydia's throat. "Oh, God, yes, I know that now. My darling Faith, alone, suffering such torment . . ."

Wally's hand was moving comfortingly against her arm, and Lydia's eyes dropped momentarily closed. Her despair was more than Wally could bear.

"Lydia, darling, you were sick. You weren't responsible for your actions. Faith isn't a child. She knew that." Wally took a short breath. "She also told me how that Indian, Broken Hand, took advantage of you . . . of your illness."

Lydia's gray eyes snapped up to his with startling impact.

"Broken Hand didn't take advantage of me."

Wally's expression stiffened at her instinctive defense of Broken Hand.

"What would you call it, then? He knew you were dazed, in an uncertain state of mind. He convinced you that you needed him."

"I *did* need him."

"You didn't! Faith would have taken care of you. He wouldn't let her see you or talk to you."

"Don't you understand, Wally? I didn't recognize Faith. I didn't know who I was or who she was. I opened my eyes, and the world was completely foreign to me. I was frightened—so very frightened—and then I saw Broken Hand. I saw compassion in his eyes, concern . . . and something else. I can't explain what it was, except to say that it drew me to him. I trusted him. With him I felt secure and safe in a world of strangers. He took care of me, protected me."

"Protected you! From what? Himself?"

"He protected me from my fears! And I had so many. . . . He spoke to me of a vision he had. He—"

"I don't want to hear any of this!" Turning away abruptly, Wally strove to control his burning jealousy. That Indian, with his Lydia . . .

"Wally, you said you understand, but you don't. I *want* you to understand, to know everything, and when you do . . . If you no longer want me then . . ."

Turning back toward Lydia as her voice trailed into silence, Wally was unable to disguise the pain he suffered. Flushed with anguish, he gripped her shoulders. His eyes were intent upon hers.

"I'll always want you, Lydia. I told you, I don't care."

"Then you must let me speak."

The depth of his inner struggle clearly reflected in his face, Wally hesitated for long moments. Finally, realizing he had no choice, he nodded.

Her eyes strangely distant Lydia began to speak. "During the time that I was in Black Kettle's camp, I could remember nothing that happened prior to the darkness, filled with pain, from which I had awakened. My awakening was terrifying. My body ached, my head was throbbing. I couldn't seem to think. I didn't understand where I was, who I was. Broken Hand was there. His gentleness calmed my fears. He took care of me. Later, I discovered the reason for the acceptance, the peace I had sensed within him. He told me of his vision. He told me I had come to him in that vision. He said he had been expecting my coming."

"Damned fool nonsense! He was taking advantage of your illness, talking you into . . . into—"

"He didn't have to talk me into anything, Wally. The visions Broken Hand spoke of were shadows of images I, too, had seen; his words were echoes of whispers I had heard within my own mind but had not understood." Lydia took a deep, shaky breath. "Broken Hand said we were meant to be together, and I believed that. I believed, and I gave myself to him . . . offered myself willingly."

"Lydia . . ." Wally's eyes dropped momentarily closed against his torment. "For God's sake, please. You were sick. You couldn't remember . . ."

Lydia's voice choked on a sob. Her beautiful face was filled with the wretchedness of the words she was about to speak.

"Yes, I couldn't remember. When I was with Broken Hand in the Cheyenne village, I couldn't remember you. But . . . but I remember everything now. That's the trouble. I'm back with you now, and I . . . I can't forget. I can't forget Broken Hand."

Wally went abruptly still. His flush faded to a startling pallor.

"Did . . . did he hurt you, Lydia? Is that why?"

"No, Wally. Broken Hand loved me."

"Loved you! He gave you up easily enough for a man who was supposed to love you!"

"No, Wally. Broken Hand didn't give me up easily."

Wally's strong frame was trembling, and Lydia knew a new despair. His voice was laced with pain.

"What are you trying to tell me, Lydia? That you love that Indian?"

Tears flowed freely from her eyes as Lydia fought in vain

for composure. When she spoke at last her voice was hushed, quaking.

"I . . . I must be truthful with you, Wally. The woman that I was then, in that camp, loved Broken Hand. But . . . but the woman that I am now loves you . . . only you."

His control cracking at her shaken statement, Wally drew Lydia flush against him. His hands moving hungrily over the familiar contours of her back, he breathed deeply of her scent, aware that his own face was wet with tears.

"That's all I want to know, darling. The rest is all past . . . all my fault. You never wanted to come to this wilderness in the first place. I'm taking you and Faith home—back to New York. We'll build that big house and start a new life."

"I don't care about a big house, Wally."

"I do. I want it for you and for Faith. If there's one good thing that came out of this damned disaster, it's the fact that I'll be able to do that now. You and Faith will have everything you'll ever want . . . ever need." Pushing her far enough away so that she might see the earnestness with which he spoke, Wally continued tightly, "And when we're in that big house, the three of us, together, we'll never mention that Indian's name again. Never."

"Wally—"

"Never, Lydia. That's all I ask of you."

Unable to bear any more, Lydia raised a slender hand to Wally's cheek. She smoothed the dampness from its surface.

"All right, Wally. Never again. You have my word."

"And I have you. I'll never give you up, Lydia. The woman that you were, the woman that you are, I love them both. I always will."

Unable to say more, Wally enfolded her tightly in his arms. Lydia relaxed against his strength, allowed his familiar warmth to sweep over her, to drug her aching mind. Broken Hand . . . she must strike his name from her heart and mind forever. She had given her word; and, in truth, she knew it could be no other way. She must force herself to forget.

*　　*　　*

Faith listened intently. The low, pained murmurs from the adjoining room had ceased. She released a tense breath. She could only hope that all was settled between Mama and Papa at last.

Abruptly, Faith turned toward the door of their temporary quarters at Fort Lyon. She did not give a thought to the fact that darkness had fallen over the fort, that most of the inhabitants had doubtless settled in for the night. She, herself, could not give a thought to sleep. Her mind was running at a reckless speed, the turmoil of the day leaving her in a far too anxious state to allow her rest.

Silently pulling open the door, Faith stepped out into the shadows of the yard. Her eyes darted around the dark stockade walls, the low buildings which lined them. When she saw the patrolling guards, her fine brows drew together into a frown. No, there was no respite from her ambivalent feelings here.

Strange . . . she felt so strange. This world to which she had returned was as foreign to her eye as the Indian camp had been only a few short months before. Why was it here and now, home with her own people, protected from any further mishap, she felt so completely alone?

Faith took a deep, steadying breath, her anxiety driving her out onto the grounds in an attempt to sort out her confusion. Ungrateful, that was what she was. She had never expected to see Papa's dear face again, to hear the love in his deep voice as he spoke her name, to feel his comforting arms around her. She had thought his love, his strength, his humor were lost to her forever. But he had been here, waiting for Mama and her to return, and his love had not changed. A heated warmth filled Faith's eyes. She loved him . . . she loved him so dearly.

But a baffling unrest still filled her mind. Papa had told her that he had struck it rich. She supposed she was still unable to comprehend the full implication of that statement. He had said they would be returning home—to New York, as soon as possible. She supposed that was best, especially since Mama was so shaken. When they returned home, were in a more familiar environment, Mama would return to her old self. And she, herself, would . . .

A sudden, unexpected step to her rear interrupted Faith's thoughts, snapping her head toward the shadowed figure approaching her. Taking a spontaneous step backward, she was halted in her retreat by the sound of Captain Potter's reassuring voice as he stepped into clear view.

"Did I frighten you, Faith? I'm sorry." His pleasant face was creased into a smile that reflected considerable warmth. Faith had taken an immediate liking to the captain who had transported her back to the fort. He was kind and extremely considerate, and the difference in their ages had eliminated a need for formality. Faith was grateful for that, but she was in no mood for polite conversation. Her smile was forced.

"No, but I . . . I wasn't expecting anyone else to be walking on the grounds at this time of night, I suppose."

Captain Potter's brow furrowed into a light frown of concern at the hesitancy in her voice. Reaching out instinctively, he took her arm.

"Is something wrong, Faith? You do know you can tell me if you need anything—anything at all."

"No, everything is going as well as can be expected, I guess. I just couldn't sleep."

His eyes moving assessingly over her face, Captain Potter appeared to become suddenly aware of his spontaneous gesture. Dropping his hand back to his side, he offered her a small smile.

"I couldn't sleep either, so I thought I'd check the guard. you never know what those—" Stopping abruptly, Captain Potter shook his head. "It's been so long since we've had even a temporary truce with the Indians in this part of the country that I think I'm finding myself unable to believe our good fortune. In any case, I'd enjoy walking along with you for a while if you don't mind, Faith."

Unable to find an adequate reason to refuse the captain's request, Faith nodded. Perhaps this was what she needed after all, an opportunity to free her mind from the vicious circle of confusion in which it whirled.

Waiting only for her consenting nod, Captain Potter took her arm and urged her out of the shadows. He spoke softly by way of explanation.

"It would be best if you stepped out into the light, Faith. The ground is uneven. I wouldn't want you to stumble and fall." His hand stroked her arm in a spontaneously comforting gesture. "You've had enough to contend with in the past few months."

Faith lifted her chin, her eyes strangely troubled.

"To be honest, William, the Cheyenne treated me very well, even if they didn't allow Mama and me to talk to each other. Walking Woman was very kind, and Black Wolf . . . he protected me from the cruelty of others." Her mind returning to the brutality she and her mother, as well as the other captives, had suffered at White Eagle's hands, she frowned. "The Arapaho who captured us sold us to Broken Hand. Broken Hand was . . . kind to Mama, also."

Suddenly realizing the young captain was studying her face intently, Faith assessed the content of her statement.

"I suppose it sounds strange to hear me talk about being sold. I hadn't given it much thought lately. We weren't truly treated like slaves. Mama and I were fortunate to be exchanged in that way."

The young captain continued to stare into her face, and Faith examined her words more carefully. Was this what it was going to be like? Was she going to have to consider each word she uttered before she spoke? Was she to be considered a curiosity by all whom she met now that she had been returned to her own people? Pausing, she waited for Captain Potter's belated response.

William Potter exerted stringent control over his strong reaction to the extremely lovely, open face turned up to his. He had never seen a more beautiful young girl. A startling discomfort tightened his stomach, and he suppressed a sudden urge to laugh. This girl, little more than a child, awakened feelings within him that set his senses reeling.

She was a child. She was disturbed and insecure after the events of the past few months. He saw that insecurity in the small frown that knit her brow when she spoke, the sober set of her exquisite features, the hesitation in her speech which he knew instinctively was not a natural characteristic. Seeing her in such a state, his natural inclination was to wrap his arms around her, to tuck her head against his shoulder and whisper assurances which would set her mind at ease, allow her to depend upon him.

But the remembered scent of the bright silk of her hair, warm and fragrant as it had brushed his face on the long ride back to the fort, was too fresh in his nostrils. The memory of the weight of her slim frame leaning against his chest, the rounded curve of her firm buttocks intimately close against him, the long slender legs brushing against his own muscular thighs, had left him far more disturbed than he cared to admit.

He studied her a moment longer in silence as she looked up to him. Her gaze was open, free of guile. But there was something about her that transcended her youth, projecting a glimpse of the woman she would soon become—an appeal he found himself unable to ignore. Dignity . . . he supposed that was the closest he could come to describing the quality that all but negated her youth in his eyes. Dignity and spirit . . .

He remembered clearly his inner response when the young Indian, Black Wolf, had delivered her to their waiting column. His own reaction to Black Wolf's possessive air had been instinctive anger. His inclination had been to spur his horse forward and personally liberate her, to take her into his care. He was only too well aware that his reaction to the return of the other captives had been of an entirely different nature. Grateful and relieved at their return, he had not suffered any of the personal feelings which had marked his first sight of Faith Durham.

In the hours since the captives had been delivered back to the fort and settled into their temporary quarters, he had gone over his unexpected response to Faith again and again in his mind. He had at first thought his intense personal reaction to Faith's return had been due to the fact that she and her mother had been given up for dead, that the possibility of their return had seemed so miraculous. But total honesty had caused him to dismiss that motivation when the image of Faith Durham's small, perfect face had returned to his mind for the hundredth time that night.

His mind too active for sleep, he had walked into the yard of the fort, surprisingly discovering the physical presence of the image which haunted him. Now, finding Faith even more disturbing than he had remembered, he was presently almost at a loss for words. A child . . . a beautiful child . . . and she left him speechless.

William frowned. Faith's expression revealed only too clearly that his prolonged silence was upsetting her. Grateful for the semidarkness which hid his sudden flush, he reluctantly released her arm and forced a belated response to her statement.

"Yes, it's more than strange to hear you speak of yourself and your mother as being sold, Faith. But you were among primitive people, and you could only expect primitive treatment. I am only happy to hear you and your mother were not mistreated."

His response caused Faith to turn away from him in silence. She began to walk, and he fell into step beside her. He sensed her annoyance, and he cursed his own awkwardness. Damn . . .

Faith was uncertain why William's words had disturbed her. Primitive . . . He had called Broken Hand and Black Wolf primitive people. She supposed he was right. They appeared to care little for the things which drove most "civilized" men—wealth, luxury. But as primitive and savage as she knew they could be, they were more honest in their feelings, more direct in their approach to life, less greedy for material things than—

"Faith . . ."

Raising her eyes when the captain tentatively spoke her name, Faith became aware of his discomfort.

"I hope I haven't offended you. It surely wasn't my intention."

Suddenly she was ashamed of herself. How could she blame William for thinking the same thoughts she, herself, had harbored only days before. She was truly uncertain when the subtle change had come about in her thinking. Had it been when Black Wolf had taken her riding, allowing her

210

to see a glimpse of the beauty his people derived from a simple appreciation of life around them? Or had it been when Black Wolf had declared his surprising feelings for her in his deep, halting tone, and had pressed his mouth to hers?

Her confusion increased by her wandering thoughts, Faith trailed her eyes over William Potter's handsome face. How strange his fair skin appeared to her now. His pale hair, lightened to a silver cast by the rays of the full moon, seemed almost colorless in comparison with the raven sheen of Black Wolf's hair; his neat, brown mustache strange when compared to Black Wolf's deeper hued, hairless skin. She remembered the brush of Black Wolf's smooth cheek against her own, the thrill it had raised deep inside her, and her frown darkened.

"Faith . . ."

William's hand moved spontaneously to her shoulder, caught a curling red strand, and he continued earnestly.

"I just want you to know how very relieved we are to have you and your mother back among us again. Through some terrible mistake we thought you both had been killed. Your father was beside himself. We were all more disturbed than I can tell you. It was deeply satisfying to have you ride back to the fort with me this afternoon." William paused, his voice dropping a notch lower. "But to be truly honest, it's now, since I've had the opportunity to get to know you a little better, to speak to you, that I realize what a truly great loss it would have been if you had, indeed, been taken from us forever."

William took a short breath as Faith's expression softened. His next words emerged with a new tone of anticipation.

"Now that Black Kettle has shown his good faith by returning you and the other captives, Major Wynkoop will be taking Black Kettle to Denver to speak with the governor. It looks like there might be peace here at last. Then your father will be able to get you and your mother situated in relative safety. It's not very far from Fort Lyon to Denver, Faith. Your father and I have become good friends, and I'm looking forward to keeping in touch with all of you and—"

"We won't be staying in Denver, William."

Startled, William shook his head.

"Surely your father doesn't intend to take you and your mother back to his diggings with him. You'd be far better off if you—"

"We won't be going back to the diggings, either. Papa has already told Mama and me that he intends to make arrangements for his claim and then take us back East immediately."

"Back East!" His sense of loss profound, William shook his head. "That doesn't make sense! Wally has business here. He—"

"Papa doesn't want Mama tortured with memories. We'll be going back as soon as he can make arrangements."

William's hand had moved spontaneously to grip her arm and Faith was startled by the intensity in his brown eyes. "You don't mean that! Your father would be a fool to turn his claim over to someone else at this point. It'll need careful developing, especially if it is as rich as he seems to expect. He—"

"Papa says his first priority is to get Mama and me back East. He blames himself for all that's happened, and he—"

"That's nonsense! There's no way to anticipate these savages. If there were, you can believe that the army would've been more successful than it has been in keeping this frontier safe. But that's all in the past, Faith. Surely, you can convince him . . ."

William's unexpected emotion increasing her confusion, Faith felt the heat of tears sting her eyes. She shook her head, her expression bewildered.

"William, how can I convince Papa of anything when I don't know what I feel or want myself right now? All I know is that Papa and Mama are attempting to put their lives back together again, and I . . . I feel so alone."

All conversation came to an abrupt halt with Faith's low-whispered statement. A muscle twitched in William's cheek as he surveyed the unexpected despair on Faith's shadowed face. Without hesitation, he drew her against him, his arms sliding around her as he pressed her head to his chest. He stroked her hair, closing his eyes to the quickening of his heart, and struck from his mind everything but the consolation he intended.

She was a child, and she needed someone now. He would content himself with being that person, no matter how very much he wished he could look forward to more.

Faith opened the door to her temporary quarters and slipped inside. She listened intently. There was no sound from the room beyond hers, and she released a low sigh of relief. Perhaps . . . perhaps all was settled now. Perhaps Mama and Papa would return to their easy manner of old and the pain would disappear from both their gazes. Then, she might be able to look more clearly to a future which now seemed cloudy with uncertainty.

Faith walked to the bed in the far corner of the room and began to undress. William had been so kind. Were it not for him, she would still be walking in the shadows, in search of relief from the uncertainty which pervaded her senses. He had consoled her, and when she had begun to feel better, he had walked her to her door and bid her a firm good night. Her cheek was still warm with the imprint of his kiss.

Faith frowned. But it was not the memory of William's kindness which filled her thoughts. Instead she was visited with the memory of a familiar, haunting visage.

We will not be separated long.

She wondered. . . .

Chapter XVI

Black Wolf dismounted with visible agitation. He was unconscious of the heat of midmorning, the insects buzzing within the tall, browning grass of the prairie, and the sound of the small stream toward which his pony moved instinctively. Relieved that he had located Broken Hand at last, he restrained his anxiety and approached the war chief who stood in silent solitude.

It had been a hard, difficult day since the prisoners had been returned. The camp was in a turmoil, the upcoming peace talks the subject of heated debates which still raged. Black Kettle and the other chiefs were adamant. They would speak to the governor, would determine the depth of his desire for peace.

But Black Wolf had found himself strangely divorced from the disputes that raged within the divided camp. The driving need for revenge which had seared him no longer lent an impetus to his days. That impetus had been tempered by the presence of the fiery-haired one who had shared his lodge and his life during the long days of summer.

Without realization, Black Wolf's hand moved to the carved band on his finger. His heart twisted with pain. He remembered the touch of Fire Spirit's slender fingers as he had helped her to guide the band onto his hand. He remembered her silence when he had explained its significance. He also remembered his own restraint when he had put her from him in the solitude of the prairie, so that he might honor her youth and innocence. He now looked back upon that time with regret. Why had he not realized that the practices of peace held little place in these difficult times? Had he claimed Fire Spirit then, she would not have allowed herself to be returned to the white man's world. One with him, despite her youth, she would have grown in his care, flourished in his love. He had been a fool, and he was now paying the price of his mistake.

His chest heaving with agitation, Black Wolf perused Broken Hand's sober countenance as the silent war chief turned to face him. He saw the torment there, and his own confusion increased. Broken Hand had disappeared from camp shortly after the cavalry had departed. He had not returned. But Black Wolf's own anxiety was such that he had been unable to wait for Broken Hand to return of his own accord. Instead, he had carefully tracked Broken Hand until he had found Broken Hand's temporary camp on the isolated prairie. He no longer worried that he would infringe on the solitude Broken Hand sought. He only knew he must speak to him.

But as Black Wolf watched, Broken Hand turned away from him, focusing his gaze on the distant horizon. His deep voice was gruff.

"I ask that you leave this place, Black Wolf. It is my wish to spend time alone . . . to cleanse my spirit."

The clear lines of Black Wolf's young face tightened with anger.

"You suffer the loss of your wife, Shadow Woman. Your heart aches, and you have come to this place to free yourself of its burden."

Black Wolf paused, his short nod going unseen as Broken Hand's face remained averted. Black Wolf continued with growing heat.

"But you will find no relief here. You have allowed the white man to take from you that which was yours by right. That knowledge is your torment. Shadow Woman entered your lodge and your heart. She is Cheyenne, and now she is with a people who are no longer her own. I bear the same torment. Fire Spirit was promised to me, and I to her. The

215

bond between us has not been severed. I honor it still. I would have her back, now, before distance can be put between us."

Broken Hand turned abruptly, his face a dark, forbidding mask.

"You speak selfishly, Black Wolf. The captives have been exchanged in a pledge for peace. You would endanger that peace and the lives of our people to put an end to your personal disquiet. Your thoughts—the action which you contemplate—are unworthy of you, as they would be unworthy of a great war chief of the Cheyenne."

"Peace is not threatened by honorable conduct."

"What is honorable to the Cheyenne is not honorable to the white man. The white man does not recognize your claim on the girl, or my claim on the woman."

Contempt registering on his handsome face, Black Wolf sneered.

"It is not my concern that the white man recognize my claim. The white man will acknowledge only those claims which he is forced to acknowledge. I will prove my intentions with my strength of purpose, the bite of my anger, the strike of my weapons if the need arises."

Broken Hand's slitted gaze surveyed his face.

"You would raise your protest alone, without the support of your people?"

"I will do all that is necessary to regain that which is mine."

Broken Hand paused. His twisted fingers jerked spasmodically at his side and he closed his eyes against the pain which filled him. The night had been long as he had searched his heart, but the memory of the vision Shadow Woman and he had shared had penetrated his grief. A vision of death and destruction . . . a vision in which Shadow Woman played no active part . . . That vision had burned into his soul. In his torment, he had questioned the intentions of the Great Power who had seen fit to give Shadow Woman to him, only to snatch her away once more. He had searched his heart and mind, and, in doing so, had reached a plane of understanding.

Shadow Woman had come to him to put an end to the

madness of revenge which had driven him. As the Great Power had intended, Shadow Woman had returned life to his spirit, diluted the hatred which had burned within him for those of her white skin. She had also brought to him a message of the disaster which would be visited upon his people if they did not look to peace with the white man. He had seen the blood, smelled death in the slaughter of his people. It was fresh in his nostrils, the scent driving away the pain which still seared his soul. During the long night which had passed, he had determined that he would suffer the loss of Shadow Woman if his sacrifice might prevent the tragedy he had witnessed in the vision. To that end, he would suffer it willingly.

Sensing Black Wolf's scrutiny, he turned back toward him abruptly. His voice was hard with purpose.

"If you would persist in your determination to regain Fire Spirit, you will press your war alone, for I have determined that the white woman, Shadow Woman, is not for me."

The contempt in Black Wolf's eyes expanded to include Broken Hand as well. He released his breath in a low deprecating hiss.

"You would return to the lodge of Owl Woman as before, declaring all you have known with Shadow Woman nullified . . . forgotten?"

"I would honor the welfare of my people above the dictates of my own heart! It is a sacrifice your youth cannot accept as necessary."

"It is a sacrifice I could not accept as necessary, no matter the limits of my age."

Black Wolf's last low, guttural growl stiffened the harsh planes of Broken Hand's face. Broken Hand pulled his massive frame up to its full, impressive height. His broad hands twitched in an obvious attempt to control his surging anger.

"I would end this intercourse between us now, Black Wolf. My affection for the young man you are, and my respect for the warrior you will one day be, allow me to put aside the anger you have stirred within me. Instead, I will respond without anger or advice, and I will tell you to do what you feel you must, for that is the course I myself take. I wish you well. I will sing a song of prayer that you may find your way back to your people in peace."

His rage knowing no relief at Broken Hand's words, Black Wolf allowed himself one last glimpse of the hard, unyielding man standing before him, before turning away in a quick movement. He was mounted once more and riding back toward camp when he realized the full import of the path he had chosen.

Alone he would regain Fire Spirit . . . or alone he would die. No other path was left to him.

Slapping his hand emphatically on the desk in front of him, Wally Durham raised his voice in anger.

"Damn it, William, I've made up my mind! If you called me to your office just for the purpose of trying to convince me to stay in this godforsaken country, you're wasting your time! Tomorrow! We're leaving for Denver tomorrow, and we'll be taking the first available transportation back East from there! I intend to get as far away from here as I can before those savages begin filing into this fort for their peace talks."

Visibly agitated, William strode around his desk to face Wally's livid expression squarely. His light brown mustache twitched in an attempt to restrain his impatience.

"I'm telling you, Wally, you're making a mistake. You're upset, and you're rushing into a course of action you haven't fully thought out. In a few weeks—a month—you'll be kicking yourself for throwing everything up and leaving."

"I have no intention of 'throwing everything up,' William, if that's what you're thinking. And if anyone else but you offered me advice on how to run my life, friend, I'm telling you now, I'd tell him whatever I do is none of his business." Noting the flush that flooded the young captain's face, Wally shook his shaggy red head. He continued with a lessening of his instinctive anger. "But the truth is, William, you're the closest friend I've made in this godless wilderness, and I know you're only concerned for my welfare and my family's. So, I'm telling you now, I'm not a damned fool. I didn't bring my family out here, and expose them to all the hardships they've endured for the past few months, only to throw away the only bright spot in the whole disaster."

"Then what in hell are you doing, damn it?"

Appearing startled by his own vehemence, William took a step backward and raked his hand through his light, well-groomed hair in an unconscious gesture of frustration. He shook his head and finally gave a low, self-conscious laugh.

"Damn it, Wally, don't you think I know I have no right to stick my nose in your business? To tell you the truth, I can't quite believe my own gall. But the fact is, friend, I find myself inexplicably concerned for both you and your family. You have a beautiful wife and daughter, and I can understand your wanting to get them away from here as quickly as possible. But Denver is safe, Wally. You can direct the business of your claim from there, and you can—"

"It's not far enough, William." A haunted shadow passed over Wally's face. "Lydia won't be able to break free of her memories while she is still in this country."

"It's only been a couple of days, Wally, for God's sake. Give her a chance."

"That's exactly what I'm going to do, William. I'm going to give her the best chance to forget I can. I'm taking her home."

"Home." William's lips tightened, his light mustache twitching once more. "By that you mean New York."

"By that I mean New York . . . that's right."

"And you're going to sell off your claim to the first buyer. You're going to let some other person reap the rewards of your find."

"No, as a matter of fact, I'm not. I'm going to play it smart and sell a percentage of my claim to a development company run by a fellow I met just before I came back here to Fort Lyon."

"And he'll rob you blind."

"No, he won't. I'll see to that."

Appearing to have settled the matter to his own satisfaction with that short statement, Wally paused to

219

squint assessingly into the young officer's face. When he spoke again, his voice held a new note devoid of his previous anger.

"Now what do you say you tell me the real reason for all this sudden concern about my future, William. I know you don't give a damn about my claim or what I do with it."

"I told you, your family deserves the best."

"And I'm going to give it to them—the best house in New York, the best life the East can offer them."

William's frown darkened.

"That's it, isn't it? You don't approve of my taking them back East. It has nothing to do with the disposition of my claim. What in hell's going on, William?"

"I think you're making a mistake, that's all." Turning away from Wally's scrutiny, William took a few stiff steps toward the window before facing him once more. "Your wife and daughter will probably be treated like objects of curiosity back there. You know how fascinated with the 'Wild West' people are back east. When they hear—"

"They're not going to hear anything about Lydia and Faith being captured."

"You're not going to be able to keep anything a secret, not after word of the peace talks gets around."

"And you're concerned for my family's welfare, is that it?"

"Yes, I guess that's it."

"Would it be the welfare of my daughter you're concerned about the most, William?"

William flushed, and Wally gave a short, incredulous snort.

"For God's sake, William, she's only fourteen years old!"

"I know how old she is." William's flush darkened.

"Well?"

"Well . . . she won't stay fourteen forever."

Wally shook his head again. A low laugh escaped his lips.

"I think you've been stuck out here too long, William. You've forgotten how people think in the civilized world."

"No, Wally, I think the trouble is I remember only too well." Again raking his hand unconsciously through his fair hair, William flashed Wally an apologetic smile. "If you think I'm not as embarrassed as hell about this whole thing, you're wrong. But the truth of the matter is, Faith is a beautiful girl who's going to be a beautiful woman. By this time next year she'll be well on her way, and I kind of thought I'd like it if I was somewhere close by when that happened. She likes me, Wally."

Wally laughed again.

"That's understandable. I like you too, but that doesn't mean—"

"And I like her. She's only been at the fort for a few days and she already talks to me, confides in me."

"She's only a child! She thinks of you as a friend!"

"That's all I want to be—for now."

Wally's jaw dropped ludicrously. His incredulous expression slowly changing, he stepped forward with a sudden thrust of his chin.

"Damn it, William. You're looking at my daughter with lecherous intent!"

William's expression took on a sheepish quality.

"I wouldn't call my intentions lecherous . . . exactly."

"Oh, hell!" His anger disappearing as quickly as it had appeared, Wally wagged his head in amazement. "This is one conversation I didn't anticipate having this morning." His mind shifting momentarily to recall the air of restrained formality and tension which had grown up between Lydia and himself, he took a deep, troubled breath. The eyes he raised to William were filled with uncertainty.

"Look, William, you're a damned nice fellow, even if you are a little crazy, so I'll tell you the truth straight out. If Faith were a little older, I'd be only too happy to see your interest in her. But right now it's a bit hard to take. I've got enough trouble straightening out my own life, without thinking of my daughter growing up and . . ." William was holding his gaze squarely, and Wally was again stricken with a sense of incredulity. Hell, the man was dead serious! Wally continued with determination.

"But the fact is, we're leaving for Denver tomorrow, and as soon as I can sign the papers with that fellow I told you about, we'll be starting back East."

"You're making a mistake, Wally."

"Mistake or not, we're going."

William's lips tightened. He took a deep breath.

"Considering what you now know, do you have any objections to my continuing to see Faith?"

"No, just as long as you remember she's a child who's gone through a trying experience. She thinks of you as a friend, and I want things to remain that way."

"You have my word."

"That's good enough for me."

Wally extended his hand toward William, finally smiling as William shook it firmly. His tone was tinged with irony.

"This is a hell of a mess, William, isn't it? I have no choice but to try to put the whole of this last year behind me."

"And if you don't succeed, will you come back?"

"I'll face that decision when the time comes."

"Will you be joining us at Major Wynkoop's dinner party tonight? He's really giving it in your honor—because you're leaving."

Recalling the long, silent meals he and Lydia and Faith had shared since they had returned to fort, Wally frowned. Yes, Lydia needed to be in company—away from her thoughts for a while.

"Yes, we will."

The door was closing behind Wally's broad back when William faced for the first time the admission he had voiced to Wally. His own sense of incredulity was no less severe than that Wally had experienced a few minutes before. In the midst of a bloody Indian war, with a tenuous peace all that stood between an Indian nation and the U.S. Cavalry, he was lovestruck by a fourteen-year-old girl and unable to get her out of his mind! What was more, he was faced with the reality that she would ride out of his life, perhaps forever, at sunrise the next day!

William grimaced with self-disgust. Hell, if he wasn't such a damned selfish bastard, he'd be glad Faith was getting away from the situation that threatened to develop. But the truth was, all he could think was that Faith would soon grow into womanhood, and he would be too far away to do anything about it!

At a sudden knock on the door, William's head snapped up. His gaze was met by a young soldier who delivered a crisp message.

"Major Wynkoop would like to see you, sir."

Picking up his hat, William stepped forward with a low, relieved breath, grateful for escape from his thoughts, if only for a little while.

His decision made, Black Wolf sat in front of the temporary hide shelter he had erected. Night had closed over the silent, endless prairie which surrounded him, but Black Wolf's thoughts were far from his self-imposed isolation. Instead, he pondered his preparation, wondering at its adequacy.

He had returned from his talk with Broken Hand earlier that day, his sense of determination profound. It had been the will of Black Kettle and the other chiefs to seek peace with the white man, but there was no peace in his heart. Instead, conflict raged within him. He touched the ring on his finger as he had many times in the past days, and he remembered the warmth of Fire Spirit's hand beneath his. The days had been long and filled with unrest since he had last seen her. He wished for no more than her return to his lodge so he might face the future with her at his side.

Black Wolf frowned. He had presented a pipe to White Bull to request his aid. White Bull had accompanied him to the sweat lodge. There the medicine man had prayed over him and consecrated his shield so that he might emerge unscathed from the confrontation to come. Black Wolf had then purified his spirit with sacrifice. He had then come to this camp and formally lighted his pipe, offered it to the sky, the earth, and the four cardinal points. He had sung his songs, made his prayers, and spoken his vows. He had done all this so he might enter on this important venture with the support of the Great Power. For he wished nothing to go wrong. He knew the importance of that which he was to do. He knew his life could be forfeit. But he also knew he would accept no less than total success.

He would bring Fire Spirit back to his lodge.

His pipe was done, and Black Wolf put it down. He lifted his eyes to the night sky, his gaze trailing the twinkling lights that illuminated the velvet blackness. He had made his vow that Fire Spirit would share this camp with him the next night, would watch the sky with him as he did now. He had also made his vow that he would lay her on his robe under these stars and put aside her youth and the restrictions he had imposed upon himself. He would then take her to his body, worship hers with his own, make her a part of him.

He would keep her separate from his people, remaining alone with her until all strangeness disappeared between them and she welcomed him fully, with eagerness, when he took her body. When they were truly one in body, one in spirit, he would return with her to his people, and he would ask them to rejoice with them.

His heart taking wing, Black Wolf took a last look at the sky above him.

Tomorrow, when night again came, he would take Fire Spirit in his arms. He would know the peace for which his spirit cried, and Fire Spirit would lie content against his heart. It would be.

"It is my impression that the petition Governor Evans sent to the friendly Indians in June, calling upon them to come in and encamp near the posts where they could be watched by the troops and kept out of hostilities, has at last borne fruit." His expression pleased, Major Wynkoop continued briskly, his eyes scanning those gathered at his dinner table. "According to that circular, the Cheyenne and Arapaho were to come here, to Fort Lyon, and the Kiowa and Comanche were to go to Fort Larned. Both camps of Indians would then be maintained by the troops. I think we can prepare for a heavy concentration of Indians nearby in the forthcoming weeks, because I do believe Black Kettle to be serious in his efforts for peace."

Low mumbles of assent echoed around the table. Her

hand trembling, Lydia lifted the fork to her mouth. The aroma of the juicy beef reached her nostrils, and her stomach jerked convulsively. Forcing herself to take a dainty bite, she lowered the fork back to her plate, and shot a quick, self-conscious glance around the table. Her eyes touched on Major Wynkoop. She was relieved to see that he had not noticed her short lapse for he continued enthusiastically.

"I'm presently making arrangements to take the chiefs to Denver as promised. I'm also readying the fort for a distribution of supplies as promised by Governor Evans's circular. I admit to having great expectations. Peace, ladies and gentlemen . . . we may yet see peace."

Hopeful that Major Wynkoop's encouraging word would continue to hold his guests' attention, Lydia chewed with quiet determination. Until he had begun speaking, she had been the uncomfortable recipient of many curious glances, and she was grateful to be relieved, if temporarily, of their weight. Lydia trailed her eyes around the table. Captain Potter's eyes had left Major Wynkoop and were intent upon Faith. The young captain had not sent more than a few polite glances in her own direction during the entire evening, for which she was intensely grateful. Lieutenant Pierce and his wife, Martha, were quietly discussing the merits of Governor Evans's proposal with Wally. She released a low, relieved breath, and then turned her head toward her right, her gaze jerking to a stop as it met Isabel Walsh's scrutinizing gaze.

Lydia swallowed nervously under the woman's avid stare, jerking her head away as the small morsel of food caught in her throat, almost choking her. Tears flooding her eyes, Lydia raised her hand to her lips, covering her mouth as she coughed hoarsely. She struggled to catch h er breath, her face flaming as all eyes turned in her direction.

"Lydia, darling, are you all right?"

Concern evident in his expression, Wally turned in her direction. He rubbed her back with his broad palm as she fought for breath. Smiling encouragingly into her eyes as she nodded with embarrassment, he waited only until she had regained a semblance of control before turning back to the other members of the small dinner party. To avoid calling attention his wife's obvious discomfort, Wally resumed his conversation with Lieutenant Pierce, and Lydia was filled with gratitude. Dear Wally.

Lydia took a deep, shaky breath. She had attempted to scoff at the apprehension with which she had entered Major Wynkoop's quarters for this dinner party; but now that she was here, she found that her anxiety was well founded and it soared anew. Was this the way it was going to be each time she entered a room—scrutinizing looks, concealed appraisal, questions hidden behind curious eyes?

Isabel Walsh . . . she had, indeed, been the worst of the lot. Her small birdlike eyes had examined Lydia intently from the moment she had walked in. She could almost see the questions forming inside the woman's brain. Even now the woman pinned her with her gaze, and a voice within Lydia raised itself in a silent shout.

Yes . . . yes, it's all true! I did indeed live with an Indian war chief! I did function as his wife! Yes, he made love to me! No, he was not a brutal savage, but a tender and gentle lover! Yes, I loved him in return—truly loved him! No, I would never have left him had I not been exchanged as part of the terms of Black Kettle's peace! Yes . . . yes, I miss the peace of the Indian camp where Broken Hand's protection shielded me from prying eyes such as yours!

"I've heard it said that a few high-ranking officers don't approve of Governor Evans's offer."

Wally's statement elicited a vigorous exchange, but Lydia was unable to follow its course. Her hand trembled more severely, and she dropped it to her lap. Her raging mind allowed her no respite as she fought to bring her breathing under control. Oh, God, would this evening never end!

Lydia was still struggling with her ragged emotions, the sound of Wally's low voice rumbling in her ears, when a broad hand moved to cover the trembling fists she clenched in her lap. She lifted her eyes, realizing for the first time that Wally had not missed a word of his response to Major Wynkoop even while his hand had moved reassuringly over hers, soothing the tight knots of discomfort. Tears of gratitude flooded her eyes, and Lydia blinked them back with fierce determination. She had embarrassed Wally enough tonight. She would allow him to suffer at her expense no longer.

Straightening her back determinedly, Lydia held her face averted from Isabel Walsh's stare. She withdrew one small hand and picked up her fork. Wally's hand slipped inconspicuously from hers and she picked up her knife and cut another piece of the rapidly cooling beef. She raised it firmly to her lips and slipped it between her teeth. Her eyes intent on her plate, she missed the sharp glance Lieutenant Walsh dispatched toward his wife, and the annoyed twitch of the woman's lips. She also missed the cooling of Faith's flush and the encouraging glance William shot into her troubled eyes. But most important of all she missed the love obvious in her husband's eyes as he took advantage of Lieutenant Pierce's prolonged response to glance in her direction.

Her hand still warm from Wally's covert caress, Lydia swallowed once more. She had been grateful for her isolation from the inhabitants of the fort since her arrival two days before. Due to Wally's consideration, she had spoken only to Major Wynkoop who was attempting to obtain information about the Cheyenne camp; to the quiet, considerate Captain Potter whose main concern appeared to be Faith's adjustment to the world of the white man; and to Dr. Holstan, who had pronounced her physically fit despite her extreme mental agitation.

In truth, she was certain if she had been in a better mental state, she would have found amusement in the manner in which Captain Potter deferred to Faith, in the way his eyes traveled her lovely, if troubled, face. Unconsciously, Lydia's eyes shot to Faith's hand. The carved band was gone. She released a silent sigh of relief. She remembered only too well Black Wolf's proprietary stance as Faith had stood beside him. No, that would never do for her Faith . . . her beautiful, spirited Faith.

Lydia's hand rose in a self-conscious gesture to the upward sweep of her dark hair, as a new thought struck her. Yes, soon Faith would be wearing her hair up, in a more adult style than the childish coiffure she now assumed. It seemed almost a shame to confine those outrageously brilliant curls. Lydia's eyes lingered pensively on the silky length of her daughter's hair, the sudden memory of Black Wolf's gaze lingering on the girl in a similar manner returning to haunt her mind.

Yes, Wally was right. They needed to be away from this country where memories would allow her little peace, where the caprice of hostile forces could so easily upset the balance of ordered lives. And she wanted to get Faith to safety.

The unexpected pronouncement of her own name jerked Lydia from her thoughts and she looked in the direction of the smiling Martha Pierce. Momentarily unable to catch the gist of the smiling woman's comments, she shook her head in confusion.

"I . . . I'm sorry, Martha. What was it you said?"

Her expression sincere, Martha repeated her comment patiently, her eyes moving to the soft green cotton Lydia wore. "I said you look extremely lovely in that dress, Lydia. I am so pleased someone has been able to wear it at last. Unfortunately, I outgrew it before I finished making it, and there was no one within this fort of the minute proportions to wear it." Patting her expanding waistline which revealed only too clearly the child expected within the next few months, she continued with a smile, "As a matter of fact, I outgrew it long before this happened. I fully anticipated seeing it languish in my closet along with other garments of a size I'm afraid I'll wear only in memory now. Now that I see the dress on you, I know it has found its proper home at last."

Flushing at the obviously sincere compliment, Lydia smiled for the first time, unaware of the reaction her smile worked on the other members of the small party. She was about to respond when Isabel Walsh interrupted with a smile far less sincere.

"Yes, I suppose you must be terribly relieved to be free of that dreadful buckskin garment you were wearing when you arrived. Barbaric . . . wearing the skin of an animal against your own."

228

The silence that fell over the dinner table did not inhibit Isabel, who directed her gaze into Lydia's paling face. "I suppose it must even feel strange eating with forks and spoons, living under civilized conditions again. You must tell us what it was like living in a wigwam . . . or whatever it is those savages call their houses. I understand you lived with a war chief and he—"

"Isabel!"

Her eyes snapping to her husband's livid face, Isabel frowned. She turned a quick glance on those around her.

"Really, John! I'm only expressing everyone's natural curiosity. I'm sure Lydia doesn't mind. She—"

"Why don't you ask *me* your questions, Mrs. Walsh?" Faith's soft interjection turned all eyes in her direction. "Mama hasn't quite recovered from the indisposition she suffered. On the other hand, I can tell you all you want to know. Go ahead, ask!"

Isabel Walsh's eyes snapped in Faith's direction. Her thin lips pressed into a tight line, she eyed Faith with obvious malice. She opened her mouth to speak just as Lieutenant Walsh rose quietly to his feet.

"That's quite all right, Faith. Isabel and I must leave now. I'm afraid little Jennifer has been having nightmares. We cannot afford to allow her to remain alone for long. Eight-year-olds are not very self-sufficient, you know."

"John, I'm not ready—"

"Oh, yes you are, Isabel."

Taking her arm firmly, Lieutenant Walsh raised his annoyed wife to her feet. Bidding polite goodbyes, he ushered her firmly toward the door. Isabel's well-padded frame had cleared the doorway when he turned formally toward the remaining guests.

"My sincere apologies."

There was silence as the young lieutenant closed the door behind him.

Faith looked back toward her mother, aware that the gazes of all around the table followed. She was about to move to her mother's side when William took her arm, quietly restraining her. Annoyed, she shot him an angry glance as Major Wynkoop began to speak with obvious embarrassment.

"Mrs. Durham—Lydia—you have my most sincere apologies for the inexcusable conduct of the wife of one of my officers. I can only hope you will not judge us all by her outrageous behavior."

"Major, Lydia and I . . ."

Still numb from the humiliating scene which had ensued, Lydia felt the first prickle of life return to her frozen lips. No, she could not allow Wally to bear the full burden of this humiliation alone. Suffering as much for his despair as for her own, Lydia touched his arm lightly, halting his intended statement. He turned immediately toward her, his brow tight with concern.

Taking a deep breath to slow the rapid fluttering of her heart, Lydia shook her head. She forced a smile to her lips.

"No, please, Wally. I . . . I suppose I shall have to become accustomed to outrageous behavior if I'm to survive." Her eyes suspiciously bright, Lydia held herself stiffly erect as she continued quietly, "Major Wynkoop, I appreciate your concern, but please continue eating. Peace should, indeed, be celebrated. I consider myself fortunate indeed to be here to celebrate with you."

Carefully picking up her fork, Lydia lowered her eyes to her plate and stabbed dutifully at her food. A brief silence was followed by sporadic bursts of careful, light conversation. Lydia monitored its tone with silent deliberation.

Relieved when it had returned to normal a short time later, she sipped cautiously at her coffee. since the discomfort had finally passed, she turned toward Wally to find him gazing intently at her. A smile trembled on her lips, and Wally swallowed with visible difficulty. His hand reached out to cover hers, and Lydia looked away. She could stand little more.

When the evening finally came to an end, Lydia stood at Wally's side at the doorway to Major Wynkoop's quarters. Her lips parted with surprise as that military gentleman took her hand and raised it formally to his lips.

"You are a true lady, Mrs. Durham. It is my pleasure to have made your acquaintance."

Unable to speak because of the lump that filled her throat, Lydia nodded. Turning, she slid her trembling hand under Wally's arm, and grateful for his strength, she walked out onto the grounds of the fort.

Her eyes intent on her mother's narrow, erect back, Faith bid the other guests good night and stepped out into the darkened yard. A touch on her arm raised her eyes to William Potter's sober expression.

"I'll walk back to your quarters with you, Faith."

Nodding, Faith was still preoccupied as William fell into step beside her. When he spoke again, the unexpected anger in his voice raised her face to his in surprise.

"Well, if your father had been having any doubts as to the wisdom of returning to New York, Isabel Walsh effectively canceled them tonight. Damn her! She's made John's life a living hell since she arrived at the fort. Too bad the Cheyenne didn't take her in their last raid. We'd all be better off!"

Faith could not suppress a spontaneous snicker at William's unexpected statement. His face softening at her amusement, he finally smiled as well and Faith released a tense breath. Her eyes followed her mother and father as they disappeared through the doorway of their quarters, and her step slowed. William was quick to pick up the cue.

"Yes, I agree. It would be kind to allow them some time alone together right now. I'm in a mood for walking. How about you?"

Faith nodded in silent concurrence, and they strolled for a few minutes before Faith felt William's arm slide casually around her shoulder. She looked up to his face, but he avoided her gaze as he urged her closer to his side. When he spoke, his voice was colored by a strange note she could not quite ascertain.

"Are you pleased to be leaving for Denver tomorrow, Faith?"

Caught off guard by his question, Faith hesitated.

"I . . . I suppose I am, William." Unexpectedly, Black Wolf's image flashed across her mind, and her hand moved to the spot the flat carved band had occupied on her finger. It felt strangely bare.

William maintained his silence for some moments, and Faith frowned at his unexpected hesitation.

"I suppose you have many friends back East . . . friends you're anxious to return to see."

William's question was unexpected, and Faith considered it thoughtfully. Surprised to find no other face appeared to supplant the image of Black Wolf which hovered in the corner of her mind, she shook her head.

"No, not really, William. I was away at school much of the time. My closest friends were there, and when my schooling ended, I saw very little of them. We moved in different circles, you see."

Faith's revealing flush tightened the line of William's lips. So that was the way things had stood. Suddenly sympathetic to the driving desire which brought Wally west to seek his fortune, William shook his head.

"And yet your father believes you and your mother will be happier returning."

"Papa is anxious to get Mama away from here . . . away from . . ." Her voice fading, Faith raised her shoulders in a light shrug. "Away from things which might happen . . . like tonight."

William's voice dropped a notch lower.

"What about you, Faith? Do you want to leave, to go back East?"

Faith shook her head. "I'm not concerned about what people will say about me, William. I don't really care what people think. But Mama does. She's having a very difficult time right now. Papa and she—"

"What about *you*, Faith?"

"I guess I'll be going wherever Mama and Papa go."

William's arm tightened spontaneously around her shoulder, and Faith leaned comfortably against his side. She liked William Potter and his easy way. She liked him very much.

"I'll miss you when you go, Faith."

Faith's response was quick and sincere.

"I'll think of you often, too, William. Somehow, I think the few months I've spent here on this Western frontier have impressed me more deeply than all the former years of my life."

Faith sensed William was not pleased with her response, but she was uncertain as to the reason. They were walking in silence when the door to her quarters opened and Wally Durham stepped out into the yard. His eyes touching on Faith and William, he stopped short.

William's arm dropped from her shoulders as Wally declared quietly, "You should think about retiring shortly, Faith. We'll have to be up quite early tomorrow."

"Yes, Papa."

Turning without another word, Wally closed the door behind him. Within moments, Faith was standing in front of the doorway, a smile on her lips as she raised her face to William's sober countenance. She extended her hand toward him, noting the tightening of his frown as he accepted her friendly handclasp.

"Goodbye, William."

William took her small hand.

"I won't say goodbye tonight, Faith. I'll see you tomorrow before you leave."

Faith's smile brightened.

"Oh, I'm glad."

She did not question the warmth that lingered as she turned and walked into the well-lit room behind her.

Wally stood in darkness relieved only by the sliver of moonlight streaming through the window of the room. He stared down at the face of his lovely, sleeping wife, grateful to see that she had at last slipped into restful slumber. He glanced back to the large, upholstered chair where he had slept for the last few nights, relieved that this would be the last night he would spend in discomfort.

Silently, being careful not to awaken her, Wally knelt

233

beside Lydia's bed. His eyes moved over her lovely face, flawless and serene in sleep, and his gaze lingered, seeking a physical sign of the change which had taken place within her. No, if there was any change at all, it was only that she was more beautiful.

Wally released an unconscious sigh of frustration. His lovely Lydia, the only woman he had ever truly wanted, and he did not feel free to love her though his body and heart cried out for her. The absence of intimacy between them was not because of any lessening of desire on his part. To the contrary, he wanted her now more than he had ever wanted her before. But Lydia's spontaneous tensing, the hint of panic in her eyes when he took her into his arms, spoke more clearly than the words she suppressed. He could not make himself ignore her silent confusion and despair, no matter the depth of his need.

Wally took a deep breath, suppressing his compulsion to touch her. It was this place—this damned untamed wilderness—that was keeping Lydia's memories of the time she had spent away from him fresh in her mind. Everything would begin to go back to normal once they were on their way home. Yes, when Lydia was home again, she would return to herself.

Wally's gaze lingered on Lydia's smooth, clear brow; the long, dark lashes which brushed her cheek; the faultless line of her profile. He paused. She was mumbling in her sleep, forming silent, unintelligible word. He stiffened. Broken Hand . . . Her lips had clearly formed that name.

A burning jealousy coming to life inside him, Wally fought the urge to wake Lydia from her dream. He did not want her thinking or dreaming about the savage who had stolen her from him. He had long since faced the painful realization that Lydia's heart was no longer his alone, but he was determined to change all that. Once Lydia was away from this barbaric land, back in familiar environs, she would be able to dismiss that Indian from her mind, just as easily as the silent Indian had dismissed her.

Wally frowned. Lydia's restlessness was returning. She was twisting and turning in her sleep, her mumbled words becoming more pronounced. No, he could not bear to hear her call that savage's name again.

In her somnolent anxiety, Lydia pushed aside the light coverlet that shielded her body from his eyes, and Wally felt the tension inside him increase. The simple sleeping garment she wore did little to hide the flowing line of her body, the rise of her small, rounded breasts. His eyes moved to the shadowed delta between her slender thighs, and the beat of his heart rose thunderously in his ears. His body ached to assuage itself within its moist warmth.

With startling vividness, the image of Lydia seated on the horse in front of the hard-faced, impassive Indian returned to his mind. That Indian had taken Lydia to his bed. He had known the delights of her body, experienced the beauty of her willing response. The knowledge was a deep, burning ache inside him.

He had not touched her since. But it would not be much longer. When they were safely away from this place, he would take her in his arms again, and he would love her with all the feeling stored up in his yearning, aching heart. He would teach her to love him again, and he would never lose her. Never . . .

Lydia was quiet once more. Forcibly restraining himself, Wally rose to his feet. He no longer sought to read the words her slender lips formed in sleep. He would torment himself no longer. They would leave this place tomorrow morning. It could not be soon enough.

Faith scanned the front yard. The sun had risen only a short hour before, but the fort was alive with activity. The coach which was to take Mama, Papa, and herself to Denver was loaded and waiting. Major Wynkoop had put in an early appearance, said his goodbyes, and retired to his office. But he had not left before he had spoken personally to the guard of five soldiers he had assigned to accompany the coach to Denver. The only person who had not yet put in an appearance was William, and Faith was keenly disappointed. Somehow, despite their short acquaintance, she considered William a friend.

Her eyes intent on the coach as the buckskin-clad, shaggy-haired driver made a last-minute check on the traces, Faith fought to dismiss the panic growing inside her. It was a panic which had come to her during the night, a strange sense of impending loss. Her hand moved to the finger which had borne the carved band, and she took a deep shuddering breath. A strange compulsion had caused her to temporarily place the band on her finger the night before, only to hear her father's deep voice in her ear.

"Take that ring off, Faith!"

As her eyes had snapped to his pale, hard gaze, he had continued harshly, "Never put it on again, do you understand me? I will not allow you to wear it, to remind your mother or yourself of the time you spent in captivity. You will strike that time from your mind!"

She had obediently followed Papa's orders, but her rebellious mind had not been so easy to control. Throughout the long night, she had sought to avoid the recurring, dark-eyed visage which allowed her little peace. In truth, she could not fathom the strange twists of her own nature. When she had been in the Indian camp, she had thought of little else but her desire to escape. She had fought Black Wolf's domination with every ounce of strength in her body. But now, when she was indeed back where she belonged, a part of her longed for a freedom she had not before recognized in her "captivity."

She remembered riding on a swift-footed Indian pony across the vast, endless prairie; she remembered the wind rushing against her face, pulling at her hair. She remembered Black Wolf's strong arms around her, supporting her; his broad chest warm against her back. And she remembered lying on her back, her arm brushing warmly against Black Wolf's as the sun warmed their skin. She remembered talking uninhibitedly as he had listened in silence, and her own fascination when he had done the same. She remembered Black Wolf's strength as he had raised her to his feet drawn her full against him. And later, as they had walked under the shield of darkness, she remembered the tight wall

236

of Black Wolf's body as he had pulled her flush against him. He had worked magic with the touch of his lips. She remembered his pledge to her, and she fought to suppress her sense of loss.

"Faith . . ."

Turning abruptly at the sound of her name, Faith looked into her father's anxious face. She bit down sharply on her lower lip to still its trembling. No, she didn't want to leave here . . . not yet. All was not finished between Black Wolf and herself. The rings . . . did he still wear his? They had not truly said goodbye.

"Faith, get into the coach, dear."

Swallowing tightly, Faith gave a short nod. She had taken her father's hand when an abrupt voice to her rear turned her toward William's anxious face.

"Wally, I was delayed with a problem. I would appreciate it if you would allow me a few minutes."

A short nod his only response, Wally mounted the steps of the coach and sat beside Lydia's stiff form. He turned his back toward William and Faith and took Lydia's hand in a gesture of reassurance.

Giving her father and mother only the briefest glance, William drew Faith a few steps back from the coach. His expression was tense, and apprehension touched Faith.

"William, is something wrong?"

His low laugh bore a touch of irony.

"Wrong? No, Faith. What could be wrong?"

"Oh, I thought . . ."

William's brief smile dismissed her words. His fair complexion coloring unexpectedly, he raised a hand to her shoulder and took a brilliant curl between his fingers.

"I should've asked you to cut off a curl so I might keep it for remembrance. I'm sure within a few months I'll begin to think I imagined this wild color."

The first trace of a smile returned to Faith's face.

"I hadn't thought you would forget me so easily. I've come to think of you as a friend."

William's hand moved to cup her shoulder. Stroking the rounded curve thoughtfully, he paused before answering.

237

"Yes, we are friends, Faith. And, as a friend, I would like to exact a serious promise from you. I promise not to forget you, and I want you to promise you won't forget me in return."

Faith's smile faded at William's unexpected sobriety. Her statement was correspondingly sincere.

"I won't forget you, William."

The burnt sienna of William's eyes snapped measuringly up to hers. He nodded, almost more to himself than to her quiet response.

"I'll see that you don't."

Sliding his arms around her, William hugged her tightly for long silent moments. Drawing back at last, he lowered his mouth unhesitantly to hers. His kiss was firm and hard, stealing her breath. A small laugh escaped his lips at her startled expression when he released her at last.

"Goodbye, Faith."

Taking her firmly by the arm, William assisted Faith up the steps to the coach. The door closed behind her and the coach jerked immediately into motion.

Faith raised a small hand in farewell. She realized William was one more person she would never forget.

The long, buffalo grass swayed with movement barely distinguishable from the ruffling of the hot summer breeze. It moved again as Black Wolf adjusted his position in a spot of observance outside Fort Lyon. He had arrived late the day before. He had secreted his mount in the closest cover and begun to observe the military fort. Unexpected activity had erupted in the yard of the fort as dawn had creased the night sky, and his interest had increased.

The reward of his endeavors had come quickly. The gates of the fort had opened to reveal a coach waiting to depart. His dark eyes had scanned the yard, picking out the figures he sought. He recognized the tall, red-haired man who was Fire Spirit's father. The man deferred to Shadow Woman who stood beside him, catering to her needs when she appeared, once again a white woman in clothing and demeanor. But his eyes fastened on and remained on the slight, fiery-haired figure who stood nearby. His heart beat tumultuously in his chest. His gaze consumed her, the girl-woman who was indeed his own.

He watched as the commander appeared and spoke briefly before directing soldiers to the rear of the coach. Five . . . there were five soldiers assigned as guards. He frowned. He saw the red-haired man help Shadow Woman inside.

Black Wolf watched the approach of another military figure. It was the same man who had so eagerly taken Fire Spirit on his horse after he had been forced to give her up. He remembered the man's subdued eagerness, and a new heat came to live inside him.

Through slitted eyes, Black Wolf watched as the officer spoke to Fire Spirit, as she raised her face to his. Stiffening, he saw the soldier take Fire Spirit into his arms, and then press his mouth to hers. Faith did not protest the intimacy, and Black Wolf's anger turned to rage.

The officer released Fire Spirit and helped her into the coach. The driver slapped the reins against the team's back and the coach snapped forward.

A low grunt of satisfaction escaped Black Wolf's lips as the officer was left behind in its dust. He consoled himself that the officer had taken but a taste of the nectar which would be Black Wolf's for the remainder of his life. He had made his decision, and it made little difference how many men attempted to stand between Fire Spirit and himself. He would make her his own. It was meant to be.

The afternoon sun was high, bringing the temperature within the dusty coach to a breathtaking point. Perspiration trickled between her budding breasts, and Faith brushed unconsciously at the tickling sensation. It had been a long morning, and there was no relief in sight from the growing heat. As it was, Faith was only too well aware that her hair was adhering annoyingly to her neck and that her dress was stained darkly in an ungenteel manner. With each passing moment her desire to escape the rocking, dust-filled torture chamber was becoming stronger.

The irony in the situation struck Faith unexpectedly, and she had an absurd desire to laugh. Escape . . . Wasn't that exactly what she and Mama and Papa were doing . . . escaping? And if that was so, why did she suddenly wish so desperately to call this journey to a halt?

Suddenly ashamed of her selfish feelings, Faith looked toward the seat across from her, her brow knitting in concern at the lack of color on Mama's beautiful face. Had she forgotten how Mama suffered because of circumstances over which she had had no control? Had she forgotten how desperately hard Papa was working to try to bring Mama some peace? No. She was only too aware that the situation between them was strained. Papa's eyes followed Mama everywhere, concern written in their depths. And Mama . . . what was she thinking? Did Mama's thoughts persist in traveling back to the Indian camp as uncontrollably as her own?

A chill moved down Faith's spine despite the escalating temperature within the coach. She wanted so desperately for things to be well between Papa and Mama again. Perhaps it was just too soon.

Faith's eyes moved back to the rolling terrain outside the window. The land was a brilliant gold in the light of the afternoon sun. She supposed she should say that she—

The sudden lunge of the coach as it dropped into an unexpectedly deep rut threw Faith unexpectedly from her seat. Grasping her arm firmly, her father lifted her back to her seat with a soft exclamation.

"What in hell . . . ? Faith, are you all right, dear?"

"Yes, I'm fine, Papa."

His eyes snapping to confirm her mother's well-being, Papa then turned to the window of the coach to call out in an angry tone.

"Driver! What in hell's going on?"

In answer to his shout, the coach began to slow, pulling over to a small stand of trees. As it drew to a shuddering halt, buckskin flashed past the window as the driver jumped to the ground. His explanation curt, the graying, bearded driver jerked open the door.

"Can't do nothin' about the holes, Mr. Durham. But it seems to me that tempers are gettin' stretched to the breakin' point with the temperature risin' the way it is. This looks like as good a place as any to stop for a while and get some relief under them trees over there. We ain't likely to find a stand any better than that nowhere along this road."

Nodding, Wally reached for the basket which lay on the seat beside him. At Faith's simultaneous grimace, he smiled wryly.

"Food may not seem too appealing right now, Faith, but it may look better to all of us before the hour has passed. In any case, I think it would be best if we followed the driver's suggestion."

Not waiting for a response, Wally moved to step from the coach. Turning, he offered his hand to Lydia and then to Faith, helping them down from the coach in turn. Lifting the basket from the ground, he took Lydia's arm and supported her swaying movements, his concern obvious.

"Lydia, are you all right, darling?"

Her own discomfort forgotten in the face of her mother's apparent bout of weakness, Faith reached out to steady her mother as well.

"Mama—"

"I . . . I'm fine." Taking a deep breath and pulling herself erect with a supreme effort, Lydia attempted a smile. "Really . . . I'm fine. My legs are just a little stiff, that's all. I'll be all right in a few minutes."

Faith's hand dropped to her side as her father took full control of Lydia. She realized her mother didn't want attention drawn to her, so she thought it best if she just watched in silence, and then . . .

"Miss Durham, ma'am."

Turning to the unexpected voice at her side, Faith looked into the heat-flushed face of the burly sergeant. She saw his eyes move assessingly toward the spot where Papa was helping Mama to seat herself comfortably.

"Yes, Sergeant?"

"Mr. Durham seems to be busy right now, but I just want

241

y'all to know that my men and me will be nearby if you need us for anythin'."

Reading the true concern in the trooper's eyes, Faith attempted a smile.

"Thank you, Sergeant. I— We appreciate your offer."

"It's my pleasure, ma'am."

Tipping his hat, the sergeant turned away and Faith released a low sigh. Turning, she walked toward the spot where her mother and father had finally settled themselves. Yes, a little respite from the grueling journey was what they all needed. In an hour or so, when the worst heat of the day was beginning to fade, they would be able to resume their journey with a new outlook. And then this strange unrest inside her would disappear. It would . . . she knew it would.

Black Wolf crouched low, seeing but unseen from his point of observance. He gave a short deprecating snort. Five soldiers to guard the coach, and not a one of them had seen him following so close on their trail. Black Wolf frowned, his eyes moving over the temporary camp. Fire Spirit's father had taken Shadow Woman to a shaded spot. The white man's concern for his wife made him oblivious to all else. Black Wolf suppressed a flicker of satisfaction. Yes, Fire Spirit was left more or less to her own. . . .

Black Wolf's brow moved into a frown. A soldier approached Fire Spirit and spoke with her, but the conversation was brief. Returning to his men, the soldier gave orders which set his men to take resting positions on the ground a short distance away. The driver of the coach was lying beneath a nearby tree, and Fire Spirit was returning to the side of her father and Shadow Woman. A low frustration rose inside him. His heart cried out to the slender figure who walked so aimlessly in the temporary camp. Come . . . come to me, Fire Spirit. I will take you back to my people, and our time together will truly begin.

His heart beginning an escalated pounding, Black Wolf attempted to restrain his impatience. There was a need for caution. The heat of the day would soon take its course. His time would come.

A strange restlessness would allow Faith little peace. Glancing beside her, she saw Mama's eyes were dropping closed as she sat on the blanket Papa had stretched out beneath a tree, her back propped against its trunk. Noting her scrutiny through heavy lids, Papa smiled. Yes, he was as relieved as she that Mama was finally resting. Faith had no doubt that Papa, himself, would be slipping off to sleep in a few minutes.

Faith's gaze wandered toward the spot where the buckskin-clad driver snored loudly. It lingered briefly, only to move on toward the guard. All were sleeping, with the exception of the one young fellow on guard, and even he looked as if he had difficulty keeping his eyes open. Faith's frustration increased. Only she was unable to put aside her sense of unrest . . . the strange prickling on her spine.

Glancing away, Faith trailed her eyes along the sur-rounding foliage. Yes, this was the greenest copse they had passed in the many hours on the trail. Papa had disappeared into the foliage a short time before, to emerge with fresh water from the stream the driver had indicated he would find. Perhaps if she washed her face and hands, refreshed herself . . . In any case, it would be better than sitting here, watching everyone else sleep when she had no inclination to do the same.

Drawing herself quietly to her feet, Faith paused. She had no desire to awaken either Mama or Papa. Mama was exhausted, the strain she had suffered during the past few days having taken a heavy toll on her endurance. Faith had heard sounds of movement from Mama and Papa's room during the night. She had recognized Papa's step and realized that he had slept little during the night. He needed the rest he was now taking if he was to be strong for both Mama and himself in the days to come.

A sound to her rear turned Faith toward the young soldier

on guard. She smiled, halting him in his step as he attempted to approach her. No, she did not need anyone to accompany her. What she really needed was to be alone, for just a short while.

Turning, Faith moved into the foliage. Papa had said the stream was not far. . . .

Faith smiled, hearing the sound of the trickling water before it came into view. Cool and fresh, sparkling in the light filtering through the graceful umbrella of trees, the stream was a slender thread woven through the brief patch of green. It drew her, called to her, and Faith walked forward to crouch beside it.

Suppressed memories flooded her mind. The evening of the day she had seen Black Wolf for the first time, while she was traveling as his prisoner. He had been hard and cold. There had been a bitterness inside him which had been directed toward the color of her skin. It had been as instinctive as her hatred and fear of him. That hatred, fear and distrust had been dismissed unwillingly between them. She was truly uncertain when other feelings had begun to develop in their place. She remembered still her sense of shock when Black Wolf had taken her into his arms. She remembered his strength, the taste of his mouth as it had sought to consume hers.

Faith swallowed convulsively against her rising feelings. William had kissed her, too, with surprising warmth. But William was a friend, while Black Wolf was—

A hand suddenly snapped across Faith's mouth, stifling her spontaneous gasp. She was struggling against the arm which closed around her waist from behind, pinning her arms to her sides, when a familiar hiss froze her protest.

"Be still!"

Instinctively obeying the short command, Faith felt the binding embrace fall away as strong hands turned her toward Black Wolf's assessing gaze. His dark eyes looked deeply into hers in an attempt to read her gaze.

"When last we met I told you we would not be separated long. I have come to fulfill my promise to you."

Faith shook her head in spontaneous protest.

"No, Black Wolf, I can't! Papa—"

"Come!"

"No, I can't! You don't understand!"

A strange light flickered in Black Wolf's eyes. His voice was a low hiss.

"Yes, I understand only too well."

Momentarily confused, Faith watched as Black Wolf drew back. Her eyes widened and he raised his hand. Shock holding her immobile, she could do no more than utter a low gasp as he brought his hand down in a rapid, sharp blow to her jaw. Her knees buckling, Faith felt the rapid assault of darkness, heard Black Wolf's low, pained pronunciation of her name in the moment before she was weightless in his arms.

She was traveling quickly, the trees overhead flashing by in a rapid canopy of flickering sunlight. She felt strong arms holding her, heard the rasp of Black Wolf's breathing. She uttered his name only to feel him clutch her closer still. She turned her head, her lips brushing against the smooth, perspiration dampened skin of his shoulder. She breathed his scent, felt his spontaneous response as a deep voice shattered the silence.

"Halt! You, there, halt, or I'll shoot!"

"No, damn it, don't shoot! You'll hit Fai—"

The sharp, cracking report of a shot reverberated in the silent grove and Black Wolf jerked convulsively. They were falling, both of them, falling rapidly to the ground. Disoriented, unable to block her fall, Faith felt a sharp knife of pain penetrate her head as it sharply struck the hard-packed earth of the trail. She struggled to lift her head, but the light of day was dimming, her vision narrowing into an ever-shrinking tunnel of light. She turned, gasping as she saw Black Wolf's face. He was lying on his side on the ground beside her. His eyes were closed, his chest still. Blood trickled from the corner of his mouth, forming a small puddle beneath his cheek.

Footsteps thudded against the ground beside her, jerked to an abrupt halt. She felt gentle hands touch her, heard Papa's voice. She was still straining to see Black Wolf through the narrow pinpoint of light remaining when she heard a young, eager voice offer sharply, "He's dead, sir! The Indian's dead."

And then she heard no more.

Faith turned, and pain convulsed her. Her head . . . it hurt . . . it hurt so badly. . . . She struggled to open her eyes even as she attempted to raise an exploring hand to her temple. But her arm was heavy . . . so heavy. . . .

Finally succeeding in raising her weighted lids, she opened her eyes to a bright, sunlit room. It was unfamiliar, as was the face of the woman who reached out a hand to gently touch her forehead.

"You're all right, dear. You have a concussion. You need rest, that's all, and you'll be as good as new in a week or so."

There was the sound of footsteps and muffled voices and Papa's worried face came into view. Mama appeared beside him, her face devoid of color. Papa's hand was stroking Faith's cheek, when the image of Black Wolf's lifeless face appeared before her eyes. Gasping, her heartbeat abruptly accelerating to a heavy pounding, Faith struggled to speak.

Papa's voice was soft, laced with concern.

"Faith, don't be afraid. You're safe now. I won't let anything more happen to you, I promise you that."

But Faith did not want Papa's promises. She wanted to know . . .

Her lips were stiff, her tongue heavy, unwilling to cooperate as she fought to form words. Her panic was growing as the image of Black Wolf grew stronger in her mind. She grated harshly.

"Bl . . . Black Wolf . . ."

Papa's pale eyes grew cold. His voice hardened.

"He's dead, Faith. We left the damned savage where he fell and came on to Camp Weld."

"No . . . no!" Faith was gasping for breath, her cloudy mind refusing to accept the words Papa hissed vengefully.

Papa's pale-eyed gaze began to show panic.

"Faith, didn't you hear what I said? The Indian's dead.

246

You're safe. You don't have to be afraid anymore. Darling . . ."

Faith attempted to shake her head, to negate the impact of Papa's words, but the action increased her pain and she gasped against the rapidly deteriorating light. Mama's face drew closer, tears of understanding bright in her eyes.

"Mama . . . Mama . . . I don't want . . . Black Wolf can't be dead. . . ."

Tears slipped down Mama's cheeks. Faith felt them, warm against her own. The last flicker of light was disappearing and she heard Mama's soft voice whisper against her cheek.

"I know, darling . . . I know. . . ."

Chapter XVII

"Captain Potter, I realize my arrival here comes as a shock to you. The fact is, it has come to the attention of headquarters that certain officers have issued stores, goods, and supplies to hostile Indians in direct violation of orders. Unofficially, Major Wynkoop has been criticized for acting so foolishly as to permit Indians to approach the post against General Curtis's explicit orders, and for leaving his district—going to Denver with his 'peace council'—without orders. It is for that reason that I was relieved of my command at Fort Larned and sent here to replace Major Wynkoop. I also consider it my duty to uncover any other unauthorized acts which Major Wynkoop may have sanctioned."

The flush that colored his fair complexion betrayed Captain Potter's reaction to the new commander who had arrived a few days before, and to his new superior's criticism of Major Wynkoop. Carefully picking his words, William faced the man squarely within the limited confines of the office Major Wynkoop had only recently surrendered, standing his ground.

"I will repeat my former statement, Major Anthony. In my opinion, the Cheyenne now gathered at Sand Creek did so on the basis of the printed circular distributed by Governor Evans and not on the basis of a suggestion from Major Wynkoop. I think you will find that Agent Colley is of the same opinion."

"Governor Evans's circular extended the protection of the

248

government to 'friendly' Indians."

"Sir, these Indians consider that they have negotiated a peace. They are now 'friendly.'"

"Friendly!" Major Anthony's eyes widened with incredulity. "They have committed all manner of depredation and held the overland road captive for over a month, allowing no manner of transportation to reach Denver, yet you consider these Indians friendly? Such would certainly not be my description of friendly Indians."

"Sir, I repeat, these Indians consider that a peace has been negotiated."

"And I repeat. There has been no such peace promised to them."

"Sir, these Cheyenne came in to Sand Creek at the invitation of Governor Evans. They consider themselves under our protection!"

"No such protection was extended to them. Major Henning is in temporary command of the district of the Upper Arkansas, and he feels that punishment must be meted out where it is due."

"Sir . . ." Captain Potter shook his head with disbelief. "Sir, Major Henning does not seem to realize that it is within the Indians' power to inflict far greater losses on the whites than the whites could inflict on them."

"That, Captain Potter, is a misconception."

"Sir!"

"You are dismissed, Captain Potter. I have no further questions for you at this time."

Swallowing tightly against his distaste for the arrogant officer who had assumed Major Wynkoop's command, Captain Potter snapped a formal salute, and walked stiffly through the open doorway. He was glad to be free of Major Anthony's incessant questions, if only temporarily.

Watching the young captain until he had cleared the doorway, Major Scott Anthony turned abruptly to focus an unseeing eye toward the window and the gray, overcast winter sky. He straightened his spine, unconsciously straining to add to his inadequate height as, in his mind, he carefully reviewed the situation that presently existed at

Fort Lyon.

Yes, Major Wynkoop had unknowingly set up ideal conditions with which to deal with these Indians. Headquarters was hot to mete out punishment to these former hostiles. He himself had met with a band of Cheyenne from Sand Creek at Bent's Fort only a short time before. He had cautiously told them that he had no authority to make peace as they requested, but that if he received such authority, he would come and tell them. He had, in the meantime, relayed to headquarters information stating that there was a small band of Indians within forty miles of him, and had requested permission to attack.

Yes, the camp at Sand Creek was as good a place as any to raid if he received the permission he sought. He had no intention of seeking peace. Hell, no! He wasn't afraid of a fight like that coward Wynkoop! Major Scott Anthony suppressed a smile. All indications were that the higher command was gearing itself up for a winter campaign. Things would be happening soon, and he would be in the middle of it. And that was just where he wanted to be.

The memory of Captain Potter's flushed face returned to his mind, and Major Anthony's brow furrowed. That young captain was doubtless going to be a true thorn in his side. He was in too close agreement with Wynkoop's methods. Yes, something would have to be done about that fellow—soon.

The morning sky was gray, the air cold, freezing in Broken Hand's nostrils. His breath was visible, emerging in little puffs of mist that swirled before him. Broken Hand clutched his robe tighter as he heeled his horse to a faster pace. Winter had come to the land, but there was little peace within him, despite the quiet that reigned in his people's camp. Abruptly turning his pony, Broken Hand paused to survey the camp behind him. Over one hundred lodges, a few Arapaho beside the Cheyenne, were camped under the protection of the white man's army. He saw the shields of War Bonnet, White Antelope, Lone Bear, Black Kettle, Left Hand . . . all were gathered there.

Broken Hand attempted to dismiss the unease inside him. He had seen this scene before, the pattern of lodges spread out before him, the display of shields. He had felt this cold, sensed impending disaster. He had known all these things—seen them, felt them—through the shadowed eyes of the woman who had lain in his arms, sobbing her despair. Broken Hand attempted to dispel the gloom which colored his mind the exact shade of the overcast sky. But there had been little sunshine in his heart since he had allowed Shadow Woman to be returned to her people.

Broken Hand took a deep breath and squared the broad expanse of his shoulders. But his sacrifice had not been in vain. Major Wynkoop had held true to his word and taken Black Kettle and the other chiefs to make their peace with the white man's Governor Evans. In return his people were encamped in the bend of this river, being fed by the white man during the hard days of winter. There they would remain, keeping their peace. The frightening vision he had glimpsed through Shadow Woman's eyes would not come to pass. Black Kettle rejoiced that no more of his people's lives would be lost in a useless war.

But Broken Hand did not rejoice. There was no joy inside him.

Broken Hand's eyes returned to survey the lodge he had just left, and his frown deepened. Smoke poured from the outlet and he knew Owl Woman was awake and had added fresh fuel to the fire for the morning meal. His appetite raged, but it was not a physical hunger. Instead, he craved food for his soul, the food which had been taken from him, leaving him slowly dying within himself.

Shadow Woman . . . She had awakened his spirit, and had she still been with him, he knew he would see this camp through different eyes. He would see joy in his temporary inactivity, a future in the peace which reigned, and he would find purpose in his day. Instead, he was empty, had even been stripped of the opportunity for revenge which had formerly given his life purpose.

As Broken Hand watched, Walking Woman emerged from her lodge to make her way toward the river. Walking

Woman had suffered a great loss in her lodge, a loss related to his, and he had been drawn to her because of it. His affection for her now was stronger than the affection he bore for the silent, bitter woman with whom he shared his lodge. Owl Woman was mother of Tall Ree. To her he was bound with a tie never to be broken. He would honor that tie for the remainder of his life, but he would never take her to his sleeping bench again. Owl Woman had been the first to put aside that part of their life together. He had honored her decision, and he now found it suited him well.

Light was beginning to break through the thick cover of gray which swirled in the sky above him. The wind blew cruelly, and Broken Hand pulled his robe tighter. He turned his eyes to the winding ribbon of water nearby, assessing its breadth and level sand bed, the occasional pools which formed there. He heeled his horse to the bank and looked across, his point of observance giving him a clear view of the horses herded on the far side. He would cross the water and tend to his horses. He would not hasten to return. There was little for him here, in this camp tucked in the bend of water the white man called Sand Creek.

Faith threw back the covers and reached for her wrapper. She paid scant attention to her reflection as she passed the full-length mirror in the spacious room. She had become as accustomed to her appearance in the fine lace-trimmed nightgown she wore as she had to the grandeur of the bedroom which she could now call her own, and to the luxury of maids who awaited a summons to come rushing to her command.

Oh, pooh! She hated it all!

She was actually uncomfortable with the number of strangers who saw fit to invade her room at any chosen moment. She could not understand how Mama and Papa could stand such an invasion of their privacy. She amended her uncharitable thought. Of course, the housekeeper and the maid always knocked before they entered. But she resented them just the same.

What was more, she resented the distance their presence had put between Mama, Papa, and herself. She was of the opinion that all was not yet quite well between Mama and Papa, despite the fact that they had been back in New York City for almost two months. It had been long enough for Papa to establish them in a house she could think of only as a mansion, and to allow Mama to reestablish contact with her father who had welcomed her home grandly. She, herself, could not seem to summon the affection for her grandfather that her mother appeared to feel. No, despite her grandfather's love for Mama, he, even now, looked with disapproval on her father and on her own resemblance to him, and that held her aloof. She loved Papa too much not to suffer the slight he felt.

She knew Papa suffered another trial as well. She had seen his face when Mama drifted off into her thoughts. But she also knew Mama could not help the frequency with which memories assaulted her.

Abruptly, tears flowed hot and moist into her eyes. Faith blinked them back with determination. Three months . . . it had been three months since that day, yet she still saw Black Wolf's face each time she closed her eyes to sleep at night. But she no longer cried and mourned his loss. Instead, she salved her grief by allowing the invasion of good memories, while attempting to set away the bad. She had attempted to replace the blurred image of Black Wolf's lifeless face with the memory of days spent racing across the prairie, of the time he had held her in his arms. Her clearest memory of the last day she had seen Black Wolf was her glimpse of the carved band he had still worn on his finger.

Swallowing with difficulty, Faith walked to her dressing table and lifted the lid of the small jewel case resting there. Carefully moving aside the new jewelry her father had bought her, jewelry he considered suitable for a girl her age, Faith found the small, carved band secreted there. Her taste of the warmth and wonder in Black Wolf's arms had been brief. If Mama's and her return had not been included in the terms of peace . . .

Carefully replacing the band, she covered it with the more

conventional jewelry. It would do her no good to speculate on something that was not meant to be. Rather, she knew she would concentrate on developing the façade Papa wished her to present. It was important to him that he establish his wife and daughter in the world to which he firmly believed they belonged. She supposed it would one day become important to her, too. In any case, those few, brief months spent in the foreign world of the baking sun and rolling prairie were over and done. Her most important link to that time had been broken, and lived only in her memory. The short, affectionate letter she had received from William had only succeeded in stirring those memories anew. Oh, how she wished . . .

Abruptly shaking aside her thoughts, Faith took a deep breath and turned toward her wardrobe. The most enjoyable part of her new life was the stable Papa had purchased along with their stately residence. It was early. She doubted that Mama and Papa were yet awake, but the groom would be about and either he or the stable boy would be only too willing to accompany her on a brisk morning ride. Yes, she would go riding, and the cold, November breeze would blow her mind free of painful memories, if only for a little while.

She reached for her fashionable riding clothes. Yes, for a little while she would be free. . . .

Wally heard soft sounds of movement in the room next door. Faith was awake and already on her feet. A small smile tugged at his full lips. Well, she was one worry which had been erased from his mind.

His smile fading, he recalled the terrible fear that had pounded through his veins when he had discovered her missing as they had rested beside the trail on the way from Fort Lyon. He remembered the sound of that young trooper's voice, the cry that had left his throat when the fellow had fired into that Indian's back. He had had no thought for the savage who had lain dead on the trail. The slain Indian's body had been abandoned by his party without a second thought. His concern had been entirely for

Faith who had lain barely conscious, bleeding from a cut on her temple. He remembered the rapid swelling of the ugly bruise and her lapse into unconsciousness, the long days during which Faith had been sorely ill and during which Lydia had not left her side.

But Faith was well now and adjusting to her new life. Stocking the stable with a few good riding horses had been a true inspiration. Faith had taken to them immediately, and riding had provided her with an outlet for her surprising sorrow at the death of that persistent savage. He only wished . . .

Turning his head, Wally allowed his eyes to drift over the small, perfect features of the woman who lay at his side. If only Lydia would awaken to the new day with Faith's enthusiasm . . . Instead, he had the feeling Lydia's interest in her new life was all an act, prompted by her desire to please him. It would be different if he thought that desire was motivated by love, but he could not make himself believe that to be true. No, it was not love Wally saw in Lydia's eyes. Rather, it was guilt . . . and shame.

His heart twisting in his chest, Wally reached out to stroke a silken wisp back from Lydia's smooth cheek. How many times did he have to tell Lydia that he loved her, that he did not hold those days spent in the Indian camp against her, that he had dismissed them from his mind? Did she sense that the last of those statements was untrue? Jealousy still gnawed at his innards, especially when he knew Lydia was drifting in a sea of memories back to those long summer days she had spent away from him and in the arms of another man. But he knew Lydia was guiltless, even in her loving acceptance of that savage. All he truly wanted was for her to forget him, to strike that Indian from her mind. But accomplishing that was not going to be simple.

Lydia's lushly trimmed lids were beginning to flutter against her cheeks. She was awakening, and Wally felt a flash of regret for the intrusion of the world which inevitably ensued upon their awakening. He had a sudden, selfish desire to eliminate all others from their world, so there might be just the two of them as there had once been. To start over from the beginning once more, to eliminate the past year from their lives . . .

Daydreams and wishes. They would never be reality. Reality was Lydia, here . . . now . . . lying beside him.

Lowering his head, Wally brushed Lydia's parted lips with his own. Oh, God, how he loved her. He had not truly looked at another woman from the day his eyes had first touched her. He knew he never would. There was no woman more beautiful, more desirable, more appealing to him. During the time of their separation, even when he had thought her dead, he had not sought to bring his body release with another woman. He had wanted only Lydia, and without her, had been content with no one.

Eyes of shadowed gray rose to his, and Wally swallowed with difficulty. Even now he was uncertain how Lydia had come to love and marry him. He was certainly nothing special, had been nothing more than a poor relation of her cousin Mary's friend. There had been so many eligible young men who had sought her hand, but she had favored only him. Oh, God, and he had let her down so badly.

"Wally . . . what's wrong?"

Wally's voice was filled with emotion. "Wrong? What could be wrong, darling? You're here in my arms, and I'm kissing you."

The shadows of bottomless gray grew deeper. Unable to bear the darkening of recollection in her eyes, Wally covered Lydia's mouth with his. His kiss this time was rougher, unconsciously seeking to force away those deepening shadows with the dawning of desire. His hands moved beneath the fine silk coverlet, finally throwing it back with impatience as it hindered his hungry touch.

The broad palm of his hand swept the fine lace straps from her shoulders, moving with efficiency to expose the tender swells of her breasts. The rosy pink crests called to him and he covered them warmly with his lips, sucking and drawing them deeply into his mouth. The taste of Lydia excited him, drove him wild with desire. He was shuddering with his insatiable hunger for her when he became abruptly aware that Lydia's need did not mirror his own. Instead, she had stiffened under his loving attack, her face tightening as panic flickered in her eyes.

No, this was not what he wanted from Lydia. He wanted complete, loving surrender. He wanted the response that had always been his for the asking, the response he had gotten rarely in the months since her return. He wanted it, needed it, badly.

Taking a deep breath, Wally raised a trembling, freckled hand to Lydia's cheek. He cupped it gently, his lips trailing across her satin skin.

"I love you, Lydia. Everything . . . everything else pales in contrast to that love. In the time we were apart, I lay awake at night, reliving every moment we had spent together. I remembered the way you felt in my arms, the way you came alive under my touch. I remembered the way your body quivered and moved when I kissed the hollows at the base of your throat, when I touched your breasts, your soft sounds of protest when you could stand no more."

Lydia's breathing was quickening and Wally felt a new hunger come alive inside him. He trailed his lips against hers, his tongue tracing their smooth curve before slipping between to taste her intimately. He was drinking deeply of her sweetness, his mouth fondling, nibbling, caressing the hollows of her mouth. His hand was moving warmly against her flesh, smoothing, seeking. The warmth of her thigh met his touch, and he heard Lydia's spontaneous intake of breath.

He swallowed her unintelligible murmur with his lips as his hand met the warm nest of her passion, tangled in the moist curls. His knowing touch met the moist bud of her womanhood, and he fondled it gently. Her reaction was immediate, but he would allow her no respite from his deliberate arousal. Her breath was heavy against his lips, her slender body trembling, and he drew back, his eyes consuming the passion written on her beautiful face. The shadows in her eyes were no longer haunted, but burned with desire; and he reveled in his victory over the memories which haunted her. But his victory was not complete . . . not yet.

With slow deliberation, he stroked her more intimately,

his own breathing becoming erratic as her passion grew. She was shuddering, quaking on the brink of fulfillment, and Wally paused. His own tightly controlled emotion was reflected in the tense planes of his face, the heaving of his broad chest, the harsh rasp of his voice as he responded to Lydia's mumbled protest.

"No, darling, not yet. I want to hear you say the words. I have to hear them. . . ."

"Wally, please . . ."

"Tell me you want me, darling. Tell me you need me as much as I need you. Tell me you love me—only me."

"Wally, you . . . you know . . ."

"Say it, Lydia."

A small tear squeezed out the corner of Lydia's eye, but she ignored it as it blazed a ragged trail into the gleaming strands at her temple.

"Oh, Wally, I do love you . . . I do. Please don't doubt that . . . ever."

"Tell me you want me, darling."

"I want you, Wally. I want you to hold me, to love me, to keep me with you for the rest of my life. And in return, I promise to love you just as much, to give—"

Unable to stand any more of her quaking response, Wally covered Lydia's trembling lips with his own, his mouth sinking deeply into hers as he brought her to wild, shuddering climax with his loving touch.

She was still trembling, her breath coming in deep gasps, when he rolled atop her, his broad, tightly muscled body pinning her with his weight. The staff of his manhood sought the quivering nest beneath him, slipping inside to sheath itself in her moistness. The low gasp that escaped him was echoed by Lydia's own, and a surging elation came alive inside him.

Lost to his passion, Wally plunged deeply, his passion soaring as Lydia raised herself to meet his thrust. He drove deeper, again and again, their joining becoming more breathless, more consuming. With a last, searing thrust, he touched the heart of her passion and the ripple of ecstasy that shook Lydia released the thunder of his own.

Gasping, loving, holding her close, Wally lay in the aftermath of their lovemaking, knowing Lydia's fulfillment had been no less than his own. He pulled her closer still. He had dispelled the ghosts that haunted her, if only for a brief time. Eventually he would know their ultimate conquest.

But for the time being, he would content himself to love her, love her, love her. . . .

It was dark, and bitter cold. An attempt to restrain his shuddering was to no avail as Captain William Potter urged his mount forward across the frozen ground. He looked around him, over the barely discernible landscape of a rolling prairie covered with short grass. All was silent, except for the sound of seven hundred men mounted and pushing relentlessly forward.

William shot a quick glance in front of him: Major Chivington, his huge outline dwarfing all others who rode beside him; Major Anthony, satisfied at last that an attack had finally been authorized; Jim Beckwith . . . But the old trapper was having difficulty in guiding them. He was cold, too cold to function. A sharply barked command sent a trooper back to the ranks to return minutes later with another man to take over the job of leading the column.

The silent march continued, and William shuddered with the thought of that which was to come. Major Chivington's arrival at Fort Lyon had been ominous. In retrospect, he realized there could have been no other reason for the gathering of such a force as had accompanied Major Chivington, and no other reason for the secrecy under which the major had traveled. Enforcing a command of silence for the entire duration of his march, Major Chivington had reportedly gone so far as to close the river to traffic when he had reached Booneville and had even held back the mail for fear that news of his force's movement would reach the Indians and thus allow them to escape. At Bent's stockade on the south side of the river, he had reportedly set up and left a guard to see that no one left the ranch to warn the Indians. From there he had marched to Fort Lyon, again

259

throwing out a line of pickets to stop anyone who might attempt to leave.

His stomach churning, Captain William Potter had immediately recognized the significance of such secrecy and the gathering of such a huge force. Major Chivington and Major Anthony were marching to Sand Creek and the gathering of Cheyenne there. They were one in their sense of purpose. Annihilation.

William shook his head with disbelief. His arguments had been to no avail and had actually been looked upon with disgust by many of the action-hungry new arrivals. He had heard the whispered comments as he had been ordered to mount and take his place among his men. Coward . . . Indian lover . . .

This whole incident was a nightmare—U.S. Cavalry attacking a peaceful camp of Indians who had been guaranteed government protection. Helpless, unprepared, unsuspecting, they would be caught in their sleep, cut down and slaughtered. No, God, he could not be a part of all this . . . but he was.

Despite the bitter cold which numbed his extremities and had brought him to a state of constant shuddering, William felt perspiration dot his brow. They would be arriving at the Indian camp soon. It was almost daybreak. . . .

Broken Hand was restless. He twisted on his sleeping bench, drawing his sleeping robes higher on his shoulder against the cold which had penetrated his lodge. But he could find little comfort from a strange sense of unease which assailed him. Rolling to his back once more, he looked to the small piece of sky visible through the smoke outlet above him, and he released a short breath. Dawn . . . the sun would soon be rising and a new day would begin.

The sound of stirring on the sleeping bench to the far side of the fire drew his eyes toward Owl Woman. She met his gaze, her eyes moving to the fire which had begun to burn low. Throwing back her sleeping robe, she moved quickly to add new fuel in performance of the ritual of never-ending women's work which would doubtless be performed all around the camp within the hour.

Sparks rose as Owl Woman stirred the glowing embers. The fire flamed anew and Owl Woman sat back on her heels, her lined face devoid of emotion. Moving to her feet in silence, she adjusted her robe and took up the container near the doorway. The cold did not eliminate the need for living water to start the day, and Owl Woman was well versed in her duties. Quickly lifting the flap, she disappeared into the semidarkness and Broken Hand closed his eyes. The new day stretched before him in his mind, devoid of challenge and joy—gray, like the dawn—like all the days which would follow.

A small frown furrowed his brow, and Broken Hand's eyelids lifted once more. Reaching down, he placed the flat of his hand against the ground. The ground trembled with the echo of many hooves. He had not realized buffalo were so near.

A sudden shout, the echo of many more, sounded outside his lodge and Broken Hand rose from his sleeping bench with a start. He raced to the doorway and threw back the flap, his eyes focusing on the fear in Owl Woman's eyes as she ran from the river, calling his name. She was pointing toward the line of mounted soldiers in the distance, thundering toward them.

His heart beginning a wild pounding, Broken Hand glanced toward Black Kettle's lodge as the chief emerged, confusion in his gaze. Black Kettle raised his hand in an attempt to stop the rapidly escalating panic as his people emerged from the lodges around camp, their eyes on the approaching cavalry. A brief signal from Black Kettle sent his wife back into his lodge. Moments later she placed in his hand the American flag he had received in council many years before. Quickly running it up on a lodge pole, Black Kettle fastened a white flag below it as a sign of friendly camp. He stood his ground, confidence reflected on his face. The soldiers would recognize his signal. His people were at peace.

Broken Hand remained immobile in the growing light of

sunrise. No, it could not be! He had seen this scene all too clearly before. . . . His eyes shot to the distance. The lines of cavalry still approached. The sounds of gunshots reached his ears as a group broke off from the main troop and moved to cut off the horses herded on the far side of the creek. Broken Hand turned to search the prairie around them. Surrounded . . . the cavalry had broken into groups which were surrounding them. His eyes dropped briefly closed. It had come, the realization of Shadow Woman's vision. It had all been for naught—his sacrifice, his loss—except that Shadow Woman would be spared their fate.

Broken Hand looked to the rise of land from which Shadow Woman had viewed the slaughter to come. He saw her clearly in his mind, watching him. Had she seen his death in the horror of her vision? He found he cared little, but the lives of others . . . perhaps they could be saved.

Running back to his lodge, Broken Hand took up his gun. Turning quickly, he raced back outside to stand at Black Kettle's side. Some of the warriors were running out toward the pony herds, while others in the camp rushed about in growing terror. Black Kettle called out to them, exhorting them not to be frightened, telling them that there was no danger.

The troops were reaching camp. Abruptly they were firing into the mass of men, women, and children gathered there, and all began to scatter and run.

The dead lay all around him; Owl Woman lifeless on the ground, her eyes staring blankly up at the gray morning sky. Firing as he turned, Broken Hand broke for cover. He was still running as a ball hit him in the hip, and he staggered with pain. All but carried by the terrified throng which surged into the dry bed of the creek, Broken Hand stumbled and fell, finally managing to draw himself into a pit dug in the high bank of the stream. Taking careful aim, he fired at the approaching soldiers even as he faded in and out of consciousness, but the killing continued. Women and children's cries rang in his ears as the soldiers shot without mercy.

Blood, death, slaughter . . . Shadow Woman's vision brought to life, and the bloody horror raged on.

The shooting had stopped when Broken Hand again came to consciousness. He peered cautiously out of the deep pit in which he lay, and a low gasp escaped his throat. Bodies of the dead and dying lay scalped in the bed of the stream; mutilated beyond recognition, others were losing their life's blood to the trickling water. The troops had retreated, returned to the camp. Slowly those secreted began to emerge from hiding. Shivering against the cold and loss of blood, the surviving wounded staggered up the creek bed in an attempt to cut a path above the captured camp. A woman wavered weakly beside him, and Broken Hand took her arm. Her face was slashed and bleeding, unrecognizable. She clutched a dead child in her arms, and continued walking.

At the sound of hoofbeats, Broken Hand raised his head, his finger tightening on the trigger of his gun. Two, three, four horses, mounted by his own people. The wounded woman was taken from his grasp, the dead child discarded despite the woman's outcry. Broken Hand took a deep breath, the last of his strength slipping away with the blood that continued to stream from his wound. He would not last much longer, but he cared little.

There were other hoofbeats to his rear, and Broken Hand turned. His breath caught in his throat as he met the eyes of one whom he had given up for lost. He called out, his voice emerging on the frigid air as a harsh rasp.

"Black Wolf. You . . . you have returned."

The familiar dark eyes were filled with pain, sorrow, and a new light of burning hatred. Broken Hand felt Black Wolf's touch, heard the sound of his voice as the last light disappeared from his sight.

"Yes, I have returned."

Faith glanced upward at the gray, overcast sky. Her mood

as dark as its threatening color, she spurred her mount to a faster pace. She adjusted her fashionable riding coat, impatiently tugging at the narrow waist of the garment and chafing at the voluminous skirt which so impeded mobility. The high, silk top hat and muslin veiling, which fashion also dictated, was little protection against the cold which stung her ears and touched her cheeks with vibrant color. In truth, she wore the ridiculous ensemble to please Papa. He had been so proud of her when he had seen her in it. He had raved so, going so far as to say the contrast of dark blue against the brilliant color of her hair took his breath away. An unconscious smile curved Faith's lips for the first time that day. Papa was so prejudiced, and he wanted so desperately for her to be happy, to forget the events of the past year which were burned so vividly into her mind. He wanted it for her almost as much as he wanted it for Mama.

A familiar sadness touched her senses, and Faith sniffed unconsciously. The air was cold, and the tip of her nose had gone numb. Snow . . . they would doubtless have snow by evening. Its bite was in the air, its clear scent unmistakable. But she did not feel the keen anticipation with which she had formerly faced the first snowfall of the year. Strangely, it merely increased the sense of foreboding which had prevailed upon her the week long.

Turning, Faith shot an unseeing glance toward the young groom who rode slightly to her rear. Davey was a nice, patient lad, only a year or so older than she. He was dark, slender, of medium height, and youthful in appearance; but he was efficient in his work, honest and trustworthy. She liked his shy smile, his polite manner, and she liked him. Papa was lucky to have Davey in his service.

Papa had not been so fortunate with the household help. Faith suppressed a niggle of impatience. If anyone were to ask her opinion, she'd say straight out that the main lot of their household servants was untrustworthy and gossipy. The only servants whom she would trust out of her sight were the housekeeper, Maida, and her own personal servant, Nellie. She was well aware of the knowing shift of the maid Rosie's eyes each time Mama entered the room, each time

Papa deferred to Mama in his considerate way. It was obvious that Rosie had heard the talk about Mama, and it was equally obvious that she was anxiously looking for some juicy information to pass along to her acquaintances. She had also heard the buzzing between Rosie and Vera, the cook. All conversation had stopped too many times when she had entered the kitchen for her to believe the exchanges had been innocent.

Those knowing glances had often rested on her as well, but she cared little for herself. Wagging tongues could not touch her. She would not allow herself to be intimidated by them, but she worried for Mama's sake. Mama bore a heavy burden of guilt despite the love Papa showered on her. Faith had begun to wonder if Mama would ever be free of its weight.

Faith frowned. She had at first thought Papa insensitive to the servants' attitudes, but she had then reasoned that perhaps she was being unfair. Perhaps Papa had indeed noticed, but did not want to institute any more changes while Mama was still attempting to adjust. Faith nodded, the thought giving her a new sense of satisfaction. Yes, Mama was Papa's main concern right now. She would say nothing for the time being. She would speak to Papa when the time was more appropriate, and they would begin to get their lives in order. Perhaps then she would begin to feel less uneasy.

Durham house was drawing into sight through the corridor of trees. Strangely, her first glimpse of its graceful columns sent a shiver of apprehension down Faith's spine. Its peaceful appearance in the early morning light contrasted sharply with the tension which had plagued her since she'd awakened.

There was a flash of movement in the doorway. Maida . . . straining her eyes in Faith's direction, anxiety evident in the stiff movements of her abundant form. A tight knot of fear began to squeeze the breath from Faith's lungs. Something was wrong—dreadfully wrong.

Snapping a short command to Davey, Faith abruptly spurred her sorrel forward. Her unexpected action startled the silent groom, but the sound of his mount's hoofbeats remained directly to her rear as she urged her horse to an even faster pace. She was abruptly certain that Mama needed her, and she wanted to get to her. She wanted it desperately.

Within minutes Davey was lifting her to the ground, and Faith paused to attempt to bring her own anxiety under control. No, she could not allow Mama to see her in such a state. If something was indeed wrong, she would only add to the confusion . . . frighten Mama more. Taking a quick, firm breath, Faith turned to the staircase. The anxious housekeeper awaited her at the doorway, her heightened color accelerating Faith's heartbeat anew.

"Miss Faith, I'm glad you're back. Your mother . . . Mrs. Durham is very upset. She—"

"Where is she, Maida?"

"In the morning room, with Mr. Durham."

Tearing off her ridiculous hat as she ran toward the morning room, Faith pulled the door open and stopped short. Her mother's small, fragile frame was outlined against the sun streaming through the large windows behind her. She was holding a newspaper in her hand, her eyes fastened with a frightening stare at the front page. His broad face mirroring his frustration, Papa stood nearby. He reached out toward Mama, but she shuddered visibly, her voice grating on the unnatural silence.

"No, don't touch me."

"Lydia, darling, please . . ."

"No, I don't want you to touch me. I don't want anyone to touch me."

Suddenly realizing Faith was standing in the doorway, her mother turned toward her with a start. She held the newspaper out toward Faith, her voice quaking.

"Faith . . . I told him. I warned him, but he didn't listen to me. It's all here, in the newspaper, but I saw it before it happened, saw it clearly—"

"Mama, who—"

"I can't say his name, Faith." Her eyes wide, unnaturally bright, Lydia swallowed with obvious difficulty. "I promised your father—"

"Lydia, I didn't mean . . ."

Lydia's head jerked back toward Wallace Durham.

"Yes, you did. You didn't want me ever to mention his name again. Well, he's dead now and I can't tell Faith."

"Mama . . ."

Faith shared her mother's pain, experiencing it as vividly as her own. Her throat tightened and she moved spontaneously to Lydia's side. Afraid she might push her beyond her tenuous control, Faith reached tentatively for the newspaper her mother held rigidly out toward her. Her eyes searched the front page, a caption midway down suddenly jumping out to meet her eyes.

CHEYENNE CAMP DESTROYED
BY MILITARY ATTACK

"It . . . it's all there, Faith, everything I saw. Black Kettle's camp was in the curve of the winding creek—Sand Creek—Arapaho camped nearby. The cold . . . the snow in the air . . . the soldiers coming at dawn, taking the people by surprise. I saw Black Kettle in front of his lodge. I saw warriors, women, and children on the ground, bleeding. . . . Owl Woman was dead, Faith. Walking Woman, too. There was blood everywhere! And I saw . . . him! I saw a bullet hit him, and I saw him fall. I saw his blood draining into the ground as he fought to drag himself to his feet. Oh, Faith, he was trying to run and I saw him fall again, and then I saw the soldiers riding after him, firing, firing. . . ."

Faith's arms were around Mama's narrow shoulders. She was holding Mama tight against her, comforting her. She raised her eyes to her father's pained expression, saw his despair. And she saw something else. Jealousy . . . yes, it was jealousy. She shot her father a pleading glance. Mama could not improve under the promise he had extracted from her. She needed to speak of her memories in order to dispel them.

Tears spilling from her own eyes, Faith clutched her mother closer. Her voice was a halting whisper directed into her father's torn expression.

267

"Mama, Papa didn't mean what he said. He didn't mean you could not say Broken Hand's name."

Her mother was suddenly rigid in her arms, and Faith felt panic assail her. Abruptly jerking from her grasp, Lydia shook her head violently.

"No . . . no, I told you not to say his name. I promised never to mention him again. Never to—"

But Lydia could say no more for Wally's arms suddenly enclosed her in a fierce grip, straining her tight against him. Tears flowed freely from his eyes as his hand moved possessively against the upward sweep of her hair.

"Lydia, darling, I didn't mean to hurt you. I love you. I want you to put the past to rest, not let it eat away at you until you're consumed. Say his name. Broken Hand . . . his name was Broken Hand, wasn't it? Tell me . . . go ahead. Tell me exactly what happened, what you saw. I want to hear it all—all of it."

Stiff with apprehension, Faith watched as her mother drew herself back from her father's clutching grip. Faith swallowed the sob which rose to her throat. The torment on Mama's face was hard, so hard, to bear.

"I do need to tell you, Wally. I need to tell someone so I can be helped to understand why he didn't listen to me, why—"

"Yes, darling, tell me."

Papa was drawing Mama toward the wide seat at the base of the window. He was sitting beside her.

"All right, Lydia. Tell me all of it, from the beginning."

Mama's voice began in a low, halting whisper. She was looking into Papa's eyes, eyes that shared her pain, eyes filled with love. Faith could stand no more. Turning quickly, she stepped back into the hallway and closed the door behind her. Her eyes caught Rosie and Vera hovering with anxious ears in the shadows of the corridor to the kitchen.

Faith voiced a sharp command.

"Get back in the kitchen, both of you!"

When the two fled from sight, Faith took a deep, shaky breath. She started resolutely across the spacious entrance hall and then went up the great, winding staircase.

Broken Hand dead . . . Owl Woman dead . . . Walking Woman dead . . . Walking Woman . . . Sweet, dear Walking Woman. Gone, all of them. A blurred image returned to her mind with startling vividness. Black Wolf, lying on the ground beside her, his eyes closed, his chest still. Dead. He, too, was dead. Oh, God, why . . . why did all this have to be?

Abruptly, Faith was running. Gasping for breath, she reached the top of the staircase and turned down the hallway. She burst into her room and closed the door behind her to lean back against it, tears streaming freely down her face. Why did this have to be?

A bright winter sun beat down on the heads of those assembled, but the air was crisp and cold, negating its warming effect. Nonetheless, the council beside the creek the white man called White Butte, progressed in lowered tones. The Cheyenne war pipe had been sent first to the Sioux and then to the Northern Arapaho. Black Wolf watched in silence from his place of observance on the outer ring of braves. His youth held him outside the circle of seasoned warriors, but he would not be held there long. His eyes moved to the familiar figure among the many seated in council. Broken Hand, his robe shielding the wound which still troubled him, did not submit to his pain. The heat of vengeance burned all other thought from his mind.

Notably absent was Black Kettle. He had already turned away from the council. The deceit of the white man had not deterred Black Kettle from the path of peace. Nursing their grief, eighty lodges would move south with him, away from disputed territory. They would take no part in vengeance.

Black Wolf pulled his robe close around him. Sorrow had been purged from his mind. All had been taken from him by the white man . . . his past, his present. Black Wolf's hand moved, unconsciously touching the carved band he still wore on his finger. With a promise of peace, the white man had also taken from him the one who was to be his future. He had attempted to regain her, but she had turned against him. She had forced him to strike her, to subdue her so he might take her with him. Then he had been shot, left for dead, to be consumed by the animals of the land. The white soldiers had then broken the peace and slaughtered his people. Few remained, but these few would make the white man feel their presence.

Black Wolf's heated gaze moved over the men assembled as the council progressed. Cheyenne, Dog Soldiers, Spotted Tail's and Pawnee Killer's bands of Sioux, and the Northern Arapaho. Soon one thousand warriors would be assembled, warriors who knew the need for revenge, the need to rid their country of those who would destroy them.

The talking was done. They would make a great raid along the South Platte. From there they would move north to Powder River and join the Northern Cheyenne and the Oglala Sioux. The white man would feel their wrath.

Black Wolf took a deep breath, and his heart began to pound as the pipe was passed around the circle. A hard smile turned up his lips when the last man had smoked. Elation filled his heart and mind. There was no other course. It was done. There would be war.

Chapter XVIII

1865

"Step up onto the stool. That is right, *mademoiselle. Vite, s'il vous plaît.* Monsieur Durham has sent his carriage with the message that he awaits you at home. I do not wish *monsieur* to think that I have detained you too long. *Non.*"

Not able to suppress her amusement at the pleasant, middle-aged couturière's flustered state, Faith stepped dutifully onto the dressmaker's stool in the small, fashionable boutique and turned toward the mirror. The awe with which so many now beheld Papa never failed to amaze her. She was at a complete loss as to how anyone could be taken in by the stern glance Papa sometimes feigned, the gruffness he forced into his voice when he desired immediate action. Surely, anyone could see the warmth and humor which lay beneath the surface, the gentleness which was so much a part of his nature.

She supposed the notoriety Papa had achieved in the business world since the turn of the year had as much to do with this astounding new attitude evidenced toward him as did his position as eastern representative of Tin Pan Mining, the company to which he had leased his claim. She shrugged her narrow shoulders. Yes, the power which accompanied the advent of wealth did inspire respect and fear in some hearts. But Madame LeClair's veined hands were trembling. Her anxiety was sincere. Faith's smile faded. Papa would not wish to shake this woman's poise so completely.

Compassion stirring her youthful heart, Faith placed her hand lightly on madame's bent shoulder, raising her spontaneously to the brilliant azure of her gaze.

"Madame, please, don't upset yourself. Papa knew my fitting was for four o'clock, and he himself ordered that you fit me for six new dresses, did he not? Papa is so well versed on fashion, and so concerned that his only daughter be suitably dressed, that he will understand how much time it takes to set the hem on a garment as voluminous as this."

Relief flickered in madame's small eyes and Faith turned toward the mirror, experiencing relief as well. She surveyed the bodice and skirt on which madame was working so diligently. She was not particularly dedicated to fashion, but she had to admit this outfit pleased her. Yes, Papa would indeed approve of the high collar which encircled her neck so modestly. She knew only too well that he was a bit uncomfortable with the changes which were coming about in her body. To be truthful, she herself found them a bit overwhelming. It had seemed that overnight the childish flatness of her chest had swelled to form full, firm breasts.

As her dresses had grown rapidly tighter in that area, Papa had commented drily, "Faith, it seems that you've not only inherited your grandmother's coloring, but her womanly proportions as well. If that is so, you will one day be a truly formidable woman."

She had grown in other ways as well in the past months. An inch in height had seemed to stretch the immature proportions of her body, curving them in a definitely feminine fashion to accent the minute proportions of her waist and the surprisingly round curve of her derrière.

Faith considered the reflection of her new proportions thoughtfully. As bemused as she was by the obvious, she failed to notice that the advent of maturity had begun to fashion other, less blatant changes in her appearance as well. She had overlooked the fact that her face had begun to take on the smooth, chiseled contours of a woman, that its new graceful lines accented the perfection of features which marked her only resemblance to her mother. She had been conscious of the small frown which had furrowed her mother's brow just that morning when she had arrived at the breakfast table, fiery strands of hair hanging loose in a casual fashion. Somehow, Faith had no patience for the upswept fashion her mother had recently decided was suitable for her age.

Soon to be sixteen . . . but surely she was not yet a woman. She was not truly ready for all being a woman entailed. She had met no young man who inspired more than annoyance in her in the months since her return, although many had shown an interest in her. They were all so immature. Faith's hand moved unconsciously to her finger. All sign of amusement left her face as she massaged the vacant space which had once been covered by a primitive band. She had been a child then, but the stirrings inside her had been far in advance of her years.

Faith flicked her eyes momentarily closed. That time was over and gone. She no longer wished to indulge in grief. Both Mama and she had put it aside. Mama was happier than she had been for a long time and she . . . Yes, she was happy, too.

Shaking her mind from the path onto which it had strayed, with new determination, Faith assessed the ensemble she wore. Yes, the white batiste of her blouse contrasted beautifully with the deep rose bolero and skirt. The ecru lace on the epaulettes that graced the long, full sleeves was the perfect trim. She moved her hips, admiring the flow of the funnel-shaped skirt and the ribbon bows that trimmed the hemline, dusting the tips of her shoes. She moved a hand to her waist, noting that madame had fit the broad, buckled belt perfectly to its narrow expanse. She smiled for madame's benefit.

"Papa will be very pleased."

A nervous smile flashed across madame's face and she returned to her work. Her response was muffled by the awkward position she assumed to turn the hem.

"Ah, *mademoiselle,* Monsieur Durham is a gentleman, to be sure. I know of no other man in this city as generous as he with his wife and daughter. So many come to my shop, their purse strings tightly clutched, eying my sketches with

273

suspicion. But your father seeks—yes, demands—nothing but the best. I would not like to lose his patronage because my helpers have been simultaneously stricken with *la grippe* for the past three days."

"Oh, I don't think you need worry about that, madame."

"Yes, but I understand the pressures your father suffers daily. It doubtless makes him tense at times, annoyed by petty delays. The bulk of his fortune is tied up in the West, is it not? He doubtless fears that the Indian wars which progress so painfully will interfere with his business plans. Especially now that this sad War Between the States draws to a close, I am sure he would like to feel his own affairs were settled as well. And the news this morning . . . the decision to have a committee investigate the Indian problem and the disgraceful massacre . . . all the witnesses that will be called—"

"The massacre . . ."

"*Oui, mademoiselle,* the one at Sand Creek. That officer—what was his name?—Major Chivington? Ah, yes, I have seen butchers like that before. My country has seen the like many times."

"Madame, please."

Appearing to note for the first time Faith's sudden pallor, Madame LeClair reached out a tentative hand to touch her shoulder. Her face flamed.

"*Pardon, mademoiselle.* I did not think . . . I had forgotten."

A new tension moving inside her, Faith swallowed tightly. Perhaps Papa had sent the carriage and requested her early return for a reason. Perhaps Mama . . .

Her face draining of its remaining color, Faith nodded briefly.

"Do not upset yourself, madame. But I must ask that you finish the hemline of this dress without me. I think you are correct. Papa might be impatient for my return. Should you need me again, I will be only too happy to make another appointment."

"*Oui, mademoiselle* . . . of course."

Madame LeClair's narrow face pulled into tight lines of

anxiety, but this time her distress went completely unnoticed. Other anxieties, other images filled Faith's mind. . . .

"I *will* go, Wally. I *will!*"

Facing her husband squarely within the confines of their room, Lydia raised her chin determinedly. Her small hands fell to her sides, to brush the green velvet gown which brought to dazzling life the latent specks of green in the eyes she fastened so intently upon his.

"No, it is not to your benefit to attend this hearing, either as a witness or—"

"I have been asked to testify, Wally, summoned by a joint committee of Congress to give my view of the attitude of Black Kettle's camp toward Black Kettle's proffered peace. Surely you don't believe I could refuse, allow detractors to be heard while I remain silent! Murdered . . . they were all murdered, Wally!"

Wally's complexion flushed darkly. He took a moment to attempt to control his rising anger. Things had just begun to go well, so very well between Lydia and him . . . and now this. He shot a sharp glance toward the letter Lydia still held in her hand, his frustration soaring. Had he arrived in the foyer a few minutes earlier, seen the official-looking document lying on the table, he knew he would have dropped it casually into the inside pocket of his well-tailored blue suit to be read at a later time. It would have mattered little to him that the missive bore the seal of the Congressional committee which had sent it, or that it was specifically addressed to his wife. His reaction would have been an instinctive attempt to avoid just the type of confrontation which had ensued the moment Lydia had read the damned request.

Lydia was still staring at him, awaiting his response. He dared not tell her how he really felt, that he would not have given a damn if the whole Indian nation had been exterminated in that raid on Sand Creek. As far as he was concerned, they were savages, every one, with no exceptions.

They were the same bastards who had taken his wife and child from him, touched them both in ways he could not begin to understand, and then coldly returned them to him when Faith's and Lydia's usefulness had ended.

And they were the same savages who had attempted to steal his daughter from him again. That attempt had been thwarted by a young trooper's quick hand, and it had meant nothing to him that a young Indian had been left dead on the trail. He took a deep breath. For the life of him, he could not understand his daughter's grief when she had finally emerged from her unconsciousness and had learned of the Indian's death. But Faith had gotten over it. She was young, and she was strong . . . just like his own mother. He was grateful for that.

And now this whole thing was being stirred up again, just when Lydia was beginning to forget. . . . That damned letter, received a short hour before . . . Lydia's reaction had been so intense that he had immediately dispatched the coachman for Faith. He had known that he would need someone, someone who would be able to understand Lydia while still maintaining a hold on reality. Damn it, why was Faith taking so long to return!

The heated intercourse which had ensued between Lydia and himself had sent her up the broad staircase at a run and into their room. He had followed her to debate the same theme and get nowhere. No, he did not want her to go to Washington, to relive the time spent in the Indian camp again. He wanted her to forget those months. *He* wanted to forget them before his jealousy consumed him.

Wally paused. Lydia was still waiting for his answer. He ran an anxious hand through his thick ruff of hair. Broken Hand . . . how he hated the sound of that name. He had only been fooling himself. That damned savage still stood between Lydia and him, his memory a silent specter lurking in the back of her mind. With a sudden certainty Wally knew that were the Indian not already dead, he would most certainly kill the savage himself if he ran across him again. But fate had taken the opportunity for that revenge from him, leaving his fury unsated.

276

His chest heaving with suppressed emotion, Wally stared darkly at his wife's ethereal beauty. No, he could not allow her to glimpse the emotions which warred inside him. She was not to blame for her condition, and she did not need to add his jealousy to the already heavy load she carried.

His response was offered quietly, with tight control.

"Lydia, those Indians are dead and gone. What is done, is done. Responding to the invitation to testify will only call attention to you."

Lydia's rigidity increased. She gave a short, hard laugh.

"So the truth is out at last. You are not as concerned about me as you would have me believe. Instead, you are concerned about the gossip, about giving wagging tongues more ammunition with which to continue the speculation which begins each time my back turns to a crowd."

"Lydia . . . you know that isn't true."

"But it is!" Stepping back from Wally's extended hand, Lydia shook her head, stirring the gleaming raven curls drawn so severely back from her exquisite features. "I . . . I thought I would never be able to refuse you anything, Wally—not after all that happened . . . the things I did."

"I don't want you to talk that way, Lydia."

"I . . . I don't suppose many other men would have taken me back, knowing I had lived with—"

"Lydia." Wally's voice was warning in tone. He would be able to stand little more.

"But you did, Wally. And you've loved me with no lessening of ardor despite my transgressions."

"Lydia . . . God . . . you didn't know what you were doing."

"But this time I can't bow to your wishes. I can't, Wally. I could not live with myself if I refused to speak out against the butchery of innocent people."

Wally's voice exploded in rage as he stepped forward to grip Lydia's narrow shoulders.

"What possible good could you do at those hearings? You know nothing about Sand Creek, except what you read in the papers."

"I saw it, Wally."

"Lydia, for God's sake! What do you think people will say if you tell them you saw a vision? They'll think you're crazy—that your captivity affected your mind!"

Lydia suddenly became still. Her stillness accented the sudden tremor which shook her low rasp.

"Is that what you think, Wally, that I'm insane?"

The low protest that escaped Wally's lips was instinctive, as instinctive as his tight embrace when he crushed Lydia close against him. He closed his eyes against the swell of emotion that left him temporarily unable to speak.

"Wally, do . . . do you think I'm insane?"

A low, grating laugh escaped Wally's throat.

"No, I don't think you're insane. Oddly enough, I think I'd find all this easier to bear if indeed that were so. The truth is harder to take, darling."

"The truth?"

"You've never stopped loving that savage, have you?"

"Wally, that's not true!"

Abruptly disengaging herself from his arms, Lydia drew herself back. The silver lights of her eyes were bright with denial.

"It's just that . . . that I cannot allow what happened at Sand Creek to be accepted as unavoidable. Wally, I knew those people. They were like us—wives and mothers with children, husbands and fathers. They were slaughtered."

"They were enemies who had slaughtered our people as well."

"They were protecting their way of life in the only way open to them. And then when they were offered peace—"

"Lydia, darling, you don't know any of this for sure."

"I'm sure, Wally."

"Lydia . . ."

The pain in Wally's voice tore at Lydia's heart, but she was resolute. She raised her chin in unspoken determination.

"And I'm sure of another thing as well. I'm going to Washington."

"I will not consent."

"Then I'll go without your consent."

An unexpected knock at the doorway drew Lydia's eyes in

its direction. A harsh response opened the door to reveal Faith's uncertain expression.

Lydia took a deep breath. Her eyes were bright with sadness.

"You'll go with me, won't you, Faith?"

Faith's eyes moved in anxious confusion between her father and mother.

"Where?"

Lydia's eyes flooded with tears.

"To Washington, Faith. There is some business we must finish up—both of us."

Extending her arm, Lydia waited until her daughter walked to her side. She had curled her arm around her daughter's narrow shoulders when she felt the warmth of familiar arms encircle them both. Lydia closed her eyes against Wally's whispered words as his breath brushed her hair.

"No, Lydia. There is some business we must finish up—for good—the *three* of us."

Lydia's breath was coming in deep, jerking gasps as she fought to retain her rapidly waning control. She slid her arm around Wally's back and held him tightly in return. Yes, the three of them. Wally had said it all. She could say no more.

"Thank you, Captain. Now, if you will tell us please, exactly what troops participated in this attack on the Indian camp at Sand Creek."

His posture militarily correct, his expression calm despite the realization that much hinged on his testimony, William sat in the stiff chair in the huge, official Senatorial chamber. He was well aware that the eyes of everyone in the room were trained on him, assessing him. He was being carefully scrutinized, taken apart piece by piece to gratify the numerous personal motives of those gathered there for the Congressional inquiry which had made headlines across the country.

He had been prepared for just this situation. For that reason he had paid particular care to his always-meticulous appearance. The dark blue uniform, precisely tailored to his lean, well-muscled frame, was freshly cleaned, bearing not a single blemish. Its brass buttons gleamed, as did the braid at the brim of the hat he held in his hand, and the high, polished boots which fit snugly against his legs. His fair hair was freshly cut, his light brown mustache trimmed neatly. He had checked his appearance carefully before leaving his quarters earlier that morning and was satisfied that he appeared to be an intelligent, well-trained Army officer. That was exactly what he was, and he intended his appearance to add credibility to the testimony he was giving so readily.

The horror he had witnessed, and in which he had taken an unwilling part, needed to be documented. In the time since the atrocities had been committed on that terrible day, his attitude toward the Indian had undergone a drastic change. With bitter irony he recalled his previous assessment of the native people of the West—inhuman savages with a lust for blood. How well that same description fitted the men wearing cavalry blue that dreadful morning.

In his mind he had come to cherish the hope that in testifying at this hearing, he would ensure that such a massacre would never again take place. It was also his hope that speaking of the events would help to purge them from his mind, at least to the point where he would no longer see the bloodbath of the year before almost nightly in his dreams.

William's eyes met the level, probing stare of Senator Hartfield Morris. He was well aware of the reputed skill of this well-known, middle-aged legislator. The man's appearance belied his sharp, analytical mind which was so suited to his position. Of medium height and considerable girth, he was gray-haired and balding. A drooping mustache covered his upper lip, appearing to add more weight to his already sagging, heavily jowled face. Although well dressed in a dark blue double-breasted jacket with fashionably narrow lapels and revers, and matching trousers well tailored to conceal his rounded paunch, the senator appeared to be a pleasant, extremely harmless old gentleman. William knew nothing could be farther from the truth.

William responded to Senator Morris's question, taking particular care to be precise.

"The attacking force consisted of the Third Colorado Regiment and a battalion of the First Regiment, both brought to Fort Lyon by Colonel Chivington; and the Second Battalion of the First Regiment, and twenty-five more men, those under Major Anthony's command, of which I was a part."

The eaglelike stare of the legislator remained on his face, but William did not flinch under its weight. Senator Morris was obviously forming a very important question in his mind. William waited with growing impatience. The previous, seemingly random questions, which had elicited the first portion of his testimony, had obviously been geared toward specific points. He had answered them all honestly, but he was truly uncertain as to the reception his statements had received in his inquisitor's keen mind. He had a feeling he would not have to wait much longer to find out.

"Captain, your previous testimony had established the size of the Indian encampment as well as the size of the force which attacked it. As you know, it was Agent Colley's accusation of treachery against a peaceful camp at Sand Creek, published in the Missouri *Intelligencer* in January, which instituted our subsequent investigation. Everything you've said so far at this hearing confirms the statements obtained by Major Wynkoop when he was sent to Fort Lyon to take the testimony of the soldiers, scouts, and officers under Chivington's command. For purposes of clarification, I would like to restate in simple terms your declarations, if that is all right with you."

"That's fine, sir."

"All right. You've told us here today that Major Anthony and Colonel Chivington both were aware that the Indian encampment was peaceful, that the Indians considered a peace to have been negotiated."

A small muscle ticked in William's cheek.

"That's correct, sir."

"According to Colonel Chivington's statement, and those

of the officers of the Third Colorado Cavalry, the killings were done in the heat of battle . . . it was the Indians' lives or their own. Were you witness to actions that could be construed as anything other than the usual practices of war?"

"Yes, sir."

"Tell us about them please."

Discomfort beginning to color his face, William took a deep breath. He frowned, his cheek ticking again as he prepared to speak.

"Sir, I would like to reiterate a point I made earlier in my testimony. Five hundred Cheyenne and Arapaho were killed. Two-thirds of that number were women and children. The fight lasted a good part of the day. When it was over and the last commanding officer had called off his men, the soldiers started back down the creek toward the camp. It was then that they began scalping the dead lying in the bed of the stream and cutting up the bodies in a manner that no Indian could equal. The Indian bodies were so badly mutilated that they were unrecognizable one from the other.

"I was witness to the scalping of these Indians, as I was to the murder of Indian women and children who begged for pity, yet were coldly killed. I was told by some officers from the Third Colorado Cavalry that Lieutenant Richmond, their officer, personally killed three women and five children who had been captured. They said the prisoners had screamed for mercy while Lieutenant Richmond coolly shot one after the other and then scalped them. His men were aghast at the barbarity of his actions. I was present when a corporal of the First Colorado Cavalry stated that he saw a major in the Third Regiment blow out the brains of a little Indian child, after which the major scalped the body. I saw an old Indian woman wandering about, unable to see because her whole scalp had been taken and the skin of her forehead was hanging over her eyes. A soldier's bullet put her out of her misery. After the attack was over, other soldiers took a captured half-blood, Jack Smith, and killed him in cold blood. Only the intervention of a few New Mexican scouts saved another half-blood from the same fate."

William paused, obviously affected by the horrors he had described so vividly. The sober-faced senator took the opportunity to interject a pointed question.

"These atrocities, Captain Potter, you are certain they were committed with the sanction of commanding officers Major Anthony and Colonel Chivington?"

"Sir, it was well known in Denver, and by every soldier who marched with Colonel Chivington from Denver, that the Colonel's orders were to 'kill Indians, to kill all, little and big.'"

His jowled face hardening, Senator Morris eyed William keenly. William's discomfort was apparent in the beads of perspiration which had appeared on his forehead and upper lip, in his obvious effort to retain a calm demeanor. The senator pressed relentlessly.

"And you, Captain, where were you while all these inhumanities were being enacted?"

"Sir, Major Anthony was aware of my protests against the attack. I had been very vocal, insisting that the Cheyenne and Arapaho camped at Sand Creek were there in peace. I came under heavy criticism for my position. I was ordered to my place at the head of my men, much in disgrace. Major Anthony obviously did not trust me to follow his orders with regard to attacking the Indians themselves. He sent me and the men under my command out to cut off the herd of Indian ponies at the far side of the creek. Sir, the men of the First Regiment under my command took the horses and obeyed orders, but I can make the unequivocal statement that my men acted kindly, and played no part in the scalping and mutilating, and no part in the murder of helpless prisoners."

Hard, dark eyes met William's sober brown. The austere senator stared into his face for long, sober seconds before nodding.

"Captain, I think I speak for my associates here at the hearing when I say I appreciate the candor of your remarks. You have been extremely cooperative throughout testimony which it was obviously difficult for you to give. I assure you that I, personally, sympathize with your distress. I am sure had I been witness to such heartless and inhuman conduct, I, too, would have been loath to live through it again, if only in the retelling of the details. I would like to state, for your benefit, that the testimonies of several other witnesses to this attack confirms your statement. The men of the First Regiment, under your command, are cited as blameless regarding the atrocities perpetrated. For this you have my own personal admiration and gratitude for conscientiously leading your men."

Pausing once more, Senator Morris gripped the lapel of his well-tailored suit with a puffy hand. He flashed an uncharacteristic smile briefly into William's perspiring face.

"One last question, Captain. With regard to the Indian horses under your responsibility, what was their number and what disposition was made of them?"

William's lips tightened spontaneously in remembered anger. His sandy lashes flickered briefly.

"The Indian herd numbered four or five hundred ponies and mules, sir. The day following the attack, I was relieved of my responsibility for them and they were distributed to Colonel Chivington's 'boys.'"

"They were given to Colonel Chivington's men . . . as their own personal property? They were the property of the U.S. Government, were they not, Captain?"

"Sir, I was informed by Colonel Chivington himself that the herd and its disposition were no longer my concern."

Senator Morris's brow furrowed in silent response to William's reply. He advanced to stand directly in front of William's chair.

"That will be all, Captain. And, thank you." Unexpectedly extending his hand as William rose to his feet, he smiled.

"I would like to say that it is my pleasure to have met you, Captain Potter. The United States Army is fortunate to have you in its service."

The stress of memory making him unable to match Senator Morris's smile, William returned his hearty handshake.

"Thank you, sir."

Senator Morris turned to address the committee as William strode toward the exit from the chamber. The sound of Senator Morris's deep voice was still echoing in the room as William pulled open the door and stepped into the corridor. Closing the portal quietly behind him, William released a deep, silent breath, relieved to be dismissed at last. But his hesitation was brief. Taking up his rapid step once more, he moved toward the main entrance of the building.

So intent had William been, that he had failed to notice the pale woman who had been seated to the rear of the balcony in the official chamber. She had been supported by the strong arm of the red-haired man at her side as she had wept in silence. Nor had Potter seen the auburn-haired young woman seated beside him, although her tear-filled gaze had not left his person for the duration of his testimony.

Unaware of all but his profound relief, William pushed open the heavy outer door and stepped outside. He breathed deeply of the fresh air, one thought pushing all others from his mind. It was over . . . over. The damned, foul deed, the massacre at Sand Creek, had been truly exposed at last.

His face moving into somber lines, William walked briskly down the front steps and onto the street. Within minutes he was putting the Capitol far behind him.

William Potter moved with a measured step among the conversing groups at the unexpectedly elaborate dinner party. The glass in his hand was half-filled with an amber liquid, and he sipped at it absent-mindedly, not really conscious of its taste. His eyes moved over the luxuriously furnished dining room, taking in the massive mahogany furniture, carved with a superior craftsman's touch, and the attractive buffet spread on an endless expanse of lace. Silver . . . crystal . . . punch in a great, glittering bowl, and champagne being served on silver trays by smiling servants.

He wandered into the living room. Soft music trailed from a string quartet positioned sedately in the corner; low laughter rose from smartly dressed guests gathered in impromptu clusters; diamonds sparkled on daintily gesturing hands; bits of stimulating conversation reached his ears as he passed one group, and then another. William suppressed a caustic smile. The life of a public servant was obviously not one of self-denial. Senator Morris lived very well.

Pausing in his thoughts, William gave a low, self-deprecating laugh. He was not being very fair. It was common knowledge that Senator Morris had a great personal fortune. The family business, fabric mills, had been turned over to his oldest son when he had decided to pursue a career as a government representative. Obviously his choice had been well received by those in his family, who seemed to be sound people from what William had seen of them. Mrs. Morris, a pretty woman who, unlike her husband, was of an age that was difficult to ascertain, had a cheerful disposition, and Morris's younger son, Herbert, a fellow of some nineteen years, was exceedingly friendly. The Morrises's daughter, Sally Anne, an extremely attractive young woman, was a true delight. Indeed, the entire Morris clan had gone to great lengths to welcome William Potter to this reception in their Washington quarters, at which many of the famous of the time circulated. Potter was extremely grateful for their consideration. He had just one question. What in hell was he doing there?

A sudden tap on his arm caused William to turn to meet Sally Anne Morris's bright smile. Small and blond and extremely pleasant, she had an almost pixielike appeal which was difficult to resist, with her round brown eyes and small features. He smiled in return as she leaned toward him with an air of confidentiality.

"Captain, am I correct in assuming that you are temporarily free of the 'curious' who have been plying you with questions about the wild frontier most of the evening? You do realize that you are the only person qualified to answer with authority many of the questions we easterners have about the gold fields, striking it rich, and the beauty of the West we've heard so much about."

His smile broadening, William nodded. Yes, Sally Anne Morris was definitely a very nice young woman.

"I was not aware of that fact upon entering this room, Miss Morris, but I most certainly am aware of it now. I have been answering so many questions since I came that I find I am still holding my original drink, and have had time only to consume half of it in the full hour since I arrived. That is definitely below my average pace, I would say."

"Oh, please call me Sally Anne so that I may call you William. I do so despise formality. In any case, I'm not quite sure whether your comments reflect favorably or unfavorably on our hospitality. Good heavens, it was not our intent that you should be so pressed by the instinctive curiosity of our guests that you find yourself without an opportunity to partake of refreshment." Sally Anne's smile quirked playfully, "But I hope you don't expect to make up for lost time now that I have you in my clutches. I, too, have many questions, which I'm sure you've only answered seven or eight times this evening. And I don't expect to be any more generous than the others or to let you get away too easily."

William eyed Sally Anne's pert, golden curls and sparkling eyes. Her light skin was fine and clear, her smile warm. He most certainly would not suffer in her company. His smile reflected his thoughts, and Sally Anne brightened as he responded, "All right, fire away."

Sliding her hand through the crook of his arm, Sally turned him toward the dining room. "Come, it seems our guests are doing more drinking than eating tonight. The dining room is fairly empty. Since you've mentioned that you haven't eaten yet, and neither have I, I think we can find a nice quiet spot where we may talk and do just that." Sally Anne wrinkled her small nose as her confidential tone dropped a note lower. "There are also some very comfortable chairs in the corner of the dining room where I may rest my weary feet." She paused. "You will not mind being tucked into the corner with me for a little while, will you, William?"

Beginning to enjoy her game, William shook his head.

"Most definitely not, Sally Anne."

"Oh, that's good, because I most definitely intend to keep you occupied for a while."

William smiled.

287

"I have to admit that your statement sounds intriguing. Dare I ask how you intend to keep me occupied?"

Sally Anne's round eyes widened in exaggerated innocence.

"With questions . . . of course!"

William's low laughter was spontaneous. He was actually beginning to enjoy himself. He patted the small hand still resting on his arm.

"All right. Once we're settled in those comfortable chairs, you can ask away, but turnabout is fair play, you know."

They had reached the buffet table, and Sally Anne had slipped her hand from his arm to reach for a plate, only to turn back toward him in true surprise at his statement.

"Turnabout . . . what possible questions would you want to ask me, William? I'm afraid you'd find little of interest in the charities I work to support, or in the political receptions I've helped to organize."

William accepted the plate held out to him, and took up position behind her as Sally Anne began to peruse the table.

"Well, we could start with the reason for my being invited to this lovely party tonight. When I left the senatorial chamber yesterday afternoon, Sally Anne, I can truthfully say I did not expect I would hear from your father again, much less receive a social invitation."

"That just goes to show how little you know about your country's politics, William . . . and how little you know about Senator Hartfield Morris."

William's smile dimmed.

"You're telling me I was invited here tonight for political motives?"

Sally Anne's expression sobered unexpectedly. Her reply was candid.

"Not quite. But Papa is a very dedicated and sometimes devious man. He was very impressed with your testimony, William. Your statements carried even more impact in light of the statements received as to your conduct during and after the attack at Sand Creek. It appears that other than Major Wynkoop, you were the only person with courage enough to speak out against the action planned against that peaceful community of Indians."

William shook his head.

"It didn't do much good, did it?"

Sally Anne hesitated as she reached toward a tempting display of canapés, frankly considering his reply.

"No, it didn't then, but Father is determined that it will now."

"Meaning?"

"Meaning, Father is much impressed with you, William. He considers you to be an honest, intelligent young man of obvious integrity. He feels you are a credit to the uniform you wear, and he feels there are too few about whom the same can be said. He was certain that inviting you here tonight, exposing you to other influential members of Congress, would serve to add weight to your testimony and a subtle pressure to see that those who do not represent our country as well as you are removed from positions of authority."

William's reply was direct.

"Your father is aware that Colonel Chivington's time of enlistment has already expired, that he is out of the reach of the Federal Government now that he is a civilian."

"Father is not so much concerned with matters of individual punishments as he is concerned that such an affair should not be repeated."

William smiled for the first time since the beginning of their serious exchange.

"Well, then we are two men with the same purpose, Sally Anne. I am happy to join the ranks of your father's supporters."

Sally Anne's small face creased in a smile.

"Oh, I am so glad, William. Your orders will keep you in Washington for a few months, is that not true? Father says that the Department of the Army has temporarily freed you of service at Fort Lyon and is considering you for another post. I admit his statement meant little to me prior to tonight, but I find that since meeting you I am extremely pleased at the prospect. I should very much enjoy getting to know you better, and I—"

289

Abruptly pausing in her conversation, Sally Anne shifted her eyes past William's head, toward the entrance to the living room. Her gaze narrowed in silent assessment as her voice dropped to a familiar tone of confidentiality.

"Ah, I see we have several late arrivals. . . . No, don't turn around, please, William. I should not like to see any more of our guests turning to stare than have already. The poor woman . . . she is the talk of Washington, she and her daughter. She gave testimony at the hearing today. She was unusually candid, considering the personal nature of some of the questions. I admit I was startled that Father should have invited them." Sally Anne shook her head in obvious incredulity. "Can you imagine . . . she was actually given an Indian name? I believe they called her Shadow Woman."

Almost unable to believe his ears, William turned abruptly, despite Sally Anne's admonition. Spotting the red head touched with gray which rose an inch or so above the throng at the door, William released a low gasp. The crowd shifted, and Lydia Durham stood clearly in his sight. His heart beginning to pound, William stood stock-still. Sally Anne had said there were three. Surely that meant . . .

Wallace Durham turned unseeingly in his direction, as if in answer to William's silent scrutiny. His brow furrowing in annoyance as the squeeze at the door became suddenly tighter, Wally reached behind him to urge a slender figure to his side. A young woman with brilliant red hair a shade more glowing than his own . . .

Oh, God . . . Faith!

His plate forgotten on the table, his companion left in his wake, William was walking toward the living room at a pace that was just short of a run. His breathing rapid, disbelief still chipping at his mind, he was firmly moving guests aside, clearing his path toward the entrance to the room. He had almost reached the three who were being politely welcomed by a smiling Senator and Mrs. Morris, when a brilliant azure gaze locked tightly with his.

Faith's choked cry pushing him past restraint, he took the last few steps to her side and swept her into his arms. His face buried in her gleaming, upswept curls, he pulled her closer still, his voice low with emotion.

"Faith . . . I can't believe it. You . . . here."

Faith was trembling . . . or was it he? Only certain that he loathed to separate himself from her, William pulled back at last. His eyes moved hungrily over the beautiful face turned up to his. Faith . . . dear Faith.

"William, I can't believe it is you. When Papa told us we have been invited here, I was uncertain whether I wanted to come. And then he told me that the senator intended to invite several of the witnesses to attend. I couldn't believe . . . I didn't want to think you would also be here, in the event that you would not. But William, you are here . . . you are."

Her arms encircling him in spontaneous warmth, Faith moved close against him once more and William swallowed against a sudden flare of emotion. He was whispering softly against her hair when he became conscious of silent scrutiny and turned. Wally's broad grin met his eye and William gave a short, elated laugh. He released Faith with obvious reluctance to extend his hand warmly in his friend's direction.

"Wally . . . Lydia . . . I can't tell you how happy I am to see all of you. I didn't know you were in Washington."

"We asked Senator Morris not to publicize the fact that Lydia was going to testify, William, for obvious reasons." Wally paused, his smile growing wider. "Damn, I'm happy to see you."

"And I'm happy to see you, too, Wally."

Lydia stepped forward unexpectedly, to briefly take her daughter's place in his arms. Startled by the warmth of her greeting, William had little time to react before Lydia drew back. Her smile acknowledged his surprise and William shot a quick glance toward Faith. Yes, of course . . . the cautious Mrs. Durham had effectively nipped in the bud the speculation which obviously abounded amongst the avid spectators. She was a mother, protecting her beautiful daughter's reputation.

"Of course, I knew that the three of you knew each other, but I had not realized how close was the association."

291

Senator Morris's low tone interrupted them, turning all eyes in his direction, drawing the four of them back to the present. Wally's reply was immediate and instinctive.

"William was of considerable comfort to me while I recuperated from my wounds at Fort Lyon, Senator. As far as I'm concerned, I owe the return of my wife and daughter directly to Major Wynkoop and him, and you may rest assured I will never forget it."

Turning to face William with a raised brow, Senator Morris shook his head.

"So, more marks to your credit, Captain. You are quite an impressive young man."

"Wally is too generous, Senator."

"No, I am not. And I do thank you, Senator, for your invitation and for the opportunity to meet with William. In the confusion which has ensued since we arrived in Washington, we were finding it extremely difficult to get in touch with him. I would not have wanted to miss the opportunity to talk—"

"Yes, and it is inconsiderate of me to keep you standing here in the doorway, when I'm certain you have many things to discuss with your old friend." Turning, the gray-haired senator signaled a uniformed servant who hovered nearby. "John, bring some refreshments . . . and the table in the corner, have someone clear it for my guests here, please. This is, after all, their night."

Sincerity glowing in his dark eyes, Senator Morris turned back toward them, his gaze touching each of his four guests with warmth. "Please, enjoy yourself."

Nodding, William followed behind Wally as he escorted Lydia toward the table in the corner. But his mind was far from the striking couple who walked in front of him. His hand at Faith's narrow waist, he urged her forward, chafing at the curious stares which pinned him. His eyes moved to Faith's face, and he saw a similar frustration. Damn . . .

William's earlier frustration had made a tight knot form in his stomach. Still seated at the small table in the crowded

292

room as the party progressed around him, he turned once more toward Faith. She sat at his side, and abruptly conscious of his scrutiny, she looked up into his face with a smile. A sudden surge of emotion tightened his throat. She was magnificent. Those great light eyes and that flawless skin . . . Her small features, always lovely, seemed to be refined even further by the new, graceful contours of her cheeks. Could it be that her hair had taken on an even brighter hue, that the dark sweep of her lashes had become even more lush? Even in the demure taffeta gown she wore, it was obvious that she had become a woman. Was it possible that the passage of a single year could have wrought such a startling metamorphosis?

Unable to get his fill of looking at her, William held Faith's gaze in silence. It was hard for him to believe that she was entirely unaffected by the changes evident in her physical appearance. Surely she realized not a man in the room could take his eyes off her . . . including himself.

William's frustration mounted. Reaching out under the table, he took the small hand resting on Faith's lap and enclosed it tightly in his. Her hand gripped his tightly in return, and William's heart skipped a beat. He had to get her away from here for a little while, so they could talk and he could tell her . . .

William's attention turned back to the rumble of small talk as another guest stopped at the table to engage Wally in conversation. It had been a long hour, punctuated by curious eyes and by the polite questions of a steady stream of guests who had seen fit to extent their compliments on both his and Lydia's testimony. Valuable time was passing. His own circumstances were presently so uncertain, his time so limited, and there was so much he wanted to say to Faith. . . .

William began to feel the press of panic.

Rising abruptly to his feet, he took the opportunity afforded him by Wally's conversation with the very vocal Senator Umbridge. He turned toward Faith.

"It's gotten a little stuffy in here. I think I'm ready for some fresh air. You haven't seen Senator Morris's garden yet, have you, Faith?"

Faith's response was immediate as she rose spontaneously to her feet.

"No, I haven't. I would enjoy seeing it immensely."

"It's rather cool outside, dear. I don't think—"

Interrupting her mother's response, Faith reached for the shawl which rested on the back of her chair.

"I'll be quite comfortable, Mother."

Relieved as Faith took his arm, William led her toward the French doors which opened onto the garden. In truth, he had only had a small glimpse of the garden when he had entered the Morris residence. Its main appeal was exactly that which had obviously stirred Lydia Durham's disapproval. Privacy. And he needed that privacy with Faith, if only for a few minutes. He needed it desperately.

William politely escorted Faith through the doors, his heart pounding. He was only too keenly aware of the tenuous control he maintained on his suddenly soaring emotions. He shot a quick glance toward the beautiful young woman who walked at his side, and his heartbeat escalated to thunder in his ears.

Grateful for the shadows which kept them from the sight of prying eyes, William turned abruptly to face Faith. The light from the room beyond shone on her perfect features, and he shook his head in wonder at the wealth of emotions this young girl-woman evoked inside him. When he spoke his voice was hoarse with emotion. His words came straight from the heart.

"I've missed you, Faith—very much. And I want to kiss you. I want that more than I've ever wanted anything in my life."

Faith's smile was tremulous.

"I've missed you, too, William. Yes, please do kiss me."

The almost childish candor of her reply touched him deeply, and he drew Faith into his arms, lowering his mouth to graze her lips lightly with his own. Her mouth was soft, sweet. The taste of her exhilarated him, creating an urgent need for her in him. He kissed her again, his arms sliding around her slenderness, urging her closer. The palms of his hands moved against her back, fondling its contours, fitting her intimately against him as his kiss deepened. He sought instinctively to separate her lips, pulling her closer still.

The firm swells of Faith's breasts were warm against his chest. He groaned at the intimacy of the contact, his hand moving to tangle in her upswept hair. Faith's lips separated at last and he tasted her mouth fully. The wonder of the contact awoke in him a soaring hunger.

"Faith . . . oh, Faith . . ."

His mouth was devouring hers. His grip was unyielding. Holding this girl-woman in his arms, tasting her sweetness, making her his and his alone . . . it was the dream he had carried inside him for the long year they had been separated, the long year during which he had begun to think his dream never would be realized. But Faith was in his arms now. . . .

William's arms were straining her closer. His mouth was moving intimately against hers, separating her lips, when panic began to invade Faith's senses. The warm glow of William's presence was beginning to freeze inside her. She was truly uncertain what had happened, why things were suddenly seeming to go wrong.

She had been as frustrated as he by the steady flow of visitors at the table, the lack of privacy which inhibited their conversation. William's hand had slipped into hers as he had sat beside her, and she had gripped it tightly, needing the contact to steady her strangely shaken emotions.

She had not remembered how handsome William was. She had not remembered the pale glow of his hair, the clarity of his fair skin. She supposed that was because his fairness had appeared pale to her in contrast to Black Wolf's vibrant coloring. Black Wolf . . .

She had shrugged aside the painful memory and clutched William's hand tighter. The brown-eyed gaze which returned to touch hers again and again was alive with a familiar warmth which appeared to soar to an encompassing blaze when he spoke her name. It touched her deeply. She wanted to talk to him. She had missed the closeness which had developed so spontaneously between them in the few short days of their acquaintance. In the year since that time, she had not met anyone with whom she had felt so relaxed, to whom she could speak so easily. She had missed him terribly.

When William had suggested a walk in the garden, she had all but jumped to her feet to accept his invitation. Then he had taken her into his arms, and his lips had touched hers as they had the day she had left Fort Lyon. She had enjoyed the gentle pressure of his lips against hers, until that gentleness had begun to change.

His arms were straining her closer, becoming more demanding. His mouth was crushing hers, forcing apart her lips. He was kissing her more deeply, and Faith was beginning to feel a strange sense of violation.

Black Wolf had kissed her like this, but there had been no sense of violation then. Oh, no, she had gloried in his touch, leaned into his embrace. She remembered Black Wolf's ragged voice, his trembling restraint when she had opened her mouth to his. She remembered the promise in his eyes when he had slipped the carved band on her finger. She remembered her own trembling hand and Black Wolf's steadying touch as she had slipped the band onto his finger in return. And she remembered the night by the river, when she had silently wished Black Wolf would never let her go.

The pain of memory shook her, and Faith's sense of panic increased. She did not want William this way. She wanted a friend . . . only a friend. She needed someone to talk to, someone who cared.

William's body was reacting predictably, swelling to meet the wild surging of his emotions, when he first sensed Faith's restraint. She was beginning to stiffen in his arms, to withdraw from his kiss. A warning bell sounded in the back of his mind, stifling his instinctive reaction to pull her closer still.

What in hell was he doing? Damn it all, Faith was still little more than a child, and he was frightening her.

Tearing his mouth from hers, William decreased the compelling pressure of his embrace. Refusing to relinquish his possession of her, he continued to hold Faith close, resting his cheek against her blazing curls. Yes, the passage of a year had made a great difference in Faith's physical appearance. Her body had matured enough to stimulate him more than that of any woman he had ever known, but in other ways, she was still a child.

Patience . . . he need maintain patience. His instinctive desire for Faith had been honed to a fine point by the experiences of his twenty-six years and by the women he had known. Faith had no such experience. Her innocence had obviously been respected in the Cheyenne camp, despite the speculation which followed her. For that he was supremely grateful. He remembered the jealous pain which had assailed him when he had temporarily suspected differently. The young Cheyenne's attempt to recapture her, the attempt which had resulted in the young Indian's death, had left him sorely suspicious. But whatever the fellow's reasoning, he had paid for his unwise actions with his life. Strange, even while suspicion had run rampant in his mind, his desire had not diminished one iota, and it was now clearer to William than ever before that he wanted Faith under any conditions. What remained now was for him to make her want him as much in return.

Damn, it was not going to be easy. He must control his ardor, make it take a back seat to common sense. He must reestablish himself in Faith's life, and he must do it quickly. He could do that only if his new orders did not come through too quickly, for he would have to pursue a fairly intelligent plan to arouse Faith's deeper affections. Oh, hell . . . love . . . he wanted her love.

Drawing himself back with supreme control, William gave a short, self-conscious laugh, but Faith was not smiling. Regret flickered across the concern on his face as he raised his hand to stroke her cheek.

"Faith, what's wrong? Did I frighten you?"

Faith made no response, and William began to feel a touch of panic.

"You're not angry with me, are you, Faith?"

Still no answer. Faith attempted to turn her head to avoid his assessing gaze, and William released her reluctantly to cup her cheeks with his palms. His eyes moved over her sober face with concern. No, he could not have alienated her so completely—so quickly.

"Faith, answer me. Have I offended you?"

Faith shook her head.

"No . . . it . . . it's just that you're different, William. Somehow you're different."

William's responsive laugh was touched with discomfort.

"Different? I suppose a year changes people in certain ways, but not significantly so. Where am I different . . . in what way that makes you uneasy? Tell me, so I can make you feel better about it. I want things to be the way they were between us, Faith."

"I don't know. I did miss you this past year, William. I thought of you many times, you know." Her sober eyes intent on his, Faith continued softly, "I wished I could talk to you. Papa and Mama were so absorbed in each other . . . I had no one left to talk to but you. When I saw you again, I was so happy. And I was proud, William. Mama, Papa, and I watched your testimony from the gallery."

"You were there, in the chamber when I testified? I didn't see you."

"Papa and Mama thought it would be unwise to let you know we were there. Papa felt it would be a distraction, that you might feel inhibited by our presence, feel a need to soften your words if you knew Mama was there."

"Your father is a wise man."

"Yes, and you're a brave and honest man. You said everything so well. Mama and I were all but overcome. When you were done giving your testimony, I wished I could go to you and hug you."

"I wish you had."

"But I didn't mean for things to be like this . . . I mean—"

"Are you trying to tell me you don't want me to kiss you, Faith? Is that it?"

Faith was momentarily silent. Her eyes were moving over

298

his face with an open intensity that set his heart to pounding anew. Compelled by need, William brushed her slightly parted lips with his.

Faith's heavy dark lashes fluttered against her smooth cheek in the moment before she again raised her eyes to his. A small smile cracked her lips.

"I like it with you kiss me like that, William. It makes me feel warm and good inside."

William gave a short laugh at the candor of her reply, his love for her swelling inside him.

"Well, I guess that's a start, anyway."

Suddenly serious, William dropped his hands from Faith's cheeks and stepped back. Taking her hand, he drew her to a nearby bench. Seating her gently, he sat down beside her and tilted up her chin until her eyes firmly met his.

"Faith, I suppose we should talk, so you can understand."

"Oh, yes, William. I enjoy talking to you. I feel I can tell you everything that's in my heart . . . that you really care."

"I *do* care, Faith. I've cared about you from the moment I first heard about your capture."

"But you care about all the captives that were taken. I saw you with the children who were returned with us, and the two ladies who were brought in the day before we left. And you were such a good friend to Papa. He—"

"It wasn't the same, Faith. And it wasn't my friendship with Wally that made me care about you." Without his realizing it, William's hand had slipped to Faith's shoulder, to caress that gentle curve.

"Faith, you were beautiful a year ago when you were still a child. The first time I saw you, I knew you would be special to me. We talked and I grew to know you were far more mature for your age than many women I knew. I didn't want you to leave Fort Lyon. I fought with your father to make him change his mind, but it did no good. When you rode off, I suppose I suspected I might never see you again. Then Sand Creek happened, Faith, and my memories of you were all mixed up with the tragedy there."

Faith's hand moved spontaneously to his chest. William flicked his eyes briefly closed against the thrill that moved

299

down his spine as the warmth of her palm penetrated his coat. He reached up to hold her wrist fast. Then he gave her a quick smile, his white, even teeth in pleasant contrast with his light brown mustache.

"Well, the truth is, I suppose I overreacted when I saw you here tonight. I wanted to be with you for a little while. I wanted to hold you, and I wanted to kiss you. But things got a little out of hand." William again laughed shortly. "The truth is, Faith, I still want to hold you and kiss you, but I won't if it will stop you from wanting to see me again."

Faith's light brows furrowed into a frown as she studied his words. God . . . she was actually considering turning him away. He'd been a damned fool, frightening her.

Faith's great blue eyes moved to meet his in silent contemplation, and a tremor of apprehension moved down William's spine. His hand tightened spontaneously on her wrist. He saw her flicker of discomfort, but he could not make himself release her. Her eyes left his at last, to trail along his cheek before finally settling on his mouth for long, disturbing seconds. He could feel their intensity and he swallowed tightly. Damn it, didn't she realize what she was doing to him?

"Faith . . ."

"I want to see you again, William. You're the only person I do really want to see."

William released a deep, silent breath.

"And I don't want to make you unhappy, so you can kiss me if you really want to."

William suppressed a low, silent groan as he struggled to smile.

Unconsciously, he slid her hand away from the rapid pounding of his heart up toward his mouth. He pressed a light kiss against her palm, his breath catching at the response that the simple intimacy stirred inside him.

"All right . . . if you promise to tell me when I'm making you uncomfortable."

Faith's expression was sober.

"All right."

William's arm slipped around Faith's shoulder, and he

drew her close to press a light kiss against the throbbing pulse in her temple. He held his mouth there for long seconds. He liked feeling Faith's life force pulsing against his lips. He wanted to know her more intimately still.

The sound of a sudden step at the doorway behind them turned their eyes in its direction. Wally hesitated for a few moments, his broad form silhouetted against the light from the living room, before he turned and urged Lydia out into the garden. He shot Lydia a short glance.

"You were right, darling. It is a little cool out here." Directing his next words to William and Faith as they rose to their feet, Wally smiled a little more broadly, "But I suppose you two didn't notice the chill, did you?"

William attempted a sober response.

"No, we didn't."

"Well, in any case, I hope you've finished your talk, because Lydia and I have decided we've done enough socializing this evening. Are you ready to go, Faith?"

Realizing William still hadn't released her wrist, Faith nodded tentatively. "Yes, I'm ready."

Wally raised his heavy brown brows.

"Well, William, are you going to let her go or do I have to break that death grip you have on my daughter's wrist?"

A small smile cracked William's sobriety as he released Faith's hand.

"I suppose I'll let her go, as long as you all promise to join me for breakfast tomorrow morning."

"We'll be happy to join you for breakfast, William." Wally's smile dropped away. "We'll be returning to New York later in the day, you know."

"No, I didn't know." William shot Faith a quick look. He couldn't lose her now, not after he had found her again.

"What are your orders, now that you've finished testifying, William?"

"I'm on my own until my situation can be reassessed. Confidentially, there's talk that I may be reassigned to work with Major Wynkoop in handling Indian affairs. I'd be very pleased if things worked out that way."

"And that means?"

"That means I'm free as long as I can be reached by the Department of the Army when I'm needed."

"Free to travel to New York?"

William's heart skipped a beat.

"If I have an invitation."

Wally turned toward Faith for the first time. His gaze was keenly assessing.

"Shall we extent this fellow an invitation, Faith?"

"Wally!"

At Lydia's short exclamation, Wally turned to take in his wife's startled expression.

"You needn't worry, darling. I know I can depend upon my daughter to give me an honest reply." Turning back to Faith, Wally raised his brows in a characteristic expression. "Well, what do you say, darling?"

Feeling the weight of Faith's perusal, William turned back toward her once more. His eyes held her startling sober azure stare. Time stretched into eternity until she responded with a soft nod.

"Yes, do invite William, Papa. I would very much enjoy his company."

Releasing a tense breath, William turned back toward Wally. His broad smile elicited Wally's short laugh.

"Consider yourself invited, William."

William's smile stretched farther.

"Consider yourself accepted . . . and I do thank you for your generous invitation."

Taking Faith's arm, William turned to follow Wally toward the Morrises' living room once more. His hands lingered on Faith's shoulders as he helped her with her wrap. When she turned to face him, he dropped his hands to his sides.

"Tomorrow morning, Faith."

A small flicker moved across Faith's face the moment before she raised herself up on her toes and pressed a light kiss against his lips.

"Yes, tomorrow morning, William."

His eyes flicking toward Wally as Faith turned, William caught her father's surprise. He also saw the instinctive

302

tightening of Lydia Durham's finely drawn lips the moment before she bid him a quiet good evening.

Watching from the doorway as the Durham carriage pulled away, William realized he wanted nothing more than to take his leave as well. He frowned with sudden impatience. He had been enjoying himself prior to Faith's arrival, but the moment Sally Anne Morris had indicated that Faith had entered the room he had . . .

Sally Anne . . .

His eyes flicking momentarily closed in sudden embarrassment, William turned to search the room for Sally Anne's small, petite figure. He owed the pleasant young woman a profound apology.

William did not need to search long. With hasty steps he moved directly to Sally Anne's side. A heated flush suffused his fair complexion under her direct appraisal.

"Sally Anne, I must apologize for my boorish behavior. I'm afraid the shock of the Durhams' arrival struck all other thoughts from my mind."

Sally Anne shook her curly blond head.

"I don't know what you mean, William."

"Leaving you in the midst of our conversation, when you had gone to such trouble to make me feel welcome . . ." His eyes darted to the buffet table where he had left his filled plate. Of course, it had been cleared away.

"Oh, that . . . You needn't trouble yourself, William. I hadn't realized you and the Durhams were such close old friends. I gather this is the first time you've seen them since you returned."

"Yes. Wally and I did become fairly close while he was recuperating at Fort Lyon. He believed his wife and daughter dead for so long. Of course, when we both found out that they were indeed alive—"

"You seemed particularly pleased to see his daughter. I believe her name is Faith, is it not?"

William's face flushed more darkly.

"And, of course, you didn't have the opportunity to meet Faith this evening because I monopolized her time so completely. Again, I apologize."

303

"No need for apology, William. The girl is obviously very fond of you."

"And I of her."

"She's a very beautiful girl."

"Very beautiful."

"And very young."

"Very."

"Not *too* young, do you think?"

"I sincerely hope not."

"And if she is?"

"Then I shall have to wait for her to grow older, I suppose."

Sally Anne's smile broadened at his frankness.

"I think Faith Durham is a very lucky girl, despite the difficulties she experienced. I do wish you luck in your suit, William. How much longer do you expect to be in Washington?"

"Just until tomorrow afternoon."

"Tomorrow! Father was of the impression that you were temporarily on leave without assignment. He had great plans for imposing upon your time so that he might further the cause we discussed earlier."

"Your father is correct, Sally Anne, but I've been invited to travel to New York with the Durhams tomorrow so I might spend some time with them. I could not refuse their offer."

"Could not or *would* not?"

William gave a short laugh.

"You read me well, Sally Anne. The truth is for your ears alone, if I might request that indulgence. I intend to make good use of that time at the Durham residence. When I leave, I hope it will be with the full consent of her parents and with a promise from Miss Faith Durham that she will accept my hand in marriage."

"William, the girl can be no more than sixteen or seventeen. Surely you see that—"

"She is fifteen, and I see only one thing, Sally Anne. I love her."

Stunned by his own declaration, William reached out

spontaneously to take Sally Anne's small hand.

"Once again, I offer you my apologies. I don't know what's come over me. I'm sure my amorous pursuits are not of the slightest interest to you. I only hope that my obviously confused state of mind will show you that my oversight earlier was unintended and much regretted."

Sally Anne's smile warmed at William's obvious embarrassment.

"Your numerous apologies are accepted, William, and I do wish you happiness."

Sally Anne's smile faded as William disappeared through the doorway a short time later. She turned at a touch on her arm.

"Oh, Father . . . It's unfortunate that William had to leave so early, isn't it?"

Hartfield Morris's keen eyes assessed his daughter's uncharacteristic frown. His full, white mustache twitched.

"Before you could succeed in getting to know him a little better, is that what you're saying, dear?"

"Father"—Sally Anne's eyes narrowed at his tone—"let me warn you now. Any attempt at matchmaking is useless. Captain Potter has already given his heart to someone else."

"The Durham girl is a child."

"You don't miss anything, do you, Father?"

"I would have had to be blind to miss the way William looked at that girl. Whether he realized it or not, he's certainly set tongues to wagging. His behavior wasn't very wise. Now the gossip and speculation which followed the mother will follow the daughter as well."

"A man in love is seldom wise."

"Fiddlesticks! You give up too easily, dear. I consider myself a good judge of character, and the like of Captain William Potter is not likely to come your way too soon again."

"I agree with you, Father. I'll admit that I found William very interesting . . . in fact, I found him a truly lovely man whom I would have been very interested in knowing better.

But he's leaving Washington tomorrow, and even if I didn't know how he feels about Faith Durham, I would think that puts him out of range of my dazzling personality. So"— lifting her chin, Sally Anne forced a smile—"I suppose I shall have to check to see if the champagne is holding out. And I suppose, after avoiding Jerry Thornbush all night, I shall have to allow him to catch up with me."

"Jerry Thornbush!"

The knitting of Hartfield Morris's heavy gray brows adequately bespoke his reaction to her statement.

"Father, Jerry is the son of Senator Thornbush, and from a very prominent family."

"And he's a fool like his father."

"Father!"

"Don't let Captain Potter get away, Sally Anne."

"Father, I don't think the choice is mine."

"And if it were?"

"That would be an entirely different matter, but—"

"H'mmmm."

Turning away in exasperation, Sally Anne had not gone two steps when a familiar touch stopped her short. She turned, and fixed a brilliant, artificial smile on her lips.

"Oh, Jerry. I've been looking for you all evening."

Ignoring her father's glare, Sally Anne slipped her dainty hand under the arm of the beaming Jerry Thornbush, and slowly walked away.

The drums were beating, echoing back from the high hills around him as Black Wolf stood in the semidarkness at the outskirts of camp. His robe wrapped around his shoulders against the bite of the wind, Black Wolf strained his eyes to the hill nearby where the pony herd grazed. Yes, the wealth of the Cheyenne and the Sioux had grown in these days of war. The herd on which he trained his eye was vast. The number of his own animals, amongst them, was great. Plunder from many captured wagon trains was abundant, and his people were eating well.

He glanced back toward his own temporary shelter amidst

he lodges of the Cheyenne. They had seen the last of the white man's soldiers for a while. Criers had passed through he camps to announce that they would remain four days onger to rest their ponies, and his people had known relief. Separate but a part of the great force, his own people raveled with the Sioux, and with them they would remain until the white man no longer threatened their land.

Black Wolf frowned as the drumming increased. The moon was full. There would be dances tonight in every part of the camp. But no amount of plunder, no number of animals would make up for the loss at Sand Creek. And no manner of celebration would bring joy to his heart once more.

As Black Wolf watched, a slender figure separated itself from those moving within the camp. It stood staring in his direction for long moments before beginning to approach him. Black Wolf's frown darkened. He did not speak as Deer Woman came to stand close beside him.

A deep sadness stabbed at Black Wolf's heart. Deer Woman was no longer the smiling young woman who had flirted so outrageously with him in summer camp a year before. Joy had left the sober eyes she raised to his, but she bore scars from Sand Creek which were far more noticeable than that loss. Black Wolf's eyes dropped to the jagged cut which distorted Deer Woman's cheek, extending from the corner of her eye to her chin. The marks of a white man's saber, like the marks she bore on her chest and back, were wounds which had, indeed, almost ended her life. He remembered well the blood which had streamed from her gaping wounds as he had lifted Deer Woman from the creek bed on which she had fallen.

There had been many, many lying beside her. He had helped to lift them to the horses caught by those of his people still able to function. It was these survivors who filled this Cheyenne war camp, and it was these survivors who relentlessly sought their vengeance.

Black Wolf's gaze continued to dwell on Deer Woman's sober countenance, and Deer Woman's lips twisted with bitterness.

"Your eyes do not find pleasure in my face, Black Wolf. The white man has taken that joy from those who look at me."

Black Wolf's dark eyes flickered briefly. He raised his hand to the jagged line which marked the skin of his temple, memory flicking back to the day he had awakened to find himself lying in a pool of blood. It had been the day Fire Spirit had been lost to him.

"Our scars are similar, Deer Woman. They serve a noble purpose. They remind us of the treachery of the white man, of the need to rid our land of his presence. They are a gift of the Great Power so that the memory will not fade."

"I give no thanks for this 'gift'!" Deer Woman's eyes sparked with anger. "It is this 'gift' which has turned your eyes from me."

A deep sadness swelled inside Black Wolf. He remembered sunlit days of summer when Deer Woman played a more subtle game. He remembered his amusement, and his admonition to Fire Spirit to save him from Deer Woman's steady pursuit. He wished he could remind Deer Woman that the affection she sought from him had never been in his power to extend to her, that despite himself, his soul cried out for one whose skin marked her his enemy, one who was lost to him.

Instead, Black Wolf reached out the hand which had touched the scar of his own wound. He traced the ragged line on Deer Woman's cheek with his fingertips as he spoke soft words of comfort.

"This mark does not distort your beauty, Deer Woman. If you feel less than you were before, it is because bitterness fills your heart. The bitterness is reflected in your eyes. It replaces the warmth which shone in them before. It is the same bitterness which has taken the warmth from my heart and left me empty. I do not have the power to restore that which is lost to you. My nights are filled with the memory of Walking Woman, lying slain, her body cut and bleeding from countless wounds; the memory of those who lay beside her, their blood draining into a great common pool on the dry creek bed. I am plagued by the memory of the long night

308

which followed, during which those still alive slowly succumbed to the cold in their attempt to reach safety. My days and nights are filled with these visions, leaving room for little else within my heart."

Deer Woman's small eyes bore intensely into his, the first trace of the beauty of old returning with her whispered words.

"I would help you forget those visions, Black Wolf. I would bring you comfort."

Black Wolf shook his head. His hand dropped to his side and a flicker of protest registered in Deer Woman's eyes.

"The life within me is gone. It will not return until the white man has been driven from this land." Raising his head to look back toward the camp, Black Wolf focused on a solitary figure who watched them in silence. He nodded in the man's direction.

"But Spotted Elk is not so afflicted. He has mourned the loss of Silent Woman and his child, and his eyes stray to you. He sees not the mark of the white man's sword, but the face of a woman. He would restore to you all that was lost in the white man's attack."

"Spotted Elk wants only that which is yours to take. The sorrow he has suffered has not changed his heart."

Deer Woman's unspoken reference to Fire Spirit tightened the line of his lips with remembered anger. When he spoke it was with deliberate care.

"Spotted Elk is wiser than I. He does not cling to that which is lost."

Deer Woman hesitated. She surveyed Black Wolf's unsmiling countenance, a sober decision dawning in the depths of her eyes as she began to speak.

"Yes, Black Wolf, you spoke the truth. We have been touched by similar wounds which have scarred us deeply. It is a pain which we still bear, which we are powerless to dismiss. While that distress still plagues our hearts, we will suffer without consolation. So it must be."

Deer Woman's parting comment kept Black Wolf's eyes on her back for long moments after she had turned from him.

She had disappeared into her lodge when Black Wolf finally turned back to the darkening distance once more. But he needed no light for the vision which returned clearly to his mind. In an attempt to drive away the fire-haired image, he set his thoughts on the more recent past.

They had been long in coming to this place. Runners sent from camp the day Black Kettle had separated from them had finally returned with the news that their brothers, the Northern Cheyenne were encamped with the Oglala Sioux on the Powder River, west of the Black Hills. Toward them, his people had moved from Bear Lodge River, to Red Paint River, and then to Antelope Point River. They would soon reach Powder River and join their northern brothers. Wood, grass, and buffalo were abundant there, and they would winter well.

A new sense of determination filled Black Wolf, and he straightened his back as he squinted into the darkening hills surrounding him. When he again faced the white man, he would be ready. His people and he would be ready, more ready than they had ever been. . . .

"I tell you, Wally, this is a mistake! Faith is a child, and she should not be put in a position where she is exposed to an adult male's amorous intents on a daily basis! She is too young, I tell you!"

"Lydia, for heaven's sake, keep your voice down."

Turning toward her on his side as they lay in the great, four-posted bed in their master suite, Wally flicked a nervous eye toward the wall which separated Faith's room from theirs. He was not quite certain which of his comments of a few moments before had elicited Lydia's violent response. He had intended their conversation to be a soft prelude to lovemaking, but somehow something had gone wrong.

"No, Wally, I'm tired of keeping quiet."

Lydia's soft gray eyes sparked with an anger which had obviously been smoldering for long days, and Wally marveled at his previous ignorance of its presence. She shook her head, black spirals of unbound hair moving against the stark whiteness of her pillow in silent testimony to her vehemence.

"I was uncomfortable with this whole situation from the beginning. I should have spoken up sooner, but I had no idea you intended to ask Captain Potter to return to New York with us."

"Lydia, don't you think you're overreacting? Adult male's amorous intents . . . It's obvious that William is strongly attracted to Faith. He has been since he first saw her, but you certainly don't think for a minute that William would force himself on Faith, do you? I thought you liked William."

"I do."

"Well . . ."

"Wally, you must have noticed the way William looks at Faith. In the five days he's been here, he hasn't taken his eyes off her for a moment."

"Faith is a beautiful girl . . . woman."

"She's not a woman yet! She is innocent. She has not had experience with the opposite sex. She doesn't know the danger that lies in her spontaneity."

Wally's lips tightened.

"It's time for a bit of honesty here, Lydia. You seem to forget that Faith spent several months in a rather savage environment. I ask you honestly, under the conditions in which she lived, do you really believe she remained as innocent of the male-female relationship as you choose to believe?"

Regretting his words the moment they had left his mouth, Wally shook his head in an attempt to halt the deep flush that began to color Lydia's cheeks.

"Lydia, I didn't mean—"

"Oh, yes, you did, Wally. You meant every word."

Lydia threw back the covers in a prelude to arising, but she was prevented from leaving the bed by Wally's restraining hand and the contrite sound of his voice as he attempted to draw her into his arms.

"Lydia, please, I'm sorry. That was a damned stupid thing for me to say."

311

"You said what you were thinking. There's no need for you to hold back, especially when the welfare of our daughter is being discussed."

Wally drew back to assess Lydia's expression, but her face was impassive, difficult to read. He tried again.

"Lydia, I didn't mean to upset you."

"Faith is innocent, I tell you. The Cheyenne respect innocence. She was not abused in that camp. Broken Hand assigned Black Wolf to watch over her. He—"

"Black Wolf was the Indian who tried to recapture her, wasn't he?" Wally's voice hardened. "You're trying to tell me that savage respected my daughter?"

"Wally, do you realize what you're saying?"

"I'm not saying what you seem to think, Lydia. What I am saying is that Faith was doubtless exposed to much that could not be hidden behind rough, hide walls, and while she is doubtless personally without blemish, she also doubtlessly has obtained considerable secondhand knowledge uncommon to a girl her age."

"You're wrong, Wally. And even if it were true, it isn't healthy for her to be subjected to William's lustful glances."

"Lustful glances!" Wally gave a short, disbelieving laugh. "She was accustomed to seeing her own mother subjected to the lustful glances of a savage on a daily basis. While you were under sedation the first night you were returned, she carefully explained to me Broken Hand's reaction to you from the time you were captured. She begged me to understand a situation which I had no idea she could possibly comprehend at her young age. And now you're trying to tell me that—"

"That . . . that was different. It is one thing to know and another to experience. William wants Faith, Wally. He is carefully tutoring her to respond to his desire."

"Lydia, for the love of God—"

"I know what I'm talking about, Wally! I know what it is to be tutored in that way! I will not have Faith exposed to such maneuvering, no matter how honorable William's intentions."

The heat of fury rushed to Wally's face and he gritted his

312

teeth tightly shut against the jealousy which assailed him. So Lydia remembered very well being tutored in desire by that savage . . .

"William loves Faith, Lydia. What would you have me do? Tell him he has to leave, that his suit is unsatisfactory to us? Faith may not love him, but she does think very highly of him. A strong bond has developed between them."

"A bond which he intends to strengthen."

"Like Broken Hand strengthened his bond with you? Is that what you're thinking, Lydia?" Wally's harsh rasp snapped Lydia's mouth tightly shut, and he gave a low laugh. "You seem to forget, you're dealing with a civilized man in William, not a savage!"

"What makes you think there is a difference?"

Stunned by Lydia's harsh whisper, Wally was momentarily unable to respond. Standing firm on her remark, Lydia held Wally's gaze with her own, and he unconsciously marveled at her determination. She had been so disturbingly weak for so long, so willing to do anything to please him. But, God, why did she only show spirit when the name Broken Hand was mentioned? Would she never forget the man?

Wally's response was low, halting.

"Isn't it different between us, Lydia? Are you trying to tell me that it would've made no difference to you which one of us you spent the rest of your life with, me or Broken Hand?"

A flicker of pain moved across Lydia's suddenly pale face. In an unexpected movement, she wrapped her arms around his neck and held him fiercely tight. Silent for long moments, she finally drew herself away. Her lips touched his in an intimate whisper.

"No, I wasn't trying to say that. I love you, Wally. I've always loved you."

Wally's arms moved around Lydia's slender back, and he crushed her against the broad width of his chest. Her breasts were warm through the sheer material of her nightgown, but he fought the growing sense of distraction caused by their intimate posture. This conversation needed to be finished.

"Then what did you mean?"

Drawing back from him so that she might direct the full power of her silver gaze into his eyes, Lydia offered softly, "What I meant is that a man who truly loves a woman loves her in the same way . . . with gentleness and respect, no matter the designation assigned to him by those who do not understand him."

"And you are saying—"

"Black Wolf loved Faith. The rings he exchanged with her were an open declaration of his feelings. He was uncivilized according to the standards which we hold. But he also was not corrupted by the white man's civilization. He held to his code, no matter his feelings."

"And you don't trust William to do the same?"

"Wally, I could do nothing about Black Wolf's intentions when at the Cheyenne camp. Indeed, I did not even recognize my responsibility then, but I still remember my reaction to the ring Faith wore. My reaction to William's open intentions are the same. She is too young, Wally! She needs time."

"All right."

Startled by his abrupt change of mind, Lydia shook her head.

"You're saying you agree with me?"

"I'm saying I will bow to your instincts. William has been here five days. I will explain our feelings, and I'll tell him we want him to visit again, soon. But for now, it is time to give Faith some room for thought, some room to grow."

"Oh, Wally . . ."

"I love you, Lydia. And I'm tired of talking."

Wally's hands were moving against the curve of her shoulder, stripping away the sheer fabric which covered them, and Lydia leaned back against the pillow to accommodate his seeking touch.

"I'm tired of talking, too. And I want you to love me, Wally. I want it more—"

Wally's hungry mouth cut off her remaining words and Lydia accepted the anxious assault of his lovemaking. In truth, she had not stated the full extent of her objection to William's suit, because the true depth of it was beyond her

314

own understanding. But of one thing she was sure; the heavy male body which covered hers was welcome atop her. The touch of his hands was a part of her life with which she could not part; and the hard staff of Wally's passion as it pierced her brought her joy and fulfillment. And it brought her peace. In the stillness, the aftermath of the turbulent feelings it evoked, it brought her peace.

Lydia clutched Wally close and rose to meet his eager thrusts. Yes, the time for talking was past, but the time for loving was not. It never would be.

Chapter XIX

The telegram had arrived at the front door a few moments earlier, and had been delivered immediately into William's hand. Faith had moved instinctively to his side, and the sitting room which had been filled with conversation a few moments before became suddenly silent. Still clutching the telegram in his hand, William reached out spontaneously to curve his other arm around Faith's shoulders. His frown darkening, he ran his eyes once more over the bold, unyielding print.

CAPTAIN W. G. POTTER. REPORT IMMEDIATELY TO ARMY HEADQUARTERS, WASHINGTON, D.C., FOR BRIEFING AND REASSIGNMENT.

William read the Spartan message again, unconsciously unwilling to accept its content. He curled his arm more tightly around Faith's shoulders, only to become suddenly conscious of the fact that they were not alone. Unwilling to release her, William looked up to meet Wally's intense stare.

"All right, William, don't keep us in suspense. What does the telegram say? It can't be good . . . not with the way you're frowning."

Turning to shoot a glance at Faith, William became suddenly caught by her obvious concern.

"I have to return to Washington."

"When, William?"

Faith's short question taking precedence over Wally's inquiry of a few seconds before, William attempted a smile.

"Now, Faith."

"Now? You mean, immediately?"

"That's what it says."

"What else does it say, William?" Wally took a few steps forward, annoyance obvious in his demeanor. "Damn it, man, take your eyes off my daughter for a few minutes and answer me, will you?"

William jerked his eyes back in Wally's direction, and gave a short, self-conscious laugh.

"I'm sorry, Wally. But you're not as good to look at as your daughter, and since I'm going to be leaving this evening, I thought I'd store up all the looking I could."

"You certainly don't have to leave this evening! Surely tomorrow morning will be soon enough." Faith's low entreaty interrupted their exchange, her strange sense of panic reflected in her voice, "Papa, tell William he doesn't have to leave immediately."

"Of course, he doesn't." Snatching the missive from William's hand, Wally carefully folded it and inserted it back into the envelope. "After all, he won't receive this message until tomorrow morning. He can leave immediately thereafter."

"Wally—"

"You can't follow orders you haven't yet received." In response to William's frown, Wally smiled. "I'll tell Lydia to have cook add something special to dinner tonight, since dinner will be in the manner of a going-away party. Yes, I'll tell her right now."

Turning on his heel, Wally walked quickly from the sitting room. He closed the door behind him, allowing William the opportunity he sought. Within moments, William had pulled Faith into his arms.

He was holding her close against him. His eyes moved over her lovely face, illuminated by the flames of the fire flickering in the nearby fireplace. She was beautiful . . . so beautiful.

"You will stay one more evening, won't you, William?"

"Yes, I'll stay. A few hours can't mean that much to the Army, but to me . . . now . . ."

"Oh, I'm glad. I . . ."

Her response interrupted by a sound at the doorway, Faith turned as her mother entered the room. Lydia walked forward with undisguised haste, her eyes moving between Faith and William in a manner which forced William to put a distance between them.

"I hear you are going to leave us, William."

"Yes, ma'am, tomorrow."

Lydia's face revealed her solemn concern.

"We shall all miss you."

"And I, you. I will most especially miss Faith."

"And I am certain Faith will miss you most fervently." Lydia Durham's pale eyes moved momentarily toward the arm William still had around Faith's waist, and he was again struck with the thought that she did not truly approve of his association with her daughter. He had hoped to charm the unspoken objection from her eyes, to gain her approval with assurances of his honorable intentions. He was, after all, from a good family, and he was well educated and had a bright future. Despite the difference in his and Faith's ages, he had been certain Lydia would favor his suit once she realized the seriousness of his intentions. But now he was not so sure. He almost felt that had this telegram not summoned him from the Durham household, Lydia would have found a way to come between the close association Faith and he were beginning to build.

William's frown reflected his thoughts and his hand moved to take Faith's possessively in his own. Lydia's light eyes noted his small, proprietary gesture, and he again felt the weight of the beautiful matron's unspoken censure. He stiffened spontaneously as Lydia spoke, attempting to smile as she did so.

"William, dinner will not be ready for a few hours. It is a beautiful day for a walk, and I'm sure Faith would enjoy some fresh air."

318

Snatching upon the suggestion, William turned toward Faith.

"Yes, a walk is an excellent idea, don't you agree?"

Faith's face brightened.

"I'll get my wrap."

Within minutes, William and Faith were walking briskly down the cobbled street. With barely a glance for the impressive mansions they passed one by one, or for the other strollers who braved the sharp nip in the November air, William tucked Faith's arm more tightly under his, his hand moving to cover the gloved hand which rested on his forearm. He pulled her closer to his side. His expression was troubled.

"Faith, I have a feeling that your mother doesn't approve of me for some reason."

The momentary flicker in Faith's gaze confirmed his words even as Faith shook her head in denial.

"No, William. Mother is as proud of you and your integrity as I am. She—"

"I'm not talking about her approval of my performance as an officer, Faith. Your mother has openly voiced her thoughts there. I'm talking about my obvious feelings for you."

Suddenly intense, William abruptly raised his gaze to search the street in annoyance. Public . . . it was all too public for this conversation.

"Faith, is there some place where we can talk more privately?"

Faith's slender brows knit in thought.

"There's a small park used by the neighborhood children, around the corner. It's rather late in the day. Most of the children will probably be gone."

"That sounds fine."

Faith's light pressure on his arm turned him toward the opposite corner, and within moments they were walking amongst carefully tended flower beds bearing the last of the season's offerings and trees stripped almost bare by the gusting wind. William's gaze moved to the well-maintained

319

swings and children's play apparatus a short distance away, his eyes coming to rest on a line of benches upon which the last of the day's sun beat warmly. He released a soft sigh of relief. Yes, Faith had been correct. The last of the uniformed nannies was attempting to gather her charges for the walk home. Soon they would have as much privacy as they needed for their conversation. Faith's unexpected interruption of his thoughts turned William in her direction.

"Is something wrong, William?"

His step slowing to a stop, William raised a hand to stroke a flaming wisp of Faith's cheek. Desire rose full and deep within him. Faith . . . so fashionably adult in the gown and cape of deep forest green which tinted her great eyes a startling aquamarine . . . Her hair, pulled informally back from her face, despite her mother's disapproval, accented her delicate features, its tresses spewing in a fiery cloud against the sable trim of her collar and hood. She was standing close beside him, her features tight with concern. Faith . . . the epitome of all he had ever wanted in a woman. But she was not truly a woman—not yet. And he did not want to leave her, to be far away when she made that final step into womanhood. He wanted—he needed—time to claim her completely as his own.

After one more nearly frantic glance around them, William pulled Faith behind the cover of a nearby tree. With no thought to the last of the park's visitors making their way noisily toward the exit, he drew her into his arms. His mouth closed over her cold lips, warming them with his own. One of his hands tangled in the burning flames of her hair, holding her fast as his mouth drove deeper into hers. The other snaked out, slipping beneath her cape to hold her slender form against him.

Faith was momentarily unresponsive, and panic flared inside him. He needed to make her want him—only him. Pressing her tightly against the trunk of the tree beneath which they stood, William crushed his hard body against hers as his kiss deepened. A low, instinctive protest sounded in Faith's throat. But William's desire was a consuming flame. He covered her face with heated kisses, his hands

320

moving beneath the voluminous cape to stroke her soft curves. His lips devoured the soft lobes of her ears, the slender column of her neck. She was gasping and he was pulling her closer still. He needed to be alone with her—completely alone. He needed to show Faith all that a man could be to a woman, to make a claim on her that no one else could deny. He needed . . .

A soft, mirthful giggle snapped William from his driven state to look at the small, golden-haired child running down the winding walk toward them, an angry nanny in full pursuit. His chest heaving from the heated turmoil within him, William stepped back from Faith. Regret darkened his gaze as he quickly drew her cape closed, and slipped her arm beneath his once more. They had taken no more than two short steps back on the path when the puffing nanny snatched up the giggling child with a harsh reprimand.

They continued walking until the nanny and child had again cleared the exit to the park. When all was silent once more, William turned toward Faith. Drawing her forward, he seated her on a nearby bench. Pausing, he finally sat beside her. He took both her hands in his, his gaze intense.

"Faith, there are things we must discuss."

"William, I—"

"Faith, we can avoid this discussion no longer."

"William, you said you would be my friend."

William's eyes flicked briefly closed. A stiff smile curved his lips.

"I didn't kiss you like a friend just now, Faith."

"William, you—"

"Faith, I need some plain, honest answers." He took a deep, shaken breath. "You said you would tell me if I pressed you too hard . . . if I offended you with my attentions." Faith was avoiding his gaze, and William gave her a short shake. "Look at me," he said, and when her gaze once again met his, he continued softly.

"Faith, tell me the truth. What do you feel when I kiss you . . . when I hold you close?" Her eyes were great azure pools in which he was drowning, and William took a firm hold on himself. "Tell me."

"I . . . I don't know."

Faith was avoiding his gaze once more, and William felt a sudden apprehension. It couldn't be possible. . . .

"There's someone else, isn't there, Faith?"

"William, there's no one I care for any more than I care for you . . . not anymore."

Faith's qualified response brought William up short. Complete silence reigned between them as William sought to restrain his surging jealousy.

"It's that Indian—Black Wolf—the one who tried to recapture you, isn't it? Did he . . . ?"

Faith's eyes met his in sudden anger.

"Black Wolf was kind to me. He took care of me. He never hurt me."

"He's dead, Faith. The trooper who shot him made a report. They left him on the trail."

"Please . . ."

"But I'm here now." His brown eyes soft with sincerity, William leaned closer. "I'll take care of you, keep you safe; and I'll never hurt you. I promise you that."

"William . . ."

His hands tightened on hers.

"Faith, I'm leaving tomorrow morning. I don't know where my orders will take me. I suspect I'll be returned to the western frontier in one capacity or another. I'll be far away from you. But I won't forget you." William paused. "I want your promise—"

"I can't make promises, William, not to anyone." Jerking her hands from his unexpectedly, Faith massaged one of her fingers as her brow knit into a frown. William remembered the carved band she had worn when she had been returned by the Indians, and a knot of jealousy tightened inside him.

"Because you've already made a promise like the one I'm asking for . . . to someone else."

Faith was silent.

"He's dead, Faith, and I'm not."

Faith made a short jerking movement of her head. "I . . . I don't want to discuss it."

William paused, suddenly realizing the futility of their

322

discussion. He could not press her now. There was too little time to settle the matter between them.

"All right, we won't—not now."

Rising quickly, William drew Faith up beside him. He smiled.

"I think your mother was right, Faith. We should walk and talk, and do nothing more right now. The time isn't right." Pausing, he raised Faith's small chin with his hand, holding it so that her liquid gaze met his. His next words were an intimate whisper.

"But the time will come for us, Faith. It *will.*"

Allowing her a few moments to absorb the full meaning of his words, William tucked Faith's arm under his once more and drew her alongside him. Ignoring the heavy hammering of his heart, he began to walk briskly toward the exit of the park. Patience was more difficult than he had ever thought it would be . . . so very much more difficult.

The morning sun had risen only an hour before. Its glow shone through the windowpanes of the graceful Durham mansion, marking the foyer and those within it with a bold, golden geometric pattern. Meticulous in his blue uniform, his light hair glinting with a flaxen glow, William extended his hand toward Wally.

"I can't tell you how much I appreciate your generosity in having me as your guest, Wally."

"No thanks are needed, William." Wally's eyes moved meaningfully toward his beautiful wife who was standing at his side, and he smiled. "We owe you far more than I could ever say. Isn't that right, Lydia?"

Her smile sincere, Lydia extended her hand as well.

"William, Wally and I owe you much. We will never forget our debt to you."

William hesitated. He did not doubt the sincerity in Lydia Durham's light eyes, and he gave only a moment's pause to the reserve he saw there as well. Instead, he turned in Faith's direction, his hand moving to grasp hers as he bid a final farewell to her parents.

Drawing Faith firmly behind him as he walked toward the outside door, William did not relinquish his grip as he accepted his hat from the smiling maid and bid her a polite farewell. Urging Faith through the doorway ahead of him, he took her firmly by the arm as they descended the staircase. He hesitated as they reached the waiting carriage, suddenly reaching out to gather her into his arms.

Determined not to allow their lack of privacy to part them on a platonic note, William lowered his mouth to Faith's. He kissed her with great deliberation, deeply, lovingly. Tearing his mouth from hers at last, he continued to hold her close, his mouth brushing hers as he whispered an entreaty.

"Faith . . . promise me . . . you won't forget me."

The tremulous lips beneath his whispered an unhesitant response.

"I won't forget you, William. I could never forget you."

Realizing that his precarious emotional state demanded stringent control, William separated himself from Faith at last. Turning, he stepped into the carriage, and within moments was firmly seated inside. Raising his hand in silent farewell as the carriage jerked into motion, he held Faith's lingering gaze.

A deep sense of loss beset William as the carriage turned out of the street and onto the main boulevard, and he released a deep, silent breath. His spontaneous avowal made the day before return to his mind. In the solitude of the rattling coach, he renewed it with impassioned fervor.

The day will come for us, Faith. It will. . . .

General Grenville M. Dodge, commander of the Department of the Missouri, squinted assessingly in Potter's direction as the younger man lowered himself into the chair opposite his desk. Dark-haired and dark-eyed, General Dodge was heavily bearded, his expression austere. He was a formidable figure in the well-fit, deep blue uniform. William's well-concealed anxiety increased. He was ill at ease, not knowing the reason for the unexpected summons he had received. After a brief interruption by an aide,

324

General Dodge returned to the missive before him, and William took the opportunity to appraise the modest office which housed General Dodge's command. Paneled walls, comfortably worn leather furniture, and a floor-to-ceiling bookcase . . .

The Strategy of Command, was the first title amongst the countless leather-bound volumes to meet his eyes. He was familiar with that volume and many like it. He had once considered them to impart the ultimate in military knowledge. It had only taken him six months on the western frontier to realize how wrong he had been.

William settled himself more comfortably in his chair as the general spoke a few last words to his aide. He had heard much about this man. A military and civil engineer, General Dodge had accomplished the building of the Chattahoochee River bridge in three days, a feat which was now legendary and which had earned him the personal commendation of General Grant himself. After being severely wounded at Atlanta, he had been compelled to retire temporarily, but his return to the field had earned him this new post. The man's services as both a soldier and engineer were distinguished. He supposed being summoned for an interview was an indication that . . .

General Dodge's deep voice broke the silence with startling abruptness, snapping William's attention back in his direction. The general's astute gaze was trained on William's face, openly evaluating him as he spoke.

"I've heard good things about you, Captain Potter. And these days, I admit that I'm finding it unusual to hear anything good about officers fighting in the war against the savages of the plains."

The almost imperceptible flicker that crossed William's countenance was caught by General Dodge's sharp eye. His response was immediate.

"You take umbrage with my statement, Captain Potter? If so, you will kindly explain why."

Uncertain which was the most appropriate tack to take, William hesitated.

"Candor, Captain Potter. Candor would be greatly

appreciated in this interview. I've called you here today because I find there are very few accurate sources from which I may make an assessment of our progress on the plains. Your reputation has preceded you. You are well thought of, and your integrity is unchallenged. Since that is the specific reason you find yourself seated in that chair right now, I would appreciate—no, I demand—straightforward responses to my questions. You may consider it your duty to give them, because it is.

"And since I have asked for candor, I will give you candor in return, Captain. I begin by telling you that reports from our western frontier have been extremely inaccurate in the past. A case in point is that during the entire fiasco which caused me to replace General Connor in the field, I had been receiving from Fort Conner information which led me to believe that the retreats of Colonel Cole and Colonel Walker up the Powder River had been a victorious advance. There were reports of battles in which the Sioux were driven, defeated, and pursued, when the truth was that those two illustrious officers were leading their men in circles in the wilderness, that their men were starving, their animals dropping under them, and that the Sioux who were supposed to have been in retreat, were playing their own game, and playing it well."

William considered General Dodge's statement in silence. It appeared the general had removed all choice as to his manner of response. He could only hope Dodge was as prepared for the truth as he obviously thought he was.

William took a deep, unconscious breath.

"It is unfortunate that reports you received from the field have been so inaccurate in the past, General. You asked me if I resented your initial statement. I think resentment or umbrage is the wrong word to use in describing my reaction. I think it would be more accurate to say I find it painful that a man at your level of command and with your experience should use such an uninformed term to refer to the native people that inhabit our western frontier."

The sharp ticking of Dodge's dark mustache the only outward sign that William's statement had struck a discordant note, the general replied in a level tone, "That's what you're here for, Captain. To 'inform' me."

"Well, sir, I must say, your mind appears to be far more open than those of the officers you've put in command."

"Appearances are not always what they seem, Captain. Now, if you will kindly give me your opinion as to where I've gone wrong in my approach to the problems which beset us on the frontier . . ."

William paused.

"That's a tall order, but I'll try. The first mistake you make, General Dodge, is the same one I made upon assuming my assignment on the western frontier—that is assuming that these Indians are merely ignorant, blood-thirsty savages. It is an idea touted by many writers and journalists of our time, and it is entirely untrue."

"Oh, is that so?" General Dodge's heavy brows rose, his violent disagreement with William's statement obviously rigidly contained. "Am I to understand that the killing and scalping of innocent settlers are acts committed by civilized natives?"

"Sir, your own men have done far worse. I have been witness to certain commands in which Indians are considered on the same level as the animals who roam the plains. You are acquainted with the testimony I gave at the Joint Committee Hearing, I'm sure. But I would like to clarify the fact that Colonel Chivington and Major Anthony are not the only officers under your command who share the opinion that all Indians are savages. General Patrick E. Connor is another and he—"

"Yes, General Connor . . ." General Dodge winced at the mention of the name. "I'm aware of the man's ineptness."

"And of his statement that 'all Indians must be hunted like wolves,' and his orders to his men to 'kill all Indian males over the age of twelve years' with whom they come into contact?"

"No, Captain. I was aware of no such orders. But if I am to be as candid as I promised to be, I will tell you that such a statement would not have shocked me, nor would I have been in wholehearted disagreement with it after the tales of

Indian depredations which had reached my ears."

William shook his head, his lips tightening.

"That is the mentality we must fight on the plains, sir. It is the mentality which has brought us to this disastrous state of affairs on our western frontier. As to your reference to 'savages,' I should like to clarify one more point. Perhaps these people could be considered savages if judged by our rules of acceptable conduct, but theirs is a far different world from ours. In it they have established a mode of life and conduct far more suitable to their environment and needs. It is our inability to understand their way of life which had put us at odds with them. And, of course, our greed. I should also like to add that it has not been these 'savage people' who have broken the terms of negotiated peace treaties again and again until those treaties have been rendered totally useless and void. That honor has been reserved almost exclusively for those of us who are 'civilized.'"

The lines of General Dodge's austere face had deepened as William spoke, and William hesitated, uncertain whether he should proceed.

"You don't mince words, Captain. I will say nothing more at this point but that your statements are difficult for me to accept."

His brow knitting in a deep frown, General Dodge leaned forward to rest his muscular arms on the desk before him. His manner was intense.

"The information I am now to impart to you is to be considered confidential, Captain Potter. I am giving you this information only because I want—and need—your input as to the situation which presently exists on the plains."

General Dodge hesitated briefly.

"Perhaps it would be better if I regress a bit in an effort to set the picture clearly in your mind. As you know, the Sand Creek Massacre—that is what the attack is now generally called—resulted in increasing Indian raids during the winter and spring following it. In an attempt to protect the frontier from further Indian depredations, it was my opinion that it was necessary to strike some hard blows at the enemy's heartland. I admit that I am still not averse to that opinion.

In any case, to accomplish that task, I sent General Connor to attack the Indians in the area of the Powder River. As I have related, General Connor's assignment to the western frontier was a complete disaster which resulted in his replacement. Colonel Cole and Colonel Walker were poorly commanded by him, and if you are at all impressed by numbers, I will tell you that eighteen hundred men were found lost and wandering on the plains as a result of their ineptitude. Of the five hundred animals that remained with them, none was fit for service."

General Dodge gave a low, disgusted snort.

"Of course, General Connor and his staff charged these two officers with all manner of misdirection of command. But the truth is, Captain, the responsibility for directing these officers and men, totally green when it came to making war under the conditions existing on the plains, was General Connor's. He failed miserably in that regard.

"His failure resulted in the withdrawal of these troops, and at present there are no soldiers in that area of our country."

Pinning Potter with his gaze, General Dodge continued in a low voice.

"You are, of course, aware that the Harney-Sanborn Treaty guaranteed to the Indians of the northern country—the Sioux, Cheyenne and Arapaho—the land they occupied in which there was still abundant game. It was the territory lying between the Black Hills, the Rocky Mountains, and the Yellowstone River—the Powder River Country. And, of course, you are aware that the discovery of gold in Montana started miners and prospectors out in that direction from all areas of the country—accounting for the greed you mentioned previously, no doubt. The principal routes thither were accessible only a portion of the year, and an effort was made to find a new road which would greatly shorten the distance to the mines. The Bozeman Trail was selected as it is the only wagon road from Fort Laramie to the goldfields at Virginia City, Montana. As you know, the Bozeman Trail passes directly through the Powder River country ceded to the Indians."

General Dodge paused, carefully scrutinizing William's

expression. Obviously satisfied with what he saw, he continued.

"It is no secret that the government is dedicated to the precept of fortifying the Bozeman Trail. We have since attempted to make an agreement with these northern Indians for a right of way through the territory to Montana. A few of the Sioux assented to such an agreement, but the Oglala and the Cheyenne declined to sign the treaty."

General Dodge paused once more, his heavy brows deeply knit.

"Now for the confidential part. Notwithstanding the lack of permission granted by the majority of the tribes, Captain, in the spring, I intend to send General H. B. Carrington from Fort Kearny, Nebraska, via Fort Laramie, to the northwest to garrison Camp Connor and to build two new forts near the Bozeman Trail."

"Red Cloud will never hear of it, General."

General Dodge instantly seized upon William's reply.

"What do you know about Red Cloud? He is a Sioux. It was my understanding that the only Indians with whom you had come into contact were the Cheyenne and the Arapaho."

"Sir, many of the Cheyenne and Arapaho made their way north to join their northern brothers and Red Cloud's Sioux after Sand Creek. I don't have to tell you their reason for joining with those tribes."

"You're saying they know they can depend upon Red Cloud to fight all attempts at penetration of his land."

"That's what I'm saying, sir. And you can depend on it, Red Cloud is not an ignorant savage."

"The road must be fortified, Captain." His dark visage unyielding, General Dodge added tightly, "Since you are so averse to the course of action to which I am committed, I would like to hear the alternative plan of action you would suggest."

William paused in response. The discussion into which he had entered with the general had been entirely unexpected.

"Sir, I have never gone so far in my mind as to formulate a plan for accomplishing the civilization of our western frontier."

General Dodge shook his head with sudden impatience.

"Come, come, now, Captain. You must have thought of a general manner in which such a penetration of Indian territory might be accomplished."

"Sir, I can only recommend that you send men who are well acquainted with the Indians to negotiate honestly with them, men who respect them and are respected by them so that the credibility of your word and your forces might be strengthened. I don't think that General Carrington or his officers and men fall into that category. To my knowledge, they are experienced only in fighting on the battlefields of the South."

"There *are* no such men I might send as an established force that is also capable of doing the job I need done!"

"Then use Indian agents, sir, men who will know how to talk to these Indians, to command their respect."

"Men like who? Like you?"

"Sir, I would be happy to assist in such an endeavor, but I don't feel myself fully qualified to—"

"Then who, man, *who?* Time is growing short, Captain. Comes the spring, these men are going to be on their way, and I need some assurance that they will not be betrayed by their ignorance of the enemy they will face."

"Agent Colley, sir. He is a dependable man. And Major Wynkoop."

"And yourself?"

William's hesitation was obvious. He had no desire to leave the East so soon. He had other plans.

"Well, Captain?"

"Sir, if you think I would be valuable in assisting Major Wynkoop or Agent Colley . . ."

"I think the more appropriate question would be, 'Do *you* think you would be valuable in assisting Major Wynkoop and Agent Colley?'"

William took a deep, solemn breath.

"Yes, I do, General."

"It's settled then. You will leave as soon as possible to return to Fort Lyon. You will settle your affairs there. Major Wynkoop has recently been assigned as agent for the

Cheyenne and Arapaho, and I will expect you to proceed with Major Wynkoop in advance of the contingent which will be sent out in the spring."

"Immediately, sir?"

General Dodge appeared to be startled by the unexpected question.

"Am I to understand that you consider some personal commitment more important than the welfare of your country, Captain?"

"No, sir."

"I'll give you a few days, Captain. But then you'll report back to Fort Lyon and await your final orders there."

"A few days will not be—"

"A few days, Captain. You have much strategy to plan and much ground to cover before spring." Rising to his feet, General Dodge walked around his desk. He extended his hand roughly in William's direction as William, too, rose.

"Captain Potter, I do not think this will be our last interview. You may tell Major Wynkoop for me that I will expect him to keep me informed as to the strategy you and he will develop in handling our 'native people.'" General Dodge paused, his dark brows again drawing together in sober consideration. "It was an education speaking to you, Captain. In all honesty, I cannot say you have convinced me to reverse any of the judgments I have already made. However, you force me to concede that there is another fully conscientious point of view, and that there is a need for the two perspectives to coexist in settling our new frontier. I will expect that you and Major Wynkoop will exert a superior effort to perform your jobs well, and I can only hope that your influence will be felt in the Indian community. I promise you all the support I can afford to give you, and though I have not accepted your theories, I will tell you, you have started me thinking. You will hear from me again."

"Yes, sir. Thank you, sir."

Dismissed, William turned abruptly and walked to the door. He was walking down the high-vaulted hallway of the impressive building when he realized he could not be certain his interview with the general had had a modicum of success.

Oh, yes, General Dodge had listened to him, but had the general truly heard him? Well, time would tell.

William frowned in helpless resignation. His orders would take him far from this part of the country where the girl to whom he had committed his heart resided. And time would put to a severe test the softly whispered words that rang in his ears: *I won't forget you, William. I could never forget you.*

William pushed open the heavy outer door of the great stone building and stepped out into the fresh November air once more. His thoughts a tangle from which there was little relief, William started briskly down the stone staircase. It appeared his future had once again. been taken out of his hands. But he was determined that this frustrating situation would not last long.

The hunting party traveled in silence. It was not a silence demanded by fear, but by the nature of the hunt. The air was cold and clear, the sun shining brilliantly on the small party having little effect on the biting chill. But Black Wolf was indifferent to the weather as he breathed deeply and pulled himself proudly erect beneath his heavy winter robe.

The soldiers had been driven from their land, and peace temporarily reigned within their camp. His people were jubilant, but in his heart, Black Wolf did not share their joy. He knew the white man well. Greed had driven the white man to trespass on their land, and greed would bring him back. He knew their victory was temporary, that the same battles would have to be fought again and again if his people wished to hold the land which gave them life.

Black Wolf turned his eyes toward the mountains the white man called the Big Horn. The sun shone with particular radiance on the snow-covered slopes of the soaring peaks before him, blending them so finely with the clouds as to leave him in doubt where one ended and the other began. Directly in front of him, four majestic spires reached to the endless sky above him; and beyond, outlined faintly in the distance, loomed the consolation of the sacred hills. The purity of the day was so precise that Black Wolf strained his eyes, certain he could see the glory of the eagles which soared amid the towering peaks.

In the year which had passed, Black Wolf had changed much. Adversity and his close encounter with death had served him well. He was certain it had been the rage within him that had refused to allow him to perish on the prairie when he had been sorely wounded by the white man and left to die. Had he not been determined that he would not succumb to the trooper's bullet, he was certain his flesh would have been eaten by wolves and his bones would now lie beneath the snow which covered the land of his people. Instead, he had survived.

Bitter memories of pain-filled days seemingly without end, during which his greatest battle was to breathe his next breath, returned vividly to his mind. It was during those many silent hours that he had searched in his mind in an attempt to understand the reasoning behind all which had progressed. But the mystery had remained until he had once again become well and had sought to return to his people at their camp at Sand Creek.

Then the pain of the horror he had witnessed returned, and Black Wolf attempted to shut out the remembered faces of the dead. Walking Woman, Young Hawk, Owl Woman, White Bull, Silent Woman—the countless, faceless bodies which had littered the bloodstained ground. It had been then that Black Wolf had realized the reason he had been spared. He had been brought close to death so that he might stare into its face and conquer fear. Step by step the Great Power had led him to the destiny for which he had been born. He would lead his people, ultimately give his life, if need be, in the war against the white man.

Black Wolf shot a quick glance toward Broken Hand who was leading their small party. Broken Hand led him now, but that situation would soon change. When the snows left the ground and the white man again attempted to take their land, he would follow Broken Hand no longer. A war chief in his own right, he would lead his warriors to fight at Broken Hand's side, and together they would avenge the blood which had been spilled into the frozen ground of Sand

Creek. He would purge the horror-filled memories from his mind by shedding the blood of those who had betrayed his people.

But another memory prevailed, despite his most rigorous attempts to dispel it. He no longer wore on his finger the crudely carved white band which had committed him to one not of his people. He could not remember when he had cast it from his hand and thrown it to the wind, but at that moment he had cast Fire Spirit from his heart as well. The white man was his enemy, and he would not allow himself to indulge in allegiance to anyone of that tainted blood.

But memory prevailed. . . .

Putting aside his somber thoughts, Black Wolf lifted his head, his eyes moving to Broken Hand who motioned his men forward. Responding to the command, Black Wolf spurred his horse to Broken Hand's side, his eyes touching on the valley below them where a great herd of buffalo grazed in silent peace. Buffalo . . . revered by his people and slaughtered into nonexistence in the south by the white man, just as the white man had slaughtered his people . . .

Yes, memory prevailed. . . . It would keep fresh in his mind the need for revenge which burned hot and deep inside him. It would give impetus to days in which the strange emptiness inside him grew. It would give his life purpose, and for that purpose he would live.

At a signal from Broken Hand, Black Wolf drew his gun and posed, ready for the noble kill. It had become his life. . . .

Chapter XX

1867

Lydia surveyed the room with a critical eye, appraising the polished hardwood floor from which the elegant carpeting had been removed. Yes, perfect. . . . It was gleaming, but not slick to the point where it would be dangerous underfoot to the guests who would later dance upon it. She surveyed the sumptuous buffet table, taking into account the intricate patterns in which the delicacies were being placed. Then she shot a quick glance toward the table in the corner on which rested a crystal bowl filled with cook's special punch. She was certain that table in particular would be very faithfully attended. There would be champagne, other wines, and all manner of hard liquors for those who were so inclined. And at this point in time, in the kitchen, cook was putting the final touches on the towering birthday cake which would be served with a flourish at an appointed hour midway through the gala birthday party which was soon to begin.

Her satisfaction complete, Lydia touched a delicate hand to her fashionable coiffure. Aware that she looked more than presentable, she had truly given little thought to her appearance. For that reason she was not fully cognizant of the lovely, extremely delicate image she presented in her voluminous gown of ecru silk. She had paid scant attention to the manner in which the graceful neckline edged her narrow shoulders, exposing the graceful column of her

336

throat; the way the bodice of the garment hugged her slender proportions, cupping her small, rounded breasts and accenting her narrow waist. She was totally unaware that the sweep of the glimmering silk, its contrast against her smooth, unlined skin, added a new facet to a beauty which appeared only to be approaching its prime.

Instead, Lydia's mind darted to her lovely daughter who was at that moment upstairs in her room, dressing for her seventeenth birthday party. Seventeen! Lydia's eyes followed the paths of the servants as they saw to the last-minute details which were transforming the front and back parlors into a ballroom of startling beauty. But Lydia's mind followed a far different track than the narrow one in which they walked.

Seventeen! Faith was seventeen, marvelously beautiful, and this was to be her night. Lydia's elation dimmed momentarily with a sober thought. There had been a time when she had thought neither of them would see this day, most especially under the circumstances in which it was being celebrated. Lydia flicked her eyes momentarily closed against the assault of memory. No, this was not a time to look to the past. It was a night to look to the future—Faith's future—and she . . .

Her eyes darting to the staircase behind her as a familiar voice sounded in the upstairs hallway, Lydia smiled. Wally . . . His booming voice could be heard throughout the house when he was in a good mood. And he was certainly in a good mood this night. She had barely escaped his amorous intent in their room only a short half-hour before.

Aware of the sudden flush suffusing her face, Lydia turned toward the vase in the corner of the room and carefully arranged the roses until her flesh had cooled. Yes, Wally had become a wealthy man of renown in financial circles. His business acumen was unchallenged, his advice avidly sought. In the past few years he had risen from the position of eastern representative of Tin Pan Mining, to the position of president of the company. Of course, she was well aware that the success of Wally's mine had much to do with his advancement, but it was his own ability which had secured him the respect he now enjoyed.

As for Wally himself . . . The heated flush, only recently abated, rose again to her cheeks, and Lydia moved to the next flower-filled vase. No, Wally had not changed. He was still warm-hearted and loving. His pride in Faith was a living, palpable presence, and his love for her was fathomless. Lydia remembered the previous night, spent in his arms. He had allowed her little respite from his affections, and she had finally protested his avid love-making, pleading exhaustion. His smiling retort had been purred through gently caressing lips.

"We'll sleep late tomorrow morning, darling. I promise you, it will be worth the time involved."

And it had. But in the back of her mind, a relentless, sobering thought nagged. The preceding day, Wally had carefully folded and put aside a newspaper with headlines that stated Indian depredations were continuing in the West, despite intense efforts by the government to reduce them. She had been unable to ignore the blaring print and had picked up the paper to read the biased, uninformed article. Her protest had been instinctive and the resulting exchange between Wally and herself had been unexpectedly heated. Broken Hand's name had not passed between them, but it had lain on the air, an unspoken barrier between them. She had been well aware that Faith had sensed the situation, and she had regretted the effect of their exchange upon her high spirits.

Later at the theater, Faith had been joined by several eager swains in their box, leaving Wally free to devote his attention to her. His attention had been strict, unswerving, and when they had retired to their room that night, he had made love to her with reckless abandon. The new day had dawned with no lessening of his avid adoration. She was actually unsure that . . .

A warm hand slipping around her waist from the rear jerked Lydia from her thoughts with a gasp. Turning, she looked into Wally's pale-eyed lascivious gaze as he pulled her back against the hard wall of his body.

"So you thought you could sneak out on me while I was shaving . . ."

Her eyes shifting to the servants executing their varied chores with single-minded attention, Lydia uttered a low protest.

"Wally, please . . ."

Removing his hand as it crept to the side of her breast, she shook her head. "I did not try to escape you."

"What would you call it then, making sure you were suitably hooked into that alluring garment and ready to leave the room before I was adequately dressed to pursue you?"

"Wally . . ."

His eyes darting to the buffet table, Wally realized his behavior was finally beginning to arouse the interest of the young Irish girl who was the newest addition to their staff, and he stepped back. Lydia's low sigh of relief was premature for he announced in an overly loud voice, "I have a matter of considerable importance to discuss with you before our guests arrive, Lydia." Firmly taking her arm, he ushered her before him. "If you will accompany me into the study, please."

Her patience short, Lydia preceded Wally out of the dining room, across the foyer, and into the study at the base of the staircase. Turning as the door closed behind her husband, she saw the twitch of his broad smile as he turned the lock and with a great flourish, dropped the key into the breast pocket of his jacket.

In a movement too quick for Lydia to anticipate, Wally then reached out and snatched her into his arms. His low laugh was cut short as his mouth closed over hers. He was kissing her deeply, thoroughly, when the mood of his teasing kiss gradually began to change. Suddenly a deep, throbbing passion was being transmitted by him, and Lydia felt herself absorbed by the heat of its assault. Wally's hands moved over her back in great, widening circles, seeking. His palms stroked the sides of her breasts, attempting to cup the delicate mounds. Frustrated by the garment which hindered

339

him, Wally tore his mouth from hers, abruptly drawing back to glance hotly into her silver-eyed gaze. His mouth swooped down over hers once more and Lydia was suddenly swept away from the small, darkened room into the ecstasy of Wally's loving ministrations.

Uncertain of the actual moment when her gown fell from her shoulders, Lydia was barely aware that Wally had lifted her free of its swirling folds as his mouth continued to devour hers, as his hands moved with growing fervor against her skin. She felt the brush of the rug against the bared flesh of her back, moved to accommodate Wally's ministrations as he stripped away the last of her lacy undergarments, shivered as he pressed his mouth against the warm mound of her passion. His tongue was caressing the delicate slit, sending her higher and higher into the spehre of mindless emotions into which his passion had thrust her. Cupping her buttocks with his hands, he raised her to his consuming quest.

He was drawing deeply from the font of her desire when Lydia's control began to slip away. Moaning his name, she pushed at his head, her fingers twisting in an unruly mass of red hair as the aching need inside her grew. Abruptly, she was drawing him closer, tighter to her, opening herself completely to his loving hunger. Her slender body heaved in quaking spasms. She was giving to him, her body responding in sweet, shuddering convulsions to the wonder of his loving assault. Her eyes weakly slitted as the last of her impassioned quivering ceased, Lydia watched as Wally drew deeply of her loving tribute, his glance tangled tightly with her own.

Slowly drawing back from her body, Wally held her gaze fast as he drew himself to his feet. Standing over her, aware that she was helpless due to the temporary weakness of spent emotions, Wally slowly undressed and came to lie on the rug beside her. Abruptly moving her atop him, he slid himself inside her in a subtle movement, his expression changing only slightly as she released a short, responsive gasp.

Lydia closed her eyes against the sensations assailing her. Oh, God, it felt so good with Wally inside her. She shifted her body, felt his burgeoning member penetrate more deeply, and she drew in a deep, shattering gasp. His eyes intent on her face, Wally raised her with the swelling of his love again and again, his lips parting with impassioned breaths as her beautiful face reflected the myriad emotions assaulting her. They were moving together, riding the waves of passion, rising on their swells, higher . . . higher. Then, abruptly, they were falling, plunging, swirling in the undertow of vibrant emotions until they were still once more.

Lydia's fragile length was stretched out atop his, and Wally pulled her closer still. He had again won the conquest of Lydia's emotions. It was a battle which he raged lovingly, but each victory was temporary for his violent jealousy was never dormant. He could not ask, but he wanted to hear Lydia say that she loved him more than she had ever loved anyone—anyone.

Faith was seventeen . . . a woman. She would soon leave them for a life of her own. Then Lydia would no longer be bound to him by convention or by the need to maintain a home for their daughter, but only by the strength of the emotions which they shared. Wally pulled Lydia closer still. The secret that he harbored inside him burned hotly into his brain.

Broken Hand . . . if she knew Broken Hand was not dead . . . If she read the reports from the mine and the letters accompanying them, she would learn that Broken Hand had left the area of Fort Lyon to wage war in the great delta of the Platte. He had not told Lydia that her vision, which was doubtless still clear in her mind, had gone astray—that Broken Hand had not been killed at Sand Creek as originally reported, but was alive and thriving. And he would not tell her that deep in his heart he cherished a desire to see the stoic savage dead for the part of Lydia he had stolen, the part which would never be returned to him. Instead, he had endeavored to bind her to him with the ties of his unfailing passion, his undying need for her. He knew he would never . . .

At a soft knock on the door, Lydia's head snapped up. Her cheeks flushed hotly when Wally refused to release her, forcing her to remain within the circle of his intimate embrace.

"Yes, what is it?"

"Mrs. Durham, the preparations have been completed, if you would like to check them before the guests arrive. . . ."

"Yes . . . yes, Maida. Mr. Durham and I will check everything in a few moments."

Unable to suppress his smile as Lydia pushed herself free of his binding embrace and rose to scramble for her dress, Wally got up and stood beside her. Her small frown touched his heart as she turned back helplesly in his direction.

"Oh, Wally, I was completely dressed. How will I explain . . . ?"

Wally's short, lingering kiss preceded his succinct response.

. "Don't explain."

Carefully helping her into her discarded gown, Wally then dressed once more. They were walking silently up the staircase toward their room when Maida's voice sounded hesitantly from behind them.

"Mrs. Durham . . . the table . . ."

Shooting her husband a short, harried look, Lydia responded, "In a few minutes, Maida."

Wally's eyes fastened intently on her face as they reached the top step and turned toward their room, and he whispered against her ear.

"Was it worth it, darling?"

All signs of her momentary embarrassment now gone from her gaze, Lydia looked silently into Wally's eyes. Her answer was in the glow in her own, and Wally pulled her close against his side.

The door to the room beside hers clicked closed, and Faith listened in surprise. Yes, it was Mama and Papa returning to their room. She smiled. Of course, Mama had been dressed so early. She probably wanted to freshen her appearance before the guests arrived. Bending down to slip a delicate foot into her satin slipper, Faith stood up and took a deep

342

breath. Dressed at last!

Taking a moment to adjust her gown, Faith turned toward Nellie who was attempting to bring the room back to a semblance of order.

"Well, how do I look, Nellie?"

Nellie turned in her direction, and Faith's smile broadened at the girl's widened eyes.

"Beautiful, ma'am. More beautiful than anybody I've ever seen."

Faith laughed aloud.

"Nellie, you are too generous."

"No, ma'am. I'm honest."

Closing the distance between them in a few steps, Faith gave the sober-faced girl a short hug. Laughing again as Nellie flushed brightly, Faith did not bother to turn back to her mirror. She had seen all she wanted to see. If she were to be honest, she would admit that Nellie was partially correct. She was certain she was wearing the most beautiful dress ever created. Madame LeClaire had outdone herself. Declaring that blue was definitely Faith's color, the couturière had designed a dress of a shimmering ice blue, with an overskirt of a delicate white lace. The off-the-shoulder gown fitted smoothly against the trim line of Faith's torso, then flowed voluminously from a tight, pointed waist to the tips of her shoes in layer upon layer of filmy lace and ruffled blue taffeta.

Quite against her mother's wishes, Faith had spurned the fashionable hairstyle of the day, finding the tightly combed and bound coiffures too restricting. Instead, she had simply swept her gleaming red-gold curls behind her ears, secured them with combs, and allowed them to fall in riotous disarray onto her slender, white shoulders.

Faith's smile broadened. She made few concessions to styles which did not suit her, and she knew it mattered little in what manner she dressed her hair. It had become increasingly obvious to her of late that no matter how her curls bounced or flew in the wind, no matter how her clothing was draped, a persistent crowd of admirers followed her. She supposed they were sincere in their outspoken admiration, but in truth, she did not consider herself a true beauty. In her opinion her coloring was too flamboyant—her hair too brilliant in its red-gold color, her eyes too blue for subtlety, the creamy white of her skin too pale. In truth, she considered her mother the true beauty in the family, preferring Lydia's fragile slenderness to her own well-endowed stature, the older woman's satin black hair, and her pale gray eyes flecked with green and silver to her own.

But she had come to the conclusion that there was no comprehending taste. She had at first found the unexpected attention she was receiving extremely annoying. She had not enjoyed being fondled over and petted like some extravagantly spoiled house cat. And she found the heated stares which followed her bothersome, but if she were to be completely honest, she would have to admit that she had grown to enjoy the attention she drew from the young, available members of her social set.

Faith's smile dimmed. If she were to be totally honest with herself, she would also have to admit the distinct possibility that no small part of her appeal to the opposite sex could be attributed to her father's considerable fortune.

Faith walked slowly toward the dresser, her expression once again pensive. She had not forgotten that the same social set which now welcomed them had refused them recognition before Papa's pockets had become so attractively lined with Tin Pan Mining gold. Standing before her dresser at last, Faith reached for her jewel box and lifted the lid. She poked at the casually stored collection of expensive jewelry, searching for the simple strand of pearls Papa had given her on her sixteenth birthday. Yes . . . and matching earbobs. She had found the one, but where was the other?

She was digging to the bottom of the case, her hand moving against the soft, velvet lining, when her fingertips made contact with the simple carved band pushed into the corner. Her heart began to pound rapidly. She hesitated, a host of memories returning. Over and over again Faith had pondered the reason why, despite the passage of over three years, memories of her Cheyenne days continued to retain such a strong hold on her mind. In the dark of countless nights, she had finally become convinced that time and distance had added a gloss to those days far beyond the bounds of reality. Yes . . . memory had all but erased those first days spent in fear and despair. It had dimmed the sorrow she had felt upon thinking her father dead, in being estranged from her mother, and in knowing that Mama lived with and loved one of the savages who had captured them. It had also dimmed the memory of the instant animosity which had flared each time Black Wolf had ordered her about so gruffly.

Instead, memory had stressed the kindness shown to her by Walking Woman, and had burned deeply into her mind the abrupt change which had come about between Black Wolf and herself during that last month in camp. She remembered so vividly the joys Black Wolf and she had shared, that no manner of thoroughbred or well-trained mount allowed her the exhilaration she had experienced in riding on an Indian pony over the vast, sunlit prairie. And no cultured, well-educated swain elicited a response that held a candle to the shuddering feeling which had enveloped the fourteen-year-old she had been when Black Wolf had held her in his arms.

Another unvoiced question plagued her. Why was it that in the grandeur of her home, amid the love and attention of family and friends, she had never truly matched the peace of spirit, the quiet happiness, she had found in lying quietly beside an Indian youth on the sun-swept prairie, speaking intimately of their lives. No pretense . . . no sham. Nothing but truth and honesty between them. Dark eyes looking into hers with a warmth that stirred her even in memory . . . chiseled features carefully controlled . . . warm, eager lips which spoke silent volumes as they moved hungrily against hers.

Faith slipped the rough, carved band onto her finger. She smiled as it remained securely fixed in place. She had been a child when Black Wolf had put the ring on her finger, but it fit her as well now as it had then.

Her hand closed tightly over the simple carved band and a familiar ache came alive inside her. With great determination she shut away the memory of Black Wolf's bloodstained body. No, she would not allow that last memory to steal the joy from her heart. In all the years since, she had attempted to share her grief with no one. Mama had been too involved in avoiding her own memories, and she had found that she could not add to the shadows which had haunted Papa's eyes. Her newfound friends were all so giddy and thoughtless. Without the slightest trace of conceit, she had realized from the outset that she was different in many ways from the spoiled, vain, careless children who passed for young women in her social set. No, there was no one who truly understood . . . except William.

But William was so far away. She had seen him only twice since their first separation. Each time his feelings for her had been stronger, the strain of his leaving more intense. He had told her that he would not leave her a third time, when he next visited, he expected her to return with him as his wife. Faith had not responded to his low declaration, for she knew, deep inside, that nothing but a memory stood between her and William.

William's letters had been regular and informative. He had described his work with Major Wynkoop as an agent for the Cheyenne and Arapaho. He had stated that he was soon to be sent off on his own to the Powder River Country, where Red Cloud led a force of Sioux, Cheyenne, and Arapaho hostiles in the war against the white man. But he had also made her a solemn promise: he would soon return.

Faith's heart jumped to an escalated beat. She was uncertain whether she was truly ready for William's return. She did not think she was ready to . . .

At a knock on her bedroom door, Faith started and turned toward the sound. Her spoken response brought Mama and Papa into the room. The glow in her father's eyes returned the smile to Faith's lips, and her mother's proud smile brought the heat of tears to her brilliant eyes.

Within seconds Papa was at her side, his strong arms enveloping her in a breathtaking hug.

"Faith, darling girl, you are beautiful. A very happy birthday to you."

When he released her, Faith turned to accept her mother's warm embrace.

Finally drawing back, Lydia asked, "Are you ready to go down now, darling?"

Taking a moment to affix the remaining earbob, Faith nodded.

"Yes, Mama."

Situating himself between them with great pride, Wally offered each an arm. His chest swelled broadly as his two beautiful women slipped their arms under his. Within moments they were moving formally down the broad staircase toward the living room, and Faith bit back her heated, unexplained tears.

Black Wolf squinted down upon the dusty plain, his eyes following the line of the white man's wagons as they made their way steadily along the winding trail. From his vantage point high on a hill above them, he viewed the scene unfolding, his eyes darting toward Fort Laramie in the distance. With deep satisfaction he realized the train would soon come into view of the guards there. Yes, his people need maintain patience for another few sundowns, and then another victory would be theirs.

Black Wolf did not need to look behind him to survey the faces of the warriors who followed him. He did not need to read the lust for vengeance, the eagerness to rid his land of the white trespassers who violated it, which were written in their eyes. The same lust filled his heart, the same eagerness gave purpose to his life. It was the driving force which had lent him strength in the years since his people had joined with Red Cloud to wage their war against the white man.

And Black Wolf did not need to observe his physical reflection to see the changes that had come to pass within and without him during his years with Red Cloud. He was aware that little semblance of the youth he had been now remained. All trace of boyish softness had left his heart, and his countenance as well. His dark eyes, always keen and appraising, had grown cold and hard. The chiseled planes of

347

his face had thinned and sharpened into the countenance of the hardened warrior. The slenderness of youth had left his body. In its place was the strength and breadth of limb and chest which testified to his emergence into manhood. His physique surpassed even Broken Hand's in both height and muscular tone. He was content with this physical change. It reflected courage and strength which had been tested severely in the past years, and had not been found wanting. It reflected the respect with which he was held in his own camp and in that of the Arapaho and Sioux as well.

Black Wolf moved his gaze down the line of wagons snaking along the trail, a smile touching the hard line of his lips. Well over the number of thirty, the civilian train was a tempting sight. The horses and mules were many, and the plunder which the train would bring to their camp would be great. His mirthless smile broadened. He was well aware of the military law now being enforced on this trail. All civilian trains in which the number of men was less than thirty were being detained at Fort McPherson because of the threat of attack. Escorts of a like number of soldiers were being furnished should such a threat seem imminent.

A low, hard laugh escaped Black Wolf's lips. That was the reason for his presence on this hill and that of the warriors who followed him. They waited patiently to be seen. In being visible, they would force an escort to accompany the train when it left Fort Laramie. Then, when the train was a safe distance from the fort and their attack was made, their victory would be twofold. Their number would be over-powering and the wagon train would be theirs. Their capture of the wagon train would cause the loss of yet another troop of white soldiers. Such was the plan which had worked again and again against the white man. The efforts of Black Wolf's people had been long and patient in this regard, and they would continue until the government of the white man realized how costly in lives was the determination to maintain the forts which violated their land.

His squinting gaze narrowing even further, Black Wolf watched as a scramble of movement with the fort signified the sighting of the train. He waited with knowing patience until the sighting would have been reported to the commander. Shortly, he would allow himself and his men to be seen, and his plan would be in motion. From then on he would need nothing more than the patience which his people had employed to their advantage in the past. Patience and determination . . . they had been rewarding. Their rewards had filled his days, and if his nights were not yet free of memory, he had not lost the will to, one day, gain that freedom as well.

His lips moving into a firm line, Black Wolf took a deep breath. The movement of his small band would be subtle, not so noticeable as to cause suspicion of their plan. Yes, it was time for them to move into sight.

Silently raising his hand, Black Wolf signaled his men forward.

William withdrew his handkerchief. Carefully lifting his hat, he wiped at the beads of perspiration which marked his sunburned brow. Replacing his hat once more, he took a deep, frustrated breath and neatly refolded his handkerchief. He returned it to his pocket, using the time to strengthen his hold on his rapidly waning control. Damn! Another emigrant train was approaching the fort!

Finally turning to the tight-lipped commander of Fort Laramie who stood beside him, he spoke in a lowered tone.

"Damn it all, is there no end to these fool trains? Does the thought of gold blind these men to the realization that they place their families' lives, as well as their own, in very real danger by entering the Powder River country while the Indians are still hostile?"

"William, I should have thought you understood by now that the thought of gold drives some men beyond common sense."

Straightening his back with true agitation, Governor Palmer gritted his teeth. His eyes followed the cloud of dust churning up from the wheels of the approaching wagon train as he continued in the same low tone. "Damned if I know how they made it this far with the trail they're leaving behind them. Maybe Red Cloud wants to tease us with their arrival so we can send out another escort to be set upon like all the others."

Exasperation was evident on the governor's bearded face, and William frowned. He was beginning to believe his presence here at Fort Laramie was a total waste of time. Had it not been for the fact that Major Wynkoop, after months of frustration, had finally settled the Southern Cheyenne and Arapho into relative peace, he truly would not have accepted his new assignment to the Powder River Country.

Red Cloud . . . The Indian warrior was doubtlessly a brilliant strategist, and he was certainly bitterly distrusting of the white man. Not that it was difficult to understand the reason for Red Cloud's reluctance to sign a peace treaty with the white man who had violated every other negotiated pact he had ever made with the Indian, but surely the chief saw the direction in which things were heading. The difficulties of the year before had not stopped the construction of Fort Reno, Fort Kearny, and Fort Smith along the Bozeman Trail. The construction of those three forts had fortified the area with approximately a thousand men. Of course, the price paid in lives had been expensive, and now the situation did not seem to be in the army's favor.

William frowned. It was obvious that the multitudinous troops sent with the idea of an expedition against the Sioux in mind had been ineffective. Mainly infantry, they were unable to pursue the well-mounted Indian forces which appeared in the most unexpected places and were off as soon as their mischief had been perpetrated. The damage done to property had been severe. The Powder River country was again cut off from communication with the East by telegraph, while overland wagon trains and even railroad trains were interrupted. It was expected that soon the stage lines would refuse to carry passengers, and citizen trains would be forbidden to travel the trail. That time could not come soon enough for him.

William shrugged. Yes, he would be glad to see the last of the citizen trains in this area of the country for a while. It was a daily struggle just to keep the road open to Fort Smith, much less to protect the civilian trains traveling through.

"Well, if all goes the way things are pointing this year, William, we may yet have peace."

His eyes snapping toward Governor Palmer, William suppressed his surprise.

"Meaning?"

"Meaning, I know about the proposal in Congress to send a delegation straight from Washington to negotiate a peace on the Platte."

"That information was supposed to be confidential, Governor."

"Not confidential from me."

William suppressed his reaction. If Governor Palmer knew, perhaps his own expected orders to return to Washington to brief the proposed commission would not come. That would mean that he would not have an opportunity to go to New York and see . . .

"You surprise me, William. I had thought that the possibility of a strongly negotiated peace would please you."

William forced a smile.

"It does, Governor."

"I wouldn't guess it by the look on your face."

"I . . . I'm surprised, that's all. I didn't realize you had been informed of the proposed plans for a treaty."

"You must have guessed the reason why I've been notified."

William hesitated.

"That's right, William. The commission has requested that I return to speak to them about the Indian question."

"Sir, General Dodge told me expressly that he wanted my input to—"

"You are no longer functioning under General Dodge's orders. The commander of the Department of the Platte is General Augru, and he has already issued his request for my testimony."

"Sir . . ."

"I'm sorry, William." His lined face sincere, Governor Palmer shook his head. "I hadn't realized you were so intent upon returning to Washington this spring. If I had, I certainly would have—"

"You misunderstand me, Governor." Pausing, William gave a short shrug. "My disappointment doesn't stem from a desire to engratiate myself with the hierarchy of command. I'm quite satisfied with the progress of my career in this portion of the country, and the position assigned to me, much as I wish I could be more productive at the present time. My reason for wanting to return to Washington is a personal one."

Momentarily startled, Governor Palmer gave a small laugh.

"A woman? I hadn't realized you harbored tender feelings for a woman back East, William. You've not been back more than twice in the last three years if I don't miss my guess."

"Three times, sir. I had expected this visit would eliminate the need for further travel back in that direction."

"Meaning?"

"Meaning I expected to bring the young lady back as my wife."

"William, I am sorry."

Pausing, his small eyes showing an unexpected twinkle, the governor leaned forward in a confidential manner. "I should hear within the fortnight whether I will be leaving as planned. I will be only too happy to take the young lady a message."

William shook his head.

"I think not, sir."

"This young woman . . . she wouldn't be the daughter of Senator Morris, by any chance? Seems to me I've heard talk . . ."

William blinked with surprise. He had seen Sally Anne Morris when he had made his obligatory report in Washington each time he had returned, but he had not realized rumors had started as a result of his visits to the Morris residence. William's mind inadvertently presented him with a picture of Sally Anne's pert face, blond curls, and appealing smile. He had attended a few parties at which he had spent considerable time in her company. She was a cheerful, pleasant girl, but he had never thought there might

352

be speculation about a more serious relationship between them. William gave a silent, rueful laugh. He supposed that was because he had never seen anyone at all but Faith from the first time he had looked at her. In any case, he was certain Sally Anne had no illusions about his intentions. She probably would be as startled as he if such idle speculation reached her ears.

"William, I seem to have struck you speechless."

"I . . . I think you have, Governor. But before this misconception goes any farther, let me respond clearly. No, sir, the lady to whom I referred is not Miss Morris."

"Really . . ."

"And that's all I am prepared to say, Governor."

The sound of a sudden alert at the corner of the stockade turned both men's attention in its direction. A shortly snapped command by the officer in charge sent two men to their horses to ride out of the gates at a rapid gallop.

"Lieutenant!"

Governor Palmer's short summons brought the young man to his side with a sharp salute.

"Sir."

"What is the problem?"

"Signs of movement in the hills to the west, sir. Possibly hostile. I've sent two men out to get a closer look."

"*Two* men, Lieutenant?"

"Sir, a closer look and arrangements for a signal which will bring our men forward to protect the approaching wagon train at a gallop. The train is so close to the fort now, I've only sent the men out as a precaution. Those savages wouldn't be stupid enough to attack when . . ."

Governor Palmer's stiff face reflected his dissatisfaction with the lieutenant's response.

"I want a troop ordered out now, Lieutenant . . . *now!* Those savages are not stupid, but likely to do the unexpected. *Now,* Lieutenant!"

An instant alert sounded, and William stepped back, watching solemnly as the wild scramble of men and horses formed into a mounted troop within a startlingly short period. His eyes darting to the approaching train which was just beginning to become clear to his eye, William drew back a step further. He watched in silence as the troop galloped through the gates, and he nodded in silent agreement with the governor's unhesitant precaution. Both men were correct: the lieutenant, in that the Indians would probably not attack a train so close to the fort; and the governor, in that Red Cloud's men could always be expected to do the unexpected. But even while he agreed with the governor's caution, he sincerely doubted the Indians would attack the train at this time. No, if they attacked at all, it would be when the train was out of sight of the fort and more vulnerable to a prolonged siege. The governor's precaution was fine, but William feared it would only put off the inevitable—the painful, unavoidable inevitable.

Watching as the mounted troop thundered down the trail, he strained his eyes unseeingly into the distance, his mind straying far from the momentary crisis.

Seventeen . . . Faith was seventeen. He needed to get back to New York this spring. Faith was too beautiful—too desirable. Were it not for the fact that his infrequent visits to New York in the past years had confirmed that her affection for him was undiminished, and that the distance between them had only strengthened his desire to make her his own, he supposed he would have abandoned the whole seemingly hopeless affair. But the women he had known in the years between had only confirmed his conviction that only Faith could fill his heart. It was his hope that she was as strongly convinced as he that they were meant for each other.

A familiar tension tightening the knots in his stomach, William felt panic assail him anew. But Faith was now seventeen, fully a woman. Letters would no longer suffice. He needed to see her, talk to her, touch her. For all he knew, she might even now be fighting some amorous young man's ardent embrace. Or worse yet, not fighting it at all. . . .

Annoyance creasing her brow, Faith struggled in Harvey Wilson's binding embrace. Her annoyance was directed at herself as well as at the persistent young bachelor who had danced her so dramatically out onto the terrace and swept her into his arms. Determinedly dodging his searching lips, Faith abruptly submitted to the surge of temper she had been attempting to restrain.

"Harvey . . . Damn it, Harvey, let me go!"

Her use of profanity accomplished what her ladylike struggles had not, and Harvey Wilson stood stock-still in surprise. Taking advantage of the opportunity afforded her, Faith attempted to take a step backward, only to come up against the trunk of the tree to which he had pinned her. In exasperation, she directed a short, hard shove to Harvey's chest and stepped out of his embrace as he fell backward a few steps in astonishment. She had almost managed to escape, when she felt his warm hand close once more on her arm. But this time the staying pressure was gentle as it turned her back to his hurt expression.

"Faith, please. I . . . I hadn't realized I was imposing myself upon you. I mean . . . I thought, well . . ."

"What exactly did you think, Harvey?" Her eyes cold as shards of blue ice, Faith took a deep, angry breath as she appraised the man standing before her. Handsome, witty Harvey Wilson—son of the financier Harrison Wilson, and heir to his shipping fortune . . . Oh, yes, the fellow was considered an excellent catch. He had been pursuing her avidly for the past six months, appearing everywhere she did, gravitating to her side like a pin to a magnet. Marilee Stern was wild for him, but it was just her luck that Harvey wouldn't give Marilee a second glance. He had made it plain to everyone that he preferred Faith over all the other eligible young women in their set. She supposed she should be flattered. He was a young man who had everything—looks, charm, money—everything but common sense! Damn, couldn't he see that she could not stand him?

Still maintaining his grip on her arm, Harvey suddenly shook his head.

"I . . . I thought you realized how I feel about you, Faith. I've done everything but string up a sign, saying that I—"

The unexpected pain obvious in Harvey's expression struck a chord of unexpected remorse inside Faith. She was

355

being grossly unfair. It was not Harvey's fault that she did not return his feelings.

Reaching up spontaneously to cover Harvey's lips with her hand, Faith halted his intended declaration. No, she did not want him to suffer the final humiliation of complete rejection. Oh, why was it that Harvey could not see, that all of them—Bigelow Carter, Jonathan Greer, Robert Collingsford, Peter St. John, and the very stuffy Thomas Colby III—could not see, that she was interested in none of them? They were pleasant enough, but each and every one of them was so very . . . boring. Not a one of them was interested in anything more vital than the rise and fall of their company stock, or the outcome of a race between this "blooded stallion" or another. She was so tired of flattery and cautiously phrased sexual innuendo. In truth, she truly felt not a one of them was capable of an intelligent conversation. Or was it that they considered *her* to be the one who was incapable?

In any case, Harvey had been a devoted admirer, and despite her annoyance at his most recent amorous attentions, she did not want to hurt him. Her gaze still holding him silent, Faith drew her hand back from Harvey's lips.

"No, Harvey, please." The frost in her eyes melting to a more familiar softness, Faith offered a tentative smile. "You flatter me with your attentions, Harvey. You are so handsome, and so very charming."

She hesitated. She was gaining courage as the hurt in Harvey's eyes dimmed. His pleasant mouth was curving into a smile, and she took a deep firm breath.

"But the truth is, I . . . I've decided not to make any decisions about my future right now. There are so many things I've not yet done, so many places to see. Mother and I—"

Snatching upon her flimsy excuse, Harvey's grip lessened, and his classically handsome face began to relax into a smile.

"Are you telling me that you intend to take an extended tour—of Europe—and that is the reason you wish to make no commitment at this time? If that is the case, Faith, I will tell you right now that I would gladly wait."

356

"No, that's not exactly what I was trying to say, Harvey." Annoyance again nudged Faith. How could this fellow be so dense? He was going to force her to hurt him badly.

"What I was trying to say is that I . . . I've given my word to Mama and Papa that I'll not make commitments of any kind until my eighteenth year. Mama and Papa feel the seventeenth year is the time for a young woman to enjoy her youth, and the eighteenth year is the time she should start thinking of her future."

Harvey's narrow brows rose in surprise. He shook his head.

"I've not heard that outlook expressed before." His pale eyes took on a somewhat annoyed squint. "Surely your parents wouldn't be rigidly opposed to—"

"I don't intend to press them, Harvey." Gritting her teeth against the web of lies which grew more complicated each moment, Faith was beginning to regret she had not been brutally frank from the outset. As it was, she was working herself in deeper and deeper with each moment. "Since I am their only child, I would not disappoint them in that way. After all, what is a year out of a lifetime if it makes your parents happy?"

"A year is a very long time, Faith." Harvey's smooth hand began a stroking motion on her arm, and he made an attempt to draw her close once more.

"No, Harvey." Firmly removing his hand, Faith made a quick turn to stand at his side. She slipped her hand under his arm and flashed him a sweet smile. "Please, I'd prefer not to discuss the matter any further right now. I've been away from the party long enough. I wouldn't want my guests to think I had deserted them."

His reticence melting under the warmth of her smile, Harvey hesitated briefly as he moved to cover her hand with his.

"A year, Faith? But you will remember when that year is up that I have spoken to you . . . that I love—"

Urging him forward with great resolution, Faith whispered in a quiet tone, "Yes, of course, Harvey. How could I possibly forget?"

They were stepping back into the converted ballroom when the music from the ensemble tucked into the small anteroom beyond it again filled the air. Unexpectedly snatched from Harvey's arms, Faith smiled up into Walter Pierce's wide grin.

"You promised this next dance to me, Faith."

"Oh, yes, of course, Walter."

Flashing Harvey a smile, Faith allowed Walter to sweep her out onto the floor. Purposely brightening her smile as she swept past her parents who stood nearby, Faith turned to see Marilee heading straight in Harvey's direction. Suppressing a desire to cheer, she muttered under her breath.

"That's right, Marilee, go and get him."

"Did you say something, Faith?"

Her eyes snapping back to her partner's perspiring face, Faith shook her head, her brilliant eyes wide with innocence.

"No, I didn't say a thing, Walter."

"Oh, I could've sworn you . . ."

But Faith was no longer listening to Walter Pierce's droning response. His sweeping step had taken her past her parents once more to reveal the unexpected presence of Oliver Willis, her father's lawyer. Intense as always, the short, balding man's head gleamed with perspiration as his hands moved in brief, anxious gestures. The frivolity of the party was instantly swept from Faith's mind by the concern which stiffened her father's face. Mama's stance was also tense. Appearing to find the chatter around him an annoyance, Papa took the flustered barrister's arm. After a brief exchange of words between Mama and Papa, Mama looked after Papa as he ushered Oliver Willis politely toward the doorway to the foyer. Her eyes focused in that direction despite the sweeping revolutions of Walter's proficient waltz, Faith was able to see the last flash of her father's well-tailored back as he closed the door to the den behind him.

Excusing herself the moment the waltz ended, Faith managed to divert a deluge of polite invitations to dance, feigning a headache or sore feet or acute stomach distress. Vaguely conscious of the fact that this evening was beginning to make her a very accomplished liar, Faith

358

worked her way to her mother's side. She took Lydia's slender arm, startled to feel her trembling.

"Mama, what's wrong?"

"Wrong?" Her pale eyes unnaturally bright, Lydia attempted a smile. "Nothing's wrong, dear."

"Mr. Willis . . . he looked upset."

"Oh, it's nothing, dear. Mr. Willis had some important matters to discuss with your father."

"Tonight, Mama? What was so urgent that he felt pressed to come here, now?"

"I . . . I'm not quite sure." Swallowing tightly, Lydia took her daughter's arm with smiling resolution. "But whatever it is, I'm certain your father will handle it. Now, tell me, are you having a good time?"

The flash of desperation in her mother's eyes warning her not to press further, Faith offered Lydia a smile.

"Of course. It's a wonderful party. I couldn't be happier."

Truly uncertain why her statement was so grossly untrue, Faith walked beside her mother through the milling guests. Their smiles were bright, but Faith suddenly realized they were both quaking.

"Why must you go, Wally?"

Lydia's soft question rang in the silence of the paneled room as she turned the full power of her concern upon Wally. The last guests had just departed, and unable to stand the torment of suspense a moment longer, Lydia had made her way directly to the den, where Wally had remained after Oliver Willis's departure. Her soft knock on the door had received an immediate, muttered response. She had entered to see Wally seated at the desk, papers scattered around him as he frowned at the long legal document in his hand.

Her hesitant inquiry had been met with Wally's flat statement.

"I'll be leaving for the mine within the week, Lydia."

"What? Why must you go, Wally? What's wrong?"

Abruptly realizing that Lydia was shaking, Wally drew himself to his feet. Within moments he had made his way around the desk to her side. His light eyes assessed Lydia's concern and he raised a gentle hand to her white cheek.

"Lydia, you're upsetting yourself for nothing. Oliver was concerned, I admit, but he is a lawyer and things a step beyond the norm are apt to set him into a tizzy. There's nothing wrong that I can't straighten out by handling it first hand."

"Wally, please. I'm not a child. If you don't want to worry me or upset me more, please tell me the truth. Exactly what has happened?"

A soft knock at the door prevented Wally from replying. His brows furrowed into a dark line.

"What is it?"

"Papa, it's I, Faith. May I come in?"

Wally took a deep breath.

"Yes, come in, my dear."

His eyes turning back to Lydia's concerned expression, he attempted a smile. "I suppose it would be better if I told you both the whole situation as it stands." Slipping his arm around Faith's waist as she drew near, he looked down into the lovely face that mirrored his wife's concern. "You're seventeen years old now . . . a young woman, and certainly too old to have secrets kept from you."

Seating both women carefully, Wally remained standing. He walked to the dormant fireplace, then turned back abruptly as he issued a flat statement.

"It appears someone has challenged my title to the Tin Pan Mine."

Silence his only response, Wally gave a short laugh.

"Well, I have to admit, my reaction was the same. I was certain the telegram Oliver had received was some kind of a mistake. But Oliver assured me he had sent a reply, requesting confirmation of the message before he delivered it to me here tonight, at such a late hour. He had just received word that the message was, in fact, correct. Someone is challenging my title to the mine. A legal claim is being made for the present worth of the mine, and for all proceeds taken from the mine since its inception."

"Papa, this is crazy! How can someone lay claim to a mine

360

you discovered—which is legally registered in your name?"

"It's not as crazy as you think, Faith. That's why I've been going over the papers—the titles—since Oliver left. This fellow—his name is John Warren, by the way, and he's a wealthy man in his own right—claims the land on which my claim stands is part of a larger tract he has recently bought from the estate of an old prospector. It seems the old prospector registered the claim, but the records were somehow lost. Well, he says they've just turned up and he's bought them."

"Wally, could this be true?"

"No . . . at least I doubt it very sincerely. It seems to me a flimsy attempt to seize control of the mine. But I can't afford to discount the possibility that this fellow will gain the assistance of the law if I'm not present to stop him."

"Surely you can send someone ... . Oliver, perhaps."

Wally's raised brow dismissed Lydia's suggestion more effectively than words.

"Perhaps Oliver would be more effective than you think, Wally. After all, you're not a lawyer and he—"

"And he would be eaten alive by a shark like John Warren. No, Lydia, I must go myself. I'm familiar with the exact legal procedure I used to register the claim and with the precautions taken in formalizing the contracts signed afterward. Only I would be effective in facing down any of the men who may have been paid to testify falsely in Warren's behalf."

Lydia's sober face revealed her silent agreement with Wally's statement. She paused, finally nodding as she appeared to come to a decision.

"You're right, Wally. You must go. I'll be ready to travel when you are, and then we—"

"No, positively not!"

His adamant response startling both women seated solemnly before him, Wally stepped forward, his expression suddenly severe.

"I will not allow either you or Faith to accompany me."

"Wally, I will not be left behind!" Immediately drawing herself to her feet, Lydia placed her hand on her husband's heaving chest. The heavy pounding of his heart was unexpected, and she frowned with concern.

"Wally, when we were reunited at Fort Lyon, I vowed to myself that I would never be parted from you again. I will not break that vow."

"You have little choice, Lydia." His expression unyielding, Wally removed Lydia's hands from his chest. "You will remain here, in New York, with Faith."

Abruptly aware that she had no desire to return to the land where painful memories would be so strongly revived, Faith interjected quietly, "Papa, you need not worry on my account. I could stay with Marilee. She has often offered—"

"You will stay with no one but your mother. I do not wish to mislead you by making you believe I will not allow your mother to accompany me because of you. That is not the case. The fact is, I will not take the chance of losing either of you again."

"Wally, you will be risking your own life. I would not—"

"Lydia, the matter is settled. I will contact the Denver office of Tin Pan Mining tomorrow and notify them that I am on my way. You will both remain behind. I have little doubt that my business will be concluded with dispatch once I am present to challenge the claim made against me. But this journey will serve another purpose as well. It will allow me to look over the new mine our company has purchased."

Lydia stiffened. Shooting Faith a short glance, she spoke with obvious reluctance.

"The new mine . . . you mentioned that it was located near Fort Kearny. That is unsettled country, Wally. I don't like the idea of your—"

"I cannot allow your fears to dictate the course of my life, Lydia."

The unexpected sharpness of Wally's response was met by Lydia's terse reply.

"Yet you find no fault in allowing *your* fears to dictate mine."

Clamping his mouth tightly shut, Wally refused comment. He reached for Faith's hand, raising her to her feet.

"You will kindly retire to your room," he said. Then,

appearing to relent at the unintended stiffness of his instruction, Wally made an attempt to smile. "I hope you have enjoyed your party, dear, and it is my fervent wish that this small crisis has not dimmed the luster of this night for you. You were a huge success, and I am extremely proud to be your father."

"Oh, Papa . . ."

Unable to speak for impending tears constricted her throat, Faith raised herself on her toes and kissed her father's cheek. As his arms closed around her to hug her close, Wally finally set Faith from him with a smile.

"Happy birthday, Faith. Now, please, to bed. Your mother and I have much to discuss."

Shooting her mother a last, lingering look, Faith turned and walked toward the doorway. She closed the door on her mother's protesting voice, and started toward the staircase. Despite her father's wish, the elaborate celebration of her birthday had been dismissed from her mind by a growing sense of apprehension. She had the feeling, deep inside, that if Papa left them now he would not . . .

Clasping her hands together to still their shaking, Faith became suddenly conscious of the crudely carved band she still wore on her finger. She glanced down, startled by its presence on her hand. How had she . . . ? Abrupt recall brought to mind the moment before the party when she had placed the band on her finger. Her parents had arrived at that moment, and she had forgotten it.

Unable to move, Faith stared unseeingly down at her hand. A host of memories invading her thoughts, she closed her eyes against their assault. What trick of fate had caused her to wear the band on this night, of all others? Those days on the prairie were long gone. She had no desire to relive such painful memories. They had no place in her life now.

Faith's strange sense of apprehension increased and she paused to take a firmer hold on her growing panic. No! The presence of this ring had no connection whatsoever to the unexpected turn of events which had so efficiently marred the joy of her party.

Refusing to allow her mind to dwell further on the

disturbing incident, Faith walked to the staircase and began to ascend with great deliberation. Papa would go where he must in order to protect his interests. He would be fine. He would return to Mama and her shortly, and she would laugh at her fears. Yes, she would laugh. . . .

Smoke, black and choking, darkened the clear prairie air. Gunfire and the deadly, whistling rain of countless arrows traveled the breach between the opposing forces. But the gap was narrowing. . . .

Pulling his pony back to a position of safety, Broken Hand gripped the powerful animal's mane, his twisted fingers holding him fast as his slitted gaze moved to the circle of besieged wagons. He gave a low grunt of satisfaction, watching as fire spread from a wagon in the center to several others nearby. In a short time this wagon train, too, would be theirs.

Broken Hand raised his gun into the air, the familiar signal bringing responsive war cries from the warriors behind him. Within seconds, the war party was thundering down the hill toward the encircled train.

Crouched low over his horse's neck, Broken Hand fired at will, his satisfaction fleeting as yet another blue-coated soldier fell. He urged his pony forward, approaching the burning wagons at a full gallop. Pressing his mount harder, he soared strongly over the lowest area of flames, to land firmly inside the besieged circle. He swung the butt of his gun freely, downing the men who ran toward him in open attack. Then he raised his gun, firing at the packing cases from behind which bullets flew in his direction. To his rear he heard the sound of hoofbeats and the grunts of Indian ponies as they cleared the flaming breach and joined the wild, hand-to-hand foray.

The ground was littered with blue-coated bodies as Broken Hand continued his deadly assault. He was firing, striking blows, wheeling and turning—a savage, human weapon of destruction, seemingly indestructible.

His attackers were no longer assailing him in the same numbers, and Broken Hand felt victory within his grasp. He turned to see warriors now entering the breach without interference. In a second's pause, he scanned the interior of the circle. A few random shots were issuing from behind piled crates on the far side of the circle. Other than that, no further opposition remained.

Digging his heels hard into his pony's sides, Broken Hand urged his horse toward the last remaining holdout against their victory. His gun raised, he was about to fire when the bullet struck.

Almost knocked from his horse by the power of its force, Broken Hand retained his seat by sheer strength of will. Regaining control of his mount, he spurred the pony forward, succeeding in passing the final barrier of gunfire. Within moments, he had eliminated the last of the opposition.

Victory pumped through Broken Hand's veins, sending elation soaring in him. He held his gun high in the air, his cry of victory ringing over the many voices raised around him. Blood streamed from Broken Hand's chest, but he felt no pain. Enemy dead lay all around him. The supplies, which were to strengthen the hated Fort Kearny, would now strengthen his own people, and the camp of Red Cloud would grow so powerful that the white man would no longer dare oppose them.

Remaining on his horse, Broken Hand watched as his men dismounted and began to move between the wagons. His massive body swayed. The darkness which closed around him bore no relation to the smoke-filled air, and he raised a hand to the open wound in his chest. He heard a voice beside him and turned to meet Black Wolf's intense scrutiny. He did not respond to Black Wolf's words, the loud humming in his ears making them unintelligible to him.

Broken Hand strained his eyes to indulge himself in a last glimpse of the victory which was theirs. He uttered a low protest as it faded from his sight. Sound, light, feeling slipped away as unconsciousness enclosed him in its silent womb.

Lydia saw him . . . he was riding, his bold outline etched

against a smoke-filled sky. His face was painted for war, and his eyes were filled with hatred. He was shooting even as he rode. He was suddenly forcing his pony to a more rapid gallop, urging it to jump high over a barricade, coming down at last within a smoke-filled circle of wagons. Bullets whistled past him as he pressed his mount forward. He raised his powerful arms, striking blows again and again, his face twisted with savagery. His dark hair streamed out behind him, touching the expansive breadth of his shoulders even as he continued his relentless attack. And then he was struck. His massive body quaked, shivering. Blood streamed from a wound in his chest but he continued onward. He was swaying . . . swaying raggedly in the saddle. He was falling. . . .

Broken Hand! No, you cannot die . . . not again . . . not again.

He was traveling in a pale world of moving shadows. Around him were familiar faces, loved faces long passed from his sight. Tall Ree stood, strong and straight, his clear eyes watching him. Walking Woman, White Bull, White Frog . . . a crowd of countless figures milled through the vast land of shade. Broken Hand called out to them, but they did not speak. He called to the son of his flesh, stretching out his arms so he might touch him once more, but Tall Ree did not approach him. Broken Hand's distress grew, but there was no respite.

A familiar voice met his ear, calling from the distance and he turned. Owl Woman, her dark eyes glowing eerily, stretched out her arms. She said his name once more, but Broken Hand paused. The peace which glowed in the other familiar faces did not shine from her eyes. She called to him again, her cry more piteous, and Broken Hand's heart stirred in response. She spoke of her need, called him to her. He took a step in her direction, and she smiled. She urged him onward. Broken Hand did not wish to go, did not wish to feel the touch of her hands, to share her unhappy rest; but he was helpless to refuse. He took another step, only to feel a silent

366

summons turn him abruptly from Owl Woman's siren call.

A figure was starting out of the shadows, moving toward him. Broken Hand's heart leaped as his lips parted in a gasp of recognition. Shadow Woman . . . The black silk of her hair streamed behind her in the swirling mists, her pale eyes held him fast. Joy coursed through him and he raised his hand, straining to touch her.

She came to stand before him maintaining a distance which he could not breach. She raised her clear, unsmiling face to his and life stirred anew inside him. She was speaking, and he strained to hear her voice.

"Speak . . . speak to me, Shadow Woman. You are lost to me, but you are still in my heart . . . a part of me."

Shadow Woman's voice grew clearer, and Broken Hand struggled to understand. He listened intently, her low-whispered words finally penetrating the mists between them.

"Broken Hand, I came to you once before. Do you remember my words?"

Broken Hand nodded, and Shadow Woman urged, "Speak . . . speak the words."

"You told me Tall Ree was not lost to me in vain. You told me sacrifice would prepare me to fulfill the destiny of my people. You said you would help me fulfill that destiny. You would teach me and I would learn. You would give to me that which I have never known and I would give to you in return."

Shadow Woman smiled and Broken Hand felt his heart surge anew. Her clear, light eyes held his in the knowledge that only a portion of her prophecy had been fulfilled.

A low, woeful wail sounded behind him and Broken Hand turned. Owl Woman called out to him, her arms raised in supplication. But Shadow Woman's silent call turned him back to her beauty. Broken Hand's heart swelled with need. His heart was hers, this woman of the shadows. The love he had long denied lived strong inside him, and he would answer her call and hers alone.

Broken Hand raised his hand to her as Shadow Woman turned away. As she walked, his step was freed and he followed her.

Shadow Woman's image was fading, and the scent of pungent herbs reached Broken Hand's nostrils. The shadowed mists began to lift, and a song of healing reached his ears. He opened his eyes to the face of Yellow Leaf as the medicine man passed his hands over him in prayer. Broken Hand glanced around, finally realizing he had been restored to his lodge and the life that passed within it. He knew it was as it should be. He had not yet fulfilled his destiny.

Wally turned, moving until his lips were only inches from Lydia's beautiful face as it lay beside him on the pillow. He longed to trail his mouth against the soft skin of her cheek, to taste its sweetness. But he dared not take the chance of awakening her. It had been long hours before Lydia had finally fallen asleep, for she had been greatly upset by his announcement that he would leave for Denver by the end of the week. She had still not given up her effort to convince him that she should accompany him, but as much as he loved her and would miss her, he knew he would never submit to her entreaties. To the contrary, it was because of his love for her that he would not relent. His love . . . and his jealousy.

Unable to restrain his impulse, Wally slid a hand beneath the light coverlet to the curve of Lydia's waist. He drew her closer. Lydia was his, and his alone. He could not take the chance that she would find out that Broken Hand had not died in the Sand Creek Massacre as she thought. He was certain that it was only Broken Hand's presumed death which had set her free at last. If she knew that Broken Hand was alive, he had no doubt memory would again come alive in her mind, and the Indian would once again stand between them. He could not allow that to happen. As it was, here in the civilized East, far removed from the brutality of the war on the plains, Lydia would never know that her former lover still lived.

Former lover . . . Wally took a deep, pained breath. Lydia, his Lydia, whom he loved more than his life . . . He could not bear the thought of her in the arms of another. Were it not for the fact that his whole future hung in the balance due to the suit against him, he would not chance being separated from her. But the threat to his financial future could not be ignored. He had been against Dan McNulty's unexpected lease of properties in the Powder River region. Doing so had stretched the resources of Tin Pan Mining at a time when expansion within the mine was at a crucial stage. He frowned. Doubtless, that was the reason John Warren had decided to oppose his rights to the mine at this time.

Yes, he need make his presence felt in Denver. His reputation for keen business sense and ruthlessness would turn the key in his favor. After thoroughly reviewing the papers Oliver had left with him, he had realistically faced the fact that unless he went to the mine he could lose everything.

Wally's frown deepened. The only true joy he found in his wealth was the ability to give Lydia and Faith the things they deserved. Lydia now lived the life of luxury to which she had been born. He had long ago determined that he would do anything to keep it so.

But separation would be hard. It would reawaken old memories. It would leave him feeling . . .

Lydia was becoming restless under his touch and Wally paused to survey her sleeping face. In the midst of a dream, she was beginning to voice a protest. The raven silk of her hair moved against the pillow, its soft fragrance setting his senses afire even as his apprehension increased. Her beautiful lips were moving, whispering. . . .

His strong body going abruptly rigid, Wally felt a flush of jealousy suffuse him. Broken Hand . . . Lydia had spoken his name in her dream. She was speaking to him, gasping.

No, damn it! He would not share his bed with Lydia and the memory of her former lover. He would not! Moving his hand to Lydia's delicate chin, Wally turned it in his direction. His voice hoarse from the heated emotions which assailed him, he broke relentlessly into her troubled dreams.

"Lydia, wake up. Lydia . . ."

Heavy, velvet-tipped lids raised slowly, the liquid silver of Lydia's gaze meeting his. She jumped with a start, and Wally's jealousy soared to new heights.

"Yes, it's me . . . Wally. I'm the one who's lying beside you, and I'm the one who's holding you in my arms. And I'm the one who's going to love you, Lydia, until you can think of no one but me."

Drawing her flush against him, Wally covered Lydia's protesting lips with his own, eager to establish his possession of her once more. His heart pounding as his mouth devoured hers, Wally felt a familiar elation flow through his senses as Lydia's arms closed around his neck, as the heat of her response increased, as her body opened to accept him deep within her. He claimed her strongly, relentlessly, determined that she would never again belong to another.

And he loved her . . . oh, God, how he loved her. . . .

Black Wolf stood in the entrance to Broken Hand's lodge, his eyes on Broken Hand's still face. He continued his scrutiny of the ceremony Yellow Leaf practiced on his wounded friend. Three songs had been sung and the rhythmic rattling had ceased. A pipe had been smoked and sweet grass was again burning on a coal in the center of the lodge. Yellow Leaf had bitten off and chewed a small piece of medicine root, and had then blown on his hands in purification. A tea was being prepared, the warm drink suited to the wound which had weakened Broken Hand's body. When Broken Hand awakened, he would drink deeply.

The ritual continued. The sound of Yellow Leaf's voice, raised in song again, filled the lodge as Black Wolf stepped backward to allow the medicine man to continue his healing.

Hope lived again in Black Wolf's heart. Broken Hand's lifeless pallor was gone. The color of life was returning to his skin. Broken Hand would live. Black Wolf's silent anguish began to fade. The white man had taken all Black Wolf held dear save his good friend and his lust for revenge. The white man would not strip him of that friend as well.

Stepping backward, Black Wolf moved through the doorway of Broken Hand's lodge. He turned and breathed deeply of the cool, twilight air. The change of seasons had again brought life to the land, but its coming had brought a renewal of the white man's quest to conquer the land of his people. Black Wolf filled his chest with the scent of freedom. He would fight the white man with every ounce of strength within him, and Broken Hand would again grow strong to fight beside him.

Thanksgiving in his heart, Black Wolf walked into the growing shadows.

Faith fought to control the quaking which shook her. A stiff smile on her lips, she turned her eyes toward the door to the den as it opened to reveal her father's broad, familiar form. Papa was dressed in a dark traveling suit, and his expression was severe. Mama walked at his side, her eyes bright with unshed tears.

Faith's eyes snapped to the traveling cases which rested beside the front door. At that moment the door opened, revealing the coachman's ruddy face. Dipping his head politely, Frederick took the cases and turned silently toward the carriage which waited in front of the house. Faith took a deep, harsh breath. So Mama had not been successful in changing Papa's mind at the last minute as she had so desperately hoped to do. Papa was determined to go to Denver without her.

Faith looked toward her parents, her gaze catching the momentary spark of regret that shone in her father's eyes. Papa did not want to leave either of them; but most especially, Papa did not want to leave Mama behind. He loathed leaving her. His feelings were written clearly in the manner in which he held Mama's arm, the tenderness in his gaze.

Papa's light eyes rose to Faith's at last, and he offered her a short smile.

"You're too old for Mama to take care of you now, Faith, so you and your Mama are going to have to take care of each other. If you need anything, you must make certain to contact Oliver Willis. He has strict orders to jump at your commands, and jump he will, or he'll hear from me when

I return."

Releasing Lydia's arm, Wally covered the few steps that separated them and swept Faith into a tight embrace. When he drew back, he smiled.

"You're much more of an armful than your mother, Faith. You are your grandmother through and through . . . and you make me proud. Remember that, dear. And remember that I love you and will return the moment my business is completed."

"I love you, too, Papa."

Embarrassed by the squeaking quality emotion had added to her voice, Faith gave a short laugh. But Papa did not seem to notice her discomfort. He stared down into Lydia's white face, Faith's presence all but forgotten as he took his wife into his arms. His softly whispered words were meant for Lydia's ears alone.

"I love you, darling. You are my life. You must take care of yourself for me."

"Oh, Wally . . . Why won't you let me come with you? I need—"

"You need to remain safe, and here you will stay."

His mouth abruptly closing the distance between them, Wally kissed Lydia long and deeply, and Faith turned away, brushing at the warm tears slipping down her cheek. When she turned back, her father had already released her mother and he was walking toward the door with a rapid step. Not hesitating until he had mounted the steps of the carriage and closed the door behind him, he turned back with a sober expression. A short tap on the ceiling of the cab snapped the carriage into motion, and Papa raised his hand in farewell.

A soft sob escaped Lydia's lips, but Faith did not turn in her direction. She could not make herself take her eyes from her father until he faded from sight.

The carriage disappeared around the corner, yet Faith remained staring in its direction until a familiar touch turned her to her mother's tear-streaked face. Lydia's voice shook as she began to speak, all pretense struck aside in the solemnity of the moment.

"Somehow I cannot find it within myself to speak in false

372

platitudes. We have suffered much together, Faith, and we will suffer this separation together, feel its pain more sharply because of what has passed before. We both harbor fears, knowing the dangers your father will face on this journey. I can only hope and pray he will travel in safety and return to us soon."

Taking a deep breath, Lydia raised her hand to brush the tears from her cheeks. She forced a smile to her lips.

"But your Papa would not want us to spend our time in mourning his absence. Come, darling." Sliding her arm around Faith's waist, Lydia stepped back to close the door behind them. "Once before we were alone, separated from your father, and I failed you. I will not fail you again."

Proud of her mother's newfound strength, Faith took a deep, steadying breath. Yes, all would be well. They would make it so, together.

Chapter XXI

The night was dark. A small fragment of moon, the sole source of light in the stillness, darted behind a cloud to plunge the unmoving landscape into total obscurity once more. The black, velvet canopy of sky stretched endlessly over the silent lodges of the Sioux and Cheyenne, but Black Wolf no longer pondered the lightless void above him. In a restless sleep, he had slipped into the world of dreams. He turned on his sleeping bench, his agitation making him insensitive to the soft step at the door of his lodge. He did not hear the one who entered and walked to stand beside him. He did not see the female form which hesitated for long moments before moving to lie beside him.

A stirring warmth pressed close to Black Wolf, encircling him in an embrace. Gentle hands stroked his naked flesh. He felt the rise of firm breasts against his chest, the brush of seeking lips against his cheek. In the depths of his dream, the face of the woman who approached him became clearer. He saw pale skin, brilliant eyes the color of the morning sky. He saw hair which burned with the brilliance of the fire. His heart began an escalated beat. Fire Spirit had returned. Her warmth met his and cleaved to him. He clutched her close. He lay his cheek against the luxurious silk of her hair, breathed deeply of her fragrance. He stroked the curve of her back, pulled her intimately close.

But something was wrong. The familiar face in his dreams began to fade and a strange discomfort began to invade his

374

senses. His eyes struggled to open even as warm palms touched his cheeks, drawing his mouth to meet eager lips. He drew back as a soft, pliant body pressed against his own.

Black Wolf's eyes opened to the darkness of his lodge and then took in the slender figure in his arms. The long hair which spilled against his robes was dark; the soft, womanly flesh of the body which lay naked on his sleeping bench was the color of his own. The eyes, half-lidded with passion, were dark, and the lips so close to his spoke softly in his native tongue.

"I have waited long and with patience for you to speak my name with desire, Black Wolf. The seasons have passed, and many of those dear to me have passed from life to join those who went before. Even the most indestructible of us have fallen, and I have seen too often the severing of the fragile thread with which life is suspended. I am a woman full grown, Black Wolf. You do not seek the consolation I may bring you because your mind is filled with other things. You have no room within you for the love I would bring to you because you say your heart is dead, but I would bring life back to your heart."

Deer Woman's well-rounded body moved against his, openly seeking his arousal as Black Wolf strained to see her face more clearly. Sensing his restraint, Deer Woman slid a small hand down from his chest, her caressing touch moving unerringly to the warm staff of his desire. She stroked him boldly, her dark eyes moving along the handsome planes of his face, barely descernible in the limited light of the dying fire. She urged him in a voice shaken with passion.

"Come, Black Wolf. Enter my body, and claim me as your own. I give myself to you this night, and for all the nights to come so that you may find peace and joy in your heart, and bring it to me as well."

Deer Woman continued to stroke him, satisfaction beginning to grow in the dark depths of her eyes as his body responded to her deliberate provocations. Black Wolf's heart was beginning to pound, exciting a similar response in the breast pressed so tightly against his own, and he closed his eyes against the bittersweet joy. Yes, this was the release

375

his body craved, the release he had found many times. But his release had been found in faceless female bodies which had responded with practiced warmth. It had been the release demanded by a purely physical need. It had not touched his heart or the hearts of those with whom he had lain. He had not been vulnerable in those encounters, and he had derived satisfaction from that realization.

The gentle stroking became more arousing, and Black Wolf took a deep, sharp breath. He reached down, clamping his hand around Deer Woman's narrow wrist. His eyes flicked briefly closed against her whimper of protest.

"No, do not protest my staying of your hand, Deer Woman. I would not dishonor you in this way."

"Dishonor?" Deer Woman's voice emerged in a gasp of agitation. "I am not dishonored when I am loved by the man who holds my heart. I am not dishonored when he enters my body."

"You would be dishonored if this man used you solely to sate his body's physical need, knowing his heart was closed to the feeling which fills yours."

A silence broken only by close, disturbed breaths was finally severed by Deer Woman's low rasp.

"It . . . it is enough for me to provide that service to you, for it is only you I love."

The brief silence which followed was broken by Black Wolf's equally rasping response.

"But it is not enough for me."

The sudden stiffening of Deer Woman's slender body the only response he received, Black Wolf remained unmoving. Finally separating himself from her, Black Wolf moved to the edge of his sleeping bench and drew himself to his feet. He reached down to offer Deer Woman his hand. He drew her to her feet beside him and then spoke, his voice a low whisper.

"Yours is a precious gift you would squander on one who is unable to appreciate its beauty. You must leave my lodge this night, Deer Woman. You must return to your own sleeping bench and think of these things I am to say."

Raising his hand, Black Wolf stroked Deer Woman's

scarred cheek, a small smile touching his well-formed lips.

"You bear marks which speak of your bravery, your courage. That courage sings within you. There are those within this camp who look upon you with warmth in their hearts. The lodge of your mother's sister, in which you now live, would be made richer by many horses should you show favor on Standing Elk, Grey Antelope, or even Red Sun. You would bear their sons in pride, and they would grow to bring much honor to you and your husband."

Dropping his hand from her cheek, Black Wolf set Deer Woman even farther from him.

"The inclination is strong inside me to take that which you offer so generously, Deer Woman. For that reason, I ask that you leave me before I betray my own honor by betraying yours. Such is the respect I hold for you that I would suffer even more greatly in that event than I suffer in putting you from me here and now. Deer Woman, the final step is yours, for your flesh is calling to me, and my strength is waning."

Black Wolf hesitated, seeing a familiar hesitation in the female form so close to his own. His hands dropped to his sides as he awaited Deer Woman's reaction to his words. In truth, he would do no more. He had given Deer Woman the final choice so he might save her noble pride, already suffering at his expense. But he knew, should she press him further, he would take her to him. He would not humiliate her, but would then keep her with him, his wife in the eyes of those around him. But he knew this proud woman of his people would never be wife to him in his heart. For even as his body had responded to her, his heart had remained unmoved, as frozen as the waters of the stream onto which the blood of his people had drained at Sand Creek. It was a coldness which he feared would remain until his final battle and its ultimate reward.

Deer Woman stirred from her silent immobility. He felt the warmth of her dark eyes traveling over his face. He saw her trembling lips move in an attempted response. Her hand rose to press warmly against the flesh of his chest, and Black Wolf swallowed tightly. Then, with a quick movement, Deer Woman turned, reaching down to snatch up the dress she had discarded only moments before, and she was gone.

Black Wolf remained staring at the doorway through which Deer Woman had disappeared. His eyes dropped closed as his powerful body regretted the loss of her. He took a deep breath, suddenly realizing that anger was replacing the sorrow and regret of only moments before. His broad chest began to beat agitatedly. His eyes abruptly snapped open, and hatred soared anew within him.

So, this was the future to which he was condemned. The white man had stolen from him that which was more valuable than all other things—his ability to love.

With slow deliberation, Black Wolf returned to his sleeping bench. His eyes stared unseeingly toward the small portion of night sky open to his view. He thought of the revenge he would wreak . . . and the small comfort it would bring him.

Spotted Elk drew back, unseen, into the shadows of the doorway to his lodge. Another sleepless night had brought him there to ponder the perversity of fate.

Silent Woman and his child . . . The pain of their loss was not yet dormant inside him, and a familiar anguish suffused Spotted Elk's spirit. The rage he felt, however, was directed at himself. While she had lived, he had not given Silent Woman true devotion, nor had he adequately expressed his gratitude for the child she had given him. He had accepted her and all she had done as his due. Now he was haunted by the possibility that ingratitude was the reason the Great Power had so cruelly taken his family from him.

Along with his torment, other thoughts entered his mind to forbid him peace. His lust for the young white girl, Fire Spirit, shamed him. He had wanted her badly, despite the fact that she had been able to see no one but Black Wolf. And his jealousy had known no bounds, as had his determination to make the white girl his own. Not until he had suffered the loss of Silent Woman and his child did he come to realize it had been his lust that had come between Silent Woman and himself. And at that moment his lust for Fire Spirit had turned to hatred.

In voluntary exile, with those of his people who pursued vengeance at the side of Red Cloud's Sioux, he had been drawn closer in friendship to Black Wolf and to Deer Woman as well. He had accepted Black Wolf as war chief, but his friendship with Deer Woman had turned into a far deeper attachment.

But fate had seen fit to once again put him in Black Wolf's shadow. It was obvious to all that Deer Woman saw no man but Black Wolf. Spotted Elk was only too aware that she shrugged aside his own attentions while she awaited Black Wolf's slightest word.

Spotted Elk took a harsh, shuddering breath which all too clearly revealed his depth of despair. He had seen Deer Woman slip from her lodge in the darkness to go to Black Wolf this night, and he had raged at the trick once again played upon him by a fate which allowed him to desire one who gave freely to Black Wolf that which he desired most.

Unable to turn away, Spotted Elk continued to watch Black Wolf's lodge, his mind torturing him with pictures of what was progressing within. Deer Woman, courage and strength inherent in her visage marked by the cut of the white man's saber, was doubtless lying in Black Wolf's arms. Did she whisper words of love into his careless ear? Did she tell him she would . . . ?

An unexpected movement at the doorway of Black Wolf's lodge brought Spotted Elk to sudden attention. He hesitated, his eyes straining into the darkness, a low gasp escaping his lips as Deer Woman emerged, her naked body gleaming in the pale light as she slipped back to her lodge once more. The unexpected sight almost more than he could bear, Spotted Elk took a spontaneous step forward. Had Black Wolf spurned the use of Deer Woman's body? He longed to go to her, to tell her he would give all he had gained in his countless forays against the enemy, and even his life, if she would offer to him that which Black Wolf had turned away.

But, instinct telling him to maintain firm control, Spotted Elk held back his wayward emotions. He would not succumb to impulse. To humiliate Deer Woman at this time, no matter the depth of his concern, would be to turn her from him forever. He would wait and work to gain her affections. She would turn to him if Black Wolf denied her, and he would take her gladly. The lesson learned, written in his loved ones' blood, would not be forgotten.

Remorse, vengeance, and unrequited love warred in his mind as Spotted Elk walked back to his sleeping bench. He sprawled on his robes, the back of his arm moving to rest against his forehead as sleep continued to elude him. In his mind's eye he imagined the comfort Deer Woman would bring his body and the joy he would bring her in return. Yes, he would not rest until it was so.

Triumph curved Wally's full lips into a wide smile as the judge's voice droned to a stop. A loud victorious hoot broke the momentary silence which followed, and Wally's smile broadened into a grin. Hell! It looked like the whole town was going to celebrate his victory with him! John R. Warren had snaked a lot of claims away from honest men in this part of the country, but Wally's wasn't going to be one of them!

Durham turned to the short, wiry fellow at his side, even as his broad shoulders vibrated with the congratulatory backslaps of the spectators filing past. He extended his hand toward Dan McNulty, who shook it firmly, a grin stretching his mouth from ear to ear.

"I told you not to worry, Dan! That damned shark Warren didn't stand a chance against the two of us."

"I didn't doubt you for a minute, Wally!"

Durham could not help but laugh at Dan's belated confidence.

"That's not what you've been saying for the past week, since I got here. But, hell, it's over and we've won. No more's to be said."

Taking his partner's arm, Dan ushered him out of the small hearing room, still nodding and smiling in response to the congratulations of passers-by. He shot a last look in John Warren's direction. Of medium height and balding, the man regarded Durham with open animosity. With his shifty eyes and his two-hundred-dollar suit and flashy diamond ring, Warren was the epitome of a crafty thief. But he wasn't going to add money from Tin Pan Mining to his fortune. Wally walked out of the hearing room, unconsciously breathing a sigh of relief as he cleared the doorway.

It was over, and he had won, a month to the day since he had left New York. His heart skipping a beat as Lydia's beautiful face jumped into his mind, Wally gave a short laugh. If things continued to go this well, he'd have everything taken care of in much shorter order than he had expected.

Curving his arm around Dan's narrow shoulders, Wally leaned down toward McNulty's craggy face, a smile on his own.

"What do you say we celebrate with a drink, Dan? We'll go over to the hotel and get ourselves a bottle and a nice, quiet table. Then we can get down to business."

"Business! Hell, I thought you said we were goin' to celebrate?"

Wally's heavy brown brows rose dramatically.

"Dan, do you remember my wife, Lydia? You met her before we went back East."

"Sure I remember her! How could anybody forget her? Hell, she's one fine-lookin' woman!"

"Well then, you should understand when I tell you that any extended celebrations I'm going to hold are going to be strictly private and they'll be held after I get home."

"Damn it, man!" Dan McNulty shook his shaggy head. "You keep it up and I'm goin' to leave you right here where you're standin' and go across the street to visit Miss Betsey's second-floor establishment for a little celebration of my own!"

"Oh, no, you aren't!" Laughing at his partner's sudden flush, Wally steered him down the sun-swept street toward the hotel. "You aren't going anywhere until we go over the papers for that damned mine you leased in Montana."

"Damned mine!" Obviously insulted, Dan shook his shaggy head once more. "I'm tellin' you, Wally, that 'damned mine' is goin' to make make us rich!"

Wally gave a short laugh. "I'm already rich, Dan. And so are you."

"Hell, I could stand bein' richer . . . both of us could."

"Not if it means I risk losing what I've got to run after what I might get."

Dan gave a low, disgusted snort.

"What in hell makes you think that's goin' to happen?"

"It's not going to happen. And just to make sure, we'll get us a bottle, partner, and the papers you signed to lease that mine. Then we'll take it from there."

"You're a slave driver, you know that, Wally?"

"Yeah, yeah . . . Just get those papers."

Faith gripped her mother's arm a little tighter and began to propel her forward. She was abruptly unmindful of the warmth of the summer day and of the fact that both she and Mama had been strolling at a languid pace past the busy New York shops.

"Faith, what in heaven . . . ?"

Ignoring Lydia's protest, Faith urged her onward, the voluminous skirt of her own pale blue batiste crushing against her mother's sober brown gown as she attempted to squeeze past the strollers blocking their path.

"Faith . . . Mrs. Durham . . ."

Faith froze when the male voice hailed them from behind, and Lydia's startled expression suddenly went blank. But Faith's sharp eye caught the smile which twitched at the corner of her mother's mouth, and she experienced a sharp stab of annoyance at her mother's covert amusement. It wasn't funny!

"Faith . . . wait a moment, please."

Faith took a deep breath and forced a smile despite the irritation growing inside her. Damn . . . was there no peace on the crowded streets of New York? Could she never hope to escape the . . .

"Faith, how good to see you again!"

Panting from his frantic chase, Harvey Wilson reached

382

out to take Faith's hand. As he raised it dramatically to his lips, Faith's smile stiffened.

"Harvey, what a surprise to see you here today."

Noting that he had released her hand to take her mother's in a more controlled greeting, Faith surreptitiously rubbed the moist reminder of his kiss against her skirt. Then she made an abortive attempt to hide her hand in its folds, only to be foiled by Harvey's persistence as he secured her hand tightly in his perspiring palm.

"Yes, it is indeed a surprise to find you both here today. It is only by the sheerest coincidence that my father sent me down to the haberdasher's to pick up a special order. The Collinses' party, you know. Papa is having specially monogrammed shirts made for both of us. The family crest—"

"The family crest?" Faith's smile began to wilt. "I didn't realize royalty was recognized in this country."

Harvey's perfect smile grew broader.

"Perhaps not, Faith, but it does not hurt to let some know the bloodlines from which we have descended."

"Oh, yes, good bloodlines do set one apart, don't they?"

"Yes, I would say they do."

Faith's insipid smile almost a grimace, she turned toward her mother to flutter heavily fringed eyelids revealingly.

"Isn't that interesting, Mama?"

Lydia choked unexpectedly, and Faith took that as an opportunity to jerk free of Harvey's grip and pound her mother lightly on the back.

"Mama . . . are you all right?"

Lydia was still coughing, but the upward turn of her lips betrayed her amusement to Faith's discerning gaze. Stifling a smile of her own, Faith turned back to a concerned Harvey. She shook her head in silent remorse. He was such a handsome fellow . . . wealthy . . . educated . . . and such a bore.

"Harvey, it appears mother is having another of her spells. You will excuse me while I call a carriage. I would like to get her home as soon as possible."

"Oh, I hadn't realized your mother has been ill. I'll do that for you."

Raising his hand, Harvey signaled a carriage, and within moments he was handing Lydia into the worn velvet interior. Pausing as he turned toward Faith, he took her hand, his apparent disappointment causing her momentary shame.

"Faith, I was so happy to run into you today. I had thought I might steal some time with you and your mother this afternoon. I've called so many times in the past weeks and not found you at home, I was beginning to think . . ." Harvey swallowed with obvious difficulty, and Faith's shame cut more deeply. "I would so like to visit you, Faith—spend some time with you. The Collinses' party . . . do you have an escort?"

"Mama and I haven't decided if we are going to attend."

Harvey was so obviously disheartened by her reply that Faith's guilt deepened. Oh, damn . . . it was not his fault that he was such a snob.

"But should we attend, Harvey, you may be sure I will let you know."

"I would feel privileged to escort both you and Mrs. Durham in Mr. Durham's absence, Faith. Indeed, I would be honored . . . delighted. I . . ."

Within the coach, Lydia began to cough furiously, and Faith jerked a quick glance in her direction. Mama, you darling, she thought.

"Oh, Harvey, I . . . I really don't have time to talk now. As you can see, Mama has not recovered from her distress. Do call on me . . . sometime."

The hired carriage drove briskly down the street, and Faith was turning toward her mother in concern when Lydia Durham raised twinkling gray eyes to hers.

"Faith Durham, don't you ever do that to me again!"

Faith's eyes snapped wide with innocence.

"What, Mama? What did I do?"

The subtle compressing of her mother's lips into a straight line provoked a spontaneous burst of laughter. Sober a few moments later, Faith shook her head.

"Oh, Mama, what am I to do? Papa and you have been so good to me, but I am so . . . so far removed from this shallow life. In truth, I find it and all the Harveys of our 'social level' a complete bore. Is this how you felt when you turned down all those fellows who were 'clamoring for your hand' and chose Papa as Papa is so fond of recounting?"

Dark shadows flickered in Lydia's eyes as she averted her gaze momentarily, and Faith felt instant remorse for her thoughtlessness. She was a fool to burden her mother with childish problems when Mama was missing Papa so. She was about to speak when Lydia turned serious eyes upon her.

"Yes, I suppose I felt much the same way as you do, Faith. Your father was the only man who was able to touch my heart, and I thought . . . I thought he was the only man who ever would."

Faith took a deep breath, realizing her mother's thoughts had momentarily drifted back to a sunlit prairie and the circle of lodges which had once been their home.

"Your Papa is my life, Faith. I can truly tell you that I knew that, felt the special emotions which would one day make us one, the first moment he touched me. It was much the same for him." A sudden smile lifting the sober contours of her lips, Lydia continued briskly, "And I think I can make a rather safe judgment in saying that I doubt very strongly that the same level of emotion will *ever* exist between you and Harvey Wilson. But you must not lose hope, dear. Surely one of the other fellows who calls will—"

"Oh, Mama, they are all so pompous . . . so boring . . . so . . . young."

Lydia's expression tightened.

"And Captain William Potter . . . he is not so young?"

Aware of her mother's disturbing yet unspoken censure, Faith replied, "No, he is not."

After holding her daughter's level gaze for long moments, Lydia turned away unexpectedly, her expression sober. When she spoke again her tone was forced and light.

"Oh, we're almost home. I had looked forward to a longer walk and some time in the shops, but I suppose we did make a very successful tactical retreat. We'll shop tomorrow . . . shall we, dear?"

Affecting a smile, Faith quickly responded.

"Of course, Mama. I would enjoy that."

As the carriage pulled to a halt before their residence, Faith maintained her smile by sheer force of will.

Oh, Papa . . . when will you come home?

Broken Hand moved against the warmth of his sleeping bench. The heat of day had begun to build early and it was now most uncomfortable within his lodge. He raised his hand and wiped at the thin veil of perspiration which covered the lined, russet skin of his face. Then he coughed, and a sudden pain in his chest caused him to clutch his healing wound convulsively. His hand touched the medicine root Yellow Leaf had applied earlier and he gave a low grunt. The time for medicine was past.

With great deliberation, Broken Hand removed the poultice and raised himself to a sitting position on his bench. He fought the giddiness which momentarily assailed him as he strained to focus his eyes on the doorway to his lodge. The sun was full and strong. He had not felt its warmth for many days. He paused. How long had he lain on his sleeping bench, helpless against the severity of his wound? He was uncertain. He remembered vaguely the chanting drone of Yellow Leaf's prayer songs. He remembered . . . yes, he remembered Black Wolf standing by the doorway and the courage he had gained from the young war chief's concern. He remembered his thought had been that he could not desert Black Wolf when so few of his people remained to wreak vengeance. He had decided that he must—he would— live.

Broken Hand took a deeper breath and straightened his back. Slowly and with care, he raised himself to his feet. He touched his face . . . his hair. The war paint had been washed from his face . . . his eagle feather had been removed. These services had been rendered to him while he had drifted in the nether world between life and death. Supreme gratitude for the concerned hands which had tended him surged through his mind as he took his first uncertain step forward. He took a second, and then a third, a low mumble of satisfaction escaping his lips as he reached the doorway and felt the warm sun touch his skin.

He had been standing there only a few moments when a flurry of movement drew his gaze to the nearby trail to the river. His eyes touched on Deer Woman who had stopped to stare in his direction, her expression concerned. She moved quickly, disappearing momentarily from his sight behind a nearby lodge, and within moments she was approaching, Black Wolf and Spotted Elk in her wake. To their rear, Yellow Leaf walked slowly.

With great deliberation, Broken Hand stepped out of the doorway of his lodge and into the full light of the sun. His face creased into a smile which grew as the tension on his friends' faces began to ease. Broken Hand flexed his arms, his broken fingers curling into a tight fist which he raised purposfully toward the sky, and his heart warmed as a full smile broke across Black Wolf's face.

Broken Hand raised his fist higher. Yes, he was well, and his need for vengeance had not yet been sated. Truly, he had not yet fulfilled his destiny.

Wally snapped his traveling case closed. He was finished packing. His pale-eyed gaze scanned the small hotel room one last time as he lowered the expensive leather case to the floor. He took a short breath. Well, he was ready to leave. He had accomplished his work in Denver in record time, and he had to admit satisfaction at a job well done.

Wally absent-mindedly slipped his hand into the pocket of his waistcoat and withdrew his watch. He snapped open the gold, engraved lid, his brows moving into a light frown. Damn, where was Dan? He should have arrived fifteen minutes ago.

Walking absent-mindedly to the washstand mirror, Wally gave his polished image a last cursory glance. Dark serge jacket, neatly tailored trousers, a contrasting waistcoat . . . He paused to run a hand through the heavy red hair liberally streaked with gray which was reflected back at him. He frowned his annoyance at its perpetual unmanageability, then smoothed the curving brown mustache which had been acquired that year. Yes, Wallace R. Durham . . . successful New York businessman and entrepreneur . . .

Wally's full lips curved into a broad smile, and the man beneath the polished exterior shone through. Surface gloss . . . all of it. But in recent years he had come to realize its full importance in the world in which he now functioned. He had no doubt his appearance had shaken John Warren when he had personally presented his case at the hearing. Wally laughed.

He had been the same man years before when Lydia's father had refused to recognize him as a suitor for his daughter's hand. He had been the same man when he had been turned down for job after job because of the influence Cyrus Burroughs had exerted. Only Lydia had recognized his worth then, had truly believed him worthy to love her. If he were to be honest, even he had not believed himself worthy of the beautiful, sought-after Lydia Burroughs. But that had not stopped him from loving and wanting her.

He loved and wanted Lydia still . . . and he would keep her. His new appearance guaranteed that, along with the acceptance he had achieved in the society to which Lydia had been born. Lydia and Faith were a part of that world now, and he would see to it that they stayed a part of it. They deserved no less.

Damn! How he wished he were free to go home to them now. Walking slowly to the bed, Wally picked up the small leather case filled with the papers Dan and he had pored over the night before. He supposed his partnership with Dan McNulty could be considered providential. He had been so anxious to return to the East after Lydia and Faith had been returned to him years before that he now realized he could just as easily have aligned himself with a less savory character. As it was, he and Dan worked very well together. Opposites did attract, he supposed. Dan, whose specialty appeared to be running on-site production, could not resist a chancy venture with the possibility of a high return; whereas he excelled in the follow-through and marketing aspects of their operation. But now, it was his responsibility to make an

388

on-site inspection of the claim Dan had leased in the gold-fields up north.

Wally's frown darkened. Leasing a claim which was all but unworkable because of Indian activity in the area was incomprehensible to him. Why had Dan taken such a financial risk? Wally paused. No doubt Dan had been thinking the same thing when he had leased his own claim from him years before . . . a risky business with the possibility of enormous profit.

Wally shook his head. He could only hope this lease turned out as well for them. It had better. Dan had tied up enough of their working capital in the venture—so much, in fact, that he felt he had no choice but to check into the investment himself. He had already decided the strategy he would take if the claim was not what it appeared to be. He would convince Dan to liquidate the lease at a loss if need be, so that they would not sink any further funds into the venture.

Whatever the case, he was determined not to return home until his mind was at rest. He knew he would not be able to function properly with the specter of financial ruin hanging over Tin Pan Mining.

A sharp knock at the door interrupted Wally's thoughts, drawing him in its direction.

"Come in."

A harried Dan McNulty appeared in the doorway, prompting Wally to pick up his traveling case and tuck the small leather portfolio containing papers under his arm.

"It's about time you showed up, Dan. I want to send a couple of wires before I catch the stage."

"Yeah, well, I got held up." Dan's face creased into myriad lines of annoyance. "And I'm tellin' you, Wally, you're wastin' your time. That lease is as good as gold."

Wincing at his partner's play on words, Wally shook his head.

"Dan, I know you're convinced of the truth of that statement, but I must be convinced."

Ushering his partner out the door, Wally closed the hotel-room door behind him and started down the hallway at his side. Dan was still protesting Wally's intended visit to the mine as they entered the telegraph office minutes later.

No longer paying attention to Dan's nonstop discourse, Wally merely nodded his head absent-mindedly as he wrote out two short messages and handed them to the clerk. He counted out the payment and watched as the clerk sat down and proceeded to send his wires.

Dan was still talking.

William eyed with disbelief the message which had been put into his hand a few minutes before.

TO: CAPTAIN WILLIAM POTTER
    FORT LARAMIE
    WYOMING TERRITORY

PRESENTLY IN DENVER ON BUSINESS. EXPECT TO ARRIVE FORT LARAMIE SHORTLY. LOOK FORWARD TO SEEING YOU.

              WALLACE DURHAM

Wally . . . coming to Fort Laramie? Was he insane?

Glancing up and finally remembering to dismiss the young private who still stood at attention before him, William snapped a short salute. Still holding the paper in his hand, he walked toward the gates of the fort, his eyes on the patrol now readying to depart.

Damn it all, nothing had truly changed here. Despite the efforts of the government, the peace treaty recently delivered and generally ignored, it was still a daily struggle to keep the road open between Fort Laramie and the forts farther up along the line. Earlier this week a government train escorted by forty men had been attacked. A three-hour battle had ensued, until relief had reached the train in the form of two full companies and a howitzer. The train had been saved, but all the horses and mules had been captured. Lieutenant Greer had been killed and thirty thousand dollars worth of government property had been destroyed.

William shook his head in disbelief. And in the midst of this chaos, Wally was calmly declaring he'd be arriving shortly?

William took a deep breath. Well, there was one consolation. Wally would never be allowed to begin a trip in this direction. The route was now closed to all civilian travel. And it was a damned good thing too.

Taking a spontaneous step backward as the gates were abruptly swung open and the patrol rode out between them, William took advantage of the opportunity to survey the surrounding countryside. Sun drenched, golden, silent, and deceivingly tranquil . . . but he knew the silence was not benign. Instead, a dreaded malignancy grew greater each day, threatening death from behind each sun-warmed rock, each seemingly harmless rise of land.

No, Wally would be stopped before he reached Fort Laramie. No civilian could get through, not even Wally with his penchant for showing up unexpectedly. No, not even Wally . . .

TO: MRS. LYDIA DURHAM
     NEW YORK CITY

BUSINESS CONCLUDED FAVORABLY IN DENVER. EN ROUTE TO FORT LARAMIE. WILL RETURN DIRECTLY AFTER BUSINESS CONCLUDED THERE. WILL SEE YOU SOON.

                                LOVE, WALLY

Lydia stood stock-still at the base of the staircase, holding the wire that had been put into her hand there minutes before. Her pale eyes moved over the message for the third time, and she took another deep, shuddering breath. Despite all her entreaties, Wally had persisted in going into disputed Indian country. Damn him!

Swallowing hard against the lump which had risen to her throat, Lydia lifted her chin determinedly. No, she would not cry. She had shed too many tears in her life. Tears of anxiety, tears of fear, tears of sorrow, tears of despair—a litany of tears, and she was done with them. She raised her chin higher.

Without conscious realization, her thoughts went back to the sunlit prairie, the endless blue sky, the vast, infinite horizon which stretched, uncluttered and unmarred by the hand of man, as far as the eye could see. She remembered the Indian camp, lodges formed in a great circle, and the simple joy of life within it. She closed her eyes against a throbbing emotion which rose within her. Her life had been inexorably altered by the events that had happened there, and because of them she had suffered in countless ways since her return to civilization. She was happy that she had been returned to Wally, that she had again been able to know his love. But a question plagued her. Did she truly regret those days in the Cheyenne camp?

A vision long avoided materialized within Lydia's mind's eye. She sought to escape it no longer. A broad masculine outline against the open sky; black hair, lightly bound, flowing to massive shoulders; russet skin; harshly chiseled, sober features; dark eyes . . . knowing . . . loving . . . as loving as the twisted fingers which touched her skin, as loving as the strong body which worshiped hers. She remembered the touch of those well-defined lips, the strength of the arms which clutched her close. She remembered the deep timbre of the voice which spoke to her of dreams of the past, of the future, of the joy she would bring him. . . . Broken Hand . . .

Did she truly regret those days when she had functioned as an integral part of the great Cheyenne warrior, when she had shared his life? No. She regretted them no more than she regretted returning to the husband to whom she had pledged her love. In the years which had passed, she had come to accept Broken Hand's remembered statement that her advent into his life was part of a yet, unclear, mysterious work of fate. With that belief, the shame she had once felt had been dismissed.

Her shuddering abruptly accelerating, Lydia turned and began to ascend the staircase. She did not wish to lose Wally to the strange twists of the fate which had all but destroyed her life once before. Damn him! Why had he gone into disputed Indian land, risked his life? Money . . . social position . . . Wally risked his life to secure those things for her when she cared for neither of them. She had lost one man she had truly loved. She did not wish to lose another.

Lifting the hem of her lace-trimmed, ecru gown, Lydia stepped heavily onto the landing and walked toward Faith's doorway. Her daughter was dressing for dinner. They were having guests, guests whose presence Faith suffered with as little enthusiasm as she. She intended to tell Faith of the telegram. She had the deep feeling that it was essential her daughter be informed because . . .

Chapter XXII

Black Wolf dismounted and led his pony to the river's edge. He stood in silence, his eyes trailing the bright surface of the water as the sounds of summer moved around him. His Cheyenne blood was restless. Much time had passed since the horror of Sand Creek. His residence among the Northern Cheyenne and the lodges of the Sioux had been of long duration. Black Kettle's peace had kept him from the camp of the Southern Cheyenne which had formerly been his home, and in his heart and mind he was part of the Southern Cheyenne no longer. He knew the same might be said of all those who had traveled northward with him, revenge in their hearts.

But even now, as he paused on the silence of the plain, a raging dispute tore apart the camp which had become his home.

Peace ... the white man again pled the cause of peace. His handsome face tightening into hard lines, Black Wolf raised his eyes to stare unseeingly into the distance. The change of seasons had brought the white man back to their land as his people had expected. They had come to reinforce the forts which guaranteed them passage onto Indian lands, and with them had come the shedding of blood. The white man remained, but the price he had paid had been heavy.

Black Wolf took a deep breath, his jaw clamping tightly shut as he suppressed his agitation. The victories of his people had been great. No longer did the white man's

394

stagecoaches carry passengers into this land. Their stations burned and their drivers killed, the companies had withdrawn the coaches which had formerly traveled the road to the gold fields. The white commander had ultimately forbidden travel on the white man's passenger trains as well. Only those trains which sought to bring supplies to the isolated forts along the Bozeman Trail continued to risk the threat of his people's attack. He had known great satisfaction in seeing the roads clear once more, but his heart had joined that of Red Cloud when the great Sioux chief had declared that he would not rest until the three forts along the trail were trampled into the dust of the land.

Peace . . . ! The white man sought peace, but even from his position of near defeat, the white man sought to tie his people's hands with the conditions of that peace. The dispute raged on within the camp of his people. Some, weary of war, sought to influence others for peace. Others, enraged at the thought of submission to the white man, sought to drive the white man from the land once and for all.

Black Wolf, weary of the battle of words which divided his camp, had ridden into the rising sun at the start of the day. After many hours had passed, he had turned his mount back toward the camp once more. He had spoken his protest to the white man's peace, and now he waited for the decision to be made.

Satisfied that his horse had drunk its fill, Black Wolf swung himself onto the animal's back once more. Guiding his mount carefully from the water's edge, he abruptly spurred him into a gallop. It was time that he faced the decision of his people. It was time that he . . .

Black Wolf snapped up his head, his gaze moving to the rider rapidly approaching the village from the opposite direction. He strained his eyes, recognition causing him to dig his heels more deeply into his laboring pony's sides. Standing Buffalo reached camp at almost the same moment as he, and Black Wolf heard his excited shout.

Another train—a white man's train—was making its way along the trail! It was heavily guarded, but that number was small in comparison to the warriors who scrambled for their horses. Black Wolf jumped from his exhausted mount and ran with an eager step toward his lodge. Within moments he emerged, ready for the raid, his eyes snapping to the lodge a short distance away where Broken Hand stood garbed for battle.

Within moments Spotted Elk, White Hawk, and Walking Bear, others trailing in their wake, made their way to his side. Watching as a group, like in size, gathered beside Broken Hand, Black Wolf felt his blood turn hot in his veins. Broken Hand had recovered and would lead his men once more. They would fight side by side, and the white man would stand no chance against them!

Signaling his men to mount, Black Wolf jumped onto the fresh pony which had been brought up for him. Warriors, ready in an instant, surged forward in a great eager line. Another wagon train to stock their camp . . . another wagon train to add to the white man's defeats . . . Another wagon train to add to their glorious victories as they took another step toward banishing the white man from their land forever . . .

A loud war cry sounded from the depths of Black Wolf's heart as he heeled his pony forward.

A familiar alarm rang through the camp and William snapped to the window of his small office. Excited shouts and frantic whinnies sounded in the enclosed yard of Fort Laramie as soldiers and balking mounts scrambled to assemble. Within moments William had grabbed his hat and was heading out to join them. Running into Major Howland as he emerged from his office, William snapped a salute.

"Sir! The alarm—"

"Another approaching wagon train under attack, Captain. And I don't have to tell you I'm getting damned tired of coming out on the losing side of these scrambles. I've ordered out two companies again—two! We won't stand a chance of saving even a portion of that train without that much firepower."

"Yes, sir!"

Further instruction unnecessary, William jammed his hat on his head and ran toward the yard. Short, curt commands brought the man into clearly cut ranks, and within a startlingly short time William was turning back to survey the company behind him. His eyes pinned on Major Howland in his position at the head of the troops, William saw him raise his hand to bring it down in a signal that sent the force immediately forward.

Within moments men and mounts were pounding out of Fort Laramie toward a formidable, not yet visible enemy that doubtless anticipated their coming. William felt the last hope for his mission die as he urged his horse into the racing throng. There was little desire for peace here in this savage land, in the heart of the red man or the white. Damn those savages, and damn the savages they had made of the men! There was no end to this killing . . . no end at all.

Outlined against the splendor of the setting sun, the last of the supply train trailed into the fort. His eyes heavy with exhaustion, William pressed his mount to the full extent of its waning strength, aware that the men trailing behind him were also drained.

He glanced toward the wagons at the front of the train. The wounded had been loaded on the wagons drawn by the freshest animals so they had been the first to arrive at the fort, and were already being unloaded and taken to the dispensary. From his position to the rear of the column, William directed his men forward. They had accounted for themselves well, the entire force. The threat under which they had lived for so long had forged a strong bond between these men, and he had been witness to acts of bravery and self-sacrifice which were inspiring. But hand in hand with that heroism had come the death of some of those heroes, and therefore a deep despondency had overwhelmed William during the last mile of their return journey.

As the wounded were being unloaded, he spurred his horse forward. Quickly dismounting, he made his way to them. One of his men, Corporal Beale, had been shot in the neck. The youngest of the troop, no more than twenty years of age, Beale was a favorite with the men and, admittedly, with himself. He did not like to think that Beale's broad, flashing grin would be absent from formation even for a day, much less . . .

Shaking off his morbid thoughts, William made his way between the wagons, his eyes moving to the prone bodies as they were being lifted down. A familiar, dark, shaggy head drew him to Beale's unconscious form. The young man's neck was roughly bound, and the bandage was stained a deep, soaking red. William's eyes darted to the boy's chest. It was still moving. He silently gave thanks.

Retreating a step as a stretcher was brought to the wagon, William backed up against another, already loaded with an unmoving, prone figure. He turned around, words of apology on his lips, only to find them freezing there.

Oh, God, it . . . it couldn't be! The wounded man was unconscious, his face averted, but he knew of no one at the fort with hair that same shade of red.

Signaling the stretcher bearers to stop, William reached over to turn the chin of the wounded man toward him, and his heart skipped a beat. Wally . . .

Blood soaked Wally's shirt in the area of his midriff, and a bloody bandage was tied around his leg, and William felt his heart sink. Wally appeared to have been wounded several times, but that stomach wound . . . Signaling the men to continue, William fell in behind them as they carried the stretcher toward the dispensary. Anger pounded more heavily in his veins with each step he took.

Damn it, why had he insisted on coming here? How many times did he think he could cheat death? What could he possibly say to Faith . . . Lydia if . . . ? Oh, damn. . . .

Deer Woman stood in the welcoming throng as exultant warriors returned to the camp. She scanned the mounted figures, her eyes searching for one face amongst the many, her heart pounding heavily in her breast as warriors drove captured animals past the camp in a proud display.

Yes, there was no doubt that the attack had been successful. Casualties were limited. The returning warriors were not badly marked or wounded. She had seen but one lifeless body, that of a Sioux, and she knew there would be much mourning that night in the lodges of their people.

In the distance, Deer Woman saw a familiar outline amongst the many. Yes . . . there was no mistaking Black Wolf, the broad extension of his shoulders, his proud carriage. Beside him rode Broken Hand and . . .

Deer Woman's breath caught momentarily in her throat. Spotted Elk rode between them, his shoulders slumped, his head bobbing weakly. Black Wolf reached out a hand in support as Spotted Elk began to sway more obviously. Then, with a nod of his head, he signaled the men who rode behind him to take charge of the horses captured from the train. They broke from his side and Black Wolf guided Spotted Elk's mount more directly forward.

Breaking free of the crowd which watched in expectation, Deer Woman ran toward them. She saw appreciation flash in Black Wolf's eyes as he dismounted and helped Spotted Elk from his horse. Not giving a thought to the depth of her concern, Deer Woman moved to Spotted Elk's opposite side to lend him her strength. She noted the blood streaming from the wound in Spotted Elk's shoulder, and she stifled her dismay.

Black Wolf nodded in silent acknowledgment of her aid, his handsome face creased with concern. Then Deer Woman muttered a brief word to a nearby youth, and the boy raced off to summon Yellow Leaf before her eyes returned to Spotted Elk's pale face once more.

Spotted Elk's eyes met hers. His lips curved in an attempt at a smile, but Deer Woman's expression remained sober. The many considerations Spotted Elk had shown her since their arrival at this camp accosted her mind. She had responded to them with little more than contempt. But now her contempt was for herself and her frustrated love for Black Wolf which had allowed her to recognize no other but him. No matter the blemishes on Spotted Elk's past, he had been consistently kind to her. She would show him kindness in return.

They had reached Spotted Elk's lodge, and Deer Woman fell back as Black Wolf helped the wounded warrior through the doorway. She hesitated and then followed behind, moving to the side so Yellow Leaf might attend Spotted Elk without interruption. She waited in silence for his direction.

Black Wolf remained standing over Spotted Elk's semiconscious form for a moment before turning to leave. On his way out, he placed a lingering hand on Deer Woman's shoulder in silent gratitude for her aid, and her eyes flicked briefly closed at the unexpected joy of his touch. Deer Woman's flesh burned at the point of contact, and she took a deep breath, aware that her mind clung tenaciously to the wonder of Black Wolf's touch even though he had left the lodge and doubtless had already dismissed her from his mind.

Yellow Leaf was administering to his patient as Deer Woman turned back in Spotted Elk's direction, only to be startled by the intensity of his slitted gaze. Her expression unchanging, she faced his perusal squarely. She did not wish to mislead this wounded warrior. Spotted Elk had raised her estimation of him. Whereas she had previously considered him devious and unworthy of the woman whom he had called wife, she now respected him. But it was Black Wolf who held her heart in his hand. That was the way it was . . . the way it would always be. . . .

The cold hand of fear clutched at Faith's throat as Nellie turned from the doorway, telegram in hand. At her side, Mama had gone completely rigid, a fact not missed by the fashionably dressed guests whose eyes had followed them despite the light conversation in the dining room. Mama had insisted upon a strong social calendar since Papa's departure, and Faith had offered no protest for she realized that Mama was making a stringent attempt to conduct herself as Papa desired. But this night, of them all, she had no patience for Harvey Wilson's concern, no matter how sincere, or the manner in which Mrs. Wilson had murmured in her husband's ear to send him to Mama's side the moment the telegram had arrived. She and Mama did not need them—they did not need anyone. They only needed Papa. . . .

Faith held her breath as Mama extended a shaking hand to take the telegram which Nellie offered in silence. She bit her lips against her impatience as Mama's trembling fingers fumbled at the closure. She moved a silent step closer to Mama's side so she might read the message over her slender shoulder and thus be spared further waiting. Her eyes touched on the lettered words:

TO: MRS. WALLACE DURHAM
   NEW YORK CITY

REGRET TO INFORM YOU WALLY GRIEVOUSLY WOUNDED IN INDIAN ATTACK AND PRESENTLY UNDER CARE AT FORT LARAMIE. KEEP YOU INFORMED OF HIS PROGRESS.

CAPT. WILLIAM POTTER
U.S. ARMY

Shock holding her silent, Faith snapped out a quick hand to grasp her mother's arm as Lydia swayed weakly. Impatience surged within her when Harvey murmured his concern and Mr. Wilson attempted to remove Mama from her grasp.

"That will not be necessary, Mr. Wilson."

Faith's sharp admonition snapped Mr. Wilson's gray head in her direction, offense registered clearly on his austere face; but Faith raised her chin determinedly as she took her mother's arm more firmly. Encouraged by Lydia's rapidly returning control, Faith continued quietly.

"Mama and I appreciate your concern"—her eyes flicked around the small dinner party to include all present in her stiff apology—"but we need to be alone for a little while." She hesitated, the pain caused by the words she was about to speak registering clearly on the exquisite planes of her face.

"This message we have just received relates the fact that

my father has been wounded in an Indian attack." The low gasps which followed her announcement added a fluid brightness to her already brilliant eyes. "I hope you will forgive Mama and me if we retire to discuss the matter in private."

Nodding absent-mindedly to the low mumbled regrets expressed by her guests even as she turned to usher her mother toward the staircase, Faith clamped her teeth tightly shut as Harvey attempted to stay her once more.

"Faith . . ."

"Harvey, it should be quite obvious that Miss Durham does not feel our help is needed."

Mr. Wilson's remark caused regret to flicker across Faith's brow, and her eyes briefly closed the moment before she turned toward the stiff-faced Wilsons.

"Mr. and Mrs. Wilson . . . Harvey . . . please forgive my sharpness. Neither my mother nor I are quite ourselves right now, and we need to be alone. But please do not think we do not appreciate your support."

Submitting to impulse, Faith raised herself on her toes to press a light kiss against Harvey's cheek. Drawing back, her eyes dangerously bright, she reached out to touch Mr. Wilson's hand lightly with her own. Then, abruptly turning back to her mother, Faith took Lydia's elbow, and together, the two women started up the staircase with measured steps. When they reached the top, the last of their guests was filing out through the front door. Pausing at the railing, as Nellie closed the door behind them, Lydia turned to Faith at last.

"We do not truly have anything to discuss, do we, Faith? The only course of action I can take is quite clear."

Faith's heart jumped into an escalated beat.

"The only course of action we can take, Mama." She took a quick breath. "When shall we leave?"

Lydia's pale eyes flickered in sober contemplation as she weighed her beautiful daughter's resolve.

"I shall have to make preparations. . . . The day after tomorrow—we will leave for Fort Laramie then. We'll wire William tomorrow."

A tremulous wave of emotion washed over Faith, and she gripped the railing tightly. Managing to steady herself before her mother became aware of her sudden lapse, she took Lydia's arm once more as she turned toward her room. Her next words came from the well of hope which sprang to life within her heart.

"Papa will be all right, Mama. I know he will."

The prairie sun shining brightly on his erect shoulders as he stood within the fort yard, William scanned the telegram in his hand with disbelief.

"No, damn it! They can't come here!"

Raising his eyes to the young corporal who still stood before him, William shook his head, snapping an absent-minded salute as he turned to stride toward the nearest building. Within seconds, he was crossing the wooden walkway at a gait just short of a run. Not bothering to announce his entrance, he burst into the small room, startling the young operator into open-mouthed amazement.

"Corporal James, I want you to send a message—immediately."

"Yes, sir, but . . ."

Grabbing for a small sheet of paper on the desk, William scribbled hurriedly in an obviously angry hand.

TO: MRS. WALLACE DURHAM

CIVILIAN TRAVEL TO FORT LARAMIE RE-STRICTED. DANGER OF INDIAN ATTACK. STAY IN NEW YORK AND AWAIT ADVICE. WALLY'S CONDITION UNCHANGED.

CAPT. WILLIAM POTTER

Watching with obvious impatience as the young soldier read the note, William took a deep, steadying breath. Faith . . . here? No. He had the feeling her attempt to come

403

to Fort Laramie would mean disaster—disaster.

"Well?"

"Yes, sir. But I'll have to get clearance to send this telegram."

"Send it now, Corporal. Every minute counts."

"Sir, I—"

"Send it!"

Clamping his even teeth tightly shut as the young telegrapher immediately sat and reached for the key, William muttered under his breath.

"I'll get your clearance for you as soon as the message is on the way."

Acknowledging his mumbled statement with a short sidewise look, the young corporal continued sending. A few moments later the key was silent once more. The young soldier raised his head as the key began to move in acknowledgment of a message received.

"Message acknowledged, sir."

"Fine." William took another deep breath. Damn, why did he feel so certain it was already too late? "Give me that paper. I'll get clearance for you."

The corner of the corporal's mouth quirked in the suggestion of a smile.

"Thank you, sir."

Nodding, his expression severe, William turned back toward the door and walked quickly in the direction of Major Howland's office. He didn't feel like smiling . . . he didn't feel like smiling at all.

Broken Hand sat before the fire in his lodge. His broad shoulders erect, he stared into the flames, his mind traveling to other days. He felt the strain of exhaustion pulling at his frame, and he ran a hand over the scar left by his most recent wound on his chest.

Visions . . . his nights were filled with visions which would give him no peace. Shadow Woman came to him often now. In the dark of the night, she visited him, calling to him, her voice a whisper which he strained to hear, but could not. She

404

approached him, but not close enough so that he might touch her as he longed to do. With the whole of his being, he longed for her. Of all the things now past, he knew that what he had given up voluntarily, nobly, for the cause of a peace which had not come, haunted him most severely. Despite his sacrifice, peace was absent from the land and from his heart as well.

Broken Hand continued his absent-minded perusal of the flames, aware that night was closing around his lodge. He was contemplating that which was unknown to him when a step at the doorway of his lodge caused him to raise his head. Black Wolf. No relation by blood but the son of his heart.

Black Wolf's dark eyes perused Broken Hand's solemn countenance. He spoke in greeting as he lowered himself to sit beside the older warrior.

"Great is the feast you brought to camp this night." Memory of the buffalo calf which Broken Hand and the smiling youth Red Sun, had delivered to camp earlier that day brought a smile to Black Wolf's lips. "The stomachs of our people are filled from your generosity. Your name lies warmly on their lips."

But Broken Hand did not warm to Black Wolf's praise. Instead, he turned his lined face back to the fire, and when he spoke his voice was low due to the thoughts which gave him little rest.

"My people praise me where little praise is due. I have yet to bring to them that which I am destined to provide."

Black Wolf's brow darkened at his friend's enigmatic response. He waited in silence as Broken Hand continued to peruse the flames. When Broken Hand spoke again, his voice was low and halting.

"My heart is heavy, my mind confused by the visions which assail me nightly, by the sign which came to me this day."

Black Wolf's silence encouraged Broken Hand to proceed.

"Red Sun, son of White Feather, no longer has a father to guide him. His youth and hunger for the knowledge of the hunt cried out to me. As prearranged, I took him with me when I started out for buffalo in the hours before dawn of

405

this day. We took four horses, two to ride and two lead horses to pack. We had traveled for many miles when our eyes touched for the first time on the buffalo. We switched to our running horses, and carefully I checked the two pistols I had taken from the white man, making sure Red Sun readied his bow and arrows as well. I carefully instructed Red Sun to pursue the calves as I pursued the bulls which stood at a distance.

"I raced up to the herd and shot a fine bull with large, smooth horns. Then I rode on to another bull and shot it. After the second had fallen, I looked behind me and saw the first bull coming toward me. Blood was dripping from its mouth and I thought it was badly hit. I turned my horse to finish the kill. I rode alongside the great animal and shot it again. When I fired, the bull turned away, and I supposed that I had not hit it in the right place. I rode on, shooting again. Suddenly the bull made a short turn and rushed toward me. I shot at it but still it came on. I turned my horse in one direction and then another, trying to avoid it, to get out of sight, but the bull followed every turn I made.

"The boy was a long way off, and I did not approach him because his horse was not very fast. The bull continued to pursue me, and I took flight, racing across the prairie with one eye to my rear and the other to the land before me. I reached the rise of a hill and started the climb, only to see that the bull had stopped short unexpectedly. I hesitated, watching as he turned, his eyes to the rear where the herd was again beginning to gather in the distance. Abruptly, he began trotting back toward the gathering animals, and it was then that I saw it for the first time."

Broken Hand's eyes turned to Black Wolf as his thoughtful face creased more deeply. "A white buffalo cow, its color as pure as the winter snow, stood within the midst of the other cows. As I watched it turned toward me. It did not show fear, but stood in solemn expectation. The great bull which had pursued me, moved steadily in her direction, finally coming to stand guard at her side. Both animals regarded me for long moments before turning and beginning to move into the distance.

"I remained on the rise of land, pondering the strangeness of that which had come to pass . . . the great bull, protector of the white buffalo, who had been impervious to my bullets . . . the manner in which he had turned me from the cow he protected and left me breathless in his wake.

"A sign of movement on a nearby hill brought me back from my contemplation. I turned as Red Sun began to ride toward me, greatly excited. His eyes were filled with the wonder of that which he had seen. He told me of his fear that I would be killed by the buffalo which would not fall. I offered no explanation, for, in truth, I had none to give.

"It was then that we went forward to take the second bull I had killed and prepare to bring it back to camp, but my heart was not filled with the victory of the kill. Instead, I have pondered. . . ."

Black Wolf's low voice entered the void as Broken Hand's recitation lapsed.

"The white buffalo, the head buffalo, who comes from the land far to the north, where the buffalo first came to us out of the ground . . ."

Broken Hand did not acknowledge Black Wolf's interjection. Instead, he spoke as if Black Wolf had made no comment at all.

"The thought has come to me that I was like that great buffalo bull. Like him I was strong, respected by my people for my prowess as a warrior. It was I who was given responsibility by the Great Power for one who was different from me in the color of her skin. I took Shadow Woman to me, made her part of me. Like the great bull, I was separated from her. Like the great bull I was shot with the white man's gun. Like him I fell two times, only to rise again as strong and determined as before. But unlike the great bull, I no longer hold Shadow Woman under my protection, and without her I flounder at the edge of an unknown destiny. It seems to me that the white buffalo came to me today as a sign. I have searched my mind for its meaning, as I have searched my mind for the message which Shadow Woman seeks to bring me nightly in visions. The only thought clear in my mind as the great bull moved away from me with the white buffalo beside him was that together they brought peace to the herd once more."

Broken Hand squinted into the fire, his voice a solemn whisper.

"As yet it is unclear to me what destiny awaits me. I know only that I seek it anxiously. The peace which once resided within, eludes me. I seek to know it once more."

Silence being all that met his sober reflection, Broken Hand raised his eyes to Black Wolf. Black Wolf's unspoken response was written in the somber depths of his eyes.

"My heart moves with yours; my arm is at your side. I am with you."

Nellie moved around the luxurious room of her mistress at a pace much slower than her normally bustling gait. She surveyed the gleaming chest, free of clutter, the smooth, unwrinkled bed, the long mirror to the far side of the room which had reflected Miss Faith Durham's exquisitely beautiful form. She spotted a small shoe lying partially hidden by the elaborate frame, and she quickly picked it up. She paused with the pale, satin slipper in her hand. Miss Faith had such dainty feet.

Nellie took a deep, choked breath and walked to the large wardrobe at the side of the room. She opened the doors, her eyes moving over the array of brilliantly colored dresses hanging neatly within. Miss Faith had taken so little with her when she had left the previous morning, just a few serviceable gowns and the necessities for an extended trip. Mrs. Durham had done the same.

Swallowing tightly, Nellie placed the small shoe in the wardrobe beside its mate, and closed the door with care. It was strange. Despite their sympathy for Mr. Durham's unexpected difficulty, much of the household staff had all but celebrated Mrs. Durham's and Miss Faith's departure that morning. An extended absence with full pay . . . quite a holiday for the hard-working help in residence. But despite the leisurely days she was certain would follow, Nellie knew she would miss Miss Faith.

In truth, in the years she had been in service, she had never had a mistress as considerate and affectionate. Miss Faith never scolded her for her overly adequate size or for the fact that her uniforms were often ill fitting because of her expanding girth. Indeed, Miss Faith had never had a sharp word for her, not even during the first year when she had suffered under the pressure of the gossip which had followed her and her mother. And Miss Faith had shown a true interest in Nellie and in her small family, having gone as far as to send presents to her smaller sister at home during the holidays and when she had recently been ill. Yes, Nellie was certainly going to miss Miss Faith.

Pausing to give the room one last check, Nellie released a low sigh and walked into the upstairs hallway. She closed the door silently behind her, taking a moment to brush a wayward tear from her eye. Then she gave a small sniff. She was being foolish. Mrs. Durham and Miss Faith would return soon, and they would bring Mr. Durham back with them. She would pray for that day when she went to church on Sunday, and she would tell her sister Mary to pray, too. God listened so much more intently to the prayers of a child, didn't he?

Nellie was walking listlessly down the staircase when the sound of the doorbell echoed unexpectedly in the foyer. Momentarily startled, Nellie continued down the staircase, her unruly brows knitting in a frown as the bell sounded again and no one responded to its summons. Her small nose twitching in annoyance, she opened the door, her brows rising at the sight of the messenger who awaited.

Moments later, she closed the door behind her, her eyes intent on the telegram in her hand. It was for Mrs. Durham. The bright-eyed messenger boy had confided that it came from Captain Potter, all the way from Fort Laramie. Her sympathetic heart had skipped a beat at the thought that Mrs. Durham and Miss Faith had already been gone for an entire day and were, at that moment, speeding on their way to join Mr. Durham at that very same place.

Uncertain as to what to do with the message, Nellie held it tentatively in her hand. Then, remembering that the staff

409

had received strict orders to report all things of importance to Oliver Willis, who was overseeing the premises while the Durhams were not in residence, she knew what she would do.

Placing the envelope carefully on the silver tray near the door, Nellie turned toward the kitchen. She would give the message to Mr. Willis when he arrived at the end of the week. It had arrived too late to reach Mrs. Durham, in any case.

With a low sigh, Nellie hastened toward the kitchen, the telegram dismissed from her mind.

Chapter XXIII

"Surely you can't be serious!"

Her light eyes wide with disbelief, Lydia took a small step backward, only to come up against her daughter's stiff form. Faith's arm slipped around her shoulder, lending her support as she shook her head.

"Mr. McNulty, I can apprecite your concern for our welfare, but we've come all the way from New York to be with Wally. Surely you realize that we cannot remain here, in Denver, knowing Wally is so close and still—"

"Mrs. Durham . . . ma'am"—Dan McNulty's narrow, lined face became more tense as he shot a pleading glance toward Faith's unyielding countenance—"try to understand. The government closed the road to Fort Laramie and the forts beyond to all civilian traffic. The only wagon trains goin' through right now are supply trains, and they're under heavy attack from hostiles."

"But they are getting through, Mr. NcNulty, are they not?"

"Please, call me Dan, ma'am. Yes, they're still gettin' through, but at a price. Wally paid part of that price."

Lydia lifted her chin in an effort to still its trembling.

"My husband is a very determined man, Mr. McNul—Dan. And I warn you, Faith and I are determined to reach him."

"Ma'am, you don't seem to understand. I've been gettin' communications from Fort Laramie on a regular basis.

411

Wally is doin' as well as can be expected. He is temporarily out of danger."

"Temporarily? But . . . but it's been so long since he was wounded. Surely—"

Dan avoided Lydia's eye, turning his attention briefly to a paper on his desk as he offered in a low voice. "Infection, ma'am. Wally's been battlin' an infection in the wound in his leg. The wound in his chest is healin' nicely, from what I understand, but his leg is causin' fever to flare up off and on. As a result, he ain't able to be transported."

"Well then, that's all the more reason Faith and I must reach him."

His head snapping up, Dan McNulty pulled his wiry frame to its full height and walked around his desk to confront the two women closely. *Damn, how did Wally manage them?* They had invaded his office a short hour before, and he had been battling with them ever since. And to think, when they had first entered he'd actually envied Wally. Indeed, he'd been flabbergasted by Lydia Durham's beauty, hardly able to believe she had become more beautiful than when he'd last seen her, but she sure enough had.

That soft gray dress she was wearin' maybe wouldn't be much on somebody else, he thought, but on her it just about matched her eyes, makin' them look all wide and solemnlike, and makin' him want to smile and comfort her. And the young woman who stood behind her, there was no denyin' whose daughter she was, not with that bright flamin' hair and that tall, straight posture. She must've grown at least two inches since he had last seen her and now they actually stood about eye to eye. Hell, she didn't look nothin' like her Pa, not in her features . . . she never did—he remembered seeing her and remarking that same thing when she and her Ma had passed through years before—but, damn, that little stick of a girl had grown into some woman, her pretty face was so damned beautiful, she was so much her father's daughter without really resemblin' him at all.

Dan swallowed, a new heat suffusing his face as he came to stand directly in front of the two women. Damn . . . I remember tellin' Wally that I was goin' to leave him flat and go to Miss Betsey's second-floor establishment if he didn't quit talkin' like he was, he reflected. Tonight, for sure, I'm goin' to be walkin' up those well-worn stairs. . . .

Dan cleared his throat and made an attempt to clear his mind of his wandering thoughts. His expression and his voice reflected his sincerity.

"Look, ma'am, please don't ask me to do more for you than I can. I can't go against orders from the Army. If things keep up like they are right now, even that supply train that's supposed to leave at the end of the week ain't goin' to set out of Denver. Why don't you give me a few more days to get some more information for you? I'll telegraph Fort Laramie this afternoon to get a report on how Wally's doin'. Maybe he's better and they can safely transport him back."

"How can they transport him safely to Denver, Dan, when you just told me there's no safety on that trail? No, I think that would be expecting too much. I don't want Wally doubly endangered. It would be far better if I go to him." Lydia paused, her eyes moving momentarily to Faith's sober face. "I . . . I can understand that the Army might object to transporting two women, especially one as young as Faith. There is truly no need to risk her life, but surely they realize I am Wally's wife. I will accept full responsibility for myself. I—"

"Mama . . ." Her hand moving to her mother's shoulder to stay her pleas, Faith interrupted softly. "Mama, I hope you realize I will not allow you to travel without me. Papa wouldn't want you to be alone." Giving her mother's shoulder a surreptitious squeeze, Faith simultaneously lifted her gaze to Dan McNulty's face, touching him with the full power of her azure eyes. "Mr. NcNulty, I hope you'll forgive our anxiety and try to understand that we've traveled a long way and are sorely disappointed that we might not be able to to go Papa."

"Faith, I will not take no for an—"

"Mama, please."

Turning back to Dan McNulty once more, Faith continued, "We would appreciate it if you would petition the

Army for permission for us to travel with the next train which leaves for Fort Laramie."

"Miss Durham . . ."

"Call me Faith, please."

"Faith, it'll be useless—"

"But you will try, won't you?"

Hating himself for the melting sensation in the pit of his stomach—it turned him to mush as Faith continued to look into his eyes—Dan stammered ineffectually, "Well . . . I guess . . . all right, I'll try. But I don't want either of you gettin' angry with me if the Army says no."

Faith's smile brightened.

"We won't get angry, will we, Mama?"

Her eyes flitting to her daughter's smile, Lydia gave a short shake of her head.

"No. I guess not."

Taking a step forward, Faith urged her mother along as she slipped her free arm through Dan's.

"And now perhaps we can impose upon you to show us around Denver, Dan . . . to help us get situated. After all, we might have a long wait."

"It'll be my pleasure."

A tantalizing sense of pleasure moving along his arm as Faith's hand curled securely around it, Dan offered his other arm to Lydia. He waited until she moved to his side to continue politely.

"Tell me, are you settled into the hotel satisfactorily?"

"We are."

"Then maybe we should have some lunch."

The slight flutter of Faith's heavy lids sent an even stronger jiggle through Dan's midsection, and he took a deep breath as she responded.

"That would be lovely, wouldn't it, Mama? And then when we're done, maybe Dan could take us to the Army depot, where we might be able to press our petition for travel to Fort Laramie personally. And even if we are declined permission, perhaps we could arrange to have some extra supplies sent to Papa, perhaps even an extra wagonful . . . at our own expense, of course."

414

Dan took a modest step toward the doorway. Well, at least Wally's daughter was being reasonable. He liked her attitude. And he had the feeling he was going to like her company. Hell, I'm goin' to like it real well, he thought. He smiled his reply.

"I'd say that sounds real reasonable, ma'am. Real reasonable. Now if you'll allow me . . ."

Dan stepped out onto the wooden walk, his chest puffed with pride as he walked along with two of the most beautiful women in Denver on his arm. Hell, he didn't mind this. He didn't mind this at all.

Wally took a deep, gasping breath, his eyes darting to Dr. Mallory's concerned expression as the gray-haired physician cautiously removed the dressing on his wound. He clamped his teeth tightly shut against the pain shooting through his leg, his gaze shifting to William, who stood observing in silence a few feet away. Wally's eyes blurred and he blinked hard in an attempt to clear them. Anger at his helplessness stabbed at him. Damn, his fever was mounting again.

Turning back to Dr. Mallory, he asked bluntly, "Well, what do you think, Hank? Think I'm going to lose it?"

Hank Mallory's bloodshot eyes jerked to Wally's face. His limp gray mustache jerked in a telltale sign of agitation.

"You don't mince words, do you, Wally?"

Wally shook his head, gasping, as the doctor removed the last of the bandage and put it to the side. God, his leg was a mess. The way things looked now, he wasn't going to get out of Fort Laramie in one piece, much less get to check out the claim he'd been so hot to assess. Damn!

"Well, it doesn't look like there's much use in trying to avoid the truth, does it, Hank? We're all looking at a badly infected wound. And it's obviously not getting any better. I'd just like to know what chance there is of saving my leg."

"Well, let's put it this way, Wally." Pausing to reach for the basin of disinfectant, Dr. Mallory then turned back in Wally's direction. "I'll tell you that I won't take drastic steps

415

until they're unavoidable. Conditions here aren't the greatest, you know. We're low on supplies—medical supplies. I don't like to take a chance on performing surgery when I don't have what I need."

"Hell, that prognosis sounds great."

Wally's sarcastic comment was interrupted by Hank's low snort.

"Look, Wally, you wanted the truth, and I gave it to you. Now that doesn't mean that the treatment I've been using for this past week won't begin to have an effect tomorrow, and that you won't start to heal."

"And it doesn't mean that treatment *will* work either, does it?"

"I can't see into the future, Wally."

Wally shook his head. Hank's light touch was causing him more pain than he had thought possible, and he snapped sharply, "Hell, I probably would've gotten more results with one of those Indian medicine men singing over my leg than I got with all the wonders of modern science."

Hank Mallory's weary eyes rose to his.

"You know, Wally, you just might have a point there. I've seen those fellow make some pretty surprising cures. I wouldn't mind having one of them in here right now with one of those medicine bundles or whatever they call them. It sure as hell would help more than this stuff I'm using."

Wally gave a short laugh.

"No, thanks, doc. I might save my leg and end up losing my scalp. I'll stick with you."

"Well, you don't have much choice, do you, Wally?"

"Guess not."

Wally raised a shaky hand to his head. The pounding was beginning again in his temple, and he was starting to feel cold—real cold.

Dr. Mallory's eyes narrowed.

"Well, I guess I don't have to ask you how you feel, do I, Wally? You're starting to feel damned bad again . . . and I'm not about to tell you you're not in for a lot more of the same."

"Look, Hank, if you can't say something encouraging, don't say anything all, will you?" His annoyance intensifying

416

as he began to shake more visibly, Wally frowned. "And hurry up with my leg, will you?"

Dr. Mallory's response was a short command.

"William, give me those blankets over there on the chair. Our friend here's in for another siege."

His hands moving with the speed of long practice, Dr. Mallory cleaned the wound and bound it up once more. After covering Wally with the extra blankets, he went to the table and mixed a powder in a glass of water. When he turned back to the bed, Wally groaned.

"Oh, not more of that awful-tasting stuff! What's the use of it? It hasn't done me any good so far."

Dr. Mallory's mustache twitched more visibly.

"If I didn't realize that was your fever talking, Wally, you can bet I'd be saying more than I am now. But for the present, just take this medicine and be thankful that you've got it. And remember, it was your stubbornness that got you in this predicament in the first place. So don't go letting that same stubbornness keep you from the only chance you have of getting well."

Pausing to consider the effect of his words, Dr. Mallory leaned over to hold the glass to Wally's mouth. Wally drank dutifully, and Dr. Mallory nodded his head.

"That's better."

Turning back toward William, Dr. Mallory shot him a quick glance. "I think it's time to leave our patient so he can sleep for a while."

"I've done enough sleeping in the past weeks to last me a lifetime. I don't want—"

"Shut up, Wally, and do what I tell you."

Motioning William from the room, Dr. Mallory took one last look at his belligerent patient and then followed William through the doorway. He was closing the door behind him when William's low question met his ears.

"He's not doing well, is he, Hank?"

"No, not well at all."

William took a deep breath.

"Will he lose that leg?"

"William, at this point in time, I think it would be more

wise to be concerned about whether Wally's going to lose his life."

Jarred into immobility by Dr. Mallory's frank response, William shook his head.

"We . . . we can't let that happen, Hank."

"William, I'm doing all I can." Shrugging, Dr. Mallory turned unexpectedly and walked away. His low, resigned voice trailed over his stooped shoulder. "All I can . . ."

Wally's shaking was beginning to lessen. He attempted to turn in his bed, only to emit a low gasp as a shattering pain in his leg wrenched him into immobility once more. Holding his breath until it slowly faded, he took a short, guarded breath.

Oh, hell, this was a damned mess he had gotten himself into! Well, he had one consolation: Lydia and Faith were safe and secure. He had no doubt that whatever the length of his enforced stay at Laramie was, Oliver could be trusted to provide for both Durham women. It was obvious that no additional investment could be made in the northern mine Dan had leased, so the situation remained at status quo. Yes, Lydia and Faith were secure. Now all he needed to do was get better.

Wally gave a low snort. That was going to be a tall order. But he'd do it, damn it. He'd do anything he must to see his beautiful women again, to feel Lydia in his arms once more. Yes, he'd even rest like that damned Hank Mallory had wanted. Well, the truth was, he had little choice there either.

Wally's eyes dropped closed, in an attempt to shut out the pain . . . for a little while.

"I still don't know how you did it, ma'am."

Dan's lined face was drawn into almost comical lines of incredulity. With this same expression he had greeted them at each encounter since he had been notified that they had been granted permission to travel with the wagon train to Fort Laramie.

Exchanging momentarily amused glances, Lydia and Faith picked up their small hand cases. Immediately taking the small burdens from their hands, Dan followed them out the doorway of their hotel room and into the hall. As he closed the door behind them, his unconscious sigh of finality turned both their heads back in his direction. Unexpectedly, he flushed. His smile was sheepish.

"Well, I was kinda lookin' forward to havin' both you ladies here in Denver for an extended stay . . . until Wally could make it back to Denver on his own, I mean. Kinda selfish of me, I guess, but an old bachelor like me don't get much of an opportunity to sport two such pretty ladies around town." His face abruptly becoming serious, he continued in a lower tone, "And I'm thinkin' Wally's not goin' to be thankin' me for lettin' you board that wagon train this mornin'." Shooting Lydia a short glance, he protested one more time, "It just ain't safe for you and Faith."

Her pale eyes intent, Lydia turned a short glance in Dan's direction, silencing the remainder of his statement before she even spoke.

"Dan, Faith and I appreciate your concern. And you may be sure we'll tell Wally that we got permission from Colonel Carter against your advice. You're right. Wally will be momentarily angry when he gets the wire advising him that we're on our way. For that reason I've asked you not to send it until we are at least a day into our journey. But the fact is, Faith and I are going, and nothing is going to stop us."

"I'm quite aware of that, ma'am."

They descended the staircase in a stiff silence, which was broken by Faith when they touched down in the isolated lobby. She shot a short glance toward the window and the semidarkness preceding the dawn.

"I think we should hurry, Mama. Colonel Carter said the train would be leaving at dawn."

"You don't have to worry about that train leavin' without you." Dan's voice was gruff. "From what I've been hearin', them boys on that train are lookin' forward to havin' your company."

Faith's response was a low laugh. "Oh, I don't know about

that, Dan. When I asked Colonel Carter if I'd be allowed to ride horseback for a portion of the day—"

"Ma'am . . . you're jokin'."

"No, I'm not, but I think Colonel Carter thought I was. I'm an experienced rider, Dan, and I have some pleasant memories of the prairie."

The knitting of Faith's narrow brows was as much a reaction to the invasion of long-buried memories as it was to Dan's unexpectedly sharp response.

"This ain't goin' to be no pleasure trip, Faith. Sometimes I think you and your Mama don't really realize how dangerous—"

"Faith and I realize the potential danger, Dan, and we do appreciate your concern . . . really we do." Lydia's light eyes met Dan's troubled gaze, and she paused as they emerged onto the lightening street. "If it will relieve your mind, Colonel Carter has told us that the only reason he's allowing us to travel with the train is because . . . because he is aware of the dire state of Wally's health." The recent report of Wally's failing health had been difficult for her to accept, and it was even more difficult to acknowledge aloud; but Lydia continued resolutely, "And because in recent weeks hostile attacks have been confined to trains traveling from Fort Laramie to the forts farther up along the trail. In any case, this train will be heavily guarded. So you see, Dan, you really needn't worry."

Her eyes moving between her mother and Dan as they walked, Faith abruptly glanced up as they turned the corner. As the assembled train came into view, her heart beat faster, and she was aware that her mother's short intake of breath revealed a similar sense of anticipation. Faith paused. Perhaps Mama was worried and anxious to see Papa, but perhaps her feelings were mixed, too. She had been reluctant to discuss how she had felt upon reaching Denver . . . the odd, disturbing sense of coming home she had experienced as she had alighted from the coach. Strange, when she'd left this very place years before, she had not thought she would ever want to see the western frontier again. There had been too much heartbreak . . . too much death. But now, even with the realization that Papa was wounded and needed them, the confusing feelings continued to assault her.

Mama was conversing with Dan in a low tone, but Faith did not clearly follow their words. She allowed her eyes to travel along the assembled wagons. There were thirty-five or forty of them, making this train similar in size to the one on which, with Mama and Papa, she had set out three years before. Three years . . . yet it seemed a lifetime.

With sudden clarity, Faith realized that it had, indeed, been a lifetime for her. In those years she had changed from a child to a woman. And with that same, sudden clarity, she realized she had achieved a good deal of her emotional maturity as a result of her encounters on the prairie on which she was again about to embark.

With startling vividness, a familiar russet-skinned visage, long-suppressed, returned to her mind, and she experienced a sharp, bittersweet pain. Black Wolf's dark eyes seemed to capture hers even in memory, and Faith repressed her spontaneous response. Black Wolf was dead, as was Broken Hand and so many of the others who had entered her life so briefly. Yet it was strange . . . despite her depth of concern for Papa and her outrage at the wound he had suffered at the hands of these same people, her memories would not die.

Her gaze trailing from the readying train, Faith turned back to her mother and Dan once more. No, she could not share those thoughts with Mama. Mama suffered a pain of her own. Only William would understand, and she would see William soon. . . .

". . . And I must remind you, Dan, that you've given me your word that you won't send that wire until we've gotten a day into our journey."

"You have my word, ma'am."

Obviously still uncomfortable with that promise, Dan abruptly extended his hand in Lydia's direction.

"Ma'am, I'd like to say goodbye before I get you two ladies settled into the wagon. I'm thinkin' this is the last privacy we'll be gettin', and them boys over there will be strainin' their ears to hear anythin' that's bein' said, so . . . Well, I'd like to say that it's been a real pleasure bein' with you and

Faith for these few days, and I'm wishin' you safety on your journey. Wally's a lucky man."

Her light eyes filling unexpectedly, Lydia took Dan's hand and pressed it warmly.

"Dan, Wally was fortunate to have come across a man like you. Faith and I do appreciate all you've done for us."

Nodding, Dan turned toward Faith. He was so obviously touched that Faith could not restrain the warmth which suddenly suffused her. Stepping forward, she kissed his lined cheek and gave him a short spontaneous hug.

"Dan . . . thank you."

Dan's revealing flush speaking more clearly than his short, "My pleasure, Faith," Faith averted her suddenly tear-filled gaze and then followed him toward the waiting wagon master.

As she walked, she swallowed deeply, her mood lightening with the rapidly brightening sky. Yes, within a short time she and Mama would see Papa again. The medical supplies they were bringing would help to restore him to health, and they would remain with him until he was once again on his feet. And she would see William. She was seventeen now . . . a woman. She . . .

A young lieutenant separated from the group they were approaching and, smiling, started toward them. Her thoughts of a moment before slipping from her mind, Faith took a deep, sharp breath. Their journey was about to begin.

Anger burned hot and deep within Black Wolf as he stepped forward to speak. He did not feel the warm summer breeze which assaulted him, the heat of the noonday sun which shed its brilliant light on the warriors gathered in council. His smooth, russet skin darkened with the heat of the words he was about to speak. His great, well-muscled chest heaved from the agitation he suppressed as he jerked his broad shoulders erect and trailed his dark-eyed gaze over the sober Sioux, Arapaho, and Cheyenne chiefs in assembly in the great camp.

"I stand in wonder at the words that have been spoken this

day in council. My ears ring with the words of great war chiefs of my people, disbelief strong and harsh within me. Peace! The white man again sends messengers of peace. My brothers meet, and some speak in favor of the treaty which has been offered! Short . . . how very short is their memory! Do not my brothers remember? Must someone such as I recall the horror of Sand Creek, the many other treaties which the white man has violated?"

Taking a moment to draw his outrage under control, Black Wolf pinned Spotted Crow with his gaze.

"Spotted Crow speaks of a noble peace. There is no noble peace for the white man! The only peace the white man knows is that in which our people will surrender to his wants, turn away from the land to accept his way. The white man wishes to change us, make us white as he! To be thus is not my desire, nor the desire of the people of my camp. Only one peace struck with the white man will be a noble peace. It will be the peace that we *win* from him."

Turning to Spotted Crow once more, Black Wolf held the Sioux's impassive gaze with his own.

"There are within this council many noble warriors who favor peace. Spotted Crow is a noble warrior such as this. In his heart reigns the same strength of purpose as that which ruled the heart of Black Kettle as he led some of us to the white man's slaughter. So strong was Black Kettle's desire for peace that even after this great betrayal, he still sought peace with the white man. Years have passed and Black Kettle still has not found that peace. The white man continues to assail him, demanding more and greater concessions. Now even Black Kettle has finally been forced into battle in the great land to the south. Black Kettle, the most determined of us, has not been able to extract a peace from the white man who speaks peace with one face while he wields his weapon with another."

Turning away from Spotted Crow's sober countenance, Black Wolf surveyed the noble faces around him.

"We have fought hard and long in this great land. The white man has erected forts where he once promised he would not. He has allowed his people to enter where he once promised they would be forbidden. He attempts to protect their trespass on our land. He has all but driven the buffalo from the land to the south, and will soon do the same here if he is so allowed. In the long, hot days which have passed, we have stopped his progress in overrunning us. We must continue to oppose him until his forts are abandoned and the land is again ours.

"The white commander has forbidden his people to travel on the trail to the country where the white man takes the gold rocks from the earth. He allows through only those trains which bring supplies to his soldiers. Victory is near. We must continue to ride against their trains until they have no choice but to abandon their forts—to return the land to us once more. Then, and only then, will we achieve a noble peace, will our spirits again be free. But until that time we must ride against the white man, hunt him down. He is our enemy—our greatest enemy. We must remember, not forget what he has done. We must remember . . . and we must *fight!*"

Silence reigning after his impassioned speech, Black Wolf stepped back into the council circle once more. Maintaining his own silence now, he listened tensely to the other chiefs who rose to speak. As the afternoon sun began a slow descent in the sky, he assessed the moods of those around him, his satisfaction growing. When at last Red Cloud began to speak, Black Wolf felt a new elation sweep his breast. He flicked his eyes briefly closed as the dear faces of those now gone flicked before his eyes. Red Cloud's voice rang in the silence, calling for his people to continue their war against a white man who displayed no honor to the red man, against a white man with whom the only peace would be in victory.

At the completion of Red Cloud's speech, Black Wolf raised his voice with those of many others in a shouted confirmation of the path they would take. They would ride against the white man—force him from their land. They would show the white man that they would not accept a white man's peace, that they would fight for a peace which would bring them honor, or they would have no peace at all.

The council disbursed, Black Wolf strode from the small groups into which others had gathered. The need to be alone, far from this scene, was strong within him. With a brief glance toward the spot where Broken Hand and Red Cloud stood in conference, he made his way toward the pony he had tethered nearby. Releasing the animal, he mounted in a quick, fluid movement and turned him toward the rising land in the distance.

Black Wolf was racing over the yellowing prairie grass, reveling in the warm air which beat against his face, glorying in the council victory won, when the assault of a familiar visage unexpectedly entered his mind. Pressing his mount harder, he sought to avoid the glowing eyes, the fire-bright hair, but it was to no avail. He could not escape them. His anger raged anew, but this time its heat was directed at his own traitorous mind which accused him, taunted him . . . how different would all this have been had you not lost her . . . ?

"I should have known—damn!—I should have known." Crumpling the telegram he held into a ball, William threw it angrily into the corner of the room. Allowing his eyes to follow it to a bouncing rest against the wall in the far corner, William remained motionlessly staring at it for long moments. Then, abruptly snapping into motion, he covered the distance to it in a few rapid steps, and retrieved it. Unrolling the message once more, he walked the few steps to his desk and flattened the paper with his hand so he might reread it.

TO: CAPTAIN WILLIAM POTTER
    FORT LARAMIE

LYDIA AND FAITH DURHAM WITH WAGON TRAIN ARRIVING FORT LARAMIE IN A FEW DAYS. THEY WOULD NOT REMAIN IN DENVER. NOTIFY ME WHEN THEY HAVE ARRIVED SAFELY.

SIGNED DAN MCNULTY

Damn it, he should have known, should have realized when he'd first received the wire that Lydia and Faith were in

Denver, that they would not stop until they reached Wally. The knot in his stomach tightened and William raised a hand to rake his fingers through his heavy blond hair in an anxious gesture. It was his fault—his fault.

Flicking his eyes briefly closed as he sought to contain his frustration, William took a deep, steadying breath. He remembered only too clearly his first reaction when he had received Dan's first wire a few days before. Faith . . . so close . . . in Denver . . . His mind had immediately raced, canvassing the excuse he might manufacture to get to Denver to see her. But there had been no option open to him, and his frustration had soared. He had been only too keenly aware of the danger the Durham women would face should they succeed in coming to Fort Laramie as they obviously intended. But there had been little possibility of that happening. They had come so far only to be fated to disappointment. For that reason, he had not even notified Wally that his wife and daughter were in Denver. He had not wanted Wally to suffer the same frustration as he.

He had carefully ignored the nagging thought that these women had overcome great obstacles to arrive in Denver so quickly, had set aside their obvious determination to be with Wally. Had the dim hope that they would succeed in overcoming the last obstacle kept him from mentioning the telegram to Major Howland? If he were to be honest, he would have to admit it probably had. And now, because of his selfish desire to see Faith, she would be exposed to all manner of danger.

Experiencing a moment's guilt because he had not given Lydia more than a passing thought, William shook his head. Obsessed—God, he was obsessed with the thought of Faith Durham. Quickly, he reviewed the past three years, the years since his eyes had first touched on her. There had been no one for him but Faith since that first moment when he had seen her riding toward him on that Indian's horse. It had not mattered to him that she had been little more than a child at the time. He had responded immediately, instinctively, deeply to her qualities: intelligence, open sincerity, warmth and loyalty, the deep capacity for love he had sensed in her.

426

She had been so damned brave and resourceful, so unaware of her own courage. And she had been so beautiful. . . .

He truly had not thought she could grow more beautiful, nor had he thought he could become more deeply involved with her than he had been at that time. But he had, and that had increased his frustration . . . his fear of losing her. This last had allowed him to remain silent instead of performing his duty and notifying Major Howland so he might wire Colonel Carter to forbid the two women to travel to the fort.

William took a deep, ragged breath and turned toward the window, his eyes moving unseeingly over the fort yard and the tranquil terrain beyond. God . . . even now his heart was racing at the thought of Faith's arrival. A few days . . . she would be arriving in a few days.

Abruptly snapping from his mental meanderings, William drew himself to attention. He'd have to notify Major Howland immediately. The major would doubtless take steps to ensure that the train arrived safely. After all, supplies were low, and the forts up the line were in even worse shape than Laramie. And medical supplies . . . they were crucial to Wally's recovery. Pausing a moment more, William made a quick decision. He would not tell Wally of his wife and daughter's impending arrival. Durham's state was too precarious to place that burden on his mind.

Refusing to allow himself further time for thought until he had accomplished his purpose, William immediately snapped into action. He was moving across his small office toward the door when a small smile began to turn up the corners of his mouth. Well, what was done, was done. Faith was on her way here. She would arrive in a few days. And when she did, he was not going to allow her to get away from him again.

That determination fresh in his mind, William jerked open the door and turned toward Major Howland's office. He glanced up toward the sky, noting with a start that the sun had not reached its zenith. It wasn't yet noon. He gave a short, disbelieving laugh. He had only found out a few minutes ago that Faith was on her way and time was already beginning to drag. Damn, these were going to be long, hard days.

Deer Woman was quietly discharging her duties within Spotted Elk's lodge. She glanced toward the wounded warrior who lay on his sleeping bench. The slow rise and fall of his chest indicated that he slept easily and Deer Woman was content. Yellow Leaf had left an hour before, but the scent of the sweet grass he'd sprinkled on the coals of the fire lingered still.

Deer Woman crouched beside the fire and stirred the bubbling pot cooking there. Her mind was temporarily at rest. Spotted Elk was healing well. Soon he would again be able to take his place among the men of camp as he was wont to do. Amusement touched Deer Woman's sober features. She had spent much time in caring for Spotted Elk's wounds. She had seen him progress from weak silence in the days immediately following his wounding, to restlessness, and finally to impatience despite his body's truly rapid healing. But in all the time which had progressed, one thing had not changed. During his waking hours, Spotted Elk rarely took his eyes from her.

At first, Deer Woman had been disturbed by Spotted Elk's unceasing scrutiny. She had remembered only too well the days she would have been flattered by such attention, but she was intensely aware that those days were now gone. Instead, she had self-consciously averted her face in an attempt to conceal her marked cheek and its resulting deformity. But as the days had slipped by, she had ceased to hide from Spotted Elk's gaze, and had actually grown to find comfort in its warmth. She had ministered to him faithfully, but had carefully avoided any contact which exceeded the bounds of her sincere concern. During that time she had acquired new respect for Spotted Elk's bravery, for he had faced his pain and disability without complaint.

Deer Woman glanced toward Spotted Elk once more, her small smile slipping from her lips. Yes, he would soon be well, and she would no longer be needed within his lodge. She turned her eyes back to the fire, her brow creasing in a frown as she searched her heart. Yes, she would miss these days when Spotted Elk looked at her with longing. The time was long gone when she had allowed herself to enjoy such frivolities. She was no longer the pretty, flirtatious girl she had been before Sand Creek. She . . .

At the sound of racing hoofbeats, Deer Woman's head snapped up and at the same moment the alarm was given. Shouted voices . . . a wagon train . . . white soldiers making their way toward the fort the white man called Laramie!

Deer Woman rose to her feet and raced to the doorway of the lodge. Her eyes went first to Black Wolf's lodge and then into the distance in which Black Wolf approached at a gallop. Deer Woman's heart thrilled as Black Wolf neared. She allowed her eyes to absorb the grace of his muscular form as he leaned low over his horse's neck, his powerful arms holding the surging animal in control as he urged him to breathtaking speed. She watched as Black Wolf gradually reduced his mount's speed, reversing his posture to draw the beast to a snorting, pawing halt as he entered camp. Within moments he had leaped from his horse, surged through the frantic activity of warriors arming for a raid, and disappeared into his lodge.

Unable to withdraw her eyes from the doorway, she waited breathlessly for Black Wolf to emerge once more. Abruptly, he appeared. War paint marking the sharp planes of his cheeks, weapons in hand, strength gleaming on the sinewy contours of his body, and anticipation shining in the dark depths of his eyes, Black Wolf was the epitome of strength and power. Deer Woman emitted a short gasp. Yes, Black Wolf was all that her girlish dreams had ever imagined he could be. He was the man who held her heart. It mattered little to her that he felt nothing more for her than affection. She was a woman who had given her heart to one man—one man alone. That was the way it was, the way it would always be.

So intense was her concentration, Deer Woman did not sense the stirring to her rear, did not hear the belabored approach of Spotted Elk until he abruptly appeared behind her. She turned to him, eyes glowing with the wealth of feelings Black Wolf inspired within her. Pain flickered in Spotted Elk's gaze, but Deer Woman was unmindful of its presence. All else besides her absorption in Black Wolf fading, she turned back to watch as he again mounted his pony, signaling to the warriors beside him as he heeled his mount into the stream of the force which rode in pursuit of the white man's wagon train.

Watching in silence until the last glimpse of Black Wolf had faded from sight, Deer Woman became suddenly conscious of Spotted Elk's touch on her arm and his warmth close beside her. She turned to him, regret surging through her as he spoke with sincerity.

"Your heart reaches out to Black Wolf, Deer Woman, but Black Wolf's heart is closed to yours. Grief and hatred have closed it to that which you would give to him. But my heart would answer yours, Deer Woman. I would—"

Spotted Elk's impassioned speech was halted by the light pressure of Deer Woman's fingers against his lips. His eyes flicked briefly closed at the intimacy of the touch, and Deer Woman felt a warmth stir within her. Yes, this man loved, but she did not love in return. . . .

Without a word, Deer Woman turned, taking Spotted Elk's arm and slipping it around her slender shoulders as she guided him carefully back to his sleeping bench. When he was resting once more, she turned from his scrutiny and walked back to the fire. Seating herself beside it, she stirred the pot, her mind returning to the memory of Black Wolf as he rode out of sight. She knew her thoughts would not be free until he had returned in safety to the camp—until her eyes again touched on him.

Behind her, silent and forgotten, Spotted Elk held Deer Woman in his gaze.

Faith turned in the saddle, looking back along the long line of supply wagons moving on the trail behind her. Finding the wagon she sought, she raised her hand, her heart stirring as her mother returned her wave. Her throat choking with emotion, Faith blinked back the tears which unexpectedly filled her eyes. Mama was so very worried about Papa that all efforts to relieve her mind had been useless. As for herself, she knew she needed to escape her own worries for her father's health, if only for a little while. She took a deep breath and turned to the young lieutenant who rode at her side.

"Lieutenant Piersall, would it be all right if we rode out in advance of the train a little way? I would dearly enjoy a brief respite from the dust and noise." Noting the hesitation which flickered momentarily across the young lieutenant's serious expression, Faith shook her head. "Oh, I'm sorry. I don't mean to be a burden to you. It was extremely generous of Captain Hallmark to allow me the use of one of your horses, although I expect you are inwardly regretting the captain's generosity. It cannot be too pleasant a task riding after me the day long."

"You need not apologize to me, Miss Durham." A fleeting smile lightened Lieutenant Piersall's sharply boned face. "And you may believe I am most sincere when I say it is a pleasure being assigned to accompany you on your ride. To be honest, I'm the envy of the whole train. I only hesitate because I worry for your safety. To stray too far from the train would be a mistake."

"Oh, you can be sure I had no intention of straying from the train, Lieutenant." Faith shook her head with great emphasis, causing the brilliant red-gold curls which streamed loosely down her back to glimmer in the reflected light of the midday sun. Her great azure eyes were suddenly intensely sober. "I just didn't think there would be any danger involved in riding ahead a short way because the train is so well protected and scouts are riding in advance of the column. But if you think—"

"Well, as long as we don't ride far, I think that would be fine. I just wanted to caution you."

Grateful for the young lieutenant's concession, Faith nodded, her smile brightening.

"You may consider that I've been cautioned, Lieutenant. Come on, let's go."

Abruptly turning her horse, Faith spurred him forward.

Waiting only until she was out in the clear, she pressed him to a faster pace. A flicker of elation shot through her as the spirited animal lurched into a gallop, stretching out his long legs in a great, effortless stride. Unmindful of the picture she presented as she leaned over the horse's neck, her brilliant, fiery curls streaming out behind her, she urged her mount onward, cantering easily along the side of the train and into the lead. Realizing the distance between the lead wagon and herself was beginning to stretch out, Faith regretfully reined in a few minutes later. She had yet to see the advance scout, but she could not, in all good conscience, put any more distance between herself and the train. Everyone had been too kind for her to be uncooperative.

Pulling her horse back into a trot, Faith turned toward Lieutenant Piersall who had maintained his place beside her. His thin, almost homely face, was startlingly altered by his wide, unexpectedly warm grin.

"You're an excellent horsewoman, Miss Durham. I haven't see a woman ride like that since I left my father's farm in Connecticut."

"Does your father keep a riding stable on his farm, Lieutenant?"

"Yes, ma'am, he does. He's quite proud of it. He's written me that he has a new foal for which he has great hopes right now. The little fella was sired by a real beauty, and his mama is one of my father's best mares. I'm looking forward to seeing him when I get back East." A brief, almost unintelligible flicker of regret touched his expression. "I expect Nightguard will be a lively two-year-old by then, but that doesn't make my anticipation less keen. You look like you were born to the saddle, ma'am. Where did you learn to ride?"

Faith gave a short shrug. She had no intention of sharing the memories of her wild rides across the prairie with Black Wolf. No, those times were too precious.

"I was given lessons at school, and after I returned to the East, Papa bought me my own horse."

Lieutenant Piersall smiled and made a polite comment, but Faith found her attention drifting. Somehow, she had difficulty concentrating on inconsequentials this day.

Keeping her horse to a modest pace, she took a deep breath and sought to get a hold on her wildly rioting emotions. Unexpectedly, her mother's sober face returned to her mind, and Faith swallowed tightly. This journey was awakening old memories for Mama, too. The shadows now visible in her mother's eyes had been absent for a long time. But she supposed Mama had no more conquered her memories than she had. There was no doubt that a return to this wild land had brought them vividly to life. But Black Wolf and Broken Hand could not be brought back. They were gone, and with them had gone the . . .

The crack of a gunshot, then another and another shattered the sun-drenched silence, and Faith started. She gripped the reins of her frightened chestnut, darting a quick glance in Lieutenant Piersall's direction. But the lieutenant was staring straight ahead, at the forward scout who was riding back in their direction at a rapid gallop. The scout was shouting.

Oh, God, no . . .

The scout's voice became clearer.

"Indians . . . two or three hundred . . ."

Not waiting for further explanation, Lieutenant Piersall turned toward her, his voice gruff with command.

"Miss Durham, back to the train! Quickly."

But Faith needed no urging. Turning her horse, she spurred him into a gallop. The wagons were already drawing into a circle when she reached the train a few moments later. Drawing up sharply, momentarily disoriented by the unfamiliar formation, Faith made a frantic attempt to sight her mother's wagon within the dust-clouded scene. Panic was beginning to assail her when Captain Hallmark's voice reached her.

"Miss Durham, please, into the nearest wagon. The Indians will be over the rise in a few minutes. We want you to be secured."

Gunfire was now coming from the forward points over the hill, and Faith began to feel fear pulse through her. Mama . . . where was she?

433

"Captain, my mother—"

"She will be adequately protected. You've no time to find her now. Quickly, please."

Obeying the captain's command, Faith accepted Lieutenant Piersall's aid as he all but lifted her into the wagon. He followed her inside, quickly rearranging the sacks of flour and grain to afford her a position in which to lie surrounded by them. The gunshots were getting closer and he darted a quick look over his shoulder. Turning back in her direction, he frowned, his concern evident.

"This wagon should be safe, ma'am. All these sacks will be real good protection. Now all you need to do is keep your head down." His dark eyes serious, he added in a low voice, "Please do that, ma'am. None of us here needs the distraction of worrying about you getting shot. And we would worry, ma'am."

Touched by his obvious sincerity, Faith nodded.

"I'll be fine here, Lieutenant. Please . . . take care of yourself."

"Yes, ma'am. I'll be right outside the wagon if you need me."

Abruptly, gunshots were ringing around them, and the sound of war cries reached her ears, sending a raft of chills down her spine. Faith lowered her head, covering her ears against their familiar ring, against the flood of memories suddenly inundating her mind.

She remembered . . . gunfire surrounding the wagon train that day so long ago . . . savage yells . . . the moans of the wounded . . . the deadly circle tightening . . . the pounding of thundering hooves . . . the choking dust. Mrs. Cummings was shot . . . dead . . . and little three-year-old Mary was alone . . . frightened and crying. Mama had been frozen with fear, and she had seen the child preparing to dart out from under the wagon. It was then that she had run out to save Mary. The Indian pony had come up behind her and she had been taken. Mama had tried to help her, and she had been taken, too.

Papa . . . shot in the chest, bleeding . . .

Faith lifted her head. The hoofbeats were getting louder,

the shots were ringing nearer the wagon. War cries . . . savage . . . more savage than she remembered, sounded near the wagon. Oh, God, it was happening again!

Faith buried her head in her arms. Fool . . . she had been a fool to ride out ahead of the train. She had been lulled by the sunlit serenity of the day. Steeped in memories she had altered to exclude this horror, she had been lulled into a sense of safety by the size of the force around her. But the Indians outnumbered them—two hundred the scout had said—and Mama was alone! Was Mama afraid—frightened enough to suffer a return of the confusion which had paralyzed her mind? Was she safe?

A hoard of doubts assailing her, Faith momentarily rose to her knees. She paused, about to go seek out her mother, only to remember Lieutenant Piersall's warning. No, she could not burden that conscientious soldier because of a foolish move. She would have to remain where she was.

Lowering herself to the floor of the wagon once more, Faith winced as the bullets rang closer and the sounds of battle rose around her.

Time passed, marked only by the furor which increased outside the wagon. Confined as she was, she was entirely unaware of the direction the battle was taking, and frustration began to blossom hard and tight within her. Gasping shouts . . . cries of wounded soldiers . . . right beside the wagon. She heard the thudding of running feet, the grunting sounds of struggle, and she could stand the suspense no longer.

Lifting herself slightly, Faith struggled to raise a small portion of the canvas cover, finally succeeding in securing herself a small opening through which she could view the inner circle of wagons. She gasped.

Firing was rapid, being conducted from behind hastily stacked crates. She searched the immediate area for Lieutenant Piersall and was relieved to see that he was firing from a position close beside her wagon. She uttered a short prayer of thanksgiving. But others had not been so fortunate. Two still, lifeless bodies lay exposed within the circle. Emotion choked her. Only a short time before they had been smiling, joking troopers without a care in the—

Suddenly freezing, Faith saw that one of those troopers, a young, fair-haired fellow was moving! He was groaning, blood streaming from his chest as bullets snapped the ground around him. He was alive . . . but he would not be for long. Surely one of those bullets would strike him if someone did not move him into cover. He would be . . .

A sudden flurry of movement directly in front of her wagon lowered Faith's gaze toward Lieutenant Piersall once more. He was drawing himself to a standing position, looking toward the wounded soldier. Oh, no, he was going to . . .

Suddenly Lieutenant Piersall was running. Within seconds his tall, slender form was bent over the groaning soldier. He was dragging the wounded man back toward the wagon, even as the firing became more intense. He was almost to safety. . . . He was . . .

Another barrage of shots sounded, and Lieutenant Piersall jerked abruptly straight. An expression of sudden bewilderment on his rawboned face, he stood immobile for endless seconds, only to be struck again. The second shot knocked him roughly to the ground beside the man he had attempted to save.

Her eyes wide with horror, Faith remained motionless, her gaze pinned on the rapidly widening circle of red on Lieutenant Piersall's chest. There was a second circle on his shoulder from which blood was beginning to puddle on the hard-packed ground. Faith strained her eyes. Lieutenant Piersall's chest was still moving. He was still alive, but he would bleed to death if he did not get help. He had been so close to the wagon . . . so close to safety. . . .

Slowly, Faith raised herself to a crouching position and inched her way to the rear of the wagon. She worked at the bolts which secured the flap with shaking hands. Abruptly, the flap fell free. No obstruction now between her and the ground, Faith took a deep breath and then jumped from the wagon. Her heart pounding in her ears, she raced toward Lieutenant Piersall's side. Bullets snapped around her, but it was just a few feet more. . . .

She leaned over the lieutenant and tried to move him. He was heavy . . . she had not realized how very heavy he would be. Suddenly, another trooper was at her side, and another. Within seconds Lieutenant Piersall was under the wagon, and the other wounded soldier as well. Rough hands were forcing her down, gruff commands were being shouted in her ear.

"Stay here, and don't try anything like that again! Take care of these men if you want to help, damn it!"

But Faith was already working at the lieutenant's jacket in the hope of stemming the flow of blood from his chest. She had no time to listen to warnings, to abide by commands. She was too busy . . . too busy.

Black Wolf leaned low over his racing pony, guiding him with the skilled pressure of his knees as he raised his gun and fired again. His bullet found its mark within the besieged circle, and a blue-coated soldier jerked spontaneously under its impact and fell to the ground. Black Wolf urged his pony onward.

Turning his mount abruptly, Black Wolf darted back into cover, then drew up his horse to silently assess the progress of the battle. A deep satisfaction filled him. Movement within the circle of wagons was lessening. Many soldiers had fallen and lay wounded and dying, openly exposed to his people's bullets. He trained his gaze on a wounded soldier so exposed. As he watched, another soldier ran to the wounded man's side, and Black Wolf raised his gun and fired. The second soldier fell, and Black Wolf felt satisfaction ring through him. He and his people would strike these soldiers down, one at a time until all of them had . . .

Noting movement beside the fallen soldier, he raised his gun, his finger on the trigger, and then he froze. Disbelief crowded his mind. A slender figure . . . a woman with hair the color of fire . . . She had slipped from a nearby wagon and had run to the wounded men. She turned. . . .

The world came to a sudden, shuddering halt as the face which haunted his dreams turned fully into Black Wolf's view. More mature . . . even more beautiful to his startled mind . . . it was she! She had returned!

As Black Wolf watched incredulously, eyes as blue as the morning sky widened with anxiety as Fire Spirit futilely attempted to pull the wounded soldier toward the safety of the wagon. Bullets snapped the ground around her, but her courage did not falter.

Not stopping to question his reasoning, Black Wolf cursed the gunshots of his own people, the firing which endangered her life. He swallowed against the tension which thickened his throat.

Another soldier raced into the exposed circle, and another. His finger twitched on the trigger of his gun, but he could not fire. The three moved the wounded soldiers under a nearby wagon and returned to fight, but the woman remained with the wounded men.

Black Wolf's tension increased. Ministering to the wounded men as she was, the woman was partially exposed to the gunfire of his people. Conflicting feelings raged within him as bullets continued to snap the ground around the wagon. Anxiety assailed him. Dust clouds from racing hooves impeded his vision, and Black Wolf fought his warring feelings, straining his eyes into the grainy mist. The brilliant, fiery head was close to the face of the wounded soldier. Did she whisper to him . . . console him? A wild fury flared within Black Wolf. The bright-haired one's loyalties were openly displayed. The color of her skin prevailed.

Black Wolf's rage burned hotter as his eyes devoured the female outline etched against the dust of battle. His finger tightened on the trigger of his gun.

Faith turned from the unknown, fair-haired soldier's body. Dead . . . the poor boy was dead.

A supreme sense of loss shaking her, Faith moved to Lieutenant Piersall who lay motionless nearby. She surveyed the rapidly widening circles of blood on his chest and shoulder, his shallow breathing; and as tears threatened she choked up. He was dying, too, and there was nothing she

438

could do.

Abruptly, Faith was struck with a thought. The wagon in which she had traveled with her mother—a small kit filled with medication and bandages had been stored under the seat. Surely this wagon was similarly equipped. Bandages, tightly binding the lieutenant's wounds, would stop the flow of blood, allow him at least a chance at survival. She took a deep breath. It was the only chance the young lieutenant had.

Faith leaned down toward Lieutenant Piersall. His eyelids were flickering, and she whispered softly in the hope that he could hear her.

"Lieutenant . . . Lieutenant, I have to leave you for a few moments, but I'll be back as soon as I can, with bandages."

There was no response and Faith touched the pale cheek lightly with her fingertips. No, she did not want this very nice young man to die.

Turning, Faith began to crawl along the ground toward the rear of the wagon. The fury of the battle had not lessened. Hooves continued to pound the ground in a deadly circle around them, and the gunfire was constant. She would be exposed to that fire for the few moments it would take to raise herself over the lowered back flap and slip into the wagon. A few moments . . . a few moments to save a man's life.

Faith reached the rear of the wagon, and she paused. But she had little time to waste. She took a deep breath. In a quick, scrambling movement she cleared the underside of the wagon. She stood up and was attempting to jump onto the wagon when her gown caught on the dangling flap, holding her fast. She fought to free herself, panic assailing her as she jerked and pulled at the skirt, trying to work herself free. The savage war cries were drawing closer, the gunfire was increasing. If she did not free herself soon it would be too late!

She pulled harder. Gasping with relief as her dress tore free, she turned to pull herself up into the wagon at the same moment hoofbeats drew startlingly close. She turned, her eyes touching on the flashing movement of a strong arm as it

439

whipped out to scoop her up into the air and onto the back of a horse.

Horror and disbelief invaded Faith's senses. No! It could not be happening again—not again! Suddenly she was struggling, fighting with all her strength. Her hands curling into fists, she pounded at the arms imprisoning her, squirming to break free of the breathtaking hold as the great animal on which she rode turned under her captor's direction and began to gallop away from the train. Realizing in a few moments it would be too late, Faith made a last desperate attempt to break free. Suddenly going rigid, she attempted to slip from the horse's back. A low, grunting sound of outrage echoed in her ears, the familiarity of it sending a quiver of shock down her spine the moment before the powerful hand which had so efficiently subdued her rose in a quick, sharp blow.

Pain exploded against her chin in a shower of bright, careening colors. A sudden humming in her ears grew deafening. It drowned out the sounds of battle, the anxiety with which she fought, all else but the darkness which began its rapid assault . . . which reached up to swallow her in its silence. . . .

The gunfire became louder, closer, as William forced his mount forward at the head of the racing column. Heading a routine patrol, he had ridden out much farther than usual and had just about ordered his men to return when he had heard shots in the distance.

Aware that sound traveled for great distances on the open land, William was uncertain exactly when he would come upon the foray in progress. His anxiety profound, he was close to desperation as the charging column approached the crest of the rise.

His strong gelding laboring, William abruptly cleared the rise, his breath catching in his throat as the scope of the attack in progress was revealed to him for the first time.

In the distance he saw a wagon train assembled into a rough circle. It was surrounded, outnumbered at least two to one by the attacking Indians, and suffering greatly as a result. Mounted Indian warriors, their war cries unceasing, circled the train, firing at will. Their attack had been very effective if he was to judge by the limited fire which came from the train and by the motionless bodies visible within the besieged circle of wagons.

Pausing only long enough to allow his column to clear the rise, he sent a last look behind him. Raising his hand, he brought it down in a signal which sent him and his men charging forward.

They were riding to the aid of the train when William realized the Indians were scattering. In a manner which made effective pursuit almost impossible, the attacking circle was broadening as they drew closer, spreading into the countryside surrounding it, the Indians heading in so many directions that it was difficult to find one on which to concentrate his men. Making an abrupt decision, William charged toward the largest of the scattering groups, signaling half his men to pursue another body of Indians traveling in the opposite direction.

His mind on the band before him, William did not see the great Indian pony concealed in the nearby terrain. He did not see the Indian warrior who held his unconscious, bright-haired captive against his chest with grim determination as he made his way through the uneven landscape and melted into obscurity.

Chapter XXIV

Lydia exerted a stringent effort to control her trembling as she walked along the narrow hallway toward Wally's room. She was still in a state of shock. She had not believed Captain Hallmark when he had reported that Faith had been captured in the raid on the wagon train, and she had wandered among the survivors, expecting Faith to appear at any moment. But Faith had not been among them.

Lydia's eyes closed briefly, the memory of William's raging despair over Faith's capture returning to her mind. In him she had seen mirrored the depth of her own pain, a pain which tore at her still. But it had all been for naught. Faith was gone.

Turning her gaze toward William as he walked stiffly at her side, Lydia glanced questioningly at him. The train had arrived at the fort hours before, but she had not yet seen Wally. She had been in no condition to face him in her distraught state, and Dr. Mallory had denied her access to her husband. She realized now the wisdom in the doctor's decision, and she took a deep steadying breath. She had not realized how very ill Wally was. She breathed deeply once more. Dr. Mallory had advised her not to upset him, not to tell him of Faith's capture. She had spent the last hour attempting to gain control of her emotions, and in preparing the lie which she would be forced to tell him. She only hoped he would not see through her charade.

Placing a supportive hand on her elbow as they

442

approached the end of the hall, William paused before he opened the door and ushered her inside.

The small, sparsely furnished room was lit by a flickering lamp on the night table beside the bed. Lydia slowly approached the cot on which Wally lay, not even glancing at the silent, gray-haired doctor who stood beside it. Suppressing the gasp which rose to her lips, she was abruptly thankful that Wally was unconscious of her approach. She needed the time to steel herself against the shock of his extensive physical deterioration.

In quaking silence, Lydia moved closer, her eyes scanning Wally's beloved face. He was changed . . . oh, so changed. The broad, strong planes of his face were hollowed, shadowed by an absence of color. His pale eyes, unnaturally bright, flicked open to look in her direction, but he did not see her. His large frame appeared to have shrunk as he moved restlessly on his bed, and even the color of his hair seemed to have faded to a shadow of its former vibrant shade.

As she watched, Wally glanced again in her direction. A glimmer of recognition flickering momentarily in his eyes, and he mumbled a short, disjointed sentence under his breath. A broad grin stretched momentarily across his lips, the first sign of the Wally of old, and Lydia suppressed the sob which rose to her throat. She reached out a shaking hand to touch his fevered brow, a tremor of fear coursing through her at the heat which met her touch.

She blanched. Then she turned great shadowed eyes toward Dr. Mallory whose expression was grave.

"Doctor, he doesn't know me . . . I had not realized . . ." Momentarily unable to continue, Lydia swallowed and tried again. "You told me that Wally was very ill, but I did not expect . . ."

Lydia's glance flicked toward William, her obvious need bringing him supportively to her side. She took another deep breath.

"The medicine which has arrived on the train . . . will it help? Will he get well?"

William's hand tightened spontaneously on her arm as she

spoke, and Lydia raised her eyes to take in his tense expression. She fought to control the emotion which shook her. Faith . . . gone, she knew not where. And now Wally . . . Oh, God, she could not lose them both.

Accurately reading her gaze, William gripped her arm tighter. His low tone was filled with resolution.

"Dr. Mallory will do his best for Wally, Lydia. And I'll get Faith back from the Indians who took her. I give you my word on that."

Realizing the intensity of the feelings William suppressed, Lydia nodded, her hand moving weakly to her forehead as she glanced back toward Wally.

"Mrs. Durham . . ."

Dr. Mallory's low, gravelly voice turned her in his direction. His full white mustache twitched as he continued with obvious discomfort.

"I only wish I could tell you what you want to hear. I've already explained the nature of Wally's condition to you. I'm hopeful he'll respond well to the new medication." Dr. Mallory offered a small smile. "In any case, I know your arrival will do him a considerable amount of good."

"Even if he doesn't realize I'm here?"

A short sob rose to Lydia's lips, but she restrained it with sheer strength of will.

"Ma'am . . ."

Taking another deep breath, Lydia managed a brief smile. "If you would be so kind, Dr. Mallory . . . William, to leave me alone with my husband for a while . . ."

Catching the quick glances exchanged by the two men, Lydia felt her face stiffen. No, she did not need their care right now. She needed to be with Wally, to touch him, to talk to him, whether he was able to understand her or not.

"Of course, Mrs. Durham."

Shooting William a glance as his hand dropped from her arm, Lydia felt her control slipping away. William was suffering as much as she. There was no doubt in her mind that he loved Faith, loved her deeply. She could not truly understand the reason she had resisted that fact so strongly before. Lydia's eyes dropped briefly closed. Where was this

444

all going to end?

Lydia did not bother to watch as the two men walked toward the door. Turning back to Wally's unnaturally flushed face, she waited only until the door clicked shut behind her to move closer to his side. He appeared to have fallen into a restless sleep at last. Leaning over him, she kissed his mouth, a short sob escaping as his eyes fluttered open to focus on her face. He did not speak, and unable to get words past the lump in her own throat, Lydia leaned over to kiss his lips once more.

Unexpectedly, Wally was responding to her kiss, his mouth moving against hers. Lydia released a startled gasp which was smothered by the heated intensity of Wally's kiss as his hand moved strongly into her hair to hold her fast. Refusing to relinquish his hold even when he drew his mouth from hers at last, Wally stared at her in silence.

"Wally . . . are you conscious, darling, or are you—"

"Lydia . . . you are here. I woke up and I thought . . ." Wally's other arm closed around her with startling strength, drawing her closer. "I thought I was dreaming, and it was such a damned good dream." His trip tightened. "But I'm not dreaming, am I?"

"No, Wally, I'm here."

Wally hesitated, his eyes moving hungrily over her face. "Faith . . . is she with you? Did she—?"

"No, dear. She— I decided it would be safer if she waited for us in Denver. Dan will take care of her."

Wally gave a low laugh. "Dan will love that." His smile fading, he shook his head. "You shouldn't have come either . . . but now that you're here, I'm glad . . . very glad."

Her deceit setting poorly with her, Lydia nodded.

"Wally, I want—"

"I don't want to talk any more now, Lydia." Wally's voice was getting weaker, but his grip was unrelenting. He was pulling her down toward him with surprising strength. "I just want to hold you. Lie down beside me, darling."

Lydia shook her head in spontaneous protest.

"Wally, what will the doctor think if he comes back here and finds me lying—"

"I don't give a damn."

Within moments she was lying beside him, and Wally was clutching her close, his hands caressing her.

"Wally, your leg . . ."

"To hell with my leg."

"Wally, the doctor said—"

"Later . . . later . . ."

Wally's mouth was moving against hers. His body was so incredibly thin as it pressed against her, his face was so pale. Lydia sensed that his strength was beginning to wane. Sudden fear overwhelming her, she wound her arms around Wally's neck, lending him her strength. She opened her mouth to his kiss, thrilled at his low murmured response. Oh, yes, Wally would use her strength and he would get well. But for the time being, she would be strong enough for both of them. That was the way it would have to be.

Black Wolf stood unmoving in the shadows of his lodge. At war with his emotions, he allowed his eyes to move over the still, female form that lay on his sleeping bench a few feet away. He briefly closed his eyes as self-contempt assailed him.

This woman and he were separated by the hatred which raged between their people. They were enemies. The girl he had known during a brief summer long ago was gone, as was the young warrior who had committed himself to her. Both had been swept away by the passage of time and the spilling of blood.

Black Wolf chastised himself further in his anger. Had he forgotten that this woman had almost caused his death once before? Only his stubborn determination to hold onto life had allowed him to survive when he had been left on the prairie. Did he not realize that she had driven coldly away with her family, thinking him dead? Had he not, this day, seen the loving care she had lavished on the wounded soldier under the wagon . . . seen her whisper soft words against his lips . . . seen her risk her life in an attempt to save that unknown man?

Black Wolf took a step closer to her. This woman who lay in unconscious silence before him was his enemy. That truth was reflected in the color of her skin, the blood which flowed in her veins, the heart which beat inside her breast.

He took another step closer, and then another. He crouched beside the sleeping bench, his hand reaching out spontaneously to touch the bruise which marked her chin. He had hit her, his anger great when she had resisted him, sought to escape him. In truth, he was uncertain of the reason for the driving force which had caused him to race forward and withdraw her from her threatened position, from the bullets which cut the air around her as she struggled to get to the safety within the wagon. He had known a compelling desire to protect her—keep her safe. And once he had touched her, taken her up into his arms, he had been unwilling to let her go.

Black Wolf frowned and took a deep breath in an attempt to stave off the tumult erupting within him. His hand moved to tangle in the fiery strands splayed against the surface of the robes, and his heart struck up a new, accelerated beat as he remembered the texture of her hair against his palm. Warm, light, the strands curled around his fingers with a life of their own, glowing in the limited light.

His eyes left their brilliance and moved slowly to the woman's still face. She had not yet regained consciousness. His blow had been strong, struck in flaring anger because of her resistance to him and the danger in which she had willingly placed herself for another. Black Wolf released a short snort in acknowledgment of and contempt for the jealousy that had overwhelmed him. It raged still in him because he had seen this woman risk her life to save another man while she had allowed him to be left to die those many years before.

His heart pounding and a raging heat coming alive inside him, Black Wolf allowed his eyes to trail her face. Fire Spirit . . . with skin as light and unmarked as the winter snows . . . with eyes as blue as the summer sky . . . with lips warm and soft . . . with a mouth so sweet to the taste it drove from memory the taste of all others. Her lips were parted. He

447

longed to take them once more.

Forcibly tearing his gaze from Fire Spirit's lips, Black Wolf swept her with his glance, taking in the womanly curves which had replaced the child's body he had held in that time long ago. Child that she had been, Fire Spirit had stirred him more than any woman in the long, angry years between. Desire strong inside him, he wanted to know the woman she had become, to hold her close, to make her a part of him. Contempt, anger, and despair assailed him; and Black Wolf felt a new fury suffuse him. Enemy of his people that Fire Spirit was, he desired her. The memory of her had given him no peace. At present she was a specter within his lodge, stirring him again to know feelings he had considered long dead.

Black Wolf stared hard at the woman who had filled his thoughts so determinedly throughout the long years of separation. No, she would not again escape him. He had been a fool before, but he would not suffer the same mistakes again. She was his captive, and she would be his slave. He would use her in the ways which best suited him, and in so doing he would purge her from his mind. When he was done with her he would dispose of her as he saw fit. But for now he would enjoy his dominance over her. It would be vengeance indeed. . . .

Faith struggled against the growing light of consciousness. Familiar scents from a time long past invaded her nostrils, and fear invaded her semiconscious mind. A fire burning close by . . . buffalo robes beneath her . . . sweet grass surrounding her . . . Her skin prickled with a strange expectancy, even as her heavy lids lifted to the subdued light.

The sounds of battle were no more. In silence she viewed the small circle of sky visible in countless dreams, sky seen through the smoke outlet of a Cheyenne lodge. Cautiously, almost fearfully she allowed her gaze to descend to the lodge's interior, her heart thudding to a breathless halt as the face of a man moved suddenly into view. Faith gasped as a familiar dark-eyed gaze met hers coldly, as familiar hands reached out to grasp her shoulders in a bruising grip. She attempted to speak but could not. Surely this was a dream. . . .

A bitter amusement rose on the harshly handsome face above hers.

"You had not expected to see my face again, Fire Spirit. You believed my flesh to be consumed by the wild animals of the land, my bones to be bleaching in the sun where I had been left to die. But as you can see, that was not so."

The apparition beside her more than her confused mind could comprehend, Faith allowed her eyes to close briefly, only to hear Black Wolf's voice rasp in command.

"Open your eyes, Fire Spirit! Look upon the man who once again holds you his prisoner. And know this"—his face drawing closer until she could feel his sweet-scented breath against her lips, Black Wolf hissed—"know that I will allow you no escape. Such will not be the fate I have determined for you."

Faith shook her head in unconscious denial of the hatred burning in Black Wolf's eyes. She was confused, disoriented. . . .

"How . . . how did I get here? The wagon train . . . Mama . . ."

"The train is gone—on to the fort as was intended. But we have struck our vengeance again. You were already my captive when the soldiers arrived."

"You—you were the one who hit me!"

Black Wolf touched her chin and she winced with pain. The responsive flicker in his dark eyes was fleeting.

"You attempted to escape me."

"Mama . . . where is she?"

"I know nothing of the woman of whom you speak."

Total recall suddenly draining her face of color, Faith closed her eyes once more.

"Lieutenant Piersall . . . he was shot, bleeding to death. I . . . I was trying to stop the bleeding."

Black Wolf's face hardened.

"My bullets struck cleanly. Had not the soldiers come, that soldier's scalp would hang from my belt as well as—"

"You . . . you shot him!" Pulling back from his touch, Faith stared at Black Wolf with disbelief. "The wagon train was proceeding peacefully. There was no reason for the attack."

"The desire to avenge that which was done to us—"

Faith shook her head.

"You *are* a savage! It is true, isn't it—everything that's been written about the war here? Senseless Indian attacks . . . murder . . . scalping . . . My father lies wounded at Fort Laramie. Had he been less fortunate, his scalp might be hanging from your belt right now. Yet you are proud of your evil deeds!" Faith shook her head, disbelief flowing through her.

"If so, you would have suffered a loss which our people have suffered many times! I do not share your outrage. The outrages the white man has committed against my people have numbed me to pain."

Faith shook her head, incredulity overwhelming her. This man before her . . . she did not know him. He wore the face of the Black Wolf she remembered, altered little by the years between except in strength and maturity. The difference was in his eyes. This Black Wolf looked at her with eyes devoid of warmth, cold eyes filled with hatred. Savage . . . he was no different from the savages who had raided their wagon train that first day, the savages dedicated to washing the land with blood rather than allowing the white man to advance further upon it. The Black Wolf she remembered was a myth constructed by youthful memory, a man who had never been. She had been a fool to have spent so much of her life mourning this mythical man who had never existed.

Faith took a short breath and gritted her teeth with angry determination. She lifted her chin, unconsciously challenging Black Wolf's domination.

"Mama . . . she was on the train."

"I told you, I know nothing of the woman you call mother."

Relief swept Faith's mind. Mama had not been captured. Faith's mind raced. She would find a way to es—

His sensitivity to her thoughts startling, Black Wolf

gripped Faith's chin, holding her ruthlessly immobile under his gaze.

"You indulge in foolish dreams. You will not escape me. I . . ."

An unexpected step in the doorway of the lodge turned both heads in its direction. Faith gasped with shock, unable to take her eyes from the familiar figure of Broken Hand as he walked to Black Wolf's side. Alive . . . Broken Hand was alive! If Mama knew . . .

Broken Hand observed her coldly as Black Wolf drew himself to his feet. The younger warrior's brow darkened as Broken Hand spoke a few words in their native tongue. Black Wolf's response was brief, his reaction immediate. Even as Broken Hand turned and strode from the lodge, Black Wolf pulled Faith unceremoniously to her feet.

Her head reeling at the jarring movement, Faith voiced an instinctive protest, but her words were ignored as Black Wolf all but carried her from the lodge to his waiting horse and swung her astride its back. Within moments Black Wolf was mounted behind her, his strong arms holding her fast, his broad chest supporting her as he jabbed his heels into his pony's sides. Before Faith had had time to fully realize what had happened, they were racing from camp, a horse on a lead following.

Her eyes trained on the two horses racing into the distance, Deer Woman gripped the rough hide which framed the entrance to her lodge. Behind her, inside the lodge, her mother's sister prepared the evening meal, her small daughter at her side. The recent raid had affected the women of this lodge very little. They had chosen to remain within, away from the turmoil of returning warriors and angry voices.

Deer Woman suppressed a short, bitter laugh. Her family had not been touched by the raid this day, but she knew with bitter certainty that her own life had been unalterably changed by the events which had transpired. The red-haired woman was back in camp, and back in Black Wolf's arms

451

once more.

Her gaze returning to the distance where the two Indian ponies began to fade from sight, Deer Woman felt pain twist anew inside her. She had been working within Spotted Elk's lodge as the wounded warrior had slept, waiting with restless anxiety for Black Wolf's return. The first shouts within camp, signaling the war party's return, had brought her running to the doorway. Her gaze had searched the warriors riding in, relief touching her upon seeing Black Wolf's familiar outline among them. And then she had seen the captive he had clutched in his arms. The rapid beat of her heart had seemed to jerk to a sudden halt when she had seen the flaming color of the woman's hair.

Disbelief had assailed her as she had watched Black Wolf hand the white woman's unconscious body down to Broken Hand before dismounting to take her again into his arms. Then a hot, molten rage had begun to flow through her veins as Black Wolf had carried the white woman into his lodge. Deer Woman had been shuddering with the intensity of her jealous fury when a broad palm had closed around her arm. She had directed a heated glance up into Spotted Elk's eyes, growling her contempt for the compassion in his dark eyes. She did not desire his compassion, his concern. She had wanted only Black Wolf, who was lost to her.

She had stridden from Spotted Elk's lodge, and had not returned. Instead, she had listened and watched as anger within the Cheyenne camp at Black Wolf's captive had begun to mount. The white woman's hair marked her. There was no doubting she had been the girl exchanged for peace— a peace which had been rewarded by the treacherous killing of their people at Sand Creek. Deer Woman had heard heated voices raised against the white woman while Black Wolf had remained with her within his lodge. But even as she had watched, Broken Hand had brought two horses to Black Wolf's lodge. He had then entered, and Black Wolf had emerged with the white woman moments later.

She cursed Broken Hand and his interference! She cursed Black Wolf and his lust for this white woman! She wished them dead, knowing full well that with Black Wolf's demise would come her own.

And now she watched as Black Wolf's ponies faded into the horizon and into safety from the angry reaction which threatened his captive. Black Wolf had saved the white woman once more. Increasing her anguish was Deer Woman's instinctive realization that Black Wolf would not willingly relinquish his possession of the red-haired one a second time.

She turned from the motionless horizon. The tall, broad outline silhouetted against the glorious color of the setting sun was no longer visible to her eye. It had disappeared from her sight, but not from her heart and mind. She knew it never would.

In his position of quiet observance, Broken Hand watched as the two Indian ponies disappeared into the distance. He shot a silent, assessing glance around the camp. The wounded were being attended, animals captured from the wagon train were being settled, the limited plunder was being shared. Disappointment ranged hot and deep amongst the warriors who had seen battle that day. The arrival of the white man's soldiers had been unexpected and had interrupted a very successful raid. Righteous anger had brought heavy words down upon the head of Black Wolf's captive.

Broken Hand took a deep, quaking breath. He cared little for the appearance of the red-haired one, except for the realization that with her came another. Shadow Woman. He had not seen her, but he knew she was near. A familiar trembling beset Broken Hand's broad, eager body. Yes, his body was eager. It was eager for the beauty Shadow Woman had brought to him, eager to feel Shadow Woman close once more, to know the consolation of her softness. It was eager for the peace which she had brought to his soul, despite the adversities which had faced his people—which faced them still.

Broken Hand's hunger for the woman who had been his wife was touched by a familiar frustration. He had sacrificed the peace Shadow Woman brought him for the peace of his people, and his sacrifice had been in vain. He would not make a similar sacrifice again.

Broken Hand's eyes snapped to the flicker of movement in the doorway of a nearby lodge as Deer Woman disappeared inside. The unexpected appearance of Fire Spirit had brought hope to one and despair to another. But his own despair would soon be at an end. He would see Shadow Woman again, and would hold her in his arms. Shadow Woman was his destiny.

As the sun was setting, Faith leaned heavily against the familiar wall of Black Wolf's chest. Her pride sacrificed to fatigue, she allowed him to bear the full weight of her sagging frame, knowing an inner satisaction in the realization that the weight of her body made his journey even more difficult. But that satisfaction did not relieve her physical distress. Her head still reeled, her jaw throbbed, her body ached. The nausea which had plagued her the entire day was growing worse.

Faith bit her lip against her discomfort. She was determined that she would not allow Black Wolf the satisfaction of asking him to stop. Darkness would soon fall, and he would be forced to halt. She would be damned if she would complain.

Even as she renewed her determination, Faith realized Black Wolf was drawing his pony to a halt. Intent on the silence surrounding him, he listened, his gaze darting to the nearby foliage. Obviously satisfied at what he heard, he urged his horse forward once more, and within moments had drawn up in a small, sheltered spot beside a small stream. Too tired to react, Faith sat stiffly while Black Wolf dismounted and reached up to lift her to her feet.

He had not spoken for the duration of their journey and Faith had been resolved that she would not speak the first word. As it was, she had nothing to say. She did not know this man who murdered without regret, who had struck her so viciously. She suffered still the weight of his blow. She had no doubt her face was swollen. As time had progressed she had found her jaw stiffening more and more.

She swayed weakly. The throbbing in her jaw had extended to encompass her entire head, and nausea was beginning to overwhelm her. Bile rising to her throat, Faith raised her hand to her lips. But she was not to be spared this final humiliation. Moving quickly into the nearby foliage, Faith fell to her knees, her body jerking in deep, painful spasms until she was spent. Weakly, she drew herself to her feet, walking automatically toward the sound of water. She did not look back to see the dark-eyed gaze which followed her.

Faith was uncertain how long she remained beside the gently flowing stream. In her weakened state, she found it extremely difficult to summon the strength to wash her face, to refresh her neck and arms. She drank the water sparingly, unwilling to chance a resumption of the painful spasms, and since the throbbing pain in her jaw showed no sign of relenting, she ripped a sizable piece of material from her petticoat and soaked it in the cold water to form a compress. The relief was minimal.

Faith took a deep breath. It was time for her to go back toward the spot where Black Wolf had made camp. She could see a fire crackling in the small cleared area where they had dismounted. It would do little good to force him to come after her. In her present condition, she stood little chance of escaping. A belated curiosity had arisen in her mind as she had sat quietly beside this stream, attempting to recoup her strength. Black Wolf's exit from camp had been made almost in the manner of an escape. She wondered . . .

Faith drew herself slowly to her feet. She did not know what manner of revenge Black Wolf planned for her. From his brief speech, she could only guess that he believed she had had a part in leaving him to die on the prairie. Did he not realize that she could not have done that to the young man he had been . . . the young warrior who had so tenderly placed the carved band on her finger and had pledged himself to her with all the fervor of his youth? Did he not remember how her young body had responded to his virile strength, how her lips had accepted his?

Faith drew herself upright with the most stringent effort. No, he did not because he was no longer that young Indian brave. Instead, he was a bitter savage, filled with hate. He killed without mercy—without reason. He had shot Lieutenant Piersall, and, doubtless, the young, fair-haired soldier who had died. For all she knew, it was Black Wolf who had fired the shot that had struck her father. It had been Black Wolf, or some other savage like him. . . .

At least Mama had not been captured. She had no doubt Black Wolf had spoken the truth when he had said he did not know of her mother's whereabouts. He would only too readily have told her if Mama, too, had been captured. To recapture both women would have been a true victory. Black Wolf had said that the soldiers had come and driven the Indians from the train. So Mama would be with Papa now, and if she herself had not been such a fool as to ride out ahead of the train, she would have been with them. She would now be standing beside Papa's bed, and William would be at her side.

Faith felt an insane desire to laugh. Black Wolf's image had been a vague shadow between William and herself. She had not acknowledged it, but it had been so. And now, when she realized the full extent of her foolishness, the specter of the true Black Wolf stood between them once more. But this time his presence was too real, too threatening; and she did not know—oh, God—she did not know if she would escape him alive.

Hating herself for the trembling which beset her, Faith stood tentatively at the edge of the small clearing. Black Wolf worked beside the fire, his back to her, and she hesitated to approach. But the night air was becoming chilly, and she was tired . . . so tired.

Approaching to within a few feet of the fire, Faith sat abruptly on a small log apparently provided for that purpose. She raised her hand to her throbbing head. No . . . she could not be sick again.

Feeling the heat of an intense gaze, Faith raised her eyes to Black Wolf's unrevealing perusal. He chewed a piece of dried meat, but Faith turned her face away as he held out a piece in her direction, her stomach lurching. She shook her head. Sleep . . . she needed sleep, and then she would be all right. Swaying weakly, she made an attempt to get to her feet. She needed to find a place to lie down. . . .

Unexpectedly, Black Wolf's hands were on her shoulders, his eyes searching hers. Within seconds he had scooped her up into his arms and had walked the few steps to the place where he had spread his sleeping robes on the ground. He placed her upon them, then drew up another to cover her. She attempted to protest. She did not need the help of a murderer—the man who had shot that young soldier and her friend, Lieutenant Piersall. She did not want . . .

A rough hand stilled her attempted protest.

"Be still. Sleep."

Faith knew she was not strong enough to resist him . . . not then. But she would be. Tomorrow she would . . .

But the comfort of the sleeping robes was working its magic and she was slipping away. She would think tomorrow . . . tomorrow. . . .

Black Wolf continued to kneel, his eyes on Fire Spirit's face. She fell asleep almost as soon as her head touched the comfort of the robes. His eyes snapped to the swelling along the line of her jaw, and self-contempt touched his mind once more. A blow intended to stun had been strengthened by anger and jealousy. He had hurt her. The length of time she had lain unconscious had been his first indication of the extent of her injury. Her dizziness and the retching when she had attempted to walk had confirmed his suspicions. Rest . . . Fire Spirit need rest. Within a few days she would be well, and then his vengeance would begin.

Yet, unwilling to take his eyes from the woman who lay before him, Black Wolf indulged his hungry gaze. Fire Spirit had become more than he had dreamed she could be. The woman who had ridden in the circle of his arms this day was far different from the slender child who had ridden with him years before. She had grown in height, and in womanly proportions. When she stood beside him now, her brilliant

457

head was almost level with his chin. He would no longer need to reach down to lift her mouth to his. And the body he would hold against his own would not be a girl's but a woman's. And he would take that body, take this woman who had possessed his soul. He would take her and make her part of him. He would overcome the hatred that burned in her eyes. He would teach her to welcome him, give herself to him freely. He would do all the things he had long dreamed of on silent, lonely nights during the years which had passed. It would matter little to him that she was not what she had pretended to be, that she had left him to die without a thought of that which had passed between them. She had burned herself into his spirit, and he must purge himself of his need.

His escape from camp had been swift, occasioned by Broken Hand's warning of the anger rising against Fire Spirit. She was marked among the Cheyenne, remembered as the hostage exchanged as a symbol of the peace which had been repaid with treachery and slaughter. His people wished vengeance, but vengeance would be his and his alone.

His eyes still fixed on Fire Spirit's face, Black Wolf reached out to touch the dark bruise on her jaw. Her clear skin was marked from his hand, and his self-contempt grew stronger. No, he did not wish to inflict physical pain on this woman. His vengeance would be more subtle, loving, until all the love was gone. . . .

Lifting himself to his feet, Black Wolf walked briskly back to the fire. With practiced efficiency he wrapped the dried beef and stored it once more. He moved to the point at which his horses were tied and checked their tethers. The camp secured for the night, he moved to Fire Spirit's side. Lowering himself slowly to the sleeping robes, he lay down beside her. She resisted slightly as he drew her into his arms, but soon settled against him in a manner which renewed memories of earlier days. He held her close against him, and his heart sang. He drew her closer, breathed deeply of the fragrance of her skin, pressed his lips against the life throbbing in her temple.

Fire Spirit . . . Joy came to life within him. Black Wolf

closed his eyes against the realization that he was only truly alive when he held this woman in his arms, when he knew she was his and his alone. The color of her skin, the treachery in her heart mattered little to him as long as she was his. Purge her from him? He feared he could sooner purge his heart from his body than force her from it.

Black Wolf pulled her closer still, regretfully loosening his hold as Fire Spirit's discomfort became acute. Patience . . . he need practice the same patience he had practiced once before, but this time the patience would be of short duration. In a few days she would be well, and she would belong to him completely. His heart raced in anticipation.

Chapter XXV

Tension stiffened the planes of William's face as he stared at the Arapaho prisoner before him. He could not read those deep-welled black eyes or that stolid countenance. He could only guess what the man was thinking, and he hoped this time he was wrong.

Using the few moments it took for him to round the corner of his desk to gain control of his anger, he came to stand within a few short feet of the stolid Indian. The corner of his lips ticked revealingly as he prepared to speak again.

"You understand that Major Howland has agreed to release you only because you have agreed to act as a messenger to Red Cloud. You must make it very clear to Red Cloud that the Great Father in Washington has sent me here to speak peace with him and all your people, but you must impress upon him that I cannot speak this peace while he continues to hold one of our women captive in his camp. The woman must be returned or the treaty which has been offered to your people will be withdrawn. The Great Father will send more soldiers, and the war and the killing will continue."

Realizing he had repeated his words for the second time without receiving a satisfactory comment from White Feather, William felt frustration soar anew. Damn, the crafty Indian.

"White Feather . . ."

His heavy features flickering to show a flash of anger, the

Indian warrior shook his head.

"I will give Red Cloud your message. I can do no more."

William felt frustration surge anew inside him. Three days . . . Faith had been gone for three days. He had personally led patrols which had attempted to track the Indians from the site of the attack, but they had been unsuccessful. His Indian trackers had either been unable or unwilling to follow their route on the uneven terrain. He was only too aware that White Feather was his last hope.

His eyes flicking to the two guards who stood at the door, William returned his gaze to the slender Indian before him. For the first time he could understand those who had resorted to physical coercion to get an Indian to cooperate. He had gained permission to release this particular fellow as a messenger to Red Cloud, but he was not certain that his message would, in truth, ever reach Red Cloud's ears. He tried once more.

"Red Cloud is a brave warrior. He is respected by the great father in Washington as a leader of his people. But Red Cloud's bravery has blinded him to his people's suffering. Red Cloud's people have been at war for many years. They grow smaller in number, and their hardships become greater with each passing winter as the buffalo disappear from the land. The Great Father would provide well for Red Cloud's people when the snow covers the land. He would give blankets, food—"

"Red Cloud wants nothing from the white man. He wants only to have the white man gone from his land."

William took a tighter rein on his control.

"You must tell Red Cloud that we will talk peace . . . but first he must return the woman."

The slender Indian nodded, and William continued.

"You must also tell Red Cloud that our patience is at an end. We will expect a quick answer to our message. You must tell him that if he does not respond within the week, we will execute the Indian prisoners who remain at this fort."

The brief, revealing flicker in the dark eyes looking into his was simultaneous with William's own reaction to the words which had escaped his lips. Fully realizing he did not

461

have the authority to issue the ultimatum he had just made, William stood his ground.

"Is that understood, White Feather?"

Realizing White Feather's short nod was the only response he would receive, William waved an angry hand in the guards' direction.

"All right, Corporal Bates . . . Corporal Sykes, take this man into the yard and give him back his horse. Then escort him to the gates of the fort. I want no interference in his departure from this fort. Is that understood?"

"Yes, sir."

Within minutes the door was closing behind the two young soldiers and the silent Indian. Waiting only a few moments, William walked abruptly to it and jerked it open. He stood in silent observance while White Feather mounted the horse provided and the two soldiers escorted him to the gates of the fort. He continued watching as the Indian spurred his horse and rode furiously into the horizon.

William took a deep, determined breath. He was only too keenly aware that the warning he had issued just a few minutes before was entirely his own, but he had had enough. He gave a short unconscious snort. Only that morning he had sat back in the silence of his room, reviewing the many shifts his attitude had taken in regard to the "native people" of this wild country. Upon his arrival from the East, he had condemned all Indians as bloodthirsty savages. After the Sand Creek massacre, his feelings had taken an about-face, and he had vigorously objected to the term "savage" when used in reference to these people. The horror of that day had forced him to face the fact that the barbarism was not only on one side; and he had decided that if the Indians were to be referred to as savages, the whites deserved that name as well. His outspoken statements in that regard had earned him the position he now held—a position in which he had been so ineffective as to arrive too late to save the only woman he would ever love from again being captured. He had now come to the point of frustration and pain where he had again begun to despise the very people he had been sent out here to represent, though he was only too aware that hatred and vengeance were a vicious, unending circle.

But try as he might, William found he could not make himself think in generalities when he was so hopelessly personally involved. He could not make himself impartial, reasonable, or even fair. He knew only one thing. He must locate Faith and convince her captors to return her to him.

Determination taking a firm hold on his mind, William turned abruptly and strode back to his office. He slammed the door shut behind him and approached the desk with a rapid step. He would give that damned Red Cloud a week to make up his mind. If he did not respond by then, it would be too late, and there would be hell to pay. . . .

Branches rustled gently overhead in the warm morning breeze as Faith awakened to the new day. She opened her eyes slowly to a bright, sunlit sky, and immediately caught the scent of meat roasting over a nearby fire. Momentarily disoriented, Faith clutched the robe which covered her and then shot an assessing glance around the small clearing. When her eyes touched on the broad figure crouched beside the fire, memory returned in a swift, dizzying flow.

How many days had she lain here . . . two, maybe three? She was uncertain. She merely remembered the pain in her head, the nausea which had revisited her each time she had attempted to rise to her feet. And she remembered Black Wolf's face, sober and unrevealing, as he had ministered to her, bathing her face, holding a cup of comforting liquid to her lips.

Another memory returned . . . strong arms holding her comfortingly close against a hard male body in the dark of anxious nights . . . a deep voice whispering softly into her ear words she did not quite understand. She remembered the consolation she had drawn from that embrace, from those softly spoken words. She remembered her panic when she had awakened alone . . . her instinctive cry . . . the immediate, whispered response, and the reassurance of those strong arms that came about her once more.

Black Wolf rose without turning in her direction and

463

walked to the horses tied nearby. Faith glanced toward the morning sky. The sun had only just risen, but a bird was roasting over the campfire and a pot bubbled beside it. And through it all she had slept.

Her mind beginning to clear more with each passing moment, Faith felt a heated color rise to her cheeks. Her eyes moved over Black Wolf's tall, virile form as he tended to the horses. She indulged herself in intense perusal as she compared the man he now was to the young warrior he had once been.

Black Wolf shifted his position, his eyes moving to the distant horizon, and Faith checked her sudden intake of breath. His profile, in relief against the rising sun, was strong and finely etched. The remembered clarity of its line had been unaltered by time except that it seemed to have become more impressive in its masculine perfection. Such could also be said for his proud carriage, the broad column of his neck, and the breadth of shoulders which bespoke a maturity and strength which had only been promised in the rangy young warrior he had been. Faith's eyes trailed the outline of his broadly muscular form, moving over a well-developed chest bared to the warm summer air, lean masculine hips and waist, and long, powerful legs clad in soft leggings which clung to their sinewy length. Unconsciously, she compared his overwhelming proportions to William's tightly knit, athletic form, and a flush rose to her cheeks.

The heat still colored her skin as Black Wolf turned unexpectedly in her direction. Catching her gaze, he paused, inadvertently allowing Faith a moment to complete her silent assessment. Black Wolf's body had fulfilled the promise of the man he was to become, as had the strength of his sharply chiseled features. The softness of youth had disappeared from the planes of Black Wolf's face. His richly toned, unmarked skin was tautly stretched over well-defined cheekbones. The sharp contours enhanced the potency of the dark-eyed gaze which raked her face, and the heat that seared the fair skin of her cheeks burned hotter.

His eyes narrowing into equally assessing slits, Black Wolf hesitated only a moment before starting in her direction.

Within moments he was kneeling at her side, his palm resting against her forehead in a clinical touch. His eyes darted to hers in momentary puzzlement at the coolness of her brow. An indefinable emotion flickered across his countenance as his hand moved to her cheek.

"The heat which burns your skin does not bespeak illness. Instead, it bespeaks thoughts which you would prefer to conceal." Black Wolf hesitated, his searching gaze raising her color even more as he continued in a softer tone. "I see a clarity in your eyes which has been absent in the days past. You are well once more."

Averting her gaze, Faith nodded and threw back the heavy robe.

"Yes, I . . . I am well."

As annoyed by the heat which continued to burn her cheeks as she was by the unanticipated awareness which had come to life inside her at Black Wolf's touch, Faith shook off his hand and pulled herself to her feet. She fought the giddiness which assailed her and resisted the strong hand which moved to steady her, struggling to remind herself that this hard-eyed savage was not the Black Wolf she had remembered. He was, instead, the man who had shot Lieutenant Piersall, seeing only the blue uniform he wore. He valued only the lives of his people, and thus did not value hers. He doubtless had nursed her back to health for his own purposes, but she was determined that she would not play his deadly game.

Anger flashed in Black Wolf's eyes when she resisted his touch.

"You have been ill for several days. You will not so easily shake off your weakness."

"I . . . I am ill no longer. I do not need your help."

Pulling herself erect, Faith stepped away from Black Wolf's side. She walked stiffly into the foliage, heading toward the stream. When at last she crouched beside it, her breath was coming in deep, ragged gasps. She gratefully splashed the cool water on her face, her relief instantaneous. But she had to fight to regain control of her reeling senses. Anger flashed anew inside her at the realization that Black

Wolf had assessed her state of health more accurately than she herself had. It occurred to her that as much as she abhorred the thought, she would not be in condition to even consider escape for a few days more.

Faith splashed water against her face once more, and managed to run her fingers through her tangled hair before she realized her energy was all but spent. She hesitated, preparing herself to stand. Somehow, the effort seemed beyond her limited capacity, but she was determined she would not call for help. No, she would not fall so easily into Black Wolf's plans, whatever they were. She . . .

At the sound of a step behind her, Faith looked to her rear to see Black Wolf come to stand at her side.

"So you do not need my help."

Anger made Faith raise her chin with false bravado.

"No, I do not need your help. I can manage myself."

Black Wolf's lips curled in anger.

"And so you remain on your knees, unable to stand."

"I *can* stand."

Taking a deep breath, Faith raised herself to her feet, determinedly ignoring the darkness which began to overwhelm her, the flashing colors which began to absorb the remaining light. From a distance she heard a deep intake of breath and a harsh, guttural exclamation, and within a moment she was swept from her feet and held in strong, unrelenting arms, foliage brushing past her as Black Wolf returned to their camp with sweeping strides.

She was in the light of the warming sun once more, and the sleeping robes were beneath her. She blinked against the harshness of the bright sun that glinted through the sparse foliage overhead, her eyes finally focusing on the angry, russet-skinned face above hers. It disappeared momentarily from her sight, only to return seconds later. A cool, wet cloth was brushing her face, its moistness refreshing. Her unsteady gaze was beginning to focus when a cup was raised to her lips. She drank deeply. Tea . . . it was tea.

She had finished the refreshing liquid, was beginning to feel its steadying effects when she was released to lie back against the softness of the robes once more.

Unable to avoid Black Wolf's gaze any longer, Faith raised her eyes to his face. Startled by his evident concern, she frowned.

"It is well that you frown." Anger evident in his deep voice, Black Wolf continued sharply, "Your stubbornness has almost resulted in your suffering further injury."

A responsive sharpness rose to Faith's tongue as well.

"And you would not wish me to suffer any injury which is not inflicted by you."

His head jerking back as if he had been stung, Black Wolf hesitated long moments before responding.

"It matters not the manner in which you came to be my prisoner. It matters solely that you are my prisoner, and as such, you will obey my command. At present, it does not suit me to see you injured further. You will obey my orders and you will regain your strength. If you do not choose to obey, you will be bound hand and foot. The choice is yours."

Faith took a deep, shuddering breath. There was no doubting Black Wolf's earnestness. She closed her eyes. No, it would not serve her purpose to oppose Black Wolf stubbornly at this point in time. It would be far better to allow him to think her subservient to his wishes; then she might catch him off guard.

Black Wolf's expression was drawn into harsh lines as he addressed her.

"I would have your answer."

Faith's response was curt.

"I will not oppose you."

Hesitating briefly, Black Wolf rose to his feet. He paused, looking down at her from his towering height before finally turning away.

In silence, Faith watched Black Wolf's smooth, efficient movements as he worked beside the campfire, the rippling of powerful muscles across the smooth skin of his back. Faith responded defensively though she remained angrily silent.

For the time being, your strength prevails, Black Wolf. You are master, but not for long.

* * *

Crouched beside the fire, Black Wolf reached for the spit and turned the roasting bird. Yes, it was golden brown and ready to be eaten. He lifted it carefully from the fire, then placed it in a small wooden bowl. Turning, he sent a quick glance toward the spot where Fire Spirit rested in silence. She was dozing.

Earlier, he had turned his back on her in anger. She had defied him with the same spirit she had shown in their first encounter many years before, and in her defiance, she had almost done herself harm. Black Wolf fought to control his irritation.

Black Wolf was well aware of the changed scope of his emotions since his eyes had touched upon Fire Spirit several days before. His first instinct being a feeling of hatred and a desire for revenge, he had begun to suffer a reversal of these feelings the moment he had again touched her. In the past three days, while she had lain suffering from the result of his jealous anger, his feelings had changed even more radically. He had tended to her physical needs, and at night, had held her in his arms. During that time, he had put aside all desire for vengeance against her betrayal, and taken her back into his heart as completely as he had in that time years before. But he was not fool enough to trust her.

Fire Spirit had changed, as had he. He knew he must accept those changes and the realization that the feelings once warm and true between them were lost forever. He had faced another realization as well: it made little difference to him what obstacles stood between Fire Spirit and himself. His body cried out for this woman, this woman of fire. And he knew its cry must be answered or he would never know peace within himself. It was a lesson he had learned over the long empty years, a lesson which had been renewed in the silence of the three anxious nights past. Fire Spirit would resist him, but he would conquer her resistance. His decision had been made.

Black Wolf picked up the bowl and turned fully in Fire Spirit's direction. She had eaten little in the three days since they had arrived at this place. Realizing her need for a food more suitable than the dried meat which he consumed, he had hunted close-bye in the early hours of morning, and this game bird had been the result of his endeavor. It would serve to stir Fire Spirit's appetite, and she would eat and grow stronger. He would see the color again in her pale cheeks, and when the glow of health returned . . .

Pausing to calm his racing heart, Black Wolf started in Fire Spirit's direction. He stood over her for long moments, drinking in her beauty as she slept. Slowly, he crouched beside her. He reached out, his fingers touching the fiery curls which streamed against the sleeping robes in curling profusion. He touched her cheek, the bruise just beginning to fade on her jaw. Heavily fringed lids rose slowly in response to his touch, and Black Wolf suppressed the surging hunger which roared to life inside him as the startling blue of her eyes touched him once more. But he did not acknowledge the soaring emotion. Instead, he frowned, his voice gruff.

"You will eat now."

Fire Spirit shook her head.

"I . . . I'm not hungry."

Irritation tightened the knots in Black Wolf's stomach. He moved to draw her to a seated position and she resisted. His anger flared anew.

"You will eat now. Your languid days have come to an end."

"Languid!" Angry color flooded Fire Spirit's face. "If I have experienced languor, it was due to the blow dealt by your hand. I have not—"

"The past is done, and the future is yet to be faced. Your disability inhibits my plans. You will eat and grow strong, and we will be gone from this place."

Fire sparked in Fire Spirit's brilliant eyes, and Black Wolf gave a low snort. It was just as well if anger would give her the will to recover more quickly. He must leave this place. He attempted to lift her once more, but she pushed at his hands. Defiant, she pulled herself to a seated position.

"I told you, I don't want your help."

Black Wolf's voice emerged in a low hiss.

"It matters little to me what you want. It is what *I* want

that is now important, and I want you to eat."

Fire Spirit's eyes burned hotter.

"And if I do not choose to eat?"

"You *will* eat."

Angered further by being maneuvered into a corner by the pale woman sitting unsteadily before him, Black Wolf placed the bowl he held on the ground. Carefully, he tore a leg from the juicy bird. He raised it to Fire Spirit's face. The tantalizing aroma wafted upward and Fire Spirit's stomach gave a gurgling response. Fire Spirit determinedly averted her face, but her persistent stomach would not relent in its loud appeal.

Black Wolf fought to maintain his anger as Fire Spirit's stomach clamored more loudly to be sated, and Fire Spirit's face grew hotter. A smile twitching at the corners of his mouth, Black Wolf finally lowered the tempting morsel back to the bowl.

"Fire Spirit . . ."

No response.

Faith cursed her vociferous hunger. She kept her eyes carefully averted from Black Wolf's gaze, still refusing to speak.

"Fire Spirit, you refuse to answer me, but your stomach loudly proclaims its response."

The hint of amusement in Black Wolf's voice turned Faith's anger to molten fury. She snapped her eyes back in his direction, her voice filled with hauteur.

"You make a mistake in regarding my determination lightly. My mind is firm, although my physical appetite betrays me."

Black Wolf paused long in response. As she watched, all trace of humor disappeared from his glance. The ebony depths of his eyes were suddenly somber, holding hers.

"I have much the same complaint, Fire Spirit. My mind is firm in wishing to refuse you reentrance into my heart, but my hunger for you betrays me. To it, I am admittedly subservient."

Faith averted her face, refusing to accept Black Wolf's words. No, she did not wish to hear this unfamiliar Black

Wolf speak in this way. This man was an intruder in her life, a savage beast whom she was comfortable only in hating. She had no desire to be torn by the realization that this man, who was her enemy, still held within him the young warrior who had pledged himself to her so long ago. She did not wish to have forgotten feelings stirred to life within her. That time was past . . . over . . . gone and she . . .

But Black Wolf's hand was gripping her chin, turning her face toward his once more. Ragged emotions, mirrored in the dark depths of his eyes, reached out to touch her, and Faith struggled against them, against his words.

"Had I choice, Fire Spirit, I would have left you at the wagon train, to determine your own fate as bullets snapped around you and your life was threatened. But the hunger inside me would know no rest. I had no choice but to ride to your side, to take you into the safety of my arms. I had no choice when you sought to escape me. I struck you so that I would not lose you again."

Black Wolf's fingertips caressed the yellowing bruise on her jaw. His low voice continued to assail her with its tenderness.

"And as you suffer the irrepressible demand of your body's hunger, so do I. My hunger for you rages within me, Fire Spirit. It is a need which gave me no rest in the time of our separation, and it is a need which I have determined I will no longer suffer unsated."

Faith swallowed tightly at the solemnity of Black Wolf's words. Unable to voice a response, she felt the surging of a similar need, one that had been long suppressed, as Black Wolf bared his heart. She closed her eyes against the strength of the feelings beginning to overwhelm her. No . . . this man was her enemy . . . a murderer . . . a man who . . .

But the stroking pressure of Black Wolf's touch was putting all reasonable thought from Faith's mind. His hand had moved to her hair. He was drawing her closer. His face was so close to hers that she was drowning in the velvet darkness of his gaze. She closed her eyes in an attempt to escape, belatedly realizing her mistake as the soft lips so close to hers began an intermittent assault between his stirring words.

"As it was from the first time I touched you, Fire Spirit, your life is tightly intertwined with mine. Whatever the course of this intermingling, I will follow it. I do not do so willingly. Pain and unhappiness lie in its wake, and appear in its future, but forces other than those which I control have deemed it so. I bow to those forces, to the will which lives within me to make you mine. And you will be mine, Fire Spirit, for the same hunger which drives me, reigns within you, also. I see it in your eyes when you resist my touch. I feel it in the quaking which besets you. It is a fierce hunger, stronger than physical appetite, for it is a hunger that gnaws at the soul. Heed its call, Fire Spirit, as do I. Submit to its victory. We have both waged an honorable battle against it and lost. But in losing, we are victors, Fire Spirit."

Black Wolf's lips were tormenting her with their assault, and Faith's resistance was lessening. She was lying back against the soft robes once more with Black Wolf's hard body pressed close to hers. His lips assailed hers, caressing, sampling, tasting; and she closed her eyes against the bittersweet joy of their touch. The warmth of the sun was hot against her skin, bringing her to memories of a time long past, even as Black Wolf continued his loving persuasion.

"Remember, Fire Spirit. Let your memory slip back to another lifetime when we rode the peaceful land together. The warm summer air brushed our faces and we laughed into the wind. We rested our horses and lay side by side, discussing those things which gave us peace and happiness. I took you in my arms, and I tasted your mouth. You gave it to me much as you do now, and I took it hungrily. I take it hungrily once more."

His lips caressing hers, Black Wolf pressed his kiss deeper than before, passing the barrier of her teeth, searching the honeyed caverns with increasing ardor. He was gasping as he withdrew from her sweetness. His voice was hoarse with emotion.

"I withdrew from you then. I chose to honor your youth and innocence. But in the years since I have cursed myself countless times for adherence to a principle which has only brought me pain. My own youthful mind could not foresee a time when the world, which both of us sought to shut away, would return to come between us. But I am young and foolish no longer, Fire Spirit. You have been returned to me. You lie here beside me and I taste your sweetness. I will not hold myself from you again."

Black Wolf's hands were moving warmly over Faith's body, stirring a wealth of unknown emotions even as she sought to maintain her rationality. No, she could not allow this man whom she had looked to only minutes before with loathing . . . she could not allow him to love her. . . . But even as her mind reacted with one thought, her body responded with another, welcoming Black Wolf's touch, moving to the subtle pressure of his body, accepting the caress of his lips as they traveled the slender column of her throat.

Her mind slipping away under the tantalizing touch of Black Wolf's knowing hands, Faith moved in response to his coercion, satisfied only when at last her tender flesh was warm against his, as the rise of her breasts brushed his smoothly muscled chest. She felt the whisper of his lips against hers once more, protested their desertion as they trailed the curve of her shoulder in sharp nipping bites. She gasped at the butterfly kisses which circled the warm mounds of her breasts, their intensity growing stronger as they neared the waiting, burgeoning crests. She caught her breath sharply as Black Wolf's mouth closed over an aching bud, warming it, bathing it in searing kisses, hotly claiming it for his own.

She was soaring in a world she had not dreamed existed, on a plane of rapture unsuspected and unknown. She was clutching Black Wolf's head to her breast, encouraging his heady assault, groaning from the pleasure he stirred, an unrelenting pleasure so intense that it approached pain. She was gasping, calling for release, a fulfillment she did not quite understand. She was crying Black Wolf's name when suddenly the warmth, the beauty, was withdrawn from her, and she was alone.

Her eyes snapping open, Faith caught Black Wolf's

molten gaze as he raised himself above her. The handsome planes of his face were still, his dark eyes blazing. He lowered his lips to hers, ravaging her mouth for long minutes while he withheld the warmth of his body. She sought to draw him to her but he resisted. When she opened her eyes once more, his expression was tense, questioning.

"Do you want me, Fire Spirit? Do you want me to join my body with yours?"

When she did not respond but sought to close the distance between them, Black Wolf held her off.

"I would hear you say the words, Fire Spirit. Whatever comes to pass after this day, I would know within my heart that you desired our joining, that the hunger which burns inside me, burned inside you as well. I would hear you say the words, Fire Spirit. . . ."

Her voice sacrificed to the shattering emotion which assailed her, Faith could manage no more than a helpless nod of her head.

But Black Wolf persisted.

"The words, Fire Spirit . . . I would hear the words."

His mouth assaulted hers once more, deserting her lips to trail heated kisses along her throat, to fasten on the swollen crests of her breasts for breathless moments longer. Her low gasp raised his eyes to hers once more.

"Fire Spirit, speak the words."

Her lips were parting. Low words, seething with passion, filled the silence between them.

"Yes . . . I hunger for you . . . as you hunger for me. I would be a part of you . . . an integral part. I would be . . ."

But she could speak no more as Black Wolf lowered himself to her warmth with a low groan. The firm staff of his passion was moving against her, stealing her breath. She felt the touch of his hand against the warm, moist nest between her thighs. Instinctively, she accommodated him, moved to welcome him. She closed her eyes against the first warning pressure, gasping as he sought to enter. A low groan escaped her lips as he drove deep and true within her, as her body accepted him, closed around him, took him home.

Black Wolf was moving rhythmically within her, and she

was meeting his thrusts. She was soaring higher than before, gasping at the raging colors, the plane of ecstasy to which Black Wolf's loving had carried her. She was clutching Black Wolf close, reveling at the smooth play of his muscles against her palms, moving to the escalated rhythm of their loving dance. She was gliding higher . . . higher. . . .

Black Wolf's low voice called to her, summoning her from the ecstatic world in which she ranged. He looked down into her face, the dark mirrors of his eyes reflecting the joy, the wonder, alive inside her, and she gasped his name. Abruptly, Black Wolf thrust deep and true, his low, heartfelt groan lifting her to the pinnacle of ecstasy. He clutched her close as they plunged from the summit, shuddering, gasping, thrilling to the wonder of their love even as they spiraled into the deep, velvet abyss of total reward.

Still joined, they lay in breathless silence. Black Wolf stirred, his lips moving to hers once more, drawing deeply, fully from their sweetness. Tearing himself from her at last, he held her mesmerized with the burning heat of his gaze as he whispered in a voice laced with the breathless remnants of passion.

"I sought to appease my ravenous appetite for you, Fire Spirit, but in truth, I have only stirred it anew. My hunger rages on, Fire Spirit. . . . Sate me . . . sate me. . . ."

Emotion, wild and glorious, soared to new life as Black Wolf's mouth closed on hers, and Faith cast aside the doubts which wavered at the borders of her mind. It was a time for loving, and she gave to Black Wolf with a fervor which she suddenly realized her heart had reserved for him and him alone.

White Feather strode from the lodge of Red Cloud, his brow knotted in contemplation. Red Cloud had been firm in his resistance. The woman was not his prisoner. He could not and would not bargain for her release.

His lined face sober, White Feather scanned the great camp, noting the eyes which followed his emergence from Red Cloud's lodge. They were hostile to the message he carried. Many had been wounded and killed in the most recent assault on the white man's wagon train. The woman's life, which the white soldiers valued so highly, was nothing to his people. But he had seen the determination in the white captain's eyes. The white captain had not spoken idle words. Those of his people left behind at the fort as prisoners would surely be executed if the response was not received. The weight of their deaths would be on his shoulders, and he would not bear it well.

Turning abruptly, White Feather strode from the main Sioux camp, his eyes on the clusters of lodges set briefly apart from the Sioux. The Cheyenne warrior, Black Wolf, had taken the girl, and had then ridden from camp. He had not returned. But he knew one in the Cheyenne camp who would respond to the white captain's warning, and he would speak to that one. The woman was not worth the death of good Arapaho warriors. She would be returned and the lives of his brothers would be spared. . . .

Deer Woman ascended the slope from the stream. Her eyes touched on the Arapaho warrior entering Broken Hand's lodge and she stopped abruptly. Water splashed over the sides of the filled vessel in her hand, and the beat of her heart thundered in her breast. Speculation had run rampant within the camp as to the manner of White Feather's escape from the white soldiers' fort. His immediate conference with Red Cloud had raised a question which was now being answered. There was only one reason for White Feather to seek consultation with Broken Hand.

Deer Woman took a deep breath as satisfaction flooded her veins. The white woman . . . the soldiers were attempting to get her back. Black Wolf had separated himself from his people in an attempt to keep her, but he would not succeed. Pressure was being brought to bear upon Broken Hand, and he, in turn, would go to Black Wolf. The white woman's time with Black Wolf was limited, and when she was gone, Black Wolf would return to camp.

Deer Woman's small face tightened with determination.

She had been a fool. She had gone to Black Wolf in the dark of the night. She had felt Black Wolf's strong arms around her, felt his flesh against hers. She had been so close to that of which she had dreamed. But she had allowed Black Wolf's hesitation to deter her, his soft words to turn her away. It was only after she had left that she had remembered the softness in his voice, his tender concern. If his feelings had not matched hers, he had at least had warmth in his heart for her. He would not turn her away a second time. And there would be a second time, her decision had been made.

Careless of the water which splashed against her legs, Deer Woman increased her step in her anxiety to reach the vicinity of Broken Hand's lodge. White Feather had today begun the workings which would eventually bring her into Black Wolf's arms. And when she was in them, there she would stay.

Incredulity left William momentarily speechless. No, he had not expected this when he had seen White Feather approaching the fort carrying the flag of truce. He remembered still the elation which had flashed across his mind, the anticipation which had surged through him at the thought that Faith would soon be in his arms.

William shook his head, his eyes fast on White Feather as the Indian stood before him in the fort yard.

"You're telling me that Red Cloud refuses to return the white woman—"

"The white woman is not in Red Cloud's camp."

"Then where is she, damn it? She was taken by Red Cloud's men . . . in a raid Red Cloud led! Does your brave leader have so little control over his people that they operate without his knowledge and consent? Is he so weak a leader that his people turn their backs on his word?"

White Feather's dark eyes, unmoving, remained on William's countenance, and William felt his anger surge anew.

"You don't really expect me to believe that Red Cloud has no knowledge of the captive's whereabouts, do you?"

"The white woman is captive of the Cheyenne . . . not the Sioux."

William's chest was heaving in anger. Aware that he was standing in the center of the fort yard, within hearing of the entire force, he attempted to control his growing rage.

"If that is the case, and Red Cloud is not able to negotiate for the Cheyenne, there must be someone who will speak for them. Who is that person?"

"I have already spoken with him."

"And?"

"He says the Cheyenne hold the word of the white man in contempt. He says once before this woman was returned in exchange for the peace promised. It was not observed and his people were killed. He says he will not be such a fool again."

A muscle ticked spasmodically in William's cheek.

"Who is this man who is so foolish as to refuse to speak with an authorized representative of the United States Army?"

"His name is Broken Hand."

A low gasp from behind turned William sharply in its direction. His eyes touched on Lydia's white face as she addressed the stoic Indian in a gasping voice.

"You lie! Broken Hand is dead!"

A slight narrowing of White Feather's eyes was the only betrayal of his anger at Lydia's words as he responded gruffly.

"Broken Hand lives. The many wounds he has received at the hands of the white man have only made him grow stronger. He leads his people in war, but he has said he will not lead them to death in a white man's peace. That is his final word."

Taking the few steps to Lydia's side, William took her arm supportively. He felt her shuddering and attempted to lend her his strength, belatedly realizing that she was aware of no other but the Indian who spoke his hard, unrelenting words. He frowned. He must send her to her quarters so he might speak more freely.

"Lydia, you should not be . . ."

But Lydia was not listening. She addressed White Feather once more, haltingly.

"The man . . . the man who has taken my daughter prisoner . . . what is his name?"

"The white woman is the prisoner of Black Wolf."

William felt the shock which shook Lydia's body, and he gripped her more tightly in support even as the same shock echoed within him. He turned sharply toward White Feather once more.

"Black Wolf is dead. He was killed several years ago."

"No, Black Wolf is alive. It is he who holds the white woman, and he, alone, who would decide on her return."

"Then I will speak to Black Wolf directly!"

"Black Wolf has taken the woman away. We know not where."

A surging jealousy added new fervor to William's vehemence.

"Find him, damn it . . . or the prisoners will be executed. You have my word on that."

White Feather's gaze remained unmoving.

"I have done all I can."

A raging fury suffusing his fair skin with a heated red, William turned to the guards standing nearby.

"I have no more to say to this man. Take him and return him to the cell with the other Arapaho prisoners."

Turning his back even as his men moved to follow his command, William slipped an arm around Lydia's shaking frame. He ushered her back toward the building to their rear as she raised her colorless face to his. His low vow vibrated on the tense silence between them.

"I'll get Faith back. I give you my word—I will."

Lydia opened the door slowly. She frowned. The click of the latch, unnaturally loud in the silence of the room, annoyed her. She did not want to wake Wally. He needed his sleep, and she needed the time to talk to him without his hearing.

Lydia approached Wally's bed with caution, the small

core of tenderness inside her expanding as his gaunt face met her gaze. Wally . . . who had always taken care of her, protected her, loved her . . . And now he was helpless, and it was all up to her.

Lydia took a deep, shaking breath. He was improving, Dr. Mallory had said he was. She knew for a fact that Wally was in less pain. He was sleeping better . . . without the sharp, breathtaking twinges which turned his skin gray and made him perspire. Yes, the medication was doing its job. She gave a short, silent laugh. Dr. Mallory had insisted that her presence had done Wally more good than anything he had given him.

Lydia shook her head as a small smile flickered across Wally's lips in sleep. She resisted the impulse to kiss his lips. No, she didn't want Wally awake right now. She had come in here for another reason.

Unexpectedly, a hard-faced, dark-eyed image, clear in her mind's eye, blocked Wally's face from view and Lydia's heart stirred anew in her breast. Broken Hand . . . how could she have been so wrong? Had that dream in which she had seen his bloodstained body been manufactured by a mind which had chosen that manner of escape from the feelings which had been tearing her apart? Perhaps that was so. . . . Perhaps that was the reason why memories long suppressed had returned so vividly to her at the mention of Broken Hand's name. Even now remembering the low caress of his deep voice, the strength of his embrace, the carefully controlled power of his body as he took her to him, she was deeply shaken. And predominant was the memory of his tenderness . . . and his need.

Lydia swallowed tightly. The machinations of fate were strange, indeed. Faith . . . her darling, Faith . . . Once again Faith's life hung in uncertain balance. A tremor of fear coursed through her veins at the memory of Black Wolf, of the feelings mirrored in his eyes when they had touched on her young daughter's face. She remembered the carved band Faith had worn . . . the matching band on Black Wolf's hand. An instinctive protest arose inside her, not untouched by fear. Faith was strong. She would resist coercion to her last breath. No, she could not abandon her.

Silently, with utmost care, Lydia leaned down over her husband's sleeping face. Her throat choked with emotion, she pressed a light kiss against the subdued blaze of his hair. Loving words remained unspoken as she allowed herself a last glimpse and then turned away.

Within moments Lydia was closing the door behind her, leaving as silently as she had entered. She squared her slender shoulders and began walking down the hallway toward William's office. She did not look back.

The great golden orb in the cloudless sky began its slow descent to the horizon, casting its dying rays across the vast expanse in myriad, breathless hues of pink and silver. A silence prevailed in the small, cleared area between the weeping trees, broken only by the sounds that marked the transition from day to night and the crackle of a campfire. Drifting in a world of semisleep, Faith raised her heavy lids to the waning light of day, only to be startled as a warm body stirred beside her and a low, voice sounded in her ear.

"You would awaken in time to fall asleep once more." Abruptly enclosed against a hard, male body, Faith felt Black Wolf's lips move against her temple, stirring her hair with warmth. "You have caused me much concern this day, Fire Spirit. I have cursed the surging feelings which caused me to act unwisely." Black Wolf's arms pressed her closer. "It had not been my intention to press you until your full strength had returned, nor to declare so openly those feelings which I have held within me during the time we have been apart. But your spirit aroused me, Fire Spirit, the fire within you lighting the blaze of desire within me. Those same feelings arise again within me, and as before, my good sense bows before them."

Pulling back far enough so that she might view his smile, Black Wolf shook his head in apparent disbelief of his feelings. "At a time when my people are in a state of unrest, when our enemies seek to destroy us, it appears I can all too easily put aside the thoughts which formerly gave purpose to my life and find contentment in tending to the wants of my woman. I question myself, wondering if my contentment indeed stems from the fact that you are weak and dependent upon me, and I am thus free to love you at will, without your protesting. And I find that I do not truly wish an answer to another question which plagues my mind . . . whether you submit to me out of weakness or desire."

Not allowing her time for consideration of those thoughts, Black Wolf traced the fine line of her brow with his fingertips. His supremely gentle touch awakened a wealth of feelings inside her as he continued hoarsely.

"But if it is weakness which responds to me, then I would make you weaker still with my loving, until you have accepted me fully and completely within your heart."

Faith closed her eyes, only to have her fluttering lids assaulted by light kisses, the line of her flushing cheeks similarly adored. She uttered a short protest which was cut short by the familiar pressure of Black Wolf's lips against her own. Black Wolf's kiss deepened and Faith struggled against the emotion which clouded her mind. Yes, Black Wolf was right . . . good sense was bowing to the force which raged between them. She needed to hold herself aloof . . . to think. . . .

But her mind was reeling. Was this not the dream she had consigned to the secret depths of her mind for all these restless years? Was not Black Wolf's the face which had invaded her dreams, restraining her desires, causing her to look with disfavor on the many young men who had called on her? All except William . . .

Faith opened her eyes as Black Wolf drew back from her mouth. Appetite . . . hunger . . . She remembered Black Wolf's use of those terms. They were bright in the lines of his handsome face, in the glow of his dark eyes, as he ran his hand along the line of her chin and down the column of her throat. He was pushing aside the robe which covered her, exposing the fullness of her naked breasts. He swallowed tightly, his lips curving in a reluctant smile.

"No more the body of the slender child I first saw in the wooded glade . . . I remember you as you were then, Fire

Spirit. An angry, defiant child who clutched her clothes against her nakedness. You could not have known that I had watched you as you bathed, allowed my eyes to consume their fill of your budding breasts, your flawless flesh, the rounded curve of your youthful buttocks. In your nakedness you stirred me as had no other, and touched inside me a well of tenderness which had lain untapped within my heart. I saw then the vision of the woman you would one day become, and my heart claimed you for my own."

Black Wolf gently stroked the full, rounded globes beneath his hands. He lowered his head to press light, intermittent kisses against their warmth. "But in my most flagrant dream, I did not envision the full beauty which you have given me this day . . . the beauty of your flesh . . . the beauty of your spirit . . . the beauty of all that you are. . . ."

Black Wolf's caresses trailed her flesh. His knowing touch found the warm nest of her womanhood and he watched her growing response to his sensual stroking. He sought the moist slit beneath, found the aching bud of her desire. Gently, carefully, he stroked it to life, a slow, appreciative murmur escaping his throat as her lips separated in growing ecstasy. He pressed his mouth to hers, tasted the sweet hollows of her mouth, muffled her intelligible words of intense pleasure as his stroking increased. He felt her shuddering and a new elation transfused him. He trailed his mouth against the smooth skin of her cheek, moving to the warm lobe of her ear where he whispered in a voice shaken with passion.

"I want that beauty again, Fire Spirit. I want it to surge to life within you, to see it reflected on your face, to know that I bring to you that which no man has."

Faith's shuddering was increasing, and Black Wolf felt its wonder. He held her poised at the brink of her passion, but he needed more, much more.

Faith's eyes had fluttered closed, and he protested their abandonment.

"Open your eyes, Fire Spirit. Open them."

Responding to the urgency of his command, Faith lifted her heavy lids, to meet Black Wolf's heated gaze. His lips grazing hers as he spoke, Black Wolf grated in low command.

"Give . . . give to me, Fire Spirit. Look into my eyes and give to me all that your body wishes to give . . . now, Fire Spirit . . . now."

Her body was quaking, shuddering in heaving spasms, showing sweet homage to Black Wolf's ministrations. His eyes consuming her, Black Wolf watched passion play across her exquisite face, a new glory rising inside him as her slender body heaved again and again in loving response, until it was done.

Fire Spirit lay silent under his touch. Releasing her gaze, he had allowed her eyes to fall closed once more as he reveled in his power over this woman who was more to him than life. Raising himself at last, his own body near to the summit of passion, he poised himself above her, savoring the moment as he thrust clean and true to complete possession. Fire Spirit's low gasp sending him over the edge of control, he plunged inside her in mindless desire, knowing she was spent, realizing her weakness and knowing he, too, would soon be similarly spent.

But Fire Spirit was coming to life beneath him. She was rising to his thrusts, meeting him, loving him as fully in return as he had loved her only moments before. He was rising on the wings of a passion he had not before known. Oh, yes, this was the moment for which he had been created, the apex of life, created for Fire Spirit and him alone.

With a low groaning thrust, he soared from the pinnacle of his passion, grasping Fire Spirit close, knowing in his heart that it was she and he alone . . . that he would not let her go again, not while breath remained in his body. She was his, and his she would remain. . . .

William's eyes moved keenly over the uneven terrain. His discomfort aggravated by his mount's measured stride, he glanced sharply to his side to assess the face of the woman who rode beside him. But the fear for Lydia's safety, which was his constant companion, appeared to be having little affect on her. Instead, determination was mirrored in the shadowed depths of her eyes.

Even now, as they moved across the silent, sunlit landscape, William found he was uncertain as to what whim had allowed him to respond to Lydia's unexpected plea. But he had released White Feather as she had urged, and yielding further to Lydia's entreaties, he had lifted his threat against the remaining Arapaho prisoners with the provision that White Feather again act as messenger.

His eyes narrowing more keenly, his hand resting near his gun, William intensified his scrutiny of the passing terrain. Although he realized that neither Lydia nor he would have a chance if this meeting was indeed a trap, that did not deter him from his watchful surveillance. He silently berated himself for allowing her to expose herself to this danger, but in his heart, he knew he would do the same again. He could not abandon Faith to those savages.

Another thought hovered in the back of William's mind, but he avoided acknowledging it. He had not obtained clearance from Major Howland for this meeting. His unique position at the fort allowed him a measure of freedom, but he was only too well aware that that freedom did not include endangering the life of a civilian. He supposed he would have to account for this later to Major Howland, but he had not allowed the thought to deter him. Nothing deterred him where Faith was concerned.

A strange sense of awareness caused a prickle of apprehension to move unexpectedly up his spine, and William's slitted gaze intensified on the surrounding terrain. There was something . . . something. . . .

Unexpectedly, two horses appeared from within a small grove of trees, and William instantly reined in his mount. A low gasp escaped Lydia's lips, and he issued a low, short command which made her draw her horse up sharply. A brief glance in her direction caused a wave of shock to move across his mind. He was thankful Wally was not present to see the look on his beloved wife's face. He did not need to ask Lydia if, indeed, the Cheyenne riding toward them at White Feather's side was Broken Hand.

Lydia's eyes touched on the mounted Indian who had emerged from the wooded glade at the same moment William had issued his warning. Her reaction to the broad, familiar outline etched against the brilliance of the morning sunlight was immediate. Elation flashed to life inside her, and Lydia released a short gasp. Broken Hand *was* alive. . . .

He was riding toward them at a slow pace calculated not to stir apprehension, and Lydia's eyes consumed him. He had not changed in the years since she had last seen him. The broad expanse of shoulders was still overwhelming, his carriage erect and proud. He came closer, and his features became clearer. Hard and bold he was, the strength of his body and spirit clearly reflected in the lines of his face. It was a face she remembered clearly, with eyes which still hovered in her dreams. Now those eyes were brittle onyx, grim and unyielding, but she remembered them at other times . . . beautiful times when he had allowed her past the barrier of that shield. She remembered the glow in those eyes when she had laid in his arms. She remembered the unsuspected sensitivity which had shone clearly within them. She remembered the deep roll of his voice as he had opened his heart to her and taken her in. She remembered . . . she remembered so well. . . .

Lydia was breathless even as she remained stationary upon her horse, watching Broken Hand's approach. She wanted to look to William, to assess his reaction to Broken Hand's appearance. He had been so uncertain, so suspicious of Broken Hand's agreement to meet with them, but she had known . . . She had known if White Feather had indeed taken the message to Broken Hand, that he would not fail to respond to her summons. No, it was still there between Broken Hand and herself, the thread of communication which had allowed him to see so clearly the frightening visions which had visited her in that time so long ago. It could not—would not—be severed.

Bittersweet joy in her heart, Lydia watched as Broken Hand approached to rein his horse within a few feet of hers. His sober countenance was turned from her, his eyes unwilling to move in her direction as he addressed William directly.

"I make it clear to you, white man's soldier, that I do not respond to your summons. My heart and the hearts of my people are turned against you. The Cheyenne no longer hears or respects the word of the white man. It was only the summons of the one at your side which drew me here this day."

Lydia sensed William's stiffening in the moment before he responded with barely restrained anger.

"I am not now concerned with the peace which continues to elude us, but with the safety of a woman taken captive by one of your warriors. Faith Durham must be returned."

Maintaining her silence, Lydia watched as Broken Hand's expression grew more severe.

"I am here at the response of the one at your side. To her alone will I speak."

Impatience added a sharper edge to William's tone.

"If that's the way you want it, it's all right with me, just as long as you tell us where Faith Durham is being held captive."

Broken Hand turned for the first time in Lydia's direction, and she held her breath. She remained motionless as Broken Hand declared quietly, "I would speak with this woman alone."

"No!" William's response was immediate, definitive. "I will not allow Mrs. Durham out of my sight. Her safety is my responsibility and she—"

"I do not wish to hurt this woman."

"No, it is out of the question. I will not—"

"William, please." Lydia spoke for the first time. "I prefer to speak to Broken Hand alone, also. I'm not afraid of him."

William turned tightly in her direction.

"Lydia, don't ask me to do something I must not do. No matter how well you feel you know this man, he is our enemy. He holds your daughter captive."

"The girl is not my captive."

"But you know where she is, and you are protecting the

487

man holding her. The United States Army will not countenance unlawful imprisonment of innocent civilians."

"William . . ."

Lydia's unexpected interruption turned William's flushed face back in her direction.

"William, I will take full responsibility for my actions. If it will make you feel better, we'll dismount. You may hold both horses. Surely, I cannot be spirited away on foot."

William jerked a short glance toward Broken Hand. Seeing no objection to Lydia's comment, he took a short breath.

"All right. But you will go no farther than that grove of trees. White Feather and I will wait here. Is that agreed?"

Broken Hand's signal of acceptance brought William from the saddle to Lydia's side. Aware that Broken Hand was dismounting behind him, he lifted Lydia down from her horse. His short instructions were muttered for her ears alone.

"Lydia, if you suspect foul play, call out immediately. I'll keep my hand on my gun." His clear brown eyes reflected his concern. "Wally would never forgive me if anything happened to you . . . and I would never forgive myself."

"I'll be all right, William."

Aware that her confidence did little to reassure William, Lydia turned toward Broken Hand. Within moments he was walking at her side. An uneasy silence reigned between them until they were within the cover of trees. Free of William's scrutiny, Lydia turned to look openly into Broken Hand's face. His eyes met hers, and emotion welled warm and deep within her. Her voice emerged haltingly.

"I . . . I dreamed you were dead. You had a wound in your chest . . . here . . ."

Lydia's hand rose automatically to touch the remembered spot on the broad expanse of Broken Hand's bared chest. Her voice caught in a small gasp as her fingers touched on a ragged scar, and she continued in a breathless whisper as her eyes moved to his strong thigh.

". . . and there. . . ."

Broken Hand nodded.

"What else did you see, Shadow Woman?"

"I saw Walking Woman and Owl Woman dead. I saw you fall onto a sandy creek bed. Your eyes were closed. You, too, were dead."

Confirmation of all she had seen registered in Broken Hand's eyes as he began to speak.

"In the days following the white soldiers' betrayal of our trust, I came very close to meeting death. But I survived. I survived to curse the day I returned you to your people for a peace which did not come, a peace which turned me from the people of my tribe to join with those in this land who still sought to fight the white man's treachery."

"The actions of the soldiers that day ... they were abhorred by all responsible whites."

"And yet the white man's soldiers continue to kill our people, take our land."

Abruptly realizing that her fingers still rested against Broken Hand's chest, Lydia attempted to withdraw. But Broken Hand's crooked fingers closed around her wrist to hold her fast. Her palm rested against the warmth of his flesh, rising and falling with his rapid breaths.

"You have not been absent from my mind in the days since we have parted. I sought to expel you from my waking thoughts, but escape from the reminder of all which was sacrificed in the name of peace was impossible. Visions of you assailed me in the dark of the empty nights. You continued to call to me, to speak of my destiny."

Her breathing becoming as ragged as Broken Hand's, Lydia shook her head.

"That woman in your visions, it was not I. I know nothing of the destiny to which you refer."

"The destiny of which you spoke has since become clear to me, Shadow Woman. My eyes touched on the daughter of your flesh, Fire Spirit, and life returned to my body with the realization that you were also near. It then became clear that *you* are my destiny, Shadow Woman."

"No ... no, I am not!" Her heart suddenly pounding, Lydia shook her head with added vehemence. "I am wife to another—one who lies wounded. His wound was suffered at the hands of your people."

Broken Hand drew her closer, his strong arms refusing to accept her denials.

"No. Broken Hand, I did not come to you for this. I came to you in trust and need. My daughter . . . she is a prisoner of your people. I wish to have her released."

"Your daughter is well. Black Wolf has taken her from camp because of the harsh words being spoken against her. He keeps her safe with him."

"My daughter does not belong in your world, Broken Hand. She belongs there no more than I. As I am the wife of a man of my own people, Faith will soon be the wife of the young soldier who brought me here. She . . . she must be released."

Broken Hand's eyes narrowed as he considered her words, and Lydia held her breath. The familiar, musky scent of Broken Hand's body tantalized her. The touch of his hands on her shoulders brought too vividly to life memories of times she had consigned to forgotten corners of her mind. She was intensely aware that they stood only a hairbreadth apart. Her body trembled, aching to close that short distance between them. Broken Hand raised a broad hand to her hair, his twisted fingers moving against the upswept strands at the back of her neck. His eyes caressed her, touching her brow, the line of her cheek, her trembling lips. Lydia closed her eyes, shame flooding her mind at the strength of her longing for this man.

Broken Hand's deep voice shattered the tremulous silence between them, raising her fluttering lids to his affected expression.

"You close your eyes in an attempt to escape a truth you cannot bear to face. But that truth will follow you as it follows me. You cannot escape it."

"Broken Hand, I came to speak to you of my daughter . . ."

"Your daughter now belongs to Black Wolf."

"No!"

"Black Wolf will not give her up. The truth which lies between us was written in Black Wolf's eyes as well. Fire

Spirit is his woman."

"No, she is not! I must speak to her—to him! I must at least have a chance to tell him that she is meant for another, that to keep Faith against her will will bring the wrath of the army down upon his people."

Broken Hand's face twisted with contempt.

"Your army is ineffective against us."

"The failure to return my daughter will bring more soldiers here . . . more and more until the land is filled with blue coats. They will bring more whites to dig up the land, to kill the buffalo. They will no longer offer peace, but will fight to the death. You must not allow Black Wolf to bring this hardship down upon your people. You must tell him to allow Faith to come home."

Realizing Broken Hand had listened intently to her plea, Lydia waited as he considered her words. In her heart she knew all she had spoken would come to pass. She knew instinctively that William would not allow Faith's capture to go unpunished. In his eyes had been reflected a look she had seen in other eyes . . . before Sand Creek and the horror it had brought to Broken Hand's people. It would mean destruction to a people as proud as the Cheyenne, who would see their blood spilled into the ground rather than give up their lives without honor.

Broken Hand held Lydia's gaze unblinkingly.

"And if Fire Spirit does not wish to return?"

Broken Hand's unexpected response took Lydia momentarily aback.

"Then : . . then I must speak to my daughter, hear her speak those words herself."

Maintaining his silence, Broken Hand caressed her mouth with his gaze. Lydia bit her lips against their trembling.

"If your daughter shows the courage to speak the words, will you show courage as well?"

"Broken Hand, I . . ."

Abruptly, Broken Hand was clutching her close, welding her frailty to his strength as he covered her mouth with his. Lydia shuddered at the intensity of the feelings which shook her as Broken Hand's mouth sank more deeply into hers, as his hands searched her slenderness, caressing her intimately in the manner of days long past. She was gasping, overwhelmed by the emotions he had brought to life within her, when he drew himself abruptly from her once more. His lips warm against her hair, he whispered hoarsely.

"I will do as you say, Shadow Woman. I will speak to Black Wolf, and I will ask that you might speak to your daughter so your mind might be put at rest. I will do all this for you because you ask it of me. But I ask something of you as well. I ask that when this is done, you will speak your feelings as honestly as you would have your daughter speak hers. I ask that you tell me then in which world you belong . . . the world of the white man, where your heart knows no peace, or the world that lies within my arms. I ask you for truth, Shadow Woman, as you would ask it of me. Do you accept my terms?"

Lydia hesitated, realizing the significance of Broken Hand's demands. Taking a deep, shuddering breath, she nodded her acceptance.

His dark eyes holding hers moments longer, Broken Hand whispered in a softer tone, "I speak to you now in solemn promise, Shadow Woman. I promise you joy in my arms, joy which will far surpass that which you have known in the arms of any other. It will be a joy of destinies fulfilled, of hearts at peace. I promise to give you this, Shadow Woman, knowing you will give the same to me in return. It is our destiny . . . that which was meant to be."

Broken Hand's voice trailed away. He hesitated only a moment more before releasing her.

Emerging from the wooded area with Broken Hand at her side, Lydia met William's anxious gaze. He walked to her side immediately, his anxiety apparent. She offered him an encouraging smile.

"Broken Hand will speak to Black Wolf. He will ask Black Wolf to allow me to speak to Faith."

Nodding, William accompanied her to her mount. All were remounted when William turned to Broken Hand once more.

"We will await your message, Broken Hand. If you do not

492

bring us a response from Black Wolf within the week . . ."

Broken Hand's face darkened unexpectedly.

"I will accept no ultimatum from you! You have my word that I will speak to Black Wolf and respond to you in turn. That is enough."

His eyes darting only momentarily to Lydia, Broken Hand turned his pony abruptly. Within moments he and White Feather were riding into the distance.

Turning her gaze to William's obvious anger, Lydia offered simply, "Broken Hand will keep his word, William."

"Lydia, you trust too much. How do you know?"

Lydia's shadowed eyes turned to follow the figures rapidly fading into the horizon.

"I know, William."

The lump in her throat allowing her no further response, Lydia turned her mount without another word and spurred him back in the direction of the fort. Wally . . . she must see Wally. She needed to touch him . . sweet, dear, Wally, who needed her.

Chapter XXVI

Faith paused, darting a quick, assessing gaze around the small clearing as she returned from the stream. Her eyes touched on Black Wolf and followed his efficient movements as he prepared to break camp. Puzzlement filled her mind. She had awakened as she had the three days previous, with the warmth of Black Wolf's strong body pressed tightly against hers. In the spontaniety of semiconsciousness, she had indulged the pleasure which had swept through her senses as her naked breasts had moved warmly against his chest. She had turned to tuck her head against his neck and had breathed deeply of his scent, submitting to the startling desire to taste his smooth skin with her tongue. A chill had moved down her spine at the intensity of pleasure it had brought her, and she had snuggled closer, her pleasure increasing as she had stretched her naked length against his when his pose of sleep had been shown to be a sham.

Black Wolf's arm had closed around her then, and he had gripped her suddenly, tightly. His free hand had tangled in her hair, jerking her head back with a sudden fierceness which had startled her. Growling an unintelligible word, Black Wolf had covered her lips with his, drinking long and deep of her mouth. Her disappointment had been acute when he had abruptly drawn back from her. Despite his arousal, impossible to hide in their intimate posture, he had glanced briefly toward the position of the sun in the cloudless sky, and turned back to her.

"You are now well. We must leave this place. You will tend o your needs and we will start our journey."

Reality had then returned. Its advent had been harsh . . . humiliating. She had watched in silence as Black Wolf had disengaged himself from the tumble of robes which had been heir mutual bed, as he had drawn his tall, naked form to its eet. She had forced herself to face the pictures which had lashed across her mind . . . intimate pictures of Black Wolf's loving, of her own willing response. She had averted her face to hide the heated color which had suffused it, but Black Wolf had not been watching. Obviously intent on other matters, he had already secured his breechcloth and eggings, and was moving about camp. He had dismissed her as easily as she had dismissed the world around them during heir loving, but the world had returned.

She had drawn herself to her feet. In her anxiety to hide her nakedness, she had dispensed with her underclothing and slipped back into the dress discarded so wantonly the night before. As she had turned her back to fasten the buttons across her naked breast, her hands trembling, shame had assaulted her in earnest.

How easily she had dismissed the remembered carnage of the Indian attack on the wagon train only three days previous . . . Lieutenant Piersall's bloodstained body, her tears for Mama, her anxiety to see Papa. How easily she had submitted to the wild urgings of her body, so easily aroused by Black Wolf's touch. Wanton . . . she had behaved as a wanton in Black Wolf's arms.

She had moved toward the stream as she had been directed, and had just returned to see Black Wolf accomplishing the details of breaking camp. He did not turn, although she knew he was aware of her presence. He seemed, somehow, unwilling to face her, and that thought twisted the knife of pain which had entered her heart. She took a deep breath. Perhaps . . . perhaps he had tired of her, and would now return her to the fort. A tremor of fear shook her as another thought entered her mind. Or perhaps he was intending to trade her off to another tribe. It was a practice long accepted by the Cheyenne, and the reason why so many captives had disappeared within the Indian nation, never to be found again. No, she did not want that to happen to her. She must be returned to the fort . . . to Mama and Papa.

Closing her eyes, Faith refused to allow the image of William to enter her mind. Her emotions were too raw, too unsettled; Black Wolf's touch was still warm against her skin.

Turning toward her at last, Black Wolf motioned her toward him. He was obviously ready to leave. The robes had already been packed and almost all trace of their short idyll had been erased. She saw that the packs had been equally distributed between the two horses, and riding blankets had been placed on both animals' backs. Black Wolf obviously intended to ride separately, another sign of his sudden desire for haste. Faith's puzzlement increased.

Swallowing tightly, Faith approached Black Wolf. He did not respond to her glance. Instead, he placed his hands on her waist and swung her up onto her horse. But his hands remained upon her. She glanced down into his face, only to feel a fierce tremor shake her at the unexpected heat of his gaze.

The warmth of Fire Spirit's skin seared Black Wolf through the thin cloth of the garment she wore, and he made another attempt to still the loud clamor of his heart. He looked up into her face, the healthy color there registering in the back of his mind. Yes, Fire Spirit was well. He had felt the gradual return of her strength. It had registered clearly in her response to him the night before. Her arms had clung to him with heated fervor, her lips had returned his kisses with loving passion, her body had risen strongly to his with each searing thrust. He had given to her with the full strength of the emotions she had brought so urgently to life inside him.

He remembered still the colors of the fire playing against her pale, naked flesh, the manner in which he had trailed his lips against those flickering shadows. The warmth of her flesh drew him still.

The warm underside of her breast brushed against his hand, and he turned to cup it, to encircle it with his loving touch. Fire Spirit's short gasp turned his heartbeat to thunder in his ears. Unable to withdraw from her, he slid the flat of his hand down from her waist to the line of her hip. The curve of her flesh was unfettered by the restrictive undergarments favored by white woman. He lowered his gaze to the long length of calf exposed by the gathered hem of her gown. Her legs were bare and smooth. He remembered their strength as they had wrapped around his back, holding him tight within the intimate circle of their mutual desire. As if of its own will, his hand moved to her ankle, to slide upward against her bare flesh and trace the fluid line of her leg.

Faith's low intake of breath raised his eyes to hers once more as he continued the seeking, upward direction of his caress. Breaking contact with her gaze, he lowered his mouth, tracing the path his hand had followed, tasting her thigh, the rounded curve of her hip. Fire Spirit's lips parted in a ragged breath. His caress was slipping across the flat surface of her stomach when Fire Spirit muttered a low word of protest. But her protest went unheeded and his hand moved inalterably to the brown, sparse curls he remembered so well. She was gasping, attempting to catch her breath even as she remained motionless under this touch, when he realized he could tolerate her inaccessibility to him no longer. Sweeping her from her horse in a swift, powerful movement, he carried her the few feet to a mossy bower between the nearby trees. He placed her upon it, and within moments, he was lying beside her, his hands fumbling at the closure of her dress, at the confining skirt. Impatience caused him finally to push her skirt upward around her waist. His brief glance caught the startled widening of her eyes as he lowered his head.

Fire Spirit was speaking to him, her low voice hoarse, shaken, but he was past hearing her words. They meant little, whatever she had chosen to say. Her heart had been in her eyes in that moment when she had met his glance, and he had known he could hold himself back from her no longer.

Black Wolf pressed his lips to the white, firm flesh of Fire Spirit's thigh, indulging himself in the unrestricted taste of her. Fire Spirit's hand moved against his head in a stroking motion which inflamed his senses, and he situated himself between her legs, his hands moving to cup her warm buttocks in his palms. He looked to the warm mound of her passion and slowly lowered his mouth toward the waiting lips. He met them, kissed them, searched the tender slit with his tongue. Fire Spirit's low gasp seared him. Her slender body was quivering. His ministrations increased in fervor, worshiping her with his loving. Abruptly, Fire Spirit's slim form was quaking in deep, shuddering spasms, and Black Wolf accepted the homage of her body. He drank deeply, savoring her body's nectar, knowing it was his and his alone to enjoy, to savor, to love. . . .

Fire Spirit was silent and still beneath him when Black Wolf raised his head once more. Her face was flushed, her eyes closed. In a quick, adept movement, he stripped away his breechcloth and leggings, and grasped her dress to lift it from her. Fire Spirit's eyes fluttered open as Black Wolf lowered himself atop her. He cupped her face with his hands even as he moved himself against her moistness. Her expression was confused, and he felt a moment's regret. Unable to respond, he thrust himself cleanly inside her, his low gasp echoing hers as his body came to intimate rest. He felt the throbbing of his manhood, its rapid swelling. He felt the wonder of all that was between them, all that could be, as he held her fast with his gaze so she might read it all in his eyes. He was gasping, plunging inside her, giving to her in return all she had given to him; and the wonder soared anew.

Black Wolf was lying limply atop Fire Spirit's body, his own still quivering with passion when he raised his head. Fire Spirit's eyes were closed, her breathing was ragged. He cupped her face gently with his broad palms, pressed his mouth lightly to her parted lips. As she raised her heavy lids, he whispered to her in the stillness.

"My need for you heeds no warnings, Fire Spirit. In the gray before dawn, I was pressed with a feeling which urged me to take you quickly from this place. My determination was strong, and I moved quickly to accommodate it. I knew I could not look to your face, consider the feelings which raged within me, or I would find myself detained. I sought to follow the warnings of the voice inside me. Victory was almost won, and then I touched your sweet flesh once more. I was lost, for I could not put you from me a second time, no matter the dire warning which sounded within me."

Black Wolf again covered Fire Spirit's silent lips with his own, a sweet singing coming alive inside him as her mouth opened to his seeking kiss. He withdrew himself from her reluctantly and, assuming a crouching position, allowed his eyes one last sweep of the woman he had loved so well. He pulled himself to his feet and reached down to draw Fire Spirit up beside him. He held her close, hearing her silence, noting the manner in which she averted her gaze. Momentary puzzlement assailed him.

"There is discomfort inside you, Fire Spirit. Speak to me."

The great eyes which rose to his at last were filled with unexpected sadness.

"Your discomfort of a moment before was due to your realization that we must leave this place, Black Wolf. The discomfort which lies inside me now comes from the knowledge that there is no place where we may go. I must return to—"

"No!"

Fury flashing through his mind, Black Wolf gripped her nakedness closer. He ran his hand roughly down her side, drawing her eyes to the line which marked the meeting of white and russet flesh. His voice was low, filled with warning.

"Look at the evidence before your eyes. You see the meeting of our flesh. Your body still trembles from our joining. And as we have been joined, so we will remain. I will sacrifice all to that end. I will not let you go."

"Black Wolf, I cannot—"

His broad chest beginning to heave angrily, Black Wolf ordered sharply, "No! It is done."

Stepping back from her, he reached down for her dress. His eyes intent, he watched as she hesitated momentarily and then raised her dress to slip it down over her head. Snatching up his breechcloth and leggings he slipped them on once more. His expression severe, he took her arm and led her

499

toward the waiting horses.

Black Wolf was about to lift her to her mount when Fire Spirit stayed his hand.

"Black Wolf, I cannot . . ."

But Black Wolf did not hear her words. His head had snapped up. He was suddenly alert. Moving quickly, he walked to a spot that provided him a clear view of the approach to the wooded copse which sheltered them.

Taking a deep breath, Black Wolf drew himself erect. A frown creased his forehead at Broken Hand's approach.

"No, nothing is wrong, Wally. I'm just feeling a little out of sorts, that's all."

Wally was propped up in bed, in as close to a sitting position as he had come in the week since Lydia had been at Fort Laramie. His position made it all the more difficult to avoid his intense assessment, and Lydia turned in desperation toward the tray on the bedside table. The aroma of the hearty beef stew turned her stomach, but she forced a smile.

"Well, it looks like you're going to like supper tonight, dear. Beef stew and biscuits. Would you like me to—"

"I'm not hungry."

Her smooth brow creasing in a frown, Lydia turned back to face Wally.

"You're just starting to improve, Wally. You can't stop eating now."

"I don't intend to stop eating, Lydia. I'm not hungry right now, that's all."

His pale eyes again searched her face, but this time Lydia's attempt to avoid his gaze was thwarted by Wally's grip on her arm.

"Lydia, wait. Sit down . . . here on the bed. Talk to me, darling."

"I promised Dr. Mallory I wouldn't tire you, Wally. He said—"

"Forget Dr. Mallory for a few minutes, will you?"

A slight flush was beginning to color Wally's fair skin, and a nervous flutter moved inside Lydia's stomach. She didn't want to excite him, and it was obvious running away from him as she had for the past two days was doing just that. Taking a firm hold on her emotions, Lydia gave a short nod.

"All right, Wally. What do you want to talk about?"

"I want to talk about you." Wally's broad hand moved to her waist as she sat on the side of the bed. It slipped up her side, grazing her breast and coming to rest at the curve of her neck. He pulled her slowly closer until her mouth rested firmly against his. He kissed her slowly, lingeringly. She parted her lips, forcing her mind from all but his kiss, forcing away the image of another mouth which had touched hers, of another voice which had whispered earnest words of love.

When Wally drew back, his breathing was rapid, his color darker than before. He gave a short laugh.

"Your mind wasn't in that kiss, but it all but did me in anyway. I must be in worse shape than I thought."

Lydia couldn't resist a smile in return.

"You're in much better condition than you were a week ago, Wally. Dr. Mallory says your leg is finally on the mend."

Relinquishing his hold, Wally leaned back against the pillow. His hand moved to take hers, and he raised it to his lips. The simple gesture brought the heat of tears to Lydia's eyes, and a question to Wally's lips.

"Lydia, for the love of God, tell me what's wrong."

"Nothing . . . nothing, Wally. I think it's just the fact that I can finally let myself breathe again . . . knowing you're getting well. Dr. Mallory was really beginning to think that you were going to lose your leg, darling."

"Would that have made such a difference to you, Lydia? Would you have been ashamed to be saddled with a cripple?"

Shock colored Lydia's face, and her reply was indignant.

"Wally, how can you ask such a thing?"

"Because something's been bothering you."

"I told you, I was worried."

"No, it's more than that. What are you hiding from me? William's been extremely tense, too. Between the two of you—"

"Wally, you're imagining things."

501

"Damn it, Lydia, tell me what's wrong!"

Lydia stared at Wally's angry face in tense frustration, her mind working frantically. There was no doubt Wally was recuperating rapidly. His color had returned. The deep hollows which had altered his face so drastically were beginning to soften. Even his hair seemed to have regained some of its former color . . . or maybe that was just a reflection of the energy which now sparked in his eyes, albeit briefly. In any case, signs of the old Wally were returning. He would soon be himself, and she would no longer be able to avoid his questions. But for the time being, she was not willing to tell him of Faith's capture, or of the shadows from the past that had come alive to haunt her, to slip between Wally and her, causing her to draw back from his intimate touch.

A sound in the doorway preceded Dr. Mallory's entrance. Lydia turned toward him in silent relief as he shifted his annoyed glare from one of them to the other.

"What's going on in here? You're supposed to be resting, Wally, not abusing your wife."

Wally responded with a glare of his own.

"Look, Hank, Lydia and I are having a private conversation. It had nothing to do with—"

"Unfortunately, Wally, you aren't allowed a private life, not yet. And if you're angry with your wife for leaving the door open all day and denying you the privacy you're too weak to afford, you can blame that on me. You're too sick for hanky-panky, Wally. Even that snuggling you and your wife were indulging in is too hard on you. I've given her strict orders."

Wally's eyes snapped to Lydia's face. There he found instant relief mixed with anger as he observed her flush. He jerked his gaze back toward the white-haired doctor once more.

"You should try minding your own business, Hank. Damn it, you had me thinking—"

"That's your trouble, Wally, too much thinking and not enough resting." His drooping mustache twitching warningly, Dr. Mallory shook his head. "If you're not careful, you're going to end up back where you were before." His eyes moving toward the table and the tray that rested upon it, Hank Mallory raised his wiry brows.

"Not eating, I see."

Throwing up his hands in a gesture of futility, Wally ground his teeth.

"Give me that damned plate."

Barely restraining her smile, Lydia picked up the plate and spoon and sat carefully on Wally's bed.

"I'll feed you, Wally."

His eyes touching hers warmly, Wally gave a short laugh.

"It'll be my pleasure, darling."

A low snort from behind lifted Wally's eyes in Mallory's direction.

"Look, Hank, if I tell you I'm not going to abuse my wife anymore, will you leave?"

Another low snort his only response, Hank Mallory turned back toward the doorway. He was on his way out when he grumpily tossed over his shoulder, "And remember to keep that door *open.*"

A smile curved Wally's lips for the first time that day as he watched Dr. Mallory's stooped figure disappear through the doorway. He took Lydia's hand, staying the spoon as she attempted to feed him.

"I'm sorry, darling. It's just . . . well, I had myself imagining that you were drawing away from me . . . holding back, somehow. If old Mallory embarrassed you with his outspokenness, I apologize. I know he's just concerned for my welfare. And I apologize for thinking . . ." Wally hesitated. His voice slipped a notch lower. "I love you, Lydia."

Wally paused again and swallowed hard. "Now, how about some of that stew?"

Her own throat equally choked, Lydia gave a short nod and dipped the spoon into the dish.

Lydia emerged from Wally's room a short time later to see Dr. Mallory turning the corner of the hallway. Unwilling to call out and alert Wally of her purpose, she started to run in his direction. The sound of her footsteps turned Dr. Mallory toward her as she approached.

"What in heaven's name . . . ?"

"Dr. Mallory . . ." Taking a few minutes to catch her breath, Lydia raised suspiciously moist gray eyes to his. "I just wanted to thank you."

"You don't have to thank me for anything, Mrs. Durham." Dr. Mallory's wiry brows drew together in a frown. "It doesn't take much to see that both you and William have been under stress these past few days. I have the feeling that if you don't hear from that Indian soon, William's going to jump right out of his skin. You're tense, too—preoccupied. And, well, if a little white lie will make Wally rest easier—thinking it was me who got the idea to suddenly leave that door open all the time—I figured it wouldn't hurt."

A pang of guilt tied Lydia's tongue. As Dr. Mallory placed a sympathetic hand on her shoulder, a twinkle flashed in his eyes.

"And the fact is, Wally *is* too sick for hanky-panky, and he's too damned stubborn to realize it. It's a good thing you have better sense."

Her guilt a heavy burden, Lydia attempted to respond, but Dr. Mallory cut her off.

"You don't owe me any explanations, Mrs. Durham. God willing, things will straighten out soon, and then you can tell Wally all about it. And in the meantime . . ."

A tight voice from behind drew both Mallory and Lydia toward William who was soberly interrupting their quiet exchange.

". . . And in the meantime, we'll have to prepare to leave in the morning. I've just heard from Broken Hand."

Lydia was trembling. It had been more difficult this time to escape Wally's watchful eye. He had been suspicious when she had said she would see him later in the morning, that she was going to lie down in her room. Dr. Mallory had again

504

come to her aid, citing female problems for which she was consulting him. She had left Wally then and had made her way directly to join William. They had been riding for more than twenty minutes, and she was shaking more with each step her mount took. A premonition, heavy and foreboding, weighed on her mind.

Lydia shot a short glance in William's direction. He had suffered as much as she, but his suffering would soon be over. They would find out where they would be able to speak to Faith. They would arrange her return. . . .

Two mounted figures were waiting for them. This time they had not bothered to conceal themselves, but rode forward as Lydia and William approached.

Lydia was trembling and William's brow knotted with concern the moment he reached up to lift her from her horse. Again guilt plagued her. Faith, Broken Hand, Wally . . . her thoughts were in a turmoil.

Lydia addressed William's obvious concern softly.

"I'll be all right . . . once I know when I will be able to see Faith again."

Unwilling to look into Broken Hand's face, Lydia walked at his side until they reached the cover of trees. Then she turned sharply to face him, feeling a tremor of fear at the pain in his dark eyes. When she spoke, her voice was quaking.

"When will I be able to talk to Faith?"

Broken Hand hesitated before responding. He stepped closer, raising his hand to touch her white cheek. Lydia's anxiety rose anew.

"Broken Hand . . ."

"Black Wolf will not consent to the meeting. He has taken Fire Spirit away."

"Away?"

"He has taken Fire Spirit into the land of the north. He will not yet return to the Cheyenne camp."

"No. You must stop him! You must tell him that we want her back. We'll do anything—"

"Your words are for naught, Shadow Woman. Your daughter is gone. Do you not sense that?"

"No . . . no, I do not! You must—"

"I can do nothing, Shadow Woman. Black Wolf will return with Fire Spirit when their time together is over."

"Their time together?"

"Many years ago it was our custom when young people joined their lives, to allow them time together, apart from all others, that they might get to know each other well, to think and act as one."

"Joined their lives . . . ! But Faith has not—"

"Black Wolf has taken her to him. Rings were exchanged long ago. The contract was never broken."

"It *was* broken! Faith was too young. She did not go with Black Wolf of her own accord. She was taken captive! She—"

"She is Black Wolf's woman. He will not give her up."

Closing her eyes against the pain of Broken Hand's words, Lydia swayed weakly. Immediately, strong arms closed around her and she was taken against Broken Hand's broad chest. Submitting to her need, Faith allowed Broken Hand's low words of consolation to wash over her. She felt his touch against her back, his lips against her face. She felt his broken fingers raise her chin to give him access to her mouth, but she turned from his kiss. Broken Hand stiffened.

"You turn from me when you know your body cries for mine. Do you not see the course of your own destiny? Fire Spirit will remain with Black Wolf, and you will return to my lodge. Your heart will be at rest there."

Attempting to ignore Broken Hand's words, Lydia took a deep, harsh breath.

"I would ask you one thing more—to answer a question with truth. I must know . . . was it Faith's choice to go with Black Wolf, to remain with him?"

A long pause followed Lydia's question. His response was simple and unyielding.

"It is of little consequence. Black Wolf will not let her go."

Lydia's breath caught in her throat. Turning abruptly to leave, she was stopped by Broken Hand's low summons.

"Shadow Woman . . . think . . . think what you do by leaving. You would sacrifice your peace, throw it away."

Lydia turned back to regard him once more.

"The decision is not mine to make, Broken Hand. My husband lies wounded. He has lost his daughter this day. I cannot allow him to lose his wife as well."

"And I?" Broken Hand's voice was low. "Do I not lose all in losing you?"

The shadowed depths of her eyes suddenly clouded, Lydia was again Shadow Woman as words emerged from her lips without being summoned.

"Our destinies, intertwined, are unclear. I only know I must return."

The weight of William's intense gaze almost too heavy to bear as they emerged from the trees, Lydia walked to her horse. She spoke to him in a low, shaking voice.

"William, all is not lost. We will get Faith back."

His eyes flicking briefly closed, William nodded. They were riding back toward the fort when Lydia realized he had not spoken a word.

Her gaze intent on the distance, Deer Woman strained to see the faces of the two mounted figures who approached the camp. Her heart pounded in her breast when she recognized the brilliant coloring of Broken Hand's pony. But hope died painfully inside her as she realized that the smaller man who rode at his side could not be Black Wolf. She took a deep breath. It mattered little. She would question Broken Hand when he came. She would find out where Black Wolf had gone, when he would return. She would make her plans then.

Turning, Deer Woman moved to a position beside Broken Hand's lodge. She cared not for the glances being sent in her direction, for the tittering of foolish voices behind raised hands. She cared not that the whole of the camp knew she longed for Black Wolf and that he had taken another woman.

Her head erect, Deer Woman watched as Broken Hand drew up alongside his lodge. She saw the weariness in his face. She saw his suffering. But she was immune to all but the pain within her. She stepped forward and raised her voice.

507

"Broken Hand, I would speak of Black Wolf. I would know where he has gone, when he will return."

Turning toward her, his brow furrowing, Broken Hand hesitated before responding. He looked into her eyes and read her glance. Then his face softened, and he replied in a low tone.

"You will not find happiness with Black Wolf, Deer Woman, unless you celebrate his happiness as your own. He has taken the woman, Fire Spirit, away. It is his word that he will not give her up on penalty of his life."

Seeing the pain his words had inflicted, Broken Hand hesitated a moment more.

"Share his joy, Deer Woman, for it is the only joy Black Wolf will give you."

The low finality of his words spoken, Broken Hand moved into the darkness of his lodge.

All life within Deer Woman ceased. Drained, an empty shell, she stared forward seeing nothing before she turned and walked away.

Chapter XXVII

Sally Anne Morris walked slowly along the carpeted hallway. She raised an unconscious hand to her hair, smoothing the sweep of unruly blond curls raised from her slender neck with heavy combs. She lifted her chin with a sober expression uncommon to her usually smiling, pixielike face and dabbed lightly at the perspiration on her brow with a dainty, scented handkerchief.

Summer was always an intensely humid period in the nation's capital. The weather was the main reason even year-round residents fled the city during those torrid months, but Papa's unfinished business had detained their usual race for cooler climes this year. She had arisen from her bed that morning, her usually pleasant, unrufflable spirits dampened considerably by the sleepless night she had spent in the elaborate room which had become stiflingly airless by the early hours of morning. She had bathed and dressed, choosing one of her coolest dresses, a bright yellow batiste which accented the golden, sun-lightened color of her hair and the fragile whiteness of her complexion. Paying no heed to the styles of the day, she had pulled her hair to the top of her head and secured the damp curls with several combs. She had not paused to contemplate the fact that her coiffure was extremely flattering to her small features. Instead, her mind was preoccupied with the argument she was planning to present to her father in favor of their long-delayed departure from the city.

But the complaints which had been hanging on the tip of her tongue, ready to be voiced, had fallen by the wayside the moment she had descended the staircase and seen the envelope she now held in her hand.

A letter from William . . . Angry at herself for the manner in which her heart had leaped when she had spied his familiar script on the envelope lying on the foyer table, she had forced herself to maintain a sedate step in its direction. But, despite herself, her hand had snatched at the bruised envelope, and the fingers which had unfolded the carefully written missive had trembled.

Sally Anne took a deep breath. She had heard from William only occasionally in the years since she had first met him. Military business had brought him to the capital on a few occasions during that time, and she had shared his company at several social occasions. William was a pleasant, courteous companion. She liked looking at him, and she enjoyed his humor, his wit, and his unexpected sensitivity. She had admitted to herself, during the solitary hours when his image outshone all others in her mind, that she would enjoy much more about him if she but had the opportunity.

But Sally Anne had also admitted to herself, during those solitary hours, that the possibility of such a furtherance of their relationship was highly unlikely. Captain William Potter had only one woman on his mind, and that woman was Faith Durham. The silent admission was distinctly painful. She remembered, her discomfort not lessened by the passage of time, the first time she had seen William and Faith Durham together. The anticipation, which had been building inside her from the moment her eyes had touched on the handsome captain, had suffered a sharp and deflating blow when Faith Durham had arrived at their small dinner party. William had walked from her side without a word and promptly forgotten her existence the moment his eyes had touched on the beautiful Miss Durham. She had no doubt that he had not even been conscious of his slight until the Durhams had left. Then his embarrassment had been acute. But she had been wise enough to accept his apology gracefully. In truth, she had had no choice. He had melted her with his sincerity and unpracticed charm. In their meetings since, his effect on her had grown.

But she had been wise . . . had actually congratulated herself on the manner in which she had dealt with the relationship between William and herself. That expert handling of the situation had resulted in the warmth with which he greeted her on the occasions of his infrequent visits to Washington. It had also rewarded her with the opportunity to spend time in his company on those occasions. The result of all this splendid maneuvering had been that her feelings for William had grown out of proportion, while he thought of her with the warmth of a friend. The letter she had received from him, which she still held clutched in her hand, was proof of that.

Pausing before a paneled doorway midway down the hall, Sally Anne raised her hand and rapped lightly. A low response from within brought her into the room, her step slow, measured. A small lamp was lit on Hartfield Morris's massive desk, despite the early hour and the sun which shone through the open window of the room behind him. Its yellow glare glinted on the white-haired senator's balding pate and the sheen of perspiration visible there, but Sally had no reaction to the heat of the room or her father's deepening frown as she stood before him in silence.

"Well . . . what is it, Sally Anne? Come on, speak up." Beginning to show annoyance at her silence, he frowned more deeply. "It's damned hot in here, and I want to finish these papers before the heat worsens. If I'm at all lucky, we'll be able to get away from Washington by the end of the week, and then we can—"

"I've received a letter from William, Father."

Senator Hartfield Morris paused, his eyes sweeping his daughter's still face.

"I know. I saw it on the tray in the foyer. I've received one, also."

"He's desperate. You know he wouldn't have written to either of us, much less both of us, unless he was."

"Sally Anne . . . dear . . ." Rising from his chair, Hartfield Morris walked around his desk and reached out to pat his daughter's shoulder comfortingly. "Don't upset yourself. It will do neither of us any good to allow William's pain to affect us. It is certainly a personal tragedy for him. He is deeply enamored of this young woman, Faith Durham. We both saw it from the first, did we not?"

"Yes, Father, but . . . but he is seeking our help. A month has passed since her disappearance in Indian territory. Obviously, the forces at Fort Laramie are too small to be effective against the savages. He has made formal appeals, threats, all manner of attempts to get her back; but they've all proved unsuccessful."

"Dear, I will give you the same response I intend to give to William. I cannot help him. There is nothing I can do."

"Father!"

Hartfield Morris frowned.

"I said there is nothing I can do."

Sally Anne took a deep breath. "Father, you're dismissing William's letter without giving it the consideration it deserves. You know you can—"

"Sally Anne, Congress will not reconvene for a month. In the meantime—"

"In the meantime, Father, we can formulate a plan by which we might make our thoughts clear on the hostilities which continue to progress on our western frontier. We can bring pressure to bear. We can convince the other members of Congress that a greater effort must be made for peace with the Indians . . . or a greater effort must be made to subdue them. We can convince the other members of Congress that we must enlarge our force on the frontier, reenforce the army at Fort Laramie, give our representatives there greater power to act on their own when there is an opportunity to strike a blow. We can—"

"*We* can, Sally Anne?"

"Father, William is suffering. The woman he loves has been captured. She is gone, and he doesn't know where she is or how to get her back. We must do something."

Hartfield Morris's dark eyes pinned her.

"William is suffering. And you're suffering, too."

Sally Anne hesitated. She nodded her head.

512

"Yes, I guess I am." She gave a short laugh. "I had not expected that I would react in such a manner upon hearing my competition has finally been eliminated and that William might finally be free." Sally Anne's small face was solemn once more. "But, I suppose the truth is, he is *not* free. He will never be free if Faith Durham is not found and brought back. I suppose . . . the full truth is, Father, that I would rather see William happy with the woman he loves than see both of us unhappy. In any case, William has written to me for help, and I cannot disappoint him."

Hartfield Morris took a short breath.

"I suppose that means *I* cannot disappoint him as well."

Sally Anne gave her father a tremulous smile.

"I *hope* that's what it means."

Hartfield Morris held his daughter's gaze.

"And I hope there is something I can do. At any rate, Sally Anne, I will give it a try."

"Papa dear, may I write and tell William what you have said?"

"Yes, dear, if you wish."

The heat of the room forgotten, Sally Anne unexpectedly slipped her arms around her father's expanding middle and hugged him tightly. She pressed a quick kiss against his sagging cheek. Within a moment she had turned and slipped back through the doorway, her whispered thank you, still soft in his ears.

Hartfield Morris stood for long moments looking at the doorway through which his daughter had disappeared, aware of a strange thickness in his throat. Sally Anne had not called him "Papa dear" for years, not since she had declared herself grown and above such a childish endearment. It must be true. His little girl loved that young captain.

And her young captain loved someone else.

Hartfield Morris was annoyed once more. Why did Sally Anne make things so difficult?

The sound of a child's laughter, the scurry of small moccasined feet . . .

Deer Woman raised her head, her eyes moving from the vessel in her hands, slowly filling with water as she crouched beside the river. A brilliant morning sun warmed her, and she squinted against its glare as she watched the children at play. It was a scene she had witnessed countless times before on the sandy river bank. In their usual manner, the smallest children remained by their mothers watching as their older cousins and brothers scattered to the river where they swam and dove in the warm water. On the sand bars a short distance away some children were running races while others dug, attempting to bury each other in the warm sand. A few boys were busy at the mud bank, modeling images of animals and people from the clay, and setting them in the sun to dry.

Deer Woman gave a short laugh. How deceiving was the tranquil scene. It mimicked a peace which was withheld from them by the greed of the white man. Even now as the children played, their fathers and brothers prepared war parties against their enemy. Some would not return.

Deer Woman closed her eyes against the warmth of the morning sun. She allowed the bright orange glow to penetrate her lids, warming her, blinding her to all around her. Had the white man not come to the land it would be she who sat by the river, watching her own children play. They would be Black Wolf's and her children, and she would care for them with all the love in her heart. Deer Woman allowed herself a few more moments for her fantasy. But it was a temporary escape. She knew she must, after all, open her eyes again and return to the camp. She could not stay here, with the happy voices, with the children, forever.

Deer Woman opened her eyes and the true world returned. She looked at the children who were not her own; she remembered that Black Wolf had left with the woman he loved almost two moons before, the white woman whose presence had forced him to leave the camp. They were alone on the land, but Deer Woman knew the white woman would suffer little hardship. Would not she, herself, sacrifice everything to be alone on the land with Black Wolf?

Deer Woman drew herself to her feet and picked up the

filled vessel. Living water . . . she carried it back to the lodge of her mother's sister. She was a woman full grown and she had no lodge of her own. She was a woman full grown and she had no man of her own. She was a woman full grown and she had no children of her own. A deep unhappiness filled Deer Woman and she fought her growing despair.

She walked slowly up the rise toward camp, her eyes falling on a shadow which fell across the ground where she would walk. She raised her eyes to Spotted Elk. His returned health was revealed in the color of his face, the strength of his posture. Time had erased all sign of his wound, except for the scar which marked his flesh. Satisfaction battled Deer Woman's sadness. Spotted Elk was well. She had not returned to his lodge for many days, but she had felt Spotted Elk's gaze following her. She had turned her heart and eyes from that knowledge.

Spotted Elk reached out a hand to stay her and Deer Woman paused. His voice, when he spoke, was deep with feeling.

"I look to the children at the river with joy and pain. I remember a time when I had a child such as they, and I think that in other days, Silent Woman would still be alive to sit in the sun with my daughter playing at her side. It is then that I curse the fates that brought the white man to this land; the same fates which offered us trust in the white man's word, only to have it end in slaughter and death."

Deer Woman felt the depth of Spotted Elk's despair and she looked away only to have Spotted Elk's hand move to her face to tilt it up to his. She felt the warmth in Spotted Elk's regard as his gaze touched her.

"And then, Deer Woman, I look to the present and I see the suffering and the pain which continues, and I realize it is all for naught if life does not go on. So I must look to the future, Deer Woman, and in that future I see myself with you beside me. I see a future where you will sit by the river, with a child at your side. That child will be my child, and we will love that child together. With that child will begin the healing of the pain we both suffer, and with that child our future will begin. I ask you to give me that future, Deer

Woman, for it is only with you that I would share it. My heart cries out to yours. The man that I was, is no more. No more will I callously dismiss that which I have, for that which I would have. When you are mine, there will be no other woman for me, and my future will be yours. I ask you to be generous . . . to forgive . . . to love."

Deer Woman looked deep into Spotted Elk's eyes, and her heart stirred. But she would not put aside visions of a love lost, and slowly, regretfully, Deer Woman turned away. She walked up the slope with a measured tread. She was in no rush to return to the village. There was nothing for her there.

William wiped the sweat from his brow with the back of his arm, unconscious of the gritty red dust which scratched his brow. The fort had come within sight, and he spurred his horse to a faster pace, aware that the patrol following behind was as anxious as he to return. He and his men had conducted another uneventful sweep of the area. Strangely enough, after Faith's capture, Indian activity within the area had lessened considerably. It seemed that the attack on the last wagon train had satisfied them for a while. William clenched his teeth with disgust and bitterness. Bitter, he had become very bitter in the two months since Faith had been captured.

Negotiate . . . had he not preached that policy to General Dodge himself? Negotiate with the Indians . . . the native people of the West. Remember that they are people who have been mishandled. Had he not looked with scorn upon those who had been unable to see past their own personal losses? But he had so easily joined their ranks.

Negotiate? Negotiation had proved to be a joke as in the past. Red Cloud did not want to negotiate. He wanted to fight, to drive the white man from his land; and nothing short of that goal would satisfy him. He persisted in denying any knowledge of Faith's whereabouts. If Indians who had agreed to discuss the matter were to be believed, Faith and Black Wolf had fallen off the side of the earth.

William took a deep breath, his eyes making a last survey

of the surrounding landscape. It was well into fall, but the heat was unexpected, unusual. The weather would soon be turning colder, and winter would be setting in. Winters were bitter in this country—very bitter—even for those accustomed to their rigors. But for Faith—unaccustomed, without sufficient clothing, living under primitive conditions—this winter would be next to impossible. Strange, he was now considering the possibility that Faith's ordeal would extend for another month or more, when, at first, he had not thought it would extend for even a week. He had been so certain that sensible persuasion would bring her back. He had not expected he could be so wrong.

The troop was drawing closer to the fort, and William saw a familiar figure in the fort yard. Lydia . . . She continued to await the return of each patrol. It was as if she had a second sense that told her when they were approaching. Or perhaps she just had a friend within the guard. In any case, she was always there. Damn, he would have to face disappointment again in those shadowed eyes.

Shadow Woman . . . Broken Hand had referred to her by that name. They had not spoken to, had any contact at all, with Broken Hand since that last day, but he did not have to look hard to see that Broken Hand remained in Lydia Durham's mind. The shadows in her large eyes had darkened that day, and those shadows remained. It was as if that great Indian's image was burned there, refusing to be displaced, even by Wally.

Wally . . . Wally was nearly well. He was now able to walk almost unaided, and Hank Mallory had all but declared him cured. He still did not know about Faith. Any day now he would have to be told. He was already talking about getting back to Denver, worrying about Faith being alone in that city for so long. He had even insisted Lydia send periodic messages to Faith, and she had humored him. The messages had never left the fort, but Wally had not been the wiser.

He did not look forward to the time when Wally would be told the truth. Durham was going to be furious, but had he been in better shape, he certainly would have noticed the toll these last two months had taken on his wife. Lydia Durham,

517

always petite and of delicate stature, was now almost frighteningly thin. Strangely enough, her wasted state did not detract from her beauty. Instead, it added a quality which might almost be considered ethereal to her cameolike features, but he was well aware that Dr. Mallory was not comfortable with her physical condition.

No, it was obvious that this state of affairs could not go on much longer. Something had to break . . . something.

Turning his mount into the front yard, William paid scant attention to the acknowledgment of the guards, the pounding hooves behind him slowly drawing to a halt. He gave a short signal to Sergeant Miller who had reined in beside him, and the troop was dismissed. He never looked back. His eyes on Lydia Durham's tense expression, he dismounted quickly and walked to her side. He did not bother with the amenities.

"Lydia, what's wrong?"

Lydia attempted a smile.

"Nothing is wrong, William. I was just walking in the yard when I saw you returning. I thought I would wait to talk to you."

William took Lydia's arm and turned her toward the building behind them. He was too tired to play games.

"Lydia, just tell me."

Lydia bit her lips revealingly.

"Dr. Mallory . . . he says Wally should be told about Faith now. He says Wally is strong enough. He says I shouldn't wait any longer. Tonight, William. I'm going to tell him tonight. Dr. Mallory insists on being present, and I thought you might want to be there also."

Despite her brave front, William was only too aware that Lydia was shuddering, and William was filled with compassion. How much more would this woman be made to bear? Sliding his arm supportively around her waist, he guided her toward her quarters. He attempted a smile.

"I would very much like to be there, Lydia. I know Wally will want to ask me some questions. I only wish I had the answers."

Lydia's step slowed, her hand coming to rest on William's

arm. Her eyes held his unflinchingly.

"William, I know you somehow feel personal responsibility here, but I want you to realize that the failure to bring Faith back is not yours."

Unwilling to argue the point in full view of interested observers, William nodded.

"Perhaps not, but I'm sure Wally will draw his own conclusion. In any case, you may be sure I wish to be present when he is told. When will that be?"

Pausing as they reached her door, Lydia responded with an attempt at a smile which was no more successful than his meager effort.

"Tonight, after supper."

Nodding, William's response was brief.

"I'll be there."

Wally's face drained of color. He sat abruptly, as if the strength had suddenly left his legs, and William realized that was precisely the case. Wally was not yet as strong as he appeared.

Lydia moved to his side and Wally stared at her in disbelief. He shook his head, his voice revealing his anger when he spoke.

"You . . . you've been lying to me all this time?"

Lydia's face twisted with pain.

"No, not lying. Please don't say that, Wally. You were too ill. I could not tell you. I—"

Hank Mallory's unhesitant interjection turned Wally in his direction. His own anger was growing.

"Your wife held back the truth on my orders, Wally. Whether you realize it or not, it was not a matter of whether you would keep your leg when your wife arrived here at the fort. I did not know whether you would keep your life. Despite our encouraging words, for a long time after her arrival the infection ran an erratic course. You had several setbacks which, in your stubbornness, you refused to acknowledge. You were in no condition to sustain the shock of your daughter's capture, nor to sustain the pressure of the worry which would ensue. You needed all your energy for healing."

Wally waved his hand, shaking his head at the same time as if the motion would negate Hank's words more emphatically than his vocal response.

"No . . . no, there is no excuse for this, for keeping me ignorant of my daughter's danger. Damn it man, she is my only child! I should have been told!"

"And what would you have done? Would worry have brought her back when negotiation, threats, and the increase of patrols could accomplish nothing? Use your head, Wally."

Ignoring Hank Mallory's severe expression, Wally turned his pale eyes toward William who stood by in uneasy silence.

"Damn it, William, how could this have happened? Did you find out nothing? Where is Faith? Who has her? The Sioux? Is it Red Cloud? What does he want . . . why is he holding her?"

William's fair face paled. He was loath to say the words.

"No, the Sioux do not have her, Wally. Neither is she at the Cheyenne camp, or the Arapaho. We have had the cooperation of several of their people and have managed to conduct a dialogue with Red Cloud through them."

"Come on, out with it, William. I didn't ask who *isn't* holding my daughter. I want to know who *is* holding her!"

"She was captured by the Cheyenne warrior Black Wolf."

Wally frowned and shook his head.

"That's impossible. If you're talking about that Cheyenne who held her once before, that fellow is dead. I know. I saw him."

"He isn't dead, Wally. And he *is* the fellow who recaptured Faith."

Wally's face took on a grayish hue, and he swallowed with obvious difficulty.

"What are his terms? What must we do to get Faith back?"

"There are no terms."

"No terms? There must be something we can offer. Winter is coming on. Those savages will be needing supplies, blankets, horses—anything. I'm a rich man, William.

Perhaps the Army cannot bargain so openly, but I—"

"Lydia has made contact, Wally, conducted a personal negotiation with the only Cheyenne who would speak with us. The response was negative. Black Wolf has taken Faith away from the Cheyenne camp. He will not give her up. He . . ."

But Wally was no longer listening. He turned toward Lydia, his cheek ticking revealingly.

"With whom was your 'personal' negotiation conducted, Lydia? Who was the Cheyenne who agreed to meet with you to discuss our daughter? What was his name?"

Lydia raised her chin, her eyes holding Wally's unflinchingly.

"His name was Broken Hand."

The silence within the room acute, Wally stared at his wife's still face. Myriad thoughts assailed his shocked mind in the few seconds before he turned sharply toward the two men who stood at her side.

"I think there is nothing more we have to discuss at this time. Since Lydia is the person who has done the negotiating for my daughter's release, I think she is the one to whom I must speak. I appreciate your concern, and I would like to speak with you again later, but if you will excuse Lydia and me now, gentlemen."

"Wally, I want to tell you that I've done everything I could. I've made a formal request to Washington, telling them of the situation here, that it is dire, that we need reenforcements. I've written to every contact I ever made there to exert the necessary pressure. I've taken steps to—"

"Not now, William." Turning back and seeing William's earnest expression, Wally shook his head. "Later, please. After I've spoken with Lydia, we can formulate a plan."

"Yes, a plan . . ." William shook his head, knowing full well the futility of all the plans he had made—the many, many plans.

Wally was standing again. He took a few difficult steps toward the door.

"If you don't mind, I'd like to be alone with my wife now."

Dr. Mallory's white mustache twitched with concern.

521

"Wally, your wife has suffered grossly in this affair. She has had much pressure to bear."

"I have no intention of beating her, if that's what you think, Hank." Wally's expression stiff, he continued tightly, "And I don't think I need give you any further explanation. So if you don't mind."

Shooting Wally a hard look, Dr. Mallory turned toward the door. His stooped figure was clearing the doorway when William spoke again.

"Wally, I cannot leave without telling you how deeply I regret . . ."

Wally nodded his head.

"It seems we all have regrets, William. I will speak to you later if you are agreed."

"Certainly."

The door had closed behind William when Wally turned toward Lydia, obviously under only tenuous control. He closed the distance between them in a few steps, his hand quickly clamping on her thin shoulder. His voice wavered with emotion.

"So, this is the reason for your anxiety, your lack of appetite. You have kept all this from me. What else have you kept from me?"

"What else?" Lydia was beginning to shake under his hand, but Wally was unaffected.

"What transpired between you and Broken Hand? What did he tell you of Faith? What were Broken Hand's conditions?"

"Wally, nothing transpired between Broken Hand and me. He . . . he told me Black Wolf has taken Faith to be his woman." The spontaneous jerking of Wally's thin frame caused Lydia's hand to move to his chest. Her palm rested there, his heart thudding against its surface as she continued with difficulty. "Broken Hand told me that Black Wolf will not give her up. He's taken Faith away, he doesn't know where. She's gone, Wally."

The pain in Lydia's voice had little affect on Wally as he stood staring down into her face. His next words emerged in a low rasp.

"And Broken Hand . . . what did he say to you?"

Her gray eyes uncommonly bright, Lydia whispered a concise response.

"He wants me back."

A dozen unanswered questions were suddenly clear in Wally's mind. Rage flared anew within him as he stood looking down into Lydia's pale face. Abruptly he was clutching her close, near to crushing her with the strength of the emotions consuming him. His voice emerged low and shaken as he muttered an oath against her raven hair.

"No, he'll never have you again. Those savages have taken my daughter. They will not take my wife as well. You're mine, Lydia, make no mistake there. And we will get our daughter back. I swear an oath to you now, upon my life. I will not leave this place until Faith walks through the gates of this fort of her own free will."

Aware that the thudding of Lydia's heart echoed his own, Wally pulled back enough that he might see her face. Tears streaked her colorless cheeks, but he was strangely cold to them. He was tormented by visions of the savage who had once held her as his own . . . who wanted her still.

Slowly, with great control, Wally lowered his mouth to his wife's trembling lips. He would purge that vision in the only way he knew. It was an effective method he had used many times before.

Wally's fervor increased, and Lydia's lips separated under his. He was already beginning to forget . . . almost.

Black Wolf dug his heels into his horse's sides, spurring him to a faster pace. Simultaneously, his arms tightened around Fire Spirit, holding her fast against him as the animal took a sudden lunge forward. He felt Fire Spirit's response, sensed the lift of her heart as the crisp air rushed against their faces, felt her enjoyment of the freedom of the trail and the openness of land through which they rode. He kept his pony to its new, brisk pace for some time, his heart lighter. Fire Spirit, the woman who held his heart and filled his days . . . her skin marked her an enemy of his people, but her spirit joined them as one.

Abruptly conscious of his animal's labored breathing, Black Wolf reined his horse to a more conservative pace. They had come a long way, and his animals were beginning to become weary. They had more miles to cover before they reached their destination. A small frown worked across the sharp planes of his face, and he pulled his woman closer still. He was not anxious to arrive at that destination.

A fiery tendril flicked against Black Wolf's neck, and his frown slipped away. He enjoyed the caress of Fire Spirit's hair, the warmth of her body as it rested against his. Without a conscious decision, he had prepared the horses for travel that morning, loading the second animal with the weight of their packs. They had been traveling for four days, and Fire Spirit was weary. He had seen weariness in her eyes when they had stopped to make camp the previous night, and he did not wish to see it again. Traveling as one, he would be able to lend her his support when she tired. She would be able to doze through the long hours of afternoon as their animals trudged onward. And he would be able to enjoy the luxury of Fire Spirit's flesh against his own.

Black Wolf moved his chin lightly against the silk of red-gold hair resting beside his chin. His heart was filled with the joy of all that was Fire Spirit. Two moons had passed since he had taken her to him. During that passage of time they had remained alone on the land. Removed from the conflict which doubtless still raged between their peoples, he had sought to renew the acquaintance broken by the years that lay between Fire Spirit's and his first meeting. Fire Spirit's acceptance of him had been fraught with setbacks.

At first the difficulty had been her body's refusal of his intimate attentions. Then her mind had remained aloof from him. While their nights had been filled with a fierce, loving exchange, their days had been filled with conflict. He remembered still Fire Spirit's professed desire to be returned to her people. His refusal, his declaration that she would not be exchanged, had elicited heated words, angry accusations. He had met them calmly, with a logic which had eventually stilled her protestations.

524

Over the course of weeks, Fire Spirit's protests had become less, although he had sensed a reservation which remained unvoiced. In the dark of night he had listened to words she whispered in dreams, and his heart had been stirred by her words of concern for the man she called Papa, her entreaties to a Mama who inhabited her dreams. His blood had turned hot as she had offered whispered unintelligible explanations to a man she called William. He had spoken the name to her in a jealous rush after a particularly uneasy night of dreams, and Fire Spirit had been startled into explaining that this William was a soldier at the fort. She had told him no more, but the look in the clear eyes raised to his had answered his silent inquiries.

When the time of the second moon had passed, Fire Spirit's protests had dwindled further. As they had ridden together across the sun-swept land, he had sensed her happiness. They had hunted together, and Fire Spirit had thrilled to the chase, savored the food which had resulted from their combined efforts. They had bathed together in clear, crystal pools where the only witnesses had been the birds which sang overhead and the insects which buzzed against their skin. They had made love, slept, and made love again. Their idyll had been fulfilling, loving and complete. And it had come to an end.

Many days before, he had lifted his eyes to the foliage over his head, assessing the brilliant colors which moved, waved, and dipped in the brisk, cool wind. He had been only too aware that the warmth which had lent its golden consolation to the days he and Fire Spirit had shared was disappearing. Each successive morning had brought a deeper chill to the air. He had known the weather would soon turn sharply colder, and their carefree life would no longer suffice. They need prepare for the bitter cold which would soon be upon them. Shelter, the protection of the Cheyenne camp, would be needed, and they were forced to make the journey they had undertaken.

Fire Spirit stirred in his arms, and the scent of her skin rose to his nostrils. The scent that was Fire Spirit's alone delighted his senses. It had remained with him in the years of their separation, and now he indulged himself in its beauty. He rubbed his mouth lightly against her temple, separating his lips to taste her flesh. Without conscious intention he slid his hand from the narrow expanse of her waist to cup a full, rounded breast. He massaged the crest which swelled against his hand, his other hand pulling her tighter against him as his lips moved along the white column of her throat in light, sucking kisses. She turned her face to his, her narrow brows moving together with a soft word of protest, only to find his mouth awaiting the opportunity to capture hers.

His lips held hers for long, searing minutes as he fumbled with the buttons to her dress. Then his hand was resting against the flesh of her breast, and she was gasping. He felt the swell of his desire and his kiss deepened, his stroking touch grew more bold. Her breasts were fully bared, the bodice of her dress gaping open, but he knew Fire Spirit was incapable of protest. She was caught in the wonder of the magic which encompassed them and was helpless against him.

Black Wolf tore his mouth from hers, his eyes snapping to the wooded trail around them. Turning his horse sharply, he urged his weary animal into a shady copse nearby. Securing his mount there with a flick of his wrist, he reached up to pull Fire Spirit from his horse. She was breathing deeply, pliable to his touch; and he took her the few steps to a nearby tree. As she leaned breathlessly against it, he separated her bodice to cover the gleaming mounds of her breasts with his mouth. He drank of their sweetness, sought to devour them, his hunger so intense that he could not spare the time to totally bare her warm flesh. With an anxious hand he raised her skirt and stripped away his breechcloth. The staff of his passion moved against the warm mound he had caressed only minutes before. She was moist, eager for him and he paused for breathless seconds to absorb the flushed beauty of this woman who was his life.

Eyes the color of the sky burned him, consumed him, fused to his gaze, and he plunged deeply within her. Her low gasp, the flicker of her heavily fringed lids, set his blood to pounding, but he withheld his surging response. Instead he lowered his mouth to hers once more. Her arms circled his neck and she clung to him, and he soared to the limits of wonder. When he drew away at last, he was gasping, close to fulfillment. His voice throbbing, realizing she, too, teetered at the brink, he grated hoarsely, "You have become a necessary part of me, more important than the air I breathe. You have restored life to my soul, and it is that life I will share with you. I will give to you, Fire Spirit, as you give to me, with my love. . . ."

Abruptly, he moved inside her, and Fire Spirit tumbled from the yawning precipice of their love, ecstasy spiraling in her eyes, flushing her face, filling her. Black Wolf witnessed it all, loving her, following her in her descent until they were motionless once more.

His breathing still ragged, Black Wolf withdrew from Fire Spirit's body with regret. With trembling hands he closed the bodice of her dress, and carefully buttoned it over the rapid rise and fall of her full breasts. He lowered her skirt and affixed his breechcloth. Then, within minutes, he was lifting her back upon his horse. Remounting behind her, he pulled her back against the support of his chest.

Contented, his lips against her ear, he whispered softly, "Sleep now. Close your eyes and know that we are going home."

The sounds of night were beginning to fall over the land although the sun had not fully set. Fire Spirit still seated before him, Black Wolf drew his horse back, pausing to look down upon the great camp from their position of observance on a slight rise a distance away. The greater number of lodges were Sioux, but Black Wolf looked past them to the clusters of lodges to the side—those inhabited by the Cheyenne, and farther on, the Arapaho. His eyes moved over the activity of the camp, carefully surveying the atmosphere which prevailed. There was no sign of the frenzy which followed an attack, no strutting of outlandish clothes, no discarded plunder which signaled the return of a recent war party. Instead, all seemed peaceful within the camp.

Black Wolf listened carefully. Yes, dogs barking, voices raised in ordinary conversation, the sound of a drum calling young people to dance. Peace, however temporary, reigned, and it was time for Fire Spirit and for him to return.

Slowly, making no attempt to hide his approach, Black Wolf urged his horse forward. He sensed rather than felt Fire Spirit's tensing. She had uncomfortable memories of this camp. Her most recent stay had been filled with fear. He had been angry—bitter—and he had not attempted to soothe her reaction to the voices raised against her. He remembered her shock when Broken Hand had walked into his lodge. She had later explained that she had thought Broken Hand dead, along with many others she had known in their village those years ago. He had explained that although Broken Hand had survived, Walking Woman, Silent Woman and her child, Owl Woman, Young Hawk—all had died in the raid on Sand Creek as she had believed. Fire Spirit had not been able to hide her sorrow. He had explained that it was the deaths of these people and many more, and the memories that her appearance had revived, which had caused voices to be raised against her in the camp.

Black Wolf pulled Fire Spirit closer as her trembling increased. He had explained that Broken Hand had warned him of the danger, and had advised him to deliver Fire Spirit from it. He had also told her that Broken Hand had advised him that he would soothe the anger of the people with the solace of reason, and they would be able to return within a short period. But exile had been sweet and Black Wolf had been unable to force himself to return until the advent of colder weather had begun to make its demands.

Black Wolf straightened his back, and with pride, he faced the first questioning stares of his people. The woman before him was his woman. He was proud of her, and he would let none threaten her or speak poorly of her. She was part of him, and he would protect and defend her with his life.

Pride soared anew inside him as Fire Spirit straightened, drawing away from him to hold herself as proudly as he. A fleeting glance at her face showed that she had raised her chin in a hint of defiance, and Black Wolf was aware that she sought to control the trembling of her limbs. Yes, this woman was as proud and brave as she was beautiful and loving. He had chosen well.

Black Wolf approached the Cheyenne camp, his eyes searching the familiar faces for a hint of the reception he would receive. Apprehension moved down his spine. He drew closer . . . closer. . . .

First one smile, and then another, and at last those warriors with whom he had ridden many times walked forward in open greeting. A smile lightened Black Wolf's severe expression and he raised a hand in response. He reached his lodge, relieved to see that it had been maintained and was ready for their arrival. He dismounted and turned his head, meeting the gaze of Broken Hand who stood at the doorway of his lodge a short distance away. He nodded in silent acknowledgment of all Broken Hand had accomplished.

Black Wolf turned, his eyes touching Fire Spirit's tense face. Were these other times, he would have taken her to him in ceremony, for the village to see, that all might know this woman was his wife. This lodge was his, and Fire Spirit and he were entering the first day of their lives together within it and within the camp; but neither he nor she had kinsmen to participate in the ritual. There was no marriage blanket on which to carry her. Nor were there kinswomen to welcome Fire Spirit within the lodge in silent happiness. They were alone together, and alone together they would begin their lives.

Black Wolf met the startling blue of Fire Spirit's eyes, and held her gaze firmly with his own. He reached up, lifting her from her horse to settle her in his arms, high against his chest. In observance of the only ritual which circumstance allowed him to observe, he carried her solemnly through the doorway of the lodge so that she might enter without stepping across the threshold. Once inside, he placed her on her feet, her sobriety causing him to smile.

"You may smile, Fire Spirit. You have successfully faced down those who would raise their voices against you. You are within my lodge, and we are home. Here we will remain."

Conscious of her lack of response, Black Wolf pulled Fire Spirit close. He held her comfortingly against his body, his eyes closed against the wonder of her. He told himself all was well. She need not speak. All had been said.

In the deepening dusk outside the lodge, Deer Woman stood in silence. She had seen Black Wolf's outline in the distance, recognized it immediately, and her heart had leaped with joy. It had only been as he had drawn closer that she had seen the woman before him on his horse, the flaming strands of her hair flying in the brisk breeze. She had grown still and silent as she had watched his approach. Her heart had stopped when Black Wolf had drawn up before his lodge and a pain, deeper than any she had ever suffered, had pierced her when Black Wolf had reached up to lift the white woman from his horse and carry her across the threshold of his lodge.

For all to see, the woman, Fire Spirit was Black Wolf's woman—his wife of choice.

Deer Woman turned abruptly in an attempt to make a fast escape, unseen, unnoted in her sorrow. But she could not escape the scrutiny of one whose eyes followed her everywhere. Sober, unsmiling, Deer Woman turned from Spotted Elk's gaze. No longer willing to consider shamed escape, she raised her head proudly and walked toward her lodge. It was time to put aside a dream which would never materialize. Yes, it was time. . . .

Faith lay in silence in the darkness of the lodge, deep in the comfort of familiar robes. The sound of Black Wolf's steady breathing as he lay beside her signaled his sleep, but sleep eluded her. Instead, she stared at the circle of night sky visible to her eye, and at the bright pinpoints of light twinkling in its expanse.

Her mind moved slowly over the events, and over her confused feelings, of the last months. It was strange that the outlet to the sky above her should be so familiar, so comforting. The rough, temporary structure in which she had lived with Black Wolf during their solitary idyll had not been so formal an abode, but this lodge with its strangeness and familiarity had, indeed, been like coming home. She remembered the continuing sense of unease with which she had faced the luxurious life her father had so lovingly provided after their return to New York. She remembered the feeling of being displaced, of being uncomfortable with the people who had made such an effort to make them, the newly wealthy, welcome. She remembered how she had fought to subdue her memories of a lodge such as this, of the sounds of night which had caressed her ears, of the circle of sky over her head. She remembered how futile had been the attempt. No matter how successful she had been in her efforts during the daylight hours, memories had returned to haunt her dreams. There had been no escape.

No escape . . . Black Wolf moved beside her, his long, hard body turning to accommodate hers, curling around it instinctively in sleep. Her eyes fluttered momentarily closed at the wealth of feelings which ensued. This man, with his savagery and gentleness, his strength and weakness, with the wonder he raised inside her, had eliminated any element of choice from her mind.

She had fought him. . . . A familiar heat flushed her face at the memory of the ease with which Black Wolf had overcome her physical resistance. She had had little strength to resist his gentleness, his caring, his longing for her; for it had matched the longing raging unknown within her for so long. She knew he had reveled in her body's spontaneous response to his loving, and her anger had soared. She had abandoned any thought of overcoming her physical weakness, her subservience to the unsuspected needs of her body. Her body had surged to life at Black Wolf's touch, but her mind had remained resistant. She had continued her arguments, had pleaded to be returned to her parents. Black Wolf had been adamant. She had expressed her worries over her parents' pain, her fears for her father's health. Black Wolf had acknowledged them in silence, only reacting when an inadvertent dream had revealed her discomfort over

531

William's distress.

But despite the worries which still plagued her, her abhorrence of the brutalities being perpetrated by both sides in this war between their people, Faith had sensed a settling of her spirit. She had fought it, denied it. But now, in the silence of this lodge, she could not escape the fact that their arrival at this camp, with all the tensions which had ensued, had, indeed, been like coming home.

The warmth of tears arose beneath Faith's lids, and she fought to suppress them. Confused . . . she was confused. She wished to see Mama, Papa, William—to reassure them that she was well. She wanted to tell them that she loved them. She wanted to . . .

Long, slender fingers were moving against her cheek, brushing away her warm tears. Black Wolf was raising himself to his elbow so that he might look down into her face. In the limited light, she saw his concern, and she was angry that he might witness this temporary weakness.

"No, Fire Spirit, do not tense in anger. There are many reasons for tears, and I acknowledge your need to shed them in darkness so that they might cleanse your soul." Lowering his head, Black Wolf pressed his lips to the damp paths, touching them with his tongue. His voice was low, affected.

"I share them with you, Fire Spirit. I take them into my body. I share the sorrow you feel at the end of the life you have formerly known, and your fears at the new one which is just beginning. But I lend you my strength and my knowledge that this is the path chosen for us, the path on which we must walk to fulfillment. The knowledge is strong in my heart, and I sense its budding within your own as well."

Fighting to overcome the thickness in her throat, Faith raised her hand to Black Wolf's face. She ran her fingers along its chiseled contours, her heart marveling at the physical beauty of this man. Pleasure surged through her as she touched his skin. Black Wolf turned his head to press a kiss against her palm, and the warmth within her swelled. She attempted to speak.

"Black Wolf . . . I cannot dismiss those who love me for that which you offer, no matter my desires. They are with me still. Their pain sears me."

Black Wolf's hand was moving against her flesh, barred beneath the warmth of the sleeping robe. She felt it slip to her breast in a fleeting caress and move across her ribs to settle on the slight rise of her stomach.

"Would you seek to erase that pain, to escape it by escaping me? No, I would not allow such a remedy to this dilemma which assaults your mind. I would not allow you to separate yourself from me, or to separate me from the child which you carry within you."

Faith's heart gave a sudden lurch, her eyes widening.

Black Wolf's eyes narrowed in silent assessment, his expression lightening within moments as he pressed his lips to hers.

"Is it possible that you did not acknowledge the signs of your own body, Fire Spirit? Is it possible that you paid no heed to the absence of your monthly flow in the time we have been together?" He shook his head and let out a low laugh of incredulity. "Even if the new softness to your features, their new beauty, is not available to your eye as it is to mine, did you not note the fullness of your breasts, the gentle rounding of your stomach, which curves beneath my hand? Did you not see these things and realize . . . ?"

His voice trailing away at the shock in Faith's expression, Black Wolf slid his hand up to cup her cheek once more. Love shone from his dark eyes.

"I thought you sought to avoid speaking of this child within you, because you had not yet accepted its coming. I did not think of your inexperience. But know now, even the thought that you did not welcome this child in the same way as I, did not diminish my joy."

Uncertain of her feelings, knowing only a growing sense of wonder, Faith attempted to absorb all Black Wolf had said. Yes, how could she have been such a fool? Had her mind deliberately refused to consider such a possibility in view of the other pressures which assaulted her? But what of this child—this new life—which she was suddenly sure was growing within her? What of the blood which would flow in its veins—the blood of two different people, enemies to each other? Unknowingly, she voiced her fears aloud.

"This child will be blood of our blood, Fire Spirit. And with this child we will seal our peace. We will raise our child to know the good in our people, and to realize that it was conceived not in hatred, but in love. Tell me . . . tell me that is so, Fire Spirit."

Filled with wonder, Faith was momentarily unable to respond. She had never said the words. Despite Black Wolf's many declarations of love, she had never faced her feelings. But here, in the darkness of the home to which Black Wolf had brought her, her feelings were suddenly clear.

Yes, it was love she felt in her heart for Black Wolf. It was love which had stirred in the heart of the child she had been many years before, love which had kept alive his memory, although she had thought him dead. It was love which had brought her body to life at his touch, and it was love which filled her now as she looked into his eyes. And it was love which made her rejoice at the child which now grew within her, no matter the obstacles which lay before them. Oh, yes, it was love. . . .

The words passed her lips, were declared openly for the first time; and a thrill shook Black Wolf's body. His arms slipped around her, holding her naked length flush against him, and Faith shared his joy. She listened raptly as Black Wolf's throbbing voice broke the silence.

"I, too, love, Fire Spirit. And in my love I give you all that I am . . . all that I can be. I give to you, knowing you give to me in return, that you will be with me always."

The beauty of Black Wolf's words hung on the silence which followed, and Faith clutched Black Wolf close. For the first time, she believed.

A bright, full moon hung in the star-studded sky, illuminating the sleeping camp as Deer Woman walked along the uneven terrain in silence. Her small feet covered the ground in short, firm steps. There was no hesitation in her movements or in her mind. She paused at the doorway of the familiar lodge, took a deep breath, and, lifting the flap, slipped inside.

A movement on the sleeping bench to the rear of the small lodge caused her to pause again, for the first time in hesitation . . . uncertainty. There was movement once more, and a slender, masculine form lifted itself from the sleeping bench. Moonlight glinted on naked, russet flesh, and she felt strong arms move around her, clasping her close.

Deer Woman closed her eyes, her heart pounding. The strong arms carried her a few short steps and then lowered her to a sleeping bench still warm with body heat. Her eyes were still closed when she heard Spotted Elk speak for the first time in a voice strained with emotion.

"Open your eyes, Deer Woman. Open your eyes and look into my face."

Deer Woman heeded the deeply voiced demand. She met the heat of Spotted Elk's gaze, listened to his earnest tone.

"Yes, look into my face, Deer Woman. See there and believe the truth of that which I say to you this night. You have come to me. I accept this gift you offer. I accept it and cherish it. Know that I will keep it and you with me for the rest of our lives. I offer you my heart and my life, Deer Woman. I tell you now that no other will come before you, and the children you will bear will know no end of love."

Deer Woman's low, choking response was noted by Spotted Elk, and he paused to caress her scarred cheek.

"No, do not force the words, Deer Woman. They will come. I know that as surely as I knew you would be mine. But know, also, that I accept this new happiness the Great Power has given me with humility. I will keep it safe and secure, for seeing myself as I was before, I was unworthy. I will keep myself worthy of you, Deer Woman, now and always."

Spotted Elk's body moved to cover hers, and Deer Woman accepted his mouth. She forced from her mind the image of one who was lost to her forever, and accepted the one who would soothe the burning ache within her. She closed her arms around his neck and drew him closer. She willed away the shadow between them, the shadow of her one, true love. She closed her mind and allowed herself to respond. And then she thought no more.

Wally drew himself stiffly erect. His feet flat on the floor, he shifted his weight from one to the other, testing. An impatient flicker appeared in his eyes. Weak . . . the leg was still weak, but it was improving. Damn, how much longer . . . ?

Wally looked toward the door the moment before it opened to reveal Lydia's sober countenance. She stood framed in the opening for a few silent seconds.

"All right, Wally. It's done."

Wally released a slow breath.

"How long do you think it will take?"

Lydia shrugged. Turning, she closed the door behind her, but she did not advance toward him. Wally felt regret surge inside him. Lydia was suspicious. He had done all he could to reassure her that he merely wanted to speak to Broken Hand in person, to see if he could convince the man that he needed to see Faith . . . to talk to her. He had finally talked William into summoning the Arapaho he had used several times before as messenger, but he knew the message to Broken Hand would have to come from Faith, herself, before the damned savage would respond.

It had been another thing, indeed, convincing Lydia to speak to Broken Hand. She had been certain that Broken Hand had spoken the truth and that there was nothing further he could do as intermediary. But Wally had not been convinced.

The weeks since he had learned of Faith's recapture had been difficult ones. After a period of relative quiet, the Indians had stepped up their attacks once more. The situation was becoming dire, and there was talk that three forts farther up the Bozeman Trail would be abandoned because of Indian harassment. In addition to all that, winter was coming, and something had to be done. He could not bear the thought of his beloved Faith living amongst savages somewhere in the wilderness, inadequately clothed and sheltered during the fierce cold. He had to do something.

536

Slowly a plan had begun to form in his mind. Lydia's contact with the savage, Broken Hand, was the first step.

Attempting a smile, Wally walked toward Lydia. He came to stand within a few feet of her. Suddenly closing the remaining distance between them, he reached out and pulled her close. His brows tightly knit, he whispered against her hair.

"You know that everything I do—everything I've ever done—has been with Faith's welfare and yours at heart, don't you, darling?"

Lydia nodded.

Noting her stiffness, her withheld response, Wally spoke in a voice laced with desperation.

"I'll get her back, Lydia. One way or another, I'll get Faith back."

The click of the telegraph key was unceasing. Messages had been flying back and forth across the wire for three days, yet despite all the activity, William was as much in turmoil as before.

Correcting his posture, pulling himself militarily erect, William kept his eye on the young corporal who continued scribbling on the small pad.

The clicking ceased and the key was motionless once more. The young soldier was still writing, and William felt his patience wearing thin.

"Well, Corporal?"

"Sir . . ." He was still writing.

"What is the response?"

Turning, the young soldier held up the message, his eyes intent on William's face.

TO: CAPTAIN WILLIAM POTTER
    FORT LARAMIE, WYOMING

NO DEFINITE NEWS RE FATHER'S PROPOSAL
TO CONGRESS. OPPOSITION HAS HELD UP
PASSAGE. FATHER FEELS MORE DEFINITIVE

ACTION WILL BE TAKEN IN THE SPRING.
WILL WIRE IF ANYTHING FURTHER DE-
VELOPS.

SALLY ANNE MORRIS

WASHINGTON, D.C.

Damn!

Crumpling the hastily scribbled message, William nodded
briefly to the young corporal before turning on his heel and
striding from the room. He gave only a passing thought to
Sally Anne's efforts on his behalf. His mind was too
preoccupied.

Ineffective . . . inadequate . . . everything he had attempted to accomplish had proved useless.

They would be meeting with Broken Hand soon. Lydia
Durham's urgent appeal had not gone unanswered. The
savage had responded positively to the proposed meeting
between Faith, Wally, and himself. So William had sent
urgent wires, hoping Congress had taken a positive step that
would make it easier for him to deal with, to threaten, if
necessary, the Indians who held Faith. He had hoped to be
able to strike fear in Broken Hand's heart, for he felt that, in
so doing, Broken Hand might induce Black Wolf to release
Faith. But he had failed once more.

Faith's beautiful face flashed before him, and William
cursed his position, the army, the savages, and the whole
world which kept her from him. Even now she could be in
that savage's arms. That thought, and countless others, had
driven him near to desperation. He had to see Faith . . . he
had to. . . .

Still mounted, Broken Hand remained concealed within
the cluster of trees. He had been there since dawn, a sense of
apprehension filling his mind. It had been several months
since he had last spoken with Shadow Woman. He had
sensed a strange hesitation in her appeal to meet with him
again. It had been transmitted in several nighttime visions

since the message had been forwarded and his response returned. His apprehension had grown in the days since. As a consequence, he had arisen before dawn, gone to the lodge of White Feather, and summoned him, so that, prior to the time of the scheduled meeting, they might inspect the area in which it was to be held.

A subsequent search had revealed no danger, but Broken Hand's discomfort remained. He squinted into the distance. Three mounted figures came over the rise, and a ragged clamoring began in his breast. He had borne the recent months with forbearance. In his heart he had known Shadow Woman was not lost to him. He had known he would see her again.

The three mounted figures drew closer, and Broken Hand frowned. The father of Fire Spirit was with them. Even at a distance the white man's animosity was evident, and barely controlled, Broken Hand suspected. The young officer's presence would be a buffer between them, and he was glad. He did not wish to harm the father of Fire Spirit, the husband of Shadow Woman. No, he would not regain Shadow Woman through violence. His visions had assured him of that.

Broken Hand rode out to meet them.

A short time later, Broken Hand rode back toward the Cheyenne camp once more. Anguish filled his heart. The need to alleviate Shadow Woman's anxiety was strong within him. It was for that reason and for that reason alone that he had determined he would attempt to convince Black Wolf to allow a meeting. The father of Fire Spirit had looked to him with heavy glances, a threat in his eyes, and the army captain had voiced warnings; but these things had done no more than raise the heat of his own anger. He was outraged that those two men had sought to convince him of their superior power. Did they not realize he knew the results of recent raids, knew that the army was close to failing?

But Broken Hand dismissed his anger. It would not do to indulge his feelings. Shadow Woman had appealed to him more eloquently with her eyes than she had with her words. And her wasted condition was further evidence of her suffering. It was evidence he could not ignore.

He would do this thing for Shadow Woman.

His decision made, Broken Hand dug his heels into his pony's sides, nodding to White Feather as his mount lurched into a run. He had decided there was no time to waste.

Chapter XXVIII

Faith sent a frantic glance around the lodge, ignoring the chills which shook her. The bite in the air, which had developed in recent days, had not yet been burned away by the morning sun, but Faith suspected the tremors that shook her body had little to do with the temperature within the lodge. She unrolled the sleeping robes with shaking hands, again searching them for the missing comb. Impatience stabbed her, and unexpected tears stung her eyes. Where . . . where had she put it?

A sound at the doorway drew her gaze to Black Wolf as he entered. Then she turned sharply away in an attempt to avoid his scrutiny, but Black Wolf would not be misled. He strode to her side, unhesitant, and raised her chin so he might peruse her face.

"Why do you cry, Fire Spirit? It was your plea which softened my heart to this meeting. If you no longer wish . . ."

"No . . . it's not that. It's just . . . I can't find my comb."

"Your comb?" Pausing, Black Wolf scrutinized his woman further. Confusion tugged at his mind. This woman was fearless in the face of adversity. She had proved her mettle countless times since their return to the camp. She had gone about her activities of the day without regard for the often disapproving stares which followed her. She had held her head high against occasional taunting. She had responded sharply in return to cutting words only when the need was proven, and she had done it without fear. She had earned respect within the camp, and he had been proud.

When Broken Hand had delivered a request for a meeting with her parents, she had waited until they had been alone to plead that he would allow such a meeting to take place. He had been unable to refuse her.

Confusion again assailed Black Wolf. The appointed morning had come, and she had been restless since dawn. He had left to tend to himself, and had returned to find her searching their sleeping robes, close to tears.

"Your comb?"

"Y-yes. I wanted to comb my hair. It is so tangled, and I wanted to look nice. Papa does like to see me look nice, and I know Mama will be scrutinizing me. I don't want them to think that I'm suffering. I don't want them to think . . ."

Black Wolf's mind tightened with suspicion.

"The white soldier—the one you spoke of in your dreams—is he the one who will be present?"

"William? Yes, I suppose he's the captain White Feather spoke of."

Black Wolf's face tightened.

A few moments passed before Faith realized the direction Black Wolf's mind was taking. She shook her head.

"No, that's not the reason why I . . ." Faith stepped backward a few paces and took a deep breath.

"Look at me, Black Wolf . . . look at me. I look terrible."

Tears again welling in her eyes, Faith touched the new buckskins she wore. She had been proud of her handiwork in which she had been aided by Deer Woman, proud of the soft, pale color of the garment, the even fringes which hung from the hem and underarms, swaying gracefully when she walked. She had been proud of the elaborate beading which she had done so painstakingly. But now . . .

"This dress is too large . . . my slippers are too wide . . . and my hair is tangled and snarled."

Black Wolf assessed Fire Spirit's appearance carefully, and he saw before him a woman with pale skin colored a golden hue by the sun, with eyes bluer, clearer than the sky. He saw the beauty of small features framed by a halo of sparkling red-gold which hung past her shoulders. The clothes she wore were well cut and sewn, and the decoration was far better than any he had ever seen. *She* was more beautiful than any woman he had ever seen.

"Your parents will be pleased with your appearance. You are healthy and strong. Your health shines in your eyes."

As tears loomed more threateningly, Faith turned to search the robes once more. Sensing more to her words than their more obvious meaning, Black Wolf stepped to her side and turned the robes carefully. Finding the comb she sought, he held it out to her.

"Is this the implement which upset you so greatly?"

Unable to respond to the hint of amusement in Black Wolf's eyes, Faith nodded. Seating himself unexpectedly, Black Wolf pulled her down to a seated position between his thighs. He raised the comb and began pulling it systematically through the long lengths of her hair. His voice was deep and soothing as he worked.

"You are anxious to see your parents, to assure yourself of their well-being, and to grant them relief from their anxiety. It was for that reason that I consented to this meeting, despite the conflict between our people. But now your anxiety is increased."

Black Wolf's efficient strokes quickly freed Faith's hair of snarls, and he slid a hand around her waist to draw her back against him as he continued speaking. His hand rested against her rounding stomach and he whispered against the softness of her ear.

"Whatever the reason for your anxiety, the thought that you do not look well is without truth. Your beauty is great, Fire Spirit, greater than it has ever been. And except for matters which are beyond our control, you are content. Do not allow that contentment to be overshadowed by anxiety. Allow your parents to have peace, so they might dismiss thoughts of you from their minds."

"But . . . but I don't want them to dismiss me from their minds."

Sadness welled within Black Wolf. His wife longed for her kinsmen, and he was powerless to grant her that consolation.

Turning abruptly, Faith closed her arms around Black

Wolf's neck. Her damp cheek pressed against his, she whispered softly, "I want you and I want them, too, Black Wolf."

His sadness turning bittersweet, Black Wolf gripped Fire Spirit tighter than before, holding her immobile in his arms. A long silence was followed by the words, "Someday, Fire Spirit. You will have your wish someday."

The full measure of love in those words registered within Faith's mind, and she felt the seeds of hope take root. Yes. Someday there would be peace, and then . . .

Allowing Black Wolf to raise her to her feet, Faith smiled, determined to shake off the remnants of her anxiety. Turning, she raised herself on her toes to press her mouth briefly against Black Wolf's. She pulled away and turned. Her softly spoken "Someday" trailed behind her as she walked toward the doorway.

Wally twisted with pain on the narrow bed, his eyes red-rimmed, his face covered with perspiration. He gripped his stomach, eyes bulging, as short retching sounds issued from his throat. But he won the battle to control them.

He looked up to Lydia's worried expression. His breath was short.

"You'll have to go with William . . . without me, Lydia."

"But Wally, you wanted to see Faith . . . to talk to Black Wolf . . . to try to convince him to allow Faith to—"

"You . . . you'll have to do that for me. Broken Hand will be there. He'll help you." His lips tightening, he continued harshly, "He'll do anything you ask, won't he?"

"Wally . . ."

Wally shot her an apologetic glance.

"In any case, I can't go this way."

Wincing as another spasm all but convulsed him, he shook his head. "Where in hell is Hank?"

"Dr. Mallory is tied up with a young man he operated on yesterday. The boy is close to death."

Wally lowered his head.

"Go, Lydia. Go, will you? If you're late and they think you're not coming . . ."

A knock on the door halted Wally's gasped instructions. At a short response the door opened to reveal William's startled face.

"Wally, what's going on? What's the matter?"

"Wally's sick, William. We're going to have to see Black Wolf without him."

William's light brows pulled together in a frown. He assessed Wally's obvious discomfort. "You're sure?"

"Damn it, of course I'm sure!" His voice rasping, Wally shook his head. "Don't you think I'd be dressed and ready if I felt I could drag myself to my feet? Get out of here, will you?" Pausing for another breath, Wally added tightly, "And remember, William, promise that savage anything he wants to get Faith back."

Nodding for the sake of avoiding an argument, William looked to Lydia.

"We'd better get going, Lydia."

Turning to press a light kiss on Wally's cheek, Lydia took her wrap and headed for the door.

As the door closed behind the two figures, Wally suddenly became silent. All signs of discomfort gone, he listened intently for the sounds of their footsteps as they walked down the hallway. He waited a few moments longer, then threw back the coverlet with a snap and walked quickly to the window.

Careful not to be seen, he squinted into the bright light of morning. His heart beginning to pound slowly, Wally watched as Lydia mounted, as William got on the horse beside hers. He noticed that another soldier had been recruited to join their group, increasing it to three so their number might match that of those awaiting them. William did not miss anything. They were moving toward the gates of the fort at a moderate pace. Good . . . good . . .

Waiting only until the three horsemen had cleared the gates, Wally turned toward the nearby wardrobe. Within minutes he was fully dressed and ready. His gunbelt strapped to his waist, his rifle in his hand, he strode to the doorway, barely limping, and jerked open the door.

Black Wolf and Broken Hand, standing slightly to Faith's rear, were silent. Their small party had arrived early at the appointed spot for the meeting, and the wait had been difficult. For the first few minutes Faith had paced as Black Wolf and Broken Hand had searched the area for any sign of intended foul play. When they had both been satisfied that no threat existed, Black Wolf had returned to her side while Broken Hand had stood guard.

Faith had been extremely tense while the two men had carefully looked over the surrounding terrain. She had feared for their welfare, feared that enemies might, indeed, by lying in wait, and, realizing her fear, had been beset by a sense of confusion. It became clear to her how thoroughly her loyalties had blended. In truth, she had even developed an affection for Broken Hand. She no longer blamed him for deceiving her mother, for usurping her mother's love for her father while they had been captive. She no longer blamed him for the haunted look which had filled her mother's eyes in the years between, for she now saw that same haunted look in Broken Hand's eyes as well.

But it was understanding that had changed her attitude toward the great Indian war chief at her side—the understanding Broken Hand had exhibited upon Black Wolf's adamant refusal to allow her to return to her people, and the feeling that Broken Hand would have taken a similar stand if Mama were indeed his once more. As much as she loved Papa, and knew that Mama and he should be together, Faith could now look back on the time Broken Hand and Mama had spent together with the realization that it was spent in mutual love.

That love was in Broken Hand's eyes still. She hoped she would not see a reflection of it in Mama's shadowed eyes as well.

Raising her eyes to Black Wolf, Faith felt pride in him

surge anew. Integrity, dignity, and determination were marked in the lines of Black Wolf's handsome face. She knew he would sacrifice her to no demands or coercion, but she no longer felt trapped by his possession of her. Her hand moved to the rounding of her stomach, her mind moving to the child with grew within her. They had conceived a life and they would share in its care. Black Wolf was right. She was content. It was now up to her to make that contentment known to Mama and Papa . . . to set their minds at rest.

The two men beside her stiffened and within moments three riders came over the rise. Her heart fluttering in her breast, Faith strove to identify them. Yes, it was Mama, William, and . . . Who was the third man? Where was Papa?

Her immediate fear transmitted itself to the men beside her, and Black Wolf took her arm protectively. She felt the tension in his stance, knew his strong muscles were ready for action should the meeting prove to be a trap. But the riders were continuing forward, drawing up at last.

Her chest rising and falling with her rapid breaths, Faith swayed toward her mother's slender figure as William lifted Lydia to the ground. Mama started toward her as Black Wolf released her arm, and within a moment, Faith was hugging Lydia wildly, aware of her mother's thinness even as she delighted in the strength of her mother's embrace.

Tears were streaming from Lydia's eyes, and not realizing they streamed from her own eyes as well, Faith asked breathlessly, "Where's Papa? Is he all right?"

Faith listened to her mother's low explanation intently.

A lone rider had covertly followed the three horsemen from Fort Laramie. He dismounted behind the cover of jutting rock a safe distance from the meeting underway, secured his horse quickly, and withdrew a rifle from its sheath. He moved to the cover of a large boulder and steadied the rifle barrel upon it as he sought to frame his shot through the sight. He swallowed tightly at the sight of the slender girl in buckskins, her red hair, so similar to his own, gleaming in the morning sunlight. There appeared to be no stiffness to her carriage . . . no fear. She did not cower like a captive. On the contrary, she appeared at ease with the two Indians who guarded her. She seemed almost . . . happy. Faith, what have they done to you?

Wally shook off his consternation and forced his mind back to the task at hand. But the grouping was too close to risk a shot from his vantage point; Faith and her mother were standing in an almost perfect line with the two Indians to Faith's rear. He must wait . . . wait. . . .

Faith had stopped talking to Lydia. She was looking at William. He did not need to see William's face to know the extent of the young officer's pain. He knew it was as intense as his own, for those savages had Faith under their control. Don't worry, William. It won't be long. . . .

Wally crouched lower as Faith stepped past Lydia and walked the few steps to William. She had inadvertently cleared the way for his shot at Black Wolf. With a low, ragged breath, Wally steadied his gun. His finger moved to the trigger. He squeez—

No! Faith had embraced William warmly and and Black Wolf had walked jealously toward them. Wally's finger moved back from the trigger. Damn! He could not take such a chance. Black Wolf and Faith were too close.

Black Wolf was removing Faith from William's embrace, and Faith was turning to him, speaking softly. The Indian was making no response, except to draw her back toward Lydia once more.

Frustration forced Wally's rifle to turn toward Broken Hand. He had not planned to take this shot first, but if he could have it no other way, he would. Most assuredly, if he succeeded in hitting Broken Hand, William would make an immediate jump for Black Wolf. They would struggle, allowing him time to get to their side and finish off the work he had started. He would bring both his women home this day. *Both* of them . . .

Wally's gaze snapped back to Faith. She was still talking, talking softly. She motioned William forward, darting a pleading glance in Black Wolf's direction. Faith turned to

peak to Lydia. Her face held a soft glow, and when she
paused, Lydia raised her hand to her mouth, her posture one
of disbelief—shock. William stiffened and suddenly the
tableau below him was motionless. Suddenly Lydia stepped
forward, throwing her arms around her daughter. She was
crying, and Faith was crying. But Faith was smiling as well.
Faith was crying happy tears.

What was it about Black Wolf's stance? Something had
changed. The wariness was disappearing.

Faith disengaged herself from her mother's arms. She
turned to Black Wolf and took his hand. She pulled him
forward, her tall, slender body efficiently shielding him as
she placed his hand around Lydia's.

Lydia stood in absolute silence for long moments as Black
Wolf spoke. She appeared mesmerized by his words, unable
to move even after he had finished speaking. Abruptly, she
took a step forward and embraced the tall, young Indian.

Shocked and astounded by the unexpected proceedings,
Wally lowered his gun. Something was happening . . . something.

Faith fought to control her rioting feelings. She had
known Mama would understand when she explained that
she loved Black Wolf, and that he loved her. And she had
known Mama would be happy for her when she told her that
she was going to have Black Wolf's child. Mama had looked
into Black Wolf's eyes when he had taken her hand. She had
listened intently when Black Wolf had said that she need not
fear for her daughter's happiness or safety, that he would
love Faith and their child, and that he would protect them
with all the strength he possessed—with his life. She truly
believed Mama had known all along that this was the way it
would be.

Faith shot a pleading glance toward William. His pale,
handsome face was motionless, but there was pain in his
eyes. Her heart cried out to him. William, I didn't want to
hurt you, but, in truth, I could never love you. My heart was
already given when we met those years ago though I was still

549

a child.

Mama was releasing Black Wolf, and she could sense his relief. But the Indian taboo against mothers-in-law could not apply in this special case, not when the worlds of those within this circle had been so torn and was only now coming together.

Black Wolf was withdrawing, indicating that the meeting was over. Suddenly conscious of the fact that Broken Hand had been silent during the exchange, Faith shot a short glance toward him. His eyes were for Mama and Mama alone. Lydia was returning his gaze, her heart in her eyes. Sudden realization flashed across Faith's mind. Mama loved both of them—Papa and Broken Hand—but she could only have one.

William was turning Mama back toward her horse, and Faith yielded to Black Wolf's entreaty to mount. Faith was astride, Black Wolf mounted beside her when she thought she saw the glint of metal on a hill to their rear. She paused to consider it a moment longer.

Wally's rifle was poised. Black Wolf was mounted; in a moment his shot would be clear. Wally's finger moved to the trigger. Perspiration was pouring from his temples, his palms were wet with sweat. He would not miss . . . he could not. . . .

Faith's head lifted abruptly and she looked in his direction. Wally froze. Somehow, even at that distance, he could see the blue color of her eyes and the startling contentment within them. He looked closer as she appeared to strain to see him. Yes, there was contentment in Faith's gaze.

Contentment . . . he had not seen contentment in his daughter's eyes since those summer months years before when he had brought her home.

It came to him then, with the intensity of a blow. The truth. The truth was that his daughter had only *now* come home. This was the message she was trying to convey to him. It carried more clearly across the distance between them han it had when he had been at her side. Oh, Faith . . .

Wally slowly lowered his rifle. Shaking, uncertain, he watched as the riders split into two groups and began to move in opposite directions.

Wally took a deep, shaking breath, and then another. His daughter was leaving, departing with Black Wolf, and he was letting her go.

Chapter XXIX

1868

Spring had brought the first glitter of sun-swept gold to the prairie. It shone down on the hundreds of Indian lodges which stood in the green Platte River Valley. Huddled beneath a great army field tent set up beside Fort Laramie, the council began its deliberations. William Tecumseh Sherman, commissioned by Washington, had summoned the Plains Indians to discuss a treaty.

The exchange was frank, sometimes bitter. The Indians complained that the whites had trespassed on one of their last hunting grounds, killing and driving out the buffalo. They demanded that the three forts on the Bozeman Trail be abandoned and the road closed.

The bargaining was long and hard, but when all was done the Treaty of Laramie sealed off the Black Hills from settlement, and set aside the Great Sioux Reservation. The Washington government also offered in the terms of peace unceded Indian territory stretching roughly from the Bighorn Mountains to the Black Hills where "no white person should be permitted to settle or even pass without the Indians' consent."

Peace . . .

From his position among the chiefs, Broken Hand

watched the signing of the white man's document. He had thought long and hard since Shadow Woman's leaving. Destiny . . . what was the destiny she had brought him?

Over the long months of the winter, his thoughts had slowly grown clearer. Shadow Woman had brought him the gift of understanding. She had brought him the gift of love. She had shown him that differences between people did not prevail when love and understanding thrived.

Black Wolf and Fire Spirit had proved the truth of this new understanding. They and their newly born son would follow the tribe into the unceded territory to live their lives in peace. Together they would ride the uncluttered land, live upon its bounty, and raise their child and the children who came after him.

Broken Hand was content. He had used the gifts Shadow Woman had given him—the gift of herself and the gift of understanding. Red Cloud had refused to join the peace council, but Broken Hand had persuaded his people to attend. He had used his gift again this day in speaking the words of peace. He would use the precious gift Shadow Woman had given him to guide his people all the days of his life.

And Shadow Woman had not deserted him. She came in nightly visions, and spoke with him. She told him that she would return to this land, where her daughter and her grandchild lived, that her heart remained with them. She told him she would see him again, and in his heart, he knew they would be together soon.

Broken Hand straightened his great shoulders proudly. He took a deep breath and sensed the presence of peace. He was content in waiting. He could ask no more. He was fulfilling his destiny.

Apart from the great number still moving to sign the Treaty of Peace, his eyes fastened on them in silent observance, stood Senator Hartfield Morris. The white-haired senator's efforts in behalf of this peace effort had earned him a position as advisor to the council. He did not take his responsiblity lightly.

A short distance away, his pretty, blond daughter, Sally Anne, who had accompanied him, was not similarly engrossed. Instead, she stared intently at the young officer who addressed the guard. His instructions completed, he turned, caught her eye, and smiled. Sally Anne smiled in return and strolled slowly in his direction as he dismissed his men. She met William midway across the grass-covered field.

Slipping her arm under William's, she shot him a pert glance. She knew his surface smile hid unhappiness, and she knew the cause. But she did not allow it to cause her concern. She was confident she would replace that unhappiness with another emotion, one that matched her own depth of feeling for this handsome officer. Oh, yes, she would. She was a very determined woman.

Far away from the formal proceedings, Black Wolf sat beside a small stream. He glanced to his side, to his beautiful wife on whose lap their young son slept. Gently taking the baby from her, Black Wolf held his son in his arms for long moments while he studied the child's clear skin, only a shade lighter than his own, the black, shining hair which framed his son's full face. He saw features small and perfect, and knew that, when awake, his son would look at him with Fire Spirit's startlingly blue eyes. He and Fire Spirit had made a beautiful child, and he was proud.

Lowering his son carefully to the mossy bower beside them, he wrapped him carefully before turning in a swift movement to press Fire Spirit onto her back and stretch himself full upon her. He smiled at Fire Spirit's gasp of surprise, smothering it with his lips as he took hers lingeringly. He paused as he drew away, allowing himself to dwell on the happiness reflected on the face of the beautiful woman who was his own.

He lowered his head again, this time taking her lips with deep, soul-shaking passion. When he drew back at last, Faith gave a low, breathless laugh. Then a thoughtful expression crossed her face, and she raised a hand to trace the contours of his cheek, the line of his lips. Her heart quickened at his physical response to her caress. Her voice was low, tremulous.

"Black Wolf . . . whom I once called a savage . . ."

Black Wolf's response was tinged with the emotions which burned in his eyes, searing her.

"If that is so, then you must still my savage heart, Fire Spirit, for it is yours."

Faith slid her arms around Black Wolf's neck and drew his mouth to hers. Oh, yes, she would do that gladly . . . she would still Black Wolf's savage heart. She knew only one way.

And the loving began. . . .

FIERY ROMANCE
From Zebra Books

AUTUMN'S FURY   (1763, $3.95)
by Emma Merritt

Lone Wolf had known many women, but none had captured his heart the way Catherine had . . . with her he felt a hunger he hadn't experienced with any of the maidens of his own tribe. He would make Catherine his captive, his slave of love — until she would willingly surrender to the magic of AUTUMN'S FURY.

PASSION'S PARADISE   (1618, $3.75)
by Sonya T. Pelton

When she is kidnapped by the cruel, captivating Captain Ty, fair-haired Angel Sherwood fears not for her life, but for her honor! Yet she can't help but be warmed by his manly touch, and secretly longs for PASSION'S PARADISE.

LOVE'S ELUSIVE FLAME   (1836, $3.75)
by Phoebe Conn

Golden-haired Flame was determined to find the man of her dreams even if it took forever, but she didn't have long to wait once she met the handsome rogue Joaquin. He made her respond to his ardent kisses and caresses . . . but if he wanted her completely, she would have to be his only woman — she wouldn't settle for anything less. Joaquin had always taken women as he wanted . . . but none of them was Flame. Only one night of wanton esctasy just wasn't enough — once he was touched by LOVE'S ELUSIVE FLAME.

SAVAGE SPLENDOR   (1855, $3.95)
by Constance O'Banyon

By day Mara questioned her decision to remain in her husband's world. But by night, when Tajarez crushed her in his strong, muscular arms, taking her to the peaks of rapture, she knew she could never live without him.

SATIN SURRENDER   (1861, $3.95)
by Carol Finch

Dante Folwer found innocent Erica Bennett in his bed in the most fashionable whorehouse in New Orleans. Expecting a woman of experience, Dante instead stole the innocence of the most magnificent creature he'd ever seen. He would forever make her succumb to . . . SATIN SURRENDER.

Available wherever paperbacks are sold, or order direct from the Publisher. Send cover price plus 50¢ per copy for mailing and handling to Zebra Books, Dept. 2159, 475 Park Avenue South, New York, N.Y. 10016. Residents of New York, New Jersey and Pennsylvania must include sales tax. DO NOT SEND CASH.

SWEET MEDICINE'S PROPHECY
by Karen A. Bale

#1: SUNDANCER'S PASSION (1778, $3.95)

Stalking Horse was the strongest and most desirable of the tribe, and Sun Dancer surrounded him with her spell-binding radiance. But the innocence of their love gave way to passion — and passion, to betrayal. Would their relationship ever survive the ultimate sin?

#2: LITTLE FLOWER'S DESIRE (1779, $3.95)

Taken captive by savage Crows, Little Flower fell in love with the enemy, handsome brave Young Eagle. Though their hearts spoke what they could not say, they could only dream of what could never be. . . .

#4: SAVAGE FURY (1768, $3.95)

Aeneva's rage knew no bounds when her handsome mate Trent commanded her to tend their tepee as he rode into danger. But under cover of night, she stole away to be with Trent and share whatever perils fate dealt them.

#5: SUN DANCER'S LEGACY (1878, $3.95)

Aeneva's and Trenton's adopted daughter Anna becomes the light of their lives. As she grows into womanhood, she falls in love with blond Steven Randall. Together they discover the secrets of their passion, the bitterness of betrayal — and fight to fulfill the prophecy that is Anna's birthright.

Available wherever paperbacks are sold, or order direct from the Publisher. Send cover price plus 50¢ per copy for mailing and handling to Zebra Books, Dept. 2159, 475 Park Avenue South, New York, N.Y. 10016. Residents of New York, New Jersey and Pennsylvania must include sales tax. DO NOT SEND CASH.